Michael J. Laurence is an award-winning screenwriter and director with over a hundred film and television credits to his name.

Thomas G. Foxworth has been an airline pilot for seventeen years and has spent ten years in the international safety field. He is the author of *The Speed Seekers*, voted the best aviation book of 1976.

PASSENGERS

'The authentic crisis situations will make airline passengers cringe'
Ben Kocivar, Aviation Editor, *Times-Mirror* magazines

'*Passengers* is a rough, tough gorilla of a book. It's a book for the stronghearted, the strongminded, and those literary weaklings who can't put a good story down. The flying scenes are superb'
Ernest K. Gann, author of *The Aviator*

Also by Thomas G. Foxworth

The Speed Seekers

MICHAEL J. LAURENCE
THOMAS G. FOXWORTH

Passengers

PANTHER
Granada Publishing

Panther Books
Granada Publishing Ltd
8 Grafton Street, London W1X 3LA

Published by Panther Books 1985
Reprinted 1985 (twice)

Copyright © Thomas G. Foxworth and
Michael J. Laurence 1983

ISBN 0-586-06385-4

Printed and bound in Great Britain by
Collins, Glasgow

Set in Times

For Vicky and Lisa and especially for Jenny,
with gratitude and love.

— T.G.F.

To my wife and best friend, Barbara; to my
sons, Erik and Trevor, for their kindness
and understanding.

— M.J.L.

Preface

Chairman G. Hollis Wright watched the long armoured vehicle as it backed its way into his three car garage. Two guards stepped down from the bulletproof cab and casually headed for positions on the manicured lawn. Their guns were drawn and held unobtrusively at their sides, fingers on triggers. A car slowed and continued past the ornate iron gates as they shut and locked. Hollis was staring at the backlit trees in the direction of his Buttress empire and didn't take notice of the banker standing behind him. How could he, G. Hollis Wright, top player in the world's breakneck aerospace game, find himself in this treacherous position, he wondered; and he stared at the trees till the sinking backlight forced him to turn away.

1

Guy Anders stretched in the co-pilot's seat and yawned. The sun was dead ahead and sinking. The air was like silk. There'd been a ripple here and there sending shivers through the fuselage but for the most part the giant red-and-silver Buttress 17-10 had held firm as it thundered for New York.

Flight Engineer Carlton Hanks checked his panel for fuel consumption.

'We're thirty-six hundred pounds behind on the fuel score, Skipper.'

Captain W. B. Cosgrove, 'old W.B.', rubbed the back of his head and snapped his levered sunglasses down into place.

'Lotta head wind out there, Hanks. Lotta head wind.' He leaned forward as though he were trying to pick out the mass of air that had been holding them up.

'Estimate for Kennedy still looks good.'

The captain turned his head to the side and listened to something in the tone, a whisper in the background.

'You didn't just change the throttle settings any, did you, Anders?'

'No, sir. Haven't touched them.'

'Yeah, well it's a good machine.' W.B. sat back. 'It's a lot of entertainment for the money.'

Guy Anders was going to ask him if he thought this revolutionary aeroplane would do for aviation what explicit sex had done for the movies. But W.B.'s look was stern, American Legion, and so Guy let go of it.

'Nice machine,' said W.B.

A radio voice joined them. 'Air World Six, Kennedy landing runway two two left, weather eight hundred broken one thousand overcast, visibility four miles in light rain, the wind's one six zero variable one nine zero ten knots, altimeter . . .'

Air World Six was now some three hundred forty miles from New York.

And then Guy Anders felt it.

The vibration started at his feet, then travelled up one arm to the left side of his face. It was as though the alignment on his car had suddenly shot loose. Guy looked over at W.B., shirt cuffs open and folded back, the sun rippling out along the broken lines of his face. He couldn't decide if the old man hadn't noticed it or whether he had and wouldn't let on. He was about to open his mouth but there was a risk involved.

If he called attention to it and it turned out to be nothing, he'd lose points. He'd look weak. It had to do with the business of having balls in America. British and French pilots, Christ, even German pilots could chatter about it like rhesus monkeys picking fleas. But in the States, if you were in the leadership business, you had to be nonchalant. You had to have a ten-pound look while they were sawing your leg off. You had to bleed casually. Even Guy's seven-year-old son had picked up on it. There he'd stood inside the front door the day they'd come back to the house from the hospital. He was thin, his small frame and gentle face too young to be confronted by the reality of his mother's illness. His long corduroy pants were pulled up over his stomach, his scuffproof shoes battered at the sides as he stood there looking at his father waiting in the doorway. He was smiling and yet his eyes were wet. Still he couldn't let himself come closer. There suddenly was something sad and distant about his father – a kind of quietness that said he could no longer be disturbed. Guy who used to horse around had joined the adult world.

Guy had wanted to wrap his boy up in his arms and hold him. He wanted to touch his son's small face and tell him to let the tears flow.

'Let 'em come on down, baby, it's OK to cry. I love you, Jamie.'

But there was this knee-jerk thing about weakness and though he was aware of it, he took that route anyway and botched it and said, 'C'mere, Fonz. How about the old bear hug.' It wasn't tears and affection – a father and his son alone. It was round-shouldered and massive. Jock stuff. Couple of regular guys grinning. Jamie'd backed away from his father's outstretched arms and ran upstairs.

Guy felt gutted. My God, why was it so tough to be direct about gentle things? Had it become even tougher since his wife's death? He didn't know.

He tightened his grip on the yoke.

He had turned away from Cosgrove. Carlton Hanks swung around in his seat and casually let his arm droop on the backrest.

'She's holding her own!' he piped. It sounded a bit too cheerful, he decided. He hoped somebody would contradict him because what he really wanted to know was what was going on.

Then W.B. put his hands on the yoke and said, 'OK, Anders, let it go now. I've got it.' He checked the left side and eased the new jumbo into a slow turn. Somebody was pulling lazy contrails above going the other way. The tremor became intermittent – off, on, gone, back again. It had an ugly quality. Guy felt an ice pick of dread, as though the fire warning bell might go off. If there was one thing he was afraid of it was fire.

'I wouldn't pucker all that much over it, Anders. Sounds to me like a compressor in the hold doing overtime.' As he said it the vibration stopped altogether. Guy was amazed. Hell's bells! Have faith in the Lord! The skipper had done it. Old W.B. was in command. Guy was relieved. He was grateful. For a moment he thought he might even vote conservative next time. Maybe these old guys had something going for them after all.

Hanks turned back to his desk feeling good he'd said

11

she was holding her own. He felt secure again and thought about the steak his wife would grill when he got home.

'Now that buzz really started about an hour ago,' said W.B. 'So, Carl, just make a note of that in your logbook someplace.' W.B. had known about it after all. 'And don't make a big deal out of it. Just a few simple words in plain fifth-grade English so even the FAA can understand it or we'll all be swearin' on Bibles and writing compositions in triplicate.'

W.B. had once commanded a squadron of bombers which cut through walls of Messerschmitts and Heinkels as they went for Berlin. He'd been shot down twice and send skidding, bleeding across a highway in Belgium. He flew over France and Holland, then came home to work for the airlines. He wasn't given to conversation.

'Keep it short,' he said.

Anders distrusted and admired him at the same time. There he was in a white drip-dry shirt, a crisscross of sunburned hash marks on his neck, a look of bourbon and branch water and violence that had been tucked in over the years. Nine spires of sunlight fanned out ahead of them. Guy watched. A copper-and-gold mist lay separated from the horizon, then fused with the ground, spilling light across the earth like surf trying to make it up the beach. Guy played the opening chords of the New World Symphony in his head. He was at the opening of time – before glass buildings and announcers' voices. He was at the controls of this newest of new gleaming chariots and there were no passengers behind him. In reality, fifty-seven rows of seats, mostly nine abreast, stretched theatre-like for some sixty yards behind the cockpit bulkhead while outside four giant turbo-fans, two slung under the wings, one on each side, close in, and two more attached to the fuselage at the tail, spewed tons of thrust. The long razor-sharp wings were swept back but the tail surfaces were unnaturally small, out of proportion as if built for an aeroplane much smaller, reminiscent of the abbreviated flukes on the huge Zeppelins of another time.

'Carl, log that sunset at quarter past. Start the clock for night-time,' said W.B.

'Love that night-time pay,' said Hanks, grinning with self-satisfaction.

Oh, you dumb ass, thought Anders. You well-meaning dumb ass.

The passenger cabin was dark. The meal was over and most of the shades were still drawn. The last moments of a re-release of *The Caine Mutiny* had passed through the projectors and the screens were being tucked away. People were lying back, bloated, waiting.

The man in white slacks hadn't been able to think of an opening line to say to that green-eyed attendant, name tag ASHLEY next to an unbuttoned blouse. Now his beard was coming in and he felt gritty. His collar itched and his pants were wrinkled. The whole trip was coming to a close. The holiday mood, still palpable before the film, died with word that New York was less than an hour away. Passengers began to draw into themselves – sifting for American coins and bills, checking passports and packages, adjusting watches, finding scraps of paper with phone numbers. A baby began to scream as the lights flickered and went out.

It had happened as W.B. applied pressure on the yoke. The plane had chattered, then steadied, as he pulled his hands away. The lights came back on. Guy stared down at his panel. Mach number point eight seven, heading two four zero, then a jolt as he realized the altitude was going through thirty-six five on the way down.

'What the hell do you call that, Skipper?' Guy noticed that his teeth were chattering as he spoke. His mouth and chin were trembling. Simultaneously he understood that the whole flight deck was vibrating, the instruments shuddering. Guy grew wide-eyed for the source of it but

13

he couldn't focus. The din shackled his brain. His left hand went for the throttles but Cosgrove beat him to it.

'Now let's not get excited,' rumbled old W.B. 'We don't want to throw the passengers on their ass back there.' Cosgrove reached for the seat-belt switch and flicked it on. The muted chime drifted through the plane. An elderly woman wearing thick glasses tried to stand. 'What is it? What's happening?'

'Just some rough air, please sit down,' Ashley said as she passed her, but it wasn't anything she'd been through before. She lifted the white phone outside the galley. My God, what now? Her legs ached. She slipped out of one shoe, took a breath and tried to be pleasant.

'Ladies and gentlemen, Captain Cosgrove has just informed us that there may be some further turbulence ahead and has asked that you remain in your seat with your seat belt fastened. Thank you.'

The lights came back on, flickered, stayed on. The man in white slacks noticed Ashley's trim foot. She had nice legs. The lights suddenly grew brighter, then slammed out with a bang. The plane shuddered.

In the middle cabin the senior steward pulled away from a middle-aged couple who were imploring that he do something. They were demanding special consideration. They were the only guardians of a child who was waiting for them in New York and they had to get home. The senior steward wasn't listening. He made his way to the back, his face the colour of grey pudding. The flight was in trouble.

Ashley opened her mike. 'As a precaution please extinguish all smoking materials at this time.'

Carlton Hanks said, 'Want me to try to raise someone, Skipper?' W.B. was feeling for vibration differences between two of the throttles.

'Now, Jesus Christ, Carl. Last thing we want is to stir up the bureaucracy.'

Carl sat looking at the two pilots. 'Well, this isn't just turbulence, Skipper!'

14

Cosgrove turned. 'No, and it isn't goose shit going through the engines either! We're a little high up here for geese!'

Guy Anders was reluctant to put his hands back on the yoke. He felt cold yet there was a thin coating of sweat on his face. He tried to focus on the quivering altimeter. It was going down again and the altitude alert blinker was flashing on the panel.

'Hey, what's happening to the altitude?'

Ashley saw the passenger in white slacks coming towards her. She was no longer in the mood for small talk and found her anger rising.

'Listen,' he breathed confidentially. 'My name's Harry Peterson and I just wanted the staff to know that I've had flying lessons.' He waited for her to say something but she closed her eyes wearily.

'There is something wrong, isn't there?' he whispered.

'Please stay in your seat,' Ashley said tonelessly.

'Sure,' Harry said.

The plane reared as if it were trying to climb, then whipped sideways and shuddered with such a slap that Harry was knocked off his feet. An armrest creased his spine. Up till now he'd been sure the massive 17-10 – this new queen of the sky – would soon settle down. He'd been in turbulence before and the bigger the plane the better he'd always felt about it.

An overhead bin flew open. A shopping bag fell and swept a wineglass against the wall. A stewardess looking grim worked her way up the aisle holding on to the armrests on either side. The elderly passenger in 23A, window seat, stopped her to explain he wasn't getting channel eight on the earphones any more. All that was left, he said, was Bill Cosby telling jokes on nine.

Harry held on to a chair leg with one hand and tried to catch his breath. He was amazed at how quiet it had become. All he could see were silhouettes in chairs, passive shapes hurtling who knows where? He'd expected to hear screaming, but there was nothing. It was like a ghost ship of the dead being transported across a line. A milli-second of blinding light, the beginning crunch of a volcanic crash, would be the only signal to all on board that the line had been crossed.

Harry was staring at a patch pattern on the carpet in front of him. It had no great significance – a piece of plastic cloth manufactured in a mill, probably in North Carolina – not a last airy view from Mount Olympus, not a chorus of farewells. Just a floor. This is the way you die, he thought . . . looking at a rug.

Guy had cut his hand on something. He didn't want to get bloodstains on his clothes. In the back of his mind he reflected that they would be tough to get out. Up front he had occupied himself with the business of helping W.B., but the shaking was wearing him out. The sun was gone now. He'd seen the earth in its first awakening and was back moving through the dark depths of eternity and he wondered how many centuries it would be before he'd see a daybreak again.

W. B. Cosgrove struggled with the shimmying yoke, but the force behind it would come alive in a mammoth convulsion that tore at his hands. Carl was already reading codes to Guy, who punched them in a keyboard on the centre panel ahead of the throttles. On the small TV screen above, rows of green writing – stored procedures – flashed in sequence as if electronic pages were being flipped behind the glass.

'No help here.'

Cosgrove glanced over and grunted. He throttled back the inboard engines and added power to the outboards, hoping to rock the nose up. He also reached over his head to the switches that could shut off the inboard lift spoilers and pulled the spoiler-control lever, which again acted to raise the nose. But none of it did any good. W.B. was uncomfortable with spoilers raised. They needed the entire wing working. He slammed the spoiler lever for-

16

ward. Guy watched, enthralled. Hanks felt his throat go dry. W.B.'s eyes were slits, his mouth compressed, the veins stood out on his neck. In forty-one years of flying the old man had never been bested by a machine, but it was now a struggle between him and this unyielding force. All else had ceased to exist for him as again and again he directed the 17-10, his fists tight on the yoke, only to have it rebuff him, wrench itself loose in a gut-stunning spasm. Cosgrove was flushed, dishevelled – he had always been unflappable, not a crease in his shirt or a loose necktie – but now, with the wraithlike glow of the cockpit distending the wet streams glistening on his neck, and the closeness aggravating the sour pungency of armpits, W. B. Cosgrove was a raging man at war.

He let go of the yoke with contempt and glared down at it.

'Yah sonofabitch bastard! All right, Anders, go ahead and ask Centre for a lower altitude. I can't hold her.'

Carl said, 'There are no lights on for the passengers.'

'Yeah? Well, you can tell them for me to go piss in their hats, then!'

Hanks looked curiously forlorn, like a sodden bird whose skinny frame shows through the matted feathers, its neck extended and eyes blinking, questioning. The flight seemed to calm down.

Guy pressed his mike switch. 'New York, Air World Six.'

One of the twenty-two air traffic controllers on the floor of the IFR room at Islip, Long Island, was pacing between two scopes as he told United Airlines fifty-four to descend and maintain twelve thousand feet and American Airlines One-oh-One to change his frequency to Kennedy Approach Control. He then answered Guy.

'Go ahead, Six.' He released the mike button and sat down. There was no response.

One hundred and eighty miles northeast Guy Anders

17

looked over at W.B., still consumed with his single-handed contest to keep the plane from falling.

'How low you wanna go, W.B.?' Anders said.

'I don't give a damn,' said Cosgrove. 'Just clear us right on down. Do it now before we hit someone!'

Hanks was suddenly fascinated by the blur of shaking instruments in front of him. He couldn't read any of them. He held on to his metal table as if that would put a stop to it. Guy was calling New York.

'Six is requesting flight level two zero zero initially.'

'Unable two zero zero. Descend and maintain two four zero, I'll have lower in ten miles.' There was a pause, then, with more interest, 'You having any trouble, Six?'

'How much do you want to tell them, Skipper?'

W.B. pressed the mike switch on his yoke and drawled, 'Naw, no trouble. Just wanna get down a little early, thank you.'

The controller sensed something was wrong – perhaps the long delays between answers. He said, 'Roger, Six. I can let you down to one five thousand now. Do you want to come down that far?'

'Affirmative,' said W.B.

Guy watched the altimeter unwind and the vertical speed indicator advance from one thousand to more than two thousand feet per minute.

'Got to lift that nose: I'd settle for three degrees,' said W.B. Then, squaring himself in his seat, he positioned his hands behind the rim of the yoke and caressingly, imperceptibly, began moving it towards him. Like a safe-cracker listening for clicks, his head tilted to one side, he tried to do with stealth what could not be done any other way. Carlton Hanks watched the control come back. The rate of descent slowed to eight hundred feet per minute but the altimeter was moving down past twenty-two thousand feet.

Suddenly the 17-10 woke up. Like a sleeping whale prodded too deep and too long, the giant aircraft trembled and shook violently. Cosgrove, determined not to let it get the upper hand, planted his feet and hauled back on the yoke. He was going to overpower it. He held on, unwilling to give more ground. Incredibly the contest became even as the old man began to take back whatever the wounded aeroplane took away. But it was no match. The 17-10 insisted and there was no staying with it.

'Skipper, you're going to tear something off if you keep this up!'

Cosgrove no longer cared. He might lose the plane, hit the ocean at better than four hundred knots, but somehow he was going to have his way. 'Goddammit!' he bellowed. 'Goddammit!' It had become personal.

Carl's eyes isolated one clock on his panel. It pointed to how fast they were coming down. He watched it with dread. The numbers churning in his head said at this rate they were now going to fall short of the field.

They were coming down through seventeen thousand feet when Cosgrove snapped, 'Anders! We're going to need some troubleshooting from the company.' Guy saw fifteen thousand feet coming. They were going to go straight through it. W.B. saw it, too, but didn't say anything. 'There's your altitude, Skipper!'

Cosgrove was red in the face, straining to keep the yoke from whipping out of his hands. 'Gimme some help here! I can't level off!' Panic cut through Guy. A major air disaster had always been a possibility, something one acknowledged intellectually. But Jesus! He felt his arms go numb but he wrapped his hands around the wheel and forced the feeling down.

Hanks was incredulous. He felt detached, the scene had become abstract. He stared at the captain, then at Guy, two disembodied automatons facing their instruments, tending a machine that had taken over. The thought burst on the surface of his mind: what am I doing with them anyway? He was jolted when W.B. said, 'Call the company and get ahold of the tech centre. I need some help.'

It meant Cosgrove was through. He had lost control. There was no one in command!

Harry Peterson couldn't believe it. After all, there they were with small children on board and three nuns. He'd never seen headlines about a crash in which small kids and nuns were involved.

The seat-belt sign fluttered and went out. Ashley was working her way up the aisle holding a flashlight, asking passengers to remove their shoes just in case an emergency landing should become necessary. The passengers were quiet, somehow enveloped by their seats; more than four hundred seats headed down.

Hanks couldn't raise their own technical people on company frequency. 'Tech Ops, this is Air World Six!' he repeated again and waited. Guy scanned the altimeter, squeezed the mike button.

'New York, Air World Six. Requesting lower.' This time he had an immediate response.

'Roger, squawk eleven hundred ident. Contact New York Centre on one two six point nine.'

Then Carl's radio came to life. 'Air World Six, this is Tech Ops at Kennedy. What's your problem?'

Carl pressed the mike to his mouth. 'Tech Ops, Flight Six. We're getting some vibration on the aeroplane and we don't understand it. We'd like some help.'

Hanks expected instant concern. Instead the voice said casually, 'OK, Six, stand by.'

Stand by? The bastards! What do you mean, stand by?

Guy had reset his frequency. They were already below fifteen thousand. He said, 'New York, Air World Six heavy, out of one five thousand requesting lower.'

There was a stir in the darkened IFR room when the controller said, 'I think I got one here's in a little trouble.' The supervisor, his belt slung under his belly, turned and glanced at the scope. 'He's also got weather between him and the runway. Anyone tell him that?'

The controller opened his mike. 'Six, this is New York.

Descend and maintain one zero thousand and proceed direct Deer Park. You sure comin' down fast. Nothin' we can do for you?'

Air World's chief engineer, Vic Moudon, took the stairs from the third floor three at a time and ran into a mechanic coming up. 'Looks like we've got a bad situation,' said the mechanic as he brushed past.

'What's the problem?' Moudon called.

'I don't know.' The answer echoed up the stairwell. 'We're trying to get a description from the aeroplane!'

Carlton Hanks checked the altitude they had left and translated it in terms of minutes remaining. He leaned over his table and closed his eyes. He didn't want to sound like he was pleading but time was running out and Tech Ops hadn't come back. Carl tried again.

'Tech Ops, Air World Six. We have to get off the dime! We've got a serious control difficulty up here. We've never felt anything like it before!'

W.B. ducked his head down and wiped his face against his sleeve. 'Hold up, Carl.' He pressed his own mike switch.

'Tech Ops, this is Air World Six. Do you read? Over.'

'We have you five by,' came the answer, responding to the different voice.

'Tech Ops, we're having a problem controlling the pitch and we've got to have a few answers.'

'Six, we'll work along with you. Say your altitude and speed.'

'We're at one four thousand and showing three six zero knots.'

'Six, how are your hydraulic indications?'

'Pressures and quantities looking good.'

'What's your hydraulic pressure in number four system?'

'We're reading three thousand pounds. Looks normal.'

'Is it fluctuating?'

'No, steady.'

21

'Can you describe your control problem further?'

'There's a spasmodic vibration. I can't determine any pattern to it. Sometimes it feels like trying to hang on to a jackhammer.'

Vic Moudon rifled through a three-inch-thick loose-leaf manual on the 17-10's control logic. 'What time is it on the West Coast?'

'Five-twenty.'

'Let's get Buttress on the horn. Get ahold of Ed Boice or Dick Miller. We need somebody who can do this without the manual.'

Lightning flashed against the glass-enclosed book cabinet on the far wall. No thunder. The storm lay curled like a long grey bedroll brooding on the rim of the northeast horizon. The speaker crackled. Only part of a sentence came through. Cosgrove was saying, '. . . she starts to fight back!'

Moudon picked up the red telephone and depressed the mouthpiece lever. 'Say again, Captain.' He reached over and fine-tuned the console. Cosgrove's voice came back strong.

'I was just saying I can't pull the yoke back beyond a certain point because that's when she starts to fight back.'

Moudon looked at the others in the room and asked the plane, 'What does your control position indicator show? Are you getting elevator travel?'

'Affirmative.'

Moudon shook his head. 'It's got to be in the engines.'

Someone else in the room said, 'He's still a quarter of an hour out.'

Moudon made some notes on a sheet of paper. At the top he wrote 'Engines.'

'What about your turbine vibration monitors?'

'Negative. Normal.'

'What about your N_1? Give me the N_1 and N_2 readings on engines two and three.'

An oxygen mask dropped between Guy and W.B. Anders tucked it back in and snapped the overhead hatch. 'We're wasting time, Skipper. We're going to have to muscle this load down on our own.'

'It's not the goddamn engines,' Cosgrove groaned. He opened his mike. 'Negative on the engines! It's not an engine problem! I'm telling you it's a control problem! I can't pull her up!'

Moudon's voice persisted. 'Roger, Air World Six. Just give the N_1 and N_2 readings.'

Cosgrove held the mike a foot in front of his face and hollered, 'Now look, I don't have time to give you all them goddamn readings! I'm telling you it's a control problem! We've got something wrong in the control circuit of this aeroplane! Let's deal with that!'

There was a pause before Moudon relented. 'Roger,' he said.

'Let's have the Kennedy approach plate,' snapped Cosgrove to Anders. 'It's like all those sonsofbitches,' he continued with a snort. 'They've got one foot on the ground so they could care less. The bastards. Terra firma. "The more firmer, the less terror." They play their water-cooled calculators like harmonicas. I'd like to handcuff one of those sonsofbitches to my wrists for two weeks so he could see what it's like up here.'

'He's sixty out,' said the voice at Tech Ops.

A young engineer had Buttress on the line.

'Hello,' said Moudon. 'Who's on with us?'

Three thousand miles away Ed Boice motioned Dick Miller and Vern Locker into his glass-partitioned office on the first floor of Buttress Aerospace's yawning assembly bay. 'There's a problem on the East Coast,' he said. Then, into the phone, 'New York, this is Ed Boice. I'm flight-control designer and I've got Dick Miller and Vern Locker standing by. Both men work with me. Are you going to relay or patch us through so we can talk direct with the aircraft?'

23

'Ed, this is Vic Moudon at Air World and we'll carry you and the aircraft two ways.'

'Fire away. What all seems to be the problem?'

Vic eyed the clock. 'I'm going to have to give it to you short. Our Flight Number Six, your 17-10 licence number N1711AW, with four hundred and twenty-one souls on board, has a serious control problem sixty miles east of Kennedy trying to complete a flight from London. He can't pull the nose up. Has this kind of thing ever come up before? Anything in the area of control circuits or vibrations?'

'What kind of vibrations?'

'The captain reports it's in the pitch – in the elevator circuit. It seems to come and go but he notices it when he applies back pressure or when he tries to hold his altitude.' There was a pause on the line. 'Did you get that, Buttress?'

Ed Boice pinched the end of his nose as though he'd just come up from a swim. 'How intense is it?' Vern Locker studied Boice's pose. It irritated him and so he decided to wade right in. 'Sounds like something in the servo actuators,' he said.

Boice looked up, slowly covered the phone and to the newest member of his staff almost too carefully said, 'You're off base, Locker.' Moudon heard the muffled exchange but couldn't make it out.

'Hello, are the other two people saying something?'

Dick Miller worked for Boise and hated him. But he'd known him for so many years he could, on occasion, assume a familiar stance without too much fear of reprisal. 'Let me talk to him, Ed.' Boice, still looking at Locker, gave Miller the phone.

'New York, is this going direct to the aircraft?'

'Affirmative.'

'Air World Six, my name is Miller.'

Cosgrove was pissed. 'Well, shithouse mouse! They found someone else! Maybe they ought to get Aunt Jemima on the line! Maybe *she* knows something!'

24

Miller went on. 'What was your indicated airspeed when you first spotted the problem?'

Anders pressed the mike. 'I think we were indicating about three hundred twenty knots, Miller.'

The captain shook his head. 'No, you're wrong,' he admonished. 'I felt something before that. We were cruising at Mach point eighty-eight. There was a ripple then.' He spoke into his mike. 'Correction on that. We can't be sure.'

Miller's voice came back calm and confident. Cosgrove was beginning to like him. 'Roger, Six. What's your indicated airspeed now?'

'We've got her slowed down to about two hundred and fifty knots and we're comin' down.' W.B. handed the controls to Guy.

'Let me take a breather. I'll handle the radio. See if you can keep us up without ripping the tail off.'

'Would you mind speeding up to two hundred and eighty knots and trying a couple of manoeuvres?' Cosgrove changed his mind about Miller.

'Look, goddammit, I don't think you guys get the idea! I'm not a fucking test pilot! I want to get this sonofabitch on the ground! I got a load of payin' passengers up here. I'll tell you right now I don't have to speed her up to make her do anything. There's a whiplash in the yoke.' He took the controls back. 'I've got it.'

Locker watched Miller and admired him. The guy was all right, he thought. He was being supercool under fire. Miller persisted. 'Captain, would you mind doing a thirty-degree bank turn for me in either direction? And hold your altitude for a few seconds and tell me what it feels like in the yoke?'

Anders had been watching the radar screen with disbelief. 'Skipper, there's one piece of weather we're going to have to work our way around.' Guy adjusted the antenna to pick out the worst spot.

'Not now!' Cosgrove hissed. The flight deck had begun

to quiver so badly that it was almost impossible to read the instruments.

'Miller' – W.B. raised his voice above the din – 'I can give you one turn that'll put us on our heading for Deer Park. And that's it!'

Carlton Hanks gripped the sides of his seat and held his breath. Cosgrove started to turn the wheel to his right.

'There's ten degrees of bank,' he called. 'Here goes the rest of it.' He leaned into it, adding back pressure as he went, but as the right wing dipped down past twenty degrees, the 17-10 reared as though straining against a giant harness, then broke loose, bucking with such spasmodic force that the yoke wrenched out of Cosgrove's hands. He recaptured it and pressed the microphone. Guy could barely understand him.

'Miller,' W.B. was shouting, 'I don't know if you can hear this but we're just past twenty degrees and she's going ape! I'm rolling out!' Cosgrove released the back pressure and eased her over to straight and level flight. Guy saw the smudge on his radar screen grow larger.

'There's a big storm cell ten miles dead ahead. We're headed straight for it. Can you swing left or right, Skipper?'

'Negative. Straight and level's my only choice!'

'We're going to get our ass kicked in that storm!'

Out on the West Coast Dick Miller looked at Locker, then at Boice – who seemed all torso and no legs. His steel-grey hair had been clipped in a flat-top crew cut. His face was jowly and his mouth had a cruel twist to it. 'I got a feeling that clatter's being induced by the electronics in the computer,' said Miller calmly.

Boice raised his eyebrows, got up, thrust his thick hands into the back pockets of his shiny colourless pants and slowly eased his bulk across the room. 'Oh, really? He hasn't hit twenty degrees of bank and you can tell all that?'

Typical, thought Miller. A subtle adjustment of a detail

to suit his position. The plane had gone beyond twenty degrees of bank. Boice had become defensive about the 17-10 even before anyone had attacked it. It had somehow become a private matter.

'He rolled *past* twenty degrees,' said Locker.

'Remarkable how you can know all that,' said Boice, ignoring Locker.

Miller rested the phone on his knee. 'Ed, for God's sake, we've got to stop the rattle in the hydraulics before he breaks a fuel line. Every time we talked about beefing up the plumbing, you screamed payload. Well, if he starts to burn you're gonna end up putting the greatest payload in the history of aviation straight into the Atlantic Ocean!' This stopped Boice. Miller went on. 'We can't let them keep shaking that bulkhead back there! The fuel line goes right through it! It shouldn't but it does!' Boice looked out of the window. The room was suffused with red light, which poured in from the west. People were going home, cars streaming out through the main gate.

'So what do you recommend? That they pull the computer apart three thousand miles away from here when they're on final approach into Kennedy?'

A curtain of soft rain moved across John F. Kennedy Airport. The asphalt taxiways shone with the lights of aircraft lumbering to their positions. Inside hangar four on the north end, Vic Moudon watched the rain snake down the window. It had become pitch-black out. 'I think we better get some crash equipment out there.' He lifted the phone. 'Buttress, how are you doing?'

Ed Boice turned away from the window. 'You don't make any sense, Miller. Hold one,' he said to New York.

'Now look!' Miller said.

'No, *you* look. They're going to have this thing made! They've got her slowed down, haven't they? It's just a flutter.'

'But they can't hold her in a turn!'

A rhythmic metallic thrashing came through on the

overhead speaker. 'My God, listen to them,' Locker said. Miller looked up. There was a tremor superimposed on Cosgrove's voice.

'This is the captain. Now I don't know what you guys are up to out there but I'm going straight in from here, I'm losing too much altitude! I'm going to make one turn on final and that's it! We have to get this heap on the ground!'

Miller kept his eyes on Boice and put the phone back to his ear.

'Air World Six, this is Miller again. Would you have the engineer pull the circuit breaker on panel seven labelled "Computer Elevator Program A"?'

Boice's face turned crimson. He grabbed the phone.

'Gimme that! Disregard that, Air World! Stand by!' Dick Miller was jarred. Locker watched him struggle to subdue the rage that was mounting inside him. He was grappling with it, his anger finally dissolving into a fatigue that creased his face and made him look old. Boice glared at him. His voice was taut and narrow.

'What the hell you trying to do, Miller? You can't put that shit out on the air!'

Miller was hoarse. There was grief in his voice. 'That 17-10 out there is the problem that was never resolved in here!'

Boice pointed the phone at Miller's face. 'You better watch your ass, buddy.'

Thirty miles from JFK the sky was smeared with a billowing blue-black front that was about to engulf Air World Six. Then, like the first skips of a wave, wisps of turbulence rippled through the stricken aeroplane. Water streaked around the cockpit.

'This is it!' yelled Anders.

'Hold it. They're saying something but I can't hear them!' Cosgrove pressed the headset to one ear. Buttress was coming through muffled. The plane slipped, dived and came grinding up short. Rain lashed into it. W.B. held on. Anders tucked his right shoulder into a niche

28

next to the window, jammed his feet up high against the panel for leverage and grappled with the controls.

'Miller, we didn't get that! We didn't get it!' Cosgrove was shouting. 'Say again! Tech Ops, tell them to say again!'

Air World Six was at eight thousand feet. A bluish glow emanated from the instruments and lit the otherwise dark flight deck in a ghostlike haze.

'We're not going to make it, W.B.!' It was Carl. 'We either get the nose up or we're going into the drink!'

All Guy knew was that he'd smacked his head on something. There was a spectacular crash. It felt as though they'd hit a brick wall. He felt the sting in his neck. Then a rush of hail roared down upon them travelling to the back and away like an express train. For a moment they drifted aimlessly, seemingly without power.

'Hey, you guys! We're not going to make it in this!' Carl was terrified. His instruments had stopped shaking but he couldn't concentrate on them. He no longer understood them. He thought of the voice recorder that might be found in the wreckage. His last words would be on it. He wanted to say something to his wife.

'We can get out of it if we can steer to the left!' Anders yelled. Cosgrove took a hand off the wheel and scratched his neck. He looked surprised.

'We're going to stay right here! Look at that altitude!' It was climbing back up through ten thousand feet. They were in an updraft. It was a chance.

Anders felt himself being pushed down as the weight built up. They were going up on a roller coaster. Ten thousand five hundred feet, eleven thousand feet . . . Then they fell off the top. Suddenly Guy was listed off his seat as the plane plummeted. Just as abruptly they ground into a mountain of shale. Fingers of ice crawled over the glass. Then it happened. The yoke loosened. The middle barrier appeared gone. At the same time a red light went on overhead. Anders couldn't figure if the bell had rung at that moment or not. Which travelled faster? Light or sound? He couldn't remember. Time had collapsed. They had a fire warning.

They had broken a fuel line.

Guy's transmission came through thin. 'Air World Six!' he called out to no one in particular, 'We've got an engine fire warning on number three engine!'

Ashley had heard the bell and felt her knees go weak. She opened the cockpit door. Cosgrove sensed her presence and without turning around said, 'You be quiet. We're busy. I'll talk to you later.' Ashley closed the door behind her. The floor danced under her feet. For the first time she felt panic. She looked out at the darkened cabin. The passenger seats were tilted to the left.

W.B. was all business. He looked at Guy. 'Silence the bell.' He then pointed a finger at Hanks and said, 'Shut that mother down.' He keyed in the P.A. and said, 'Cabin staff, take your seats.' Curiously Hanks felt a surge of strength. At last there was something to do. He went down the checklist for Guy.

'Throttle idle . . . fuel control lever cutoff . . . fire handle pull . . . fuel valve light . . .'

Then W.B. put it on the line.

'New York, Air World Six! Mayday!'

Ed Boice froze. It had come through to the West Coast loud and clear. Miller was grim. His anger rose. His voice was deep.

'There it is. What the hell else do you want, a certified statement? They're coming apart at the tail! They're starting to break lines. They're shaking themselves to pieces!'

'Roger, Six,' said New York Centre. 'Squawk seventy-seven hundred. What's the nature of your problem?'

'We have a fire indication . . . we shut down number three engine . . . and I'm having control difficulties.'

'Roger. Kennedy now landing three one right. Three

one left available. Weather IFR, ceiling eight hundred broken, visibility five miles, rain showers. Surface wind three-one zero at eighteen, peak gusts thirty. Altimeter three zero one eight. Descend and maintain two thousand if able. Cleared direct to the outer marker, three one right.'

Boice had his fingers wrapped around the mouthpiece. He was staring out of the window. 'They'll make it.'

'The clock's running out,' said Locker. 'It'll be over in a minute.'

The red steel doors on building sixty-four rumbled skyward. Two emergency foam pumpers rolled out and, burning rubber as they turned, sped off for taxiway zulu separating the two long runways. Distant yellow police cars, beacons rotating, streaked noiselessly to their predesignated stations to stop all ground traffic. The field-condition light was changed from alternating white and green to red.

Kennedy International Airport was closed.

Three thousand miles away Dick Miller looked at Vern Locker, then at Ed Boice. 'You're going to let that plane go down? It's going to *go* down! You've got to tell them to shut down the computer and stop that clatter!'

Boice clenched the phone against his chest. He didn't move. He was matter of fact. 'You can't tell them the back end of that aeroplane's no good,' he rasped. 'You can't put that out over the air. You'll sink this company! You got any proof? Show me your paperwork! You put that crap out and that order sittin' fire in Germany is going to go down the drain and the twenty-six waiting for shipment to the Middle East – they're going down the drain! And the European competition, waiting for us to make *one* slip . . . will wipe us out! There'll be cancellations coming through that door all day and night!' This was the man Miller knew existed but had never seen. Now he was out in the open. Miller was stunned.

'What the fuck are you talking about!' he yelled. 'There's a guy on fire out there!'

The night supervisor in the radar room picked up the phone and rang the tower. 'You see that emergency squawk out to the northeast? That's Air World Six. He's on fire. I don't know what his control problem is but he's got one. Give him all the room he needs and give him a code thirty-three.'

'Roger, the field's already closed.'

Moudon looked out of the window. 'Cosgrove's a good man,' said Vic.

Ashley worked her way back to a woman who'd gone faint with fear. She could no longer hold her child. All she could manage was plaintive sighs. The lights above the emergency exits were on. The dark interior creaked as the plane groaned and skidded against a curtain of water. There was a hiss like air being let out of a tyre. Flames could be seen reflecting against the last row of windowsills.

'Air World Six, can you maintain your heading, airspeed and altitude?'

W.B.'s voice was calm. 'We're tryin' our best . . . clear a path for us. I don't know if I'm going in the bay or into Yonkers. Get all the emergency equipment out. Give me a vector straight for the airport. We're gonna use three one left and keep an eye on us.'

'Roger. Steer two eight zero. You've got thirteen miles to go. You're cleared all the way. Contact Kennedy tower now on one nineteen point one.'

Three high-capacity fire trucks and a third foam pumper took off for the strip alongside 31–left. Ambulances carrying emergency rescue teams and burn pack units turned on to the tarmac and moved out past the blue taxiway lights headed for the runway. A flicker of heat lightning lit the field.

The control tower operator searched the northeast but there was nothing. Rain was still falling.

'Air World Six, do you read the tower?'

Guy checked his side window. They were still in the soup. 'Roger, five by!' he answered.

'There isn't any more I can do with that fire!' Hanks shouted.

'Go in the back and see how bad it is,' said W.B. Hanks stood up wide-eyed and opened the door. The passenger cabin was grey and cavernous. But he could see the flames from where he was standing. The edge of a blistering corona was visible through a string of windows on the right. Hanks, gaunt and elongated against the green backlight coming from the flight deck, stooped towards the aft section. A smell of kerosene and a biting stench of burning metal cut into his senses.

'Oh my God, Captain,' a woman was sobbing. Hanks held her hand as he bent over and looked out of her window. Flames were streaming, then trailing away in strings of exploding globules. His armpits were soaked but he said, 'Don't worry. We'll be all right.' Carl wasn't sure how he got back to the cockpit.

'Close the door!' Cosgrove snapped. Hanks stood there, looking down over the panel, hoping to see a break in the cover . . . a twinkle of lights . . . a piece of Long Island.

'Well?' W.B. demanded.

'Captain, we've got to put it down. We're gonna burn the tail off.' Anders sat back, his arms dropped to his sides. They were in the southwestern edge of the storm. Vicious downdrafts were now sapping them of the altitude they'd gained earlier.

'We're not going to have enough height for an approach,' he said.

'Now where's that stew? I want her to get the cabin ready for an emergency landing. Shoes off, everybody bent over, arms folded. Make sure they're all ready to go down the chutes after we stop. Get everything set up back there. Right now.'

The 17-10 bored its way towards Kennedy, its meagre fund of height slipping inexorably away. The vibration was quiescent but the fire warning light still glowed, nagging the crew. For Guy Anders events blurred, over-lapped, confusing the sequence. There was a break in the clouds. The streams of water that ribboned out along the windshield were gone. There was a light below . . . a fishing vessel. It had to be five or six miles out. For a moment he thought he saw the soft luminescence projected from the city a few miles beyond – a hue somewhere above the water – but he couldn't be sure. He heard a remote voice call the tower, watched as the radio was adjusted. It was his own actions perceived through a haze. Shimmering far away the apparition that was W. B. Cosgrove was consumed in fury. He was raging against the machine, wrestling with all he had in him. Ahead the runway emerged, its lights seen edge-on, much too flat. The VASI slope indicators were solid red. Guy couldn't come to grips with the feeling that in mere moments his own well-favoured body might evaporate in the core of a searing explosion.

A man in Cedarhurst, Long Island, was out dragging a garbage can down his driveway. The street was still wet. Chill gusts rustled through the trees and made him shiver. He looked up. For an instant the thin underside of a cloud glowed crimson, then he saw what looked like a giant blowtorch in the clear. The high-pitched whine of several jet engines descended to a growl as this flaming spectacle passed overhead and again was consumed by the racing overcast. He stood there holding the garbage can. The throbbing cascaded, repeated itself in diminishing slaps. Then it was quiet.

'Holy God.'

The man remained as if hypnotized, his upturned gaze fixed, oblivious to the splashes of rain. At last he turned to go back inside. As he reached his front door, suddenly, as though someone had pulled a giant master switch, the entire street went black.

The employees' gate on the West Coast was still open but most of the people had gone home. The parking lot was empty. Miller looked at the red sweep hand on the wall clock. A siren wafted through the window and died. Boice squared his jaw.

'Best crash equipment in the world's out at Kennedy.'

The fire truck, engine running, stood cocked at the threshold. The men dressed in yellow-and-aluminium fire suits, their metal and glass visors open, looked to the east. The airport was still. Then the first indistinct flares of Air World Six's landing lights pushed through the veil, the ones to the right blurred by a splintering halo of fire. The men climbed aboard, pulled down their masks and waited. The driver gunned the machine. They were going to try to run alongside, spraying her with foam. They would have to get a head start, get the pumper up to speed.

'Take off when she passes the water tank!' The driver pressed his foot down on the gas and held the brake.

Up in the tower the controller watched the aeroplane's landing lights hanging in space, the fire whipping, billowing, changing shape . . . the plane appearing not to be getting any closer. Just lower.

Cosgrove was still flexing and sweating. It was now or never. The remaining engines bellowed as he poured on the power, hoping to lift the 17-10 over the threshold.

Air World Six roared by the water tower. The driver released the brake and the number one pumper, its red-and-yellow beacons spinning, tore into the damp air alongside 31–left. At first the truck's throbbing engine filled the night; the distant plane was noiseless. But the 17-10 closed and the thunder rose up behind them and rolled in and occupied them, holding them in an ear-splitting grip as the distance between them shrank. The three-man team manning the main hose rotated their turret to face the oncoming jet. For an instant it looked as though the trestles that held the approach lights would reach up and snag the 17-10. The truck was halfway down the runway when Air World Six swept over the threshold and collided with the ground. The sudden clouds of smoke from the tortured wheels blossomed as big as houses, then streaked away behind. Burned-rubber stink and wasted burned air punched the nostrils of the firemen. A wing dipped, the plane was enormous all at once; it lurched towards the careening truck. Its momentum was awesome, it towered over them, the angry wind from it was like a hot vortex that would swallow them all, tumble them helpless into its maelstrom. Already two streams of foam spattered on the scorched tail pipe as the plane ground down the long runway, perilously close to the edge. Somehow the pilot managed to keep it from overrunning the grass. Then it was past.

The first-class curtain swayed. They were on the ground, clusters of wheels beneath them compressed against the concrete – solid at last. A hurricane of foam lashed into the windows and hit the tail in a splattering crescendo. Ashley felt a pain in her throat. Tears were running down her face but she was smiling. She loved the captain and Anders and Hanks and the statuesque yellow forms racing alongside in their gleaming trucks. The undercarriage shrieked and moaned as the brakes grabbed, and spumes of moisture whipped off the giant cowls and over the wings as the engines strained in reverse. The passengers were thrown forward as the 17-10 laboured to shed its momentum. At last they stopped. The first note of bedlam snarled as people stood and clambered for the aisles. But Cosgrove slapped them down. He was on the PA insisting on order. 'No need to panic now. We're safe.'

Doors on the right side flew open. The steady mutter of truck engines became apparent, the real world, fresh and cool, was outside waiting for them. Orange escape chutes squirted from their slots, bloating, stiffening, and shot for the ground. Images merged . . . weird shapes in ponchos perched on fire-truck scaffolding, searchlights dappling, voices on two-way radios . . . then three outlines up on one wing escorting the first passengers to the chute that swept to the ground two stories below.

Harry Peterson stopped at the doorsill to say something to Ashley, but before he could form the words she had whirled him around by one arm and hurled him unceremoniously into space. Others crowded behind. Harry pulled himself up at the bottom, brushed his white slacks, and thought ruefully, Some vacation: spent three grand – and didn't even get laid!

Cosgrove and Anders had remained by the aeroplane. Thirty minutes had gone by since they landed, and it was empty. The trucks had gone. The only reminder of the fire was a thick, unpleasant smell. They gathered their papers and walked silently towards the Air World station wagon that sat patiently to one side, waiting to drive them back to the terminal. It was quiet now; the field was back in operation, but it was late.

Cosgrove stopped, turned around, and stood looking back at the wounded bird: its tail blackened, a big stain spreading underneath, but silver and red and still majestic. 'Nice machine . . .' W.B.'s voice trailed off. It was frayed. 'Got a computer . . . but it ain't like it used to be . . .' He turned and looked at Guy Anders. His face was haggard and worn. 'One of these days they're gonna train a chicken to fly that thing and you and I will be like the Hardy Boys. Oh, don't laugh. It's on the drawin' board.'

2

In Washington, the National Transportation Safety Board's chief aviation accident investigator, Doug Moss, had just gone to bed and turned the light out when the phone rang. They wanted him in New York. The FAA had a Sabreliner waiting for him. Washington National Airport was already closed. Christ, it meant he had to go to Dulles, thirty miles away. He tossed his overnight bag into the back of his '71 station wagon and wheeled on to 495.

The seat was cold, like guard duty used to be in the air force . . . everybody asleep and warm and him alone in the shadows in the night and the cold. 'Have to get up in the middle of the goddamn night to clean up after a couple of dumb-ass pilots,' he grumbled. 'Always have to pick up the pieces.' The engine heat came up off the floor. There was nothing ahead and nothing gaining in the rearview mirror. He was suddenly eager to get to Kennedy to start digging into the debris.

The two pilots assigned to take him to New York buttoned themselves in. Moss didn't know who they were or what they looked like, and he didn't want to know. It was too late to be pleasant. He put his bag down and stretched into the second row of seats.

'I hear that was a pretty close call at Kennedy,' said the figure in the left-hand cockpit seat. Moss didn't feel like getting into it. He was pissed that he had to risk his neck in a plane in the middle of the night because someone else couldn't do what they were supposed to.

'I hear the airline pilots' union now wants twice the pay and free vasectomies. You guys ought to get in on that. You won't get shit working for the government.' There was no response from the front. 'You want to know what happened at Kennedy? I'll tell you what happened at Kennedy.' His tone was contemptuous.

The Sabreliner bellowed down the runway. Moss crossed his feet. He always did that on takeoffs.

It was past midnight at Kennedy. Air World's operations room was jammed with the fortunate but weary passengers. The night staff, squeezing between bodies and moving from wall charts to offices, preparing weight and balance load sheets for Air World's morning departures, found it difficult to make headway. Two men in white shirts and red company ties were tracking a transparent wall display in search of another jumbo to replace the scorched 17-10. They had Los Angeles on the phone.

'What about ship 1712? The plot here says it's not scheduled to be anywhere till the afternoon.' There was a pause, then:

'Uh, she's on a maintenance delay. We're pulling a plane in from Hawaii to cover that. What about 1715 out of Dallas – Fort Worth? Why'n't you check that?'

'We did, LA. Thanks anyway.'

Two weather people and a dispatch assistant doggedly tried to follow established routine but the mob of passengers still waiting to be questioned blocked them.

It was a displaced cocktail party in overcoats waiting for something still bigger to happen, but their moment was already fading and would, in a day's time, be eclipsed by the ball scores.

Captain W. B. Cosgrove, wearing steel-rimmed glasses, was still at a desk near the wall finishing the paper work. The pen he held made him look overgrown, like a labourer at a grade-school desk struggling to complete an application, and yet he wrote neatly, meticulously. He had been staring at the last page, which had one final question on it. 'Why did you select this course of action?'

'Select, for Chrissake!' he exploded. 'You select in a supermarket when you have time!'

Guy stood behind him looking down over his shoulder, waiting to read his answer.

'That's the page they hang you on,' rumbled old W.B. 'The no-man's-land of opinion . . . mine against all those who weren't there.' Captain Cosgrove didn't move.

Guy butted in. 'Why don't you just say, "We chose the best course of action under the circumstances." Let them make something out of that.' He watched as W.B. flicked the dust off the page.

'I like it,' the old man said. He rubbed the pen on a piece of scrap, paused, his eyes deep in the distance, then slowly wrote, 'It was the only way home.' He looked at it, closed his pen and without turning said, 'They're already going to work in Europe. What do you say we get out of here?'

There was a minor scuffle as a group of ad-agency people, rousted out of bed to take the pulse of their largest client, but in fact looking for some leftover limelight, pushed their way past. Guy turned away from them.

'Good night, Skipper.'

It was finished. He sensed the tension empty out of him and a deadening fatigue rush in. For the first time he felt the grit, the grease on his hands, his stubble, and his shirt stiff from dried sweat. He shouldered his way back into the crowd to get his bag.

'Pardon me.' A young woman caught his eye. She didn't smile. 'God bless you,' she said simply.

'Good night,' Guy said softly.

Guy picked up his flight bag and turned to go. A chunky gnome of a man suddenly blocked his way. Knowing eyes peered up at him from a round face. He was holding a wet eight-by-ten photograph by its edge.

'Here you go, Cap'n. Something for the attic.' It was a stark black-and-white shot of Air World Six, badly charred, its sleekness disrupted. It looked hangdog, reproachful of those who had gotten away. 'My God,' was all Guy could say. He'd been inside that ship as she slithered to line up on the VASI lights, coaxing her across the threshold less than ninety minutes before, puckering up on his seat to keep her aloft. And here she was, pressed flat on to an eight-by-ten.

'It's yours,' said the man, his narrow eyes lit by an inner light, watching intently as Guy studied the photo.

'It's a lemon, isn't it?' the gnome challenged.

'I reckon we'll fix it,' said Guy and moved to leave.

'That's if you can *find* what needs fixin',' said the man almost triumphantly.

Guy noticed the red police pass Roundface had stuck to his shirt. It identified him as a stringer for the *News*.

'I covered the Electra,' the man persisted. 'They tore that plane apart, right down to the seats, and she was clean!' His tone became confidential. 'And then one day this little old farmer comes by and tells a story of how he'd heard all the coon dogs in the prairie settin' up this awful howl just *before* one of those Electras went in. And that's what finally tipped them off to that asymmetrical engine vibration that tore the wings off.' He leaned closer. 'There *is* something wrong with the 17-10, isn't there, Cap'n? All those columns written by Benny Reese about Buttress were right after all, weren't they?'

Guy put the photograph down on his flight bag and shrugged on his jacket. 'Seems to me we got two choices,' he said to the stranger. 'If Mr Reese was right we can refuse to fly the sonofabitch.' He blocked his cap and put it on. 'If we don't do that, we can look up the people who made it and make them do it over.' He picked up the photograph. 'I'll keep this over the mantel.'

'Compliments of the press,' said the man and he was gone.

Guy saw Hanks standing at the exit. The lanky engineer seemed thinner.

'Well, no one's gonna dismiss us.'

The night driver of the Air World crew bus didn't mention the flight. Either he knew better than to bring it up or he never heard of it.

'Where you parked?' Guy asked.

'Back of the crew lot, a walk and a half,' said Hanks.

'I'll take you over.'

'He'll drive me,' Hanks said confidently and called to the bus driver, 'Right, amigo?'

'Your family know?'

Hanks nodded. 'Yours?'

'Unless the TV's shot.'

'Didn't know you were married.'

41

'I'm not.'

Guy got off. His car stood where he'd left it, unaffected by what had just happened, hunched forward, facing the fence, mutely waiting.

He sucked in the cold air and felt exhilarated. He was safe.

At twenty-three and some four thousand miles from what had been home, Anja felt trapped. Though it was two in the morning, she was still in her jeans and button-down shirt, sitting through the suspended hours in a house still strange to her, not knowing what to do with the rest of her life. Her hair was tied up in a knot; she was petite – not small, but petite in the neat sense, what the French call *gamine* – with a delicate figure that gave the impression it could be lifted with one arm – yet with the capacity to dazzle as well. She learned of the emergency on TV and it had made her angry at Guy, even though she knew him only as an employer whose wife had died, leaving him alone with his seven-year-old son. She'd answered an ad in the European *Herald Tribune* only weeks ago and now here she sat, on Long Island, a stranger who had very nearly become the boy's only contact with the adult world. She knew tonight's close call wasn't Guy's fault but that didn't mollify her. Somehow the whole thing was thoughtless of him.

Moreover, Long Island wasn't what she'd had in mind. It wasn't that different from what she'd left behind. She'd looked forward to extricating herself from the encroaching blue haze of her small town in northern Europe and heading for the American West and perhaps beyond that to the delicate pastels and gritty mysteries of the Far East. She had spent her 'wishful youth' (as she put it) enchanted by stories of the American West from her American neighbours. The father worked at the consulate. She was proud to have adopted the American vernacular. And now, at last, she had rebelled against stolid parental caution, stuffed her red tote bag with her collection of maps – her 'Western Islands' – and answered the ad placed by 'widowed American pilot'. Long Island wasn't west but it was an improvement in terms of narrowing the distance. And the pay would help.

She had a special island in mind, elusive – only a vision, a place she imagined with no asphalt or bulldozers or telephones. She saw herself defending it.

She studied herself in the living room mirror. 'Be a good girl,' her father had admonished. She had to stop thinking of herself as a girl. Dungarees and an old button-down shirt didn't do much to help the image, but she knew that without those clothes – without any – she was a beautiful woman.

The phone startled her. Mrs Carlton Hanks identified herself.

'Listen dear, have you heard from Mr Anders? Are they coming home?'

'I haven't heard,' said Anja.

'I don't know what to think, you know?' Anja listened and waited. It sounded as though the engineer's wife had been crying. 'I don't know what to think,' she repeated, seemingly unaware she was speaking to a stranger. 'Carlton isn't that young. He's been through four or five of these now, and tonight I thought about his chances running out.' Anja held her breath, not knowing how to handle this. Mrs Hanks went on, 'But you know, he'll just walk in with those smoke and grease smells on him, wash it off, and sit down in the kitchen and wait for something to eat.'

All at once Guy was standing in the doorway, shedding the last echoes of the night's bedlam. 'Hi . . .'

'Perhaps you shouldn't worry,' Anja said absently to Mrs Hanks and hung up. She looked at Guy.

He tried to speak but his voice caught. He wasn't sure if it was fatigue or the aftershock reaction to the life he

43

might never have seen again. 'Hi . . .' What a strange and innocent sound to come from his throat after his battle in the air. 'I didn't think you'd be up,' he added quietly. 'It wasn't part of the deal we made for you to wait up for me. But I appreciate it. The ad should have said "plus overtime".'

'It should have said a lot of things. I saw what happened on the news.'

Guy started upstairs. 'Did he?'

'He was asleep.'

Guy hesitated and came back down.

Up in his attic bedroom, Jamie had tried to stay awake, forcing his eyes open every few minutes. Now he heard the two voices below and got up on one elbow. His hair was ash-blond, his cheekbones high, he was small for seven. Guy's voice drifted towards him. He lay back, satisfied. At least his father would be home for a while. Secretly he wished Guy would come up and he wondered if he should make some noise to let him know he was still awake. But he decided not to. He was sore at Guy for leaving him alone and sticking him with another stranger. He turned to face the wall. He'd wait her out just like the others before her.

Guy came into the kitchen, his face framed by the soft lamplight. He was haggard, his eyes far away, still on final approach to JFK, the smell of machinery and the cockpit still about him. For an instant Anja was tempted to reach out to him. She wanted to choke it off and smother it but it overcame her. Impulsively she hugged him and planted a short kiss on his neck; and, just as quickly, drew back, businesslike again, as she took his coat and draped it over a chair. 'That wasn't personal,' she announced, keeping her back to him. 'It was ceremonial. I made you some coffee.'

Guy put a hand on the trembling percolator. The warmth was reassuring.

Anja was pleased all the elements of the house were

back under one roof. It was the way she had found it, allowing her to feel her obligation had ended. 'I want you to know I'm glad you're back. I mean that. But I don't think you should get too comfortable or take everything in your life for granted.' She paused. 'I've been struggling with this but I won't be staying,' she declared. 'I thought you should know that.'

Guy watched her from the corner of his eye. 'That's what I call a mixed greeting.'

'What?'

'Well, you embrace somebody, set him up with hot coffee, then whack him in the head.'

'I know I'm not picking the right time. But I'm very emotional tonight. I'm sorry. We won't discuss it now. I agree you deserve that much.'

'Thank you. That's mighty thoughtful.'

Anja pressed her hands together nervously. 'You almost orphaned a boy tonight!' she blazed.

'Now there you go again.'

'Well, that's what I was thinking! Here I am, alone in your home with your son, believing that you'd never come back. That upset me. Is that abnormal?' She waited for an answer but Guy offered none. Tears clouded her eyes. 'I prayed that wouldn't happen! I've been walking between the kitchen and front door praying that wouldn't happen! And so I kissed you when you came in. I'm sorry I did that. Is that abnormal? My God!'

Guy poured a cup of coffee and waited her out.

She dried her eyes. 'What happened to you tonight?'

'Since you'll be moving on, it doesn't matter, does it?'

'I didn't mean I would leave this second. I said that so I could be honest instead of being a polite employee and misleading you. You can deduct it from my pay.' Her tone softened. 'If you want to talk about what happened, I'll listen.'

'It's OK.'

'Don't be a martyr! I can't stand martyrs!'

45

He stared back across at her. 'Somebody screwed up.'

'Who?'

He opened the refrigerator, took out the tuna fish, walked to the bread box on the counter. 'I don't know. Somebody . . . someplace,' he said vacantly. 'Some union boy down in the hangar or out in the factory, somebody bored with aeroplanes . . . committed to time and a half and a pious devotion to fringe benefits.'

'I don't know if I was afraid for you tonight or for your mixed-up life . . . with a seven-year-old I can't get out of the attic, who won't talk to me and who doesn't know you any more. Everything is all business here.'

Guy noticed there were a few last traces of tomboy about her. He bit into his sandwich.

'I never see anyone smile here except on TV,' she accused.

He frowned.

'I guess I can't blame you for it,' she said.

'That's nice. Thank you.'

'The laughter on your TV is frantic and hysterical. It's dishonest. It's fixed.'

'As you see, we're not perfect. By now you've had a chance to see the city. The Twin Towers. How about that?' he asked, chewing.

'You won't like my answer.'

'OK, we'll let it pass.'

'Those buildings aren't for people!'

Guy sat down, watching.

'All you can do in your buildings here is stand out and be exposed. The building is in charge, the human being is just an intruder. I hate things that are new and improved. I'm not in love with the great benefits of technology. You seen, you made a terrible mistake.'

'Oh?'

'You hired the enemy.'

'I think you ought to go to bed and hate everything in the morning.' Guy smiled at her, cleaning up his dish.

46

'Don't laugh at me!'

'I'm not.'

'You're being superior. I'm trying to be direct.' She considered Guy as he stood pensively watching her. Her eyes had gone grey, her voice was almost sad. 'I don't like what you do for a living.'

'I had some thoughts about that myself tonight.'

'You may not believe this, but I know why there was a problem out there tonight . . .' Her gaze fixed him. 'And I don't know anything at all about your 17-10.'

Air World's chief exec, Matt Aspinwall, had been on his way to the Cape for two days' rest. He decided to drive; he wanted to be alone to contemplate the Big Season just ahead of him. But he had got only as far as the turnpike when he heard about Flight Six struggling to make it down. So he cut across to the nearest airport, called his wife to say he wouldn't be coming after all and dragged the owner of the local air taxi service out of bed to fly him back to Kennedy. It was nearly three in the morning when he ran up the steel gangway that led to the operations centre. He was a physical man, his scalloped copper-and-grey hair impervious to the wind, the expression around his eyes between mirth and ambition. He'd been Air World's number one since it had wobbled towards bankruptcy eight years ago and he'd staked his career and the company's long-range survival on the economic magic promised by fly-by-wire and the 17-10. At fifty-one he'd already had one heart attack, but he'd set aside the shock, picked himself up, lost weight, worked out, let the sun bake some youth back into his body, and he was beginning to catch up. Now he had to remain mellow, make calm decisions, make sure the nitro-glycerine tablets were always handy in his pocket. And know that Air World, destined to be first to go worldwide with the 17-10, would climb into the black and loft him to national prominence – from there, to the head of the nationalized US airline that would, out of financial necessity after the debacle of government overreaction to economic regulation, be formed to take over the entire nation's airline operations. Matt saw it coming and he meant to survive.

He was still dressed in a mohair sweater and corduroy slacks when he opened the door marked NO ENTRANCE, EMPLOYEES ONLY. The vast circular ops room was virtually empty now; the last of the passengers had left; Matt had missed it all. The heavy door slipped shut behind him. The night supervisor turned and was startled.

'Uh, Mr Aspinwall, sir.'

Matt surveyed the clutter of cups, the empty bottles and plastic duty-free shopping bags lying on the floor and caught the apprehensive expression on the supervisor's face. Other cautious faces peered out from behind glass partitions, aware that Air World's service had been disrupted, making them all a little less respectable. The supervisor stooped to pick up a paper plate at his feet as though recommencing what Matt had interrupted.

'Let it lay, son,' he said. 'There's gonna be time enough till morning.' Matt's voice was husky; he began to discover how upset he was by this setback and he felt it in his throat.

Slowly faces appeared as though emerging in surrender from a broken stronghold. Matt had never got entirely used to being a deity; he was suspicious of the ceremony. He handed a young assistant a set of keys to the executive locker next door. 'Unlock all the booze.' Matt circled to the glass wall that overlooked the field. A lone 727 trundled through a maze of purple-blue taxi lights.

'Where is Flight Six?' Max asked.

The night man stood uncertainly in the centre of the room.

'C maintenance dock in the west hangar,' he answered. 'They wanted to keep the frost off so they could get a better look at it.' Another man spoke up sharply. 'Sir, the crew has only been able to speculate about probable cause. They left an hour ago and the last group of passengers who missed their connections were taken to the International Hotel. Mr Moudon and his people are still downstairs compiling status reports. We've got a Tristar heading in from Detroit to cover the One-oh-one to San Juan and that should arrive in about two hours.' Aspinwall moved away from the window.

'Every once in a while some unexpected thing will come trottin' in from behind and bite you in the ass. Life's like that.' A half dozen employees looking like waiters invited to sit in at a board meeting stood uncomfortably holding their cups.

'Last one to get shitfaced gets fired,' boomed Matt with a broad grin. Guarded laughter. 'Well, let's see now. Sit down.' Matt was going to organize the situation for them. 'No serious injuries, correct?'

'No, sir. In fact we came out of it looking kind of heroic. People are grateful.'

Aspinwall smiled ruefully. 'I been advised to do just about everything from putting psychics on the payroll – and after the crash at Tenerife I'm not so sure that's a bad idea – to hiring the Joint Chiefs of Staff on weekends to teach us something about contingency planning. But there's no way to avoid it. Always something's gonna bite us in the ass. Tax man does it to me once a year, but then you have to be born evil to prey on your neighbour.' The mood in the room was beginning to change. 'Look, we're the top of the heap, the best airline going anywhere. So let's not walk around with baggy knickers just because some US citizen left a lit cigar in the crapper.'

Someone ran in with the morning paper. '421 ESCAPE FIERY DEATH AT KENNEDY', read the full-page banner. Aspinwall studied it, put it down. 'See if you can get someone from Advertising on the line. I hope no one decided to yank the commercials.'

'The agency said it would be discreet to go mute for twenty-four hours.'

'Oh, Christ, this is the time we need to sell *seats*, not anxiety! Somebody call and cancel that! What about the government? Expected them to be hoppin' up and down here like fleas on a hound dog.'

'Regional NTSB's been at it since midnight and their man from Washington rolled in about twenty minutes ago. His name is Doug Moss. We gave them all some coffee.'

'Doesn't hurt to be thoughtful,' Matt agreed. He stood up and scratched his head. 'Well now, as far as I know we're still going to Tokyo and London in the morning and we're still going to be the first airline with a 17-10 exclusive, so let's call in the stomp-and-polish brigade and clean this place up.' Then, turning to the night supervisor, he suggested, 'How about we take a ride to the hangar?' It was then the night man remembered.

'One more thing, sir,' he said apprehensively. 'Flight Thirty-two won't be coming from Paris tonight. It's a 17-10 and it's been grounded.'

'It's been what?' Matt let the door slam behind him. 'Grounded? What the hell for? What happened to it?'

'Nothing happened to it, sir.' The young man looked stricken but he knew he had to cough up the rest. 'The night dispatcher won't let her come ahead.'

'He won't what! He won't do what? Where is that sonofabitch?'

'In the telex room.'

'What time is it in Europe?'

'Nine o'clock, sir. In the morning.'

The night dispatcher, his head down, shoulders hunched, was leaning on the telex for support.

Matt's voice was calm. 'How come Thirty-two isn't airborne?'

'I have to call it the way I see it,' said the dispatcher.

Matt shifted to face the man and bent down a little. 'Which way do you see it?'

50

The dispatcher didn't budge. 'The crew was sharp tonight and they pulled it off,' he said quietly. 'Six is on the ground but it's still in the air for me.'

Matt stared at the man. 'But the outcome is no longer in doubt now, is it?' It was a statement.

The dispatcher nodded to a sheet of paper lying on the corner of his desk. 'That's the voice communication between Flight Six and Buttress. Somebody who thought it was more than a simple fire was cut off.' The night man picked up the sheet and glanced at it.

'Who was it?' asked Matt in a low voice.

'I don't know.'

'What did he say?'

'"Air World Six, this is Miller again. Would you have the engineer pull the circuit breaker . . ." It became a little garbled through here, like the man wasn't near the mike, but we think he said "the circuit breaker on panel seven labelled Computer Elevator Program A." We can't be sure. Then he was cut off completely. Right here, you can see for yourself.'

Aspinwall took the sheet of paper, not looking at it. 'Yeah? So?' He straightened the page by knocking the crease out of it, continuing to look past it, to study the night man.

The dispatcher stood, earnestly facing his boss. 'It's not so much *what* he said as *how* he said it.'

'How do you know how he said it?'

'The kid who brought it up heard it.'

Matt folded the sheet, stuffed it in his back pocket. 'Now you let me get this straight. You want to shut down this whole airline because somebody got excited during a patched-through transmission while one of our planes was making an emergency descent. I think that's what I'm hearing. You want to take the ball that's taken us eight years to get to the one-yard line and hand it to the other side, give the foreign carriers a score they couldn't get any other way! Let me remind you, no one was killed! One

51

dislocated shoulder, one warm body so loaded he goes down the chute upside down.'

The dispatcher took a clipboard off the wall. 'Here's something else. Two pages of phone calls, and that's only in the last hour: everyone from Independence for Puerto Rico to Amnesty for Hijackers is taking credit for Flight Six.'

'So pull an extra security check in Paris! Look between their toes! But you let those engines turn and you bring those precious customers home on Air World!'

'Sorry, sir, I've cancelled Flight Thirty-two whether you like it or not. I have that authority.'

Matt wanted to grin. Here was a man he could understand, young and principled, both balls hanging out, and Matt wanted to let him have the moment, to give him something he could one day take to his son and tell him how he'd stood up to the boss, how he'd kept his morality intact.

'In a way, I envy you, mister. You can take a stand on what you think has to be with Air World Thirty-two, and then go home. I have to take a stand too, but without throwing in the towel – for all of us.' His voice was mellow but stern. 'Now you sign that release and you rap out a "come ahead" on that keyboard and you do it *allegro con gusto*.'

'No, sir. If you want it signed, you'll have to sign it.' The dispatcher was adamant.

'Then I guess you better get out of the way.'

The young man blocked Matt's path. 'Are you relieving me, sir?'

'You bet your ass I am.'

'Are you saying I'm fired?'

Matt paused. Then smiled. 'Hell, no.' He put an arm around the night man. 'What is this, Friday morning? Come back Tuesday. You may be a pain in the ass but I'll take that over a yes-man any time.'

Matt rubbed his hands together, found the code for Air

World in Paris, and typed. 'CDGOWAW. GO. RELEASE FLIGHT AW32. CONFIRM. ASPINWALL.'

He waited, then the carriage reset and the keys clacked an answer. 'CONFIRM YOU ARE ASPINWALL.'

He stared at the scroll waiting for something else to happen. But nothing did. So he keyed in Paris and typed, 'IDENTIFY YOURSELF.'

'I AM JEAN CLAUDE EPICIER, PARIS STATION MANAGER,' came the reply.

Matt picked up the phone and dialled the operator. 'Give me Paris,' he boomed. The fatigue seemed to catch up with him all at once. He fingered the nitro tablets impatiently and waited. After a few moments he was connected to Jean Claude Epicier.

'Listen, you French whoremaster, you release that flight, you comprenez, monsieur?'

There was a startled pause and then an American voice cut in. 'Sir, this is Captain Dawkins. I'm on the line, too.'

'Well, now, how am I coming across, Captain?'

'Five by. We're on our way, sir.'

The West Coast press had been waiting in front of the Buttress PR office when Snethler, the new addition to the PR staff, rushed in. He held a hand up against the barrage of questions as he passed.

'There'll be a press conference sometime this morning!' he shouted. One voice cut through. 'Is the 17-10 a mistake?' The babble stopped. Snethler looked scared, 'All I can say is there's nothing wrong with the plane.'

'Is Buttress responsible for pilot training?' insisted the querulous voice.

'Only to the extent we train the carrier's instructors.'

'Was pilot error or unfamiliarity with the plane a factor in the seriousness of the fire?'

Snethler thought, then a little uncertainly replied, 'Procedure is always a factor, isn't it?'

'Hey now, that's misleading,' Guy said when he saw this replayed on 'The Morning Show'. He'd dozed off on the couch, awakened with the sounds of cars leaving for work and turned on the tube. The picture dissolved to a long indistinct shot of Air World Six, fire trailing from the starboard engine . . .

'As relatives and friends who had come to greet the arrival gathered on the observation deck, with life and death still hanging one hundred and fifty feet in the air, ABS's Chris Maldino caught this remarkable sequence . . .'

Guy found the number for ABS.

'American Broadcasting System, good morning.' The voice was genuinely attractive.

'I'd like to speak to somebody in the newsroom, please.'

'TV or radio?'

'TV.'

'Thank you.' An extension rang.

'Hello. News,' came a clipped voice.

'Who is this?'

'You've got the newsroom.'

'My name is Guy Anders. I'm one of the people who flew that 17-10 you've got on the air right now.'

'Yes, sir, we've already finished our piece on the passengers.' The sound was impatient.

'I'm the co-pilot. My name is Anders.'

'Oh.' The voice became solicitous. 'Hold one, sir.' There was a click. Presently a new voice, like malted milk, came on the line.

'OK, you say you were the co-pilot? And your name, sir?'

'Anders. I'm Guy Anders.'

'Do you have any objection if we tape this?'

'No, you go ahead and tape it.'

'OK, shoot.'

'I think that Buttress spokesman who's on the air ought to re-evaluate his statement.'

'On what basis?'

54

'On the basis that he may have been shooting his mouth off.'

'Was there a specific cause for what happened?'

'I don't want to imply anything against Buttress Aerospace as yet. It's a fine operation, but they're probably human like everybody else, and so statements like that fellow is making should be taken with a great deal of salt.'

'Can we read an inference there?'

'You write what you want. But no, no inference.' Guy smiled.

G. Hollis Wright, Board Chairman of Buttress Aerospace Corporation, sitting alone at the head of the enormous polished table in Buttress's hushed boardroom, heard Guy Anders's phone conversation as it was re-broadcast for the West Coast as a voice-over against the dramatic footage of the 17-10 rolling to a stop in New York. He pressed the remote control and the TV picture died. He carefully refilled his coffee cup, sipped it, wiped his hands on the linen napkin and pushed the coffee tray to one side of the conference table. It was ten o'clock. G. Hollis Wright, white-headed patriarch of American aviation, appeared as a point of light in the centre of the dark mahogany cavern. *Business At Large* magazine had voted Hollis Wright one of America's historic leaders, comparing his visionary instincts to those of the nation's founders. Now he sat, reflective, ever so slightly wizened, but his blue eyes glittered. He punched the phone and immediately a secretary's confident voice came on. 'Yes, sir?'

'The name is Guy Anders,' Wright said calmly. 'He's a co-pilot for Air World – flew right seat on that Flight Six incident last night. I want a confidential report on his background.' The secretary started to say, 'Yes, sir,' but Hollis Wright had already released the connection.

It was now four o'clock over the fifteenth meridian. Air World Thirty-two was six hundred miles out of Paris.

Air World Six had been rolled to secluded quarters and, like a wealthy patient in the private wing of a hospital, sat waiting for the arrival of the more senior medical team.

Matt Aspinwall was still several blocks away, his cast-iron frame moving like a piston, dominating the cavernous chain of maintenance bays.

'Where the hell does that peckerhead pilot get the starch to shoot his mouth off that way on national TV! We have a rule against that, goddammit! Doesn't anybody read the memos that get sent around any more? We're in spitting distance of the biggest season this company has ever seen . . . and I was going to give the sonofabitch a medal!'

Behind him strode a freshly arrived Buttress man and the NTSB man and two Air World lackeys, the short one turkey-trotting to keep up.

'There better not be anything wrong with that ship that can't be fixed with a goddamn ball peen hammer!'

The entourage said nothing, silently heeding the pace Matt beat out for them.

A thousand miles away Air World Thirty-two knifed through high cirrus wisps pouring its swirling contrails among the quicksilver tendrils that fell behind at almost nine miles a minute. The crew, peering through green transparent visors clipped to windshield lugs, were unable to see the eastern sky to the rear that already thickened purple in the earth's shadow. The captain had taped the five-hundred-millibar weather map to cover his number two window and block the sun that relentlessly paced their flight. It was a long moment of suspended reverie in the cockpit. The crew didn't speak. One corner of the map along the window's edge fluttered slightly. The flight engineer adjusted his air vent.

Almost fifty yards behind them a passenger rubbed his stale face and, stumbling slightly on half-asleep legs, moved back along one aisle to the line of vacant-faced bodies waiting to use the rear bathrooms. There was always a jam-up after the movie finished. He spoke a quiet word to one of the flight attendants, who presently handed him an electric razor, kept aboard as a convenience. There was only the barest ripple underfoot as the plane bored onward.

In New York day workers, curious about the damaged 17-10, slowly circled the crippled jet but kept their distance. Matt Aspinwall, his feet planted like oars, hands on hips, was standing underneath the fuselage intent on work being performed inside the plane's shredded underbelly.

Doug Moss, the NTSB man from Washington, had just stepped out on to the scaffold that framed the tail above and placed a blackened piece of steel on a white sheet.

'When are these whiz kids gonna come up with something?' Aspinwall rasped.

Vic Moudon's face was slick and grey, his clothes shabby from bird-dogging the Air World Six incident for ten uninterrupted hours. 'Should have a reading sometime later today, sir.' Vic didn't like being Matt Aspinwall's lackey. He felt obligated to say something more but all he could think of was yes, sir, no, sir, you bet your ass, sir, when the fuck can I go home, sir. Instead he added, 'Real shame.' Aspinwall remained still, following the moves made above him.

High above the fifty-third parallel of latitude, the first officer couldn't tell if the captain harboured any concerns about the Air World Six landing at Kennedy. Probably not. Occasionally the old man studied the EPR gauges and touched the throttles delicately in turn, monitoring the subtle power adjustments made by the computer to account for the vagaries in the razor-thin sea that sustained them, a degree of temperature change, another thousand pounds of fuel burned.

The inboard throttles tingled his fingertips, the only expression of the plane's vast motion.

Finally it was the passenger's turn to use the bathroom. He unpeeled one of the tiny bars of soap and filled the sink with warm water, sloshing it clean first. As he studied his face in the mirror he was aware of how dimly lit the room was.

Or had it just gone dim?

He dried his face and plugged in the razor. Funny, it seemed to run slow. He checked its 110/220 switch – no, it was still set at 110. He placed the shaver next to his chin; just then its raucous buzzing grew louder. The razor was whining, becoming hot. The passenger winced and changed hands. Just as suddenly, its noise subsided. What the hell's wrong with this thing? the passenger puzzled. He unplugged it with a grunt. No telling how many people had used it before him. He splashed on some aftershave and turned the bathroom over to the next in line.

'I'll tell you this much, we're not going to take a bloody nose on this.' Aspinwall's jaw was set. He turned towards Vic and faced him full on, like a searchlight finding its mark. Vic flinched in the glare. 'Can't afford to be nitpicking at this stage of the game. So far nobody's found anything critical on that bird, right?' Aspinwall's question burned into Moudon, demanding an answer.

'Right,' Moudon echoed, surprised at the conviction in his voice.

The response pleased Matt. 'That's right,' he said as he led the group away.

A young employee approached. 'Mr Aspinwall, sir, the ad agency's here.'

Matt saw four men with expectant, apprehensive expressions waiting inside the exit. 'Ah, for Pete's sake, not here!' he moaned. One fellow, slightly more self-assured, stepped off a white minibus which disgorged easels, large covered cards, cans of film and a projector. Matt smiled. 'Ah, the bullshit brigade.'

'We asked them to rig your screening in the maintenance conference room. They're up against a deadline and they need your approval.'

Minutes later the conference-room screen was lit with a spectacular view of an Air World 17-10 punching through puffy cloud floes, then peeling dramatically away. 'These are the first answer prints of the new TV commercials,' a voice said in the semidarkness. 'We felt that Air World's old motto – "Fly the Routes of the Tradewinds" – was outmoded, Victorian. It made you sound, frankly, like you were operating the *Santa Maria* and *Pinta*, not a modern jet-propelled airline. So we've dispensed with that, and upgraded the whole effect.'

Matt Aspinwall sat motionless, his face like carved stone in the backlight. Sleek images danced before him. But behind him in stark contrast, through the partially draped window overlooking the vast maintenance bay below, could be seen the real 17-10, its blackened tail immense as white-sheathed men crawled among its flukes, and probed there.

Another two-dimensional view of a 17-10, approaching head on, giant engines spewing, slicing beneath the camera's view, rolled by on one wall. 'We've adopted a new theme and matched it to some contemporary music, quiet, elegant jazz. It's coming up. Our new pitch is – "A New Curve in the Sky! A New *Feel* in the Sky."' The music swelled. Clapping began in the darkness. At first only two people were heard to clap enthusiastically from the corner where the admen had congregated, but the

applause grew. As the clapping swelled, it seemed disso-
nant in the metallic setting, ringing hollowly, as if in
defiance of the damaged 17-10 below.

'All right, that's enough.' Matt's voice was a bark.
'Turn the lights on.'

The applause died lamely, prematurely. Matt sat immo-
bile, facing the now blank wall.

'I think your ad is not only in bad taste, I think it's
obscene,' he snapped. His voice rose. 'A new *feel* in the
sky? Feeling up who? We're not running floating whore-
houses. Go sell all the feels you want, but not with this
airline.'

The adman with long hair was stung. Faces of the others
opened in bewilderment.

Aspinwall continued, 'It's no good. You came for my
reaction, well then, you've got it in a nutshell. The whole
thing stinks.' The modish adman brushed the hair from his
eyes and cleared his throat.

'You misunderstand – '

'Yeah, and if I do, what about all the stiffs we're trying
to peddle tickets to? We're not selling sex, we're selling a
new concept of flying – '

'Your new concept of flying *feels good* to the passenger,
Mr Aspinwall, so just how – '

'I'll tell you right now. You're not saying what we want
said. Air World is providing a new day of flying. You
didn't get that in. And you didn't get in the idea that this is
a new kind of flight – a new kind of aeroplane – the first
true computer-age transport. Goddammit, you talk to me
about outmoded Victorian concepts, but your ad looks
like we're still running 707's to Bermuda. We're not
jerking honeymooners back and forth to Bermuda, we're
talking about a Global Season. We're the first ones in line
with the 17-10 – a revolution in the sky! We want to
exploit *that!* You missed the whole point.'

In the pained silence the admen threw despairing
glances at each other.

Aspinwall continued. 'Let me make it simple for you. Say you had a bow and arrow, you shot an arrow with no feathers in back. Would that arrow go straight?'

'Well, I guess not – ' the adman faltered.

'You bet your sweet ass you guess not.' Matt Aspinwall's words had a certain blunt way of crushing equivocation. 'That arrow would flip end over end. Totally unstable. But that's what we're doing here. We're flying aeroplanes like that arrow – aeroplanes with no tail feathers. Why? To get the weight and drag down, the payload up. Where it once took seventeen feet of rudder, it now takes nine. We almost cut it in half. And when you chop out all those steel beams and girders and leave them lying on the floor, they don't eat fuel that way.'

'Yes, but – ' The adman wanted to explain this sort of thing wasn't exactly appropriate for mass advertising.

'I know, I know,' Aspinwall interrupted, 'you're going to ask how do we keep the aeroplane from flipping over like the arrow. That's where the *computer* comes in. The plane wants to flip, sure, but the instant it starts to veer off, the computer sends a signal to our half-sized control surfaces. In milli-seconds they correct the plane's path, keep it straight. The plane starts off in the other direction. Another signal. Continuous. Faster than the blink of a human eye, but so smooth the passengers don't know it's happening. We've handed over the intelligence of the flying process to a computer. The technology has taken the control away from the pilot – because he could never do all these things by himself. It had to be done with electronics – *fly-by-wire*. And Air World is the first fly-by-wire airline with the 17-10. Put *that* in my ads!'

Matt underscored the numbers they were dealing with, throwing glances like barbs to the Air World and Buttress people in the room. 'For the first time in years we have an aeroplane with the chance to make real profits.'

'Pardon me, Mr Aspinwall,' said a young man who had rushed in and waited in shadows nearby. 'We thought you'd like to know: Air World Thirty-two made it from Paris OK – he just landed, he'll be on the blocks in five minutes.'

'So what?' Aspinwall grew impatient at the implication. 'I didn't know *that* was supposed to make news. Who the hell's flying it? Amelia Earhart? Do they want a medal? Look, let me say something to everyone here: get out of this trance about whether we can get across the Atlantic or not. We've been doing it several times daily for more than thirty years!'

Two miles away Air World Thirty-two nudged into its glass-walled dock. The doors slid open, hordes of people filed into the terminal. A couple of Air World mechanics waited unobtrusively in the jetway until the last of the passengers had stumbled by. The first officer, briefcase in hand and cap perched on his head, was leaving, the captain was buttoning his coat. He turned to the lead mechanic. 'Don't you guys touch nothin'! You got a great ship heah. Yawl just go flush the toilets.'

Inside the hangar Matt Aspinwall turned towards the others. 'Anybody here like that ad?'

Silence.

'OK. Now go back to your office and work up something that tells that message.' The Buttress man's bemused expression indicated he had no stake in this contest.

Aspinwall turned on him, his voice lowered. 'I gather *you* understand what we're trying to do here. I assume we're not in for any more unpleasant surprises.' He threw an over-the-shoulder glance at Air World Six in the bay below. 'I've got to *rely* on that jumbo. That plane delivers,' he warned, 'or we're all going to hold hands in the slaughterhouse.'

3

It was a quarter to three in the morning on the West Coast. G. Hollis Wright stared at the full moon, unable to sleep. He watched the string on his linen window shade turn slowly in the slight breath of air that stirred the dark mimosa trees outside.

The silhouettes of distant iron gates were indistinct at the end of his lawn. His wife's Jaguar was parked on the blue cinder driveway. He flicked on the light and fumbled on the bedside table for his glasses, reached for the green memorandum lying on his night table. Typed in capitals and spaced across the top of the front page was the word CONFIDENTIAL and below it REPORT ON FIRST OF-FICER GAVIN ANDERS, AIR WORLD EMPLOYEE #07362. The chairman lifted the cover sheet.

EDUCATION: High school diploma. One year logging in Alaska. 4 years university; Bachelor of Science Aeronautical Engineering. Class standing 234 out of 613.

MILITARY: First lieutenant, US Air Force. High student honours in flight school. Qualified pilot F-4 Phantom. 1273 hours. Crash landed Luke Air Force Base after hydraulic failure. Base investigation not unanimous as to probable cause . . .

AIRLINE: Eight years' service, Air World. Current seniority number 789. Airline Transport Pilot Licence number 1516273 with type ratings on Boeing 707 and Buttress 17-10. Currently first officer, 17-10, International Division.

OTHER: Active in Air Line Pilots Association (ALPA) and International Federation of Air Line Pilot Associations (IFALPA) air safety committees for six years. Attended government/industry meeting in Washington highly critical of certification process. Not politically oriented.

There was more, but Hollis decided to get a drink before going further. When he sat down again he read:

MEDICAL: FAA medicals: no waivers. Appendectomy at 17, broken leg when freshman in college. Medications and psychiatric counselling during wife's illness.

MARITAL: Unmarried. First wife died (cancer) thirteen months ago. One son, James, age 7. Attended by new housekeeper.

FINANCIAL: Owns home, Long Island. Outstanding mortgage of $53,700. Two tax audits in the last five years. Owed back taxes three figures. Late payment of $8,000 on wife's medical bills. No outstanding debts. Airline group insurance. Airline pension fund, vested for $54,000.00.

LEGAL: Four parking fines in last four years. One fine for moving violation (55 in a 25 mph zone). No accidents. Standard will.

PERSONAL: Drinks malt whiskey.

PRESENT: Subject Anders has been observed with journalist B. Reese, whose recent series of articles critical of Buttress was discredited.

Hollis turned back to the item of the Phantom crash landing listed under MILITARY, stared at it and then, thumbing through his private phone book, found the number he wanted under PRESS.

In Los Angeles, Ben Reese, discredited journalist, didn't know if it was the second ring or if it had been ringing for a long time. Since his forced retraction of allegations against Buttress, he'd taken to sleeping late. He got out of bed, confused, his eyes still shut, and waited for another ring to give him a clue as to which room he'd left the phone in the night before. It was on the floor next to him.

'Yeah.' Ben cleared his throat. It was *The Wall Street Journal*.

'Could we interest you in a subscription that might change the rest of your life?'

'"Might" is too risky.' Reese recognized the calm voice of an elderly colleague who used to breakfast with him when they covered the White House. 'Now that you've tromped around on my brain, the answer is yes, I'll help if I can. How you been, Len?'

64

'It's Leon.'

'What the hell's the difference?'

'Ben, I have a story fed to us by one of our stringers west of the divide. It says Guy Anders, identified as co-pilot Air World Flight Six, once made a mess of a crash landing in a Phantom. You know Anders pretty well, Ben my boy. Just how well do you know him?'

'Why the interest?' yawned Ben, scratching his back.

'The angle of the piece is frankly pro business. Anyway, all I want to know from you, true or false? If it's true, you have my word we'll draw no half-assed conclusions.'

'If you print that, they're going to put your face on a T-shirt next to mine.'

'Then it's crap, huh?'

'Of the scurrilous variety.' Ben cleared his throat again, regarded the clock and asked solicitously, 'Tell me, Len, who's your source?'

'I'm not at liberty.'

Ben glanced at the receiver with unfeigned contempt. 'I'm sorry to say I am.'

Anja was peering through the venetian blinds at the few competitive news teams, each loosely huddled, one individual checking his watch, all seemingly waiting for a consensus to develop as to whether to go or stay.

'It's like they're waiting for someone to jump,' Anja said. Her hair was knotted and stuck through with a little ornament, her figure trim and fetching in jeans and a tight T-shirt. 'I took the TV upstairs. There's somebody up there who thinks you're a new bulletin.' She took something from the table. 'I found this on the staircase.' It was the trumpet Guy had bought for Jamie in Brussels over a year ago, a classic horn, and the boy had been fascinated by it. But now the bell had been crushed, the silver mouthpiece was missing. Guy said nothing. Things had changed. That was made indelible to him before he left for his last trip to London. 'See ya,' he'd said and his son had faced him and something unspoken began to form. But it faltered and sank, then slowly reassembled behind his child's eyes. Guy saw the struggle. What he couldn't see was that the boy wanted to say that he hated and loved his father at the same time and that he didn't know how to say it. He looked betrayed, bewildered at not being able to speak at all.

They should have moved, Guy thought.

The phone rang. Guy examined the horn, placed it on the table and scooped the receiver.

'Yeah, hello?'

'Listen, Guy?'

'That's me.'

'It's going to be important that you not give any other interviews until after we've had a chance to find out what really happened to you out there last night.' The voice was unfamiliar.

'What?'

'I'm calling you as a friend.'

'Who is this?'

'I just wanted you to know.' Guy waited for more but the line went dead.

Guy replaced the receiver and stared at it. He checked the street. A camera crew was sorting through its gear.

'Who was it?' Anja asked.

'That's one thing you're going to learn about the States,' Guy said. 'You make news in this country and all the cranks head for the phone.'

'What did he say?'

'It's not important.'

Someone had turned a light on outside. Anja watched as Guy stood facing the backlit venetians. She'd seen him stand like that before . . . Was it a *déjà vu* or a premonition? She'd seen his figure like that, in a free fall above the earth, his back arched against the dome of the sky, his body caught in diagonal shards of brilliant sunshine and, like a swimmer reaching for his first stroke, trying to fly but in her dream he was trapped in a raft of metal beams and there was a pleading in his eyes . . .

Anja couldn't alter the image she had of this man, trapped, airborne, caught behind silver mesh.

The doorbell startled her. 'Will you answer it?'

Guy motioned for her to move to the side. 'Stay out of the way.' He opened the door to the people outside. It was already dark.

'Sorry, fellows, I've got no more to say,' he told them.

'Didn't you say earlier that Buttress made an incorrect statement?'

'No, I didn't say that,' Guy said wearily.

'Could you repeat what you said earlier?'

'Look, if anyone gets in touch with me with anything new, you leave me your phone number and we'll get together.'

Somebody aimed a hand-held camera at the door and tried to move into the house. Guy blocked him.

'Now, come on, I've been awake for two days. Don't do that.'

'Do you have any idea why the lights went out over Cedarhurst when your plane passed overhead?'

'I didn't know they went out.' Guy didn't get the point of the question. 'Did we start a fire anywhere?' He heard the phone ring once inside.

'No, but the power companies are at a loss to explain it.'

'I don't think I can help you on that one.'

'What will you be doing next?'

'Going to bed. I don't know if it'll help your story but I do that without any clothes on. You can come in and watch provided you don't make any noise.'

The crew stood looking at him uncertainly. Guy eased the door shut.

The thing about Cedarhurst interested him.

* * *

The phone had been replaced and Anja was working on a pizza for delivery upstairs when Guy walked in.

'Who was it?'

Anja barely heard him. The words just spoken to her by phone were jammed inside her head. She found it impossible to reduce them. Her hands spread the dough. 'I'm trying to understand something. I want to know whether I should be scared about what's going on around here or whether all this is normal. I can't get a clue from your face.'

'Crisis training.'

'What?'

'We get that in cockpit school. They exchange our emotions for checklists.'

'That's the very thing that I'm finding – unusual. No, let me be more specific. There are things happening and you're just watching them happen. There's smoke in your clothes and I don't even think you stopped to think about that. There are crank calls and you shrug. You have no relationship with your son and there you are, Cool Hand Luke on the throttle – but the right stuff doesn't work here. This is your kitchen! That's just a little of what I've been seeing.'

'Are you finished?'

'No, I think I can do better!'

'I'm certain of it.'

'It's like you're willing to do nothing and accept the worst.' Frustrated with the pizza dough she blurted, 'And what in the world are you doing running a catering service for your son?'

'I'm a soft touch.'

'It's not normal.'

'Now look, you better get something straight. I've been handling things around here long before you got here. Alone.'

'With admirable competence,' she sniped.

'So maybe you're superfluous around here.'

68

She stared at him, eyes blazing, hands on hips. 'So you think I'm superfluous?' Anja untied her apron and banged it on the table. 'Is that right?'

'It's got a good ring to it.'

'And just how long has this opinion been brewing?'

'It's a revelation – just came up on me.'

'Did you know that you're a very defended person?'

'Defended?'

'Blocked. It's amazing you don't clank when you go upstairs, you've got so much armour plate on.'

'Tomorrow you can go through your travel folders and shove off for Tibet.' The prospect of eliminating this waspish creature from his life was like tonic for the moment.

'I don't think you realize you're heading for a . . . crisis.'

'The only crisis is the one in this room.'

'You want to think about getting a little help. Find out what's eating you. I'm talking about your son.'

'He's none of your business!'

'Then why did you hire me?'

Guy looked up, surprised. 'OK, that's a fair question. That's a very fair question. I want to thank you for the question!' Guy took her by the arm, steered her through the kitchen. 'You've put your finger on it! I know now what's been eating me!' He grabbed her case of maps standing by the door and deposited it and its owner on to the stoop. 'I want to thank you for figuring it out!' He handed her her raincoat. Anja was too stunned to object. 'Let me know your next address and I'll have whatever you forgot shipped!'

A reporter started for the door but Guy shut it in his face.

Guy wandered around inside. He heard the clock on the mantel and fully expected it to be interrupted by a brick sailing through the window but nothing happened. He went into the living room and waited, standing rock-still, listening for some telltale sound.

Nothing.

He peered through the curtained window. Anja was standing in the middle of the street, facing the house, her arms folded defiantly. A battery-operated light was on but he couldn't make out what the TV people were doing. Her raincoat was draped over her shoulders like a cape; Superwoman, Guy thought. Christ. But frailer than that, too. He paced the kitchen and stuck his hand into the wet dough. He was reminded of a story he'd heard about an executive at some company throwing the gauntlet down in the boss's office, turning on his heel and marching straight into the coat closet. Tough to undo.

Guy smacked the pie dough back on to the plate, crossed to the foyer and yanked the front door open.

'OK, you can come back in!'

Anja didn't budge. 'Hell, no!'

'What do you mean, "Hell, no"?'

'I'm furious!'

'It's understandable!'

'To hell with you!'

'OK.'

'I've got conditions!'

'Fine!'

Sunguns were snapped on and shoulder pods raised, cameras aimed. A reporter took his cue and began, 'I'm standing here in front of the home of Air World co-pilot Gavin Anders –'

Anja marched past, entered the house and cut the reporter off with a slam of the door. Guy reopened it and retrieved the suitcase.

'Had your fun?' She smiled as she walked away. 'Does this mean you want me to stay?'

'I suppose it does.'

'You better be more positive about it.'

'Why?'

'Because now the only way that will happen is on *my* terms. Would you care to know what they are?'

'Yeah, OK.'

70

'"Yeah, OK" isn't overwhelming.'

'You didn't read the exclamation points.'

'First, I have to be allowed to be honest. *Neither* of us is superior. You don't pay enough to be superior.' Her eyes flashed a warning. 'Second, there are things I've noticed here in this house – in which I have to live too – that I want to feel free to talk about.'

'Well?'

'You haven't shown the slightest emotion about anything, not since I arrived, not about last night, not about your boy who won't talk to me, not about what's going on out there . . . You're like a visiting ghost. You come by to water the plants.'

Guy hung his head. 'OK, who was on the phone before?'

Anja removed her coat from her shoulders and dropped it on the table. 'He didn't leave his name. He only said, "It's ten o'clock. Do you know where the Anders boy is?"'

Guy stared at the grain on the butcher block and tried to shift this new development on to a harmless track. Anja didn't help him. He strained to hear a reassuring sound from upstairs but the house was silent. Anja watched as he bolted and heard him take the stairs two at a time. When he returned he unplugged both phone lines.

'Crank calls, huh?'

'He's OK; he's watching from the window,' Guy explained.

'The attic.'

'Best seat in the house.'

'I can see why he stays in the attic because of me. I'm the latest uninvited female who has the authority to take his clothes off. But he was up there before I came. That doesn't bother you, does it?'

'No, I don't suppose it does.'

'The trumpet bothers you, doesn't it?'

Guy studied the pot of geraniums his wife had hung over the sink two years before. 'Yes, it does.' Seeing the

71

unfinished challenge on her face, he added quietly, 'Things'll turn out.'

'Just a little turbulence.'

'Something like that.'

'The captain has turned off the seat-belt sign.'

'I'll let you smoke, too. Here, want a cigar?' He grinned, unwrapping a panatela, but sensing her disgust he stopped. 'Defensive, huh?' he admitted. He put it away, poured a glass of mineral water instead and sat down.'OK,' he relented finally, 'you're so smart . . .'

Anja gathered and smoothed the pizza dough. 'Your son stepped on the trumpet because it was around' – Guy looked up quizzically – 'and you weren't.' Guy concentrated on the bubbles in his glass. 'You're the last serious goodbye he's got left,' Anja continued. 'There's a lot that's not being said in this house. Straightforward things. The ad you placed was dishonest. "Work for American pilot and small son who are inseparable." That's what the ad said.'

'I guess maybe "inseparable" was wishful thinking on my part.'

'I'd know how to rewrite that ad.'

He resisted the first flip response that came to him. Instead he said, uneasily, 'There was a time when Jamie and I talked to each other a lot.' As he said it, he reluctantly acknowledged to himself that his wife had always been better at it than he.

'And now you're down to a checklist,' Anja said sadly. 'Some people solve problems by moving away from them. With your flying schedule you can solve at least a dozen a month. That way you never have to get to the mourning or let anyone poke your feelings.' She held her breath for an instant, then continued, 'There is something you ought to know. I'm a professional rescuer. It pisses everybody off. But that's who I am.' She waited for some acknowledgment. None came. Softly she asked, 'Did your son ever see you cry when your wife died?'

72

Guy placed his glass on the table and stood up to leave the room.

She regretted sounding too caustic but fired another salvo to stop him. 'Last night, before you returned, Mrs Hanks called. She said all her husband would do after something like that is just come home and eat a sandwich. That's just what you did.'

'I think we were both grateful we could still eat.'

'I was thinking about it when you came in – that something was missing.'

'What would you like to have seen?'

'You should have put a hand through the wall,' she remonstrated sharply.

The shoe was pinching, he was becoming exasperated. 'Maybe I would have done it the next day.'

'This *is* the next day.'

The only sound in the room was the faucet dripping. Suddenly his fatigue, her barbs, the after-echoes of Flight Six, his expanding sense of bewilderment over his son and the anonymous threats – all reached the boiling point. Anja watched wide-eyed as he placed a framed picture on the counter, spit on his fist, took careful aim and unloaded a mighty haymaker straight at the wall. A foot-wide area fractured into dust. 'Like that?' he said, turning to her with a reckless look in his eye.

'You meant that for me. Didn't you?'

'I don't know, I don't know.' Guy was having trouble keeping up.

'I know.'

'Well, you wanted emotion! That's emotion! Look at that!' Guy yelled, examining the damaged wall. 'They make these houses out of crap!'

'Why didn't you do that last night?'

He turned back to her questioningly.

'When it counted!' she implored, working the pizza dough fretfully.

Guy rubbed his fist thoughtfully, came over to where

she was standing and took the pizza dough from her. 'You're going to worry this stuff to death.' He took over, kneading it vigorously. 'I was grateful we pulled it out. How am I supposed to get angry about that?' His energy with the pizza dough had ebbed. He was slowly shaking his head.

'"Somebody screwed up." You said it last night – and you accepted it.' She delivered it as a reprimand.

'No, I didn't accept it,' he said curtly. 'I called the network. Why do you think they have this street wired? Look outside, I'm a damn celebrity! They're gonna put me on the news between a word from the Carpet Freak and a hairspray!'

'Your statement was very correct and inoffensive. You nearly genuflected. And you just did the same again! It was totally unmemorable!' She'd become provoked and excited; she wanted her disapproval to touch something inside him. 'You ate a sandwich and accepted it. I had to be angry *for* you. You didn't put any part of yourself into it.'

He bristled. 'What part did you have in mind?' He saw her ire near the surface. 'Careful, now.' A slow smile formed at the corners of his mouth. 'I need all the parts I have. I look 'em over every morning.'

'Have you looked to see where you checked your feelings?'

Guy saw defiance in her eyes. He walked a few steps into the middle of the kitchen floor, intent on his clasped hands. The hole in the wall, the prominence of it, was a badge – gratifying, yet ignoble. He looked up at her, finally relenting. 'OK . . . You're right.' He watched her helplessly, with warmth creeping into his eyes. 'Who the hell asked you to come here?' He turned his attention to the pizza, thought again of Jamie in the attic. 'What are we doing here, running a catering service?' He tried to recover, hesitating.

Anja rescued the moment. 'I'll make sure he doesn't starve . . .'

'Well, then, throw me that tie. No, to hell with the tie.' He measured the distance to the door. 'OK, so it's time to be memorable.'

Outside Guy confronted the remarkable spectacle of two additional TV mini-vans pulled up to the curb. As soon as he appeared on the doorstep, three news crews and a couple of loners moved their portable gear up the lawn in front of him. One with headphones and slightly hysterical eyes shoved a mike wearing an egglike windshield at his face.

'Sorry to keep you people waiting,' Guy began. A couple of sunguns were snapped on, momentarily blinding him.

'Mr Anders – is there another aspect to your earlier statement?'

'Mr Anders – do you have anything to add to what you said earlier?'

For the moment Flight Six and now Guy Anders were part of the TV ratings war.

'Yeah, there is something I'd like to add.' Guy waited until the cameramen stopped moving. 'That comment about procedures that Buttress PR fellow made is a crock.' One microphone came in a little closer. 'We even tried to get help directly from Buttress with a phone patch but they wouldn't give us any.'

'Is this based on some new information?'

'Nope. Just that what I said before wasn't quite complete . . . and it was too charitable.'

'Then is there something wrong with the aeroplane?'

'Yeah, there's sure as hell something wrong with *that* aeroplane. And if the rest are anything like that firebird, then there's something wrong with all of them!' He felt rash and rejuvenated as he searched their faces. 'The point I'm making to you is, there was no pilot error. Make sure you get that straight.'

There was a pause until one of the reporters asked carefully, 'Do you want to let the implication stand?'

'You're damn right I do.'

Guy nodded pleasantly, seeing that he hadn't displeased them, turned on his heel and re-entered the house. He slammed the door and stood against it, hands and feet out, facing into the living room, surprised at the depth of his breathing. Anja was before him.

'How'd I do?' he asked.

'Not bad for a start.'

The next morning Guy made his way downstairs to call Ben Reese. A can of worms had been opened; the time had come to involve an ally. Although he knew only too well of Ben's reputation for journalistic broadsides, often devastatingly accurate but sometimes embarrassingly short on proof, he had continued to be one of Ben's steady conduits. He'd got to know him at a series of air-safety hearings they'd both attended and had taken a quick liking to his directness.

'Now, how in the hell can you have the FAA that's mandated to *promote* commercial aviation to the public also be responsible for *certifying* aeroplanes these poor souls have to climb into?' Reese had demanded from everybody in a conference at the FAA.

'You're supposing that the people who run this show are dishonest,' came one challenge.

'Well, goddamn right they are!' he shouted. 'They have a very high aptitude in that direction!'

Reese had started out trying to do unbiased accounts for a news service and had searched for stories in beer joints but more than once had got his nose broken taking sides. He was the kind of journalist who could end up as a truck driver, a croupier in Vegas or a Pulitzer Prize-winner. What made Ben particularly valuable right now, Guy thought, was that the man had spent some recent time inside Buttress. He'd been developing a case against the Buttress F-19, the so-called hottest fighter in the

Western arsenal, but the exposé had backfired. Despite damning circumstantial evidence, Ben hadn't been able to make any of his findings stick, was forced to apologize in print and was dumped by his editor. Guy would offer him salvation. He found him holed up in a boathouse on the West Coast.

'The cheque's in the mail,' Ben said.

'What?'

'Who's this?'

'Reese?'

'You identify yourself and I'll decide if I'm Reese.'

'It's Guy Anders in New York.'

'Do you realize what time it is? Of course you don't realize what time it is. You don't realize you're still alive! So how do you like the 17-10?'

'Benny, in all the work you put together on Buttress, what did you find out about the 17-10?'

'It's the F-19 with seats. It's got the same parents.'

'I've been thinking about finding out a little more about it. I'd like to talk to somebody knowledgeable out there and I figured you'd know who.'

'It's four o'clock in the morning out here.'

'I've got a lead and I thought maybe you'd know him. The guy that got on the radio to us from the factory. We couldn't get him in the clear. His name is Miller.'

'First they'll put a sieve in his throat, then they'll let him talk to you. Sweet guy but he's owned and paid for right down to his bunions.'

'So what would you recommend?'

'First see what the NTSB comes up with. Sit back and wait for them to hang you.'

Guy sat on the couch. Ben's tone softened. 'Listen, take some time off to reflect. This is trouble country out here. There's a lot of pressure right now. I was on my way out of their parking lot when their number one test pilot guns by in an F-19, sets it on its tail right over the flagpole, hits the afterburners and shoots for the sun. God, he looked great.

Scare hell out of the Russians. Only trouble was, pieces of graphite and epoxy fibres start breaking off his tail and two guys come charging out of that centre building, one is Eddie Boice, lights flashing on three or four staff cars as they head out for the range. Their test jockey put it on the ground but no one's sleeping nights out here.'

'When did this happen?'

'The same day that fate was sizing you up for a dip in the ocean. Right now they're not in the mood for poachers, Guy.'

'I was just thinking that maybe between the two of us we could get some answers. Maybe it'd help you get reinstated.'

'It's nothing personal. I love you and all. But I got to hunt up some fresh adrenaline. So you put me on the back burner, y'hear? Meanwhile I wouldn't go out of my way to rattle their cage. They're sensitive.'

The noise from the assembly bay was bone-jarring. House-sized jigsaw shapes reflected miles of overhead fluorescence like ripples of green water, the metal slices nudged into proximity, steel elephants kissing, then with enormous energy fused. And the energy of that fusion assaulted the ears of mitelike men including Ed Boice and Dick Miller as they rode the elevator, hurrying to the head of the production line. Boice had been muttering to Miller all the way.

'That goddamn Air World co-pilot. Goddamn hearing on the loan extension coming up and now this too!'

The first position on the production line was tied up, they couldn't move the nearly completed 17-10 from the bay, the landing gear was faulty. Meanwhile other 17-10s behind were beginning to logjam, the production sequence was going awry.

'Everybody around here acting like it's Sunday, pulling their puds! We got to GI this place, make it shine!'

Miller, impassive, looked scholarly in his grey woollen sweater and slightly awkward in the presence of Boice's fuming. The elevator clanked like an old steam locomotive and jolted to a stop.

Boice barged out, his head bristling a warning. Overhead towered the 17-10 with no engines in its tunnel-like nacelle shells, ready to be dragged into the sunlight as though from a cocoon. Its windows were in and miles of wiring like ganglia strung through it but not yet hooked up. A truncated metal stump protruded from one wheel well and underneath pieces of the landing gear lay, huge gorilla-sized forgings, shiny posts like steel logs, and small yellow jacks holding up the plane seemed to wheeze under the weight.

A foreman, warily eyeing the oncoming Boice, spoke first. 'She'll roll today. The men are busting their ass. They're tired.'

'It's ten of ten,' Boice said evenly. 'I want that first position cleared by noon.' The words were measured, final, but the foreman didn't blink or move.

'Ed Boice, Ed Boice.' The overhead bullhorn was harsh. 'Call two six three. Ed Boice, call two six three.'

Boice was off the scaffold, on to the floor, grabbing a blue phone by the row of file cabinets that lined the production-line pathway.

'This is Boice.'

'Eddie, are you calling from the assembly bay?' It was Fenton 'Buzz' Riddick, his boss, who bore the onus of ramrodding production and who'd dumped additional duties in his lap.

'Yeah.'

'Would you come up to my office for a minute? And would you bring the Air World Six folder?'

'I'll get right over.'

Boice slammed the phone down. His face was dark. Miller frowned, his resentment raised a notch, yet still wary of Boice's sudden anger, which had become increasingly sour since their struggle over the phone patch to the stricken Flight Six.

'Well, let's go, Miller,' Boice ordered. They bolted into a long corridor, Boice at a run, his heavy footfalls pounding a drumbeat, Miller's making a staccato counterpoint. Miller wanted to stop yet his legs pumped on; the corridors seemed to snap him first left, then right. Boice reached their office and charged across it like a bulldozer. Miller grabbed the metal doorjamb to break his momentum and let himself sag into a chair. He was out of breath. His boss fumbled at a bookcase, dumped a stack of reports on his desk and pulled one folder free. 'OK, let's go.'

But Dick Miller sat impassive. 'I'm not going,' he said hoarsely.

Boice dismissed it. 'Get your ass out of that chair.'

'I don't want to play along with you any further.' Miller's face was long; the folder of IBM runs he'd been carrying sat crumpled on the edge of Boice's desk.

Boice ran a hand through the upright spikes that glistened like so many soldiers at attention on top of his scalp, which was white in the centre where the spikes were shortest. 'What the hell's bugging you?'

Miller stood, paced to the window. Somewhere there had been another time, another place where his restless talent lay gathered, fired with a vision that once seemed able to concentrate all his passion into the first stroke of pencil on paper, like Da Vinci's pure circle, an extension of the core of him, his essential being exploding in a dot. Now the dot was muddy, lost, the core hollow, the passion spent. And here was Boice, crowding him. He felt his fear subside as a rage broke through a dam deep inside him and rolled past all the restraints imposed by twenty-seven years of Friday paycheques.

He blared at Boice, 'It's time to cut the bullshit!'

It was an announcement and it surprised even Miller. He felt the pure force of his long-subdued convictions rising, spilling, and he allowed it without concern for himself.

Boice blinked back his shock. 'What the hell are you talking about?'

Miller swung towards his raincoat hanging nearby and yanked something free. In his hand he clutched a slim device like a pistol barrel with a small gleaming shaft that protruded from its chamber. He flipped it at his disbelieving boss. 'These servos are crapping up the signal to the tail!' Miller's voice was resonant, his chest an echo chamber. He was pleased by the effect, for Boice was suddenly smaller, another employee in a white shirt sweating for his groceries. Miller rolled on. 'Crap like that has no place in a four-billion-dollar project.'

Boice hunched in embarrassment as if Miller had just blasphemed in church. But Miller was transported, all his courage distilled and concentrated in this one isolated moment.

'"Save weight, low bid, chop space,"' he went on, gathering force. 'We try to warn you. But no one can tell you! So what have you got? You're into retrofit while we're still ass-deep in the first deliveries!'

'Wait a minute!'

'Don't cut me off! It's gotta be *your* show, *your* logic, *your* radio call to Air World Six; no one can get past you, you intimidating sonofabitch!' Miller felt like he was singing the national anthem.

Boice stared back, blotched and ashen, his face slack. 'I don't fucking believe this,' he said finally. 'I don't believe it. Wait, I want somebody else to hear this.' He spun around. 'Murdock!' he shouted through the still-open door. Miller stood, trying to remain firm in his isolation, but it was then he felt his rage begin to sag, to drain away from him. He went after it, chasing it internally, burrowing down, stretching but it was sinking beyond his reach. His moment was spent and the more familiar anxiety was already rushing back in.

'Go on, Miller, tell Murdock here what you told me!' Boice's jaw was thrust ahead, his eyes like pig's eyes, his face eager. 'Go ahead!'

Miller turned away from the older man who had just come in.

'It's nothing new,' Miller said.

'It's new! It's new!' Boice insisted, dancing up and down.

'It's nothing new, goddammit!' Miller screamed. The visitor, who had come in to hear a joke, looked distressed. Miller lifted his raincoat and began folding it. 'I guess you won't mind if I go home.'

Boice, alarmed, jerk-shifted to block the door, his body coiled. Then his expression softened. He nodded to the visitor to get lost, stuck his hands in his back pockets and feigned a sympathetic expression. 'Richard . . . Richard. We're all so worn out around here. Last night . . . last night I noticed I hadn't spoken to my wife in three months except to ask her to pass the salt and when I look at what's ahead I don't know how I'm going to make it.' A plea from the field first: the consummate con artist, thought Miller. He knew Boice, but the knowledge didn't help. Boice was smiling now, his voice chiding. 'For God's sake, let's not get diarrhoea just because one plane had a little trouble the other night!' Miller turned away and stood, drooped, for a long moment. He turned back and slowly draped his coat over a chair. Boice watched him, waiting to be certain the tide had turned. 'We're under attack. We've got work to do.'

Miller didn't answer.

Boice reached for the door, his mind again on the race to Riddick's office.

Snethler, the young addition to the corporate PR team, was standing in the hall. 'I'm here for my appointment, Mr Boice.' Events tumbled across Ed's mind – yes – the meeting to brief PR on technical aspects in response to media curiosity. Set up yesterday. So long ago.

'I see you got your ass in a crack yesterday. I want you to pay close attention. You don't have arthritis, do you?'

'What?'

'Then fall in and I'll set you straight along the way.' Boice broke into a trot, Snethler jolting along behind like a figure from a silent movie, running every few steps. Miller trailed, his face sullen, a spiritless heaviness to his gait as he made the effort to keep up.

'You gotta be sure you get the right story to your boss about what we're doing down here,' Boice boomed. 'You tell them this for me: the 17-10 is the best thing that's happened to commercial aviation since they built the DC-3, you got that?' Boice's grunts emphasized the point. 'The 17-10 is the *answer* to commercial aviation.'

'They're beginning to ask if we're planning any changes to the design!' Snethler panted.

'Yeah? Well, you tell them our fly-by-wire control system isn't new – except in commercial aviation! We pioneered the fly-by-wire fighter more'n fifteen years ago! Look it up!'

'Fifteen years plus,' repeated the younger man.

'Right! And you tell 'em this, too: that system is tuned – you go in now and start tinkering with it, you affect the entire system.' Boice was breathing hard. 'And here's something you keep to yourself. Anyone lays a hand on that control system means you're talking ten million a copy for starters. Total recalibration. Maybe even recertification. Then we're really in deep shit.' He turned on to a catwalk suspended high above another assembly bay. 'So you tell those sonsofbitches thinking about making changes this isn't re-rigging the cables on a goddamn barnstormer.' A burst of riveting lashed at them from the floor below. 'You tell 'em that for Ed Boice!' he called. They ran down a flight of stairs.

Boice stopped and turned as the others caught up. He put one hand against the wall and sucked for wind. 'You tell 'em the 17-10 is the *answer* to Arab blackmail, to the world's airlines sucking hind tit to the Arab oil cartel, the *answer* to impossible noise limits set by dink-town shop-keepers, the *answer* to the European Consortium that's trying to finish its own version of fly-by-wire.'

'Shall I use all of that?' gasped Snethler.

'Use all of it.'

'But suppose they ask me specifically about the co-pilot's comments?'

Boice searched the man's face, didn't respond. He turned to open Riddick's office door.

Riddick didn't beat around the bush. 'Eddie, I'm a little disturbed.'

'Yeah, what about?'

'I didn't want to call you away from what you were doing, but it wouldn't have been fair to let any more time pass without refreshing your memory. Now I know you're doing your best but the production line has been stopped since four o'clock yesterday.'

'We're kicking it loose.'

'Well, I got a little maths problem; it's not difficult, you can figure it out.' Riddick scribbled numbers on the chalkboard along one wall of his office in bold, huge writing, round figures that filled the slate, crowding the edges. 'Here's our capital outlay so far on the 17-10 project.' He wrote '4,270,000,000'. 'That's four point two seven billion. Now stay with me. As of today, we have a hundred and eighteen orders, announced and unannoun-ced, at roughly seventy million each; that's if there are no cancellations as a result of Air World Six. Of that, only nine point five million is available from each sale to repay our investment.' He wrote '118 × 9,500,000' across the middle of the board.

'Can you tell me how many more sales it's going to take for us to break even? Forget inflation, do it straight.'

Boice punched numbers quickly into his pocket calcula-tor. 'I come up with three hundred and thirty-two aeroplanes.'

'Close,' said Riddick, 'I'll buy it. But now suppose we produce only three hundred and thirty-*one*. How does it figure then?'

Boice continued earnestly, 'That means a loss of nine point five million dollars.'

'No, you're wrong. What it really means, you see, is that you'll be out on your ass.' His voice became husky. 'Now do you know what it's like to get work after forty-five? There's a club in town called After Forty-five. Call them up. They'll tell you. They're in the yellow pages.'

Fenton Riddick surveyed the hard-shelled silence between them. Then he put the chalk down. 'I want you to think about that and I also want you to start thinking about your opening remarks at the NTSB hearing on Air World Six.'

Guy Anders revelled: the April morning was as pure as a dewdrop, the cold a razor slice on his cheek, and his breath made white steam in the sparkling air. Nothing stirred on the little airport except birds and overhead high translucent clouds, light-struck ripples in a slow, stately march across the sky. The blue wings of his tandem Beechcraft T-34 were slick, their colour enriched by the sky they mirrored, and Guy pulled the plane from its hangar on to the little tarmac with mounting exhilaration. There wasn't a speck or an imperfection on it. He removed the blanket from its cowl and let a finger drift slowly along the smooth metal there, lingering, feeling in the delicate touch of his fingertip an artistry, an exactness. He always allowed himself a private moment, he could conceal it from the impatience of others; certainly his aeroplane's beauty deserved unhurried appreciation, but it was more: it was a return to something scrupulous and substantial. His destination was Washington and the FAA offices that would no doubt shed some light on the riddle of the 17-10.

Another early riser removing tie-down ropes from a Cessna nearby came over to admire the rakish ex-military trainer. 'Need a hand?' He carried a jacket, it was smudged with grease and had sharp-edged brass buttons, he was about to toss it on the wing.

'No, don't do that,' Guy restrained him gently. 'If you don't mind.'

The man was slightly piqued. 'Sure thing,' he said, and moved off.

Guy turned away. There was no room in this morning for anything careless or dangerous or ugly.

He strapped himself in the narrow cockpit, the clear bubble cranked back behind his head, and started the engine. The propeller flashed, the noise shattered the stillness abruptly, and the dawn, just moments before terraced in the murmurings of breeze and animal songs, was now whipped with urgent energy, laced with the acrid blasts of exhaust. He wheeled on to the asphalt strip and pushed the throttle forward. The Beechcraft lofted into the perfect blue morning. He surveyed the glossy smooth wings of his aeroplane and the texture of the earth just beyond, rolling by as if from a variegated, endless scroll.

It was glorious to be alone.

On the cab ride from National Airport, past the squat, dire-looking Pentagon, Guy wondered if he'd be able to interpret the 17-10 data. It had been a long time since engineering school. In ten minutes he stood in the lobby of the 'marble palace', the nine-storey white cellblock federal office building at 800 Independence Avenue which housed the FAA. He submitted his briefcase for inspection at the central information booth and phoned his contact.

'Oh, I'm terribly sorry, Mr Anders,' the secretary said. 'You were told to call from the airport when you arrived, I believe, so that Mr Merewether would know whether to come in from Bethesda, where he had a meeting this morning. But, now that you're here, I'll call him there and I'm sure he can clear his day. Check back in ten minutes, why don't you?'

Could happen, Guy thought. So he paced, walked into the small FAA museum off the main lobby, from glass case to glass case, uninterested in the exhibits, not seeing them, and at once was back to the phone.

'Oh, Mr Anders. An emergency came up. Mr Merewether had to remain at Bethesda. He apologizes and hopes you'll understand, but he won't be able to meet you after all.'

'Well, how long is he going to be tied up?' It became difficult for Guy to hide that special brand of frustration that seemed to be engendered by government workers.

'Well, I don't know; I know it's going to be through lunch and maybe through three o'clock.'

'Will he be back by three? Shall I come by at three?'

'I'd call first if I were you.'

'Now hold on. Let's the two of us go over this a minute. This was arranged yesterday. I mean, I'm not here visiting the White House Rose Garden.' There was a pause. 'Honey, you're the one who took my phone number.'

'Well – uh – ' Guy could hear her breathing. 'Uh – the emergency came up this morning, Mr Anders,' she said, regaining some composure, 'and it was too late to call you. We knew you would be on your way, there was of course nothing we could do about that. Perhaps if you'd call back at three-thirty . . .'

He left the marble palace feeling bruised. Buttress was bound to be guarded about the plane's plans, but the FAA? Who else was there? *Aviation Digest* carried meticulous details of fighters, the MiG 25, the B-1 bomber; its publisher was repeatedly hauled before Senate investigators to reveal his source; he had a pipeline. Guy checked a copy at a newsstand, found the editor's name on the masthead and phoned him.

'Look, this is Guy Anders. I was one of three crew members in the point end of that Air World flight Thursday and I was wondering if you guys had anything on the 17-10 control system you were planning to print?'

'Listen, Captain, if you can tell us how to get our hands on some of that, we'd make a substantial contribution towards your next Mercedes.'

Aviation Week & Space Technology – nothing.

Flight International – nothing.

Aeronautics & Astronautics – nothing.

After lunch Guy paced the featureless lobby of a building on K Street and had the feeling he was being watched. He locked eyes with a security guard who was beginning to look him over. Christ, he was a suspect. Everyone had become a suspect. The whole world up against the wall, pants down, attaché cases open. Then it was three-thirty. He slid into a brushed-aluminium phone booth and punched the buttons for the FAA. The secretary answered with an edge of irritation. 'I'm sorry, but he still has some people with him.'

'Is this the same conference or a new one?'

'What?'

'Listen, honey, hold the line a second will you?' Guy cupped his hand over the phone and beckoned to a delivery man in coveralls waiting in the lobby. 'Hey, friend, what's your name?'

'Andy,' he said with a look of astonishment.

'That's right, Andy, it's for you.'

'For me?' Andy took the phone. 'Hello, this is Andy, whaddaya want?'

Striding out, Guy threw a crooked-arm Italian salute, leaving a startled guard in his wake. A cab was cruising by, he hailed it and ordered the driver to take him to 800 Independence Avenue. He soon found the office, and confronted the arch-eyed secretary.

'I don't even want to see your boss.' He leaned in closer and grinned. 'I'm in Washington to see the certification design data on the 17-10, which is the aeroplane I fly. All you have to do is tell me where those papers are, and we won't need to be getting at each other any more.'

The woman disappeared, but before Guy had time to study the white, metal-partitioned government office, noticing only that she sat underneath a trio of government-issue portraits showing the lithograph smiles of the President, the Secretary of Transportation, and the FAA administrator, she was back. 'Room nine two three, ninth floor. They're in charge of all aircraft design records.'

'You become much nicer with time.'

'His office closes in five minutes.'

'That's wonderful,' Guy smiled.

A man in 923 seemed to be waiting for him. Guy leaned on the counter and nodded his greeting.

'I'm the fellow looking for the 17-10 design data.'

The man tossed a sullen look at the clock and said, 'Mr Anders, I'm sorry, but that material isn't all available at the moment.' Guy stood waiting for him to elaborate but the fellow just stared back.

'Where did it go? There's a law that says citizens have the right to see that.'

'Well, most of it's proprietary. The part that isn't is out of the area.'

'When is it coming back?'

'I'm not told everything that goes on.'

'There must be more than one copy. You're the regulating agency!' The employee raised his hands to indicate his own innocence. Guy continued, 'You mean to tell me I could be hauled up before a long green table in this building for misoperating the 17-10, yet I can't even have access to the operating standards I'm supposed to adhere to? Friend, you've got it all wrong. This is US government territory. This isn't a banana republic. You and me, we're supposed to be on the same side.'

The worker lowered a cracked plastic cover over his typewriter. 'There's nothing I can do about it.'

Guy ran for the stairs.

People had begun huddling in doorways, buttoning their coats, ready to be let out. It was almost four-thirty. The secretary he'd spoken to was locking her file. Guy leaned over her desk. 'Listen, sweetheart, would you do me a favour? Tell your boss that unless I see that data, I'm gonna have to give another interview for the media. Tonight. "Pilot's request to see jumbo's blueprints denied, details at eleven." He can call me at the L'Enfant Plaza whenever his conference is over. I'm real sorry we had to meet this way.'

He walked out, certain he'd left a smouldering fuse behind. When he reached his hotel room he found the red message light on his phone aglow. Aha, he thought, pleased with himself, maybe we're getting somewhere. The operator told him a man named Ed Boice had called from the West Coast – from Buttress Aerospace. Puzzled but now fully attentive, Guy asked to be connected. The sound of a tank crunching gravel greeted him.

'Guy, this is Eddie Boice out at Buttress. I guess we owe you and Captain Cosgrove a debt of gratitude.' Guy had no time for a comeback; Boice went right on. 'But my call really has another motive!' Boice laughed self-consciously as though confessing to a priest about drinking too much. 'We'd like to hear *your* version of that flight and we figured if you could get out here we could give you the tour, show you whatever you want and perhaps get a little play-by-play from you in exchange!'

Guy's thoughts were racing. He was certain the FAA had just called Boice. Into the phone he said, 'How do we put this together?'

'There's a five-forty out of Dulles – put you here about eight. We'll have a car at the airport. What do you think?'

'You don't beat around the bush, do you?' Guy said.

Boice laughed. 'We'll be lookin' for you!'

90

4

The rush to Dulles was harrowing. The old cliché, Guy thought, the most dangerous part of flying is the cab ride to the airport.

Now seven miles high, he thought about Boice's invitation. Companies don't invite critics in for socializing, he reasoned. He considered that, then played devil's advocate. Nobody's ever been mugged out there either. Which was probably true. But it was also true he'd fired a shot across their bow on national TV . . .

The plane descended over the mottled Sierras, haze thickening in the hollows, the western slopes coarse-grained and pink from the falling sun and they reminded him of the Chesapeake shores he had skimmed across only that morning in his T-34.

The Buttress limousine met him at baggage claim, ostentatious and serene amid the clamouring autos and hotel courtesy vans muscling their way to curbside. He sank into its unborn-English-calf upholstery, studying the appointments as they glided past the harried, frantic cops and angry cabbies and sped on to the freeway. He was whisked to the large, lit highway hotel where the dinner had been organized. The drinks and banter were in full flow when he was ushered in.

His first impression of Flight Control Design Chief Ed Boice, who charged forward to greet him with two hands, coincided with the mental image formed from his telephone voice. He was handed a tall Bloody Mary, then introduced to Fenton Riddick – 'Buzz Riddick, one of our best known pioneer test pilots'; 'Yes, I know, I was weaned on Buzz Riddick stories' – but while they were making inanities, he noticed Riddick's very female companion. She looked incongruous by Riddick's side, sunshine-bright to his grey; she was as tall as he, but what made Guy feel light-headed was the saucy red ribbon she wore in her raven-black hair. Her eyes were large, almond-shaped, they looked straight into him through all the surface layers, her mouth was liquid, the cupid's bow of her upper lip accentuated with a delicate white rim, he had an almost irresistible urge to run a fingertip over it. Her neck was long and supple, especially where the downy hairs formed at the nape, and her bare arms were soft with skin like dark cream, he wanted to brush the fleece there, he saw it and knew it would stand up electric to his touch, he pictured her thighs, he sensed her fragrance. And he stood there and his heart pounded.

They were introduced. Eyes locked on one another. Her name was Natalie Mason.

'So happy to meet you.'

They were apart from the conversation for a moment. He smiled at her.

'That's noticeable perfume – uh, I mean noticeable in the provocative way.'

'I should hope so, Captain Anders. It's to help narrow the distance.'

'Pardon me?'

'So they got you to come to the combat zone.'

'Looks reasonably peaceful.'

'Don't be deceived by your drink.'

'I'm afraid I don't follow you.'

'You may be able to follow me if you have a finely tuned nose for incipient corporate panic.'

'You're Buzz Riddick's secretary.'

'Your knee-jerk assumption tells me you're not emancipated. No, I'm not his secretary.'

'Better than that.'

'Better. But I do work with him.'

'You're upwardly mobile.'

Natalie smiled.

'Then they must have plans for you.'

'No, on the contrary. I've got plans for them.' She laughed, a joyous laugh, gave a little-girl innocent wink and twirled away. Guy stood rooted, following her with his eyes, and drained his Bloody Mary. And he looked at Buzz Riddick with new interest.

Vern Locker was there and spoke to Guy. 'Nice, huh?'

'The lass with the whiskey-sour voice?'

'Randy, twenty-eight and divorced. Uncertain property of one Fenton R. Riddick. He's been known to take unkindly to poachers.'

Fenton Riddick and Ed Boice kept Guy's glass topped off.

'So you noticed a shimmy . . . ?' Boice was smiling to cue easy entrance to the subject at hand.

'No, more like a vibration: thin . . . the kind that can set your teeth on edge. The captain picked it up before I did.' Guy decided to plumb the depths they were fishing in. 'Are you trying to corroborate a particular suspicion or is the chair still open to suggestions?'

Riddick studied his drink and looked up at Guy. 'I don't believe we'll ever come up with anything major.'

'That's reassuring to those of us who have to strap it on,' said Guy. 'Now that I'm here, I'd like to be some help. I'd like to talk to the individual who tried so hard to pull us out of the sky.'

'Who's that?' Riddick smiled.

'We heard him intermittently. His name was Miller.'

Riddick was impassive. 'Miller's good people,' he said. 'The two of us go all the way back to the Lancejet programme . . . one beautiful guy . . . but,' and his voice lowered as though he were talking behind his hand, 'frankly, straight out of a hardware store.'

'He had something in mind to get us outta there.'

'Yeah,' said Riddick, 'he had some kind of Rube Goldberg scheme. If you'd gone that route, you'd have needed a week and a hand growing out of your ass to do it.'

93

'He sounded to me like the source,' Guy challenged.

'The only source we have lives upstairs in the office next to the boardroom, and he's very protective about the product.' Riddick smiled again, raising the ante.

'Just the same, I'd like to thank Mr Miller personally.'

'Before you go, we'll make sure you get to shake his hand.'

It sounded as though Miller was in protective custody, Guy reflected. Well, hell, if they weren't going to be more forthcoming than that . . . He made a mental note to find some other way to contact Miller.

The large arched doors on one wall swung back. Dinner was served. They moved, still talking, in a group towards the doors, some taking last tidbits from the hors d'oeuvre trays, into the Buttress permanently reserved executive dining room. A profusion of burnished light cascaded from ceiling-mounted spotlights, illuminating an exquisite replica of the 17-10 perched on a delicate silver arm in the centre of the table. Guy noticed that conversation suddenly dropped away. At the head of the table, assuming his place, Fenton Riddick adjusted a sliding rheostat on a panel built into the table's edge. The lights dimmed except for one, which isolated the model. Anders was painfully alert, conscious of being an ordinary mortal admitted to a conversion rite.

'Friends,' said Buzz Riddick, 'a toast to the 17-10.' Organ music became apparent as Riddick pushed another lever. Glasses were raised.

'Mr Anders, aren't you going to join us?' Riddick was smiling. Guy was aware of a dozen eyes boring in on him. He looked around and self-consciously picked up his glass.

Later, during the meal, Natalie Mason without warning leaned over close to Guy. He felt a very wet and active tongue tip dart into his ear. Then she whispered in a voice that raised goose bumps all over his body, 'The one thing wrong with old man Riddick is that he'd rather be blown by wind tunnels.'

His ear tingled with her moisture as he turned to face her. She saw his look, it was unfeigned surprise, but to her twinkling eyes it looked like seriousness.

'Don't you ever get to think that way, Captain Anders.'

The Buttress limo that whisked him away the next morning was magnificent. Fenton Riddick's spacious office had an air of arrogance; the brochures and folders stuffed with colour pictures he was handed were ostentatious. A screen was lowered for a film – 'There's some real hot-shit flying in this' – and there was: all sun-rimmed and sparkling, macho shots of the 17-10 in flight test, some, like the V_{MU} trial when the tail was dragged smoking along the runway before the plane's sharply tilted takeoff, spectacular as a voice enumerated the statistics, the miles of wires that were strung through the ship, the months of proving flights that had taken place. A central core of egoism ran through it all. Then came the tour, conducted by two overweening engineers. They herded him to the Styrofoam and cardboard cockpit mock-ups of Buttress's low-noise future SST; they showed him exotic new traffic-situation displays and advanced flight simulators. 'Have you ever seen anything like that? Here, strap it on, fly a couple of approaches.' He even got a 'ride' in the F-19 simulator, mounted inside an enormous Ping-Pong ball – an enclosed stadium with a blinding artificial sun and a 'sky' on which could be projected scenes of enemy fighters that could come at him from any direction.

Guy was ushered into an adjacent projection room where Boice jumped up to greet him. 'We've got another film showing our F-19 mowing a little grass for the Air Force. You'll go for this one.' After the initial swell of music, Boice stepped outside, leaving Guy alone. Guy got up and checked the projection booth, sticking his face against the square hole in the wall. The 16-millimetre reel appeared to be no more than twenty minutes in length.

Guy cracked the door. The corridor was empty. He ran

from the room, trying to recall the route Boice had used in escorting him from the flight-control design section. Outside, past a huge production bay, into another complex. He couldn't recall if he'd even heard Miller's first name.

Within minutes he had located the proper area and found himself racing along a beige corridor with white-lettered blue flags above the doors. He saw Richard Miller's name, reached it in three bounds, pulled the door open. Empty. He entered anyway, looking for a phone. He'd copy down the number, call Miller later. As he was writing on a scrap of paper he heard a rustle behind him. The thin stranger in the open doorway appeared more startled than he.

'Can I help you?' The stranger was shaggy and grey with rumpled hair and an old loose cardigan.

'Hello – I'm Guy Anders – co-pilot of Air World Six.'

The round-shouldered stranger regarded him as if uncertain what to do.

'You Miller?'

'That's right. I heard you were coming.' They shook hands. Miller smiled bashfully as if trying to make up his mind to add something. 'We're still working on last week's deadlines . . . Things are pretty wild around here,' he offered, more to his desk than to Guy.

'Well, I wanted to thank you for trying to give us that big hand the other night.'

'I didn't know whether we were getting through. I remember I was doing a mixture of thinking and praying.' As he spoke, a figure passed by in the corridor outside. Miller constricted.

'We didn't get all of it,' Guy said. 'What did get through was something about pulling a circuit breaker on an elevator program, and I'm not sure if it was A. I've checked the flight manual. There's no mention of an Elevator Program A in any of the procedures.'

'. . . Legal department scrubs every word before it gets printed.'

96

'All we have in our book are three-colour schematics drawn with push brooms for paintbrushes.'

Miller laughed, and Guy sensed a tentative bond between them.

'Why Elevator Program A, Dick?'

Miller's smile disappeared. 'Is Boice with you?'

'I don't know where he is. Elevator Program A,' Guy pressed.

'. . . It was a thought, you know? Nothing definitive . . . It wasn't orthodox.'

His last words sounded bitter, but Guy couldn't be sure. 'Look, Dick, I don't know what song they're playing for me back there,' he said earnestly, 'but they sure as hell are laying on the ketchup. Seems nobody wants to put a sharp focus on what I came to find out.'

'Do they know you came down to this office?'

Guy ignored the question. 'How'd you people set up the pitch circuit in that aeroplane?'

Miller tried to orient himself.

'Precisely how did you stick those controls together?' Guy persisted.

Dick Miller's twenty-seven years with Buttress hung like a web-like mist between them. He faced his computer graphics console, seeing in the dead picture tube a distorted reflection of Guy Anders through the strands of that mist.

Guy prodded: 'Nothing I've ever been up in behaves like that.'

The room had become perfectly still. Even the milky vista seen through Miller's window was motionless.

'Is this new territory or is it something else?' Guy asked quietly.

Miller sat down in his chair, slowly shaking his head.

Guy frowned, puzzled. His tone was sympathetic. 'What the hell goes on in this place?'

Slowly Dick Miller faced him. His words were strained. 'You want to know what goes on in this place? Then shut the door.'

Guy eased the door shut, questions beginning to bloom in his mind. But Miller was already talking. It was coming in a half monotone, but half in explanation as well.

'We used to work with one idea at a time. Now that's exploded, so you have to make a lot of decisions faster than before. The number of choices we have is staggering. And the thing is, you don't want to make the wrong choices . . . because they can get expensive, and you can get . . . stuck with them. I made my objections a long time ago . . . You see, there's an open-door policy here, you can go right to the top and talk to one of the vice-presidents and make your case. But if you can't make your case stick by the second visit, you're out. And with a lot of qualified engineers waiting their turn out there, you don't go upstairs for the second visit. I went once and I was told I was wrong.'

'What's this got to do with the 17-10?'

'Well . . . this was all during that programme . . . We've had a lot of things to work out.'

'No doubt.'

'You're working on deadlines and the schedule is laid out for years down the road and you get some people around here who like to shove their weight around – they know everything – walking think tanks,' he said derisively. 'And some decisions get through that . . . well, that nobody understands.'

'*Specifically?*'

Dick Miller suddenly couldn't focus on the clouded view through his window: the objects in the room – in particular, Guy Anders. Uncertainty and chagrin expanded behind his ears like steam pistons. And, to his surprise, yearning. He felt a surge of longing for Guy Anders's freedom, and found himself wanting very much to trust him; yet he was only able to view Anders through averted, sidelong inspection. He became self-conscious at the same time that his own visage had altered, and he was angry with Anders for that and for pushing him and yet regretful that he, Miller, was able to say only, 'You get the old whipsaw of technical decisions becoming other *kinds* of decisions . . .'

'What kind is that?'

'Economic when they shouldn't be.'

'Has anything like this been decided on the 17-10?'

'There've been trade-offs.'

'Like what?'

'There are always trade-offs; there have to be.'

'What's wrong with the 17-10, Dick?'

Dick Miller searched for words that would launder his thoughts but couldn't find them, and he didn't answer.

'What the hell happened to us out there?'

Again there was no answer.

'If I call you at home, will you talk to me there?'

Miller whitened. 'Most people say it's a pretty good aeroplane.' His tone was wistful. Guy stared at him. Miller met his eyes. 'I'm not going to be able to add anything to that.' Finally Miller turned away.

Guy glanced at his watch and left. And Dick Miller stared at his desk, terrified.

Guy ran through Miller's wing of the complex, crossed the production bay, and had almost reached the screening room when he heard footfalls slapping towards him from around an approaching corner. He slowed just in time to step across Ed Boice's path.

Boice grinned a little too brightly at him. 'Just wondered where you were.' His offhandedness couldn't hide the panic behind his eyes or the flush he was trying to tamp down.

Guy pushed into the screening room. The lights were on, the film had been stopped. 'This film is a wipe-out,' he said. 'Cameraman must have shot it with his dick. I had to get some air.'

Boice stood agape.

With a crackle, Fenton Riddick's amplified voice invaded the closed space of the screening room from a desk speaker. 'Eddie, is Mr Anders with you?'

Boice stumbled to mash the speak button. 'Yeah, I found him!'

'Well, why don't you have him come on by?'

Ed Boice turned to Guy, still grinning, still eyeing him suspiciously. 'Buzz has a visit to R & D lined up for you at one – '

'And what time is the live sex show?'

Boice blinked. 'Huh?'

'Eddie, let's you and I get serious. I want to take a look at the 17-10 control system from the inside out. I thought that's why I was invited out here, as a matter of fact.'

Boice could only continue heaving for breath. The grin had apparently frozen in place. 'What was that?'

'The pitch circuit in particular – the internals – the lash-up to the computer, not the Cook's tour for shitfaced generals.'

'We'll have to arrange – '

'No you won't. No PR. No red carpet and fried shrimp. I want to see the logic in print or as she is, naked to the touch.'

Boice's grin began to unhinge. 'That's entirely up to Mr Riddick.'

Riddick was brushing his sleeves as Guy met him at the hexagon – the hub of six main corridors. Guy walked wordlessly alongside. Riddick had overheard him in the screening room and it was clear the relationship had taken on a new aspect. An awkward electricity charged the air. Neither spoke. Their footfalls clattered in the broad corridor and Guy turned slightly to study Riddick, whose eyes were narrow, pointed straight ahead. Riddick opened a door.

'After you.'

'Thank you.'

They stepped into the sunlight, squint-eyed bright, its warmth an impact. Riddick motioned Guy to a grey Porsche. They got in.

'I want to show you something,' Riddick said, acknowledging the wave of a guard. Tyres squealed as the car swept in a turn between two yellow lines painted on the broad concrete tarmac. Across, on the far side as they passed, three new 17-10s sat parked, glistening, unpainted, the sun throwing little shimmering eddies of heat from their broad backs. Nearby, adjacent to their route, a building that looked like an enormous upended metal carton rose above them. Across its corrugated front in letters ten feet tall, beige metal letters with sides but no backs, so widely spaced they were read one at a time, were the words BUTTRESS FLIGHT TEST CENTRE.

A partly shrouded fighter, pointed like a scorpion, nestled on the dark side of the next monster cube as though cradled in a huge black arm. Guy noticed, from pictures he'd seen, that he was looking at a supersecret F-19, bantam-tough and poised, cocked like an arrow at the draw, just the hint of its broad cobra afterbody apparent under the tarpaulin covers. For a moment Guy imagined himself cinched deep in its pit, reclined to take the crushing g, free to peer through his visored helmet across the entire sweep of sky, and the juices stirred deep within him. But already several test pilots had been violently killed, slammed to earth in fire and thunder in mysterious F-19 crashes. Something evil lurked there underneath that shroud, a presence, omniscient. Guy saw it fix him in its gaze, one all-seeing eye, trapped within its lifeless shell, that leered straight at him.

While he watched fascinated, Fenton Riddick began to speak. 'You look out there, Anders.' He paused as though to wait for Guy's eyes to take in the full sweep of the giant Buttress landscape. 'On the one hand it's beautiful, don't you agree? On the other hand, I can tell you, you're looking straight into the jaws of the corporate shredder.'

Riddick's car swerved into a turn, following the endless yellow dashes between two towering buildings. Guy didn't speak, but faced straight ahead.

'A company like Buttress has to protect itself,' Riddick said. 'It has its own personality. Look there, at that 17-10 rolling out. Do you know what it took to develop and produce that magnificent aeroplane? Do you have any conception? Four *billion* dollars, twenty-nine million man-hours; it would take a thousand men almost twenty years to produce that. A company that has that much financial resource invested, you understand, it can get real angry. Anyone who tries to take it on better have an electric eye in his ass.'

The car swerved, zooming past the yellow blinker, into the visitor's parking lot beyond the chain-link fence. Riddick roared between rows of cars in the sprawling lot and screeched to a stop. Guy, thrown to the side, hung on. He smiled at Fenton Riddick.

'We had a saying in the Air Force. "Gotta watch yourself in the turns."'

Fenton Riddick's face was set in an expressionless smile. 'You gotta watch yourself all the time, Mr Anders. The bus stops here. It'll take you to the airport, runs every half-hour.'

Guy got out, stood looking in at Riddick, studying him.

'You know, Riddick, just when you think you got it wired and you aren't looking yourself, some joker'll find a way to outturn you and crawl up your tail pipe. It's been known to happen.'

At the airport Guy dialled Toby, ALPA's permanent staff man on accident investigations in Washington. The familiar voice answered.

'Listen Toby, there's something cooking out here. And I think the union ought to get in on it. They know something went wrong with our flight at JFK and they're hiding it under a bowl of mayonnaise.'

'Guy?'

'Yeah.'

'I'm glad you called, I've been trying to reach you. I was just on the line with an old friend at the FAA and he was groaning, "Oh, shit, this one's going to be hard to hang on the pilots." He was joking but he was serious, know what I mean? He was referring to business as usual. Take the cheap route: hang the pilots and spare the bankers. So the NTSB's about to hit you and W.B. with pilot error and hang old Carlton Hanks up by his balls.' Toby's words filled the back of Guy's brain and something in the man's tone warned him it wasn't the stock bureaucratic threat. 'Your cockpit voice tape might be incriminating,' Toby continued.

Guy shut his eyes, trying to concentrate. The statement scared him. 'Has anyone been in touch with Cosgrove?' he finally managed to ask.

'He's on his soybean farm, won't pick up the phone. But we're on to one of his neighbours. We want him to know too . . . that the responsive reading they're setting up is going to be closed.'

'You mean closed – like in kangaroo court?'

'Closed as in closed to the press.' There was a pause. 'Guy, there could be a logical reason for all of it. The loan-extension hearing is three weeks away and a certain consensus wants commercial fly-by-wire to smell good. If it doesn't, Buttress will file bankruptcy and Uncle is going to have to eat fifteen billion plus!'

'But they can't hide the fact that something did go wrong up there! Have the mechs in the hangar come up with anything?'

'Don't quote me but right now the doors are locked. It's like the night before the school play. They're all learning the words.'

'And what are we supposed to do in the meantime?'

'We're gonna have to wait for their other shoe to drop, see what the allegations are.' Toby sounded plaintive.

'See the allegations? I'll *tell* you what they are! Careless and reckless, improper procedure, failure to consult the manual, late on calling a Mayday, improper radio discipline, failure to go on oxygen, failure to wear our hats . . . and none of that ties in. This wasn't some routine engine failure!'

'I know it wasn't.'

'We're talking about a fly-by-wire aeroplane that may not be ready for passenger service!'

'Jesus H. Christ, Guy, we can't take that position! Based on what?'

'Based on thirty minutes on the end of a fireball that no one wants to explain to me and the fact that I can't get my hands on a single meaningful drawing of the insides of that sonofabitch from anyone!' Guy's tone changed. 'Who do you know, Toby?' Toby didn't answer. 'What about the Senate whip – Searington? He's an Air Force general!'

'What do you want him to do?'

'What he does all week long! Reason with people – only for us this time. Slow things down. Keep that hearing open.'

'Never.'

'Read him the Bill of Rights!'

'Guy, listen –'

'You could go see him now,' Guy insisted. 'Find out where he takes a crap and pass a note under the door. I'm thinking we need some help!'

'That's not how we do things in Washington.'

'Well, now forgive me, but judging from what's going on here we don't have time for the way you do it in Washington!'

The federal security guard at the south entrance of the old Senate Office Building looked inside Guy's flight bag, told him Senator Searington's office was midway down on the second floor. Inscribed in the centre of the door was the Virginia seal and under it, in gold leaf, MR SEARINGTON. VIRGINIA. PLEASE COME IN. Searington's receptionist was a well-coiffeured woman in her late forties with an exuberant welcome. Her eyes examined him, seemed to look past the creased jeans and easy stance and approved.

'How are you today? How may we help you?'

Guy placed his bag next to her desk and surveyed the anteroom. There was a small woman working in the corner, the carpet was green, an elaborate glass chandelier hung above him. The receptionist waited, her eyes expectant. She tossed her hair and adjusted an earring, the bracelets on her arm jangling like the metal strips on a tambourine.

Guy pulled his wallet from the inside pocket of his Levi's jacket, opened it to his Air World ID, and held it out for her to see.

'I'm a citizen and a pilot with Air World and I'm anxious to speak to my senator.'

'Well . . .'

'I was also the co-pilot of Flight Six you've been reading about and I know the general will want to hear what I've got to say.'

The secretary smoothed the back of her skirt and readjusted herself in the chair. 'Now are *you* the one!' she cooed, as though others had taken credit for it before him. 'The senator's at the White House.' She deposited the sentence like a cardplayer laying down a straight flush. 'Would you care to leave him a note?'

Guy leaned forward, resting his hands on her desk. 'I couldn't put it all in a note. You see, I got word how there's going to be a lynching,' he said evenly.

The woman blinked.

'They're gonna lynch the crew. I'm one of the designated victims. What I want to know from the senator is why the Administration won't let the press inside to watch

105

it happen. I'd be grateful for the answer to that before I leave.'

She re-examined him. His face held no uncertainty, no particle of amiability she might play on to get him to leave, and so she said, 'Perhaps, when the senator gets back, we can work something out.' She turned away from him to face her typewriter, not seeing the words, trying to hide the look that said she knew Guy had unlaced her.

'I appreciate that,' Guy said, satisfied. Again, and with a sort of deliberate vigilance, he studied the ornate massiveness of the room, the way it overpowered the sparrowlike typist working delicately in a far corner, its air of heavy timber, its walls festooned with gold trophies and photographs of the senator and Dwight Eisenhower smiling at the camera, the senator standing on the steps of Air Force One with a grinning JFK, sitting in brooding concentration with Nixon, walking at Camp David with Reagan and the large one of the senator gloved and rugged in the cockpit of his Starfighter. There was also a group shot of people standing around the roll-out of the first Buttress Lancejet.

Guy recognized a few of the faces; the fellow holding on to the wing was a younger Senator Elton Osborne, angular, balding even then; and the shorter man next to him was G. Hollis Wright, with the look of a stern-faced abbott. Albert Searington had come the whole distance to bask in America's well-carpeted enclaves of power.

Guy sat and waited and felt his mind slip loose. Hundreds of other flights had already travelled across the scorched concrete at Kennedy and had turned around for Delhi and Singapore while his own recent moment of terror lay as a slim memory to be brushed aside. But that memory was an anchor he had to hold on to. Other headlines were clamouring for attention and the cameras that had beamed in on him at Kennedy had already spun away. Someone had once said there'd be a day when everyone would be famous for fifteen minutes, and in

Guy's reverie he could sense it had already arrived. Movie stars and presidents had been supplanted by the hijacker, the hostage, the man with the banana nose waving to his friends on the news, the Sears Roebuck couple walking up the gangway the way royalty used to . . . and so with everyone taking turns in an ever-faster revolving limelight, events once etched sharply by their uniqueness had begun to matter less. A plane going down somewhere was an irritant. It demanded time and no one had any left to give. Moon shots, underground nuclear explosions, had once been something for an audience to mull, but the audience had climbed up on stage and had become what was happening.

The secretary looked up, showed Guy a little extra leg and asked if he wanted any coffee or was there something she could do to make his visit to Washington more comfortable. Guy hadn't paid much attention to her earlier, but he noticed her now. She was middle-aged and southern and pleasant and plump and still on the active side of sex and Guy could visualize her on a bed naked, losing herself in a wet sighing afternoon in a motel room, then neatly dabbing the ends of her peroxide curls, readjusting her mottled green-chiffon dress, talking about Georgia and her sisters and the church bridge party and growing up with Jesus, who never said it was wrong to have fun and why don't we go down and get another bottle . . .

Just then the impeccably dressed Senator Searington walked past her into his office.

'See if you can get Senator Osborne,' he called to her over his shoulder.

Guy became alert. Senator Osborne represented Buttress's home state; many considered him protector of America's aviation interests.

'Sir, the senator left the building. He went over to the NTSB.'

'Damn.'

The secretary followed him inside, stayed for a moment, came back out and winked at Guy.

'You may go in, Mr Anders.'

Senator Searington changed his sunglasses to the aviator-style bifocals he was so well known for.

'I'm sorry to keep you waiting, Mr Anders. The President was running behind today and I'm afraid I only made matters worse for him.' He made it sound as though transactions concerning the President had always been of mutual interest to himself and Guy.

'How do you think I can help you?'

Guy was surprised by the man's mild manner and his effortless smile. The senator was six feet two, just over sixty, well tanned. He had Scottish good looks, his trimmed greying hair slightly askew. Al Searington was a country lawyer who knew the subways. He looked younger than the cartoons made him out to be. He sat on the corner of the desk and pointed to a blue upholstered couch. Guy sat down.

'Senator, four days ago I flew right seat in the 17-10 that almost didn't make it into Kennedy.'

Searington folded his arms and lowered his voice. 'I know you did. Mrs Searington and I followed it because she returned on the same flight the night before, and I want to say how full of admiration we both are for the crew.'

Guy eyed the older man. 'Then I've come to the right place. Maybe you can tell me why the Administration has decided to keep the NTSB inquisition closed.'

'How do you know it's going to be closed?'

'A reliable source told me it's going to be a kangaroo court.'

'Did the reliable source tell you why?'

'No, but I did some figuring on my own and I figure it'd be too costly to fix the blame on the aeroplane.'

'Too costly for whom?'

'We could start with Buttress and work our way up Constitution Avenue.'

The intercom buzzer sounded. Searington leaned down and pressed a key. 'I don't want any calls right now.' He turned back to Guy. 'That's pretty audacious.'

'I've just taken up scepticism. So far I've been to six bureaucrats sitting on steel chairs hauling in their GS pay and looking for something to do and I can't even get a paper copy of the aeroplane I get paid to fly. Just now I've come back from a ceremonial visit to Buttress, where the best they could come up with was a plate of shrimps and a gold-bordered brochure.'

'Now you can't blame them for wanting to hold on to their recipe!' barked the senator. 'Europe would take a second mortgage to find out how we put that aeroplane together. What the British and French can't hear, they can't copy!' The senator leaned forward. 'Now maybe that's why the doors are going to be closed.' His words hung in the air with a confidential timbre.

'I didn't know the NTSB worked for Buttress,' Guy retorted.

Searington's face revealed nothing. 'It's independent but responsible to our interests,' he said flatly.

'That's double-talk, Senator. It can only be responsible to its independence.'

The retaliation ignited the air between them. The senator looked at the lights blinking on his phone. Guy watched him as he screwed up his eyes, squinting as though someone had let too much light into the room. Where he once might have fallen into step with the older man, the events of the past few days had placed Guy beyond convention.

'I was wondering if you knew of a senator who might be concerned if the government were to find *against* Buttress?'

Searington scratched the top of his head vigorously. 'I think there'd be some concern in certain quarters, yes,' he said laconically.

'I have the feeling that right now the NTSB and

Buttress have their heads up each other's knickers. What's your feeling?'

Searington inspected him. Guy stared right back. The senator rubbed his face and readjusted his glasses. He settled forward, resting his arms on his knees. 'Now let's just back this up a little.' His forehead knitted and he spoke to the floor. 'Now we both been pilots a long time, and me, I've been one longer'n you're old and I've been in the Congress since before you drew your first crayon picture of an aeroplane.' His tone was calm but resolute. 'Now I know about aeroplanes and I know about the FAA and I know about the Congress and I know what Buttress did for this country when the Japs were swarming around the Philippines and shooting our boys in the water and a few fellows at Buttress rolled up their sleeves and brought their lunches in over the weekends and began pushing out the first silver snub-nosed foldaway fighters that let us get in our first licks.' He was speaking fondly now. 'They used to stop the downtown traffic so that those Buttress boys could roll their fuselages through the streets, right on to the docks, where merchant marine transports was waiting for them and the people stopped and applauded on the sidewalks as they rolled by and suddenly the air was like pure oxygen.' He got up, glanced at Guy, crossed to the window, and stood there, a silhouette against the sky.

'The people at Buttress, fallible as they are as human beings, shoot straight, and they never did give us anything less than a dollar's worth.'

'Then how about getting the doors to that session open?'

'I can't do that.' He turned away from the window. 'But I'll tell you what I will do. We'll take a picture together, me with my arm around you, and you can stick that in the pilot's newsletter.' He waited for a response, then not taking his eyes off Guy, leaned over, pressed the intercom and said, 'Get Matthew up here with his camera.'

Searington was rugged, a plainsman rendered polite by

careful grooming. Guy let the offer lie and picked up the senator's reaction instead.

'Then I'd like to recommend that you and I do our own investigation. You're a man who likes the inside track,' he said. Searington let go of the intercom key. Guy had got out of the blue couch to go to a black framed aerial view of Andrews Air Force Base hanging on the wall. He pointed to it.

'We're fifty minutes from there,' he said. 'The cover of *Aviation Week* shows they have a 17-10 waiting on the ramp. The second delivery out of six. I've never known anyone to refuse a senator who also happens to be an Air Force general a joy ride.'

Searington remained crouched over his desk.

'I've been trying to make the point I believe there's something wrong with the aeroplane, Senator. So let's you and me take her up over the bay and see exactly what she's made of!'

Searington rose and faced Guy in the half-light.

'And if they need time to set up a suitable reception for you, I'll call in sick, cancel my next trip and we can do it in the morning!'

For the moment the distance disappeared between them. Suddenly they were colleagues in a possibility. Searington liked the idea. He wished he could undertake it, and regretted he was no longer free to do so; nevertheless, the futile possibility played in his head: he *could* arrange it, and in two or three hours, by tomorrow morning at the latest, they could be pulling that 17-10 up over Cheasapeake Bay. It had drama. The senator could make news with it now or save it for later. What time was it? He checked his watch. They could do it . . . it would endanger his chairmanship of the upcoming Peck-Searington hearings on the Buttress loan extension . . . he wished that were the only consideration. He envied Guy's freedom and earnestness. He had known it in himself in combat over Chemnitz and Ludwigshafen, but he was no

111

longer a lanky fighter pilot and he had to differentiate between a nostalgia for it which was almost gone and the current realities which had since reshaped his commitments – and so he said, a bit too piously, 'No senator's got the right to commandeer a seventy-million-dollar aeroplane! The base commander won't go for it!'

'This one will if he's interested in another star! He'll go for it and kiss your ass in the bargain!'

The challenge couldn't be ignored. Searington turned and looked out at the clouds. 'We'd have to have something to go on. Look for something specific. Not just bore holes up there.'

'You have the power to make the trade-off and get us an open hearing or you can come upstairs with me, and we can do that before sundown.'

Searington leaned back and shut off the air conditioning. He spoke with hushed urgency. 'Trouble with it is, you got nothing specific to go on. You got to let go a little, boy, if you got nothing specific.' The words dropped to a half whisper as if he were telling a secret. 'We all see spooks in the cockpit! I flown with them too!' He turned and stalked towards the couch, cleaning his glasses.

Guy's voice rumbled, barely disguising his rage. 'Do I tell your girl to get us a car?'

Searington swept the Washington *Post* off the couch and slapped it back down. 'Now the paper come out every day since your accident and they been no emuhgency! 17-10s takin' off and gettin' on the step, clockin' off departure and arrival times and all nice and filled up with passengers chompin' on peanuts and lookin' down on the nimbostratus and smellin' the nice smell of new seats. Why, the only thing the 17-10 ain't got is a gold-plated shower in first class, and I'm fixin' to talk to old Hollis about that!'

'OK, you go talk to old Hollis about that.' Guy crossed to his flight bag and picked it up.

'I'm talkin' 'bout sumpin' . . . !' The senator raised his voice, but Guy cut him off.

112

'I'm talking about doing something up front right now, while both our feet are on the ground, and there's no blood spilled!'

Searington stuck his neck out like an angry rooster. 'And I'm politely suggesting you not take on the whole industry because of a leftover itch in the seat of your pants!' The senator came closer. 'But there's another point and it's something you ought to have in the back of your mind before you go out of here. You see, there are times Mrs Searington and I been overseas and we've both been ready to kiss the skin of that 747 or now the 17-10 waiting for us out there at Heathrow or De Gaulle to take us home. After all that polite food and four-hundred-year-old plumbing there she is, that beautiful hunk of metal standing tall, made at home, and when you sit inside it, it's like being back a little early.' The senator smiled and his tone was smooth. 'But they's another side to all this,' and his smile fell abruptly. 'Most often, when an Italian or a Dutchman looks up at a jet contrail passing overhead, he's looking at a piece of Seattle or Long Beach, and though that may be a subtle way of advertising, it's nothing any of us want to lose.' He turned to the window next to his desk and gazed out. 'We've already settled down in front of the Japanese TV set, our pants are made in Taiwan, our shoes, Mr Anders, are coming in from Spain, the Japs and Germans are running up and down our highways and the national debt gets worse every year. So we don't want to be too fast to turn against our own products.' Albert Searington took hold of the armrest on his swivel chair and sat down between the American and Virginian flags.

'There's a process here, mister,' he continued. 'I've learned over the years there's a process. You cross that process and no one here's even gonna let you state your case.' Almost gently he added, 'You go for a little piece at a time in this town.' He smiled and reached for the phone. 'Now, let's you and me get our picture taken.'

Guy's voice was deeper than he expected. 'I get the feeling somebody's paid for you in full.' They were both aware of the thousand-day clock silently turning on the mantelpiece.

Albert Searington didn't move. He slowly recradled the phone. 'I think you better get out of here,' he said softly.

Guy turned and pulled the door open. A thin fellow holding a camera stood outside the doorway. An older man carrying a floodlight stood behind him staring at Guy.

'You fellows are next.' Guy greeted them with a flourish. 'Go ahead in and set up. And screw in the wide-angle lens if you have one. You may want a shot of the senator talking out of both sides of his mouth!'

5

Guy traced Ben Reese from the Coast to New York to Washington to a rooming house behind the Capitol and told him to meet him at the Senate Coffee Shop.

'Jesus H. Christ, you didn't say *that* to Albert Searington!' Ben exclaimed. 'You can't talk to a senator that way.'

'I need a second pair of hands.'

'Put an ad in the paper.'

'Somebody with experience in dealing with these people.'

'Somebody successful.'

'Right.'

'Then shove off.'

'Somebody who might be sympathetic,' Guy persisted.

Ben mopped up the remains of his fried egg and hoisted his glass to his eyebrows. 'So they're going to wipe your nose in it,' he said.

'I could use a road map.'

'I don't have any road maps,' Ben said. 'I always went

114

by instinct and instinct isn't equal any more to the electronic circuit.' He refolded a paper napkin and wiped his mouth. 'The Buttress F-19 is the biggest piece of flying shit ever to come out of an American hangar and yet the computer printout says she's terrific. Sixteen guys killed so far because they can't keep it up or put it down, and yet my retraction in print is proof that the computer in that aeroplane and the people who make their bread from it are right.' The storms that once washed over him clouded Ben's eyes, and their force had permanently pleated his face. He was tanned and the sun had lightened the edges of his red-blond hair, but he looked tired and older than his forty-nine years.

'I'll offer you this: if I were you I wouldn't bother with Searington. I'd get busy with people who could get me a verbatim of the final ride into JFK. Find out who said what out in the open – words that can be used against the crew.'

'The cockpit voice tape . . .'

'There are two. The original's at the NTSB. One copy's at the underwriter's office. Intercarrier writes all of Air World's insurance. And if it were me I wouldn't bother with the NTSB.'

As Ben spoke, Guy became aware of another figure in the room, a tall man buying a refill for his lighter.

Ben noticed the figure too. 'I'd also keep an eye out to see if I were growing a tail.' He nodded towards the stranger. 'Now, I can't prove any of this because if we lifted his ID it wouldn't say Buttress on it. But that's who he works for and he's here on no other business than to see what you're up to.' Ben produced a crumpled ten-dollar bill. 'Ten bucks says he'll split if you go for the door.'

Guy reached down and covered the bet. 'You'll forgive me if I have more faith in people than that.' He checked the distance to the exit, suddenly stood and made his move. The stranger grabbed his change, turned on his heel and hurried to the door. Guy whirled and crashed into the man, who backed off and apologized.

Ben pocketed the bet.

Guy sat down. 'That could have been an accident.'

Ben disagreed. 'You're not sceptical enough . . . I charge by the hour and you're not telling me what's on your mind.'

'We need to get that hearing open. And we can do it with facts.'

Ben passed a fresh cigar under his nose. 'Go out and sit on top of the obelisk and look down at Arlington and at the cabs filled with ambitious little bastards plucking at the public trough and find out how this game is played. And then tell me about facts. I wasn't wrong about the Buttress F-19 but I'm unemployed.'

'You got your facts mixed up with fortune-telling. Answer me this. Who's so goddamn keen to keep those doors shut?'

'Warm bodies concerned with proprietary interests, classified materials, national security – physical and economic – and there's one more . . .'

'The loan guarantee . . .'

'And the European competition. Washington doesn't want to put the blueprints of our last shot at worldwide aviation dominance on the public record. And you're the goat.' Ben took a drag on his cigar. 'They're going to pack Cosgrove off to memory lane and set you and Hanks up for suspension. And a month from now they'll be picking their noses, telling themselves the 17-10's safe! And they'll only get away with it in a closed room.' He let the smoke curl around his brow. 'But you won't pry those doors open with facts. The game here isn't played that way.' Then, smiling wryly, he continued, 'You want an open hearing? I'll get you an open hearing.' His face folded, became malevolent. Guy studied him cautiously. Ben shifted towards the steam table and shot a subdued whistle through his teeth. Morton Judd, the bespectacled, rapidly greying ABS Washington correspondent, was paying for a hot roast beef platter. Reese gestured for him to come over. He wore a navy-blue Savile Row suit and his curly hair was plastered down at the sides as if he'd just come from the barber.

Morton Judd had been aware since childhood that he was not a natural, but he'd worked seven days a week and mastered his material. His bullet-hard, nonstop virtuoso performances during national crises had earned him tacit acceptance if not love from his colleagues. He'd always enjoyed being with Ben, who in the early years had treated him as a friend even when no one else had.

Ben shoved the debris around on the small table to make room and introduced Guy.

'Come on and sit down.' Judd moved the salt and pepper aside and slid in behind his tray. 'I need a favour,' Ben said. Mort winced, tucked a napkin in over his tie and cut into the roast beef.

'What kind of favour?'

Ben reached over and took his fork away. Morton Judd looked up and recentred his glasses.

'I want you to make a call to the Hill for me. I want you to call Albert Searington.'

'You must have some two-hundred-year-old whiskey you want to get rid of.'

Reese shot a glance at the next table, then said quietly, 'I'm going to give you something that'll put you three weeks ahead of the Washington *Post*.'

'And then what – ten years in jail?'

Ben took the cigar out of his mouth and bent the ash off on to his plate. 'How did Searington vote on the Freedom of Information Act?'

'Affirmative.'

Ben reset himself, scraping his chair on the floor. 'OK, now this same proponent of open access to information, this same cocksucker who speaks of Thomas Jefferson as though they were cronies because they're both from

117

Virginia, now thinks it's better if the government investigation on the smoking 17-10 this man helped land in New York Thursday should be held in secret!'

'You still chasing up and down those runways?' Judd asked ruefully. Then, looking pained as though by indigestion, he added, 'I can lose ten Nielson points just being *seen* at this table.'

'But you haven't asked me *why* he wants it closed, you bastard.' Reese shoved Judd's tray aside and moved closer. 'So they can ram the loan guarantee through three weeks from now with no questions left dangling!'

Judd checked Guy for verification, then to Ben said, 'You don't know that.'

'I can't afford to know different and neither can you, unless you've taken to wearing an anchor up your ass.'

Guy watched the two, the one squeezed in by his collar, trying to assess the validity of this street intelligence, the other in his worn military shirt and epaulets looking more like a foreman on a highway construction gang.

'Morty, I want you to call Searington and tell him you're doing a piece on the validity of the Freedom of Information Act and how you just heard the NTSB is going to smother the hearing on the near-miss at Kennedy and would he care to comment.'

Judd held his breath.

Ben's eyes coaxed like those of a teacher waiting for a clue to sink in but Judd wanted the rest of it.

'It's coronation time!' Reese moaned encouragingly as though Judd had almost got it. 'The 17-10 has finally made it to the gate! They're perfuming the streets! They're shining St Patty's bell to ring in our newest ambassador and they want Anders and anyone else who might have embarrassing questions to ask dead and they're going to see to that by hanging him and his friends in the basement!'

'You've been reading tea leaves again,' said Judd.

'No he hasn't,' Guy broke in. Judd's eyes flicked back

118

and forth across Guy's face. 'There's a picture of Searington and my boss and "old Hollis", as he called him, on the wall of his office. The three of them are standing around a Lancejet and my guess is they weren't discussing the critical Mach number of the swept-back wing.'

'My father once took a picture with Adolf Hitler,' said Judd.

'But I don't figure you have that hanging on your wall,' Guy replied.

'Searington's got contraband in his closet,' Ben added.

Judd glanced up under his thick eyebrows. 'That's a guess,' he said. 'That's more of your rotgut instinct.'

'Then what's a Republican senator who's an Air Force Reserve general doing sitting on open disclosure? What the hell do you want, corroboration from the New York *Times*? The serial numbers of the cheques he's cashed at the supermarket?'

'That's dangerous!' Judd warned.

'But what if it's true, you dummy? I'm handing you a wedge on a silver platter to find out!' Ben rose and tried to get Judd out of his chair. 'Come on, for God's sake, I'll do the same for you when they replace you on the tube with a doe-eyed girl from the Midwest.' Ben stuck the cigar back in his mouth. Judd got up. 'Besides, I hear they're getting pissed with you. You're not laughing it up enough on the news any more!' Reese tossed Guy the fork. 'Anders here will eat your dinner for you.' Ben dug into his shapeless trousers, came up with a coin, pressed it into the correspondent's hand and steered him towards the coin box. 'I'm telling you, they'll give you a new hairstyle, stick your face on a billboard and give you a crack at "The Today Show".'

They squeezed past the last table. Ben held the correspondent by his arm and, like a coach with last-second instructions, gave him the play.

'Now you're on a tight deadline and you know how valuable he's always been and you just want to know his view because there are some people who want to crucify him on TV because of the way he's contradicting himself,' Ben prompted, 'and you're on your way over with a camera crew and you sure would like his clarification.' Ben took the receiver off the hook and placed it in the man's hand. He looked into Judd's face and smiled, his eyes alive with excitement. 'And you won't have to leave the building. I just want you to sow the seed. Searington will do the rest. Make an appointment for two-thirty. That's when you'll be having your hernia fixed. Your secretary will call and cancel with regrets. Will you do it?'

Judd pulled his napkin away from his tie. 'It's been rough on you, hasn't it, Benny?'

Ben's face softened. 'I'm out of credentials.'

Judd slowly nodded. He shifted his gaze to the floor. 'I get nervous when I lie, so beat it.'

Ben let go of his arm. He smiled and lingered for a moment. 'That's good,' he said, beginning to enjoy the image of the dramatic effect the phone call would have. The jukebox began tootling a piece of Dixieland. Reese took a breath and ambled back to the table, his head bobbing to the beat.

'They're going to open that hearing so wide they'll have to hold it in Yankee Stadium!' He cracked his knuckles, looked back at Judd on the phone and sat down. Guy was smiling.

The sky was loaded. Office lights were going on early under a cold new rain. Despite the low scud Guy flew his T-34 from Washington National, where he'd parked it two days before, back to Long Island. He found the house empty. The fatigue returned and washed over him as he stood at the refrigerator, eyes shut, drinking milk to calm his exhausted insides. He fell into bed with his shirt on. When he awoke it was eleven. Both Anja and Jamie were gone.

He padded into the kitchen.

No messages.

Damn.

He thought of phoning crew scheduling to see if he'd been replaced, but decided to drive out and check the roster in person. He realized that if he were not disrupted he'd be back at the controls of another 17-10 in less than seven hours.

The shadow of an idea on how to get his hands on the Air World Six cockpit voice tape had started to form. He'd think it through on his way to the airport.

He reached Kennedy just before twelve. At crew scheduling he found his name listed next to Flight Five – the evening departure for London. The captain would be Roger Beaucamp. Shit.

He went to his locker and changed into his uniform. Next he took a small Lanier cassette recorder from his flight bag and stuffed it into his jacket. When reaching for his hat he noticed the photograph given him the night of the fiery landing. There was the scene frozen as in his memory. Tipping the picture to reduce the glare, he studied the soot path the fire had taken. Surprising how much of the plane had been engulfed.

Then he noticed something new.

He folded the photograph reflectively and slipped it into his inside pocket.

Outside a car horn blasted him back to the sidewalk. He heard a girl laughing. He recognized Synova, a stew he knew slightly, sitting in her powder-blue Stingray looking eighteen, only she was twenty-two and had already flown for a year, happy to get away. She'd worked Flights Five and Six, the London–New York route. He recalled her sitting in the cockpit jump seat on a flight coming home, her knees together, leaning forward, her chin in her hands as she told about herself, her high school in Florida and the suffocation of hearing about the church from her father, who was a minister, and sitting in cars with guys who were going to sell insurance or work for IBM and how she loved to drive into the country by herself, shut off the engine and wait for a UFO or God or a stranger, and then she wanted to hear about everyone in the cockpit, where they came from, why they flew, what they thought. She was a tomboy with them but she was soft and graceful, too, and that's what Guy thought about in the cockpit. And she had watched Guy, sitting confident and relaxed in the right seat, and she'd decided then and there that she wanted him.

She looked at him now and said to herself, Now I know what I'm going to do today.

'You coming or going?' she called.

Guy looked at her and said to himself, Now I know how I'm going to get that tape. He came down to the car. She was tanned, wearing a white blouse.

'I'm coming but I'm going too,' he smiled. The breeze lifted the end of her hair against her mouth.

'If you don't know if you're coming or going, get in and take some time to think it over.'

Guy pulled the door open and got in. She eased them away from the curb and gunned down the ramp. Guy leaned against the door to watch her drive.

'Where we going?'

'To soft and mysterious places' – she feigned an ominous tone – 'where neither of us has ever been before.' She laughed and tossed her head to look at him. Her eyes glowed softly, unafraid. The Stingray flowed around the plodding lines of cars on the Belt Parkway, occasionally riding the shoulder, churning dust, overtaking the oncoming waves of horizons.

'I need a collaborator,' Guy tempted.

Synova glanced at him, his hair whipping in the wind.

'What kind of collaborator?'

'To help take something away from some boys in black hats *while* they're looking at it. It'll be a little like making love in public without anyone noticing.'

'I once thought of doing that on a commuter train,' Synova smiled. 'If it doesn't work could we end up going to jail for it?'

'Oh, yeah.'

'Then let's do it.'

Guy told her they would have to move fast. He directed her on to the Cross Island Parkway, then the turnoff that fronted a shopping mall, where he had her pull into the parking field.

He got out, locking the door. Synova reangled the rearview mirror so she could see herself, unaware of the beat-up Plymouth that pulled in two rows behind her.

Minutes later Guy returned with a rectangular black case, which he placed carefully on the back seat.

'The shortest distance to your place,' he commanded. They drove under the elevated on Roosevelt Avenue, Synova trying to stay even with a clattering train overhead, inching closer to the truck in front, squeezing past yellow lights that threatened to turn. Guy hollered instructions to her through the din. She would not be able to go with him, he shouted. She would have to wait at her house.

'What do I do by myself?' she cried. Did she know how to operate a Lanier? She thought so. He pulled the pocket-sized recorder from his jacket and placed it between them.

'And I'm going to need your car, too!'

'Never!'

'Then let's call it off and drop me at Hertz!'

'You can have the car!'

A red light stopped them. The screech above diminished as the train jolted away, allowing soft rays of sun to slant back down through the metal beams. The beat-up Plymouth that had been trailing them pulled up directly behind.

'I was going to get your clothes off,' she said quietly.

'Don't let go of that idea just yet.'

They drove to her building and she got out. Guy slid in behind the wheel.

123

'I'm going to need a ride to the airport, so don't go away.'

Synova pouted. 'Don't let anything happen to this,' she appealed, holding on to the open door.

'Stay near the phone,' Guy said.

She threw the door shut. Guy cleared the traffic on his left and pulled away.

With luck he'd be in Greenwich just past two.

The Intercarrier Life and Casualty Company had been around for a hundred years but wasn't old any more, at least not by appearance. The lobby was a cast stucco cavern with a huge rustlike smear spread across one wall signed at the bottom in stilted letters. The orange carpeting was deep, the lighting from high overhead indirect, and in the epicentre of this rotunda, which was silent except for the discreet bubbling of a distant indoor waterfall, was a round white formica desk that encircled the receptionist. She was a young woman in white with her hair up. Her eyes were blue orbs that filled the rimless glasses hanging over her nose. They gave her the look of an expectant fish and seemed to detach themselves to inspect Guy's uniform from an inch away.

'I'm here to see the chairman,' Guy stated as though in conclusion.

'Is he expecting you, sir?'

'No, he's not.' Guy placed his arm on the desk to make sure his three stripes were in evidence.

'Your name, sir?'

'Anders.' She depressed a sequence of push buttons on her console and nestled the phone to her ear.

'There's a Mr Anders here to see the chairman. The gentleman has no appointment.' Guy caught her attention, pointed to the orange house phone and winked at her encouragingly.

'Let me speak to her,' he whispered. He took the receiver, shielded it from the receptionist.

'Hi, you his secretary?'

'Yes, I am,' said a polite elderly voice. The receptionist cut herself off the line.

'Listen, I'm a first officer with Air World and I need only a few minutes of the chairman's time.'

'Yes, well, that wouldn't be possible without making an appointment first.'

'Could you put him on the line? What I have to see him about is urgent.'

'Sir, he's not in his office.'

'Is he at lunch?'

'He will not see anyone –'

'Is he in the building then?' Guy insisted.

The secretary paused, then her voice came back; it had gone brittle. 'Sir, he's in the gym in the executive fitness programme and cannot be interrupted.'

'Right, well, I understand that and I appreciate it. Tell him I'll write for an appointment.' Guy hung up and turned to the receptionist.

'Which way to the gym?'

The gym was on the third floor, set behind a room like an air lock, stark and small, with deck chairs around the wall. Through the glass in the door Guy saw the stationary bicycles and treadmills in place. On each machine was the shape of a man churning methodically, the slow pistons of tugboats; all were wearing identical gym clothes with the Intercarrier logo, flags fluttering from their smokestacks. A loud voice from behind startled him.

'Who are you looking for?'

Guy spun around but there was no one in the room with him. It was a deep voice, Jamaican, Guy thought.

'I'm here to see the chairman.'

'This floor is off limits, sir. You may want to contact his secretary.'

Guy realized he was having a conversation with an overhead speaker.

'I've been through that. My mission here is critical.'

All at once the doors opened with a burst of steamy

125

haze and body odour. Amid the efflux stood a muscular black man in tight T-shirt, grey sweat pants and sandals. His upper arms had the supple fullness of a prize-fighter's.

'Come on in.' It was the same voice but unamplified this time. Guy suddenly felt the heat crawl all over him with tiger's paws. The room was large, padded, oddly quiet. He missed the exuberant yelling and slap of sneakers one subconsciously associates with gyms. Instead there came only the rhythmic *swish-swish* of the treadmills churning, interspersed with heavy breathing. Half a dozen men were working with single-minded intensity.

There was a hospital-eerie feel to the place. A dimly lit four-bed cardiopulmonary resuscitation room was adjacent, door open, and Guy could see the ominously apparent defibrillators looking like white electronic units with loose Mickey Mouse ears strung to them. And here, across the threshold, executives like separate gods were in training, but each with one eye on that room – a brother-hood trying to shove one another into the electric fence.

On the other side of the main room was the massage area. A flab of meat lay like a beached whale on one table, while a block-faced man with slant eyes kneaded the prostrate mound as if probing for bones. Nearby a white-haired man sat in a Jacuzzi. Guy had a hunch, walked straight to him and knelt down.

'I helped save you two hundred and fifty million dollars in death claims last Thursday – not to mention another seventy-odd million you would have had to pay for the hull had we missed the runway. I want a half hour of your time in exchange.'

The chairman looked at Guy with the cold assessment of a field marshal. Guy met the older man's look and prevented it from gaining any advantage. The chairman refused to break off the engagement.

'Is there anyone else who should be in on this?' he asked, trying to dislodge water from his ear.

'Anybody who does any decision making on aviation matters.'

The chairman gazed out at his executive vice-president on a bicycle. The executive vice-president had sweat running off him in lakes. The chairman called his name.

'Any man that's carrying the kind of weight and responsibility of these boys you see here has to spend seven and a half hours per week right here or they don't get paid,' the chairman confided. The executive vice-president wiped his face on a towel handed him by the black trainer and hunkered down. The chairman had Guy introduce himself and waited for him to continue. Guy surveyed them both, then spoke.

'I'll venture a guess the product liability claims that this industry is exposed to presently exceed its net worth.'

Silence except for a jogger's pounding footfalls and the burble of the whirlpool.

'You ought to know,' Guy went on, 'that you're underwriting a sick aeroplane.'

The executive vice-president waited for the chairman to respond and when he didn't, carped, 'Which aeroplane is that?'

'The 17-10.'

The executive vice-president spotted a quick gain. 'You're talking about a brand-new aeroplane that's just been declared safe,' he ordained.

'According to the FAA,' responded Guy. 'But you tell me, was the FAA regulating or was it promoting?'

The executive vice-president reacted as though Guy had made a ghastly error on his chessboard. He waited for Guy to retrieve it. Finally he spoke. 'That would be contrary to integrated thinking!' he crowed.

Guy cringed at the executive jargon. The VP continued to lecture that the 17-10 had been through the system and granted birth with appropriate certification. There was something chilling about him – zealous yet peaceful, as though caught in the spell of an alien faith.

127

The chairman, who had come up through the streets, recognized something basic in Guy's rebellion and with a reproving look advised his vice-president to be quiet.

'Go on, Anders.'

'I want you to help me break through the protective ring that has that plane surrounded.'

'That's a lot to put on the table at one time,' declared the chairman.

'Maybe,' said Guy. 'But if I'm right and your insurance is based on publicity instead of facts, it could leave you holding the bag.'

The chairman watched Guy with narrow eyes, then turned away with an abrupt motion and splashed hot water on to his face. 'Engine fires are a hundred dollars deductible, aren't they, Eugene?' he ventured offhandedly. The second in command chortled appreciatively. Guy eyed the two of them warily.

'If you believe that was an engine fire we flew, maybe you better get a second opinion.' He removed the eight- by-ten photograph from his inside coat pocket and unfolded it.

'I want you to look at this.'

'I need my glasses.' The chairman hauled himself from the pool, grabbed a towel around his nakedness and took the dark-rimmed specs held out for him by the prizefighter. The exec vice-president touched a light switch in the heart-rescue room. Guy spread the photograph flat on the bed. The second in command adjusted an overhead spotlight.

'That's the aft end of the aeroplane and that's the starboard fuel shroud drain situated in front of the number three engine.' Guy touched it lightly with the blunt end of a pencil. 'Look closely around the rim of it. Part of it's melted and lost its shape. The lip is frayed and curled inward. Now if all we had was an engine fire, who the hell started this one eight feet further forward?' The chairman pulled the picture closer. Guy waited. 'If there were *two* fires or at least one *preceding* the engine fire, you may be into a little more than a hundred dollars deductible.'

The chairman looked up.

'What do you want, Anders?'

'I want the cockpit voice tape of that flight. You go along with me and I'll see that you get better data to work with before you hang any more of your underwriters out on the line.' He looked up at them. They stared back. 'All I need is a room, a pencil and a pad of paper.' He pointed to his bag. 'I brought my own playback, just in case yours is busy.'

The chairman frowned in the direction of his heir apparent, took the wall phone off the hook and picked out his extension.

'The cockpit voice tape, Air World Six, JFK last Thursday, bring it to me. And bring some paper.' He put down the phone. 'I can't let you have it,' he said, 'but I can let you listen to it here provided one of us is present.'

The door shut with a sigh. Guy was alone in the cool heart-rescue room. He unsnapped the black case and placed the new tape deck on the night stand next to the white phone. He then took his business card and carefully folded it into a four-sided cube with half-inch-high sides. He picked up the phone, got an outside line and dialled Synova collect so that there would be no trace of the call on the company's records.

At that moment, outside in the visitors' parking lot, a man stood leaning against the blue Stingray, his head tilted back strangely, asymmetrically, seemingly enjoying the end of the lunch-hour sun. Another car started up and drove to the exit. As soon as it left the property, the man turned around, opened the hood of Synova's car and drew a thin wire from a tiny box which he attached to the underside of the hood, threaded it up the windshield and embedded it into a white claylike grouting tamped around the edge of the glass. Then he eased the hood back down.

Twenty-six miles across the bay, Synova placed the Lanier recorder next to the earpiece on her phone and waited. She could faintly make out what was going on on the other side. She heard Guy tell her, 'Don't touch the phone and don't hang up till I do.' Synova didn't answer, but watched fascinated, witness to an as yet undisclosed event.

The exec VP, red-faced from the workout and looking refreshed and tanned against his pinstripe, came in just as Guy placed the receiver on top of the white paper cube positioned between the disconnect buttons. To the casual eye, except for the lit extension light, the phone had not been disturbed. The exec VP handed Guy a yellow pad and a flat ten-inch box containing the tape.

Guy opened the box and slipped the tape out of its aluminium wrap.

'What is it you hope to find?' asked the executive.

'The language of gremlins,' answered Guy as he snapped the tape into place. 'The background sounds, an "instant replay" in greater detail. Part of the answer of what went wrong and when it went wrong is on that tape. We just have to find it.' Guy finished threading the quarter-inch tape, set the speed at 1¾ IPS and turned up the volume. The vice-president stood uncomfortably, blocking the door as though to prevent Guy's escape.

Guy hit the fast forward lever to be sure they had the right tape. He stopped the tape and pressed 'play'.

Synova heard a few seconds of what seemed like static. Then she recognized Guy.

'How low do you wanna go, W.B.?'

'I don't give a damn. Just clear us right on down. Do it now before we hit someone!'

'Six is requesting flight level two zero zero initially.'

'Unable two zero zero. Descend and maintain two four zero, I'll have lower in . . .'

Guy rewound the tape and started it from the beginning. The vice-president, fascinated, watched Guy with new admiration. The chairman slipped inside the room and stood listening. Guy wrote on the yellow pad and eyed the white paper cube that held the receiver above the disconnect buttons.

Outside the building, the man who had wired the Stingray sat waiting in the Plymouth.

The tape began leaving the building as surely as if Guy were carrying it out under his arm.

Synova glanced at the clock next to her bed. It was just past three. Guy had to be on board for London in less than three hours.

Guy watched the reels turn and heard the whine of the landing gear going down again and he heard chips of voices mingled with static. The chairman and his number one were riveted. There was a terrible groan from Cosgrove's throat. Involuntarily Guy's arm flexed as if to pull the plane up over the threshold and in doing so his hand knocked the telephone receiver off its paper perch and on to the table. The executives were startled. The paper cube fell harmlessly to the floor. Guy recradled the phone. He would not have the landing but he had enough to have analysed by a lab he might be able to reach through a source in London.

The tape stopped.

'Shall I rewind it?'

'Do you have enough?' asked the chairman.

'It's a beginning. And I'll keep my word to you. I'll copy you verbally on anything I find out.' Guy handed them the tape and resnapped his case. He smiled at both of them and said, 'Meanwhile, if I were you, I'd handle requests for new insurance . . . gingerly.'

The Stingray ignition chattered and sent a surge of power through the car's innards. Guy turned out of the parking lot and took the centre lane of the boulevard that curved to the east. It was just past three-thirty; he felt euphoric. Although made over a telephone line, a copy of the recording was in his possession, and that was a start.

Traffic increased. He found himself boxed in, slowing down, moving past the roadside stands that became more numerous at the edge of town. The traffic in front cleared. He settled back and caught a glimpse of the red needle moving past sixty.

He didn't notice the Plymouth that now hung with him in tight formation.

Guy moved the Stingray into the fast lane. The driver of the Plymouth held his position in the centre. Next to him on the seat was a small black box sprouting a six-inch antenna. He lowered his window a crack, slipped the antenna through the opening.

Guy saw a distant overhead marker but the split-second process of interpreting it was interrupted by the ear-splitting report of close thunder, and his view ahead splintered into a thousand jagged sections. Inches from his head, sharp bits of destroyed windshield speared back to imbed themselves into the seat. Instinctively he ducked and jammed on the brakes, gripping the wheel to keep the car straight. He didn't see the Plymouth streak by. When he looked up the Stingray was stopped, ticking over, and for the moment the road was empty. The windshield immediately in front of his face was ballooned six inches into the car, shattered by a thousand white veins, but it had held. Nine inches away was a gaping hole with edges like shark's teeth.

The same thing had happened to him years earlier when a kid pegged a snowball, hitting his windshield and exploding it with an impact of sixty miles an hour. This had been something like it. Perhaps it was a rock, he thought, a ricochet off a truck tyre. But he was surprised that he hadn't seen it coming. Briefly it occurred to him that he could have been maimed for life, blinded, his career ruined, and he shuddered. Then he thought of Synova. He pulled her car over and worked feverishly to free the bits of windshield, then drove it slowly to her place.

Synova's apartment was on the ground floor of a subdivided onetime mansion that overlooked Little Neck Bay on Long Island Sound. Her carpeted living room was a gallery of posters and Turkish hanging lamps picked up on trips abroad. The place was neatly furnished with suede pillows, a beige couch and two beanbag chairs facing a room divider filled with quadraphonic components. John Denver and Sinatra were on tape, playing in concert.

Guy stood in her bathroom and put drops in his eyes. The Lanier on the sink was turned to full blast.

'. . . thirteen miles to go,' it crackled. 'You're cleared all the way.' It was the controller's voice. 'Contact Kennedy tower now on one nineteen point one.' The recording was remarkably clean. Guy shut it off. Synova had been quiet. She was upset about the car.

'No telling what might have happened if you'd been sitting there, too!' he called. But there was no need to shout. She was behind him leaning against the door frame, her features sharpened by the backlight coming from the living room window. She stood impetuously, yet graceful, just as she had done in the cockpit. She wanted to play. Guy's eyes were smarting from the drops.

'Keep them shut.' Her voice was enticing. 'Go on . . . tilt your head back and let the nice medicine do what it's supposed to. Don't look yet.' An oscilloscopelike line crawled down on the insides of his eyelids. He heard the light switch followed by her silky command. 'OK, turn around . . . now open and tell me what you see.' Guy blinked and waited for his eyes to adjust to the subdued light. She was standing, her white blouse in her hand, posed like the featured nude in *Playboy* leaning provocatively against the door frame. Europe and London were far beyond her living room window, beyond the bay. Her apartment was warm. He led her to the bedroom where the twilight sculptured her body in smooth halftones. She was exquisite.

'God Almighty, I'm actually going to miss the flight!'

'Only until the taxi comes,' she said, working to unbutton his shirt.

A muted horn sounded the moment she said it. Guy moved the curtain. A yellow cab, its roof light on, was parked behind the Stingray. Synova sat down on the bed and pulled the rumpled bedspread against her.

'I've had a fantastically lousy day,' she sulked. Then her face softened. 'I thought it was going to be more like Bonnie and Clyde.'

'I'll be back Monday morning,' Guy consoled.

Synova reached over, took a key from her dresser and placed it in his palm.

'What's this?'

'Your season's pass.' Her eyes glistened. She added, 'I'm happy you got what you wanted. I really am.'

Guy stuffed the Lanier into his shirt pocket and took her hand.

'By the way,' she said, 'just before you came, there was something on the news.'

'Oh?'

'They said your hearing's going to be open to the public.'

Captain Roger Beaucamp, settled in the captain's chair, surveyed the computer-generated flight plan, head tilted back, squinting down through his Ben Franklin spectacles. Guy Anders, buckled loosely in the right seat, had always felt an estrangement flying with Beaucamp, who had never moved comfortably to Guy's earnestness. Beaucamp's right eyelid had begun to twitch as he peered around the cockpit from within his bricklike face. Without meeting Guy's eyes, he announced, 'Way I put it together, you weren't much help to W.B. the other night.'

Guy leaned forward to adjust the course and heading readouts on his horizontal situation display. 'You ready for the checklist?'

'I don't know what your game is, maybe trying to earn some outside pay, whatever. Just you remember, some of us don't mind working for this outfit. Some of us aren't too keen about anyone taking a leak on Air World. And

134

I'm not overburdened with enthusiasm for the choice of co-pilot crew scheduling has dumped on me tonight.'

'That's called fate, Rog.' Guy forced one of his kid grins.

'If you decide to push your slander against this company any further, some of us might move to stop you. Now this flight will be operated strictly by the book, Mr Anders. Is that understood?'

'Absolutely, sir. Are you on some sort of personal slowdown programme I should know about?'

Beaucamp eyed him for the first time.

Guy met his eyes. 'Would you also like ruffles and flourishes when I call ATC?'

'Your assignment in my aircraft is not locked in cement – '

'We got ourselves a long haul coming up, Roger,' Guy reminded him. 'Computer says six hours and twenty-three minutes to London. Maybe we oughta establish a truce.'

'*You* will make the takeoff and landing. That way I can watch you. You'll use standard operating procedures throughout it. If a matter of judgment comes up, I expect you to keep your mouth shut. If it's a matter of safety, well, then, of course . . .'

Guy was not surprised that the captain had given him the takeoff and landing. It was common pilots'-lounge knowledge that Roger Beaucamp had become afraid to fly.

Guy noticed Beaucamp's twitch had spread to his hands. The wheel glistened where he touched it. He could picture Beaucamp vividly in about five years, a suddenly very old man, irascible with palsy.

They swung on to the long runway, the same one Guy and W. B. Cosgrove had landed on the night they caught fire, but there was hardly enough time to think about that as Guy took the throttles and pushed them forward. The 17-10 swept down the runway and slipped steeply into the moon-mottled sky. The landing-gear locks rumbled and

Guy banked the 17-10, watching the diamond-lit world fall away, the view expanded, and he sensed in that instant how one's cares evaporated and became as formless and ephemeral as the misty silver clouds that now flashed past the windshield.

Guy turned. An amber glow bloomed from the panel and just as quickly extinguished. Only Beaucamp noticed it. His eyes were white in the darkness.

'Hey, wait a minute. That was a warning light.'

'Where?'

'It's out.'

Guy swung back in his seat. 'Which one?'

Beaucamp pointed to the elevator control differential 'out of limit' light, now benign. The flight engineer checked the circuit breakers. Everything seemed in order.

Roger was mustering the effort to posture. 'I want us to keep an eye on it.'

'We're still within shouting distance of New York,' Guy declared. 'And I'll be perfectly frank with you: I'm not exactly game for a repeat of last Thursday.'

'Ah, shit, Anders. Get over it, huh? We don't need your jinx. The light's out and we're going to London.'

The distant lights of Boston fell behind, then the western edge of Nova Scotia. The lights below were sparse; Halifax slipped by on the right. Beaucamp hadn't spoken for an hour. Occasionally he grunted and shifted in the captain's seat. He seldom said much, and tonight he seemed particularly morose and walled off; the mood of hostility which had launched this flight was palpable. Guy was prepared to wait him out.

Yet Guy felt a passing edge of sympathy for the captain. Roger Beaucamp had spent his Air World years notorious as a stickler for whatever Air World policy, procedures or edicts found their way to his company mailbox, a true Air World fascist. It was slightly pathetic, Guy thought, that

136

Roger Beaucamp had invested so much energy into kissing middle-management ass, hoping earnestly for a desk job and at least a token title – chief check pilot, anything – and yet had been totally ignored, left to grow old and wither, two hundred numbers down on the Air World seniority list. Here he sat, twenty-nine months left to fly until his sixtieth birthday, putting in his time, hating it, maintaining his defiant loyalty almost as if by reflex.

Beaucamp had welcomed the 17-10, the opportunity to turn his motor functions over to a robot, to let a black box take over the operation, in the meantime reading his weekly trade journals, looking for a clue to the day when all he had to do was sign the logbook. It was common knowledge he'd busted his last simulator check and needed much prodding and assistance to pass after two retakes. Only four more simulator checks till he retired.

The 17-10 sped by the fiftieth meridian more than seven miles high. The moon was a ball with substance but no weight as it slid past, as though flying itself, its orbit accentuated by the jet's eastward motion, which doubled the earth's rotation. A carpet of clouds lay so far below it seemed part of another entity, removing the sense of weight from the unseen earth, and gave Guy the feeling he had been totally disconnected from his mother planet.

When Roger spoke, Guy thought at first the words had come from the radio.

'Anders, some of the boys and I, we took a vote on what you did on the tube. There's an opinion . . . I want you to know I'm not the only one . . .' He let the words hang, ugly in the close dark space between them, peering through the dim-lit shadows, unable to tell if Guy had heard.

'Hey, Rog, you're free to trust that black box that's parked under your ass. That's up to you – '

'Stepping in shit is an accident. Drawing you as a co-pilot was an accident. I don't want to step in shit again.'

'Before, when you said I wasn't much help to W.B., you

137

got me a little warm. And then when you said I was on the take, I began to get uncomfortable. Now you've got me angry.'

'If you don't like the conversation up here, you can get out of my cockpit and sit on your ass in first class. We can handle the rest of this trip alone. Of course, once we get to Heathrow, we'd hang you for mutiny. I'd get a lot of applause for it.'

Guy stared at the steadily changing light segments flashing on and off to form the numbers, the navigation computer output. 'Rog . . .,' he said at last, 'I don't mind your being a devout company prick. I never try to interfere with a man's beliefs. But I'm a natural-born heathen. The only religion that fires my interest is the truth. But that's the damnedest thing to come by.'

Roger didn't respond.

'For example,' Guy continued, 'this aeroplane doesn't belong on a runway.' He turned to the captain. 'And neither do you.'

Beaucamp sat hunched as though trying to hang on to his tight little world.

'Certain people,' Guy went on, 'when they reach a certain age, they become afraid to fly. Some hit the bottle, they climb into the cockpit with lots of chewing gum to hide the stink. Some others keep a calendar – like prisoners do in jail – counting the days to retirement, counting the takeoffs and landings that are left – staying awake at night, wondering if they can get away clean, with no screwups and in one piece.'

Beaucamp's right hand, resting on the throttles, gave a particularly violent spasm, like the jump one sometimes makes just before sleep.

'What do you think, Roger, in your vast experience, you ever hear of anyone like that?'

'You're stepping mighty close to a mutiny, Anders. No captain has to take that kind of talk.'

* * *

The 17-10 sped eastward. The first long rays of the still unrisen sun made the immense upper bowl of sky deep blue, and soon a brighter segment in the distance indicated the precise location of sunrise. Soon it was full daylight, it had come upon them too soon, as always, before they were ready for it, sour stubble on their chins and congealed empty paper cups stuffed into the sack behind the throttle pedestal. Guy's body complained that it was only 2 A.M., yet here was pristine dawn. The mantle of clouds below, like the tops of some infinite creamy pudding, became red, then almost at once blinding white, as suddenly the sun burst over the rim and speared its intolerable brilliance straight at them.

At that moment, the warning light which had blinked shortly after takeoff blinked again, then extinguished. None of the crew, busy avoiding the sun, noticed it through their red-rimmed fatigue.

The chime sounded that indicated a message on high-frequency radio awaited. Guy punched the chime off, switched on the hf monitor. 'Station calling Air World Five, go ahead.'

The voice was distant and wavering behind mountains of static. 'Air World Five, climb so as to cross ten west at flight level four one zero, go ahead.'

'Air World Five, stand by.' Guy turned to Beaucamp, who turned away.

The flight engineer said, 'Gross weight's fine, we've burned off enough fuel. It's a plus-five day, but we can make four one zero easily.'

Guy, mystified by the old man's lapse, prodded, 'I'm sure they'd like an answer some time this morning, Captain.'

Beaucamp remained silent.

'What should I tell them, that we need a little more time to think it over?' Guy spoke to the back of Beaucamp's head as though to a child who's been roughly shaken.

Beaucamp said, 'I don't want to go up.'

'Somebody westbound needs our altitude.'

'I don't give a shit.' Beaucamp's voice was gravelly, clogged with the early morning. 'Make the other bastard go up.'

'They're too heavy to get up that high by ten west, coming out of Europe.'

'Well, fuck 'em then, let 'em go down. We're staying here.' Beaucamp was intransigent. His face had the consistency of spoiled lard.

'Shanwick, Air World Five,' said Guy into the mike. 'Request remain at flight level three seven zero.'

'Unable, Five. You must change altitude. You can have four one zero or two nine zero.'

'Air World Five, stand by.' Guy turned again to Beaucamp. 'You don't have much of a choice. You want to go down to twenty-nine? That'll cost you a lot of fuel.'

Beaucamp huddled ever deeper in his chair, his head again turned away from the other crew members.

'All right now, goddammit, this is a safety matter. This isn't some simulator ride you can bust. And walk away from.'

The sun, already high in the sky, bore into the cockpit. Beaucamp turned on Anders. 'Did you forget? This is your leg . . . Let's see what kind of move you'd make.'

The authority behind the words was empty. He'd been unable to rid himself of Guy's earlier offerings. Had he become that transparent? Without looking round he shifted slightly, as a child might in sleep. After that he didn't move.

Guy regarded Beaucamp with a certain pity. Then he pressed the mike button and said, 'Shanwick, this is Air World Five, we're out of three seven zero, climbing to four one zero.'

The pilots noticed the amber elevator control differential 'out of limit' light almost simultaneously, the same one that had blinked on momentarily shortly after takeoff.

They had already begun their letdown, more than a hundred miles west of London. As the giant jet descended past the height of the uppermost reaches of cloud, it began bouncing slightly in air chopped and parcelled by convection. The crew had the impression of being strapped to office chairs suddenly loosed to roll over sharp cobbles. Each fluffy cloud was the soufflé top of an invisible cauldron, stirred by accumulating calories radiated from the patchword griddle three miles below.

The weather radar, its desk-sized antenna in the ship's bulbous nose, was on to pick out particularly sticky spots; the water droplets suspended in these clouds reflected the radar's strong bursts of microwave energy causing multi-coloured blips to form on the scopes in the cockpit by the pilot's knees. No prudent man flew too near these blips. Even the boldest pilots had learned to respect them, to do what was necessary to thread their way around and past them, for they marked the areas where the most intense vertical winds inside the clouds rubbed and sheared against each other. Sometimes the blips would grow and gang up on the scope in vicious lines, great guards and tackles of the sky crowding shoulder to shoulder, solidly, leaving no space to squeeze by, sending their ragged, wind-torn edges to curl and twist in the scope into loops and figure 9's that could rip the wings off the most solidly built aeroplane. But today they were widely spaced and for the most part benign.

The 'out of limit' light began blinking.

'I don't recall that light's supposed to *blink*,' said Roger Beaucamp slowly, nodding towards it.

The flight engineer raised his eyebrows to the expanse of circuit breaker panels on the curved roof of the cockpit. Guy turned towards the electronic data storage tube and called up the flight control system page.

'"Pitch modes A or B – select alternate,"' he read, pointing to a guarded toggle switch on the centre instrument panel.

141

Beaucamp threw the switch a couple of times. The light blinked out momentarily. Then it came on steady and glared at them. They were more than fifty miles from London's Heathrow Airport. Despite the light, the aeroplane flew normally.

The engineer ran through the alternate procedure, rechecking circuit breakers and the flight control computer self-test monitor functions. The warning light refused to go out.

A mighty cumulus loomed, one of the morning's few buildups, blinding white against the perfect blue. Not yet a full-fledged thunderhead, at fourteen thousand feet it nevertheless towered well above the 17-10. Guy leaned forward and switched ranges on the radarscope, from the fifty- to the twenty-mile scale. A faint hazy patch of greenish light glowed in his scope. He increased the intensity of the range rings, showing that the cloud centre was nine miles dead ahead. Idly he wondered if they'd have to request vectors to deviate around the cell. Heathrow approach control, issuing commands to several dozen planes, seemed distinctly indifferent.

'Air World Five, turn left heading zero seven zero, descend and maintain nine thousand,' said the approach controller.

'Left to zero seven zero, down to nine, Air World Five,' acknowledged Guy. He wheeled the massive ship into a graceful turn merely by twisting a small cursor knob on his directional indicator, looking through the window as the towering cloud fell off behind the right wing, no longer a factor for them to consider. Absently Roger Beaucamp reached down and switched the weather radar to standby, shutting off its intense electronic emission.

Abruptly the 'out of limit' light extinguished.

'What the hell did you do?' queried the flight engineer as he turned from one of the circuit-breaker panels.

Guy glanced over his shoulder, not sure it was he who'd been addressed. 'Nothing,' he said, made defensive by the engineer's tone. 'Just turned,' he added in explanation. 'We're going down.' He faced back forward and pushed the altitude select switch on the AFCS panel after dialling in '9000'.

The aeroplane descended with utter smoothness.

Beaucamp shrugged beneath his shoulder harness, regarding the 'out of limit' light in its rank, now opaque and inoffensive. 'Looks like it solved itself.'

The flight engineer muttered something, looking helplessly at his open book.

'Air World Five, turn left heading zero four zero, radar vectors to the ILS final approach course runway one zero left, descend now to four thousand.'

In the distance the Staines reservoirs shimmered like silver spoons. The clouds and turbulence were behind. It was clear all the way into London.

Guy called the IFALPA office from soot-stained Liverpool Street Station. Colleagues in the London-based International Federation of Air Line Pilots Associations had in the past used an electronics firm somewhere north of London for their own investigations into safety matters, but Guy couldn't remember where it was.

'Chelmsford,' the woman said on the phone and she identified it further. She also promised to call ahead to announce Guy's need for an urgent and secret conference with the firm's senior expert on flight recording analysis.

The ride to Chelmsford took an hour in a clanking, worn carriage lined with heavy doors that slammed in a fusillade as it jerked through the frequent stops in the shabby blight of London's eastern environs. Shortly before ten Guy found himself standing in the slightly rumpled foyer of an old mansion with high ceilings. He was presently taken into a large room surrounded by shelves of oscilloscopes, tape reels jolting in broken tempo, banks of computers with bundles of wire snaking

143

between the work tables. A lanky, almost gaunt professional man with suspenders under his apron greeted him in a soft burr. His welcome was subdued, yet he was clearly intrigued to meet the actual co-pilot of Air World Six.

'I'll just shut the door. I'm told you wish our meeting to be confidential.'

'I would prefer it.'

'We're alone.'

Guy freed his Lanier and placed it on the table. 'This is a copy of the Air World Six cockpit voice tape including our end of the phone patch from the Coast. I'd be grateful if you'd scan it for me, perhaps break it down in this more objective atmosphere.'

The professor surveyed Guy with guarded interest, the hint of a smile forming. 'Look over here, Mr Anders . . . Come this way, please. I think we've already gone a step ahead of you.'

Guy watched the older man. He picked up his tape and came around the table to join him.

'First of all, we don't require your cassette. We already have our own copy of the recording, obtained – well, let me say, very shortly after your incident.' He flicked on a bank of oscilloscopes.

Guy was intrigued. 'And we get hung for having a CIA.'

'Let me say only that our own aeronautical consortium is interested in all aspects of operational experience with fly-by-wire. We are building our own aeroplane, you know . . .'

Guy watched him adjust the levels. 'How'd the crew make out?'

'The voices were a hindrance. By dropping them out and enhancing the background noise, we've been able to deduce a great deal more about what actually happened to your 17-10.' The elderly man walked to one of the lit wall panels. 'We have a scanner here, we've done a thorough spectrographic analysis of all the same patterns, both inside and outside the cockpit – engine noise, airframe

144

vibrations – an entire spectrum of frequencies, any one of which can be isolated and examined in this room. Let's have a look at your tape. We can do it with your cassette.'

The professor pressed a lever, spinning Guy's tape in fast forward.

'All right, at any point in the tape we can hear the engine noises in the background . . . Now look here . . .' He switched the speed to 'play'. Mountains of tall grass could be seen moving across the scope in waves. Suddenly the image exploded in violence. 'Sorry, that's just someone talking, you see why we wanted to get rid of it . . . Here we can determine the characteristics from engine number one; in fact, we can even discriminate the low-pressure spool from the high-pressure spool – N_1 and N_2 I believe you call them. We can tell the exact number of revolutions each is making, and from that it's a simple matter to deduce the precise thrust output of the engine.' The old man leaned back, a broad grin of accomplishment on his face. 'I won't go on; let me say that by careful analysis we can isolate both spools in all four engines: they were just enough out of sync, although for a critical portion of the flight engines number two and four were difficult to separate, they were turning at almost identical speeds. Of course, it was engine number three which later caught fire.'

Guy stared at the rippling grass on the scope.

'Now come here, please, Mr Anders.' He crossed the room and shut off the overhead lights. 'The next part is a bit difficult, or was for us. But we are positive we detected definite airframe vibrations in our analysis, vibrations which are distinctly different in character from the normal. Let me show you a run from our own tape. We can stop the action on the scanner – by the way, let me hasten to add, all of this has been analysed digitally – in fact, it was our digital computer that picked out the abnormal airframe noise – Well, now, look here.' Guy stared again at the scope, trying to glean the subtle difference the professor was so eager to point out as he cued new images on to the scope. 'It's a rather low frequency, relatively speaking, I mean. It begins to abate here. But, ah, not quite. It returns.'

'And this, then, has taken you directly to the cause,' Guy said hopefully.

'No, we are not quite sure of that, but we're exploring several different ideas. I'll show you briefly one of these which may show some promise.' The professor turned off the scanner and crossed to another part of the room. 'We've also obtained a readout of the flight data recorder. I must admit, we did have a bit more trouble getting hold of that in a timely fashion, mind you, and we were concerned it wouldn't be in a form accurate enough for our use . . . However, we have confirmed the readout. Now, what we've done is to reference the two tapes to a common time frame, the cockpit voice recorder and the flight data recorder. We can plot the maximum peaks of airframe noise together with the aircraft heading and track, altitude, airspeed and ground speed; the navigation information goes straight from the inertial navigator into the flight data recorder, of course, which makes it particularly convenient.' He flashed another grin. 'Come look here.'

The professor walked to a massive drafting table and threw back the cover to reveal the surface overlaid with a huge map, the outline of Long Island in light blue. Guy recognized it as very accurate, including the exact layout of the runways at JFK Airport. The whole was under an orange grid network, like a stretched net stocking. A black line traced an uneven curve across the chart. Guy could see at once that it represented the flight path of Air World Six.

'Now, here we've referenced those odd airframe vibration peaks I showed you, via the flight data recorder, directly to this geographical plot. Let me explain: the flight data recorder allowed us to draw in the exact flight

146

path of your 17-10 during its approach to JFK; this was even corroborated with stored radar plots from New York Air Traffic Centre. Here, you can see precisely where you flew. Once having the geographical plot, it was a simple matter to indicate just where the worst airframe vibrations occurred.' He pointed to various places on the plot, and Guy bent over to scrutinize, straightened and whistled softly, impressed. He would have to get Ben Reese on the phone at once. These people were into hard science, playing catch-up ball with facts instead of PR.

For the first time Guy understood the aggressiveness of the competitive game that was being waged. He felt suddenly as if he were standing in a war room inside the Kremlin, listening to something still classified to his colleagues at home. And he felt vaguely uneasy: the amount of irrefutable information was dissolving the last remnants of his hope that Air World Six had been a fluke.

He considered his host. 'I'd like to know why you're telling me this.'

'My dear Mr Anders, what would we hope to gain by keeping it quiet? If we could, we'd advertise what we've found. It wouldn't help the American position and that is a decided bonus for our side. I'm chauvinistic enough to cheer that, but then, that's only human, isn't it?' The professor watched Guy. His expression was detached. 'We have gone one step further,' he continued quietly, 'which may interest you . . . Let me overlay this extra sheet on the plot. Now *this* is a plot of storm activity the night of your arrival into JFK. The information came from stored data transmitted from weather satellite photographs, for which we have the exact time. We can see quite clearly the location, size and movement of significant weather, especially the thunderstorms, that is, the intense electrical activity. It seems that on cursory analysis there appears to be a correlation between the airframe vibration peaks and your proximity to thunder-storm activity – in other words, the location where your 17-10 would be most likely to acquire an electrical charge.'

'The fatal weakness?'

'We're reluctant to jump to any snap judgments. I would say to you, however, that the military is looking into the possibility of disrupting fly-by-wire fighters with electrical jamming of the computer; it's called inducing *electronic corruption*. In your case, the thunderstorm proximity may be purely a coincidence.'

'You wouldn't have suggested a connection if you thought it was a coincidence.'

'Perhaps not. We wanted to ask you if you noticed any pattern to the flight, any susceptibility to the weather?'

'We were too busy. Couldn't see the storms except on radar, no way of telling where we would have been most likely to pick up the strongest static electric charge. We avoided the most intense cells, which are the only ones that show up on our scope in the cockpit anyway.'

'Any lightning strikes or St Elmo's fire, anything of that sort that seemed to cause the controls to react dif-ferently?'

'No, nothing like that. The controls were difficult all the way in. The captain did most of the flying, but he was fighting it all the way.'

'Of course. None of this proves anything as yet. We're looking only at symptoms – not causes.'

'This time of year, three, four flights a day ride along-side thunderstorms – some of them cut right through – all of them without incident. What you're showing me doesn't wash.'

'Perhaps they're still on the safe side of the statistics.'

'What do the statistics tell you about us?'

'They may point to servo valves with large null bands, out of phase with the computer's output. Slippage of that kind doesn't happen simultaneously across the board.'

'Then you expect a recurrence?'

'We don't have enough to go on. We must face the possibility there's no correlation between outside electrical disturbances and your control difficulties at all.'

'There's one question that's still unanswered. Where on the aeroplane was the vibration exactly? Can you target that?'

'Oh, dear.' The professor laughed. 'That's asking a bit much. But I can tell you we're fairly sure it was somewhere in the tail. We can't be sure just where. It was difficult enough isolating that frequency as it was.'

'And our voices in the cockpit – '

'The voices in the cockpit are totally unimportant, Mr Anders. I can assure you of that.'

'That's it, then?'

The professor paused. Guy sensed an internal debate going on. Finally the professor said guardedly, 'There's one more thing. Were you aware all the lights went out in Cedarhurst almost immediately when you passed overhead?'

'So I've been told.'

'It may be coincidence – or it may be related to your flight in some mysterious way.'

Guy waited. But the professor motioned to the door. Guy turned to go.

'If I could have some of your notes to take back with me, to help in my defence before the government, I'd be forever in your debt.'

'Ah – it's a bit difficult, you see, we haven't put our material into finished form. But – perhaps we can put a few things together for you that will demonstrate, at least, that there are certain – ah, aspects other than flight procedures that warrant further scrutinizing.'

'I'd appreciate whatever you can let me take.'

The professor peered at him carefully. 'You realize that Stateside response to any presentation of this material might be particularly harsh to you.'

'I'm aware of that.'

'Then I see no reason why we can't let you use these partial findings.' He led the way to the door and stopped. 'There is a war going on, an economic one to be sure, but as deadly for some people as World War Two was for others. One of these days you'll have to decide which side you're on.'

'I'm not on any side.'

'That's idealistic. But in the present economic reality it may no longer be possible to remain that pure.' The professor smiled. 'Now, if you don't mind waiting a few minutes, we'll get our copy machine going and put a packet together for you.' The professor extended a sinewy hand with a vicelike grip which surprised Guy. 'I'd keep a sharp lookout.'

Anja was reading on the patio when the phone rang. She let it ring three times while she tried to finish the paragraph; then, annoyed, she put the open book down and went inside to answer the phone, leaving the door ajar. It slammed shut just as she heard a man's voice she didn't recognize.

'Yes?'

The man explained he was a friend of Guy's, a pilot colleague. 'I talked to Guy just before he took off for London, and he mentioned he thought you ought to go out more and I told him about a party in the city my wife and I are going to. We wondered if you'd be interested. We'd be pleased to have you join us.'

'What party – who did you say you were?'

The voice continued disarmingly. 'It's a party given by Melissa – the model whose story's featured in today's *Post*. She's been on a dozen covers, does the Sundown cosmetic ad. It's at her brownstone on Seventy-third Street. Guy said he was sorry for being away so much and "Why don't you see if Anja would like the evening out, she's sure to enjoy it." He had meant to tell you about it. So – will you join us there?' Anja could sense that he finished the question with a smile, yet she shuddered. She had an impulse to hang up, but she went on listening.

The voice continued after a pause, but not insistently. It mentioned Guy again. 'We ran into each other about a month ago in the crew parking lot. You had only been with him a short time. He was rechecking his car to make sure the lights were off. Said he couldn't face another dead battery in the middle of the night like last month!' Anja remembered the incident, the phone calls. Only a friend could have known about that. She began to relax. 'You'll enjoy it,' he said. 'I promise you you won't feel out of place being unescorted, if that's what you're thinking.'

'Well, I don't know . . .,' Anja said, torn. 'I don't have the night off but I suppose it can be arranged . . . if the sitter is available . . . I'll need to make a call.' She was flattered Guy had expressed thoughtfulness for her, pleased that he'd be that concerned for her to get out on her own while he was away.

'If you decide to come, your invitation will be at the door. We'll meet you there, Amy and I – Amy and Jack Vickers. You can ask for us downstairs as you come in. But don't look for an Air World patch!' He laughed a merry, unprepossessing laugh. 'It's the brownstone next to the private French school between Park and Lex on East Seventy-third.'

Before Anja could say goodbye, the caller hung up, and in the cataract of silence that inundated her she stared for a long time at her own, solemn reflection in the kitchen window. The moment reverberated away, its echo hung like the faint scent of flowers in a bowl. The house was hushed, utterly motionless. Yet she felt as if a gust of wind had sprung up.

* * *

Melissa's party was in full swing when Anja was ushered in. She saw at once that it wasn't at all what she expected. It occupied all three floors of the Manhattan brownstone, and gave the impression of being an open house to all manner of glittering and gaudy people. No one appeared normal, they were either astonishingly beautiful or grotesque; all modes of expensive and outlandish filed underneath Melissa's pale-green awning while passersby gaped with dull expressions and wide eyes as if those entering were attending a premiere, which, in some ways, they were.

Anja, fresh and graceful, turned heads as she shouldered her way into the foyer, where a short woman was taking coats. She wore Olde Worlde lace and spoke with a refined Teutonic accent, barely audible in the flux of people pouring in from long, cream-coloured automobiles and luxurious black limousines. Melissa's having 'a few friends over', they'd said. My God, there must be nearly three hundred people here already, Anja thought. There was no record of Jack Vickers at the door. The attitude was one of: shrug, enjoy yourself. And for Anja, upon seeing the turbulent opulence that swelled and expanded inside the surging rooms, there was no turning back. Two bars were in full swing, one on the first floor, another on the third; a man in crushed velvet was pouring from a steady succession of cases of Lagavulin and Chivas Royal Salute, while silver trays of Dom Pérignon were being lofted by waiters through the crowd. Anja found herself alone in a moving sea of people who all seemed so much larger than ordinary people she knew: faces were larger, tie knots were larger, tits were ever so much larger . . . The colours were vivid and garish. She turned to find herself being peered at much too closely by a stern-faced woman with long, metal insect antennae sprouting from a silver helmet. Large purple nipples stood out like tawdry emblems from the open aluminium fishnet that lay slung across one shoulder. Anja twisted away but could hardly move. Then she felt warm breath on her neck and a hand on her flank, and confronted the smooth, androgynous face of a boy in ruffles and cinnamon-coloured tux. His face seemed vaguely familiar, but the expression was sardonic, master over slave. Anja grabbed him by the wrist. 'Don't touch unless you know how to do it,' she said and pushed him away.

She was crushed up against the staircase by a steady horde trying to get to the third floor, where the wildest action was supposed to be. Melissa herself was up there, overseeing all, Melissa the Beautiful Person, the Melissa who would sleep with anyone of power and influence, as long as they could pay the price – which was invariably formidable.

Up there was the hall of purple, the black light and incomprehensible music of the day in a room done up with mirrored lamps that swivelled, and roving spotlights. Two groups of gyrating, half-dressed singers took turns slinging spumes of sweat and strident dissonance that jarred the room; both had been flown in by private jet, one from London, the other from the Coast. There seemed to be a constant flow of people from Palm Beach, Rome, Ibiza, Bariloche, Newport . . . The scene became wilder, faces springing like pop-up peacocks at a shooting gallery, two former senators' wives, filmmakers, romantic egotists she'd read and wondered about, gone before she could study them, trendy novelists in the surf of people, corporate chairmen drooling after some young nooky while their wives were out yachting somewhere. She overheard one burly fellow in pinstripes arranging for the Sister Set from West Berlin, two incredibly lovely models with calculating resourcefulness who came to Melissa's to select a discerning and very wealthy man and hire themselves out as twins to drive him berserk for a couple of nights . . . Some of that was already in progress. Anja glimpsed a short, rotund man with a scar on his cheek – someone said he had once saved the Saudi chief of state from assassination – disappearing into a side room with an over-lipsticked six-and-a-half foot redhead known to millions of TV viewers – but not for her chief talent.

Anja retreated to the second floor, into a quiet corner of respite, where the thinkers, the philosophers, the people who had recently run away from Europe to sit and write back in the Hamptons, were clustered. At least here, in the slightly more subdued and serious atmosphere, she might find a moderately intriguing conversation. She tood a drink from a passing tray, and moved through the crowd.

It was only then that she became aware that his eyes were once again across the room. She had noticed them first in the living room downstairs, as distinct as beams of light in the haze. The eyes disturbed her. He had the lithe, feline spring of a thirty-year-old Marathon runner but he was older, probably forty. The skin on his forehead was smooth, pulled tight as a rubber mask over the front of his skull, his hair was blond. He wore jewellery, a gold rope chain, rings, a bracelet, it was all lavish; that bauble on his chain, she reflected, is probably worth more than Guy's house. But it was the eyes. She couldn't look straight back at those eyes, they seemed to insult her.

She knew he had noticed her. She half expected, if not a frontal assault or even a lunging flank attack, at least a graceful offensive manoeuvre. She should have known better. He would wait, bide his time, he would make her come to him. She had to catch herself: he had already planted the seed in her mind.

The bits of conversation she heard and overheard about him billowed past her. 'He's a lifelong skier,' rootless words that conjured romantic images: dark night wartime ski missions, every atom crouched and alert to the enemy's presence, dissolved their sepia frames into the expressionless goggled faces of men crouched and alert on Olympic ski jumps, visions that slipped past like the subdued clink of Gstaad or Chamonix or Kitzbühel where suave men in white turtlenecks set up deals, manoeuvred constantly, all in undertones. 'He's dabbled in politics – you know, the International Monetary Fund – ' 'No, he's a salesman.' 'Of course, darling, but it doesn't matter if it's ballbearings or cosmetics; it's not the product, don't you see, it's the *leverage*.'

'He had a yacht . . . .' 'Yes, it's lovely – eighty-five feet, I think – quite comfortable, really.' And Anja visualized how such deals were implemented, the skier slipping his yacht alongside others at the quay, all of them softly bobbing in unison, the yachts of presidents and Greek shipowners, and dope runners posing as writers, the yachts of other deal makers and of entire corporations. 'Come on over for a drink.' A friendly hail among men of equal stature, an arrangement as casual as a backyard lawn party but among men as cunning as cat burglars. No appointment calendars to contend with, no special audience to be arranged. Just: 'Hi, come on over for a drink.'

And then she was alongside him.

'Good evening, Anja. Enjoying yourself?' The voice was smooth as rare liqueur.

Anja felt her heart pump, she was startled hearing her own name, but didn't reveal it in her tone of voice. 'It's like a bazaar, isn't it? Have we been introduced?' She regretted sounding nervous and stuffy.

'Formal introductions seem to be anachronisms, redundancies, especially at a place like this. I'm Maximilian. You won't mind, will you, if I continue to call you by your first name?' The skier smiled, but only with his lips. The eyes remained almost insolent. Anja became physically aware of being admitted into his aura, the insulated space in which he moved. It was as if his body enclosed some cloaked but luminous lodestone which emitted a glow, an influence that shielded him from the frenetic clashes, or magnetized those he would calmly reach out and lure.

'This party,' he began, casting an almost disdainful glance around the room, and looking back at her with his

155

piercing and arrogant eyes, 'is a microcosm of all that matters in our modern world. Here you have potentates and paupers, but they all have some slice of the pie; it's a kind of autonomous, absolute power elite, you might say.' He smiled again, and it made her shiver slightly. 'Take a look: intellectuals, whores, gangsters, industrialists, beautiful people, money people, nobility – and ugly people, too,' looking straight into her, a hint of confidentiality in his eyes. 'All are tyrants in their own way, over their own piece of the domain. But in here – a little Switzerland.' He smiled again, more engagingly. 'Look there, the district attorney is here, eating quiche Lorraine from one side of the plate. The Mafia don is eating from the other. Ah, but both have left their guns outside. That's always understood at Melissa's.' He paused to sip from a glass of champagne, his eyes studying her constantly over the glass. 'Outside, outside is warfare. The streets of business are in fact dark streets of war . . . The irony is the higher one gets, the closer to one's aspirations, the more uncomfortable and unpleasant it can become. Everything assumes a different character; people become afraid to bring in the milk. The maid of an executive who crossed the system brought in the milk one day . . . only it was plastique . . . The newspapers said it was a propane gas explosion, they couldn't find enough of her or the family in the mess to say it wasn't. Most people just aren't capable of understanding it.' He brushed 'most people' off with a note of contempt.

Anja looked straight back at Maximilian, bringing herself to confront his eyes, and making her voice heavy with sarcasm said, 'And over in one corner of the forest the little bunny sat meekly watching the master juggler with the golden hair spin a scene from the Wunderschön fairy tales by Somebody-or-Other Andersen.'

The skier, who had just motioned to a passing waiter, tilted his head back and laughed. He turned to take another glass of champagne from the tray, offering one to her. She declined, smiling in mock benevolence, and said, 'But you go on . . .'

'Anja, forgive me.' His eyes became bright and piercing once again, separate from the flow of words. 'Enough of ugly parables that insult you, especially now, when in a very real way you haven't yet reached what you're after and yet, at the same time, not entirely sure you want to look any further; one can sense it all combined in a subtle, delicate look about you.'

She felt suddenly exposed as if he'd seen something private within her.

'It doesn't take a clairvoyant to see that you relish new flavours, new sensations, new experiences . . . or perhaps something more serene than that.' His eyes almost twinkled in the kaleidoscopic light. They were extraordinarily deep-set, but alert, as if endangered, forced forever to peer out guardedly from behind a rock. He watched her and said nothing and felt a passing gust of regret at having to use her – that conditions weren't different. How shining and incomparable she would have looked on a mountain pass, the texture of her cheeks framed by the primeval ice four miles high . . .

'Let me tell you briefly about what I do. I deal in attraction.' He smiled. 'I buy and sell for the most prestigious perfumeries in the world. I realize the combinations, I even help create them. Such incredible scents . . . You know, the sense of smell is the most provocative . . .'

Anja felt fully awake, the first time all evening, perhaps the first time in weeks. The mesmerizing words, the piquant, gamy odour, of Maximilian the skier had seeped past his barrier to work its influence, drawing her inside his aura. The giddy thought occurred to her that if right now, this instant, he were to take her into a bedroom, she would submit and go with him. The difference between Maximilian and other attractive men was the awareness in his eyes, his intense awareness of her, as if he were

157

probing the innermost back of her skull. It didn't matter that the eyes may have been turned on to a thousand other women, or that they all may have reacted similarly. That was beside the point. He was looking at her, and he knew. She saw that he knew and her legs went weak, she could almost feel his thick fingers finding out how wet she was. But he smiled slightly, just at the corners of his mouth, and let the moment pass.

'How long ago since you left Europe?'

Anja felt as though he were escorting her off the edge of a high building. She scrambled back to safety. 'I never told you my name, yet you knew it.' It didn't sound as resolute as she wanted it to.

Maximilian nodded towards the crowd at the front door. 'I heard it in passing. But I've said too much already.' Anja couldn't remember her name being mentioned at the front door.

'Do you know who the Vickerses are?' she asked.

'No, I don't know them,' the skier said, smiling.

'I don't know what they look like.' Anja shrugged.

'You were going to tell me how long it's been since you left Europe.'

'I wasn't.'

'I'm afraid I've startled you then. I am from Munich. You're from somewhere north and west of there – though you might be international, living here and there. You're here permanently then . . .'

'I have a visitor's visa.'

'What sort of business are you in?'

'I demonstrate vacuum cleaners.'

A genuine smile played around his eyes. 'I didn't mean to push. I'm only interested.'

'I'm afraid I'll just disappoint you.'

'I don't think you realize it, but there's no way you could disappoint anyone.'

'You don't know how wrong you are. I suppose you'd say I'm indirectly in the aeroplane business.'

'Here in the States?'

'Yes.'

'On a visitor's visa?'

'I said – indirectly.'

He had caught her. He was either a lawyer or something akin to a medium.

Anja studied her hands. 'The truth is I'm an *au pair* to an airline pilot.'

'International?'

'Yes.'

'What's his name?'

'Donald Duck. That's a personal question and it's none of your business.'

'You're right. It's just that I have so many friends in the flying business –'

'I thought you were in perfume.'

'Not twenty-four hours a day. I've always enjoyed aviation. I've been around the world thirty-one times. Yes, I have. I thought I might have flown with him or run into him.'

'Maybe you have.'

'At Melissa's last party, perhaps.'

Anja tried to read some meaning into his eyes but they remained open with curiosity. She looked down. 'Well, his name is Anders. Guy Anders.'

'Doesn't ring a bell . . . You know, I've always wondered why anyone would want to drag unappreciative passengers around. And they can be unappreciative.'

'In his case I don't believe they're unappreciative.'

'People will only appreciate flight the day the pumps go dry. Excellent minds are already planning against that day,' the skier said and leaned closer. 'The time has come to bring back the Zeppelins!'

Anja laughed, shaking her head, a twinkling laugh. But the skier merely arched his eyebrows.

'No, I'm perfectly serious. Consider the Arabs here at Melissa's. Now we certainly don't want them to become

159

our lords and masters. But that's what's happening. A 747 consumes almost a hundred barrels of petroleum every hour! The Concorde burns up the same amount or more but only carries a third as many passengers. Things are getting worse, not better. Millions of barrels of expensive oil spewing out the tail pipes of these monster machines every day. And the Arabs have it all tied up. Do you know how much money is in this room?'

From within his oasis Anja looked out to survey the two dozen or so people who decorated the room like lavish drapes. 'It probably changes by the minute,' she said, smiling.

The skier sipped his champagne. 'You can depend on that: the pound goes down – the franc goes up – and they make another half billion in forty seconds! But we all pay. A ticket overseas on the Concorde costs more than two thousand dollars. Soon it'll be twenty-seven hundred, then thirty-eight hundred, who knows where the insanity will stop? And finally there's going to be only one drop of oil left. And the whole world's going to be fighting over that one drop of oil – each country will need it to last another thirty seconds – the whole world at war over a milk-bottleful of oil.'

Anja wanted to escape the skier's rising intensity. She searched the remote sea of faces hoping to alight on a familiar pair of eyes . . . she listened for her name . . . but the man in front of her raised his voice and persisted.

'The answer to this dilemma is *helium*. Stop the speed. We've achieved enough speed. We have to regain sanity and go back to the simpler days.' He could see a certain interested expression in her eyes. 'That's right,' he continued, 'back to the days when people had time for gentility, time to converse and listen to each other. Nowadays we only hear each other as passing echoes, everybody's in such a rush . . . I'm serious about helium. The Zeppelins stopped because they couldn't get helium. But that's not true today. I know where there are millions of cubic feet of helium stored, just waiting,' he said, almost whispering. His voice had taken on a confidential, enthusiastic tone. 'If we could get that helium, we could get the Zeppelins up again. Give people a graceful way of moving around.'

'Go backwards in time,' Anja said, smiling tolerantly, a bit on guard because of his insistence and the bizarre idea, but attentive.

'Try to imagine how it would be! Travellers would come and go calmly. The Zeppelins were virtually noiseless. They're clean, like enclaves of how things used to be. Make people feel special when they travel.'

Despite the outrageousness of the skier's spiel, the litany was pleasing to Anja, and she took another glass of champagne.

'Somebody's got to buy up all the helium to be ready for the big day when the world comes to its senses,' he continued. 'What do you think?'

Anja laughed out loud.

'Mark my words, the Zeppelins will fly! People will travel in splendour again. And we could be in on the ground floor. Wouldn't that be something? People will go for it – you'd go for it! And somebody will definitely put it together. So why not us? All we have to do is corner the market on helium!'

She cocked her head to study him more closely. He was absolutely serious.

'I have a plan,' he said, his momentum in full stride. 'We'll be partners. We'll go fifty-fifty. What do you say to that?'

As he spoke, Anja sensed that his eyes and voice were integrated, not separate as before. She had become distrustful, yet enchanted enough to have him make his point. 'How would we put out hands on all that helium?' She dared him to explain it.

He took her hand firmly in both of his, and held it. 'That part's easy. Just open your beautiful eyes and look around. There must be fifteen people in this room alone who could float a whole new Zeppelin industry. Our seed money is sitting right here in front of us! All we have to do is pick it up! Look at that fat Arab. Wouldn't it be remarkable if he knew he was about to finance his own competition!'

Anja pulled her hand away. 'Now don't start anything because I asked you a question!' The skier had turned and was proceeding towards the Arab. Anja was wide-eyed. She could feel her heart pump as she followed. The conversation and the action had slipped into the surreal but it excited her. She watched almost rapt as Maximilian turned coldly serious. His eyes were again separate from his spoken words, and suddenly he was holding a deck of cards which must have been in his pocket. He riffled them with one-handed virtuosity. With supreme confidence he stepped before the chubby, insolent-looking Arab who had been gaming in the corner.

'Fifty thousand on the nose – one hand.'

The Arab surveyed the skier as he would have a loathsome beggar. They studied each other. Finally the Arab reached beneath the folds of his clothes, and took out his own deck.

'My deck.'

Maximilian signalled to a passing waiter. 'Drinks for everybody,' he said, 'and' – motioning to an empty chair in the corner – 'a chair for my lady.' He brushed a crumb from the tabletop, cut the deck with an expert flourish and dealt, swiftly.

Anja watched, disbelieving, trying to follow the mutterings of the two men, who now looked as venomous as highway robbers as they threw their cards back and forth. She was suddenly afraid for Guy, flying somewhere in his 17-10, his features so different from the self-assured, imperious faces at the game before her; Guy's eyes so full of candour next to these relentless marbles. Yet Guy seemed as a pale memory just now. Anja watching the game's intensity, thought about what real power means to some men. She squirmed, conscious of having been on a budget all her life, while out here, in the periphery she had never visited, people slogged through a swamp of money. But what she didn't fully understand was the *power* and how it was taken or ordained. And she wondered if Guy Anders understood it any better than she did.

Suddenly her attention was refocused on the table before her. The game had ended. The Arab was shrugging, handing the skier his marker. Maximilian stood up, taking the note together with his drink. Anja watched it as through a window, wanting to back off, but swept away by the crowd. Maximilian steered her to a quiet corner of the room.

'It's really incredibly easy,' he said as he busily scribbled something into a long, leather-bound booklet.

'What are you doing?'

'I'm writing you a cheque for twenty-five thousand dollars – half of our seed money.'

'But –'

'Since you're on a visitor's visa and have no work permit or social security number, I'm going to make this out to your boss. Fifty-fifty means twenty-five with three zeroes.'

'I can't take that, it's ridiculous!'

'He can cash it, pay the tax on it if he's so inclined and give you the proceeds.'

'It was only a joke,' she said. The pale-blue cheque lay untouched on the mantel.

Maximilian placed the slim chequebook in front of her, indicated the stub from which the cheque had been torn and gave her a pen. 'You sign here and your share is official, my partner. It's aboveboard and fair. Oh, it's all selfish, I assure you. This will make it possible for me to see you again. One day we'll get together and bring grace back to our world – and begin that helium business.' Maximilian smiled. 'And let's not feel too guilty about any of this. By Monday our Arab friend will be back in the

Gulf, biding his time till he can jack the oil price over the next intolerable threshold.'

Anja signed her name and returned the pen.

'I'm delighted you joined me.'

Slowly she reached up, touched the cheque, slid it towards her. It was payable by Parfum de Grace, 31 rue Hugot, Paris.

'Don't misplace it. It's worth precisely what it says it is.' The skier straightened himself. 'I'm expected upstairs and I've overstayed. You're very lovely and I've enjoyed our first moments together.'

Then the energy between them passed, evaporated in the tinsel vapour. She looked up and he was gone.

She stood holding the cheque and felt her legs go weak again. There, stretched and twisting in the prismatic light, the purples, reds and greens, as though seen through a revolving stained-glass window, was Guy's carefully written name, and the figure '$25,000'. The sensation came upon her like a laugh, a laugh that starts down deep in the belly and rises slowly, the sort of laugh one doesn't relinquish but holds on to and feels, and savours it all. And so it was with the cheque. Outside, the world awaited her, the boy asleep at the neighbour's, his father away on a trip, dirty cups and saucers in the sink. Outside nothing had really changed. But here, inside, in the aura of the skier's crater-deep eyes, she had felt the giddy tingle of being charged. And she wanted to linger within it.

She held the cheque for a long time. The pounding of the party, the phalanxes of overweening, puffed-up faces all jabbering, swirled around her, and she felt their subtle ostracism. The party had not abated and no doubt would not for hours, but Anja now felt estranged, and as she stood there, a little cold, she didn't know why she had begun to feel depressed. In her purse was a cheque for twenty-five thousand dollars. But the enthusiasm had fled. She was aware only that a headache had developed above her eyes, making images even more blurred than they had seemed. She went to find a bathroom; she needed aspirin and an escape from the noise. She opened the door, only to reel back at the vision of a swarthy man sitting in the soapy bathtub, busily scrubbing his feet. He looked up at her with a mild, quizzical expression, and smiled. Two leather suitcases sat by the bathtub and an open overnight case was on the toilet with items spread about.

Anja turned away and pushed her way outside. She had to find a taxi. The damp coolness came as a relief. She walked towards Fifth Avenue, glancing back once. The windows of Melissa's brownstone seemed to be eyes fastened on her. An awning rustled and she jumped with fright. She couldn't shake the feeling of being at the end of a gunsight.

Anja stood outside the brilliantly lit but silent Air World terminal enjoying the moment of respite. It was four-thirty in the morning. Less than five hours had passed since she had left Melissa's party. Guy, due to land hours earlier, had been delayed by a baggage handlers' strike at Heathrow. The new arrival time was now set for five.

She vaguely heard the dying wail of an arriving jet on the far side of the terminal. Minutes later, Guy walked quickly past clusters of dishevelled passengers hauling their belongings to the curb and stepped outside. All at once he was home, with the sensation of returning from a cold mission in space back to the fresh simple welcome of the earth. He nearly jumped at the blast of a horn that sounded in the general stillness. Synova again? No, it was Anja in her beige raincoat standing next to the station wagon, her hair loose. She seemed vulnerable.

'Well, I'll be . . .' He was pleased at the sight of her – and at the prize from England in his bag. He pushed his hat back and smiled and he seemed boyish to her as he strutted away from the exit. Her face softened.

An Air World employee ran out and handed him a small envelope. 'This was on the bulletin board, chief.'

Guy tore it open and unfolded the message. 'Guy,' it read, 'Call me. Urgent. Synova.' There was a lipstick smear on it. He folded it, tucked it into his shirt pocket and pushed his way clear.

'So England went well,' Anja greeted him.

'Yes, indeed.' Guy rubbed his neck with deep satisfaction. He closed the door on the passenger's side and she slowly eased the car on to the exit ramp. She didn't speak until they had left the airport.

'I'm glad for you.'

'Thank you.'

'I really am glad for you and that you think things are working out. As for me, I can honestly say I've had a hell of a time – with the emphasis on the hell. I hate ending a day with unfinished business . . .'

'What in the world are you rattling about?'

'I'm trying to tell you something diplomatically and I know at the wrong time but your social friends frighten me.'

'What friends?'

She ran a stop sign. It distracted her and she forgot Guy's question. 'My diplomatic statement to you is that I want to give you two weeks' notice from right now.'

'Two weeks from five in the morning?'

'I'll be counting the hours.'

Guy watched her drive. She was saucy and at the same time like a child in a dream, sitting high, taking charge. 'I thought you'd at least wait till you and Jamie managed to talk. You thought you'd have an influence.'

'I think I've failed at that. Someone else will do better. I'm sure of that.'

Guy felt regret nudge his weariness. 'Well,' he managed after a minute of silence, 'I want to thank you for giving me the two weeks. I'll look around and place an ad.'

'I'm sorry,' Anja said.

Guy noticed the pleasant scent of her perfume mingled with the odour of cigarette smoke that came from her raincoat. 'How come you've picked me up?' he asked.

'My sweet nature. The salary doesn't cover it.'

Anja drove, intent on the rhythmic thump of the tyres crossing the tar separation lines in the highway. 'Despite everything, I'm probably going to miss you,' she said. She saw him close his eyes as they sped through the peace of the countryside not yet fully awake. She didn't know if he heard her some minutes later when she said, 'OK, I'll make you a deal. You don't have to write the ad just yet. I'll wait till I get your boy out of his hideaway. But it'll be two weeks from that day.'

Guy opened his eyes. Anja slowed the car and looked at him.

'I'd really like to call a truce.' She said it gently.

'Truce,' Guy agreed.

She pulled the car over to the shoulder of the road and took Maximilian's cheque from her bag. 'I think you'd better put your name on the back of this before I lose it.' Her voice was uncertain.

Guy took it from her, wiped his face, held the cheque to catch the passing lights. He saw his own name as the payee. 'What is it? . . . *Twenty-five thousand dollars!*'

Anja told him about the previous evening's call from Vickers.

'I don't know any Vickers.'

She'd been fearful he'd say that and now the hint of alarm she'd felt during her talk with Maximilian blossomed into a growing dread. When she finished telling him about the party, Guy was watching a woman different from the one he'd hired. Her defiance was muted. She was terrified and she looked younger.

Guy studied the cheque again. 'I don't even know if we should cash it.'

'I have a feeling I've done you some harm tonight,' she said.

'No one gives away this kind of cash.'

'I know.'

They sat in silence. Guy finally said, 'Which has to mean there's something else going on.' He slipped the cheque into her handbag and tilted his head back against the headrest. Anja drove towards the house.

'Ben Reese tried to call you in London but you'd already left.' She glanced over at his reclining figure. 'The hearing is scheduled for Monday.'

Guy looked up at the sky. The moon was still out. Despite the intrusion of the strange cheque and Anja's decision to leave, he smiled.

Inside the foyer of the house, Guy dug through his pockets, removed some foreign change and came up with the rumpled note Synova had left for him at the airport. The pencilled word facing him was 'Urgent.' He dialled the number. The line rang half a dozen times before a sleepy voice answered.

'Yes?'

'I'm sorry about the hour. I got your note.'

'Listen – ' There was a pause while Synova swallowed.

'Yeah?'

'Listen, Guy, you know the windshield that smashed when you came back from Connecticut?'

'Yeah?'

'It wasn't an accident. Someone tried to kill you.'

6

Senator Searington was sitting back, his feet on a chair, enjoying his breakfast coffee. The story on the second page of the *Post* was headlined 'PRESIDENT TAKES DELIVERY OF NEW AIR FORCE ONE.' Beneath it, there was a fine three-column picture of the President shaking hands with his personal pilot. The freshly painted 17-10 was clearly in view behind them. The caption read, 'The Buttress 17-10. Latest Flying Command Post for Our Commander-in-Chief.' The senator smiled, put the paper down on his lap and looked out of the window. It was a perfect morning on which to start the hearing.

It was ten after nine at the Sheraton Hotel in New York. Participants and spectators to the NTSB hearing were still milling about in the early-morning mustiness of the Grand Ballroom looking for their designated seats. Guy Anders stared at the picture of the 17-10 and the President in a copy of the *Times* Hanks had given him.

'Timing's an accident,' Hanks said drily. 'Just a god-damn coincidence.'

Guy handed the paper back. 'There'll be another picture tomorrow. When he reads what I have to say, he'll be yanking up and down on a pogo stick.'

Five long tables draped in green felt had been arranged in a rectangular pattern around one end of the room. Printed white placards set at the edge of each table identified its active participants. At the head of the room was the main dais, which would be manned by members of the National Transportation Safety Board. The young chairman, Merle Tarpender, stood behind it, resetting his watch. Alongside the other members, he looked tanned and fit. Directly opposite him, some twenty feet away and in front of the spectators' section, were three long tables in a row. The one on the left was designated AIR WORLD, the Buttress table had been placed next to it in the centre, and the Air Line Pilots Association had been given the table on the right. The FAA had the fifth table, which closed one end of the rectangle at the far left. Three young lawyers were already in their places looking comfortable. In the centre of the wide space flanked by the large tables was the witness stand, a metal chair facing a card table covered with the same green felt. Next to it, provision had been made for a court stenographer.

Vic Moudon stood behind horn-rimmed glasses at the Air World table arranging pages in a loose-leaf binder for Matt Aspinwall. Ed Boice placed a pile of folders on the Buttress table and snapped the locks on his attaché case.

The news that the hearing had been forced open had got around, so an overflow crowd of press people had gathered in the hall and a call had gone out for additional seating. Two men in green work clothes arrived pushing a wheeled rack of metal folding chairs between them.

Anja was seated on the aisle in the front row of the spectators' section. She had insisted on coming, 'eager,' as she put it, 'to see Anders lay them out.' She had forsaken her jeans and the standard shirt and sneakers for an eye-opening pale-green dress. Guy was unprepared for her transformation into elegance. He was on his haunches beside her, his flight bag nearby, vaguely aware of someone kneeling down trying to face him, taking a bead on him. Then the blinding light from a flashbulb drained the colour from the room and he waited in darkness listening to the babble. Slowly his sight returned and he saw Anja smiling at him.

'I met Ben Reese and I like him,' she said.

Craning his neck, Guy spotted Ben through the crowd, a Danish in one hand, licking his thumb and collating press releases spread across a metal-legged wooden table against the wall.

'What'd you do with the cheque?'

Anja patted her pocketbook.

Guy barely moved his mouth. 'Let me have it.' He hoisted his flight bag, which contained the 17-10's personal cardiogram, made his way with the effort of pushing through a crowded subway train, trying to avoid the occasional calls of greeting that accosted him from around shoulders and over heads. He handed the cheque to Ben and told him how he got it. Ben stared at it with some disbelief, then held it closer, his eyes coming alive with growing recognition. Guy left it with him to make his way back to the ALPA table. On his way he passed Boice, who was thumbing through his briefcase. Guy stopped and faced him.

'Bring your sales brochures?'

Boice threw him a sideways glance. 'Got your pilot licence?'

Chairman Tarpender handed a roll of breath mints to an assistant and indicated to Moss that it was time to start. Matt Aspinwall sat, slid his chair closer to the Air World table and clasped his hands in front of him. Vic Moudon was already seated. Eyes straight ahead, Aspinwall said to him, 'This may be where we find out what we really paid for.'

Papers were shuffled and stacked for the last time and voices lowered in anticipation. The ballroom door opened again. Someone was entering, straight and tall and so slowly that people felt compelled to turn towards him. As he came into view silence fell; Captain W. B. Cosgrove was standing in the light, surveying the arena.

Quickly Vic Moudon stood to greet him. Cosgrove was dressed in a pale checked jacket and matching pants, shopping mall slick, but the effect was rendered strangely subdued by his stalwart presence.

He saw Moudon and waited. Moudon came close and, conscious of the stillness, tried to whisper his welcome.

Crow's-feet deepened around the sides of W.B.'s sun-parched skull. 'What?' he frowned.

Moudon looked around to see how much louder he could go without being overheard. He knew he was being obsequious but, unable to change course, cleared his throat and went on.

'We should have had it ready sooner, but we have a scroll back at the office signed by Mr Aspinwall that acknowledges the company's gratitude to you for Flight

Six.' Moudon gritted his teeth hoping the captain would smile, maybe give him a friendly tap on the arm and go away. But W.B. just watched him with shale-grey eyes; then, without a word, he crossed to the ALPA table and sat down in the chair between Guy and Toby. He nodded slightly to Hanks and turnèd his attention to the green table at the end of the room.

Guy leaned over to Cosgrove.

'We've got a little outside help that's going to surprise you. You may be home by this afternoon.'

Cosgrove, not understanding, didn't move his head. 'Well, it's their show,' he said. 'Let's see what they come up with.'

Merle Tarpender adjusted his microphone, stared at each table in turn until the last murmuring died.

As Tarpender opened the formal hearing, Doug Moss's thoughts drifted. Idly, through the words, he watched Guy Anders – and hated him. He followed his thoughts back to his own days as a flying cadet. Through his years at college he had worshipped the jet aces of Korea, dreamed of being lionized like that, imagining that a set of those silver leg-spreaders on his breast would make up for his acne and awkward manner. And he marched down the campus pathways defiantly shouting 'hup-twos' and went into the Air Force only to fly. Memories of the warm wetness of Florida mornings filled with the pungent smell of aeroplanes could still stir him deeply, evoking something of an almost visceral anticipation that lofted him above the mundane bureaucratic quagmire already engulfing him.

Moss thought of that day, shortly after he had taken off solo amid the tumescent clouds to practise landings at an outlying field. He spotted the grass strip and landed, taxied back, and began his takeoff run. Noting the earth's dampness, he horsed the aeroplane free of the muck as soon as the wings signalled the first nod of flight. His plane staggered into the air, nose high, barely flying, the elevated snout blocking the forward view, and he carefully pushed over to gain speed. The view in front expanded – and there, in all its horrifying import and brutal rivet-shadow clarity, was the grotesque array of power lines that webbed the sky. The shock of seeing those lines slapped squarely across his face changed his whole life in a split second. He realized it was hopeless to go under them and probably impossible to go over, but he yanked back – he had to try – instinct and terror enabled him to hold the aeroplane just on the shuddering edge of stall – no way to guess how close he came – but then he couldn't lower the nose to sag for vitally needed speed because a stand of trees not far beyond the power lines blocked his path. So he pointed the ship down abruptly and piled it up in the remaining grassy space. They found the aeroplane demolished but Moss was only bruised. He had mistaken a farmer's private strip for the outlying field he intended to use, and for this sin he was washed out, banished from Air Force pilot training, and castigated unmercifully for his extreme personal stupidity. It didn't much matter then because the stark horror of those few brutal moments had drained all joy from flying. It persisted and fuelled his nightmares for several months.

His subsequent Air Force duties were drudgery and demeaning, he hated them and counted the days until he could shed them, and he developed a deep resentment for the hierarchy. But he still looked up whenever a plane flashed overhead, feeling dwarfed as he stood with his neck craned, the idea of being up there more remote, and the ache more exquisite than ever.

Now he was in the air safety business, at another hearing watching a man with the same casual air of contempt that the fighter jocks of his fantasy affected, their top buttons always undone, cool smiles on their faces. He'd seen them often after that day, strolling by; he had to salute them and call them 'sir'. Guy was one of their ilk.

Tarpender called Ed Boice to the stand. 'I'd like to turn to the flight-control system in the 17-10, if I may, Mr

Boice. You have been called as an expert witness in this area, with the hope that we may be able to probe into some specifics. Could you give us a simple explanation of the Buttress 17-10 flight-control system?'

Ed leaned back in the small metal chair and for a moment the look of an evangelist drifted across his features. 'Active controls – control-configured vehicle – fly-by-wire – call it what you will – is new to passenger aircraft but isn't hard to understand. Used to be pilots could push or pull on their yoke in the cockpit – half a city block away from their elevators and rudders – with a direct lash-up of one to one or two to one or ten to one, using heavy push rods and cables. We've replaced all that in the 17-10 with a wire – like a telephone wire – which goes to a computer, so in the 17-10 the pilot no longer has a direct connection to the wings or tail. When the 17-10 pilot moves the control yoke or presses on the rudder pedals, he's really just dialling in a set of instructions to the computer – we call it the Automatic Flight Control System computer, or AFCS – you may have seen that term in the supporting documents – and the computer, in turn, figures out the exact rate and angle to deflect the ailerons or elevators or rudders to produce the manoeuvre the pilot wants, say a turn of a certain amount, something like that.

'Well, now, Mr Chairman, the great advantage of all this is that since the computer can wiggle the tail surfaces so fast to keep the manoeuvre exact and smooth – and *independent* of the pilot's yoke and rudder pedals – it allowed us to build much smaller tails, save weight, cut fuel costs, increase profit for Mr Aspinwall sitting over there.' Ed was smiling, a confident look on his florid face, obviously pleased with himself.

Tarpender consulted a yellow legal pad on which he had scribbled notes, then looked at Boice.

'Can you tell us what provisions you have made for possible failures, Mr Boice?'

174

'We've developed a highly survivable system, Mr Chairman, by imposing extremely severe design constraints.'

'Could you elaborate on that?'

'Let me assure you, Mr Chairman, the chances of a glitch in our system are so remote they can be ignored. We solved that problem on the F-19.' There was a catch in the room. Boice seemed to gasp for a moment, as if groping for something else to say.

Ben Reese looked up as Boice tried to recover. On his pad Ben scribbled the words 'WHAT PROBLEM?'

Tarpender smiled. 'Yes, Mr Boice,' he said helping him. 'If we could return to the 17-10 – '

'Since then,' Boice was already continuing expansively, 'we've imposed a strict failure-immunity index . . . we've adopted new reliability management assessment techniques . . . consistent with acceptable-risk parameters . . .'

Anja looked up, startled by the phrase 'acceptable-risk', but Boice had already barged ahead.

'. . . Malfunction detection and diagnosis in information paths is through the application of analytic redundancy . . . In the 17-10 we have dual fail-operational channels based on an integrated network of microprocessors for data acquisition with digital filtering – '

'Thank you, Mr Boice,' Tarpender interrupted. 'I'm fascinated, of course, with your description of an obviously advanced control system.' Again he smiled at Boice. 'But I'm now interested in returning to the computer interaction with the pilots and their procedures.'

'Yes, of course, Mr Chairman,' said Boice, adjusting the microphone on the small table before him. 'What we came to grips with at Buttress is that the pilot, whether he knows it or not, doesn't really give a damn – uh, doesn't really care, Mr Chairman – what the elevator surface at the tail does. He's interested only – or he *should* be interested only – in what the aeroplane does.' Ed had adopted a condescending, grating tone. 'So the AFCS computer may be wiggling the elevator up and down rapidly, but the pilot won't feel any of that up front. The computer will give him exactly what he expects to feel – and, Mr Chairman, I must say that sometimes I wonder about what I do . . . 'cause no matter how hard I try to give the pilot what he wants, I'm not sure I know what it is he really wants to feel!' Ed shot a look at the ALPA table and rumbled into laughter. A roar of guffaws rolled through the room. Tarpender pounded the gavel.

'I can see the pilots are upset,' Boice said, still grinning as the laughter died. 'Well, in all fairness, there's something that should be said. If it wasn't for the raw courage of those three men at the ALPA table in an unfamiliar situation, I guess we'd all be sadder today.' There was a scattering of applause which Tarpender cut short. 'Nevertheless,' Boice went on, 'these are hearings to determine facts, and no matter how courageous, the actions of these pilots require further scrutiny. Buttress Aerospace Corporation believes that the crew did *not* follow the procedures set forth by our operating instructions. We at Buttress are angry because through insinuation and inference, a very serious and growing set of aspersions is being cast on the airworthiness integrity of the 17-10. We expect that from these hearings will come the true facts, Mr Chairman, and in order to do that these hearings ought to be concentrating on the testimony of the crew instead of hanging Buttress by the neck by implication. We repeat: there is absolutely no evidence whatsoever that anything is remotely wrong with the 17-10!'

With a clatter as his metal chair crashed to the floor, Guy Anders stood and in a voice that carried through the ballroom like a thunderclap shouted, *'That's a lie!'*

The words hit with the shock of a lightning stroke, stunning the room. Only Ed Boice's face was in motion, reddening. 'I won't condone interruptions,' he gargled. 'You'll have your turn, Anders.'

'I'll take my turn now, Mr Boice. Because there *is* hard evidence that proves you're a liar – and I have it right here!'

176

Anja looked at Guy in wonder. Gushers of voltage galvanized the ranks of reporters in the rear. Flashbulbs began to pop in a dynamo of silent explosions. Before Tarpender could think of what to do next, Guy raised his hand and, holding up the English report for all to see, called out, 'This is a spectrographic analysis of the cockpit voice tape from Air World Six that proves beyond doubt there is something wrong with the automatic flight-control-system pitch channel in the 17-10!' He slammed the inch-thick report on the table with a thud that resounded in the shocked silence of the chamber.

Ed Boice looked as if he'd been shot. Sweat stuck out on his scalp. Matt Aspinwall went rigid and looked towards Tarpender like a drowning man seeking rescue. The uproar began in earnest. Guy noticed the Buttress table was in total disarray. At the main dais, Doug Moss had reared back in disbelief, his fingers clutching the table's edge. Again Guy raised his hand and the swelling murmurs tapered off.

'Not only that, but I for one hereby refuse to fly any 17-10 for any reason until it's fixed. And *that's* for publication!'

Pandemonium reigned in the hearing room.

Aspinwall rose to his feet, the volcanic pressure giving his face the colour of raw meat. Anja laughed out loud and embraced Mrs Hanks next to her as Carlton sprang up at the table, all six feet three of him, Adam's apple pulsing under an incredulous grin. A large contingent from the Airline Passengers Association broke into cheers. Captain W. B. Cosgrove looked at his watch and patted his jacket where his discount ticket home nestled safely in the inside pocket. Maybe he could get an early plane out. Tarpender was on his feet banging the gavel.

'Can we have some order here, please?'

Ben Reese surveyed the scene, a half smile forming on his lips. He sat motionless in his slouched position, calmly watching the commotion about him. A two-man team, one shouldering a camera, moved in on the Air World table. Aspinwall saw them only as silhouettes against lights pointed at him. He barged past the glint of a lens, knocking the camera back into the cameraman's head. Moudon stumbled over his chair and caught up alongside.

'Who the fuck is that guy?' Matt demanded. 'I don't need any social action workers or bleeding hearts at a time like this – get him the fuck out of town! Get him away from the press! Send him out of the country! Get rid of him!'

Vic ran alongside him, his words jolted by the uneven pace. 'You can't, Matt, you'll have a pilots' strike on your hands!'

'Well, then, give him a vacation for eight weeks; I gotta get my Big Season started. Better yet' – and he lowered his voice as he pushed through the mob – 'he seems to know how to read a graph, transfer him to the outback, put him on our technical assistance programme, make him an instructor to those jigaboos. The cocksucker will think it's a promotion!' Matt raced down the steps out to the lobby.

A crowd pressed in around Guy. Several people were standing on chairs. Reese found Anja outside the circle of commotion working her way towards him.

'Knockout in twenty-two seconds of the first round. The customers want their money back,' she giggled.

'We're going to have to go out the back,' he said. 'Wait in the kitchen.'

Cameras were held above the mob pointing down at Guy, who was trying to be agreeable. The clamour was split by the rippling static of flash-bulbs, erupting like heat lightning through the haze. A squabble of questions rose to a shrill peak, one overlapping the other. Guy waited for one to ring in the clear.

'What's in the report, Anders?' 'Who gave it to you?' 'Does it apply to the whole fleet?' 'Who did it?' 'Is it stolen?' 'Will this generate a pilots' strike?'

'I can't speak for the Air Line Pilots Association.'

More shouting. One voice broke through. 'Would you recommend no one fly the 17-10?'

'I have nothing against test pilots strapping it on.'

'How will you pay your bills?' The questioner's face was superior.

Guy's eyes were like hard-cut diamonds. 'One at a time,' he said tightly.

Laughter.

'Is there any correlation between the F-19 and the 17-10?' The question was perceptive, the questioner obviously picking up on the same thought that had shot through his mind during Boice's reference to the F-19.

'Mr Boice will have to answer that for you.'

'How would you feel if Air World were to default on its summer bookings?'

'A lot of people would be hurt – none fatally.' Another crisp sputter of flashguns. Then Ben was at his side.

'OK, the zoo's closed.' He took a lighter from a young woman and relit his stogey. He reached out and helped an older man down off a chair. 'There's another show down the hall. Some *Homo erectus* named Aspinwall. He's already plugging in a mike. On your way! Ben returned the lighter.

Guy relaxed, letting himself be jostled as the tight huddle broke up. He grabbed his bag and grinned at Ben. 'Kiss me. I'm a passenger,' he said. 'I've got one more copy in here and when that baby's gone to the insurance underwriter, I'm going home. I'll let Morty Judd fill me in over some old malt whiskey.' Ben laughed as he urged Guy ahead of him through the double doors that led to the kitchen. Excited yelps and the clatter of dishes slapped off white tile walls as the hotel crew moved along aisles of platters, readying them for an upcoming luncheon. Anja surprised Guy as she threw her arms around him and held him tightly. He stood there smiling, holding his bag.

'What the hell are we doing in the kitchen?' he said, looking into her face.

Slowly she let go and looked at him, seeing him, yet not hearing a sound, a wisplike image she would always own; a moment between them . . . He had laid down the gauntlet. There were tears on her face. 'That hug was not ceremonial.'

Ben shuffled to break the spell. 'Hey, what about me? I taught him everything he knows!' Anja let go and kissed Ben on the neck. Ben wrapped one arm around her and held her affectionately. 'Where'd you get a girl like this, huh? If I had my youth, I'd buy a new shirt and take her away.' There was a sudden frantic stampede outside the kitchen doors, another breakout from the hearing room. Ben chuckled and shook his head, visualizing the scene outside. 'Like a cherry bomb going off in a chicken coop!' His eyes twinkled and again he laughed, listening to the sound of commotion as more footfalls pounded by the other way. 'Like a raid at a circle jerk,' he said, his look like that of a contented old tomcat stuffed with fish. 'Oh, man, you gotta savour these moments.' He leaned back luxuriating in the recollection of the turmoil and looked at Guy, his face slowly straightening, becoming serious. 'But from here on in, you're going to have to use back doors and service elevators, because now you've got them mad.' Ben didn't move. The words were suddenly there, a barrier across the trail to Oz on which they had all been dancing a moment before. A brief hubbub on the other side of the doors rose and vanished.

Inside the ballroom, Merle Tarpender glanced at Anders's document, just handed him by an aide. Doug Moss tapped the gavel and leaned down to the thin table mike. His voice echoed in the already rapidly clearing hall. 'This hearing is recessed and will resume at the convenience of the chairman.'

In the kitchen Ben fixed Guy with an uncompromising look.

'Now it's their serve.'

Out in Central Park the blond man with the skier's suntan jogged with an even pace, working up a good sweat. His rhythm was that of a well co-ordinated athlete, his body straining forward in the calm of the cool morning air. He had nearly reached the Seventy-second Street turnoff at Central Park West when the beeper on his belt sounded, alerting him to call in. Without changing his stride he veered slowly to his left and ran towards the exit.

The heat in the hotel kitchen was oppressive. Neither Guy nor Anja spoke. The giddy relief Anja felt only moments ago was being broken into particles, blown apart. She searched Ben's face for a flicker that would betray the joke but his expression was matter-of-fact.

'They won't be able to afford Guy any more,' he said.

'Say it more directly.' Anja's voice was unsteady.

Ben watched her with a grave, tired expression; it was in that instant she understood. She tried without success to force the black bubble forming in the deep pool of her mind from slowly expanding, rising up, to burst into newspaper images she had seen of Robert Kennedy in another hotel kitchen minutes before he was shot.

'They may rely on something less than that,' Ben said. 'That cheque you signed for wipes him out. That fine spectrographic analysis he just dropped in their laps will be on a garbage scow by morning.'

Echoes of Melissa's party drum-rolled through Anja's head and the sting of guilt at the confusion caused by the skier washed over her. Guy's face suddenly seemed whiter. She saw him struggle to find his voice.

'You'll have to spell that out for me.'

With lightning-fast flicks of a stiletto-like knife, a Japanese chef carved exact squares of meat from a lean side of beef behind them. Ben pushed himself away from the wall and eased Guy back a step. He reached into his shirt pocket for the pale blue cheque and held it up for both to see.

'This,' he said gently, 'is what's known in the trade as a "shield" because no matter how close a blockhead like Anders here gets, he's tainted and can be discredited. This one has relatives. It's the second I've seen. The first was presented to a kraut who didn't like the F-19 because more were planted in the ground than were operational. He had incriminating data. But he accepted the cheque as half of what was jokingly described as a down payment to go into the helium business.'

Anja blanched at the mention of helium. Ben held the cheque in his sights.

'When it was shown that the apparent source of the cash was a British aircraft manufacturer eager to hawk its own wares, his opinions were dismissed as industrial sabotage. He's back to driving a honey wagon.' Ben extracted a well-rubbed three-by-five photograph from his pocket and held it up for them to see, and there, from between his weathered fingers, peered the smooth arrogant face of the skier. Even from the dull photographic paper the eyes arrested Anja with their separate magnetism. Guy frowned, sensing her stunned reaction, and struggled with the pang of understanding.

'The name of the man you met is Anton Jasovak. You check me out. Anton set up his mark – that's you, sweetheart – to go along fifty-fifty with a joke. "It would be a gas to go into the helium business." Sounds interesting over some booze. Then he sharps a shill. It's a setup and he sticks half the win in the mark's pocket, a present of the down payment. The money comes in a straight line from Buttress.' He turned to Guy. 'Buster, right now you couldn't give nooky away on a submarine.'

Guy poured two fingers of cooking wine into a coffee mug.

'Buttress launders the money through a perfumery in Paris and if you dig behind that, you'd find it's an apparent front for the European Skybus Consortium. Complete with an honorary board of directors made up of decomposing members of Europe's aviation industry who are very pleased to receive stipends for what they believe to be a reputable perfumery. A female acquaintance of First Officer Anders takes a cheque for twenty-five grand in his name from the opposition to start up a helium business? Of course not. Anders has been paid off directly by the European competition to smear the good old Buttress name.'

'Prove it.'

'I did an article on it. Unpublished. I was ahead of my time.' Ben gave them a wry look. 'But you've given me a reprieve.'

Guy reached for the cheque. 'We'll tear the goddamn thing up.'

Ben held it away. 'In the first place, she signed for it and that would be tough to explain.' Anja covered her eyes. 'No, we're going to let it go through.'

'Tear it up and I'm clean.'

'Jackass! If we prove Buttress wrote this cheque, you'll be immortalized.' He smiled. 'You could run for President.' He flipped the cheque, placed it facedown on the cutting board, unclipped a pen from his shirt pocket and handed it to Guy. 'Your name goes right there, just the way Jasovak wrote it.'

Anja watched the two men who suddenly seemed like dark abstractions. Her gullibility at having allowed the skier to affect her to the point where she signed her name filled her with dismay and self-reproach. And despite Ben's assurance that the cheque could be used to advantage, she didn't believe it would be that simple. Ben examined Guy's signature. 'We're going to need a notarized Xerox copy of both sides to support the fact that this cheque existed. Next Guy deposits it to let the smear go through. I then have to find the fellow who hands these out – '

'Jasovak.'

' – and prove that he and his perfumery live at the end of Hollis Wright's chain.'

'And if we don't cash it, the British analysis flies.'

'Baby, criticism of GM written by Ford never flies.'

Anja hardly heard what they were saying now. She was distracted and had to locate the source of it. She tried to capture the thought that was trying to surface. She knew she was angry with herself – but no, seeping past that anger something else was disturbing her. It was something Boice had said that no one had questioned – like a gross remark overlooked in polite company, no one had challenged it – something unspeakable that was casually accepted in the name of necessity. Then she remembered what it was. She turned to leave.

Guy's mouth moved. 'Where are you going?'

'I'm really sorry about what happened.'

Guy wanted to calm her dismay but the echo of the moment had lassoed him.

'I have to pick up your son,' she said.

Both men stood as though rooted amid the harsh yellow spread of an industrial cloud bank. Guy folded the cheque and slipped it into his shirt pocket.

'It was so simple when we were kids, huh? What happened, Ben? What's the standard?'

'You've got to be impeccable. The evidence has to have the stamp of divinity on it – pure.'

'Like the faces of the dead.'

'That's pretty divine. Only we don't want to let it get that far, do we?'

Toby, his hair askew, burst inside and, locating Anders, stood still while the doors flapped shut behind him. He blinked, a nervous tic.

'There are questions I'm supposed to answer out there.'

184

His face was ashen. 'You compromised me. I don't even know what you put on that table!'

There was a scuffle in the hall and again the kitchen doors flew apart. A reporter lurched on to the stone floor and pointed at Guy. 'There!' A tangle of bodies stumbled through the opening.

The Japanese chef, a twelve-inch meat cleaver dripping with gristle clenched in his hand, stepped before them, blocking their way. He planted a greasy fat fingerprint squarely into the reporter's silk necktie.

'What the hell do you think this is?' he threatened. 'Somebody call security.' A hush came over the kitchen. Nobody moved. 'Get out,' he said. Then he looked at Ben and Guy. 'You too.'

'I think he means it.' Guy was deadpan.

Ben stepped lightly towards the back stairs and nodded to Guy. 'You first.'

'We'll come back later when you're not so busy,' Guy said soothingly over his shoulder.

'You know you're interfering with the First Amendment,' Ben smiled, then bolted after Guy down the steps at the rear of the kitchen that led to the dark subterranean corridors beneath the hotel and out towards the street. Toby stood flat-footed, checked the crush at the door and bounded down the steel steps after them. He caught up as they trotted, then walked swiftly along a grimy, poorly lit corridor that smelled of garbage and disinfectant.

'You got us out on a limb.' Toby's voice reverberated down the length of the underpass. 'If what you have is that big, let us in on it.'

'We'll get you a copy.'

'That statement you made in there, you're on your own. It has nothing to do with ALPA. That's how I'm going to put it. We're not going to rubber-stamp you.'

Guy threw a look of mild disgust towards his colleague, whose face was contorted by the shadows.

'That's up to you. Convene the committee if you want,

but there's not going to be room for a six-month study this time.'

'Are we in this or not?' pressed Toby.

'In.'

'Then let go of the ball.'

'Toby, I can't,' Guy asserted.

'Then I'm heading home.' Toby's tone was one of utter finality.

Guy stopped. He felt sympathy for the beleaguered man, shut out, left standing alone. He took two steps towards him and put his arm around Toby's shoulder.

'Toby, what I really need now is what you can't give me.'

'Like what?'

'A walkout.'

'A walkout?' Toby was incredulous.

'Slowdown, stand-down, a strike. Oh, Jesus, if we had that, they'd have to come clean. They'd *have* to talk, convince us on *our* terms, show us how they put that bus together from the inside out!'

'Aspinwall would have an injunction before sundown. You're getting a lot of people bent out of shape.' Toby stepped away again.

'Toby, we've got the jump this time!'

'You *had* a jump,' Ben corrected.

'You've only got a hunch,' said Toby. 'Since when do we go in without facts? Ben here went in without facts. What the hell's going on? Is he contagious?'

Guy stared at Toby like a sergeant exhausted from shepherding a contrary recruit through the front lines. 'What do you want to do, wait till you have to pick through the pieces, dig a flight recorder out of a sidewalk? Is that the *only* way?'

'It took us fifteen years to build some credibility. We put a lot of people back to work, cut the rope from around our own necks. And we did it with science. We beat the FAA and the NTSB and the manufacturers through maths.

And if you've got something – if you're right – we can do it again!'

'Toby,' Ben interjected gently, 'there's no time for footnotes and correct spelling. Right now they're heading down the hole and pulling the hatch shut. We want to keep it open.'

Toby stood, staring at them, his face set, resigned.

'If ever you want help, hit us with facts. Give us crossplots on a graph, things people can study. Until then you're a Committee of One.' He turned and headed up the stairs. The echoes of his footfalls diminished and finally they were gone.

Ben stood there like a flat-nosed bear shrouded in the shadows. He turned to Guy. 'Welcome to the war.'

'Goddamn.' Guy breathed it with the inescapable knowledge that the other side wouldn't stop until he was out of their way.

The ballroom had already assumed the quality of an empty railway station. Only trailing pieces of conversation and the occasional chair scraping echoed through the hall. Ed Boice leaned over the Buttress table, where his three assistants waited in embarrassed silence. All the other tables had been abandoned except for a few stragglers collecting their papers from the litter. Ed was shaking, his thick arms were out in front of him for support, the hands were red, the fingertips, pressed hard against the table, where white. He was talking, not to any of the three who listened with abject raptness, but to where his eyes stared, two feet in front of him. 'Work your brains out to put these boy-scout airline pilots into the middle of the next century . . . Give them the Rolls-Royce of the sky . . .' Ed's knuckles clamped harder. Sweat poured from him. 'We *are* failure-conscious, for Chrissakes . . . Look at the problems we solved . . . and now they're fighting us on fly-by-wire. Fucking bastards don't understand it. Ungrateful scum!' There was an awkward pause. Without acknowledging his colleagues, Ed Boice slowly turned to go.

Anja was standing in the open space between him and the door. He stopped at the sight of her.

'You used two words,' she said, her voice carrying clearly.

His fury unabated, Boice perceived her as though through gauze. Slowly he recognized her as the woman who had been with Anders, now standing before him, serene in her own separate sovereignty.

'"Acceptable risk",' she said. 'I'd like you to tell me what that means.'

Boice stood at a slant as though facing an uphill climb. 'You tell Anders I meant what I said about the courage of the crew,' he rasped. She sensed he had the capacity to be rude just then but held it in check. For that she almost liked him. He remained mute but the churning inside him was audible to her and for a moment she felt compassion for him.

'Those two words,' she coaxed.

He knew he should have passed over them in an open hearing. And now it came as no surprise that they had already returned to ring again through his head even before he'd left the hearing room. He glared at her. 'It's part of the purchase price.'

'It means a certain degree of risk – a certain number of deaths – are acceptable.' Her voice was steady. She waited.

Boice didn't answer.

'It means that, doesn't it?'

Boice looked away, as if to go. Anja stared at him.

'I thought so,' she said.

Matt Aspinwall stood facing an array of hand-held TV cameras. A cluster of microphones converged towards his chin. His hands were in his pockets. Vic Moudon stood slightly behind him trying to look nonchalant, but he felt his eyeballs protruded too far and his lips were dry. He had an urge to check his fly but felt the eyes behind the lights were upon him. He settled for staring at the floor. Matt was talking. He was polite enough, smiling, aloof, but irritated by some of the probing and baiting from the smart-ass reporters.

'We have one thousand two hundred and twenty-six crews at Air World. Forty-six have been checked out on the 17-10 and we're currently checking out eighteen per month. There have been no other complaints.'

'What was your immediate reaction to what your man Anders said?'

'I thought of the passengers who were fortunate enough to have picked him and Captain Cosgrove to bring them home. My feeling is that any pilot who's done what that man's done deserves a rest.' Aspinwall liked being blunt.

'What information does he have?'

'For all I know it's the phone directory.'

'Is your implication, sir, that he's unstable?'

'My implication is that I haven't yet seen what he has.'

'He said that what he had was proof that the automatic flight-control system has a problem.'

'Problems provide us with opportunities to improve. If there's a problem, we'll fix it.'

'Will this affect the status of the 17-10s Air World has on order?'

'No effect.'

'Is the 17-10 safe?'

Aspinwall smiled thinly. 'We didn't buy a pig in a poke.' Then his demeanour turned serious. 'Lockheed, Boeing, Douglas, the French and the English, the best there is, all compete for our business. We had a free choice in an open market.'

'According to your advertising your Big Season is about

189

to start. But so far Air World has only six 17-10s in service. Even if you ran them twenty-four hours around the clock, you couldn't handle the bookings that have already been made.'

Matt rubbed his chin. Behind the puffy exterior there was a steel cable in his gut. 'We've got another six 17-10s being readied for delivery from Buttress. And another six after that. Maybe you ought to get yourself a calculator and work up how many passengers those deliveries represent.'

'It seems impossible to believe your capacity will be equal to the requirement. The 17-10s are late.' The reporter was tenacious. 'Do you think, in view of this, the government will give Pan Am the route authority, let them handle your traffic?'

Aspinwall looked at the reporter a long time. Despite the florid jowls, his face had the sharp aspect of a dangerous reptile. 'The route case has been decided, and like many others in the past, it went against Pan Am.' Matt Aspinwall's tight mouth pursed. His eyebrows cocked. 'You can rest assured the government won't reverse that decision,' he said knowingly. 'Our equipment will be at the gate. Period.'

The reporter paused, his mind flailing not to be shut out. 'One last question, Mr Aspinwall. How does the pilots' union figure in all this?'

'It doesn't.'

'They could make trouble.'

'Not with impunity.' Aspinwall smiled sardonically and turned to go. Another reporter broke in with a piping voice.

'Would you say W. B. Cosgrove is an unusual pilot?'

'He's capable.'

'What did he say after he landed?'

'Three Hail Marys.'

Somebody in the back laughed and that defused the put-down. The reporter who asked the question began to smile

190

wanly. Aspinwall left. Moudon checked his fly and followed his boss.

The interview had concluded.

7

Ben Reese hailed a cab and piled in after Guy. 'There's something across town I want you to look at,' Ben said and ordered the driver to head west.

'Later,' Guy said, tapping the second copy of the spec analysis he'd just dumped on the hearing table. 'I have to get this over to the insurance company.'

Ben waved it aside. 'Never mind that now and listen up. That bastard in there just vindicated me. I've been right all along.'

'Which bastard in there are you referring to?' Guy asked.

'Boice. There *is* a connection between the F-19 and the 17-10. They share the same problem. Boice just owned up to it.'

'Should I be surprised?'

'You're not surprised?'

'No. Where's your backup? As I recall, you're not too well known for proof.'

'That's what I want to show you. It's written in German in plus and minus signs.'

'No doubt one of your impeccable sources.'

'No, smart-ass, I don't read German.'

'As far as I know, you don't read plus and minus signs either.'

'It's a Luftwaffe report commissioned to explain why the F-19 has been shaking itself to pieces over Düsseldorf and Ramstein. I never got to use it. You're right, I don't know what it says. But if there is a connection, then that report may just tell you why you had so much trouble getting into JFK.'

191

'You know anybody who reads German?'

'That's where we're headed. She's on Riverside Drive. Teaches at City College. She's got the file.'

'How'd *she* get the file? How'd *you* get the file?'

'From the German Embassy.'

'The German Embassy!' Guy exclaimed.

'Pipe down!' Ben scowled. Then his expression changed. 'There was this young girl there. Ursula. No, Gisela. It was Ursula or Gisela. I paid her for my stuff.' Ben's eyes twinkled. 'I'd go back and buy her a drink if I could but I'm fresh out of credentials. Persona non grata.'

'You have a document like that on Riverside Drive?'

'That's right.'

'And you still wrote what you did?'

'Riverside Drive came too late. Besides, what I wrote wasn't wrong.' Ben ticked it off on his fingers. 'Union-weary workmanship – that was the lead-off. Flaws introduced on the production line, blind reliance on computer analyses of parts that had never flown before, middle management's silence in the face of mismanagement, pissing in its britches for fear of the axe, Buttress building planes that self-destruct to prime its replacement pipeline. We even documented the fact that Buttress would end up getting paid twice for every F-19 it delivered.'

'It wasn't fact.'

'It was self-evident.'

'You didn't document it.'

'We had figures.'

'You made them up.'

'I filled in a little,' Ben smiled. 'And I figure the odds are still on my side.'

The cab swerved to avoid a bus. They were a dozen blocks from the hotel ballroom.

'Wonder what they're doing back there now,' Guy mused.

'Right now they're tear-assing for home. They've got to re-synchronize their crib sheets. Or did you think you put them in a moral dilemma? Look, there's no reason for both of us to do this.' Ben checked the street number, unclipped his pen and scribbled an address on the inside of a matchbook. 'Here. The woman you want to see, here's her name. Look her up in the phone book. You go handle it alone.'

'She doesn't know me.'

'Call her up, make an appointment. Tell her to read you the Luftwaffe report.' Ben rapped on the cabby's partition. 'Pull over here.'

'Where're you going?'

'You deal with the plus and minus signs. It wouldn't mean anything to me anyway. I'm going to get my hands on the guy who sells helium.' Ben opened the door and held it ajar. 'I want you to know I wasn't fooling around back there in the kitchen. It's not hard to make people disappear these days. The going rate for a guy like you is ten grand including a two-digit percentage for inflation.'

'I reckon they've spent some of that already.'

'They can afford overtime.'

'And what about you?'

'They've already cut my tongue out. That doesn't mean I'm off their list. Just that if they knock off a newspaperman they piss off a few hundred others who pick up the scent and that can get sticky.' Ben clambered clear. 'Keep in touch.' He slammed the door.

Guy called Riverside Drive and got no answer. He then called home; the threat made evident in the hotel kitchen that morning had heightened his concern for Anja and his son. Nagging tugs of premonition had begun to weigh him down. When Anja answered, he stood galvanized by what she said. There was dread in her voice. An unlabelled package had been placed in the doorway of his house. Guy asked her to describe it. It was cardboard, looked heavy and it had not come with the mail. She didn't want to sound paranoid but she felt certain it would go off. She was unable to say more.

Guy didn't recall stepping out of the phone booth. He believed he'd told her to stay clear of the front door, to take Jamie and herself out back. His head was reeling. Slowly he realized he was staring at a powder blue Stingray waiting nearby. He recognized Synova behind the wheel the same moment she hit the horn. She was in her prim stewardess uniform, waving at him.

'I went to the hearing.' Her smile was easy and confident. 'I followed your cab.'

'You got the windshield fixed,' Guy said absently.

'The police want to talk to you.'

Guy watched her mouth and squinted through the glare from the chrome. He gripped the second xerox copy of the English spectrographic analysis and was aware of her saying something but he couldn't follow it.

'You look distracted,' she frowned.

'I've got a report to deliver,' he heard himself tell her.

'Well, you're not driving this car again.' She blew him a kiss. 'Where's it going?'

The buzzing in his head cleared and he saw Synova smiling at him. 'The Intercarrier insurance people in Greenwich – the chairman or the president only. Nobody lower.'

'Give it to me. I'll take it.'

'Really?'

'I swear. I'm trying to make points. Now get in,' she smiled.

'I can't.' Guy scribbled the address. 'I've got to go home.'

She looked at him quizzically, her expression unresolved.

'Something's come up,' he said helplessly.

She shook her hair loose, recovered and cocked her

194

head. 'One of these days, Anders, I'm going to get your pants off.'

When Guy came up to the house, the front door was open. As he entered, he saw Anja standing in the kitchen doorway. The cardboard box was on a table in the foyer, its cover torn apart, a copy of the thick annual *A to Z Discount Catalogue* he received once each year protruding in plain evidence.

Anja's hands covered her eyes. 'I'm embarrassed to death,' she said. 'I saw there *was* a label on it after all. It was delivered by Parcel Post. But I believe in warnings.'

Guy noticed Anja's suitcase standing in the corridor.

'I think your needs have changed,' she continued, 'and I'm the one responsible for that. You need an armed guard and I don't think I can fit into that. I don't want to be anyone's unlucky omen. You make me angry a lot but I couldn't stand to see you hurt.' Her eyes were glistening.

Guy saw that her case of maps was packed too. 'So it is goodbye.'

'While we're both ahead. You're going to need to find a better friend.'

'I've got friends.'

'You haven't got friends.'

'There's Benny Reese and I'm working on others.'

'Who?'

'There's the folks at Buttress and the NTSB and the FAA and my brothers at ALPA. I'm trying to save their ass. They just haven't picked up my mating call, is all.'

'The damn thing about it all is, you got me involved.'

'Oh?'

'I mean in your problem. Which I can't be responsible for.'

'Right.'

'But I am to a degree. I should never have answered

195

the phone that night. Then I wouldn't have signed my name and the cheque would never have been written.'

'It hasn't hurt anyone yet.'

'But it hasn't made your day either. Let's face it Guy, I've been an intrusion.'

'No, you're a novelty.'

'I'm a distraction.'

'I guarantee you you're not that at all.'

'Well, that's a very lousy thing to say!'

'Oh, for Chrissakes! You're a distraction in the . . . provocative sense, not in the wrong sense. Now that I've said that, I think we should take a moment and put things in better perspective. Suppose I put some extra money in your envelope.'

'What for?'

'Well . . . extra services.'

'You can't buy that!'

'What?'

'It's not for sale!'

'Don't flatter yourself. I've never paid for it. You're confused.'

'You're telling me!'

'Look, Anja, you distract me like a ball of fire – like an attractive hand grenade. With you in the house I'm more awake today than I've been in the last thirteen months and that's good. There's a lot going on and I'm glad there's someone pecking at me even though I don't know how to appreciate it. It doesn't mean I'm ungrateful. If you want to go, I'll put you on a plane and I hope you'll write Jamie and me and tell us about your island.'

'Oh, shit,' Anja said, tears sprouting at the corners of her eyes.

'Now what?'

'I don't want to get involved with you. I thought you'd be older and fat. Your ad sounded fat. I want to keep a distance. This was supposed to be a job with hours like an office.'

'We'll keep it distant.'

'I called a cab already and that makes me feel guilty.'

'About what?'

'About chickening out! I promised to help you and I haven't done that yet. It would be easier if I had. Then I'd be gone – like a storybook character leaving a gift behind and never returning –'

'Would you like to say goodbye to Jamie now . . . or are you undecided?'

'Don't you understand? I'm undecided!'

The horn outside signalled that the cab had arrived. Guy hoisted the suitcase and took it to the open front door. Anja stood uncertainly.

'Jesus Christ,' she said through her tears.

The cabby jumped out of his hack to take the bag.

'Sorry, Fred,' Guy apologized. 'We got the flight mixed up. Won't be needing a cab.'

'Oh, OK, Mr Anders.'

'Sorry.' Guy tipped him.

'No sweat.'

Guy shut the door and set the bag down. 'I've made your choice for you because you owe me something.'

Anja refused to look at him.

'Your promise was that you wouldn't leave till two weeks after you got my son permanently out of that attic. And we'll keep it distant,' he added.

Anja held on to the back of a chair and stared out of the window until her eyes dried. She recovered and spoke again; her words were soft. 'And I'd like to help you and Ben. I've already got an idea how.' She said it like a wish.

'All donations on behalf of the passengers will be greatly appreciated.'

It was early afternoon. Anja was back in her dungarees and button-down shirt. The man who had been watching

Guy's house followed her and saw her go into the local library.

By daylight Melissa's brownstone crouched morosely amid the curling eddies of morning-after streets and the stink of garbage cans. Collar up, Ben Reese climbed the stone steps and punched the doorbell twice. The house remained silent. Only a dog passing by spoiled the empty aspect of the sidewalk. Ben flicked the ash from his cigarette and shoved against the door, which, to his mild surprise, opened easily; he wasn't sure if it had been pulled open at that moment by the broad woman in maid's uniform who stood looking disinterestedly up at him. Ben nodded, then strode past her into the dim-lit foyer still littered with debris. Shrugging, the maid turned away to face the mess. Ben picked his way towards the purple-carpeted stairway and reached the landing just as Melissa appeared above.

A towel draped her head and a half-open cassock of rich brocade flowed loosely over her otherwise undressed body. Ben noticed the chipped polish on her fingernails, the raw cuticles, the brittleness of her hands. Her shoulders were slightly too square, her calves slightly too muscular in the harsh morning light. Ben stood admiring the excellent architecture of her face, a technical perfection. Yet it was with a flicker of regret that he saw as well the absence of that inner glow which the jolting journey away from youth and towards ambition extinguishes, an absence to mar and spoil the beauty. The unpainted face was tough, the large agile eyes sizing him up, a squat dishevelled man under a froth of curly hair. He stood framed by a colourless sunbeam which caught the tendrils of cigarette smoke rising slowly above his head. His face, she saw, was like the butt end of a cross-grained telephone pole but the knowing eyes arrested her; she found Ben strangely lovely to look at.

'The name's Ben Reese – '

'Printed, published and disgraced,' she said archly.

Ben pulled at his lower lip, his searching eyes rooted to her. 'Come down here, I want to show you something.'

Melissa descended the stairs with stately grace. Ben fished out a mottled photograph of the blond skier from the inside of his mackintosh, and held it out to her.

'His name's Anton Jasovak . . . a.k.a. Maximilian . . . a.k.a. Little Orphan Annie . . . I need to find him. I think you can help.'

Her face flickered. 'What makes you think I know anything about this man – '

'I'll take the short form,' Ben growled with muted vehemence. His eyes tightened. 'So let's cut the cute bullshit. You've cleaned his pipes too often.'

'I'll take ten per cent of your royalties, Mr Reese,' she said coolly, her expression remaining fixed.

A crooked smile twisted the corners of Ben's mouth. 'I'll gladly give it to you. But since I don't have any royalties – at the moment – I'll have to give you . . . something else.' He returned her gaze blandly but squarely.

'What's my advantage?'

'The intimate knowledge that Maximilian is dangerous. Perhaps it's time you used that.'

'Sounds like a prediction of trouble.'

'The smart money never put all its chips on a single number. I'm suggesting you spread your risk.' Ben blew a stream of smoke past her face.

The maid went scurrying out carrying a load of garbage.

Melissa's luminous eyes probed him from point-blank range. Finally she said, very evenly, 'Try the Aldwych on East Eighty-first between Park and Madison. An exclusive establishment, you might not – '

'I'm familiar with it.'

Ben didn't budge. Almost as an afterthought he added softly, 'No second thoughts, OK? Don't try to warn him.

199

Because if he's not at the Aldwych, why then I guess I'll have to come back here for round two.' The capacity for ugliness lurked in the creases around his eyes.

She moved a half step closer to him. 'What's the payoff?'

Ben bent over to stub out his cigarette in a jade-lined ashtray on the Chippendale table next to the landing. His other hand slipped inside her cassock. She didn't object. Her eyes were steady as his rough hand traced the sculpture of her body. It lasted only a moment.

Then he said simply, 'I'm the payoff.' Ben half smiled, stepped back with a nod, turned and clattered from the landing. The heavy door slammed shut behind him.

Melissa remained standing as if transfixed, staring at the emptiness.

On a deserted piece of sand-strewn road four miles from the Jones Beach obelisk, a junked car stood facing the ocean, an unclothed mannequin propped behind the wheel. A lone figure nearby squinted obliquely in both directions and listened. Satisfied, he peeled a puttylike substance from a packet and tamped it carefully around the windshield's edge, delicately sculpting it so that it was thicker under the left wiper than at the ends of the frame. He lifted the hood to make a final adjustment, then closed it gently.

He dried his hands with a handkerchief, slipped behind a dune and took from his toolbox what appeared to be a TV remote control. He held it over his head so that it pointed towards the car, waited for a rising breaker to crash towards the beach and pressed the trigger. The sharp clap of an explosion was muffled by the sudden roar of surf. A puff of smoke rose and was dissipated by the wind.

The figure clambered over the dune to check the results.

The rehearsal had been a success.

The windshield was gone, as was the mannequin's head.

The body had been blown back, ragged edges of plaster streaming from its throat.

For three days after the hearing Guy was unable to reach the translator on Riverside Drive; her phone went unanswered. Guy first faced the impasse with a mixture of frustration and elation: frustration because he couldn't rid himself of that quality of muted tension common to prizefighters between rounds; elation because it gave him time to duck away and be together with his son. He and Jamie drove to the Aquarium, both looking forward to a quality of brightness, an expectation of a small adventure, but to their mutual bewilderment they bounced along the Belt Parkway in unbroken silence. Guy realized it was his own preoccupation that created the mood. Despite Anja's advice and his own intent, he didn't know what to say.

Jamie reached across the seat and touched Guy's hand, but he never took hold and squeezed back. Instead he moved away and reached for the wheel, telling himself he had to control the car. He was mortified by the devastating nature of this reflex yet he knew he couldn't retrieve it.

For two hours they walked past the glass tanks at the Aquarium, past the sharks and the whale tank and coloured tropical fish. Guy read the wall plaques out loud while his mind travelled back and forth over the true nature of the silence between them, over his long absences, about which he felt guilty but for which he had no solution. He thought about the pain that would get loose if they did talk. The pain was in his throat and it frightened him. He was certain that if they started, the flood that would follow would overwhelm them both. Yet he vowed somehow to end the estrangement and bridge the impasse between them.

On the afternoon of the third day Guy reached the

translator and was at last seated in the living room on Riverside Drive. The German woman who had taken on Ben's report was in her mid-fifties and elegant. The room was large and well stocked with dark, old furniture, not at all musty but rather imbued with a patina of *beau monde* and a certain quiet dignity. Guy, in a large, richly upholstered wing chair, was left alone with the report while the woman disappeared to make tea.

The English translation was neatly typed in double-space and stapled to each page of German text. The first page began:

A preliminary evaluation of the reliability of the F-19 flight control system was undertaken as a primary issue since this system is flight critical. The complexity of the control system configuration caused some concern and was specifically addressed by our evaluation staff . . .

'God almighty!'
Guy's eyes raced farther down the page.

. . . distributed information processing hierarchy centred around a fault-tolerant digital computer, a system designed to satisfy the minimum stability margins, failure immunity and invulnerability requirements of the United States Air Force MIL-F-9490 Flight Control Specifications . . .

During flight evaluation of the F-19 weapons system under operational conditions, test pilots have encountered intermittant control surface vibrations . . .

Reese, for God's sake, you were at the one-yard line!

. . . and rapid concurrent degradation of flight stability and control . . .

He turned to the next page and read:

Upon review of data assembled from initial evaluation of three fatal accidents in eleven days, a preliminary assessment has been reached that excessive demand on electro-hydraulic servo valves may induce control surface flutter independent of pilot input. Based on this assessment, a request has been made for the manufacturer in the United States to modify the authority of certain electro-hydraulic servo valves in accordance with . . .

The woman appeared with a silver tray of tea. She started to say something but hesitated, noting Guy's concentration.

Guy skipped a paragraph because the terms *electronic corruption* and *17-10* seemed to leap up and assault him from the middle of the page. His eyes raced back to the beginning of the sentence.

The degree of susceptibility of the digital flight control system to electronic corruption has not yet been fully assessed although a relationship between regional computer signal processing and main computer signal degradation has been theorized. The causal factors of such effects are subject to further analysis. The state airline Deutsche Luftgesellshaft AG, which has the similarly equipped Buttress 17-10 civil transport currently under evaluation, has been requested to advise this authority of details of any events of flight control system degradation which they may experience.

Guy stared at the line, then the date on the original page of German text underneath. The question had been framed months *prior* to the flight of Air World Six! He went on to read:

Upon compliance of the manufacturer with the requests from this authority for modification, a series of comprehensive F-19 flight tests will be undertaken to explore the entire flight envelope (note to Mr Reese: is 'envelope' used correctly in this context? I could find no other word. HB) It is expected that the conclusions reached as a result of these tests will be forwarded to the Air Ministry, Bonn, by no later than five months from the date of this report.

The report Guy held had been dated well before Christmas, which meant that if the schedule had been adhered to – and he knew the Germans were reliable in such matters – the results were already available! So here it all was, in a quiet eighth-floor apartment on upper Riverside Drive. And if the Germans *had* uncovered a common weakness shared by the F-19 and the 17-10, it would finish Buttress.

'Would you care for some tea?'

Guy raised his eyes. She was smiling, offering him a cup.

'No . . . no, thank you,' Guy said, standing up, shuffling the report into its manila envelope. 'You've been very kind . . . but I must go.'

Buttress workers who happened by the 'hexagon' veered to favour the left corridor wall, mild alarm registered on their faces at the commotion outside Fenton Riddick's conference room, and they hurried on. Any moment Buzz Riddick would appear, they said over coffee and doughnuts, to lop off some heads. Ed Boice tapped only a few shoulders, the meeting would begin at 1100 hours in Riddick's room, the place they called 'the Tank'. Ed's face was still haggard from the last twenty-four hours, the nightmare hearing and the trip back from DC, unpleasant and bumpy all the way. They'd lost his suitcase, to top it off.

They filed glumly in to arrange themselves in inconspicuous order around the conference table, an anonymity of white shirts. Normally all the section chiefs and foremen would be there crowding the room – hydraulics, electronics, flight controls, power plants, wind tunnel – a room for forty people including two or three grim-faced women, for Riddick liked to run the proceedings like cabinet meetings. But today it was more exclusive. Ed Boice, Dick Miller and Vern Locker were seated at the table along with but four or five others, fresh pads and sharpened pencils before them, and at the far end were

Buttress chief test pilot Gus Helmsdorf and his assistant, Jake Blasingame.

Gus Helmsdorf had been one of the great Luftwaffe fighter aces, though it was seldom acknowledged. With his new title, 'Director of Flight Operations', Helmsdorf now spent a lot of time behind a massive polished desk in a long room studded with framed paintings and models of Buttress aeroplanes. Only one model in that room wasn't a Buttress product: placed on the second shelf down in the bookcase behind his chair, where it often went unnoticed by visitors, was a twenty-five-centimetre sterling-silver Me.109 with tiny engraved swastikas. No one knew for sure how many Allied planes Helmsdorf had bagged flying those things. He'd flown in Adolf Galland's hand-picked Messerschmitt *Jadgeschwader*, where any pilot with fewer than a hundred kills was a malingerer. Gus flew combat every day for four years – three of these before he was twenty – except when he was in hospital; the last time he was shot down it took half a squadron of P-51s. That was over the Great Müggelsee just east of Berlin in May '45, and the Russians got him that time and threw him in prison camp. Ten years later and forty pounds lighter he was repatriated and shortly thereafter was sent by the new Luftwaffe to the States to check out in Starfighters. But he arranged a job with Buttress as chief test pilot and stayed on the West Coast. His given name was Sigismond but few knew it and of those who did, no one dared use it. When he was called anything, it was 'His Majesty' and always behind his back. For as long as anyone currently at Buttress could remember, Gus had always made the high-visibility flights, the cameo appearances. He'd flown left seat on the first flight of the 17-10 and he flew the range record from New York to Sydney nonstop with Jake riding shotgun and the chief pilots from eight airlines standing in the cockpit, crowding to see over their shoulders. And Gus, still the fighter jock after all these years, could strap an F-19 on to his lean old ass and pull a tolerable number of g's.

A few other staff people pushed themselves deep into chairs that lined the walls. The red light outside in the corridor flashed: CONFERENCE IN SESSION. DO NOT ENTER.

No one talked as they waited. And Helmsdorf was the first to observe Buzz Riddick as the inner door by the head of the table opened, paused ajar while the boss finished last-minute orders to someone unseen, then pushed open.

'Good morning, gentlemen.'

There was a murmur of reluctant greeting.

Riddick sat down, arranged some papers in two piles before him, then looked up to survey the faces around the table.

'OK, so the honeymoon's over. Some unfortunate things were said in Washington.' Everyone in the room knew the words were meant for Boice. 'There's been a lot of pressure. From here on there's going to be more and since I prefer dealing with reality, we might as well accept that and get on with it.' He slowly stirred the coffee that had been placed in front of him. 'As you know, there's a man named Anders in New York who won't fly the 17-10 any more. That's not for us to worry about. That's his ass.' He poked through the pile of kneeboard flight data cards stacked on the table. 'We're taking Prototype Two upstairs at thirteen hundred. Gus will fly it. Jake will ride shotgun and Ed will monitor on board. Vern, you'll be down in telemetry.' He nodded to Ed. 'OK, Eddie, it's your show.'

Boice took over. 'The NTSB wants a spectrographic analysis of their own to play with. We're going to make it for them and we're going to put some candy in the bowl they never expected to find.' The words were tough, the right tone for a coach.

Gus Helmsdorf remained aloof. He shifted slightly in his chair as Boice launched into the details. Miller sat back and stared at the table.

'We have ninety-six independent telemetry channels and laser-guided photo-theodolite trackers – and special recorders mounted at eleven different places in the aeroplane. We're going to bypass certain functions of the computer and see if we can duplicate the conditions of Air World Six.'

'That shouldn't take all day. The New York press closes three hours before we do,' said Riddick significantly.

'Then we're also going to run some tests using mismanaged flight procedures to see if the crew could induce the problem.'

'I don't think that's going to be productive,' said Miller.

A pencil dropped. Riddick rotated his coffee cup and pressed a wet ring on to the table. He looked at each person in the room before he said:

'What do you think *would* be?'

The words had the effect of turning on a loudspeaker in the room, its presence tremulous, hot in the air, waiting for the first blast.

'You know, there's a difference of opinion in this room . . .' Miller faltered.

'Want to narrow that down?' Riddick was almost affable.

'The test may lead to biased results,' said Vern Locker a little too loudly, sparing Miller.

'What bias?' challenged Ed Boice.

'There's the added question of *external* influences on the computer,' replied Locker coolly.

Boice smiled. 'If you're making an obtuse suggestion there's any other computer problem, forget it.'

Riddick fixed Locker with a stare, admonished him sternly. 'The only question we've got today is to check the pitch-channel programmes and tweak up their interaction with the hydraulic components. That's where the Air World Six problem lies.'

Locker sat back, chastened.

'We've been into anti-jamming techniques on the F-19 for months,' added Ed Boice solicitously, trying to recover the mood. 'We've got that system under control –'

'Yeah, but no way should we continue to use the same hydraulic servo valves,' said Locker, still defiant.

'If it needs to be addressed, we'll get to the bottom of it,' said Riddick.

Suddenly Dick Miller stood up, grabbing the table edge with clenched fingers and glaring at a disbelieving Riddick, transported on a giddy exultation as he shouted, 'The fact is, we're in a lot of trouble, aren't we?'

Boice was about to answer but Riddick stopped him. Miller was shaking.

'What kind of trouble is that, Dick?' Riddick said dangerously. Helmsdorf locked his fingers together and studied his hands. Miller stood looking at the fluorescent lights reflected in the table. He could start out and thread the trouble all the way back to the first days when they had discussed design alternatives. Somewhere they had made a wrong turn and no one had said anything. But it was too late to go back. They'd have to find a way forward. He brought his eyes up to face Riddick's and he struggled not to look away.

'Go ahead, Dick. You're among family. What kind of trouble are we in?'

Dick's voice trembled. 'It's not the plane we started out to build.'

Riddick thought it over. 'No plane ever is, is it? They gain weight, change their appearance, fulfil some promises, break others. Or do you have something more specific you want to say?'

This is how careers end, Dick thought. No big deal. No escorts to the car waiting at the sidewalk, but in a split second, the end of the line, the last Friday paycheque just ahead, the pension still beyond reach. His voice was barely audible. His eyes were bloodshot.

'You're going to hang that crew no matter what, aren't you?'

Riddick looked at him until Dick had to turn away. 'You better sit down. We're not spending a hundred G's plus this morning to hang anyone.'

Boice finally felt he had the green light. He was livid. 'The crap I had to chew on in Washington belongs on your plate, too. That aeroplane doesn't just belong to me! Look at the title on your door and tell me you had nothing to do with it!'

Riddick grimaced as though puzzled. 'Maybe I misunderstand,' he said. 'The credit belongs to everyone in this shop. And I think it best if we continue to think of that credit in the positive sense.'

Miller tried to speak but the words died, now deferential to the cold-faced Riddick. He sat down and felt the sweat that had gathered under his arms and spread across his middle. The room was a marsh, he loathed being mired here, his strength evaporating like spume.

Riddick motioned the onlookers closer. They were colleagues, after all. The mood was skittish but Riddick took a deep breath, painted a smile on his face like the moon emerging from behind a cloud.

'Boys, we're here to make fly-by-wire go. Period.' He sat hunched over, his hands clasped in front of him, and waited for the words to sink in. He then calmly stacked his papers into a neat pile, looked around with a brief nod and disappeared into his inner office, leaving an aftermath of quiet disarray. Miller's ears were red and the others averted their eyes, making a pretence of gathering their papers, Locker especially glum and awkward as he fumbled with the coffee maker. 'Coffee?' he said, all the while addressing the square-cornered metal coffee jug, the type used in airliner galleries, which was always plugged in by a side table in Riddick's conference room. Most of the people who had sat through the outburst were too shaken

209

for coffee and it was with relief they escaped, suddenly in a hurry to finish preparations for the test flight, now set for takeoff in less than two hours.

The 17-10 waddled across the concrete, squat wheels revolving slowly. Some birds flapped wildly away and a small jackrabbit skittered across the taxiway into the grass, not pausing to look back. The nosewheel went several metres past the runway centre line, then careened on its corners as the plane swung round to line up. Ed Boice was standing in a half crouch behind Helmsdorf in the left seat, and marvelled that when the plane stopped, Helmsdorf had it pointed down the white dashes, not six inches off centre. Takeoff clearance came through the overhead speakers and Helmsdorf didn't delay. The four throttles went smoothly forward and the 17-10 started to move ahead in earnest. Boice had to grab the rim of the captain's chair with both hands to keep from being thrown over backwards. The dashes outside rushed at them, the momentum built. Somewhere far away the engines whined.

'Rotate.'

Helmsdorf gave the yoke a firm tug, the nosewheel unstuck, then he reduced the pull until the orange pipper on the grapefruit-sized attitude indicator before him was precisely on eleven and one half degrees nose up. The only signal that their mass had left the earth was the click of the cockpit landing gear lever unlatching as, fifty metres away, the tree-like struts, free of weight, extended.

'Gear up.' Helmsdorf let the nose come up until it was pointing exactly nineteen degrees above the horizon. The jet seemed to shed its bulk, leave lethargy behind and acquire slim grace. Like a rapier it stroked the sky. Boice always loved this moment, watching the ground fall swiftly away. The two pilots, sitting in ridiculous reclined positions facing steeply upwards with unchanging, serious expressions, didn't notice.

They soon gained their height, established contact with the various ground stations, did some slow, lazy turns to enable squinting men below time to calibrate the trackers, white telescopes moving automatically in their mounts as they kept the 17-10 continually in the cross hairs. Voices were undertones, stripped of identity by the squelch of radio or interphone, giving chopped-off commands or acknowledgments. Quickly the various computer programs were verified, the pilots making scribbled notes on kneepads to supplement the telemetered data now being stored in mountains of computer printouts below. In the aeroplane's cabin, stripped of plushness and resembling a metal-ribbed basketball court, teams of engineers positioned like telephone operators monitored the recorders set to reproduce the spectrographic analysis of the aeroplane's every pulsebeat.

The tests proceeded quickly. The men jotted their notes, coordinated with the ground. All was as expected: a clean bill of health.

'We're ready for the crew procedures runs, Ed,' said Jake, glancing over from the co-pilot's seat as Helmsdorf banked steeply to head back uprange.

'Computer's all put back together, programs verified,' came the report from the flight-test engineering supervisor in the cabin.

Boice licked his lips, riffling through a black, three-ring binder at his station.

'Right.'

They climbed, just to start back down again, Helmsdorf intent on duplicating the descending path and increasing speed recorded on Air World Six when the flutter got bad. In the scrub-covered ridges miles below, cameras with long lenses were fixed on the 17-10, guided by sensors locked on to one of the light beacons on top, bottom, and wing tips, all invisible to the straining, upturned eyes of men in sunglasses.

'He's gonna be pushing it; watch those telemetry channels.'

'Compensating for any miscalibration in the Air World Six recorders.'

Edge-punched green computer paper erupted rhythmically from the machines, gathering in stacks. Huge tape reels spun on their consoles. The telemetry hummed.

'Here he comes.'

The 17-10 shuddered and groaned. But there was no flutter. Everything was letter-perfect. Helmsdorf's face was grim as he rolled the 17-10 into a sharp turn and hauled it in a wide arc across the test range. A couple of flight test engineers in back stuck their faces into the cockpit. 'Hey, what the hell are you trying to do?' Their faces were the colour of ashes.

'Get your asses back there and strap in,' commanded the chief test pilot.

Again Helmsdorf rocketed the 17-10 into a percussed dive, the Santa Ana mountains filling the windshield. Boice's eyes were wide, he was holding his breath, his face was in a leer. 'Watch the recorders,' he shouted into the interphone to the engineers in back. 'Call out any vibrations!' The jumbo screamed down.

'This will pop some rivets,' said Blasingame laconically from the co-pilot's seat.

Ed ignored the remark. He was intent over Helmsdorf's shoulders on the flight instruments. 'Try that rolling pullout once more!'

Helmsdorf twisted the yoke. His touch was as light as a surgeon's but the occupants felt their guts sag as if a dam had burst on top of them. Blasingame was calling off the g readings. The wing tips flexed like drawn bows.

'Now give me the lateral input,' said Ed excitedly

through his teeth, hanging on with all his strength. 'Watch for the flutter!' he called into the interphone.

Helmsdorf gave the yoke a sharp pulse sideways. Just his fingertips held the gunmetal handgrips, unpainted and covered with dials and pickoffs for the test. The 17-10 gave a strong lurch, throwing the engineers in back hard against the arms of their stations. But there was no flutter.

'No negative indications,' came the voice of the flight-test engineering supervisor from somewhere aft. He sounded shaken, even through the interphone. His team sat stoically before their monitors, but tense, conscious of every subtle note played in the howl of wind past the cavernous hollow tube in which they sat.

Ed Boice flipped the pages in his black notebook. 'The next test calls for the rolling pullout again, but I need more g and this time I need an elevator pulse during the turn.' He was virtually licking his chops.

'It's no dice, Ed,' said Helmsdorf over his shoulder. 'I'll do one or the other, but I won't put this ship through that. She's not built to take it.'

'We're so close now, do it!' bellowed Ed. His voice was belligerent.

'*Negative.*' Helmsdorf spat the word sideways through curled lips.

'Then dive it! We have to prove that Air World SOB exceeded the design envelope!'

'I'll go to V_{NE} – that's it!'

'You have to go past V_{NE}! We have to find out what that chatter was!' Ed's voice was desperate. He felt suddenly lightheaded, there was a moment of elation as just before a head-on collision – the conviction that man can outwit fate, come out whole on the other side.

'This isn't an F-19!' Ed could hear Helmsdorf's German accent become thicker. 'I won't do it.'

'You have to do it! You have to go past V_{NE}!' Ed Boice was a man transported. His jugulars stood out like cords.

'Now you hold on and listen to me,' admonished Jake sternly. 'The Air World crew never went that far. Their flight recorder proves they didn't get anywhere near V_{NE}!'

For a moment Boice was speechless with rage. He ran his hand across his mouth. Then, with great control, he said, 'You have to repeat the last test. I want you to do it again.'

The giant jet scythed in a graceful curve, a silver shark fin slicing a perfect crescent on the delicate, scar-free sky.

'You'll get one more run like the last one,' said Helmsdorf softly, 'but that's all we're going to do.'

'Well, then, give me a pitch pulse instead of an aileron pulse.' Ed sat back and readjusted the black notebook on his lap.

Helmsdorf picked up the PA mike from the pedestal, identical to the Air World version. His flat voice boomed through the vacant cabin, 'All right, one more time, here we go.' Then he radioed the ground tracking stations. 'Telemetry one, stand by for one more run.'

A ripple of fear raced through the six silent men strapped to their seats in the cabin, looking at their oscilloscopes. To the flight-test engineering supervisor in the rearmost seat it seemed like being trapped inside a subway tunnel and, as the aeroplane banked to begin its dive he thought of falling, somebody's pushed you off the platform on to the tracks and your leg's broken and you can't crawl out and you hear the train coming. Booming closer. And all he could do was concentrate on his video tube. To his assistant alongside it seemed like being a gunner again in the war when the bullets start coming at you and to him the video tube was like the breech, you've got to concentrate on the bullets you're pumping back, think of nothing else, then he too felt the heaving as if the very earth had opened only it was the awesome jet lurching – watch that screen – but before he saw anything he heard it first, the guy at the wheel's gone berserk, he thought wildly, then the others heard it too, the screech of tortured metal as the subway wheels grabbed for track and missed, an express train sailing gracefully off the tracks, hurtling into space . . .

Then the supervisor saw the hydraulic pressure fluctuating on his monitor and felt his throat go hot.

'Pressure's fluctuating on A system!' he tried to say but his voice wouldn't work. It caught and stopped and that frightened him. He tried to swallow and he cleared his throat and finally he bellowed the message through. 'Pressure fluctuation on A system!'

He looked again.

'We're losing hydraulic quantity! Abort the test! Abort the test!'

'*Don't abort it, goddammit!*' screamed Ed Boice in the cockpit. 'I need that pitch pulse!'

'We're losing fluid! We have a hydraulic leak!' The desperate intercom overrode everything else.

'It's the A servo valve!' interrupted another voice from the rear. 'She's let go! We've lost the A servo!'

'We gotta find that flutter!' beseeched Ed through crushed teeth. 'Keep going till you find that *flutter!*'

'. . . *a leak!*' echoed the voice of the supervisor.

Sunlight spilled in luminous Niagaras, dripping in scintillas from the scimitar-like wings of the 17-10. It was docile again, landing gear extended and reaching for the earth like the open claws of an eagle, all its metal feathers stretched and gripping the air until it relaxed with a sigh. Helmsdorf cancelled reverse thrust, eased up to the hangar, cut the engines. The final whine died away, lost over the rim of the desert. Ed Boice sat recessed in the shadow of his station, chewing a cigar slowly. It was unlit. The black notebook lay closed where it had fallen on the cockpit floor beside him.

* * * *

215

Ed Boice walked back to his office. The building was strangely quiet. He had the feeling of starting from scratch, as though this were the first day of the project when he had given the green light to Personnel to open the gates and begin hiring, and notifications had gone out to subcontractors telling them they had been selected to compete for the 17-10's sub-assemblies, and the bays were still empty and the paper work was spread all over the plant. He now carried the hobbling sense that there was something wrong with the 17-10 and that it wasn't the crew. He didn't want to think further than that for the moment. He eased back into his chair; he had to concentrate now on holding on to his strength, to persevere. What lay ahead would not be pleasant. Presently he dialled Greenvale, the man who made Buttress's servo valves. A woman answered.

'I want to speak to Greenvale.'

'Who's this?'

'Boice, Eddie Boice from Buttress.' There was a click, some muffled mumbling, then a bright 'Eddie?'

'Did you read the papers?' Boice asked.

'What?'

Ed closed his eyes. 'Don't horseshit me. We've got trouble, big trouble.' Boice waited but there was no response. 'You've been paid for servo valves and we don't have them. You hear that? The ones you sold us leak like two-cunted cows pissing on a flat rock!' Again there was no answer. 'I'm going to be at your shop at seven in the morning. We got to start all over!'

'I have appointments – '

'Cancel them!' Boice cradled the phone and stared at the wall.

More than a day had gone by since Ben Reese had spotted Jasovak on Madison Avenue in the Eighties. But the helium man had not gone back to the Aldwych, his roost in New York according to Melissa. Somehow Ben lost him. Now Ben was elbows-on in a booth of the deli opposite the hotel eating yet another Nova Scotia salmon sandwich. It was raining and he hadn't been home except for a few hours in the middle of the night. He knew Jasovak was somewhere nearby, and he fully expected to see him; when suddenly Jasovak did appear through the smoky plate glass standing catty-corner across Madison Avenue, Ben almost choked on the onion. He went for the door as Jasovak was crossing, leaping to dodge the shower thrown by a bus that wouldn't slow down. Jasovak disappeared into the back seat of a taxi.

Gone again! Reese wondered if he could stomach another salmon and onion when the roof light of an unoccupied cab appeared. An elderly woman saw it simultaneously but Ben was quicker.

'Dollface, this is an emergency.' Ben pushed in. The driver was an old-timer with a cloth cap. 'Head downtown on fifth,' Ben barked through the screen. Jasovak's cab turned across town and was blinking left at the corner of Fifth. His own cab had fallen in directly behind.

'How far down?' fussed the cabby with the tone of long suffering.

'I'll let you know when I find the address.' The light changed. Jasovak's driver was more aggressive. 'Just get the lead out.'

The asphalt gleamed with pale broken light, the wipers slapped, spreading grease across the windshield. Traffic was heavy, nobody was moving fast, it was easy to sit back and watch the other cab prowl down the avenue. Finally it stopped as they reached Fifty-third Street.

'Here!' shouted Ben.

'What?'

'This is good enough.' Ben shoved six dollars through the hole.

Already Jasovak was across the street, scurrying from the rain. He paused to grab a newspaper, then darted into the subway. Ben quickly ducked into the entrance on his side of the street, taking the steps two at a time. It was a descent into an airless cavern that smelled of pickles and urine, dim in the pale glow of bare sixty-watt bulbs. Ben fished for a token, his eyes adjusting to the subterranean murk, and pushed through the clammy turnstile. He spotted Jasovak wedged into a phone booth.

The platform trembled with the violence of a train lurching past. Ben pushed his face close to the broken mirror of a vandalized gum machine, watching Jasovak's reflection. The echoes of the passing train dissolved with the whine of a ricochet, but the tremor began again as another train approached. Jasovak's back was to Ben, he appeared to be writing something next to the phone. Ben wiped the mirror with the edge of his fist to study the scene more carefully. Jasovak had scribbled something near the edge of the box and now left the booth as the train pulled in and slowed to a grinding stop.

Ben reached the booth in a dozen bounds and plugged a coin into the slot. His eyes had never left the mark Jasovak made. Seven digits – a phone number. Quickly he dialled. People streamed from the halted train. The other end was ringing. Already the embarking crowds were swirling, pushing their way into cars. A click as the phone at the other end was lifted.

'Bronx Zoo . . .'

Ben wheeled, then slumped against the side of the booth as the train slouched ahead. He smiled ruefully at his last helpless glimpse of Jasovak, back turned, newspaper open.

Ed Boice sped for an hour amid the legions of impatient drivers that coursed in streams along the freeway, past the smoggy outskirts, out to Greenvale's plant, the kind of low, featureless building one can see all over the United States, off the six- and eight-lane highways. Two hundred feet square, one storey, a clever logo over the front entrance but weeds growing next to the truck bay in back and little jail bars on the windows. Out back abandoned crates and pallets and boxes rotting, like rusting tumbleweed.

Greenvale was in his office waiting for Ed Boice. Pacing next to his wooden desk, pacing the threadbare carpet where the seams showed and already smoking his third cigarette. The secretary brought something in, smiling in his direction but not meeting his eyes. She was old and fat like a grandmother; there were no young women in Greenvale's shop. Greenvale crushed out his cigarette, put his hands in his hip pockets and squinted through the window. He felt resigned and ready for the Buttress muscle coming down to kick his ass. He'd worn out the nervousness of this morning when his bowels ran and he had no taste for breakfast.

Ed Boice marched in, uncivil and curt, and slammed a glistening grey servo valve on Greenvale's desk. 'Here's one of your midget servo valves. Straight off Air World Six,' he badgered. 'So we're gonna review the quality control you ran. I don't have any time to waste, so let's get this on the test block.'

Greenvale picked up a folder from his desk and cast a baleful look at the back of Ed Boice's neck. He felt a shot of defiance surge through him. He'd always been meticulous, ever since he'd cut his first element for Buttress, no, even before that, ever since he'd started in his basement seventeen years ago. There he could control his overhead; he could work the hours he wanted. But his wife couldn't stand the racket his machines made, so he had moved his work into an empty garage down by the industrial park. There were a couple of minor payoffs and too many

219

underbids just to break in, and now he had two hundred and thirty employees and no hair. Greenvale had always been a faithful Buttress supplier; he took pride in the things he made for them, even did some prototypical work for them when they were first setting up the 17-10. But he could barely cover his overheads. At 5 P.M. he always said to his matronly secretary – or to himself if she'd gone – 'Boy, it's tough to earn a living . . . isn't it?'

The slim servo valve was installed in the maze of the test rig. The engineer at the console ran the pressure up to four thousand five thousand psi, one and a half times the normal.

'This programme is nothing but harassment,' said Greenvale severely. 'You only pay x, but you want double-x quality. Well, I'm working on a two per cent margin – '

'I don't wanna hear about your two per cent margin. How you do it isn't my problem. All I know is you have a contract with Buttress Aerospace!'

So now Buttress might pull the plug on him. He lit another cigarette as if by reflex. There must be fifteen thousand subcontractors all over the States, and several more overseas, all the myriad bits and pieces flowing from the four corners of the map like those coloured lights in jukeboxes, all spilling together into 17-10s. So many strands, metal threads on a giant loom. What's one thread more or less to them? But Greenvale knew what it was to have one of the aerospace giants cancel a contract. *Clang*, like a steel door slamming. He sucked a bellyful of smoke and glanced at the test rig. He had no room to manoeuvre, costs were clobbering him, he'd cut it too thin this time. Even if all they did was change the requirements by one millimetre, after all his inventory was in, all that expensive, specialized stuff, he'd get wiped out; he couldn't give that stuff away for a pack of cigarettes. One mistake by his workers on the line, one step screwed up in the production sequence: wipe-out. And even without a wipe-out all he had left over was enough for the payroll. Month after month. Greenvale had had two bleeding ulcers.

'I know your contract from memory. Do it for less! Produce it faster! Make it do more! I'm still trying to produce the goddamn things to do something, but you're asking too much of them.'

Boice didn't answer.

The servo began to quiver in its maze of pipes. The needle on the pressure gauge flicked nervously.

'I've been giving you whatever you asked for. But I can't work magic. They won't do all the things you need – it's impossible!' The engineer watching the servo from the console looked alarmed, as if he wanted to duck.

'Maybe they shouldn't be produced in this crummy shop! Maybe we shoulda sublet the whole thing to some-one on the East Coast!' Boice's voice shook.

Greenvale wasn't seeing the servo straining in its leashes. He was looking beseechingly around the thing he'd built up over seventeen years and wondering why the fuck he'd hung on. Why hadn't he stayed in the pizza business with his brother, back in Tallahassee? Life was simple next to that old blacktop highway with the diner a quarter mile away and the old ramshackle gas station. So why the hell did he hang it out here? The lure of the West Coast – the Gold Coast –

'Just keep watching,' Boice commanded.

'No one can produce more than they've been given.' Greenvale fought back, a note of desperation there. 'You want the moon but you can't get the budget. Get the lead out! Watch the price!' he grumbled.

Underneath there was a pang of recognition. Each man had the sensation of looking into a mirror.

'Push the parts out, get the planes out, eat the overtime – ' accused Greenvale.

'Don't make me bleed. You begged for the contract –
on your fucking knees!' Boice countered.

Greenvale defended his servo. But he had kids in
school, a son looking to keep him in Dartmouth. It was
more than that; if he'd cut a few per cent in the quality it
was so he could *live*. It had to do with being respectable,
with having someplace to go in the morning at nine. Even
more, to have the leverage of being able to say, 'I'm doing
business with Buttress.' It had to do with holding his head
up when he was mowing the grass and his neighbour
walked past, or when his wife looked at him across the
dinner table. Just a couple of per cent to keep the
mortgage going, to keep a few expenses under control.

His wife had seen the anguish on his face and asked, 'Is
there any way I can help, honey?' It was a rhetorical
question because she spent all her life making casseroles,
because what could she do, make a servo valve?

'What do you use to make the seals?' Boice was
shouting. 'The stuff breaks, it disintegrates – it turns to
gum – it turns to glue! That's not rubber, that's glue! It's
shit!'

'You forced me, you sonofabitch.' Greenvale loosed his
own anger. They were like two bull icebergs now in
collision, but both on the same course, impelled by the
same current, each diminishing equally, each aware of
extinction.

There was an ominous wisp of smoke rising from the
servo valve. The pressure fell off, but regained. The
needle on the gauge jerked.

'Did you ever think what it would look like from the
inside of a jail cell?' Boice was yelling now, his face taut.

'You're crazy!' Greenvale fought for breath.

'You have liability!' Boice screamed.

And then the first leak appeared. Boice suddenly
yanked the control away from the subcontractor's engineer and rode the test to high. Greenvale made a feint

towards the console, then turned his back in a crouch. All at once the servo exploded with a shock that made the foundations rumble. The noise and fury of a fire hose of blood assaulted them as the crimson hydraulic fluid spattered in gouts through the lab.

'Shut it off – shut it off!' Greenvale was grasping for the control panel.

'You son of a *bitch*,' screamed Ed Boice. 'You know what you've done to us! You sold us shit and kept the change! Look at that!' It was an orgasm of hate.

The two of them stood in the dying reverberations, facing each other, Boice out of breath.

'I'm gonna wipe this place up! We'll come in here with fucking bulldozers!' Boice was bellowing so hard tears were forming in his eyes. And filling the creases in his face. It was a threat, but it fell between them like a plea.

Greenvale stood, looking back at him, his face a knot of agony, seeing Ed's vision get blurry, feeling the hot salt sting in his own eyes.

'It's gotta be corrected, goddammit, or you're going down the drain.'

Inside the Buttress design offices the air conditioners were already working overtime. Dick Miller dreaded these days, which were coming more frequently. The joy had fled, somewhere far away over the hills, the hills of his youth that once stood in sharp relief. Now, even on the best days, only a faint thickening could be made out through the milky pollution. There'd been a time when shiny aeroplanes with rows of glistening rivets – the kind of aeroplanes kids collected pictures of – lofted into a tingling blue from the small factory airfield backdropped by the broad green brushstrokes of the hills, daubed with yellow fields. Everybody grinned, shook hands, spoke in first names, felt proud. You remained outdoors, looked up, caught a sun flash from the plane's silver wing far overhead. Standing there, neck craned, you realized if you dropped the Rosetta stone with your future inscribed into that blue vault, it would fall upwards forever. The test pilot wore a leather jacket in those days; he might even have had goggles. He'd say the rudder was a little stiff or the wobble pump didn't transfer the fuel and two or three of us could roll up our sleeves and tackle a problem like that. We caressed those aeroplanes. Even Ed Boice was mellow and enthusiastic in those days.

But now enormous concrete runways shimmer in grotesque heat mirages behind miles of chain-link fence. Miller felt a sudden compusion to flee. Ed Boice was coming towards him wearing the same narrow bow tie he always wore, and his Air Force P.X. low-quarters ($29.80 for both feet). His belly was hanging out, his keys jangled from his belt, and his pens stood in a menacing row in their plastic holder in his shirt pocket. Outside, in the distance, another 17-10 took off.

'It's time to roll up our sleeves and get some work done around here. We've got a couple minor problems I want cleaned up before the loan-guarantee hearings kick off in the Senate.'

Miller's face was expressionless. Boice pushed some of Miller's papers aside, brusquely bit off the end of a fat cigar. He spat it out but didn't meet Miller's eyes. 'Washington's asked for some material. The control system may get the beady eye. We just gotta make sure it's clean. The only thing I'm concerned about is the elevator-control actuator. Perhaps it could stand some beefing up.'

'You think the rest of the system can stand up to scrutiny?' Miller's indignation rose up in his throat.

Boice peered at him like a marksman. 'Those people don't know a servo valve from a tit wart! They couldn't tell if they're looking at a blueprint upside down. But

224

they can read these!' He slapped the folder he carried in the centre of Miller's desk. 'FAA reports of hydraulic leaks. We have to unload the servo valves with a tougher actuator. That's where the leaks are cropping up. We're going to get upgraded servos; I've already seen to that myself.'

'That's good, but we both know a heavier actuator isn't going to do it, don't we?' Miller's challenge hung tensely in the tepid air. 'There wouldn't *be* any leaks if there were no vibration first.'

'Not necessarily – '

'It's *vibration* that's shaking those servos to pieces. If there's any feed-back distortion – or any other stray signals from the computer – no servo on earth can react fast enough. They'll go out of phase, the whole tail end will go ape.'

'You better check the calendar, mister. We're eight years down the track! The computer, the fly-by-wire, the electronics are all fucking immaculate!' Boice spat the words out with a cloud of foul cigar smoke. 'I'm talking about adding beef to a couple of hydraulic components. That's all! No more!'

Outside the heat blazed across the acres of white concrete. Another Buttress 17-10 minus engines and airline paint was tugged from the final assembly hangar, emerging as though from a cave to take its place in the row of 17-10s awaiting delivery across the ramp. They sat poised, a pack of shimmering metal beasts, the heat rising from their distended bodies like some ethereal sweat. I can't feel as if I fashioned any of this, thought Miller. Instead of a row of aeroplanes he saw a row of Ed Boice's computers like livid black hearts beating. He turned to face Ed Boice. His words came quietly. 'We both know what has to be done – '

'If you're going to start that shit again – '

'I want you to listen for a minute. All three hydraulic

systems depend on one support. I don't care how many separate systems you have for backup, if they all come together at one mounting like they do on the 17-10, you've destroyed your fail-safe. Those lines are routed through the floor here and they almost touch each other. If there is any stray vibration at that mounting, all three lines let go. Where's your precious redundancy then? The fuel lines for both aft engines pass right alongside, for Christ's sake!' Miller felt a shot of strength. He felt giddy. 'You crack a fuel shroud drain or, worse, a fuel line – '

'We're in a time vice. We're about to get our ass kicked. This is all we've done, you and me, for the last eight years. It's opening night, and politely as I know how to say it, I'm asking for a small change.'

'What you're saying is that you want me to Band-Aid the control system with a new actuator.' The words were almost inaudible.

'I didn't say "Band-Aid" it.'

'What the hell do you mean then?'

'It's no goddamn Band-Aid!'

There was a hard pause. Then Miller said simply, 'It *wasn't* the crew of Air World Six, was it?'

Boice snapped the light on over Miller's drafting table and smoothed the blueprint there. 'Let me lay it out for you. I didn't come in today to argue. You've been listened to as much as anyone around here.'

'. . . I wasn't emphatic enough . . . was I?'

'That bulkhead mounting is built like a stone shithouse already,' Ed said in a more placating tone. 'Besides, it won't be a problem, with a heavier actuator to take the shocks.'

Miller remained calm. He was still peering out of the window but now he was seeing nothing. 'You're asking too much,' was all he could say.

Boice's impatience flared. 'If you can't do it we have plenty of people who can.'

Miller ignored the threat. He just stared outside, his face jagged.

'Dick, we both know if won't be done nearly as well if you're not in the picture.'

It was an offering.

Ed Boice took a long drag on his cigar, flicked the ash into a paper cup half full of cold coffee on the table. 'It all boils down to something very simple,' he said, resuming smoothing the blueprint. 'The only reports the FAA has on the 17-10 are of leaks in the elevator-control actuator. We can beef that up. Right now it's a moving actuator, travels back and forth along a rigid piston, we had to use flexible hydraulic hose because it does move, right? You're going to redesign a *fixed* actuator, let the piston move instead, use rigid stainless-steel plumbing. You should have just enough room to fit that in.'

He waited.

'You have to agree,' Boice admonished, 'stainless-steel pipes are safer than flex hose. Look, we can get fix kits out to the airlines fast. Get new actuators installed in the ships down on the assembly line before they roll out.'

Miller was no longer listening. A festering had intruded and he longed to leave Buttress . . . but he didn't know how.

Matt Aspinwall hunched forward over his desk. From underneath his scowl the grey eyes darted across one of the Plexiglas charts that covered the huge wall opposite his desk. Vertical crimson columns lined the chart, each resembling a thermometer that measured the progress of every individual Air World 17-10. A horizontal blue line which sliced across the vertical bar represented the start of assembly; orange, the mating of wing and fuselage, capped by engine-on-dock, first flight and delivery, all spaced with ever-decreasing intervals in each aeroplane's progress towards service implementation. Across the entire board with unalterable inevitability stretched a horizontal green tape near the top marking the beginning of Air World's coming Big Season. So far only four 17-10s were operational. But Matt needed eighteen and the distance to the broad green stripe for the others wasn't closing fast enough.

Matt felt the shortness of breath which had become increasingly familiar during the last few weeks of preparation and trial. He faced his broad telephone console, punched the well-known sequence and soon heard in the squawk box the clear ring of Hollis Wright's private line. The secretary told him in a polite but infuriatingly offhand manner to 'wait a moment, please.' Matt sat motionless except for his eyes, which continued to rove the Plexiglas.

Hollis took the call on his red scramble phone. He heard Matt's voice, a civil crust over a wellspring of barely restrained fury. Hollis sat back unruffled, cast an impatient look at his desk clock, then smiled to answer Matt as a father might deal with a recalcitrant schoolboy.

'Good grief, Matt. Don't you think I can imagine sitting on your side of the desk, for Christ's sake?'

'You've started to crowd me, Hollis. I'm looking at the calendar and it doesn't make sense any more. I've got to see fresh planes coming out of the west. I've got to start seeing them in twos and threes.'

'Matt, for God's sake, we've got the place running wide open. We've started replacing the light bulbs around here faster'n the coffee – '

'I'm not interested.'

'We're fine-tuning the ship, Matty, cleaning the windows, giving you refinements that weren't even called for.'

'I don't want your refinements, goddammit. I want the planes I paid for. I've got crews standing by and bookings piling up. The Big Season is all over the tube. It's on every billboard I could buy!' Matt's words cut through in a welt of wrath. Then with an edge, he added, 'I hear the prototype European fly-by-wire Skybus is almost ready to roll out.'

There was no comeback. Matt decided not to speak but to wait. Hollis's retort was flat. 'Let me tell you about the line outside our main gate,' he said. 'It's been there for months. TWA, Singapore, United, KLM – all trying to figure how they can beat you out of the first exclusive.'

'That's crap. I still have a few inches to move around in. I'm looking at a cheque here on my desk for signature, it's in eight figures – the quarterly payment. Twenty-seven million dollars, due to leave by courier tonight. I expect to see three 17-10s touch down at JFK twelve hours from right now.' Aspinwall pressed the sweep hand lever on his stopwatch. Then he added with menace, 'Or we'll pull out the rug. We'll stop payment. You see, Hollis, there's a fuse burning. And I think it's only fair we each hold half the stick.'

There was a pause at the other end. Then Hollis said soothingly, 'There's no need for anyone to provoke a heart attack, Matty. If you'll look out of your windows you'll see another delivery land any minute.'

Matt heard the disconnect and stared down at the unsigned cheque. He swivelled for a view of the runway. A 747 with a strange foreign paint job rotated on runway 31L, tucked its forest of wheels into the wells, and arched ponderously for altitude over Jamaica Bay. Matt pressed the key which connected him directly to dispatch. 'I hear we're due some aeroplanes.'

'Just one, Mr Aspinwall. Delivery flight one-eight-alfa-whiskey due on the blocks at twenty-three past the hour.'

Matt snapped the switch. One lousy delivery; he would hold on to the cheque. Let Hollis sweat . . .

Then he saw it. Unmistakable with its crimped tail and bulbous fuselage. It made a beautiful approach to runway

4R, steady and firm until the simultaneous white puffs from the main gear trucks as they contacted asphalt spoke silently of its return to earth. Matt watched it taxi in towards the Air World ramp, an empty ship needing final refurbishment before he could launch it with passengers. It rounded one of the bends in the inner taxiway, moving deliberately towards the outermost parking place, which was the one underneath Matt's office at the Air World terminal complex. As it turned the corner on to the Air World tarmac Matt got a full view of the resplendent new Air World paint job, but his feelings remained flat.

At that moment Vic Moudon knocked and entered, slightly out of breath and agitated. Before Matt could speak, Moudon held up a video cassette saying, 'Got you a preview of tonight's news, something I think you ought to see.' Moudon headed straight for the main console of Matt's closed-circuit video system.

Matt cast a glance over his shoulder at the 17-10, its nosewheel now within a few feet of where it would stop on the smudged yellow block almost directly below his vantage. A man in freshly laundered overalls stood near the yellow mark making brisk come-ahead motions with a pair of orange paddles to the pilot. A second mechanic kept pace beneath the left wing tip making sure the way remained clear. Crews in neighbouring bays might get away with sloppiness, but here they were as sharp as drill sergeants. Here they were fresh even if they were dead. For when they worked directly under Matt's window, they tucked in their haemorrhoids.

Matt was suddenly startled by a trumpet blare. Wheeling around, he saw Moudon fiddling with the Betamax at the wall console; the drapes hummed, and there, looking huge and close on the video screen, was the nose of the first European fly-by-wire Skybus glistening under ten thousand factory lights. Triumphant tones swelled from two dozen shiny band instruments bobbing in unison

230

underneath a raised temporary dais built of two-by-fours and hung gaily with crepe-paper bunting in the national colours of the four consortium nations. The plane turned slowly before the lens, distorting as it grew close until it revealed its diminutive tail, a configuration much the same as that of the 17-10. A British narrator was breast-beating in monotones. Moudon's nasal voice was louder.

'It's the rehearsal for the roll-out ceremony of the prototype fly-by-wire Skybus. Right here what we're looking at happened twelve hours ago,' he emphasized. The newscaster's voice rose above a burst of applause and described the quadripartite handshake among the beaming aviation ministers, who could be seen on the dais holding their clasped hands aloft like four gloating prizefighters.

Matt watched it for a moment longer, then pressed a switch on the remote control on his desk and shut the picture off. He felt his mood pull clear of the deep grey that had enveloped him. So it would be one 17-10 at a time, would it?

'I want you to make copies of that tape and send one each to Pan Am, TWA, American, United, Delta and Eastern – just to broaden their thinking – and send one to Hollis Wright with my compliments. When's their roll-out?'

Moudon faced him with a serious expression. 'In four weeks.'

Matt fingered the stems of his reading glasses and turned them to reflect the light from the ceiling. 'I want you to send a telegram to Great Britain and congratulate the Prime Minister and send a copy of *that* to Hollis.'

8

The atmosphere was carnival-like. Men jostled, wet clumps of hair falling over their ears and collars in the electronic heat of the press room. Chaplin, the Buttress director of public affairs, strode to the podium with its plastic hotel logo in place. Above the dull brown of false wood his ruddy face appeared too vital, his curls brittle, an aluminium plumage flickering in the light. Those closest to him might also have noticed the hesitation in the cast of his eyes. Just a flicker.

Chaplin suddenly produced the Vaseline smile. 'Good morning, ladies and gentlemen.' The Buttress press conference, called to respond to the accusations levelled by Anders in New York, was under way. 'I have a couple of announcements before I take your questions. Contrary to some reports, it is anticipated that the 17-10A will continue to be delivered to Air World at the rate of three new aircraft per month, with further anticipated acceleration to six per month in the near future.' He knew the sentence had a built-in escape; all his sentences had built-in escapes. No one could be held to account for anticipating. 'Despite some other reports with respect to the supposed sudden fast leap to completion of the European fly-by-wire Skybus, Buttress still maintains a very substantial flyable hardware and sales lead which, according to present calculations . . .' Present calculations might have to be set aside for future calculations. His patter faltered but picked up and carried on while his mind raced.

Lately his work had become a struggle for him. He had begun to regret the years he'd been away from journalism, ostensibly to inform other journalists, but in cold fact to fight them. He remembered when he left them and

232

crossed over. It had happened at that lunch so long ago in the old Buttress boardroom in the centre building; the genteel conversation over fillet and wine, then being measured with drowsy eyes in the silence of the after-dinner cordial, and finally, having passed, being escorted – or was it delivered? – to his own glass-enclosed corner of the inner sanctum.

He'd finished his preamble though he wasn't exactly sure where he'd stopped. Three or four reporters were crowding each other to get his attention. Their questions came at him in harsh waves.

'Is the 17-10 going to be grounded?'

'Have you determined what was wrong with Air World Six?'

'What's to prevent another Air World Six from happening under the same conditions?'

Chaplin eyed the regiment of questioners coolly and fitted his answer neatly through the barrage, letting his words dance across the no-man's-land between them like charmed Mercuries.

'As a direct result of Air World Six, selected parts of the pilot's operating manual are undergoing a more fully integrated feasibility review to forestall the likelihood of indeterminacy on the part of the operating crews with respect to a complete understanding of all backup modes of the fly-by-wire controls.' Chaplin smiled indulgently and sipped from the glass of water on the lectern. Other questions were coming but he hadn't finished. His voice was soothing. It burbled and purred as though it could, by its quality, round the rough edges of the issues thrust at him. 'Air World Six would not have happened the way it did if it had been fully understood by the crew and handled properly from the outset and not allowed to go so far . . . and we at Buttress, in our desire to continue to merit and even strengthen the trust we've earned over forty-five years in the air transport business, are instituting preventive adjustment in all information-retrieval aspects available to the crew, who, after all, bear the final responsibility in flight . . . We make no bones about it: fly-by-wire isn't simple but it can be trouble-free. And let me emphasize, this function will be computerized in the 17-10B. We've designed a new central warning system, which we call CWS, and computer-stored checklists with video-tube readouts. The press of a button by the pilot will call up a TV picture of the entire procedure, vastly simplified; we've taken into account ergonomics, pilot work load and stress parameters, and automated much of the backup so that this kind of procedure will never go off the track again – '

A young woman under a frizzy ball of red hair not unlike an Afro was standing. Her eyes were savvy and wore no makeup. They arrested Chaplin; he tried to recall where he'd last encountered her.

'Sir, your man in New York City during the Air World Six hearing said something about a problem that had existed on the F-19 that had been *solved* on that aeroplane and the implication was that it also existed on the 17-10. What problem was he referring to?'

Chaplin resumed his studied smile. He had not expected the question but he was ready for it. 'Well, as you know, the fighter and the 17-10 are both active-control aeroplanes. With that in mind, there was thorough evaluation of feedback strategies, how much force the pilot feels up in the yoke. Our flight-control computer is advantageous in that it allows minor adjustments to provide the sort of feel he would expect across the entire flight envelope consistent with the size of the aircraft.' His voice then held a deep *ahhh* – like a musical fermata – a breathless pause promising a payoff before he resumed the mannered tempo: 'The 17-10 does have a common bond with the F-19. Military fly-by-wire came first so, yes, there's bound to be a generational relationship.'

Gradually Chaplin became aware of another familiar face, one with deeply concerned features. In contrast, his own face was benign, its inquisitiveness lost. He no longer liked it. It had become flabby and so he wore heavy horn-rimmed glasses and had taken to looking severe to feign a position. He turned to a man half out of his chair trying to keep his papers from falling off his lap, but the frizzy-headed woman wouldn't let go. Her voice belted up at him stridently.

'Is Buttress presently involved in a design change on the 17-10 – and I'm referring to the hardware itself – as a consequence of recent events? I refer to the fiery landing of Air World Six and the statements since made by the co-pilot of that flight.' The woman remained standing.

'The safe landing of Flight Six has been taken into account along with hundreds of other perfectly safe flights, I assure you. As to statements made by the co-pilot, all crew experience adds to our knowledge – but our progressive enhancement programme predates the co-pilot's statements.' He looked around the room for a reaction to the words *progressive enhancement*. Detecting nothing out of the ordinary, he went on. 'One problem we have encountered, and this is mutual in terms of the F-19 fighter and the 17-10 transport, is that the automatic systems are so reliable that our human factors people have had to consider the problem of crew complacency, which is a kind of by-product of the American Sky God complex.'

He was smiling. Did the reporters hear the lines he spoke? Faces seemed transfixed. The words came in streams, interweaving, like shallops where brooks converge, doubling over each other.

'I want to dispel the notion that thinking stops with the delivery of one of our products. In this instance we have initiated a programme of post-delivery progressive enhancement which borders on the area of customer options.'

235

His eyes scanned the rows of faces again. The new definition had been fully introduced. The euphemism had now been mentioned a second time. He adjusted his glasses and recognized a German correspondent standing next to a cluster of cameras.

'Are these "progressive enhancements" or "customer options", as you call them, deemed mandatory by the FAA?'

'No, they are not.'

For a moment no one spoke. Then the man with the concerned face, a former colleague, stood. His voice was gentle yet deliberate as though having to fetch his thoughts to the fore with great effort. 'Chappy, can we simple folks out here construe the meaning of the words *progressive enhancement* to mean *fix* as in mend, repair, rectify, redo, rebuild, and if so does that imply something was wrong which needed mending, repairing, rectifying, redoing or rebuilding?'

Laughter swept through the room. Chaplin tried to laugh along but couldn't and kept his head down instead. He adjusted the microphone and leaned into it.

'We have undertaken an enhancement which can be construed as progressive – an extra progression if you will.'

'Did I hear you say *one* enhancement or several enhancements? What did I hear?' His friend cupped a hand to his ear.

Chaplin knew what was coming now. He was at a chessboard with one piece left and a queen, a rook and two bishops were closing in. But he wasn't cornered yet. They would have to come get him. He placed his hands calmly on both sides of the lectern.

'You heard me say *one* progressive enhancement but in the context of an overall product assessment. I haven't personally investigated this – it's in the hands of our very capable technical department, the Buttress flight-control

236

design staff – but I assume that one progressive enhancement may have several elements.'

His old colleague looked at the floor. 'If there are that many elements that need enhancing, does that imply something was wrong?'

'Absolutely not.'

'Might go wrong?'

'Negative.'

'Then why not leave well enough alone? I've known artists and writers and architects who improved their things till they made a mess out of them. If the 17-10 is that good, why do you have to do so much enhancing to it? Did anybody send in a letter and complain? The passengers didn't sign a petition, did they?'

'I don't know that I can be that frivolous.'

'I'd rather see some directness myself.' He looked hard into Chaplin's face. 'What is it that's gone wrong with the 17-10 that suddenly requires you to fix it?'

'*Wrong* is improper. The undertaking of a progressive enhancement, which is in the nature of an ongoing improvement, in no way implies that there was anything wrong.'

His one-time colleague picked up his coat, then with sorrowful eyes turned his back to the podium and on his way to the rear of the carpeted room announced to the crowd, 'I would characterize that as quibbling mixed with a good-sized dose of horseshit!'

An explosion of laughter and applause punctuated his remark. Chaplin was determined to reclaim control.

'The word *fix* carries an insinuation which can be damaging to a manufacturer – '

'Are you blackmailing me?'

Chaplin shrugged. 'Write whatever you wish. But I suggest you check with your publisher first. He may ask you to produce some evidence for what you have in mind . . . I think Ben Reese would advise the same.'

The laughter had died.

'If you don't believe me,' Chaplin challenged, 'take a hike out to Dulles. There's a 17-10 parked there. You're free to climb through it.' Chaplin cleared his throat, smiled out at the gathering and took a breath to go forward. He never really noticed the room slowly beginning to empty. 'We've felt it incumbent upon the organization to innovate beyond the contract to better satisfy the desires of our customer airlines . . .' His voice continued and he thought how, as a journalist, the pay had been inadequate, the deadlines were murder, the meals were often cold and uncertain. He remembered the harassment . . . Then, too, he remembered the involvement. Finally when he looked up, the assembled members of the press were nearly all gone. No one had come back to him with a question. So he stood there as the room cleared, the bile rising in his throat.

Melissa nestled closer, burying her head into the deep broad shoulder of the man lying on his back next to her, his chest heaving slightly. They remained like that for several minutes, recovering. Finally she spoke.

'That wasn't a bad payoff.'

Ben Reese grunted and let his fingers slowly move back and forth over the lowermost base of her back. She sighed, enjoying the stroking. She could tell he wasn't tired, nor would he soon sleep. But she felt too comfortable in this moment to let him go just yet and snuggled against him. His hand came up to rest on the loose hair by her cheek, to hold her to him. It was an act of calmness, like a pause; yet she sensed that some unseen mainspring inside him was being wound, a turn with every breath he took. His eyes were fixed on the ceiling.

'Before you go, there was a message waiting for you. To return a call.'

He looked at her, frowning.

'Here?'

Abruptly she pulled herself to a sitting position and reached for a pad on the bedside table. 'The maid took it.'

Ben sat up. He studied the scrawled message.

'Mr Ben Reese. Please call 382–5968.' That was it. No signature.

As he punched the numbers he became aware of the letters above them. He stared at the fifth digit, stopped and chuckled to himself. Melissa was perplexed.

'What's the matter – why don't you finish?'

Ben got out of bed. Taking the phone from the table, he held it up to look beneath it, then very gently placed it on the floor. He searched the room, grabbed a white antique chair next to the vanity table and brought it near the bed.

'What are you doing?'

'Take the sheets off the bed and tie them together at the ends.' She hesitated. 'Go on.'

Melissa wrapped her brocaded robe around her nakedness and pulled the rumpled sheets from the bed, letting the blanket fall to the floor. Her fingers fumbled as she twisted the sheets and knotted them together. Ben meanwhile slid the nearest of two Persian rugs close to the phone and tested the rear legs of the chair on it, pushing against the chair's back in short jabs. It didn't slip.

'Now give me a loose end,' he barked without looking around. In utter bewilderment, she placed the sheet into his open hand. Ben quickly knotted it around the top rung of the chair.

'Now get into the bathroom.' His fingers flicked. She did as she was told.

With one hand Ben grasped the sheet, holding the chair in a tipped-back position, and kneeling, adjusted the phone carefully underneath so that the '8' – the last digit of the unsigned message – was directly in line with one of the elevated front legs. Still holding the chair reared back,

Ben slowly moved away, placing one foot carefully behind the other, lengthening the stretch of the sheet between his body and the chair hand by hand. He reached the heavy chest of drawers against the far wall, shoved his shoulder into the opposite corner, crouching, burying his head close to the dark mahogany. Melissa was in the bathroom, peeking around the edge of the door, still quizzical.

'Get back in there.'

She quickly disappeared. Ben tried to recall the Hail Mary, couldn't; and then let go of the sheet.

There was a roar like a howitzer. The wall came apart as the explosion twisted the room into tissue paper. For the instant before his eyes failed the black wood of the chest had gone pure white. Only then was Ben aware of the crushing punch which had cracked his whole body hard against the bureau. His ears rang with a sirenlike echo that wouldn't let up, like a stuck alarm.

'Ben?'

He barely heard Melissa's call, which intruded along with the impression that his sight was slowly returning, but of that he couldn't be sure. The world was blotted by whiteness, an opaque cloud of plaster dust which filled the space and stung his eyes. As it cleared Ben perceived, as if through murky water, the gaping hole in the wall by the bed, shredded with the ragged ends of torn slats, raw where the plaster was missing. The phone and the chair were completely gone.

'That son of a *bitch*!' Ben grimaced.

Melissa emerged from the bathroom looking chastened and suddenly very young. Finally she ventured, 'You want Jasovak again, don't you?'

Ben was still staring at the enormous maw where the side of the bed had been. 'This time I'm going to break his balls!'

'In that case, call the Aldwych . . . and ask for Kovaks.' The warbling shriek of a siren bit the air, coming closer. 'What do I tell the cops?'

Ben pulled her panties from the vanity-table mirror where they had landed and slowly rubbed the fine silk texture of the crotch between his fingers. His old face crinkled like a prune. 'Tell them we had a blast.' He scooped up the armful of his clothes and bolted for the stairs.

Hitching his jeans and shoving down shirt-tails, he burst from the front door and made it unnoticed into the alleyway. Protected by the darkness he took a minute to button up, then cut through the back way across to the avenue and found a lone cab which took him to a limo agency in the upper Forties east of Lex. Today Ben would need his own wheels; he'd have no time for cabs. One long Cadillac had just rolled in after an all-night party and the driver, a gaunt old Italian in frayed tux, was flopped out on the stained office sofa under a city final edition of the *Daily News*. In the garage another man was tossing parabolas of cold water from a chopped-off hose over the car. Ben entered that way and stepped into the office. Soon he had the driver revived and seated in the limo headed uptown on Park.

Ben sank into the plush rear seat, letting his gaze drift lazily across the netting of blue-grey haze which lay curled around the base of the city, prepared to commit murder and be arrested for it. The gleaming limo coursed northwards, catching the green lights in even procession. No one was out except a rise-and-shine executive standing behind his dog with a paper bag.

At Seventy-ninth Ben leaned across and muttered to the driver. The limo stopped and Ben got out. He told the driver to follow but to remain a block behind. The phone booth on the street corner diagonally across from the Aldwych was damp and smelled of urine. Ben dialled the hotel and asked to be connected to Mr Kovaks. The line rang half a dozen times before a man answered in a tight voice that stumbled with sleep. Ben listened for a moment seeking more, then hung up without saying a word, satisfied his quarry was inside. He sighed and shoved a fresh cigar between his teeth. No doubt there would be a lot of waiting. The toughest part, Ben figured, putting the cigar back into his shirt, would be not being free to find a john.

It was after the fourth container of black coffee from the take-out deli that Ben finally caught sight of Anton Jasovak, leaving the Aldwych under heavy skies still grey in the early hour. Ben trashed the paper bag with the remaining two coffees and moved towards the limo. Jasovak carried a thin leather attaché case. He glanced at his watch, then at the sky which promised to brighten, and began to stroll north on the west side of the avenue, stopping to look at a sculpture displayed in the window of an art gallery. All at once he stepped off the curb and flagged a cab which veered in front of an oncoming bus to pick him up. Ben stepped into the limo and followed. They drove in convoy up the East River Drive, over the Triboro and into Queens.

The smell of La Guardia Airport had a sour bite to it.

Ben paid the driver. 'Go get some shut-eye.' He headed for the shuttle and caught up with the Washington line with just minutes to spare, but the agent was growly and the clashing decor matched his own mood. The Coke he'd grabbed on the run tasted like gunmetal.

Aboard the 727 Jasovak saw Ben take a middle seat three rows behind the forward bulkhead. The morning sun, not yet fully awake, was a brown yolk struggling through the banked flood of industrial pollution, high-lighting the maze of scratches in the tiny window. Ben heard the engines spooling up, their whines rising and overlapping out of phase. The aeroplane filled com-pletely, the last breathless stragglers forcing their way in with the kerosene exhaust fumes. Abruptly the 727 moved to the platform runway and screamed and lofted, streaking upward into high bubbly cumulus that rode the purple haze layer like a fleet of clipper ships under full sail. Ben looked away from them and the washed blue sky above. He faced dead ahead, his eyes shut, waiting. Jasovak had helped wreck his career, he thought, and now the time had come to pay him back.

Disembarking at Washington National fifty minutes later, Jasovak lost sight of Ben in the flurry of coats from the overhead rack. Both jolted through the crowded terminal, slowed by converging streams of passengers flowing in from other gangways. Outside, taxis were inching past in a continuous double queue. Ben caught sight of Jasovak's cab when he bundled into his own. He held three tens up for the driver, a young African, to see.

'Thirty bucks says you don't lose sight of that cab.'

'Point him out.'

'Green and white with the Virginia plate.'

Melissa had got away early for the Hamptons, leaving her apartment to police investigators and workmen. For the first time in her high-stakes career, she was deeply afraid. Waiting at the toll booth, she studied the broken polish on her fingernails. She was certain she had gone too far with her casual betrayal of Jasovak. Her silver Mercedes purred evenly, breaking out of the city, and was cruising eastbound on the brinelike surface of the Montauk Highway before noon. She'd arrive in time for brunch and a languorous afternoon in which to round out her St Tropez tan.

Finally Melissa breathed deeply, enjoying the aroma of the sea. She gunned the 450-SL, relishing the sensation of power and speed – she'd had the road virtually to herself for some time except for one car far behind, neither diminishing nor growing in size. Melissa was cruising at seventy; nevertheless, the distant car slowly began to fatten in her rear-view mirror; a brown sedan. It came to within a hundred feet of her, drifted to the outside lane. Melissa gripped the wheel with both hands, holding her course and slowing slightly to allow the vehicle to pass. But the expected blur didn't appear. She adjusted her side mirror.

The driver of the other car pulled twenty feet closer and lowered his window. Melissa turned her head for a glimpse just as the man pointed an object into the air above his car. Suddenly alarmed, she flattened the accelerator. At the same instant the other driver's finger found the recessed button and pressed. Melissa's windshield exploded.

Both her hands were still gripping the steering wheel as the headless Mercedes wheeled off the highway and bumped to a halt in a potato field.

The West German Embassy seemed to crouch behind its black iron fence with the forbidding aspect of a Thuringian wild boar, little eyes alert, bristles on edge. Stolid but ready to spring. Guy pushed through and entered the foyer, where he told the receptionist he needed to visit the press information office. A uniformed guard standing nearby watched him. The woman made a call and directed him to the self-service elevator, which took him to a stark scrubbed cell with walls so thick a thrown grenade would bounce back like a tennis ball. They met the floor in curves, affording no crevice in which to jam a bomb. From either side overhead the miniature Cyclops eyes of two TV cameras peered down at him.

The elevator clicked shut behind him and Guy faced two young men in white shirts and ties who looked like management trainees except that each wore a shoulder holster bulging with an all-too-apparent weapon. The thinner man sat behind his colleague as if to cover him.

Guy slid his passport and Air World ID card through the glass slot.

'Who do you want to see, sir?' asked the heavier one through the microphone, glancing from the photo up to Guy's face.

'It's something between myself and a woman in press information who works here.'

'Her name?'

'It's either Gisela or Ursula.'

'Is this of a personal nature?'

'That's right. Someone she knows well just died.'

Guy and the young man stared at each other. The second guard's face remained impassive.

'Wait.'

He kept Guy's credentials and reached for a phone. Guy turned back to the closed space, surrounded by bulletproof glass and reinforced concrete. He wondered if all apartment houses would someday be emblazoned with bulletproof guardhouses. He visualized long lines of people waiting to collect their keys only after interrogation and a positive ID check with central files.

'Mr Anders?'

Guy wheeled. The interior security doors opened on silent bearings to admit him. He knew he'd been searched with magnetic metal detectors hidden in the doorframe.

He was taken to a spacious room with barred windows where a double-chinned man sat behind an almost completely cleared desk. He made a brief gesture of straightening his blotter, then performed a symbolic rise to attention as though warding off an unspoken challenge from the stranger who lounged, feet apart, observing him.

'I am Rolf Messer. What may we do for you?'

Guy had expected the hauteur of the overlord but not the precious Oxford accent. He sensed now that he had been cast as the subordinate, and though the words were polite they were patronizing. When Herr Messer smiled, he smiled thinly.

'I have read about you in several languages,' he said, returning Guy's passport and ID card. 'You are notorious.' It was meant to be a joke but it was edged with sarcasm.

Guy caught the slight. 'Which, as my father who fought across Europe told me, is better than infamy.'

Messer didn't blink. 'Why are you here?'

Guy held his gaze, sensing a hole in the armour. 'Ben Reese is dead.'

Messer drew back as though hit by a gust of wind.

'Reese?'

'He left something for one of the women on your staff who helped him.'

'Natural causes?'

'Would you suspect anything else?'

Messer tried to match Guy's nonchalance but couldn't. 'I'm shocked to hear it.' He knew at once it sounded arch. He struggled to regain composure, but summoned instead an overbearing posture. 'You are aware we have the opinion that certain Buttress products are as bad as Reese wrote they were.' Surprised by the unsolicited salvo, Guy eased away from the wall.

'How bad *do* you think they are, Rolf?'

The sudden assumption of familiarity caused Messer to stiffen visibly. He'd been sternly raised in a place where people lived together under the same roof for years before dropping the formality of *Sie* and adopting the familiarity of *du*. He was also offended by the fact that Guy wore no necktie.

'There wouldn't be a single 17-10 on German soil if it weren't for your State Department,' he said tersely. His bearing remained aloof.

The statement penetrated and grew with the impact of an alarm in the centre of Guy's brain.

246

'Talk to me, Rolf.' He checked to see if they were alone. 'Come on, declarative sentences, one after the other.'

'I am not free to speak as a private citizen.'

'Of course you are. Now say it again. I heard you say the State Department, "my" State Department – '

'The woman you wanted to see,' Messer replied and started to move away.

Guy blocked him. 'The State Department.'

The two faced each other. The German spoke more confidentially.

'It has not been a free choice. The price of our defence is sometimes larger than the published amounts.'

'Can we work together?'

'No. Our methods are not yet American.' There was the possibility it was meant as a compliment but it came across as a rebuke. 'We cannot wage our fight in the press, and you, Mr Anders, are hot.' He paused. 'Now if you will follow me.'

Messer escorted Guy into a smaller office and somewhat awkwardly approached a stylishly dressed young woman behind a desk. She stood quickly. Her long hair swept forward from the back over one shoulder. The attaché spoke to her, Guy noticed, in the same patronizing tone he had first adopted with him.

'One of your acquaintances is the journalist Reese?' The innuendo was plain. She tried to appear bewildered but Messer did not soften his words.

'He's dead.'

The girl jumped as if she'd seen an animal spring from the curtain. Her face went ashen white. Guy felt sheepish and sorry for her.

'Do you mind if I speak with her alone?'

The attaché was plainly not pleased but acceded.

Guy took the girl to one side. She searched his face and was drawn by the sympathy in his eyes.

'Did Ben ever hurt you in any way?' he asked softly.

'My God.' She tried to remain poised but her hands shot up to her face. 'On the contrary.' Guy turned to see that the German was not in earshot, then took her hand.

'Shut out what you just heard. It's not true. You can scream later and no one's going to blame you for it but right now I need you.' He heard her breath catch. 'Benny wants you to have this.' He produced an open envelope and let the girl glimpse the wad of currency that bulged from within it. 'But,' he continued, 'he only wants you to have it if you give me the latest report on the F-19 – the update of what you gave him.'

Again the girl blanched. 'I can't give that to you.'

'Then a second report does exist!'

'Yes, but it isn't here!'

'Where is it?'

'Senator Osborne has it.'

Guy fought to reject the words. 'Osborne?' He glanced to see if Messer had heard.

'He has to keep Germany in check,' she whispered. 'The planes come from his state. You're a day too late. He was here yesterday and made a terrible row. We can't talk any more now.'

The attaché reappeared and approached with an air of impatience. 'Excuse me please, I have a meeting to attend.'

'Sure.'

Guy smiled wanly at the young woman who stood immobilized, her face crossed with distress.

The attaché escorted Guy briskly from the office into the corridor through the double security doors which slid back into their wall recesses with a well-oiled rush and into the bomb-proof armoured reception tomb.

'Mr Anders?' The voice came through the squawk box. It was the thin guard in the white shirt seated behind the bulletproof glass partition. He was holding the micro-phone.

248

'Telephone for you, sir. The caller says it's urgent.'

'Who is it?'

A bolt of utter astonishment unhinged the attaché's grim-set features when the answer came.

'It's a Mr Reese.'

Guy threw an apologetic shrug towards the confounded attaché as he took the phone proffered through the horizontal glass slot. There was an echo to Ben's voice, which was breathless and more insistent than Guy could remember.

'I'm at Dulles. I've got the bastard cornered!'

Guy pressed the phone closer to his ear, glancing towards Messer. 'Now which bastard is that?'

'The helium man! Jasovak!'

'Well, Ben, that's fine, but –'

'He's inside the Buttress hangar!'

Guy didn't answer.

'Guy?'

'Does he know you're there?'

'It's a setup. I'm the cat at the end of his string, but I don't give a shit!'

Guy felt a sting of scrutiny from the three Germans as if a nest of vipers had retracted but were all fixed on him.

'Uh, listen, Benny, keep your head on a swivel, huh?'

'I'm having trouble covering the exits.'

'I don't like it.'

'What?'

'I said I don't like it.'

'I've got a long lifeline. But I could use some help. We need proof he was here. And he's offering it to us!'

'I'm the wrong choice. I'm a self-serving witness. It'll be his word against yours.'

'Not if he leaves here in an ambulance! There'll be a record of that. Do you want me to set it to music? Are you listening?'

'Yeah.'

249

'I'm in the north perimeter road. I'd have asked the cops, kid, but I don't think they'd understand.' The disconnect was abrupt. Guy handed the phone back through the slot.

The attaché was standing next to the elevator. His expression was one of utter disdain.

'You have an explanation?'

Guy crossed to the exit, stared hard at the floor, then threw one of his kid grins at the German. 'Reese?' he said. 'He . . . uh . . . just came back from the dead.'

Guy dismissed his cab and walked the last quarter mile along the perimeter road until he saw the chocolate-brown Buttress hangar which squatted against the far boundary of the vast airport acreage. It was low-slung and solitary, a steel-and-stone sumo wrestler whose arms on either side contained a deck of offices; the centre corrugated belly could enclose two 17-10s. Near the edge of the large concrete ramp alongside, Guy found Ben near a row of oil drums.

'The sonofabitch is inside,' Ben greeted him. They stood watching the dimly lit bay across the concrete as though looking into the deceptive stillness of an enemy stronghold. Parked nearby, in the centre of the concrete ramp, was the immaculate prototype 17-10 now used for Cook's tours and fly-by-wire briefings for foreign dignitaries and the world's aviation press. The day's last procession had filed through its innards, tracing lines of silver-encased wires to the hydraulic drive units, then back to the gun-blue metal shield which housed the plane's computer. The ship was empty now and temptingly accessible, touched only by the breeze. Sitting alone, it had the compelling quality of a live electromagnet.

Bees droned in the ankle-deep weeds, an out-of-sync snarl that grated on the ear. There was no sign of life.

'What are we gonna use for witnesses?'

Anton Jasovak observed them both clearly from his vantage. Neither was moving as he watched and he thought of lighting a cigarette but didn't in case the flame might reveal his position. He adjusted himself to ease the pressure on his back and wiped the windowpane, which had developed a circle of condensation from his breathing.

At that moment Guy and Ben saw one of the doors in the string of offices on the second tier open and a figure in coveralls emerge. He walked quickly to another door and disappeared.

'Hardly a crowd,' Guy observed.

Ben mopped his face with one hand. 'There isn't going to be a polite way of doing this.'

Guy hesitated. 'The last time I decked anyone was in high school for stealing my hair tonic. I had to do social conduct all over again.'

They left the partial refuge provided by the oil drums and went inside. The afternoon light was failing, letting thick crimson planks fall from musty skylights through the overhead rafters to intersect the floor in shimmering oblongs.

'Where do you suppose everyone went?' Guy's voice was hushed.

Ben scanned the second-floor balcony, but behind the bare steel railing which extended to the rear on both sides it was deserted. A phone rang somewhere in the hidden reach of the massive cavern and went unanswered.

'He's got to be in one of those rooms,' Ben said, surveying the narrow wraparound ledge above them. 'Let's go.'

Guy took the metal stairs on the right two at a time; Ben's pace on the left was slower. At the top they faced each other from far ends of the balcony like poised aerialists half a city block apart. Closed office doors

251

waited in a row along the darkening length between them. Ben flexed, then with an explosion of pent-up brawling rage he kicked the first door hard into its compartment. It crashed against the metal partition inside and bounced back with a reverberation that still echoed when the report from the second door being smashed open cut through. Ben crouched as he advanced, ready to overpower any trap, anticipating the jack-in-the-box if Jasovak were to spring. Door after door banged open in a frenzy as he moved along the passageway. Guy, more deliberate, was slinging open his fourth door when Ben reached him. The last unopened office stood between them. Ben twisted the doorknob to its stops, motioned for Guy to step aside, reared back and kicked the door towards the centre of the room. It rebounded almost shut again, but even through the narrow opening it was apparent that this cubbyhole too was deserted.

They stood looking down the length of the jail-like corridor. All that could be heard in the echoing aftermath was the slow creak of an overhead beam. Guy fully expected to see activity on the vast floor below, perhaps a platoon of helmeted workers racing to surround them; but the floor was vacant. Even the lone figure in coveralls had vanished. Guy turned back to Ben.

'You were a little loud, don't you think?'

'I wouldn't know,' Ben said. 'I've got a tin ear on one side and I want to share it with somebody. That bastard tried to blow me away this morning.'

He looked back over his shoulder at the row of empty offices.

'A standoff.'

At the bottom they emerged from the stairwell on to the bare hangar floor. Jasovak watched them, two insects in the open, making their way outside. Guy took one last look around.

'You know what? I'm going after the new German report. I know where it is.'

Ben ignored him. 'There's only one other place he can be.'

Almost as one, they acknowledged again the parked 17-10, caught behind the slant of a crimson sun still visible on its tail. Without speaking they separated and headed for the prototype, approaching it from two sides.

A man in rumpled mechanic's coveralls climbed out of a cherry picker he'd just parked and headed for the hangar. Guy changed course to intercept him.

'How ya doin'? Where is everybody?'

'Early day. Lot of time owed.' He leaned towards him confidentially. 'Place was cleaned out by eleven.' The mechanic looked off at Ben who had stopped, still facing the 17-10. 'If you missed the press tour, they start up again in the morning. But if you wait till I get my lunch, I'll show you around.'

Guy looked at the plane, then back at the mechanic, and nodded slowly. 'OK, sure.'

The mechanic returned to them from the hangar carrying a wrapped sandwich and a short thermos. With unspoken reserve they let themselves be escorted towards the jet. Shadows grew like long thin strips of dark moss from under the wheels to stretch far across the ramp. They were under the wing tip, less than fifty yards from the gaping pit that cut into the junction where the wing bridged into the fuselage. The main wheel-well doors, located aft of the landing-gear struts, normally were closed, even on the ground, over the huge, bomb-bay-like access areas that housed the multiwheeled bogies when retracted. Yet they were hanging open like scoops and, unlike the rest of the plane, were unpainted. Ben, whose attention was elsewhere, hadn't noticed. Guy could see the pipes and forged trunnions like steel stumps that connected the wheels to the aeroplane. The fuselage was low-slung, even a few inches lower than the early Boeing transports. The plane hummed. Some sixth sense tingled inside Guy; outwardly he remained calm.

The mechanic accompanying them offered to go inside to release the metal stairs at the rear. Without waiting for a reply, he stepped under the open wheel well and reached up to place his thermos on the aluminium ledge inside the cavernous wall where the giant assembly of wheels would be stored in flight. Ben, now curious, started after him. All at once, in one blinding instant when every nerve end blazed, Guy understood. He knew what he had to do but it was as if his body had mired itself in chains. In slow motion as though refracted through a glacier Guy saw the mechanic's smile falter, his eyes widen, the colour begin to drain from his face. With the force of a torpedo Guy lunged into a violent horizontal dive, pushing all his strength against slabs of stone. Everything was in stark precision, the mechanic's terrible expression, the slick grey hair combed in waves beginning to fly. The hardness of Ben's knee intersected his arm and they fell away just as the edge of the raw metal scoop bit into the mechanic's side between navel and nipple. Guy saw the man's body jostle as lightly at first as if he'd only been tapped on the shoulder – the look of surprise, the wince beginning on his lips before his face disappeared into the well. Then his legs contorted, his feet lifted from the ground. In that microsecond maelstrom the man's coveralls even brushed against Guy's own bare hand.

He felt rather than heard the shock wave of the giant wheel-well doors as they crashed shut just above his head. Then he was aware of the warm gallon of gore that gushed over him from the severed body, which had been chopped in two as neatly as if by a guillotine.

Guy and Ben lay sprawled on the asphalt with the wildly thrashing torso and legs in their ragged, spoiled coveralls draped over them. One shoe continued to lash out painfully, catching Guy in the kidney. With effort he disentangled himself, sliding on the mass of blood and vomit that had emptied from the mechanic's opened belly, and he thought of the mechanic's head and chest and arms sealed inside the closed wheel well five feet above him. Grunting and spitting, Guy shed the gruesome thing, its kicking diminishing into spasmodic twitching, the full horror of it not yet upon him. Very slowly, through the line in the fuselage where the two closed doors met, warm coffee dripped to mingle with the blood.

Guy and Ben stood quickly, holding their dripping arms away from their bodies. Several seconds passed in queer and utter silence. Already the protective screens of shock and detachment had begun to drape their psyches.

'Jesus . . . ,' Ben muttered.

'So much for the sanctity of newspapermen.'

'What the hell happened?'

'I've got to get in there. Somebody has to be inside the cockpit!' Guy took a step but his shoe, full and squishing, shot out and almost threw him. At the same instant he knew there would be nothing inside the entire aeroplane except the dead man's head and torso. No one could have observed them from the cockpit. The control must have been remote – a signal triggered from a vantage point overlooking the area.

Ben stood staring at the fluid bits of human waste running in rivulets across the harsh concrete texture. Curiously, it wasn't this manifestation of violence which troubled him. It was the profound corroboration that he was playing for keeps.

Both of them heard the squeal of rubber and swivelled to see the red tail-lights racing towards the perimeter road into the murk.

'Guess I've been outfucked again,' Ben muttered.

'It could've been worse. As it is, there's only one fatality.'

Ben stood rooted, eyeing the distant car. His voice came barely audibly but each word was distinct. 'There's going to be another one. I can promise you that.'

Guy and Ben searched for a place to change their clothes without being seen and headed for a trailer used as a day room by the construction gangs working on a highway extension. Neither the police nor airport security had shown, so they managed to leave the field without being seen. They washed the worst of the gore off their clothes and Ben took a clean pair of Levi's hanging in one of the lockers. They both knew the execution had missed. It had been meant for one or both of them.

'I'm through with this cat-and-mouse shit,' Ben swore. 'Hell with chasing Jasovak. The root of this stinkweed's stuck in the heart of Paris.' He would leave for France and specifically for Jasovak's bogus perfumery as soon as he could get a fresh set of clothes. There he'd crawl in with the morning mail, pull a stickup and take off with their articles of incorporation.

Guy crossed to a well-lit motel-diner in search of a phone. The time had come to confront Senator Elton D. Osborne, recipient of the second and supposedly hot German report on the F-19. From a pay phone in the foyer he talked his way through the Senate switchboard to Osborne's secretary saying he wanted to see the senator on an urgent matter indirectly linked to national security. 'This evening if at all possible.'

Her answer shook him. 'I'm afraid that's impossible, sir. The senator has just left for Germany.'

9

Ben Reese barked at the wall phone next to the bar but was barely able to make himself understood. Happy Hour was in full swing and Ben had Morty Judd on the line.

'It happened less than three hours ago!'

'It's an accident story,' Judd repeated.

'It was no accident.'

'A mechanic getting killed isn't news.'

'He was cut clean through like rump in a butcher's shop!'

'We already got a lot of death on tonight's show. It could affect the balance.'

'*Balance?*'

'We're hemmed in by thirty minutes.'

'And you jam it with crap! Reptiles wearing hats in Florida isn't news. That was on last night.'

Judd sighed. 'We have an obligation to the lighter side.'

'According to who?'

'People invite us into their lives for enjoyment.'

'You've got them caught between calamity and hysteria. You're all insane!'

'Well . . . that could be.'

'I want you to think about something, Mortimer. When Ed Murrow started all this, he never figured on the Eleven O'Clock Laugh-Along!'

'I admired Ed.'

'You're a patronizing sonofabitch.'

'I really have to go now.'

'So you won't do it?'

'Your timing stinks, Reese.'

'What you mean is, we picked the wrong day for a guy to get killed.'

'What?'

'I said the dumb bastard who died picked the wrong day to do it!'

'Well, if it had happened yesterday, you would have had a better shot, Benny. That's our reality.' There was a pause. 'Otherwise I'd like to help.'

Ben smashed the phone back into the wall. A messenger stood facing him holding a thin envelope.

'What the hell do *you* want?' Ben rasped.

'They said you were Mr Reese.' He proffered the envelope. 'Your ticket to Paris.'

Ben fished a crumpled dollar bill from his trousers. 'I appreciate it.' He folded the ticket and was shoving it into his shirt pocket when the waiter pirouetted by on bent legs with three tankards of beer on a tray. Ben swiped one and with a nod to the crowded bar, roared, 'The Fourth Estate is going to hell!' The place smelled of fried shrimp and dowager carpet, all those smoky smells mingled together with the blood colour and brass doorknobs, and the heavy mahogany bar with the massive curled edge, a perfect imitation of the ones in the Senate cloakrooms. Ben wedged into the leather booth under the pictures of Everett Dirksen and Sam Rayburn, next to Guy and Toby.

'Did you guys know that news was a matter of supply and demand? They already got today's quota of murders. We got a guy cut in two on a tarmac, but he's too late. He might have made it yesterday. They were short on guys cut in two yesterday.'

'Now look,' said Toby. 'I passed up dinner to get over here. So let's get it over with. There was an accident. How does that impact the union?'

'That chop was no accident, Toby,' said Guy.

Ben added, 'The trouble with you, Toby, is that no one ever twisted your nuts in anger. You see, this isn't thesis time at college. We were targets out there today, but don't ask me to prove it.' Ben lifted his stein. 'Here's to the cat-and-mouse game. I'm not playing any more.' He took a swig and stuck his nose close to Toby's. 'Did you know Buttress is in the French perfume business? I bet you didn't know that.' He noted Toby's perplexity. 'Well, stick around. It's a camouflaged fact being protected by murder. It's going to take another killing to prove it.'

Toby was taken aback by Ben's ferocity.

'Toby, see if you can follow this,' Guy said. 'I can't produce it, but it exists. There's a German report out criticizing the F-19 and apparently the 17-10.'

'How do you know that?'

'We have a source at the German Embassy.'

'The German Embassy?'

'Proven reliability.'

'The best money can buy,' Ben added.

Toby struggled to speak. He pried the words loose with great effort. 'I believe you. I've always believed you. I want you to know that.'

'Then let me at least get what's been going on into the *Air Line Pilot* magazine. Send it around. Attach a questionnaire for anybody who doesn't believe me. I'll answer every one of them. I swear it.'

'Guy, I can't print allegations.'

'I'd like to see us pull a strike over this!'

'More than half the guys flying 17-10s would never go along. They'd have to downgrade to smaller equipment and they make more money flying the 17-10. They won't agree there's anything wrong. Besides, we're in the middle of next year's contract negotiations – '

'Next year! Next year! You have *power!*' lashed Ben. 'Go back to that parade of hijackings. Every government in the civilized world was paralyzed. Then you people finally got off your backsides and said the hell with it. And said we're not going to land in the countries that give these cocksuckers sanctuary. And whaddaya know? We got

259

legislation. And all the charts and studies about hijackers and how short or tall they were and whether they had moustaches, all that went into the incinerator.'

'I can take a stand on anything with facts,' Toby began in pale tones. Guy cut him off.

'You're hopeless. We're out there getting shot at and you've got your nose stuck in a dictionary trying to figure out what a bullet is!'

Toby's face was twisted in genuine pain. 'All right,' he relented. 'I'll try to see it your way. I'll think about it.'

'Reese!' The bowlegged waiter was holding the phone in the air. 'It's for you!'

Ben pushed his way free, stepped sideways around a neighbouring table and took the receiver.

'Yeah?'

A lilting feminine voice he didn't recognize greeted his ear. 'You don't know me but I know you get laid at Fourteenth and K.'

Ben rubbed the top of his head. 'I used to.'

'They know a lot about you down at the Press Club. Like where you eat.'

Ben's features crinkled into an appreciative smile.

'Who's this?'

'You know where Guy Anders is?'

'Anders?' Ben asked, slowly deflating. 'He's ten feet away.' Ben caught Guy's eye. 'It's for you.'

'Me?' Guy came over, frowned at Ben and took the receiver. 'Yeah?'

'Yeah yourself. It's Natalie Mason.'

Guy needed a vector. The voice was warmly familiar but no corresponding picture came. The silence prompted her to jog his brain.

'Buzz Riddick's Girl Friday.'

'Black hair . . . blue eyes . . . red ribbon.'

'The same.'

'My ear is still wet.'

'I have something I must show you. I'm at the May-flower – in ten oh one.'

Instinctively Guy faced outward, away from the mirrors, towards the door. He sensed a palpable change in the presence of the room. A new danger had been introduced. 'Meet you in the bar across the street instead.'

'Fifteen minutes?' She sounded a little breathless.

'Half an hour.' He hung up and stood for a minute thoughtfully. Then he returned to the table, unclipped his pen and scribbled something on a napkin. 'I have to leave. If I'm not back in two hours I want you to start looking for me here.'

Ben glanced at the scrawl and shoved the napkin in next to his ticket. 'And if *I* don't make it back from France, call Judd. He'll put it on the news unless there's a lot of other people missing at the same time, in which case I'll lose out.'

At the Mayflower, Guy pushed into the lobby, cutting across brittle chandelier reflections laden with slowly drifting dust. After a minute's wait the receptionist appeared.

'I need a room for tonight.'

'Certainly, sir. Do you have a reservation?'

'Nope.'

The clerk looked indifferently at the registry card on which Guy had scribbled, 'Thomas Latimer. World Wildlife Fund.' Then he turned and searched the rows of room-key slots.

'How will you be settling your bill, sir?

Guy laid down seven ten-dollar bills. 'Cash.'

'Yes, sir. I thank you and here's your key.'

Guy was on his second Blood Mary in the bar across from the hotel when Natalie Mason entered. He spotted her half hidden between two other people, framed in the revolving doors. Standing to greet her, he recalled that moment at the Buttress dinner when he first saw her, a recollection not so much intellectual as in the rush of animal arousal that gripped him at the sight of her. She was wearing a dress the colour of rich cream and tailored to cling in the right places. Her raven-black hair was tied back in a brush with the same saucy red ribbon, giving her an impish quality. Her eyes were nervous, her voice quick as she placed a thin leather attaché case carefully by the chair he held for her.

'It's such a surprise to find you in Washington,' she smiled.

'Seems you knew where to look.'

'I was hoping . . .'

She seemed thinner than he recalled from his visit to Buttress.

'If you're here, Buzz Riddick can't be far away . . .'

'It wouldn't go well for me if anyone found out I was here.'

'What have you got to show me?'

'We're too visible like this.' She'd tilted her head back. Her mouth was perfect and he succumbed to his original temptation, reached up to her face, and let his fingertip trace the delicate rim of her mouth. She merely leaned closer, half closed her eyes and inclined her face towards him, enjoying the sensation. Her mouth parted slightly. Guy could feel her warm breath and see her long slender neck disappearing into the loose folds of her dress.

'Riddick wants me dead,' he said, still running his finger softly along her upper lip.

She didn't move her face.

'They tried to kill me,' Guy went on, watching her expression. 'He'd do anything for Buttress. Wouldn't he?'

262

'Let's talk about it,' she said in a dusky voice. 'But not here.'

In the elevator Natalie pressed '10'. Guy felt like the old man standing stiff and self-conscious in *American Gothic* exposed to the lobby until the doors swished shut. As they started to move he reached over and pressed '8'.

'What are you doing?'

Guy studied her for three floors before he spoke. 'You're one of the smoothest women I've ever met.' He brushed his lips close to her mouth, not touching but close enough to feel her soft exhalation. Two more floors went by. 'But you might also be bait.' The elevator stopped and the doors opened.

Guy found 814 and turned the key. He let Natalie through, slipped the DO NOT DISTURB sign over the outside doorknob and twisted the lock shut. The room was small, with only a few feet of space between the walls and double bed that dominated it. Natalie placed the leather attaché case in the shadow next to the bureau.

'A little cramped,' she said, and sat on the edge of the bed.

'Riddick won't know we're here. Only you and me.'

'You're melodramatic. He's got meetings all over town. I won't see him till ten. He's having cocktails with the vice-president after he leaves Searington, and he has to call on Senator Peck as well.'

'Plans can change.'

'I can't imagine why you wanted to rent this broom closet when Riddick has a suite upstairs.'

'Is what you want to show me in that case?' He made a move to get it for her.

She grabbed his hand, stopping him. 'I've played it your way so far. I'm the one who's taking the risk.' There was an edge of harshness in her admonition.

'OK, let's start again,' Guy said. 'You called. The door's locked. No one knows we're here. Riddick's a fool

263

for letting you out of his sight and I'm pleased he did but I've had my fill of runarounds in this town, so maybe you better just get to the point.'

He saw the hurt in her eyes and she waited, allowing it to diminish. Slowly she settled back on the bed and held her hand out to him. He joined her and watched as she placed her face close to his. Then, her eyes still wide open, still fixed on his, she gave him her wet tongue. She took his hands and placed them on to her breasts, letting him feel the rigid nipples through the fabric. As she did, the red ribbon pulled loose letting her hair come undone and fall in sleek raven cascades across her shoulders. She pulled him down, took one of his hands in hers, placed it deep between her legs, opening, and his fingers were on the smoothness of her thighs and then the thin cloth of her panties, wet with her nectar. She moaned, pushing her body brazenly at him, his fingers probing through the hair at the edge of her panties, beneath into her hot wetness. Gently he opened her.

'Oh God let me feel what it's really like . . .'

She was grabbing at his pants, hard, pulling and tearing. The smell of her body mingled with the pungent scent of dried sweat on his clothes. He had trashed his ruined underclothes. Suddenly she had him free, and her mouth was on him. She went at him hungrily. He grabbed her hair and yanked her head back hard so that she was looking up at him. Her eyes were pleading and full of challenge, the most intense emotion wreathed her face.

'I know what you want,' she said huskily. 'I can get it for you. I can get you anything.' She looked wild, her hair draped over her shoulders, her dress crumpled and spoiled, one bare leg raised over the bedspread.

The texture of the bedcovers came up through his shirt. Her body pushed him down, she was tugging, she had one of his legs free from the trousers. For a blinding moment he felt a kind of panic, as if all of Buttress were crouching

264

over him, pinning him down. With her back to him she tussled with her own clothes, throwing them in heaps on the floor. Finally naked, she pushed herself on her haunches over him again, and he knew in that instant that even Riddick had never seen her revealed like this.

She perched herself up to take him again into her mouth but instead he pushed her body firmly away from his face, down over his chest. He lifted her slightly, the wall of her back falling white like a flux to her spreading soft buttocks, now protruding towards him just over his belly, her hairy fount between them clearly visible to him. His hands were on her buttocks, guiding her. She saw him arching underneath her and she watched fascinated as the fistlike penis, as wide as the space between her open legs, probed into the sticky lips which lay back to receive it, watched as her body yawned to accept him, and she gasped as she felt him fill her. He grunted and pulled her to him, his hands on the soft bottom roundnesses of her, pulling her harshly on to the hilt of his moving penis. He twisted one arm to get a look at his wristwatch, check the time against his deadline for Ben. He was strong. He knew her rhythm, he moved with it, endlessly . . .

She was moving like a machine, her hair falling loosely to his knees as she rode him up and down with a kind of growing vengeance, and looking down all she could see of him was hairy legs and his feet, and the two sets of genitals which had embraced in a detached dance of their own. She began to feel that none of this had anything to do with her, his urgency seemed so compulsive yet oblivious too and she felt a desperate estrangement engulf her.

All at once with a short cry she lifted up to free herself, letting him flop sleek and loose. The cold air startled him.

'What are you doing?'

'I can't see you this way. I need to see you . . .' Her breath was heaving but it sounded close to tears.

'What's going on?'

She had turned herself around to lie down beside him, pushing her head near his. 'Oh, God, I thought it would be different with you . . . I really didn't want to take it on the run like this . . . Everybody else I know, they're all people who can only yank orgasms out of each other's brains in a frenzy.'

'I thought – '

'I don't blame you.' She snuggled closer to him, she felt much smaller to him. 'I don't want it like this with you.' She lay there, the sound of her breath in his ear.

'Hey . . . .' He was looking at her, slightly puzzled. With the backs of his fingers he stroked her cheek.

'I'd like to feel comfortable with you,' she said.

He didn't speak but lay there, feeling her warmth next to him. Behind the stillness of the room and the steady breathing he heard the insistent intrusion of the daily industrial conflict outside like a drum roll in the background. Slowly it stilled, receding.

'Guy?'

'Yes?' His face seemed sympathetic in the half-light.

'It's OK now.' She whispered it to him. She paused, huddled in his arms. 'Please . . . fuck me.'

For a long time he held her. Gently he kissed her. She was ready for him and she smiled and she felt him again, this time with wonder at the fullness of it and the warmth and beauty. Again he matched her rhythm, she moved with him, feeling again the growing waves of intense pleasure, and they melted into her.

Then, suddenly all the waves closed in, all coming at once. She was lost, conscious only of the fullness building in the pit of her belly. Her teeth sank into him and her fingernails, she wrapped herself around him, enclosing him, clutching him with her mouth her arms her legs, shaking, knowing in that moment if Riddick or even her mother were to walk in on them she couldn't stop, she'd stay just like that, knotted to him, coming and coming and coming.

All at once she felt his body surge rigid above her, she heard his voice uncoil and rise up in his throat, an incredible sound, gasping, groaning, an aboriginal sound she had never heard from a man, his thrashing unleashed like an engine gone wild, almost too strong to bear, until with white-hot flushes he erupted into her.

'Oh . . . That's . . . beautiful . . .'

He threw an arm across his face, contorted, eyes rolled back in his head.

'Oh, shit.'

A rush of revulsion swept through Guy in the aftermath of the shattering orgasm. Images of his dead wife and now even Jamie and his *au pair* tried to push through but he turned away from them. He felt cold and acutely aware of his nakedness and moved to cover himself.

'I've never had it like that,' she said.

Guy grasped his knees and avoided her face.

'I've wanted to help you ever since I first saw you,' she said.

'I'd like to believe that.'

'You could have had me the first time we met, right in front of Riddick, in front of his whole crowd. All I could think of all evening was you, filling me up.'

'I'd like to believe that, too.'

'You can have more proof, if you're able.'

They laughed. 'Right now I'd like to see what you have for me.'

She retrieved Riddick's attaché case and placed it on her lap. Her breasts were incongruous next to the grey papers she lifted for Guy to see.

'Here's a copy of a transcript of a phone call from Buzz to Al Searington,' she said, as if she were primly clothed up to her neck behind a big desk. 'Buzz is informing the senator of the roll-out plans for the European Consortium

Skybus. Buttress is very anxious to have the loan hearings done and finished with positive results before the European roll-out. He's going to be spending a lot of time in Washington – trying to get the hearing dates moved up.'

'There's no letterhead on this memo. How do I know it's authentic?'

'Trust me,' she said.

'Is this it? That's all?'

'No, it isn't. There's something brewing with at least one subcontractor. Certain components have been coming up substandard.'

'Which components?'

'I have no idea. But here's a juicy memo discussing the theoretical impact of retrofits. If you cut through the jargon, what they're talking about is delay and that's something they can't afford.'

Guy took the Xerox copy and studied it.

Natalie shut the lid of the attaché case. 'There are a number of people who'd go a little insane if they knew you had that.'

'What do you know about a guy named Anton Jasovak?'

'Never heard of him.' She hesitated. 'We have a Jackson Van der Vac.'

'What's he do?'

'Runs the commissary.'

'Does he ever leave the country?'

'He hasn't missed a day in twenty years.'

Guy let it go.

'There's a German report,' he said.

'There are two,' she countered. 'The latest one yesterday is a declaration of war. It's making a lot of noise. I haven't seen it but people are angry.'

'Besides Riddick, who else?'

'The entire executive suite. It's got them all scared. There was a meeting last night and we were warned not to

268

discuss anything that goes on in the plant. Husbands were told not to discuss anything with wives.'

Guy tried to figure the reason for this unsolicited windfall. 'Why are you telling me all this?'

'When we met you took me for Riddick's secretary.'

'A chauvinistic mistake.'

'There was a small celebration at Buttress when I was hired. There I was, at the start of the equal-rights awakening, a female ushered into a male roost, fussed over as though I were a Nobel laureate, promised the future and then, as all tokens are, used and passed over. Several times. As has been accurately reported over the centuries, women don't enjoy being promised things and passed over – that's professionally and personally.'

'Riddick?'

'He's part of the problem, runs his own fiefdom.'

'And has a permanent wife after all.'

'I'm not sure I'd be upset if Buttress disappeared from the Stock Exchange. It's very basic, really. They seek advantage by taking it. I want to take back some of what they took, but with interest.'

'A pound of flesh.'

'Measurable in dollars-and-cents benefits . . . to another company. And perhaps in turn to me.'

'That's ambitious.'

'No, calculating.'

Guy noticed the gooseflesh on her arm. 'And you're scared.'

'I'm glad you didn't say "ruthless". Yes, scared. Now that you know . . . my deepest secrets, is there anything else you'd like?'

'The German report.' Guy felt he was overstepping but he went on anyway. 'I also need the control system schematics on the 17-10. The real stuff. I want one look at the certification data on the pitch circuit. I want to look at their original thinking.'

Natalie stared at the lid of the attaché case. 'Even if I could get it, how would I get it to you? The mail's out and you can't show up.' Natalie pulled the sheets closer to her. 'There's the Xerox phone.'

'There must be two dozen places here and in New York where we could set up a line.'

'I don't know if I can get close enough to what you want.'

'Whatever you can do.'

Neither of them spoke again. Both were aware of the risk she would be taking.

Dick Miller reached his house while the sun still threw strong light on the westward-facing terraces that bordered the freeway. His small Cape was one of a row of houses slotted uphill among others clustered in from the ocean, all set back in the valleys in rows which now reflected like a sequence of mirrors. The guy next door was already home watering his wisteria and wetting Miller's too because it was so close by. They had grown a foot in a month, it seemed. Time is a murderer, thought Miller.

It hadn't been so long ago Miller could joke about still being on the sunny side of fifty. Hell, he could remember being on the sunny side of forty; that didn't seem so long ago. The valley looked prettier then. But what do you joke about at fifty-one? Being on the sunny side of sixty – there's no punch line in that. He'd gotten his twenty-five-year pin and his pension was going up at two grand a year for each five years he put in. He'd get 9.6 grand per year in nearly worthless dollars if he went all the way until he couldn't walk. He reflected on his 21.8K in the pension fund. Not counting Sandy's three grand she'd been stashing in the cookie jar for the last few years.

Ed Boice wasn't much older than he – couple of years if that. Certainly no more. Ed's son was a volunteer fireman in one of the towns out this way, Miller seemed to recall. One of those rednecks with a big belly like his old man and a phony police beacon on top of his car. Well, that's his hard-on. He wondered what the omnipotent Boice had saved up. He wondered if, amid all that electronic brain-power, the idea had ever occurred to Ed Boice. The thought of an ex-control design chief selling soft ice cream or collecting tolls gave him a vengeful satisfaction.

Miller's wife's name was Sandra. They'd always called her Sandy even though her hair was black. The first time Dick ever saw her, sitting across from him in a trolley car, her hair hung down in glossy waves with little blue highlights like anthracite. Her eyes spoke back to him across the crowd, grateful and patient. But she'd worn her hair too short for too many years. He'd never liked it short. He'd said it looked 'pert' to make her feel good and hide his disappointment. Now it had gone slightly ratty. And her face had become permanently crumpled with concern. But they seldom spoke of their concerns unless they had to do with repairing the screen door or redoing the driveway.

He didn't go to change into his old clothes when he came in. This disturbed her. And his withdrawn de-meanour disturbed her too. He seemed not to have noticed her at all, but she held back mentioning her pique. It might just upset him further. He's been so touchy recently, she thought, and she resolved to tread lightly and hide her feelings of rejection. 'I'm not hungry,' he'd said over his shoulder as he passed by the kitchen. She'd made him a tuna fish casserole. She'd thought of opening a bottle of wine to go with it, but changed her mind; save it for Saturday Maybe he'll unwind a bit by then, and we can celebrate the weekend. The hope didn't cheer her, however.

She dished out the dinner, and called. She had to call twice more and this irritated her. Finally he came,

271

gravely, still with his tie close around his neck. She tamped down the alarm that tried to rise in her throat over the dark bags under his eyes. His face was white, his hands looked dreadful. He still didn't seem to acknowledge her, but stared down at his plate. Dusk had settled like a heavy curtain. He picked a few bites from his plate, lost interest. She sensed with a rush of anxiety that something was troubling him deeply, and she yearned to find the key that would release it from him – from both of them. She had no way of sharing the terrible churning that was torturing his stomach. The kettle boiled. She poured the coffee, placed the full mug before him. It was his favourite mug, the yellow one with the big handle. He seemed to look past it with a vacant stare. Instead, he began softly to pick at his knuckles.

He sat like that, and she, her eyes on him, pleading, and neither of them spoke. Finally she turned half away from him and looked beseechingly at the wall. He sat on the edge of the chair, feet apart, stooped, looking down at his hands between his knees. Only his hands moved, incessantly, over and over.

'I wish you'd stop that awful picking. I can't stand to see your hands so sore.'

He looked up at her. The neck was too small to support the head; the filaments there stood out like bands. Her wiry hands clutched the wooden chair back.

He didn't speak.

'Why don't you eat, Richard? You must finish your dinner. You hardly touched your food.'

'I'm not hungry. I told you.'

'I wanted so much for you to have a nice dinner. Oh, Richard, sometimes I just don't know what to do with you.'

She shook slightly, a birdlike flutter underneath the pink terry-cloth robe. She had gathered the folds across in a double thickness but the robe still swallowed her, as if by excess she could insulate her fragility.

'I'm going back to the plant tonight,' he murmured finally.

There was no sign of acknowledgment. Her eyes were on the uneaten meal, congealing and loathsome.

'I said I'm going to do some more work tonight. I'll be driving back to the plant.'

He made no move to go. He seemed to be concentrating on his hands. A minute passed. Two. He began to shuffle in his chair, his eyes downcast.

She was watching him now, her eyes full of pain, looking up at him from the kitchen chair. The grandfather clock slowly ticktocked from the shadows of the hallway. The house was dark and silent except for the harsh kitchen light. He looked into her eyes deep in their sockets, the lids large and raw.

'It must be important,' she said tonelessly. It was a virtual whisper.

'I have to design a fix for the 17-10,' he said matter-of-factly. 'I have to get it done very quickly. I don't know how I'm going to finish. I don't know if what I'm doing is good enough. But I have to go and find out.'

She looked helplessly at him. She was thinner than he remembered. She looked drawn in her faded robe. He couldn't recall seeing her become an old woman. My God, she's old . . . when did that happen?

He turned away, towards the dark hall, jamming his hands deep into his trouser pockets to suppress their trembling. It had seemed so spacious and fresh here when Lynn was a child, back when the house was new, the picket-fence dream house of their early marriage. Now the hall was as narrow as the entrance to a cell, the linoleum on the kitchen floor was cracked, the hall carpet at the doorway colourless and threadbare. The only sounds were the clock and the sounds of their breathing.

* * *

273

Dick Miller had sought the evening at his office to work out his task in solitude, untrammelled by the pace of the day. But now the silence had weight. When had he last been here at this hour? He'd forgotten how the building's aspect changed by night: the walls were not friendly, they glowered. He tried to force his attention on the details of the new actuator but couldn't. The sounds and shuffles of daytime were as essential as sharp pencils.

He hadn't been aware of Vern Locker's entrance. The younger man stood in the doorway wearing jeans and canvas shoes. His shirt ballooned over his belt from sitting in too many positions. 'Hello, Dick,' he ventured. 'Kinda late, isn't it?'

Dick welcomed the chance to throw his pencil and template down. He stretched, tried to stifle a yawn, but was unsuccessful. 'Can't let go of the job, huh? Got to learn to let go,' he observed.

'Grinding through some futuristic stuff on the F-19A,' Locker said. 'Direct force control – sidesteps without pointing the nose. Decoupled modes – fixed-attitude manoeuvring. Stuff like that.'

Miller's eyes were wistful. They were not fixed on Locker and the young man sensed this. He began to feel the awkwardness of having intruded when Miller smiled and spoke. 'When I had more hair I used to comb it the same way you do. I was just as full of piss and vinegar when we were designing the first jet peashooters that went to war in Korea . . . I had the same enthusiasm then, I lived for that design . . . the Lancejet . . . a great design . . . I watched it grow into hardware downstairs . . . then they finally put wings on it, and I watched it roll out.' He looked directly at Vern Locker, a mellow cast softening his haggard features. His eyes moved past the young man, and back to the window.

'They said that snub-nosed sonofabitch wouldn't fly. It wouldn't have the stability, it wouldn't have the manoeuvrability, it wouldn't have the speed. And we were loading weight on that thing, it seemed another hundred pounds every two hours. And the challenge was when we loaded on one hundred to strip off two hundred – for every step backward to take two steps forward. And we ended up with a good design. But there were a lot of late nights – hell, we didn't mind then.

'And I remember the night before we rolled her out. Christ, nobody slept that night. She was going to be rolled out the next morning at eight; nobody went home the whole night, we stood around down on the final assembly floor talking to each other and went back and forth to the machines taking candy out, eating candy all night and drinking coffee, some guys brought in some beer. And – I think once every hour and a half we went out there and took a look at her, sitting there quietly by herself, all shined up – flick a piece of dust off her, y'know – ' His voice had become strangely hushed. Vern Locker remained absolutely motionless, Miller's eyes were lost in the distance. 'Yeah, we'd look at her again, climb the ladder and look down into the cockpit – stand back and look at her like an artist does, at a painting. Then, by six o'clock we're all pretty bleary and I stretched out next to a radiator somewhere, on a phone book – put my coat over me, slept for an hour. We heard the people start coming in to work, cars arriving, generals coming in for the roll-out, you could hear the cars being parked all over the place. And when the curtain went up there we were, standing right next to the wing – it was incredible.'

Miller stopped talking. He sat still as stone, his eyes on the dim lights from the faraway hills. A moment passed. He turned to face Locker.

'But – ah – I've lost track of all that. I – uh – I don't stand by the wings any more. I don't stay up all night. If it rolls out that's all right and if I read about it in the paper that's OK too.'

275

Dick Miller stepped around his desk, rearranged some papers, softly chewing his lip. Vern Locker didn't speak but remained pensively by the wall. Miller was drawn to the window, where he stood, head lifted, thumbs through his belt. Without turning he spoke again, softly.

'I don't know what the hell I'm doing here. You know – uh – there was a time when I thought I was going to go somewhere and now I realize I got less time comin' to me than I already took. And the security I worried about for tomorrow – I hadda have all that security – job security – Who needs job security? I need *time*. Can you get time security somewhere?' It was almost a whisper. '*You* want job security. But me? My daughter's grown, she's out of sight. All I need is to make ends meet. Hell, the pension'll take care of that. I've got a few bucks saved.' His liquid eyes swept the tiled ceiling, the small blackboard on the opposite wall. 'You know, sit around, go fishing. So I don't need job security.' He turned towards Vern Locker, who sat rapt, unmoving. 'But I want some time. And there's no time left so what am I doing here? . . .

'I was thinking the other day, maybe I – ah – ought to give this up. I've always thought about – uh – doing something else instead . . . I think I – uh – I'd like to change the whole scene, you know.' His eyes had turned back towards the phantom shapes of the hills. 'I'd like to drive into a town and park the car and walk up to a strange house that I've never been in before. And there's a girl in there . . . young girl, twenty years old, she's lying there on the bed and she's naked . . . and . . . there are no complications and . . . she knows how to soothe me and she's not going to hang any bills on my ass or problems or involvements. It's just gonna be cool and quiet . . . and it's gonna be great. And that's what I really long for . . .' His voice trailed off. Locker sat mute, almost reverently.

Abruptly Dick Miller turned, a sheepish grin on his face, his eyes downcast as he fumbled with his pencils. 'I don't know if you know what I'm talking about . . . but, anyway, thanks for coming in and listening . . .'

Vern Locker's look of attentiveness was crossed with uneasiness as he turned to leave. I can't say he's off his rocker, the tousled young man was thinking, but there's something wrong.

Dick Miller remained stock-still after Vern Locker left, staring out past the drawings that littered his desk. He stood like that for several minutes, stock-still except for his raw hands which moved slowly in front of him. Then he opened the long centre drawer, fumbled until he found a business card Ben Reese had given him some months ago, and began dialling numbers on the phone. He listened to the start and stop of the distant phone. He was afraid of the coming night. Like so many nights before he knew he would lie awake, sweating with terror . . . wide-eyed, heart pounding, terrified . . . but not sure of what. Of not being able to compete any more? Of not being accorded even a modest nod of approval for his excruciating effort? Dick Miller listened with growing uneasiness. What would he say if Reese answered? Could he bring himself to say there's a design problem in the 17-10? How would he frame it? What details could he give, he'd have to go into the microfiche files, come out with a truckload of stuff, he'd have to go so far back it would be like trying to thread your way through the phone system to locate the first phone ever made . . .

Phones. Dick Miller held the phone to his ear as if immobilized. He'd grown weary. He'd pushed all his life to get ahead, to climb the slope to reach that plateau upon which he could stop to catch his breath before moving on. But there were no plateaus – just the slope, which was there every morning, just as steep as it was the day before. And if he didn't climb it – my God, he would slide all the way down to the bottom again . . . and he'd be too far down to come back. Then it would only make sense not to look up any more . . . because his exhausted arms would no longer reach . . . and it would only make sense to look down . . . and then, with a grateful smile, to die. He would be grateful to die. Dick Miller smiled as he regarded the noisome telephone. He hung it up and turned away, towards the window and the darkness outside. The thought of dying warmed him.

10

There was a feline quality about G. Hollis Wright as he glided into his heavy oaken chair at the head of the table. The immense boardroom was hushed; only one or two nervous men moved silently behind to take their places. Hollis Wright waited as though camouflaged, peering at quarry. He was impeccably dressed, in tones that merged with the carpet and drapes that blanketed the room. The only colour was the red scramble phone that sat near his elbow.

On the table's far end stood a stack of twenty-by-thirty-inch cards with an easel mounted on the floor beside it. Hollis could remember the undercurrents of eagerness when it had been a conference to convince the board that a successful programme could indeed be launched. A programme called 17-10: the saviour of the 1980s. He already knew what was on the cards that lay neatly piled on the polished mahogany. Continue with the 17-10B. In the face of European competition. In the face of escalating fuel prices. In the desperate need for airlines to re-equip. He could sense the nervousness running across the room.

Hollis nodded to his corporate vice-president and general manager, Civil Transport Division, to begin the pre-

278

sentation. The vice-president started through the cards. One card was a market analysis for the 17-10B, airline by airline. 'An analysis of Air World profitability leads us to believe that Air World may no longer have prime customer potential, unless their specific requirements for the 17-10B are renegotiated.' Detailed descriptions of manpower requirements and escalating tooling costs for expanded use of nonmetallic graphite-epoxy structures for the 17-10B flowed through the room. 'We have made certain cost assumptions. We are now refining realistic cost targets. It appears that our cash requirements for the 17-10B will now be one billion dollars before the first plane is delivered.'

'I didn't come to hear an apology for the 17-10 programme,' Hollis whispered to the stern-faced Fenton Riddick sitting alongside. Motioning slightly with a nod of his silver mane, he stood up and, stealthy as a cat, glided from the room. Riddick followed him. In Hollis's private anteroom the chairman turned to face the granitelike character whom he had personally handpicked to ramrod the 17-10. Hollis had known Riddick would roll up his sleeves, get his fingernails dirty. He'd taken to him instantly in their first conversation, which, both knew, had been in reality a deadly earnest interview for big corporate stakes, and he'd liked it when Riddick had said, 'You need more balls on the transport programme, Hollis. I'm just the guy who can kick those flying cattle cars in the air.'

Hollis eyed Riddick now with a mild expression. 'I think I'm going fishing.'

'Looking for big game?'

Hollis raised his eyebrows. 'It's just that I feel the need for some time away with Mrs Wright, that's all. Sit on the fantail of *Scorpion* and cast for a little mahimahi for a few days. Of course,' he offered as though the words were an afterthought, 'I'll want Matt Aspinwall to be along with me. I'm sure he and Mrs Aspinwall would enjoy the expedition.'

'No doubt.'
'Arrange it.'

On the East Coast Matt Aspinwall fingered his nitro-glycerin tablets and tried to subdue his abrasiveness. Vic Moudon looked too alert with his fresh haircut. Strangely, it accentuated his Adam's apple, and the effect disgusted Aspinwall. He'd had a bad night. Two dozen oysters Rockefeller had given him heartburn, which at first he took for angina, and the fright had left him sleepless and edgy. He swallowed the nerves down with his slug of morning coffee (home-ground imported Tanzanian) but felt the irritation of the day as sharply as the sticky wool of his turtleneck.

The luncheon meeting had not gone well. Intense discussions concerning 17-10B financing had resolved nothing. Matt had grabbed the tablecloth and clamped Moudon's stringy arm in his grizzled paw. With his ballpoint he scribbled figures on to the executive damask, lining some out, going over others so sharply he almost punctured the linen. Moudon nodded like a tethered goat.

It was a full-blown staff review to bring Aspinwall up to date on the status of negotiations with Buttress. Staff members scrambled to flash a hastily assembled group of charts showing the effects of all conceivable changes of contract provisions which might be considered by Buttress. Aspinwall waved the cards away with an impatient gesture. 'OK, OK, I've got the picture,' he growled, slipping his pen away, looking balefully into the expectant frozen expression of every person at the table. Some of them were having their first experience in the executive dining room and were finding it not altogether enjoyable. 'Moudon, you stay here. The rest of you can go. *Vamoose.*'

There was mixed pique and relief as the half dozen staff

men pushed their chairs back and shuffled from the room. 'Take your coffee with you if you haven't finished,' Matt called after them. No one dared interrupt his flight from the room. As soon as the door had shut, Aspinwall turned on his trusted aide and barked, 'Now I'll tell *you* what we negotiate with those cocksuckers.' He hunched forward, fists clenched in front of him. Matt Aspinwall's negotiations were never written and always made where there were no observers or staff members to make notes. He'd always found the freedom to disclaim in private what his staff had negotiated in conference to be a powerful weapon.

'Some provisions of our present contract with Buttress must be cancelled. We substitute later growth components – 17-10B technology – but delivered earlier. I know goddamn well Buttress is ready to go right now with the 17-10B, but instead they're holding the government up for ransom. And jeopardizing our Big Season in the process. I don't give a shit about their precious loan extension if it kills our Season. I want better delivery and return options.'

'Buttress doesn't need to meet our requi – '

'Make no mistake about it. Buttress needs Air World. They need us bad. Without us the 17-10B doesn't fly . . . and without the 17-10B, Buttress is on its knees. Now I want the return options in writing. Six copies on plain paper. No letterhead. No Xerox. All originals, all to me, just like always.'

'Yessir.'

'This morning I was invited to go fishing for a few days as the personal guest of Hollis Wright on the Buttress yacht. Gonna take Mrs Aspinwall. Enjoy some quiet sunshine.'

'Yessir.'

'These options are to be restricted inside here. The staff shall not know. The Buttress negotiators shall not know. Two copies go with me to the yacht.'

'Yessir.'

'If we have any spies in here I'll crucify you.' There was a moment of forced laughter.

'Yessir.'

'Now burn this goddamn tablecloth.'

Fenton Riddick was seated on Senator Albert Searington's broad blue couch, leaning forward, bare arms on his knees, his hands folded with knuckles pressed together draining blood from his fingers. The air in the closed inner office had the quality of quiet that follows an earsplitting explosion. Riddick watched the senator stride from behind the white standing screen, the kind seen in hospitals, and waited. Searington had just swallowed four aspirin and shut off the tap. He drained the last of the water from the plain glass and placed it on a folded white hand towel which lay on the corner of his desk.

'How many hours of operational proof do you have so far?'

'We broke four thousand last night,' said Riddick. 'And we're accumulating almost a hundred fifty more each day.' A rich tan extended across Riddick's chest, partly revealed by his open shirt which had bold, carmine-coloured stripes.

'And during these four thousand hours there's been a marked incidence of hydraulic failures on the aeroplane.' It was spoken as a statement, not a question.

'Not true.'

'Well then, would you characterize them as routine?'

'I won't characterize anything that hasn't occurred.'

'Then what do you think it was that made that aeroplane vibrate and shake itself out of control on its approach into Kennedy?'

'We can only offer conjecture at this time.'

'I for one would like to hear it.'

'There are several modes of maloperation including

procedural error, and even direct pilot-initiated control input can account for what happened.'

'Pilot-initiated control input – I haven't heard that one before. Did the crew initiate the fire as well?'

'Engine fires are nothing new to aviation, Senator.'

'What you're saying, then, is that in your entire experience with the 17-10 there has never been a justification for alarm.'

'That's correct.'

'And that view naturally would be corroborated by your test pilots.'

'You'll have to ask them – but I believe they'll bear that out.'

Portents of a hot summer wafted through the room. Cherry blossoms had already faded, tourists in T-shirts crowded boulevards outside the cathedral window, air conditioners throbbed in the background, even at this late hour. Riddick took a deep drag on a cigar thick as his thumb; Ed Boice had given him half a dozen.

'In other words there was no hint during the manufacture of the aeroplane that it might harbour a design deficiency.'

'There is no deficiency, past or present. That aeroplane is clean. Period.'

'As clean as the F-19?'

'You're talking apples and oranges. You can't compare the demands made on a fighter with those on a transport.'

'So you had no warning. No one knew anything about Flight Six into Kennedy. No one ever imagined it.'

Riddick's brow was crossed with pique at the grilling. 'Of course not – '

'You're a bald-faced liar, Mr Riddick.'

Riddick's expression challenged the senator. 'You'd better explain that.'

'In March of last year you called a meeting which was attended by your test pilots as well as Mr Boice and Mr

283

Locker and three people from Buttress flight-test centre and the range controller and you told them of your concern about the unexpected behaviour of the 17-10 and that you hoped the transport wouldn't follow the flight characteristics of the F-19, which is its predecessor in every respect insofar as the basic design philosophy is concerned.'

'Where the hell did you get that?'

'Is that your response?'

'I'm serious. Where did you get it?'

Searington merely leaned back and surveyed Riddick. 'Those are the kinds of questions that are going to be asked.' He smiled thinly.

'But there's no basis for that statement.'

'Senator McDermott has a way of inventing things that sound as though they have a plausible basis. He works from the plausible situation, introduces it as fact and then slips in the false premise. Most people don't notice it.'

'A fishing expedition. They have nothing concrete to go on.'

'I don't know that. And you can't take Senator Peck for granted, either.'

'I'd prefer it if you'd said *we* can't take him for granted.'

Albert Searington placed his thumbs in his vest pockets and watched Fenton Riddick. He'd heard what Riddick had said perfectly clearly but was giving himself time to let it register. And the implications as well. He studied his man, searching for that spark of trust, but found it lacking. He began to play Riddick in his politician's creamy tones.

'The loan hearing is going to be murder. You're going to be up against people who got their training back in the sixties and who've had nothing to piss on since the nuclear accident at Three Mile Island.'

'So we have to hold our breaths for the refuse left over from Vietnam, get on our hands and knees to explain ourselves.' Riddick gestured impatiently and stood up and paced towards the window. 'My people have passed out facedown on the production line at four in the morning! We put in years of overtime – for what, to be summoned here to have ourselves checked for fleas? Let them look up our asses?

'She's a magnificent aeroplane.' Riddick glided to the heavy carved-walnut sideboard and poured from a crystal decanter of whiskey. He walked back to the window, handed Searington a tumblerful, and sipped from his own. 'It's less than a man's lifetime since those guys jumping around in old films strapped themselves flat on their bellies in wood frames and we've taken that and put four hundred paying passengers into velvet seats . . . feed them steak dinners and move their asses along at nine miles a minute and burn less fuel per person than the family car. And we're doing it with the help of a computer that lets us beat the Arab cocksuckers at their own game of extortion and gives our airlines a fighting chance to survive with a three per cent profit. Sure the clutch sticks once in a while and the windshield wipers grab because we're in the predictable shake-out mode. So what? We never said we were fortune-tellers!' Riddick took a deep puff from his cigar and chased it with a swallow of the senator's twelve-year-old Glenlivet.

Searington put his drink down on the folded towel next to the empty water glass. He hadn't drunk any. 'The technology got ahead of us – didn't it, Buzz?'

Riddick was stunned. He slowly lowered his glass. The room was sweat-hot, the air conditioner hummed. A fly cut through the still space between them. 'I'm not ready to concede that.'

Searington hunched forward and cast his eyes dead on Fenton Riddick as though lining him up for a missile attack from his Starfighter. 'Level with me. You're covering areas that need attention. You need that money because the clouds lifted and you found you're wading in deep shit!' He didn't budge. Riddick felt uncomfortable but it passed. He sipped the last of his scotch and turned back to face the senator, smiling reassuringly.

'All we need is a vote of confidence and a night's sleep.'

Searington decided to close in and make his point. 'The country can't afford to have you standing in deep shit,' said Searington. 'I can't afford it, either.' He walked back to the window and looked out over the vista. 'I put a great many eggs in one basket and you guys are beginning to shake that basket around. I gotta be frank with you, Buzz, you're not the only people on the street building fly-by-wire.'

'You'd better go home and feel around in your safe, Albert, and think that one over.' There was a pause. Riddick continued, 'And there's something else we want you to think about. We want to narrow the room for mischief before our loan-guarantee hearings get started. Hollis wants you to move the hearing up.' The room seemed fraught with unseen energy despite the hushed tones, a battery of hidden guns poised, awaiting the lanyard.

Searington seated himself behind his desk, between the US and Virginia flags. 'It'll look suspicious if we move the hearing up. The plain fact is that in this corner of government some people look to the private sector to foot the bill – the entire bill.'

'The plain facts are we've already sunk four billion private dollars into active controls. That was money we didn't have but we got those fly-by-wire sonsofbitches off the ground. And a lot of people are benefiting from that . . . Buttress can't stop now.'

'It's the airlines who buy your aeroplanes. Let them pay.'

'This is too big for them. They're murdering themselves with cut-rate fare wars.'

286

'What do I say to constituents and critics about a new date? There's a groundswell of opinion that'll be against us being a party to another bail-out loan.'

'There are ad agencies that are getting pretty good at converting that. You'll have to sell the enormous potential return on investment.'

'Concorde was a government programme. You tell me what the fucking return on investment was to the governments who funded that programme!'

'We're not talking only about government return on investment; we can't neglect the personal side.' Riddick took a thoughtful drag on his cigar.

'I've got good people on the committee and they're not all rubber stamps. They don't all think the way I do.'

'You've got to move the goalposts up thirty yards.'

'I have a certain regard for those people and so far we've been able to work together to iron things out and stay together as a family, but I can't promise it.'

'You can't promise it? How long do you expect Osborne to sit on the fucking krauts?'

'You're talking to one member of the committee!'

'I'm talking to the Senate whip! I'm talking to the senior minority member of the Armed Forces Committee! Mayberry wants government health care, tell him to suck wind! Della Beck wants mass transit, tell her to get lost! McDermott was arrested in a whorehouse in Taiwan! Bogen has been logging time with a psychiatrist! MacMurray was seen kissing toilet seats in the Pentagon –'

'Where the hell did you get that?'

'I can't prove it,' Riddick smiled. 'But it's plausible. What the hell do I have to do? Teach you your business?'

Searington grinned in spite of himself. For a moment he saw Buzz Riddick standing before him again as he had those long years ago, draped with a yellow Mae West, cinched in his tight g-suit like an olive-drab ballet costume with buckles, accenting the same lean frame. The hair was thicker then, the face unlined and more openly roguish. His best squadron commander. And the gunsmoke-blackened Lancejets were lined up in the background.

'I should have remembered. Buzz Riddick. The best that ever showed in Korea. One hundred twenty-three missions. There are a lot of people who came back who still owe you.'

'We have no quarrel with each other, General. Just don't cop a plea. I feel comfortable. I feel secure. I'm in the office of the Senate whip!'

Searington had been Riddick's mentor in those rugged days of swift simple justice, but the student had long since graduated. And now he held the loaded pistol in their shadow duel. Riddick's blue eyes flashed and he smiled and looked immensely pleased with himself and took a final long drag from his stogie, then mashed it out in the ashtray on Searington's desk. The assumption of prerogative offended Searington. Still the brash devil, Riddick.

'I have to leave here with more than a promise. Either that or we're all going to Matty Aspinwall's funeral. He won't own up to it right now but he's taking off light. Right this minute he's twenty per cent behind the eight ball.'

'I'll do my best.'

'Just as long as we understand each other.'

The senator glanced away from Riddick. The next line was difficult and he didn't know quite how to frame it. Finally, still looking towards the window, he said quietly, 'I'm having some trouble with the new method of payment.'

'Senator, we always pay upon delivery.'

DAY ONE – FORENOON WATCH – SIX BELLS

Scorpion II bobbed gently at the quay, the sun bright on its superstructure. In the mid-1960s it had replaced the old spoon-bowed, frame-sided *Scorpion I* built for Buttress brass back in 1929. But the tone of unhurried opulence had been preserved aboard the newer craft even at the risk of contravening the modern fast-paced ethic. Hollis Wright's large cabin was in readiness, a stage set with lean furniture, fully equipped with the ermine trappings of the corporate gladiator. Hollis Wright still thought of himself as strongly handsome, and making his final arrangement for Aspinwall's visit, he was convinced of it. *Scorpion II* was appointed to accommodate his penchant for the expected luxuries, all neatly arranged for delivery in the correct sequence. Nowhere in sight was there a single indication of aviation, and this obvious absence occasionally puzzled visitors; no aeroplane models decorated the sideboards, no aeroplane portraits hung on the mahogany-panelled bulkheads. Hollis Wright had sold bulls in Argentina to get his start. Matt Aspinwall had come to Air World as a finance man who had muscled through. Aeroplanes were abstractions to these men, functional articles, nothing more, and if others perceived aesthetic qualities on which to lavish nostalgia or regard, it was their time wasted. Wright and Aspinwall had come together as two potentates to lock horns over ledger sheets.

Their wives kissed as they met on the quarterdeck. Mrs Aspinwall, thin and so brittle it seemed as if the sharp wind off the sea might crack her eggshell countenance, yet retained the last traces of resilient sexuality. She opened her mouth in an overdone smile nervously, the haggard lines under her chin betraying the strain of nursing Matt Aspinwall through his ramrod drive to power. In contrast Mrs Wright was plump with smooth round features, untroubled and well powdered, with a fixed wistful set to her mouth, a face as pure as that on an oval cameo and just as oblivious to the charging concerns of her husband's life.

There to fetch the hand luggage were three servants. To Matt they were throwbacks to the Georges who once served on Pullmans, dressed in little white waistcoats, and there was a bartender to serve the Southern Comfort highballs, and two maids. The number of servants aboard seemed oppressive to Matt, who wanted to be able to stretch without elbowing a deferential stranger, stretch and breathe the clear Pacific air and let it renew something vital within him.

As Hollis led the Aspinwalls on board Matt could feel the pressure build behind his eyeballs. For a moment he grabbed the rail and hesitated, hoping Hollis wouldn't notice. It reminded him all too vividly of that black day three years before when suddenly the pierce of a lance inside his chest staggered him, forcing him to his knees, where he grabbed the parking meter, heaving for breath, his face ashen, his fingers white and slipping as they clawed his tie knot . . . then, shaking, straightening it. 'It's OK – just indigestion,' he had barked to the vice-president with him, detecting on the man's face concern not for his boss's welfare but that he might be called upon to undertake an unpleasant task. 'Must've been the oysters . . . goddamn heat, humidity.' He knew he seemed depleted struggling like that and he hated it, his jowls tight, and he knew all too well what was happening to him. Slowly he had regained his feet and his composure. 'I'm OK, goddammit.' And he had managed to walk on. That night he was in intensive care. And as he moved on towards the cabin belowdecks he gritted his teeth hard as he had done on that day and fingered the nitro tablets in his pocket.

The sight of the back of Hollis's slick white head bobbing cocksurely as he led the way down the ladder made Matt want to reach out with both hands and grab hold and shake. He wanted to shake Hollis so hard he'd make the aeroplanes fall out of his ass. Instead he must feign politeness, a pretence that made him doubly impatient. Smile at the ladies. Geselda Wright was speaking to him. 'Oh yes, isn't the weather nice? Hollis had them fix the pump . . . now we don't have to worry about the bilge overflowing . . . all the staterooms have been done up with new curtains. Don't you like them?'

Matt had to grab his nitro. He felt the arteries in his neck bulge. Here I have a worldwide airline that'll go bust if Hollis doesn't deliver and this woman is talking about the fucking curtains!

DAY ONE – AFTERNOON WATCH – THREE BELLS

The fat boat bore towards the open sea. Details of rocky coastline merged and became indistinct. Presently the large rolling seas beyond the shoreline's farthest promontory stung the bow with chill slaps as they rumbled past. Hollis Wright sat coiled in his chaise longue on the open rear deck, the strong features beneath his white mane creased with an expression that could have been cynicism, wisdom or arrogance. Matt, in shirt sleeves, was in the chaise longue beside him, relaxed but wary, the coarse hair on his forearms standing in the wind like curled barbs of rusty wire. Hollis acknowledged the silver tray placed before them, nodded curtly to dismiss the waiter, and gazed out across the distant knife edge of blue on blue. He spoke without looking at Matt.

'I remember our first jet transport, Matty – the 17-06 – a financial disaster. Near crippled us. The design was right but our loss on that programme was more than our entire working capital. We had powerful men – in our credit institutions, on my board, on my working staff – all saying, there, that proves it's impossible to make a profit with jet transports. "Jet indigestion" they called it. The first time the old tried-and-true formula of more speed plus more seats equals more profit broke down. But you know what I did? I said *no*, goddammit, it means we open our eyes, gentlemen, and learn what problems to avoid in the *next* programme. Then came the 17-08. Another cost monster – a real bastard. But that's an investment a corporation like Buttress has to make in learning the business. We can't be dismayed by temporary losses – '

'To a certain extent those losses can be expected,' interrupted Matt. Abruptly he replaced the tumbler of bourbon from which he had been sipping. At that moment he devoutly missed the huge Dutch cigar he then would have waved with a flourish. Had to give them up after his heart attack. They'd been made especially for him in Amsterdam and always looked dried out and had an offensive musky odour. But he didn't have one now as he looked squarely at Hollis. 'Like me you've learned to apply strict controls – or you should have. If you run into unanticipated costs now, any kind of redevelopment, you could drown, and pull a lot of people down with you.' He let it hang like the cigar smoke of old.

'We're strong, Matty, we have a strong divisional organization,' Hollis smiled. 'Our military division, our missile division – all strong. Submarines, radar ranges – '

'Submarines won't make it for Air World. Transports has to make it on its own.'

The conference was under way.

DAY ONE – AFTERNOON WATCH – FIVE BELLS

The stewards had just cleared the table and refilled the bourbon tumblers. The women were below, talking, trying to ignore the strong motions of the boat which made drinking tea difficult. On deck Matt put his hands

292

behind his head. 'I want you to put yourself in my shoes, Hollis. You've got the imagination. My office is forty-nine metal steps above the tarmac at Kennedy. I look to the West for the best in the business and for this reason I depend on you.'

Hollis listened.

'It was Air World who got your 17-06 off the ground first, back in fifty-eight. They said I'd go broke for sure. I showed 'em. Inside of a year all the other lines were beating a path to your door. But that first coupla years, they were rough.'

'That's bullshit. You were never scared to make the big move that promised big profit. That's why you came back to us for the 17-10.'

'I'm not tied to it.'

'The price of fuel says you are.'

'There's no law down yet that says I've got to buy American.'

'It's chaos out there today. Only giants can bring order out of chaos.'

'It's more than chaos: it's a life-and-death situation. I'm beginning to wonder if you can deliver, Hollis. Your programme is going to murder me.'

Hollis sipped his bourbon. 'My programme won't. But the competition will. *They'll* murder you.'

Matt studied Hollis, searching for a clue as to whether Hollis himself thought he could outdistance the economic threat.

'We've given you something new with the 17-10,' Hollis continued. 'We're giving you the advantage of electronics. Let computers replace tails and make wings thinner, let them run the engines for fuel efficiency.'

'You haven't been listening, goddammit. We can't tolerate the delays. I sell a commodity. An aeroplane seat is a commodity on the move. I have to deliver it when promised and I have to resell it often enough to keep it

293

moving and pay my overhead. Break down my dependability in doing that and you'll break my balls. However you make it, Hollis, whatever you call it, I have to depend on it. It's gotta be there. We have a contract, you and me, and I expect that contract to be lived up to in all its aspects. I don't want any more explanations. I can't fly your goddamn explanations.'

Hollis lubricated his throat with a fresh cocktail and grabbed a handful of hors d'oeuvres. His tone became remonstrative. 'You're confused. We're not giving you explanations. I personally went out and got you the only engine that could deliver. That took some doing but that's not an explanation – that's a gift. And you know full well the day you fall behind my performance guarantees – even by one per cent – you can come to me. And I won't say it's not my beef, that your argument is with the engine builder who will tell you the engine's OK, that it's Hollis's plane that's too heavy and run you around in a circle. You know where to come. Our place. Right here. Where it's been ever since we were building goddamn *cropdusters!*'

'You're right, Hollis. We got a terrific contract.' Matt Aspinwall studied his adversary. 'And I will look you up, but not because you're so virtuous. It'll be for our mutual self-interest, won't it? We have – a certain brotherhood. It has nothing to do with whether we love one another or not.'

DAY TWO – DOGWATCH – SEVEN BELLS

The day had started badly. Matt pushed his no-letterhead position papers across the breakfast table. They came too suddenly; Hollis exploded. Matt retorted in a pique, 'Turn this skiff around. Let's not waste each other's time any further.' Then the fish hadn't cooperated. Now, they were waiting impatiently for supper. It was that nether hour between cocktails and dinner. The boat creaked gently in the long swells under a pure sky loaded with brilliant colours as the sun dipped.

'If I were you I wouldn't be too sure about me buying your 17-10B.' Matt decided to push Hollis a little further.

'We've studied your fleet requirements, Matt.' Hollis was informal but deeply serious. 'Parametric studies based on your own figures for your ten busiest city pairs. We know just how many 17-10Bs you're going to need to keep going. We'll extend some credit to you, but I'm not going to give you those aeroplanes.'

'I'm beginning to toy with the idea of dumping the 17-10 altogether after this year's Big Season.' Hollis laughed but Matt read his agitation. 'You can't even build the B without that government loan.'

Hollis was momentarily stung. It passed. One of the nation's grittiest free enterprisers, G. Hollis Wright. It rubbed him against the grain that money for Buttress projects in the past had come in large measure from exorbitant government expenditures on military projects. Now this – *the loan* – the government carving out a share of civil fly-by-wire development. Yet Hollis was an opportunist, as exploitative as any riverboat cardsharp. He screwed up his eyes. 'You're getting rotten advice. You see, more than Buttress is at stake on that loan,' he said quietly. 'The entire nation's industrial leadership is at stake. There's always some asshole somewhere beating a drum, out to sink you. Billy Mitchell sank a battleship once and made his point for air power. What he didn't understand was that battleships in those days kept the steel industry going. And that kept the whole USA going. *And that wasn't wrong.* They *had* to shitcan him. Well, it's the same today. We're in the battleship business. And we won't let any torpedo runs against us go unanswered. We're gonna put some broadsides into a few bleeding hearts on the Hill to educate them that Buttress is more

295

than aviation: it's the cutting-edge reality of Yankee industrial supremacy.'

'If you can't educate them, you shitcan them.'

Hollis looked straight at Matt and smiled like a Chinaman. 'You bet your ass.'

'But you see,' said Matt coolly, 'shitcanning them won't really help you at all if I don't get the rest of my fleet on time.'

Right there Hollis wished Aspinwall would croak. Then all he'd have to do would be to wrap him in a flag and dump him overboard. Then he'd have all the time he needed; time to think . . . time to repair the 17-10.

DAY THREE – MIDWATCH – ONE BELL

It was late, the deck was silent. The stillness closed in on Matt with the force of a knot constricting his heart. He wanted to yell but didn't dare. Instead he tried to stifle his heartbeat, convinced that any small noise would have the effect of shattering a huge plate-glass window; a blade of grass falling would reverberate with the shock of a cannonade.

Leaning over the ship's rail, searching the horizon, Matt could picture the sandbox where he'd played as a child, making a wooden aeroplane out of a crate and two boards, then sitting in the sun, feeling it fly. Ever since then he'd committed his life in the ever-accelerating quest, unaware of time passing, hearing the incessant call to succeed, unimpressed by the fact that the final reach could only occur in death.

The darkness became deep as the stars. Night stretched away beyond all man's cares into the perpetual cold. The cold crawled through porous layers of wool gnawing with an immobility of fingers and toes as if snuffing distant beacons in the night, one by one. Shivering, Matt huddled deeper into his turtleneck. Finally the sharpness cut through even to the marrow, making a coldness of the inner being. One was powerless against it; one would be crushed under its silent, motionless mass. Matt looked one last time across the stillness and felt the touch of something gentle but alien, not venal, not greedy. The thought of being the commander in the sandbox returned. He'd rather be that person again, now, with the realization his own life had not so much further to go. A man on his deathbed thinks of the sandbox . . . Matt wanted to cry.

'Matt? You on deck?' It was Hollis from below.

Matt stifled his feelings. He had made his commitment. He would rejoin Hollis Wright in the struggle to achieve. For that, after all, was his goal. Even if it killed him.

DAY THREE – FORENOON WATCH –
FIVE BELLS

The late-morning sun rode high and hot. Matt had had enough of the *Scorpion II* and more than enough of Hollis's forced intimacy. He was angry. He and Hollis had retreated below, into Hollis's private stateroom. The three portholes were bolted open, but the heat was oppressive. Matt sat down, put his clenched hands on the polished-onyx writing table between them and faced his adversary.

'Let me give you a solemn goddamn promise, my friend – just so there's no misunderstanding. You keep on with this feint and parry and I'm going to Europe. I'm going straight to the VIP lounge at Heathrow Airport, I don't even have to go into town. And I'll sign a one-page order for fifty European Skybuses. If I do that, you can stick the 17-10 – A and B – up on Fisherman's Wharf and run tours through them.'

The ensuing silence was broken only by the crackle of bugs on the electric-net bug killer. Each report signalled the end of a life with a noise like the sharp snap of a spine.

'You're insane.'

'They'll have a brass band out.'

'You back away from the 17-10 now and you're dead.'

'We've made promises. We've advertised them. I intend to keep them.'

'I didn't like the tone of the note that accompanied your last payment.'

'We've got a good Xerox machine. That note will be stapled to every cheque we send you.' Matt leaned forward grimly. 'It would be in the best interests of both our companies to settle right now on the most workable contract specs.' It hung in the close space like a threat. Matt placed his no-letterhead memo on the table where it lay in conspicuous isolation.

'You're obsessed and you have to watch that. You have to get closer to what's going on, put your nose in the middle of reality.'

'You don't make those goddamn deliveries as specified in pages fifty-six to seventy, I'll block your pipeline.'

'You have no time for Europe.'

'I'll get an injunction. I'll print every page of that contract in *The Wall Street Journal*.'

'You're a one-man shop. That's your problem. You have no depth in management. If you'd had a brain trust, your timing might have been better.'

'I'm tired of your deception.'

'The only difference between you and success is your obstinance: you try to bull your way through, shove the calendar around.'

'We took your word.'

'We warned you not to go headlong with your Big Season promotion, but you couldn't wait.'

'You signed the deal.'

'You had to jam it all in during Matty Aspinwall's lifetime.' Hollis let it fly as though from a bazooka.

'You spell that out,' Matt choked.

'You can't will your way ahead of the reasonable order of things. You might strain yourself.' The implication was clear.

Matt stared across the space at the man who had reached out and grabbed it all. His breath came fast as though by breathing hard he could accelerate the deliveries, the profit expansion, the career leaps that kept him tossing at night.

'You'd better start changing your ads, Matty. Slow things down.'

'We've got three and a half weeks left.'

'You can't force the clock. You've been selling false expectations.'

'I'll print wall posters of Flight Six on fire!' Matt's arms were flexed. Hollis merely smiled at his petulance.

'American companies used to deliver!' Matt shouted.

'Pearl Harbor is dead, you dumb bastard.'

'There's loyalty.'

'There are other loyalties. There always have been.'

Matt started to say something but Hollis knocked his words aside with his fist.

'You launch from Kennedy – but we've got contracts with England! (Hollis punctuated the enumeration with his brown fingers, bursting from his fists one by one) France! (finger) Germany! (finger) Japan! (finger) Saudi Arabia! (finger) Egypt! (finger) Israel! (finger) China! (finger) Soviet Union! (finger) *Count them!* You won't find Buttress in your grade-school geography book . . . because our allegiance is bigger than that.' Hollis enunciated each word deliberately. 'We *have* no boundaries.' He pointed through one porthole towards the Buttress ensign fluttering from the bow. '*That's* the flag. You see,' he hissed, 'we don't care which side buys or which side wins.'

His face was like the edge of a smelted steel ingot close to Matt's. *'We own them all.'*

'Tell that to the Senate!'

'I will – from the private phone in the Oval Office! Next Tuesday!'

Matt pointed to the paper on the table. 'There's still a contract.'

Hollis brushed the page on to the deck with a contemptuous pass of his hand. 'I don't need your contract. The country doesn't need your airline. What do you think I've been trying to tell you for the last three days? *Wake up*, Matty. Save your life. You're just one mouse in an international rat cage.' Hollis's expression was defiant. Matt glared at him. 'Take us to court,' Hollis said. 'Print whatever you want. Your finish line's in sight, Matty.' He could see the rage beginning to alter Matt's features. 'You go broke, we'll have a different paint job on your airplanes overnight. You see, the point is, it makes *no difference* if Air World doesn't fly!'

Matt half stood in helpless fury. For the first time he had the awesome sense of being trapped. His epiglottis worked to choke back bile. His eyes smarted.

Hollis was shouting. 'We supply you but you have to wait for it! Right now you're sucking on an empty tit! The flow is coming, goddammit!'

Matt mustered a comeback with all his strength. 'Yeah, is that so? We feed off you? *We suck you? We don't count?*' His voice was strained, barely, controlled, tears of rage glistening on his face. His eyes had grown white and glassy. With one continuous motion he stood up completely, unzipped his fly and loosed a swollen penis which flopped obscenely on the table between them.

'You suck on this, you bastard!'

Hollis surveyed the display with calculating eyes. Then he grabbed the sides of his chair, pushed it away from the table, stood, turned his back, and slowly walked away.

'You'll be back to suck on this because your loan is dead if we pull out!' shouted Matt in a breaking voice behind him.

The summit meeting had come to an end.

DAY FOUR – MORNING WATCH – EIGHT BELLS

Matt lurched down the steep gangplank alongside his wife, who steadied him around the waist with both hands. She wore a beret and a man's shirt and waistcoat. At the bottom Matt turned and for a moment looked back at *Scorpion II* while his wife rubbed his cheek with her hand in the slow stroking motion she'd use on a baby. Matt didn't seem to notice. He flicked one hand to his cheek unconsciously as though warding off a fly. The Wrights had followed the two of them to the pier and Geselda Wright smiled benignly, waiting for them to go.

'Matty was upset,' Mrs Aspinwall said to her, returning the smile. It was a smile produced by moving only the sides of her mouth, drawing them tight. 'I know he didn't mean all those nasty things he said . . .' She looked back and forth between them. 'You know how we both feel about you.'

The final hugs between the women were stiff. The handshakes between the chairmen were correct.

Hollis didn't smile. His face didn't soften at all. 'You'll be back Matty.'

The Wrights reboarded the yacht.

When they were out of earshot, Matt turned to his wife with a choleric expression and breathed, 'That cocksucker.' It was his benediction.

She squeezed his hand, pulling him away to the open door of the waiting limousine.

* * *

At first Guy wasn't sure if it was the phone or the doorbell. He found himself up on one elbow, opening his eyes in the blackness, and realized it was the phone.

Jesus Christ. It wasn't yet four in the morning. He reached across the nightstand, knocked a cup to the floor and flound the receiver.

'Yeah?'

'It's Natalie. Guy?'

'Yeah. What's going on? Natalie?'

'Are you awake?'

Guy swung his feet on to the floor. 'Hold it.' He hit the light switch. 'I want to be sure this isn't going on in my sleep.' The neighbourhood was absolutely still. 'OK, I'm sitting up. Two feet are on the floor. I'm on the phone and it's four o'clock in the morning.'

'I can't stay on the line. I want you to find a Xerox phone at nine forty-five in the morning your time and call me.' She read him a number with a West Coast area code.

'I don't have a pencil. I need a pencil.' He felt around on the night table and came up with a quarter. He decided to scratch the number into the wood floor. 'Say it again.'

She repeated the number. 'Guy?'

'I'm writing it. What's the time out there?'

'Tell me that you're awake and that you understand me.'

'I'm awake and I understand. I don't know what I understand, though.'

'Listen closely. I've got all the papers you want. I've got the German report.'

Guy stared at the number on the floor. 'You're joking.'

She hung up quietly.

Guy touched the numbers he'd scratched into the varnish – just to be sure the call had occurred.

* * *

Merle Tarpender noted several conspicuous empty chairs at key tables, as he gaveled the resumption of the NTSB hearing on Air World Six to order. Ed Boice had failed to reappear for Buttress and likewise Matt Aspinwall for Air World. Once again FAA Administrator Nick Muskgrave was absent from the FAA table just as before, but perhaps, knowing Nick as he did, that was understandable. The FAA's three lawyers were again in place but this time more wary, less self-assured. The other quite obviously empty chair belonged to Guy Anders, and that surprised him.

Tarpender read into the microphone from his stack of three-by-five cards, perfunctorily reminding the assembly that this was a fact-finding body, not a court of law. That they'd take up just where they'd been forced to adjourn. He sensed Moss becoming agitated at his elbow.

'Is there something you'd like to add, Mr Moss?'

'Yes, Mr Chairman. There is one difference in the continuation of this proceeding. During the short recess our engineering staff had the opportunity to perform a scientific evaluation of the spectrographic analysis introduced by co-pilot Anders and we're convinced it is seriously misleading. A more recent spectrographic analysis received from Buttress flight test has been analysed by us and confirms the weaknesses of the one forced on the board at our last session. So I suggest, Mr Chairman, that we pick up the hearing as though the co-pilot's analysis never existed.'

Moss paused to sip some water, sample the reaction. He was being obsequious, he knew, but he was also gloating inside. Let Anders show up late – for Moss felt sure Anders would arrive. By then there'd be no thunder left. Tarpender was nodding thoughtfully.

'Thank you, Mr Moss – '

'Mr Chairman, with your permission, I'd like to begin by calling Captain W. B. Cosgrove as the first witness.'

Tarpender was relieved to have Moss take charge, and deferred to him.

W. B. Cosgrove approached the witness stand purposefully and pulled the metal chair slightly away from the low table so that he'd have room to cross his legs when he sat. His head was erect, his long veined hands steady as they lay one on top of the other in his lap.

'How long have you been with Air World, Captain?'

'Since nineteen forty-six. Captain since nineteen fifty-one.'

'How much flight experience do you have?'

'Roughly twenty-eight thousand hours. One thousand six hundred twenty-four transatlantic crossings.'

Moss's eyebrows shot up at the precise enumeration of the transatlantic crossings. Cosgrove didn't seem the type –

'How old are you, Captain?'

'Fifty-nine.'

'How much money do you make in a year?'

W. B. Cosgrove recoiled.

'Well?'

'Is this a proper question, Mr Chairman?' someone at the ALPA table shouted.

'If you won't answer that,' Moss interjected, 'then would you tell this board how many days you work in a month.'

Cosgrove began to redden. The freckles stood out on his head.

Moss continued, 'Isn't it true that you are paid approximately one hundred and thirty-five thousand dollars a year for working an average of eleven days a month – '

The sharp crack of a pencil breaking in Tarpender's hands stopped Moss. There was a flurry at the head table as Tarpender shoved a note towards Moss telling him to change his tack. Moss glanced at the note without altering his expression, then peeled the first two sheets from his yellow pad.

'Captain, I'd like to get right to the events of the night you were in command of the flight in question.'

W. B. waited wordlessly.

'Were you in contact with Buttress?'

'We were.'

'And that was because you didn't know your own procedures and needed help – was it not?'

Cosgrove raised his hand. 'You do yourself a disservice, Mr Moss. We were having problems not mentioned in any flight manual or on-board information system.'

'Then it's obvious to me, sir, you don't know your own book.'

Cosgrove didn't flinch. Someone at the ALPA table made a note.

'What did Buttress tell you precisely, Captain Cosgrove?' Moss sneered.

'They weren't much use to us. They wanted some turns, some manoeuvres. Not practical under the circumstances. Mostly they came in garbled.'

Moss flipped a page of his pad. 'In reconstructing the events of that flight, I want you to tell this board why you didn't reset all the electric and hydraulic trim system and pitch mode circuit breakers!'

W.B. stared at Moss. 'That takes time,' he said finally. 'What would it have gained? We didn't want to interrupt circuits that were working for us. Besides – we were busy.'

'Why didn't you deselect the alpha-sensitive AFCS pitch mode, and outerloop functions like altitude acquisition and altitude hold?' Moss was flipping the pages of his pad.

W.B. looked incredulous. Then, with the sonorous quality of a father whose patience has been tried, he said, 'They weren't engaged to begin with! I was flying the ship manually – or trying to!'

305

Moss didn't acknowledge the answer and read off the next question. 'Why didn't you monitor the stabilizer setting on the instrument panel or try to engage the alternate electric trim motors – '

'Of course we monitored!' W.B. had grabbed the edge of the table and seemed about to come out of his chair. 'It wasn't a trim problem; it was a basic control problem!'

Moss didn't look up but continued to read from his pad. 'Tell this board, Captain, why you didn't select hydraulic override by engaging the air-driven hydraulic pumps on the backup pneumatic system off the number two and three engine bleeds?'

'I repeat to you, sir, it didn't appear to be a hydraulic problem. Our pressures were steady – '

'"*Appear* to be"!' Moss looked away from his pad with a scowl of triumph. To his right he saw that Tarpender was watching with curiosity. 'Captain, we're here to determine what *was*, not what appeared to be.' Moss flipped over one more page of his pad and with his lips projected guppylike towards the mike but with his eyes lowered, refastened on to the written question, he spoke loudly, 'Kindly tell this board why you failed to go through the manual trim reversion checklist as specified in the alternate operating procedures of the FAA-approved manual you are required to carry aboard at all times!'

'Jesus Christ, that procedure takes twenty-five minutes to do in the best of conditions. I had the aeroplane on the ground in fifteen – '

'Aren't you required to demonstrate proficiency in that procedure in the simulator during periodic refresher training?'

Cosgrove was leaning forward but his set features had regained the odd calm of a man able to maintain his dignity after being slapped across the face. Then, to the consternation of the gathered assembly, W. B. Cosgrove slowly stood. Even Moss fell hushed before the tall presence of the veteran captain. A flashbulb popped, then another. Cosgrove waited. Tarpender hid his face in his hands. An attorney sitting next to Tarpender coughed and began to stammer something that sounded like an apology. His voice was choked. W.B. cut him off.

'I want to say I appreciate the invitation you have given me to come down and to testify. In fact, I thought this could be an important hearing and I looked forward to an answer or two for what we went through. I have now witnessed two sessions of this particular investigation, and I want to remind you all that I have not been a critic of this aeroplane. But if you have to defend it this hard, maybe you got something to hide.' The lawyer cringed with anguish as the old man spoke. 'Seems to me,' W.B. continued, 'you people up at that table have made a lot of noise about a crew that managed to save the lives of four hundred and twenty-one passengers.' Applause was incipient but W.B. would have none of it. 'And how well I know you all got the power to take away my pilot's licence. Or you can stick some wet-eared gummint inspector into my cockpit jump seat with a big black notebook and a probe up my butt. But if you think either of these is the right answer, I just hope you're mighty sure. Not for my sake, 'cause I'm going to be outta there before long. And 'cause I got plenty of other things to do – like my farm – which I like almost as much as flyin'.' He paused and slowly looked around the room. 'But for the sake of a flight that has not yet left the ground.'

The solemn hush of a church filled the chamber. W.B. looked back at Moss. His expression was as bland as that of a pope. 'Now, if you don't mind – I don't care to stay any longer.'

In the shambles of the moment, Tarpender leaned to Moss and whispered sharply, 'We're going to have to get some control back. From here on, I want you to subpoena these sonsofbitches. Then let's see who walks out.' He paused. 'And you'd also better make sure your homework's done.'

'What do you mean?'

'You better get up to the Buttress computer facility in Connecticut and find out just how clean that computer is.'

11

The salesman at the Xerox office told Guy his request to receive a single document by phone from the Coast could be handled as walk-in business at the midtown office, and now, at quarter to ten in the morning (six forty-five, LA time) Guy stood next to the telecopier waiting for Natalie to pick up the phone. He was relieved when the familiar huskiness of her voice came on the line.

'You were awake after all,' she said.

'Ever since.'

'I'm all set on this end,' she declared calmly. 'But there's a lot; I don't know if I can send it all.'

Then the human sounds were gone. Guy slipped the receiver into the special receptacle and imagined Natalie, alone in the early morning, handing the guts of her company away. Soon the first page was clear and Guy held it up. There was no letterhead. It was merely dated and headed:

TRANSLATION OF THE GERMAN-INDUSTRY REPORT
SUBJECT: BUTTRESS AEROSPACE FLY-BY-WIRE CONTROL SYSTEM EVA-
LUATION
      1. F-19 FREE WORLD ACTIVE-CONTROLS FIGHTER, THIRD
      EVALUATION
      2. 17-10 ANALYSIS

Guy scanned down the neatly indented, double-spaced introductory paragraph, noting it was in appropriately conservative governmentese style. Though primed for surprise, he was completely startled by the following words:

Buttress design philosophy for both the F-19 and the 17-10 is considered to be *premature* . . . It is strongly recommended that the state airline Deutsche Luftgesellschaft AG re-evaluate its design specifications for the Buttress 17-10 civil transports on an urgent basis . . . Supporting discussion follows. Specific recommendations concerning the 17-10 appear after the F-19 analysis . . .

Guy stared at the words for almost a full minute. Two more pages had dropped free. He placed the page he was holding facedown in the open manila folder on the desk beside him and grabbed the next sheet.

Each F-19 uses 4,987 pounds of graphite-epoxy which represents 41% of its total structural weight. If built entirely of metal, the aeroplane would be 2,432 pounds heavier . . . Although the use of very large graphite-epoxy pieces in both primary and auxiliary structures represents a 20% saving in structural weight, a 46% saving in part count, and a 53% saving in recurring cost, there is considerable concern over *safety* . . .

Guy threw the page in the folder and grabbed the next sheet from the tray. His eyes travelled down to the second paragraph:

Luftwaffe flight trails have established serious problems with the graphite-epoxy composite structure. These are:
1. Surface erosion
2. Inadequate lightning strike protection . . .

The words scalded Guy. The 17-10 also used graphite-epoxy, especially in the tail, but up to now, no one at Air World had done anything but praise the new space-age material. His eyes returned to the page:

3. Moisture absorption into the material, which changes its chemistry and degrades its mechanical properties. This has resulted in occasional in-flight breakages . . .
4. Release of free fibres from the material into the local environment. This poses a *severe hazard* to on-board electronic computers due to the high electrical conductivity of the microscopic fibres, and is discussed in detail elsewhere in this report . . .

Guy reread the last sentence, amazed that he was looking at it in print. The next sheet lay waiting . . . and suddenly Guy knew he was staring straight at classified data:

The F-19 flight-control system main computer together with four regional computers is designed to meet the most stringent requirements of military specification MIL-9858C using microcoded bit slice microprocessors and programmable logic arrays, enabling direct control of processor data paths . . . The main computer is capable of *20 million operations per second* . . .

Guy whistled out loud. He'd read the rest later; he already saw the heading on the next page: ELECTRONIC CORRUPTION. Sudden recollection of the professor in England flooded back, the suspicion that *electronic corruption* had to be at the source of his own close call at Kennedy. The subhead read: EXTERNALLY INDUCED ELECTRONIC CORRUPTION. He read:

Sources of externally induced electronic corruption likely to disrupt operation of the flight-control system include:
1. Lightning strike.
2. Outside radiation, such as would be associated with the near-term effects of nuclear blast. The radiation effects caused by intense sunspot activity have been considered but are deemed inconsequential at this time.
3. Hostile electronic jamming. This is still under *intense evaluation* . . .

310

It was now clear to Guy that Ed Boice had lied at the hearing. The problem of electronic corruption had not been solved after all!

On the West Coast Fenton Riddick had awakened early and wondered why Natalie was nowhere in the duplex apartment. Squinting in the semidarkness, he'd got up and checked the downstairs kitchen and the bathrooms. Puzzled, he'd driven to the plant. And now, as he saw her on the fourth floor, her back to him, feeding pages into the Xerox telecopier, he understood.

In New York the next heading Guy saw was INTERNALLY INDUCED ELECTRONIC CORRUPTION and the paragraph underneath read:

Sources of internally induced electronic corruption likely to disrupt operation of the flight-control system include:
1. Aeroelastic interaction.
2. Free fibres released from the aeroplane's graphite-epoxy composite structural material as the result of fatigue, erosion, impact, or fire.

The release of free fibres is considered to be the greatest source of hazard at this time. Investigations continue in conjunction with recently experienced progressive failures of the fly-by-wire control system which have resulted in the loss of sixteen F-19 aeroplanes and the deaths of nine test pilots. The overall causal factors in these incidents is not well understood as of this date. Despite the claim made

The next sheet had not been released into the tray. It seemed overdue; the copy machine had stopped. Guy pulled the page free with a gentle tug. Only the first few lines had been printed:

by Buttress that fibre optics improved the system's invulnerability to electronic corruption, in at least one crash the release of free fibres from the aeroplane's composite structure into the local environment was determined to be specifically

311

The rest of the sheet was blank.

Guy waited.

Good God, they had Hollis Wright on a scaffold!

The copy machine remained silent. Puzzled, Guy considered picking up the phone.

'What's going on?' he asked the attendant.

'Other side hung up,' he shrugged.

Guy stared at the slot. 'No way . . .' He checked the number and redialled. As he waited for the reconnect he rifled through the pages in his manilla folder. He wanted to cheer, he felt like a sweepstakes winner trying not to react in public. The wall clock told him the NTSB hearing would be well under way. He smiled. He'd have it closed down before lunch! Then with a shock he realized that without the Buttress letterhead no one would ever believe it was valid.

At last someone picked up the ringing West Coast phone. He heard a male voice. Immediately he was suspicious.

'I was disconnected,' he said simply.

'Who's this?' came the metallic reply.

'Isn't this . . . ?'

Silence ensued. Both men listened through it. Guy tried to pick up the background – some sound of Natalie.

'Who am I talking to?' Guy knew his question was futile.

The distant phone clicked dead.

When the secretary told FAA Administrator Nick Muskgrave that Hollis Wright of Buttress had attempted to reach him, Muskgrave felt a swell of anxiety. The messages that inevitably awaited his return from lunch often panicked him and it took increasing amounts of courage to face them. Recently the feeling of being overwhelmed had become worse and Nick had increased his intake by an extra half pint to get through the afternoons. And now even the press was after him – especially a certain syndicated columnist who had alluded to 'handshakes behind the barn' as being the most plausible explanation for unresponsiveness and insensitivity within the FAA. The writer had been discounted for not being more specific, but at this point in time Muskgrave didn't want to hear from Hollis. He had been advised by Fenton Riddick that certain things were being changed on the 17-10 and he didn't understand what they were. Moreover he'd become convinced that his phone was tapped even though the electronic sweeps were clean. He turned slowly through volume three of the original 17-10 certification, which ran close to nine hundred pages, and waited for Hollis to come on the line, swallowing hard when he heard Hollis in the desk speaker.

'Glad you called back, Nicholas.'

Muskgrave swivelled in his chair and shut his eyes. 'I understand there are changes in the works. I haven't been copied in on them.'

'That's what I wanted to talk to you about,' said Hollis. 'We're not going to have time to go through the ritual, so you're going to have to trust us.'

'I've always trusted you, Hollis, and right now I'm looking through the certification. It's open on my desk. Maybe we weren't thorough enough if you're making changes.'

'I'm not sure I understand that.'

'We all got our necks on the block here. I want to know what's going on.'

'We have no secrets from each other, Nick. But this time I want you to leave it alone. We'll do it our own way.'

'If you're making changes we may have to make them mandatory.'

There was a palpable delay before Hollis responded. 'I don't agree with that and I'm sure you wouldn't either if we could talk face to face. I'm thinking of Matty Aspinwall and what that kind of publicity would do to him.'

'Hollis, we never had any trouble . . . I want to know what the hell you people are up to.'

'If it were major we'd have come to you. It's an improvement, something we planned for the 17-10B. We're putting it on the A, that's all.'

'If you're horseshitting me, Hollis, then for God's sake let me in on it now.'

'I'll personally send a message describing the change by courier tonight.'

'OK, but I'm relying on you.'

'Get some sleep.'

'I'll pass on whatever you've got to my northwest region man, Devlin. He's a good boy.'

'Say hello to the kids, huh? . . . Oh, and by the way, we want you to know we're proud of how you're doing.'

'Hollis?'

'We're all pleased you're off the wet lunch.'

'What?'

'Keep your bottom drawer locked.'

It was approaching ten-thirty and the meeting at Intercarrier Life and Casualty was well under way, a high-level meeting with men from several countries in attendance. The director from Belgium sat between the technical man at the head of the table and the two Lloyd's directors from London on his left. Suddenly the door burst open and the chairman, carrying a thick folder, strode in.

'Sorry to break in on you.' The chairman's manner was solicitous as though he should have asked permission to join them. 'There's something I need to bring to your attention.' He held a folder aloft, then handed it to the senior man present. 'It's the spectrographic analysis of the Air World Six cockpit voice tape done by the British. If what I've read here is true – even if we dismiss half on the grounds of European vested interest – there's a hull loss of seventy million waiting for us. And if that machine happens to be carrying a convention of doctors, a whole planeload of earning power, we can multiply that by a factor of twenty. Open-ended if it falls into a city.'

The chairman studied each of their faces in turn.

'Now, then, that's just part one,' he continued. 'What I'm about to say must not leave this room.' He gestured to a young man sitting in his shirt sleeves. 'Shut that window.' To a man next to him he said, 'Pull the phone connection out of the wall.' The men complied and sat down. A hush fell around the table. Finally the chairman spoke. 'I refer you to a localized power blackout at Cedarhurst, Long Island, that occurred shortly after Air World Six made its approach into Kennedy. Cedarhurst lies in a straight line with the final approach course to runway three one left.' He leaned forward. 'We have reason to believe that this blackout and the approach of the 17-10 when it was on fire are connected.' He waited for the reaction to subside and held up one hand to stop incipient questions. 'When I know more, you'll know more. But I want you to be aware of it, because the implications could be very serious for us. Consider a transport catching fire over the Pentagon – or move the scenario over a nuclear power station and write your own ending. The way I see it, this puts us ass-deep in lawsuit country. And we're not talking about repainting a dinged-up wing tip. We could very possibly be talking about suits to cover losses of productivity from entire industries hit by blackouts. We're talking about hundreds, maybe thousands, of businesses going down as the consequence of a single event.'

The chairman waited. The silence attested to the consensus in the room.

'That's a lot of premiums, boys.'

* * *

315

The small elevator took Hollis down to the sub-basement of the White House, where the President had installed his own woodworking shop. Whenever he could, but particularly after lunch, the President would go downstairs to revitalize an antique or to work on one of his wood carvings. It was the way he relaxed and, as he confided to his closest aides, it was also the way he managed to keep in touch with what he termed the more basic values of life. Hollis was escorted past a uniformed guard into a shiny grey corridor which opened on to a row of offices. All were closed except the one at the end. As they approached, the sound of a power tool could be heard there.

'The President is always downstairs at this time of day,' said the escort. 'I don't think the Joint Chiefs could make him change that.'

The President didn't look up when Hollis entered. He was bent over his lathe in deep concentration. The escort backed out deferentially and Hollis stood inside the doorway, watching, for almost a full minute. Finally the President switched off the tool and looked up. Without shaking hands he reached for the unfinished back of a wooden chair. It was of superb quality. 'I'm making a set of two for the Lincoln Room. How do you like it?'

Hollis held the ornate assembly for a moment and handed it back to the President, who carefully placed it to one side. Then the President reached into a drawer. 'Here, my friend, you'd better wear these goggles.'

Hollis brushed them aside.

The lathe spun again, sending streams of sawdust into the close, oil-odoured atmosphere.

'Is this what our taxpayers pay for?'

'Don't get too indignant, Mr Chairman. You haven't paid a cent of tax in six years. These chairs will please the tourists, the connoisseurs – and me.'

'I didn't think you'd have the time.'

'I didn't think so either until I took a look at my

priorities. It's amazing how many solutions you can find in polishing the grain on one of these pieces. What's on your mind?'

'You've been losing points in the poll.'

'How'd I do last week? Am I still behind on NBC?' The President laughed as he bent to sight along the axis of the piece he was finishing, his expression hidden by the bulbous goggles he wore. It made Hollis uncomfortable not to be able to judge the reaction to the words he spoke.

'It's time we got serious about your re-election,' he said impatiently.

'You didn't come here to talk about the election.'

'Everyone thinks you're doing a fine job. Your campaign for national honour and brotherly love is first rate and we're proud of you for making that stand.'

'Cut the preamble, Hollis. Ninety per cent of the people who come to see me wear me out with preambles. Here, hold this.' Hollis was handed the cut-off end of a dowel. 'Use your time more wisely. You came to talk about the 17-10 and, time permitting, the F-19.' The President was stooped over the lathe, neck stretched towards the whirring piece of wood. The chisel bit. Chips flew. Hollis felt them sting his cheek. Instinctively he blinked and spun his head.

'Go on, Hollis.'

'I need to borrow the prestige of the presidency.'

The President halted the lathe and wiped the sawdust from his goggles. 'The prestige of the presidency is not for loan.'

'It's all coming to a head. I can't say I'm really concerned but we have to walk into the loan hearing with the trump hand.' Hollis hadn't meant to sound so alarmed. He swallowed and tried to control his voice, but the high-voltage pressure at the plant had begun to seep into his office, even – despite his attempts to keep it in perspective – into his sleep. His best troops were starting

317

to show shortfalls in performance, now, on the eve of their toughest battle. Almost complete 17-10s were mired at their berths on the assembly line awaiting last-minute installations, most particularly the beefed-up actuator fix being put together by Ed Boice's people. 'I don't think we want to underestimate the other fellow,' Hollis said more evenly. Again the blade caught the edge of the wood sending a thick veil of dust into the air between them.

'What?'

'I said I'm not really concerned!'

'OK!'

'Our plant is running eighteen hours a day!'

'What?'

'Turn that goddamn thing off!'

The President squeezed the switch.

'We can't afford to have the plane grounded!' Hollis said too loudly.

'Be specific.' The President readjusted the piece of wood in the lathe. Hollis resisted an urge to spin the President around.

'I came here because a man has to rely on certain – expectations.' The President noticed that Hollis's voice had a husky, cracked quality. 'We've got an annual report due out any day loaded with deficit because of all the money *we* poured into fly-by-wire. Four billion five to recover and eight years riding on the outcome of that hearing. No man wants to show up for that without having a pretty good idea of the outcome.'

'I thought Al Searington provided you with some cover.'

'The man is burned out. He wants to go home to Virginia where his wife bottles rhubarb and salute the flag every morning.' Hollis coughed.

'If Al turned you down, he had no choice.'

'I want you to move the loan hearing up by two weeks,' Hollis said.

318

'It's not your custom to be this nervous.'

'The Germans have come up with a report that could be damaging.'

'So I've heard.'

'It's a broadside. Wild stuff. Accuses us of everything from short weight to incest.'

'And how do you plead?'

'The British and French want Bonn to get behind the Skybus. The Germans are nitpicking us on commas.'

'And you want me to tell them to cut it out.'

'Better than that.' Hollis's words got stuck in his throat. He grumbled as if to clear away some phlegm but the nervous catch was obvious to both of them. 'I want Bonn to buy twenty-five additional 17-10s and I want them to do it by the end of the week.'

The President could not recall seeing Hollis so agitated before. He pushed his goggles back on the top of his head, yellow headlamps in his thick hair, tousled like a boy's. A delicate haze of sawdust rode the fringes of his temples. 'Well, hell, we can do that with a phone call! Let's see, that's probably close to a billion and a half dollars. They'll be only too happy to part with that on my say-so!'

'They buy now or we starve them on missiles. Maybe pull a few troops out. I don't care if they cancel that order the day after the hearings close. They can do whatever they want with it. But at least the loan will have some accounts-receivable support. Not only will we be backed by the US Treasury but by a billion-plus-dollar order from the Fatherland.'

'No dice, Hollis.'

Hollis stood nonplussed, frowning at the President. 'Goddammit, I have a right to walk out of here today knowing that the loan is secure.' His words were beginning to quake with irritation.

'I'm not sure you have that right,' the President said quietly.

'I don't want to have an argument here.'

'There's no need to. My dear friend, you ought to know how I've become concerned about other things. I've become genuinely concerned about the little guy.' The President stopped and stroked the piece of wood on the lathe and savoured the words. 'The little man.' And he was smiling.

'I want you to go to the Germans.'

'You're mixing free enterprise with foreign affairs.'

'Don't you turn holy on me! We *are* foreign affairs! I'm not suggesting anything new!'

The President pulled his goggles down and snapped on the lathe. 'We've gone the distance on the 17-10. We bought Air Force One from you and publicized it, gave you the presidential seal. We sold a lot of F-19s for you, took your quality on faith. So don't come around here as though you're owed something.'

Carefully he eased the chisel up to the slowly spinning wood, conscious of Hollis's discomfiture behind him. 'How much do you care about what you turn out? I know how your wallet pines away, but I'm talking about Hollis Wright, the man.' The lathe shone, the wheels on its ends were ringed with little beads of light. The President removed the piece of wood from its chucks, held it at arm's length, turning and assessing it along all its edges. Then he brought it closer, gave it a light stroke with his hand to flick away some clinging bits of sawdust, and held it out for Hollis to see. It was one of the posts for the chairback. The intricate ropelike pattern that wound around its length was perfect. 'That's craftsmanship. Are you into *craftsmanship?*'

'Your lease may not be renewed.'

'I can accept that. But this presidency is not for sale.'

'Not for sale?' Hollis was shouting. 'You don't have a fingernail left that belongs to you! We chose you, briefed you, bought you a bigger campaign than a goddamn new detergent, and you're not for sale?'

The President's tone was soft and controlled. 'A man's perspective changes in this office. After the clawing to get here stops, a man will listen to himself, and for the first time since childhood, I've had a chance to listen.'

'And what have you heard?'

'Every man writes his own profile in critical times. So I'm doubly grateful to you because you've given me two opportunities. First, you helped put me here, that's true. And now you've given me the chance to find out who I am and I'm not going to miss out on that!'

'There's no way you can hide from your responsibilities down here.'

'Hollis, suppose we went ahead and twisted the German arm and they bought twenty-five more of your machines. Do we guarantee their payments, too?'

'You know the answer to that! It need never come up! They can renege the moment the loan is extended!'

'Remarkable. You're remarkable. You company fellows are always the first to scream against social welfare. Well, what do you think you are? You're nothing more than a goddamn vagrant with a king-sized tin cup in your hand waiting for the working taxpayer to keep you afloat!'

'Our condition is temporary.'

'Every debt-ridden rummy on skid row will tell you his condition is temporary! He's only there between seasons! You were granted the loan once and you're in deeper now than you were before!'

'We're one company competing against the combined efforts of several countries!'

'I can name sixteen countries that have smaller budgets than you do.'

'We're the first with breakthrough technology in the West!'

'Don't delude yourself, Mr Chairman. The F-19 is a

321

piece of shit. You know it and I know it. It's only a matter of time before it blows up in our face.'

'I'm asking for your help.'

'You've had my help.'

'It's not enough.'

'The country has other priorities.'

Hollis's fingers tightened around the dowel in his hand.

'Good day, Hollis.' The President faced Hollis. His neck was flushed.

'We're going to miss you and the First Lady . . . but we have our priorities, too.'

'Get out.'

Dick Miller had already put in an hour at his computer graphics console, seated before a large video screen on which his new actuator grew in an outline picture composed of slightly jagged green lines. As he moved knobs on the keyboard below the screen, the picture jumped through a contortion as though an invisible hand behind the tube were turning it from side to side. Every once in a while Dick touched the screen with a light pen. The tip was bright with an internal luminosity, and when it touched the televised image, he could examine a certain cross section of the pictured actuator or cause it to cycle back and forth, and see instantly in the row of readouts projected beside the screen the figure's length, volume, area, deflection under load and other factors. He worked slowly, struggling to pull his attention together. The computer would store the geometry of whatever shape was depicted, and when Dick had decided on the final form, the stored information would be data-linked by direct communication to the computers which operated the automatic machine tools that shaped and fashioned the finished pieces from raw blanks of metal.

He leaned back and closed his eyes, shutting out the

screen which glowed impassively before him, its thin lines jiggling every so often, a dozing cat waiting to be called. Dick was conscious only of the sound of rain outside, the delicate crescendo of rain patter in his ears while he blanked out the dull white room with his eyelids. The rising-and-falling sensation of the sound was that of an engine and he was floating, riding on the strength of it in his reverie towards a glowing spot far away when Vern Locker intruded.

'It's a crock, isn't it?'

Miller hauled himself to sit up straight and prepare for the demands the younger man would impose. He waited for a long time before speaking. 'How you doing, Vern?'

Vern placed his coffee on the file cabinet by the blackboard and leaned against the wall, hands buried in his pockets. 'How's it coming?'

'We're on the last leg.' Dick nodded towards the screen.

Vern slouched forward and peered at the picture. 'Looks a little like putting a splint on a runny nose.'

'Well, it may not be ideal but it's not a bad solution. We've gone to a tougher piece here in the tail.' He stared at the screen. 'A tougher ram to control the elevators. A tougher servo to take more pressure. Put together they could handle an earthquake.'

Vern studied Miller's absent expression. Then he said, very gently, 'I think a man I know called Dick Miller could shoot that argument down – if he wanted to.'

Dick turned and stared at him as if Locker had kicked sand in his face. Vern became alarmed by the vacant cast to Dick's misfocused eyes. The only sound was the soft slap of rain pelting the windowpane. Finally Dick seemed to rouse himself. He turned back with the frown of a man just waking from a nap in the sun and peering at a figure blocking the sun from above, squinting to recognize him . . . slowly he shifted towards the video console

323

again, where the waiting cat dozed with half-open eyes, regarding them both through nervous lids.

'Here it is now,' he said, speaking to himself. 'Ready for product assurance – ready for *hardware*.'

'You're bullshitting yourself, Dick –'

'It's – it's not bullshit, Vern.' There was a trapped desperation to the pleading in his eyes. 'The aeroplane's elastic behaviour is completely accounted for . . . We made a dynamic analysis of all the cross-coupling derivatives . . . hundreds of simulations . . . we worked *eight* years . . .' Dick suddenly turned full on Vern, his open hands out, his face tragic. He was struggling to say something but the words were choked. Vern had the impression of seeing a man disappearing beneath the sea.

12

Guy saw the trumpet lying on a fanlike display of sheet music in the window of the guitar shop of Forty-fifth Street. It was a beautiful silver Besson, a jewel of a horn which produced a gentle, rounded tone, sweet yet distinct and pure and so he bought it to replace the trumpet that had lain broken in his son's room.

It was almost dark when he pulled into the driveway and shut the engine. The neighbourhood was calm. A TV set was on next door. Blue light could be seen flickering in long fingers across the neighbour's ceiling. Guy stuck the present under his arm and let himself in through the back door, a habit he'd got into ever since the press had set siege to the front of the house. Anja was in the study perched cross-legged on the divan, surrounded by stacks of books, trying to finish the page she was on. The white extension phone lay next to her.

'There's been a car circling the block.'

Guy set the package down and pulled his tie free. He took a glass and poured himself two fingers of scotch. 'What kind of car?'

'A Plymouth, I think.'

'How do you know it was circling?'

'It had two men in it. I saw them first about five. The third time I got suspicious so I brought the extension in here. I think it stopped about a half hour ago.'

'Where's Jamie?'

'Upstairs.'

Guy shut off the light and opened the front drapes. Except for a neighbour lugging an attaché case home, the street was deserted. 'Could have been anything.'

'But it wasn't anything.' Again Anja pictured what Jasovak had told her about the maid who had reached outside for the bottle of milk. 'To some people, death is just another strategy,' she said.

Guy sensed the chill that overcame her as she spoke. He looked out the window, shading his eyes to block the dim light from the hall. 'Buttress isn't Murder, Inc.' He said it more to hear how it sounded than out of conviction. 'A fellow named Hollis Wright runs it, not the mob.'

Anja placed the book aside and unfolded her legs. 'Whether it's animals with broken noses or close-shaven executives in plastic shoes, the result's the same. The only difference is the executives have public-relations people.'

Guy let the drapery fall and sat down. 'I think it might be a good idea if you and Jamie left for a while.' He had a vision of them sitting safely deep in a forest somewhere.

'Why should we?'

'Did they stop to look at the house?'

'Only once. They were waiting for something.'

'Then they left.'

'And came back.' Anja turned the page of her book. 'I wonder why Ben never used this. Did you know that Buttress has an economic right to kill passengers?' Guy checked her expression. 'There's a law right here – if you read it slowly – that allows a certain number of passengers to die at any time at all, only it says nothing about whether the people who wrote this ever asked the passengers if they wanted to go along with it. So I wonder who wrote it.'

'It doesn't mention Buttress, does it?' Guy was distracted.

'No, but it's the blanket licence that Mr Boice was referring to at the hearing. He called it "acceptable risk" – not his risk, mind you, but my risk which he finds acceptable.'

'There are lawyers who can probably argue for that,' Guy said absently.

'Only from the safety of their living rooms.'

The headlights of a car hit the drapes and seemed to hold, then moved on and disappeared.

'Suppose I go around and see who that is?'

'It wasn't the same sound.'

They sat like that on the divan in the shadows, their voices subdued. Guy swallowed the rest of the scotch.

'It's like war, isn't it, all this?' she said. 'Lights out, like the Irish against the British, a blackout somewhere . . . What's in the package?'

'Something for Jamie.'

'He and I had a fight today.'

'About what?'

'I tried to get him to move back downstairs to his room. I tried to use my influence.'

'What happened?'

'I didn't have enough influence. He's locked himself in.'

'Why the hell does everyone have to be at war?' His voice sounded distant.

'What you need is an island. You ought to look through my brochures, pick somewhere with soft white sand and no cars or telephones.'

Guy paused. 'I had two islands once,' he said wistfully, 'and not that long ago . . .' The comment interested her. 'One, right here . . .' The words trailed off. 'The other . . . well, flying used to be the other . . . as pure as your white sands. And now we're all in the trenches.'

It wasn't so much what he said but how he said it. It was a dimension she hadn't seen in him before, and it moved her.

Guy wrestled the aluminium ladder off its pegs in the garage and toted it to the side of the house. Fully extended, it allowed him to look out over much of the surrounding neighbourhood. From a position even with the second floor he could see a kid on a moped two blocks away, but there was no one else in sight. He climbed to the dormer facing his son, who was sitting on his father's old military footlocker scraping the white stencilled letters off with a key. The window was held firmly ajar by nails Guy had put in from the inside for safety.

Balancing gingerly on the swaying aluminium, he leaned across the sill. 'Hi, I was passing by and I thought if you had nothing to do, we could shoot the breeze. I heard you had a fight.'

Jamie frowned.

'Listen, Jamie, why'n't we talk about it? Do you want to tell me what she did?' Guy had to adjust his stance to prevent one foot from going to sleep on the rung and to get a better grip on the windowsill. 'Would you come over by the window?'

The child didn't answer.

From his improved vantage, Guy tried to pry the nails on the inside of the frame loose so he could raise the window but he couldn't get enough leverage. 'Hey, sport, give me a hand here before this ladder takes a walk.'

Jamie watched his father but didn't get up.

Guy recognized his own seriousness in the familiar

327

gravity beneath the soft blond brow. 'What happened between you two?'

The boy shook his head. 'It's not important.'

'Hell, yes it is.'

Jamie busied himself with a loose shoelace.

'It's important to me . . . Did she beat you? You getting enough to eat? Tell me.'

'No.'

'Try.'

His son wiped the side of his eye and Guy watched him struggle to stifle the moan building in his throat.

'Come on, Jamie.' Guy's tone was gentle. 'It must hurt to try to do everything by yourself up here . . .' He leaned across the sill, on tiptoes, ignoring the ladder's sway, thrusting his head into the room.

The boy faced him and wiped his nose on the shoulder of his T-shirt. He took a deep breath and held it and wiped the other side of his face.

'Let it go,' Guy urged.

The boy struggled. He looked intently at the floor, hoping that the coming moment wouldn't happen. The words exploded with a terrible pain.

'I miss Mother.' His voice shook loose, he let the anguish fill his throat as the sobs came.

Guy felt the sweat on his neck being dried by the breeze and he stood on the ladder peering through the small open space, unable to reach in. His mind groped and his stomach churned and softly he offered, 'It's been pretty rough without her, hasn't it?' He felt the pain when he said it but it came out not as sympathy but as a statement of fact. He faced away towards the neighbourhood searching for something else to say. The terrible irony was that the boy's mother would have known precisely how to handle it. Guy put his face close to the window. 'Jamie, open the window for me, will you?' Guy grabbed helplessly on to the dormer. 'Son, listen, I'm

328

going to rip this goddamn window out because I love you.'

Jamie was looking down at his smeared shirt.

'Jamie, I loved your mom when I hadn't met her yet and when we were introduced the first time, we talked about you and we hadn't met you yet. You see, a lot of times I don't want to look at the bridge down at the pond over there because that's the way she used to come home. Can you hear me? And once, when we had an argument – she took a walk by herself out there and she looked very small and I felt like a creep and I went out and told her I was and she laughed.' Guy looked down at the front of the lawn, struggling to remember. 'She used to stand in the front here in the evening working on her flowers until it got too dark because she knew there wasn't much time left. She planted most of those fir trees over there and when she wasn't too strong any more, she used to take hikes with you between the trees and you insisted on wearing her orange backpack and she told you you were doing miles.' Guy was smiling but there were tears in his eyes. 'And you weren't around but when she left for the last time to go to the hospital, as we were crossing the bridge out there in the car, she asked me to stop and she looked back at the house and she waved at it.' Guy had to stop to bite his lip. 'Oh, my God, kid, huh? You see, Jamie, I loved her very much. We should have moved but I didn't want to say goodbye.'

The breeze rustled the leaves behind him and Jamie stood staring at him. Guy smiled back through his wet eyes. 'What the hell are we doing talking like this? We're relatives!'

Jamie wiped his nose. 'Anja isn't one. She's not a relative.'

'No, she isn't.'

'I want her to leave. You can tell her. She'd listen to you. She can be gone by morning. I know how to cook. All you have to do is leave me enough cans and stuff when you're not here.'

'And what about the nights? What would we do about the nights?'

'I'd leave the TV on and wherever you were we could talk to each other on the phone. You wouldn't be disappointed.'

'Sure, we could do that,' Guy said, groping for an answer. 'But there's a dumb law you can't do it on your own till you're twelve.'

'Nobody'd have to know.'

Guy pulled the still-wrapped trumpet from his belt and placed it on the cabinet inside the window. 'This plays at least five tunes the first week, and you know, another five the week after that. All it needs is some kid to blow into it.' Guy took it out of its felt sack and set it down on its bell. It gleamed in the light. 'Go on, take a look at it.'

Jamie wiped his face and came closer. He picked it up and seemed about to consider it. But he merely jutted his lip and slipped the horn back into the felt. He hiccupped and sighed unevenly. 'I don't want it.'

Guy's attention was distracted by a dull-brown Plymouth slowly heading up the block. As it passed a streetlamp, he could see two men in the front. His voice was hoarse. 'Good night, Jamie.' He spoke gently but he was angry now, angry with how life had so unpredictably interfered with him, angry with the medical profession that hadn't been able to do anything to save his wife, angry with himself for having believed for so many years in the Fourth-of-July verities and the commencement speeches of his high school and college graduations.

He watched the stripped-down Plymouth through the trees as it came to a stop below and noiselessly he backed down the thin rungs. His fury rose at having been used for target practice before and now it had come to his front door. Head pounding, he knew he had to put an end to it. He was convinced at that moment that he could bend the aluminium ladder with his hands and he knew, too, that

330

he could tear the doors off that car, drag the two men outside and overwhelm them. He jumped away from the last few rungs, shoved a cluster of branches aside and headed directly for the front of the car. Suddenly, his rage was set adrift. The two men lounging on the front seat identified themselves as cops. One of them flicked the map light on and read from a sheet of scribbled notes. 'Your name Anders?'

'Yes, that's right.'

'We've been asked to keep an eye on your place,' said the man reading from the paper. 'You're a pilot with Air World out of Kennedy International? And you live at this address?'

Guy kept his distance from the car door. 'Right so far.'

'You know about any threats on your life, Mr Anders?' The cop folded the paper weightily and tucked it into his inside coat pocket. His question was supposed to be friendly but came out as though he had asked, 'You have any idea how fast you were going?'

Guy didn't know how much they knew and there was something that suggested they might not be cops at all. If they were phony, they played their parts well, their clubfooted English diligently straightened at the edges, their beery ruddiness politely restrained by their suits. 'How about one of you boys calling the precinct and telling them where you are – just in case they never heard of you.'

The one driving kept both hands high on the wheel. 'I guess maybe you've had a reason to be a little suspicious, then, huh, Mr Anders?'

The driver's partner unhooked the mike and squeezed it. 'Car One Three Zero.'

'Go ahead, One Three Zero,' came the electronic bark.

'Yeah, we're still at the scene of our last assignment.'

'Ten-four, we've got that, One Three Zero.' He wearily rehooked the mike.

331

'So who's been trying to kill you, huh, Mr Anders? Maybe if we kicked it around down at the station house we might come up with a profile.'

'Who said anybody was trying to kill me?'

'Well, you see, this friend of yours . . . Synova' – and the cop smiled – 'she's been talking to us.'

'What did she tell you?'

'We saw her windshield. She's what you call the type that could make a lot of males jealous. We figured it was about four ounces of plastique probably set off with a firing device by somebody driving along next to you. It should have removed your head.'

'Why don't you check her boyfriends?'

'We did. You know anybody who might be the perpetrator of this kind of thing, Mr Anders?'

'I haven't got the slightest idea. But if you'll give me your card, if anything comes to mind, I'll call you up.'

The one in the passenger's seat produced a white card. 'You don't have a side business, do you? Anything where you have a contract with a union? Maybe a little labour dispute?'

'No.'

'Well, we just want to let you know that we're on this, Mr Anders, and you know, if you can remember anybody you might have pissed off in the last six months, give us a call.'

On his return from Paris, Ben called from JFK and said he was certain he was being followed, that he had to show Guy something devastating – but at a busy location, somewhere where crowds would provide cover. Gimbels seemed as good a place as any. Neither man said anything till they stepped on to the escalator. Ben wore a worsted suit, tight across his shoulders, the lapels French cut. Guy was spellbound at Ben's foppish, misshapen appearance.

'What the hell is that?'

'I bought it,' Ben declared. 'It's my disguise. Goddamn thing itches . . . it's giving me hives.'

The suit appeared to be held closed by a large fist from inside.

'Stop grinning,' Ben admonished. 'Before we go any further, you're going to have to write me a cheque. This thing cost a bundle. The dollar isn't worth shit in Europe; besides, you're employed, I'm not. I'm going to need some bread if I'm going to keep this up.'

Guy nodded in agreement. They came to the second floor. Ben instinctively checked over his shoulder before the two of them started up again. Once between the walls enclosing the moving stairs, Ben handed Guy his Adidas bag.

'I've had some success.'

'What'd you come up with?'

'Something that'll put Toby at his ease. He wanted facts. I got him facts. And I got you cleared on that cheque, which we can now prove was written by Buttress to tie you to the competition. So right now I'm hotter than an unauthorized leak from the Pentagon. I went through customs on all fours trying to pass for an Afghan. Ask that guy over there if they sell bulletproof vests.'

They passed counters of crystal as they headed for the next escalator.

Guy looked inside Ben's bag. 'Maybe one of us is wired. I don't know if they're tracking us with lenses or parabolic mikes, but they keep running me off the road. Natalie Mason is the girl who called me at the bar in DC. She's Riddick's trustee. She got up early one morning and fed me the preamble to the Luftwaffe's opinion on the F-19, a kind of lead-in to their verdict on the 17-10. Jesus, it's murder. The transmission went dead midsentence at the part where Hans began elaborating on the F-19's vulnerability to electronic corruption. I've called back several

333

times. According to Buttress, no one named Natalie Mason ever worked for them.'

'She got caught.'

'And now here, a day later, I get this in the mail.' Guy handed Ben a Mailgram. It read: 'YOU ARE INVITED TO ATTEND DEMONSTRATION OF AFCS INVULNERABILITY TRIALS AT BGR COMPUTER FACILITY, COCHOGUE, CONNECTICUT . . .'

'Coincidence,' said Ben.

Ben and Guy got off and walked through the lingerie department.

'So I called,' Guy said. 'The press isn't invited, no one from ALPA, no one from Air World, no one from the FAA, just a few "distinguished critics".'

'They mention me?'

'Do I let it pass or do I go?'

'Leave town.'

'Seriously.'

'I'd screw the old glass eye into my buttocks and waddle over. The glass eye's important, you see, because you could turn up missing, too. Apparently there's a precedent.'

A saleslady approached. 'Are you being taken care of?'

'Not as well as we'd like, sweetheart,' Ben winked.

The woman took it as a salacious crack and ducked in among the bathrobes.

'OK, Benny, we have privacy. Shoot.'

Ben opened the carbon flimsy of a letter relating to the perfumery's registration he'd dug up in Paris. The raised letters at the top of the sheet identified it as having been sent by the Washington law firm of Kolmar, Swinburne & Stapleton. It read: 'Dear Toni, Thank you for helping us with the registration, I am grateful and look forward to a long association.' Where the signature should have been there was only a scribbled notation – the abbreviation for 'James'. The fluorescents along the walls made the engraving on the letterhead stand out in sharp relief.

'It turned up in the basement of the Hôtel de Ville,' Ben said. 'It took a whole night of dancing the boogaloo, a nature diet of refried beans and a baksheesh. It was in a box marked dead storage.'

Guy said nothing. It was after they'd marched around and were headed for the next floor that Ben grew impatient.

'Well?'

'It wipes out the illusion I had.'

'About Buttress.'

'No, about you.'

'Me?'

'This is no better than the conjecture you got canned for!'

Ben stared at Guy like a coach watching his own man running towards the wrong goal. 'It's proof! You're looking at proof!'

'Of what?'

'It's got an engraved letterhead – '

'It's circumstantial, you dumb bastard! This is a carbon copy of nothing.'

'It's the law firm that represents Buttress!'

'Reese, you're a pestilence! You're a goddamn tragedy because you're in the wrong business! Sure it's incriminating. Of course they're one and the same. But you can't bring this into a court of law! It doesn't prove anything! Lawyers aren't prevented from having as many clients as they can get! You have to *prove* a connection exists!'

'The connection is obvious!'

'We know it – you and I know it! But it isn't enough! Where's the Stateside lawyer who set this up? This James somebody. Find *him* and get him on the witness stand, have him cross-examined – '

'I'll get it in the papers,' Ben said brightly.

'No! Jesus, Ben, how did you get to be a journalist!'

'You're looking at an open-and-shut case!'

335

'You should have been looking over transoms in divorce cases! You can't bring this to a newspaper!'

'I brought us back a goddamn fact!'

'You need the *witness* to make it a fact – whoever it is that signed this letter! Until we have him we have nothing!'

'You're an ungrateful bastard. I turned the French bureaucracy upside down . . .' Ben stared dejectedly down at the crumpled piece of paper in his hands. Finally he refolded it into a small square and shoved it back into his shirt pocket. 'Well, that's the best I can come up with as a short-order cook.'

'I hate to have to ruin your day.'

'I'll get over it. You see, there's this lady I know in a cool brownstone. She sleeps on satin sheets. She has a velvet ass.'

'There's something else that happened while you were away. Natalie isn't the only one that's missing.'

'I wasn't gone that long.'

'They only just pieced it together.'

'Pieced what together? What the hell are you talking about?'

'The lady you know in the brownstone.'

Ben knew what was coming but didn't want to hear it. 'I know, she moved. There's a hole in her wall.'

'Melissa's dead, Ben. It's been in the news all week.'

Ben took back his Adidas bag and said nothing. He stood there on the fourth floor, blinking at the rows of glass counters.

Guy Anders spotted the two-mile-long asphalt runway at Cochogue, Connecticut, stretched alongside the shoreline of Cochogue Bay, just before it slipped beneath the wing tip of his T-34. He banked well offshore over Long Island Sound and studied the layout more carefully from thirty-five hundred feet. The entire complex had been carved from dense woods. The voice from the control tower cleared him to land and added, 'Land immediately or stay clear, at least one five miles offshore. We have an F-19 test aircraft launching in three minutes for multiple low passes.' Guy banked steeply to set up a left-hand pattern, dropped the gear, flew a short base, dropped full flaps and made a pretty touchdown, buttoned her up and turned off at the first intersection.

A tall raw-boned man with aviator sunglasses emerged from the austere corporate building painted in Buttress tan and greeted him. 'Jim Pierce,' he said, shook Guy's hand and led him to an observation chalet set up alongside the runway. Half a dozen men with craned necks and glinting sunglasses stood searching for the eighth prepro-duction F-19 as it circled to the west. A jamming unit had been set up on the ground nearby, a tanklike vehicle chocked just off the runway. Atop its flatbed trailer the radar-guided antennas swivelled in their mounts, huge eyes with no pupils, following the fighter. Inside the trailer the ECM jammers were activated. Unseen electron beams pulsed skyward.

'So this is where electronic corruption meets American ingenuity,' Guy said above the noise coming from the squawk box.

'Your consuming interest is well known,' Pierce smiled.

'It's a subject that's dear to my heart,' Guy smiled back.

'It's a fairly recent interest, I'm told.'

'You're dead on.' Guy watched him out of the corner of his eye. 'Ever since I saw the German report.'

Pierce didn't flinch.

The F-19 was directly overhead, firing its afterburners. The air for half a mile grew long spiky bristles and the men stood pinned watching the two lavender-diced plumes of fire diminish in a vertical arc far above their heads.

'Did you hear what I said?' Guy prodded. 'I have eight

pages of the German report in my possession. What's your emotional feeling about that?'

'There are still six passes to go,' Pierce said, studying a developing graph.

'Are you deaf? I've got them in an envelope with a stamp on it!'

'What?' Pierce grimaced as though disturbed by a troublesome bug.

'You might pass that along to whoever told you to pump me to see how much I know.' Guy watched expectantly.

'I think maybe you've got your appointments mixed up.'

'No' – Guy shook his head – 'I don't think so. You see, I have these classified pages of what the Germans don't like about your computer. Am I getting through to you?'

'We've got some hard evidence inside that may answer your concern.'

Guy surveyed the crew at the jamming console. 'Now you fellows didn't arrange this li'l old party just for me, did you?'

Pierce didn't answer. He led the way across the runway and escorted Guy into the main building. Once inside, Guy blinked and peered. Another man stepped out of the shadows. It was Doug Moss.

'Well, whaddaya know? Whaddaya say, Douglas?' Guy threw him one of his kid grins.

Moss looked as though he'd eaten too many prunes.

'You didn't have to come all this way to find out what I know, Douglas. You only had to *ask* me if those eight pages got through to me.'

'What pages?'

'I would have told you without this smoke screen.'

'I'll play if you tell me the name of the game.'

Guy smiled. 'How about "war"?'

'Doug's here for a closer look at the flight computer,' said Pierce.

338

'Sorry to burst your bubble, Anders. This may jolt your paranoia but the NTSB is interested in all aspects.'

Guy followed the two men through the heart of the complex where white-gowned women in long rows were performing painstaking piecework on tangled fragments of microscopic quilt work. Pierce led the way up a metal staircase and on to the third-floor balcony of a full-sized hangar. In the centre, dominating the space, was an F-19 suspended by insulated cables and surrounded from the cockpit aft by huge pale-green coils like smooth metal intestines. It was the mechanism capable of drenching the aeroplane from any angle with powerful magnetic fluxes and to accelerate particles through the fighter's innards.

The three men stepped up to the railing overlooking the scene below.

'OK, Jim, tell me the good news.'

Pierce leaned against the barrier and began. His voice reverberated in the hollowness. 'The main flight-control computer occupies only four hundred cubic inches, weighs only fifteen pounds and consumes only a hundred and fifty watts of electrical power. We're talking about one thirtieth the volume, one fifteenth the weight and cost, and one eighth the power-supply requirements of the first digital fly-by-wire computer that flew in a NASA F-8 fighter back in 1974.'

'OK, look, no offence, Jim,' Guy interrupted, 'but skip a few pages and go right to the part where it gets sexy. I've already had the guided tour. On the other hand, I don't want to deprive you, Doug.'

Moss waited for Pierce to continue.

'Electronic corruption is of no consequence to flight safety and we've proved it,' Pierce went on. 'We've proved it right here with the F-19!'

'Excuse me, I don't mean to interrupt again, but I didn't come here to learn about the F-19 – unless of course it has certain handling characteristics that apply to the 17-10.'

Pierce paused, examined his hands in silence and pressed on. 'We've perfected techniques in the way these aeroplanes are put together – fibre optics for data distribution, radiation-hardened circuits with circumvention techniques using vertical parity in the memory – some very specialized and classified techniques. Electronic corruption in any event is of serious interest only to military applications.'

'That's not true, is it?' The handrail seemed to be trembling slightly under Guy's fingertips. His eyes roved over the chamber with its exotic machinery. He moved a few steps away, circling the arena. 'Look, Pierce, you'll have to forgive my impatience, but my decision to accept your invitation was not frivolous. I'd like you to start the next sentence with the 17-10!' he directed. '"The 17-10 is susceptible . . ."'

Pierce ignored the taunt. 'We're into magnetic-bubble technology for nonvolatile storage!'

'How about it, huh, Jim? Stuff the ritual and tell me about the 17-10! Moss here wants to hear about it! He came all the way from Washington to hear about it! "The 17-10 is susceptible . . ."'

Pierce stepped around the railing and into a wire cage that would take him to the fighter. 'We're using two-hundred-and-fifty-K-bit bubble domain three-hundred-nanosecond dynamic random access memories on *single chips* for mass storage!' Pierce persisted. His voice echoed through the cavern. 'We're about to surpass the density of the human brain!'

'Back page of *Fortune* last January! See, I already know your advertising copy! I want to hear about the 17-10!'

'We achieved base-line design freeze and verified all the support software for Buttress here at BGR!'

Guy came across a square-shaped red phone recessed in the wall. He lifted it off its cradle and blew into it.

Instantly his breath boomed throughout the building. Pierce looked up, startled, but didn't connect the sound.

'We had to develop an entire higher-order language, do all the verification and validation,' he shouted. 'All unique to the Buttress flight-control system architecture!'

Guy's voice bellowed through both sides of the entire BGR complex. 'Tell me about the 17-10!' The workers in white in the unseen far wing were dumbfounded. 'Start the sentence with "The 17-10 is susceptible . . ."' The voice reverberated.

Pierce nearly fell out of the cage. 'Put that down!' he yelled. 'That's the disaster evac line!'

'Tell me about the 17-10!' The voice blared through the complex. 'Tell me what's wrong with the 17-10!'

'That line isn't private!' Pierce tried to clamber out of his rig.

Guy released his grip on the cradle. 'Stay put and start talking to me about electronic susceptibility on the 17-10 or we go back on the air. No more canned soda pop!' Guy squeezed the lever. 'Yawl stay tuned,' he said grinning. 'Hello, out there!' He could hear his voice slap around the entire structure. It probably carried across the runway, too. 'There's more coming!'

'Jesus Christ!' Pierce yelled.

Moss was fingering the door uncertainly.

'Hold up, Douglas,' Guy called. 'Well, what about it, Pierce?'

'Put that goddamn phone down!' Pierce was standing uncertainly inside the cage.

Guy waited him out. 'OK, Jim, let's forget it. You've given me what I came for – and more directly than I really had a right to expect.' Guy reslotted the red receiver. 'Douglas, do you mind if I join you?'

'What?' Moss was startled.

'Well, you look like you're leaving.'

Moss was fingering a set of car keys. 'I – have to get back to La Guardia, make the twelve o'clock shuttle.'

'I can get you out by eleven.'

'I've got a rented car outside.'

'Jim here won't mind returning it for you, will you, Jim?' Pierce said nothing. Guy crossed to Moss, took the car keys from him and set them down on the counter. 'Mr Moss will be coming to La Guardia with me in my T-34,' Guy said to Pierce. 'So I think it would be a good idea to tell whoever's in that F-19 up there I've got a hotshit government employee with me. I don't want any trouble over Long Island Sound!' Guy squeezed Moss's arm. 'I can have you there in less than an hour, Douglas.'

'You needn't take the trouble.'

'No trouble,' Guy smiled. 'Besides, it's time you and I had a talk. You're not blind to this charade. What I have to say might broaden your perspective.'

Moss glanced at Pierce and checked his watch. He didn't look up when he said, 'I'll be right out.' He ducked into the men's room but didn't approach any of the half dozen urinals that lined the wall. Instead he went quickly to one of the washbasins opposite and stood before it, leering at himself in the mirror. Moss was shaken by Anders's confrontation but at the same time surprised at the strong urges which impelled him to fly with Anders: the unquestionable convenience, the seductive lure of the small training aeroplane itself which, since the spectacle of the F-19 flyby, had raised a wellspring of perverse temptation in him, a disturbing pull his mind tried to reject – but couldn't. He leaned closer to see his reflection and with the thumbs of both hands pulled the lids away from his left eye and stood scrutinizing the insides of his eyelids. He remained like that for several seconds. Then, abruptly, he ~~snapped~~ his hands to his trousers seams, standing up ~~straight~~ at the same time, tucking his chin into his neck. ~~He~~ swivelled slightly to double-check that he was alone. That assured, his right hand described a deft arc that was both graceful and surreptitious as it hoisted a silver-trimmed leather-covered flask to his lips. The bourbon blasted his throat with hot raw gurgling sounds as he threw back his head and drained six straight ounces. He wheezed for air and ran his left shirt cuff roughly over the glistening red gash that was his mouth. Then he replaced the flask in its holster, straightened his tie and stood back from the basin. He was ready to fly.

Guy helped Moss sort out the straps in the rear cockpit. The parachute straps were stiff but they were an inconvenient necessity: the chute doubled as cushion in the bare-metal bucket seat. Then came the shoulder-harness straps with fittings that clanked as Guy connected them to the lap-belt attachment. If he smelled the booze he didn't let on, and Moss, embarrassed by the rough physical closeness of hands reaching past his hips to tug the lap belt tight, tilted his head and held his breath. Finally he was cinched in so snugly he thought he couldn't take a deep breath – unnecessarily snug. Anders was climbing into the front cockpit, untangling his straps. Moss could look straight over the top of his instrument panel at the back of Anders's head, and that made him squeamish, as when forced to endure the graphic details of an unpleasant movie.

Guy hollered 'Clear!' The starter whined and with a sharp-smelling gust the engine roared into life. Soon they were at the departure end of the asphalt runway. Moss located the tachometer on his panel during Guy's run-up, saw the needle quiver as the mags were checked. Guy pulled the prop through and made a couple of other checks before throttling back. Suddenly his voice was hot and prickly in Moss's ear.

'Intercom check. How do you read?'

Moss pushed the button he'd been shown. 'L clear,' he responded.

'OK, Mr Moss, get yourself all tensed up because here we go!'

It was only then Doug Moss realized he couldn't cross his legs for takeoff. The dual-control stick between his knees was in the way.

The little sapphire-blue aeroplane tucked up its wheels, lofted into a pure, robin's-egg sky and banked steeply towards the west to point along the axis of Long Island Sound, which spread as a mottled diamond surface beneath them. Moss felt the g's pile on during that first turn and sucked in his breath at the unpleasant sensation of his stomach sagging into his groin. He tried to tense the disused flab there and grunt through his teeth, but the noise he made was offensive and the effort disagreeable. Now the wings were level again and the widening vista spectacular. Moss was perched up on his parachute pack, his elbows out from his sides resting on chest-high metal rails, his head bobbing inside the clear fishbowl canopy which afforded an unaccustomed panoramic view in all directions. The sensation wasn't altogether unpleasant now that he was getting used to it; a slightly giddy feeling as the little aeroplane rode the eddies, little unseen furrows of air to chop at, or breach and bore through, and it all hearkened back to something he'd tried to bury forever in the past. The engine had settled down to a reassuring, deep-voiced throb and he almost forgot Anders sitting directly in front of him five feet away. Instead he was thinking how nice it would be to get home early – even beat the rush-hour traffic – and he was gazing idly past the instruments on the little panel nestled over his knees, the altimeter slowly winding around as they climbed, the other needles comfortably motionless in their proper places. But these he found boring and he peered out over the geography of Long Island on his left. Smoke from the Northport power-station chimneys lay in a huge grey wake as from a motionless ship and it spread slowly southward to blanket central Long Island in a flat, thick haze.

He checked the time. Good. They would be landing at La Guardia in probably fifteen minutes – certainly no more than twenty.

'Doug?'

Moss glanced up at the hairs on the back of Guy Anders's neck.

'There's something I've wanted to talk to you about. I heard you treated W. B. Cosgrove pretty shabbily the other day. It got me pissed off. I mean, to think you actually have the balls to sit there and tell a man like W.B. how he should run an aeroplane! Do you really know what it's like to spend half your life in the sharp end of one of these things?'

Moss felt his mouth go dry. He had suddenly forgotten to enjoy the scenery.

'Tell me,' Guy continued, 'where do you get off flying your goddamn mahogany bomber, talking down like that to a man with forty years' experience in aeroplane cockpits? Making judgments about what goes on up here . . . I think if you want to talk that way you should maybe get some firsthand knowledge.'

At that instant Moss felt his stomach grind heavily on its way nonstop towards his shoes. The character of the T-34 had overturned from placid to vengeful, it had real fangs and they were bared. Moss tried to brace himself but didn't have time. Guy kicked the plane into a hard bank and hauled back on the stick. She shuddered violently like an old washer with one leg gone – Guy could feel it coming, almost . . . almost . . . *now* – and the T-34 slammed over the top into a savage, nose-down spin. Moss had lost all sense of up and down, the side of the cockpit jammed heavily into him, all he knew was that the horizon had gone crazily ape like a giant windmill out of control. The T-34 was pointed straight down, rolling viciously, slamming Moss from side to side like a limp doll. Guy booted the rudder, Moss felt the control stick bang into his knees painfully then hit the stops, right back in his gut. All at once he was looking straight up into the sky.

'Now you look, Mr Moss, you get back to Washington and you do your homework. I know you haven't done your homework!' Guy could barely force the words from between his clenched teeth as he piled on more crushing g. 'Now this is what life can be like up here – '

Shadows swapped ends inside the cockpit, the instruments looked foolish behind their circular glass dials, meaningless white needles twirling in different directions on the panel which a moment before had been darkened in shadow, now was flashing sun reflections like a dozen blinding lights converging into his eyes. Moss twisted in the straps and was confronted with the remarkable and terrifying sensation of seeing the entire geography, fields, woods, rivers, and Long Island Sound planted squarely over the top of his left shoulder. He groped to hang on but his hands had no strength and the seat was shooting out from under him . . .

Moss was completely lost in space, he'd stopped trying to keep oriented, he was making terrible grunting sounds, lost in the shriek of engine sounds and wind sounds wailing in an appalling moan, he wanted out but couldn't find the latch. He couldn't possibly bail out, that would be even more unimaginable. The stick snapped back again and Moss was smashed into his seat, his cheeks pulling his eyes shut. Then he was catapulted forward into the straps he'd thought were too tight, thrown so hard that the top of his head bounced with excruciating force into the canopy. The inside of his head exploded. They were whirling upside down, Moss felt his head snap back and he was horrified to be looking straight into the smokestack of a huge ocean vessel directly above him. Details of its wake

346

were instantly blotted by a spray of stinging grit that assaulted his eyes; it was dirt from the cockpit floor that had fallen upward to fill the space around his head and blind him. He felt the straps dig deeply into his chest, he felt his guts heave and then he was only dimly aware of his bourbon-soured shrimp salad lunch spewing out of his mouth in wet lumpy spasms.

'Arrggh! Arrggh!'

Guy had his pocket tape recorder running. He glanced into the rearview mirror and saw the agony on Moss's vomit-splattered face, and for a moment he experienced a trace of genuine pity. He'd seen only one other person who looked so absolutely miserable in an aeroplane – and they'd washed him out of pilot training on humanitarian grounds. But then he punched into another steep dive, picking up speed, and hauled back again into a hard climb, rolling the T-34 on to its back and pushing with all his strength out the other side. At first Guy had just smelled the puke. Strange, the horizon tumbling violently outside had nothing to do with the upheaval of revulsion that swept in a gust past his stomach. A detached, oddly quiet part of his brain was able to reflect, even amid the jack-hammer thudding of air beating in solid waves against the stabilizer, that motion had never made him queasy – only the close, stuffy proximity of another man's regurgitation. Even as the T-34 hauled itself from another percussed, groaning gyration Guy felt wet flakes strike his neck. Throwing a glance over one shoulder he saw the Plexiglas canopy around Moss was spattered on the inside in a foul ochrous arc above his head. Moss's face had gone bilious and slack, it looked flatter, mashed into his neck by the heel of an unseen granite hand. His mouth drooped, sweat poured from him, his hands clawed like those of a drunken swimmer but there was nothing to grab. Guy was working hard, sweating too, winded from the strain of gritting and grunting against the hard g forces to keep his stomach from exploding, taut muscles in his arms aching from combat with iron might in the controls. Then he ducked and shoved the stick forward with both hands. When his left foot jerked out against the shuddering rudder pedal, Moss had the wild sensation of being a boulder swept from a cliff, hurling into space, pursued by the cannonade avalanche of pain bouncing on the ledges, all gathering, ricocheting as he crashed towards the sea. His pleas were lost in the shriek of wind that tore at every rivet of the struggling plane. Guy himself had a sudden moment of alarm that in his zeal he may have asked too much.

'Gimme a hand!' he yelled. 'You went to flight school!'

Moss was totally helpless. He tried to blink in the loathsome blackness, his vision went blood-red as the sun and negative g slapped across his face, but the roller coaster was plummeting completely off the tracks again, this time straight through the guardrail, and his ass was four inches off the seat.

'Holy shit!' hollered Guy. 'She's out of control! I've lost it!' His words were loud and filled with dreadful panic. The plane hurtled in a fierce tumbling gyration through the sky.

'I can't control it! I can't control it!' Guy's voice pounded through the interphone.

Moss was crying out, the fear searing his brain. 'Oh, my God, no! . . . No! . . . God! . . .'

And then Guy had the wings level. Long Island was back in place on the left, and La Guardia was less than fifteen minutes away. He glanced at Moss's face in the rearview mirror. Moss looked destroyed, reduced to pulp as if by a battery of fists. Guy couldn't help feeling refreshed and charged; even as the cockpit filled with the reek of vomit, he felt cleansed. His voice came through the interphone with sudden confident clarity.

'That's how it feels, Mr Moss, to be in the sharp end

348

when one of these things goes out of control. And goddammit, W. B. Cosgrove and I had as much control over Flight Six coming into Kennedy as you just had over this little joyride. The difference is, this was for fun, Flight Six was for real. Not to mention the four hundred and twenty-one passengers!'

Then Guy opened his canopy, letting a small hurricane of cool, fresh air flow in a welcome rush across their faces.

The remaining fifteen minutes of the ride were spent in silence except for Guy's clipped communication with La Guardia approach and the control tower. He taxied quickly to the general aviation ramp and cut the engine. Moss sat exhausted, sodden with foul liquids from collar to cuff. As Guy reached in to assist him with the straps he let him see the mini-tape recorder strapped to his belt.

'I have a recording here,' he said. 'Something to remind me of the interesting discussion at BGR this afternoon – and of our short ride together, which might provide some fun someday.'

Moss stared at Guy. It was the ultimate indignity. 'OK, Anders, you've made your point – '

'You remember this, Mr Moss: my job's still up there. Your job's down here. You get your ass out of this cockpit and you get it where it belongs, back in the *tail end* of the 17-10. You take a good, hard look back there, and you find out what's wrong with that blueprint. When you find out what it is, you'll have the secret to the whole thing. Don't talk to me about pilot egos, Mr Moss. Talk to me about science!' He leaned closer despite the odour. 'I'll give you forty-eight hours to do some meditation. You'd better say your mantras – and if you don't have any fresh ideas for me by then, we'll talk again . . .'

Guy climbed down. A couple of airport attendants he was slightly acquainted with were standing a few feet away, curious, but making no move towards the T-34. Guy went over to speak to them.

'The fellow in the back lost his cookies coming in here. Give him some rags and a pail of water. He knows the rules.'

13

The cubelike Buttress buildings on the West Coast stood facing the sun, their shaded sides ending in razor-edged sharpness at the corners. The grass had been freshly clipped and the sprinkler system was on, arching hoops of mist in scalloped layers along the length of the complex. There was nothing in the plant's external appearance to suggest anything unusual except the large number of cars that had been left overnight in the parking lot.

Inside the main facility, sixteen gleaming aerodynamic shapes in various stages of completion thrummed, their cockpits glowed with a red-and-green incandescence, spaceships being readied in their first hangar. Three completed 17-10As with Air World speed striping and logos faced the still-closed sliding wall, obediently waiting for Miller's fix, which was taking longer than expected. A massive logjam of successive 17-10s was now crowding in oblique angles, one behind the other.

Throughout the three-quarter-mile-long assembly floor, supervisors and selected engineering teams remained overnight to remove the actuators and servo valves that had already been installed. This was their second night away from home. By morning of the third day a number of teams found themselves with nothing to do. Predictions on when the new hardware would arrive changed by the hour and concern spread when the rumour surfaced that Miller was having serious difficulties. Clusters of men, their ties off and shirt sleeves rolled up, sat in the gloom of half-lit hallways speculating about the upcoming loan hearing, concurring that the President and the Congress had no real alternative any more. In all likelihood, they reasoned, the decision to continue the loan had already been made and so they agreed the future was stable and that it would carry them to retirement. Others gathered on balconylike tiers that fringed the silenced assembly line and spoke in subdued tones, like neighbours milling on a sidewalk at midnight in the wake of a calamity. Rumours had begun to circulate. There was clouded talk of a possible merger, about Fenton Riddick being on the way out, that Hollis Wright hadn't been seen in the building for a number of days, that a split had developed among the members of the Buttress board over the cutoff of 17-10 deliveries on the eve of the Peck-Searington hearings and that Hollis had been asked to resign.

Up on the fourth floor of the East Wing, Fenton Riddick was still seated in his captain's chair, pages of the translation of the final Luftwaffe report on the F-19 spread across his desk. He stared at them now in the harsh shaft of light pouring between the drapes behind him and found the place where the 17-10 had been mentioned as the fighter's civilian descendant, inheriting the same design characteristics that had caused so many losses to the Luftwaffe. It was an arrogant piece, meticulous but gloating, and it was damning. If ever it found its way into the press . . . Riddick stood and pulled the drape back with a snap. The implication was malicious. The fighter and the transport had different missions. Nevertheless he would have to locate Chaplin, make him privy to the German report and rehearse him with a cover story should a leak occur.

Riddick was certain the phone was going to ring the instant before it did.

'Had your breakfast?' It was Hollis Wright.

'No, sir, I haven't and I think I'll pass it up.'

'I'm told nothing left here last night.'

'You were told right.'

Hollis sounded pained. 'Buzz,' he whined, 'I wonder if it wouldn't make good sense if the two of us were to sit down and take stock?'

The question was rhetorical, of course. Riddick would have to agree it was a good idea but he wasn't prepared to deal with Hollis. He felt sick to his stomach and his eyes were caked at the corners. 'When did you have in mind?'

'Suppose I order up a tray of coffee and eggs and have it waiting for us on the fifty-yard line.' The fifty-yard line was the designation for the centre of the assembly hall. 'Say in about ten minutes?' Hollis didn't wait for the reply.

Riddick marched down the quarter-mile-long corridor in the bowels of the building, fumbled for the dog-eared production schedule folded into his back pocket and pulled it free. All of the week's delivery deadlines had been missed and the week coming up would be no better. It was impossible to work any harder and he decided not to think too far ahead. His shirt had become rancid but he no longer minded his own sweat for it was the badge of his effort. His world had become the close darkness of front-line battle in which no time could be taken for thoughts of comfort – not until the victory was clear. For a moment he allowed himself to reside in the image of George Patton and he saw himself standing on an icy country road, determined to get the frozen line moving again.

In two minutes he reached the main floor facing the metal jungle of spars and pulleys and walked slowly along the centre stripe. The whole assembly line was at a halt. An eerie presence pervaded the huge assembly hall; incomplete jumbos rose above him on both sides, perched liked winged Victories in flight. The arena, though enclosed, had the vastness of a jet airport, so large it had its own haze, its own weather. He arrived at the fifty-yard line clearing, identified by a Raiders banner strung from an overhead cable, and stood nonplussed, facing the spectacle of Hollis Wright seated at a room-service-style table on wheels that had been rolled into position at the centre of the intersection. It was properly bedecked with fresh tablecloth, flowers and two glistening settings; in attendance was one of the two white-jacketed waiters who normally worked upstairs in the kitchen next to the boardroom. His deportment was correct, Riddick noticed, but his self-consciousness here uneasy and apparent.

Some of the people who had remained overnight and a number of the early birds stood watching to see what would happen next. Riddick put a hand through his hair, shutting out the implausibility of it. The waiter held the chair for him. Despite the pressure Hollis appeared rested, his suit impeccable, his tie expensive silk.

'Best way to jam a rumour is to demonstrate some evidence to the contrary and do it out in the open,' he said, looking like a celebrity who knew he was being watched. 'You're supposed to have cleaned out your locker and, according to reliable word from the boiler room, Hollis Wright has been asked to go fishing. I figured we had a right to some equal time. Sit down.'

'Why don't we wave at the people?'

Hollis pressed a pat of butter into a roll. 'No point in having meetings upstairs, is there? We can't see anything from upstairs. Right here is where we derive our inspiration.'

The waiter patted a portion of scrambled eggs on to a clean white plate.

'Save the eggs,' said Riddick. The waiter withdrew the plate and slid it on to a bottom shelf behind the tablecloth.

'Then pour Mr Riddick some coffee.' Hollis didn't look up when he said, 'Are you still inspired, Buzz?' He leaned closer and his face became flushed. 'I want to see every last one of these aeroplanes out of here by the end of the week.'

Riddick studied Hollis's baby-pink face. There was no hint of mirth, the words were meant, one behind the other, the way they were spoken. 'And suppose I told you that I have to add seven, maybe eight, days to the schedule?'

Hollis took a forkful of eggs, chewed on it, then wiped his mouth with the napkin. 'You were the iron man who could do it all – debate the fine points of a contract or a blueprint, negotiate or kick ass. You see, the reason I called' – and Hollis sounded pained again – 'is that we now have less time than you or I thought we had yesterday!' Hollis turned in his chair and surveyed the scene behind him. 'I want you to gain a couple of days for us over the next ninety-six hours.'

Riddick stirred his coffee and laughed, a laugh of exhaustion which fell away from him in waves, bringing tears to his eyes, developing its own momentum, and he began to enjoy it. 'Oh, shit, oh, dearie me, said the man in the quicksand, this is unjust!' Fenton howled and pushed himself away from the table, wiping his eyes; Hollis waited impassively until the laughter wore itself out.

Riddick stared back at the chairman. 'You're talking about six days in four *with* the actuator fix or without it?'

'The fix is only important insofar as the Germans are concerned.'

'Wrong. It's going to come up at the hearings.'

'No one at the FAA has said anything about it being mandatory.'

'And if it becomes mandatory?'

'It won't.' Hollis laid his fork down and pushed his plate aside. 'The FAA is going to roll over and play dead for Miller's fix.' The waiter poured a drop of cream into the chairman's fresh cup of coffee.

'Well, I'm going to get that new actuator on board – and to do that, I've got to stop the production line.'

'Any delay's going to make it look like we've got second thoughts.'

'And if I don't do it, Buttress's backside is unprotected.'

354

In distant rings around them the rubberneckers had converged, blue-shirts accumulating to line the metal-railed tiers row by row like silent flocks of birds alighting on phone lines.

Hollis acted as if he hadn't noticed the growing ranks of men. Riddick swung his head slowly, uneasily. Hollis looked at his watch, reaccosted Riddick's attention. 'I'm concerned about Miller. I hear he's coming up with blanks. Should we hire someone else to crack the whip?' Hollis fixed Riddick with an unmistakable challenge. 'I mean I'll leave that decision entirely up to you, Fenton.' His tone became solicitous.

Riddick resented Hollis's cool authority. 'If you're serious about the six days in four then I'm going to cut this short.' Riddick stood. 'How free am I to hire?'

'You call the shots.'

Dick Miller sat watching the computer-graphics console but he wasn't seeing the now rather tired green cat in the screen. Instead, a swirl of images flooded his mind. He saw himself screaming through the night at that inaccessible cockpit to pull the circuit breaker on Elevator Program A and through the glare of his futility he could just perceive Ed Boice on the quest of a deficient servo valve and all the images washed and smeared together . . . Predominating, as though he had eyes in the back of his head, was Fenton Riddick's well-barbered smile constantly encouraging him to perform more acts against their own best interests and he knew the price for a can of soup on the table was a chain around the soul, links which over the years would corrode and tighten, merge into a mass too tight to shed. And was it Fenton Riddick berating him again, saying why don't you finish? He opened his eyes and looked at the screen. Why can't you finish, Dick Miller? Thirty-three hours had gone by and he had sat at his console trying to work his way past the impasse, calling up abstracts of ram-actuator configurations, forcing himself to look at their consequences under different flight modes, and he was not satisfied.

It was with a stab of anxiety that he noticed the phones had begun to ring. It was daylight again and still he was undecided. A young machinist who had come by to check in with his boss smelled of shaving lotion and soap. He'd been home, Dick thought, and he carried none of the burden.

'No need for you to stand there,' Dick said as he copied a readout. 'It won't happen any faster.' The tone in the room changed and Miller knew that Fenton Riddick had taken up a position directly behind him; the man's agitation quickly choked off the breathable air.

'I want to know what's going on around here.' Riddick said it softly. 'I want to know where Boice is.' Three people in an adjacent alcove took their feet off the chairs.

'He went home,' Miller said without turning around. He did not add that Boice had sat watching, deferring, as he put it, to the talent in the room.

Riddick's face, usually ruddy, seemed on the verge of powdering into chalk. 'I thought you were cutting metal! Why aren't we cutting metal?'

'We're not ready to cut metal,' said Miller.

'What the hell is going on around here? You've got fourteen million feet of floor space tied up! We've got four ferry crews scratching themselves in the locker room waiting to take something to New York!' Riddick yanked an adjoining door open revealing two men asleep under their drafting tables. 'What the hell is this? A flophouse? A goddamn Chinese flophouse!' One of the men on the floor struggled to focus but before he could get his mouth open to say something, Riddick tossed the door shut. His face was knotted in anger.

'How would you like me to put it?' he rasped. He

addressed the group, including the young machinist, but the words were meant for Miller. 'We've got sixteen 17-10s downstairs trying to cross the finish line. Their total worth if they don't is zero. Zero divided by two hundred and seventy thousand on-site employee salaries is zero! We've got competition. If you read *Time*, the Europeans have made a move for the inside rail. We've had outsiders and insiders try to sabotage us. We've been wise to it. The day shift has just come on and if we can't find something for them to do, we're going to have to pay them for playing with themselves again. This is a business, Miller, not a goddamn research lab endowed by a grant! You're being paid for a service!'

Miller sat back and rubbed his knuckles into his eyes.

'What are we designing, fine art?' Riddick demanded. 'The company isn't interested in fine art!'

Miller shut the console off and stood a little uncertainly. 'You can go fuck yourself.' He lifted the sweater off the back of his chair and took his glasses off.

'What are you doing?' Riddick's tone was sharp, incredulous.

'You can't talk to me that way.'

'Hey, there's people waiting!'

'You can't come in here and lecture me, goddammit! You can't do that, you sonofabitch. You're in a hurry, well, there it is! Take a seat! *You* work it out!'

One man began a careful search of his empty shirt pocket for a cigarette. The light was snapped on in the Chinese flophouse and could be seen under the door. Miller hesitated for a moment, nodded self-consciously to the chief tool-and-die man and, his mind made up, left the room.

Riddick caught up with him as he passed the glass-enclosed security office next to the front door. 'What do you say we go out and get shitfaced?' Miller headed down the steps. Riddick reached out and caught him by the arm.

'You have my apologies up front. You can go home if you want, that's up to you, but first I'm buying us a cup of coffee.'

Miller pulled his arm free.

'I'm asking for two minutes.'

'The coffee machines are dry.'

'Then we'll split a bag of peanuts.'

'We're not cattle you can kick around,' Miller glowered.

'I can understand your feelings.'

'Can you?'

'Two minutes?'

Miller slowly turned and came back up the steps. 'We're people. I know I'm not as outspoken as some of the others in this building but I've earned some dignity around here.'

'Of course you have. You're entitled to it.'

'Don't you patronize me, goddammit.'

'I've given you my apologies, haven't I? What else would you like me to do?'

Miller stopped.

Riddick came back to him. 'Listen, why are we standing out here talking to each other like this?' He guided Miller into the food dispensing alcove next to the elevator. 'Dick, almost thirty years ago, you and me, we've had parties. Thirty years of perfect roll-outs. Everybody in this place has gone crazy. I'm crazy, too. Look at this, they cleaned out the peanuts. Nobody around here's had a good night's sleep in weeks! We're zombies! You can take that into account.' He put his arm around Miller and ducked down to face the mirror in the coffee machine. 'Look at us. The two of us look like a couple of panhandlers straight out of the Klondike. You look like a cactus with ears. Dicky, this isn't us! This is a temporary condition! I know what you want, but we can't start all over. This is the plane we've got and she's magnificent! All it needs is that little extra muscle in the tail. You can't go home now! Dick Miller can't go home and leave someone else to do it – someone else who, at their best, wouldn't be as good as you when you're asleep! You couldn't live with that. I'll have a car drive you home. Go back in and give the boys something to work with. You could do it in fifteen minutes!'

Riddick found the Buttress personnel office deserted. It was eight-fifteen in the morning and no one was in yet. That irritated him. Charts comprising the names and jobs of those to be laid off in the event the extension of the government loan failed were spread across the desks. Riddick scooped them up and dumped them into the trash can. The door opened and the director of personnel appeared holding a white paper bag containing coffee and Danish. He was startled to see Riddick occupying his office and gestured that he'd be glad to wait outside until Riddick had finished. But Riddick waved the offer aside, put a finger in his ear and returned his attention to the phone. Presently someone answered.

'Who's this?' Riddick snapped. There was a muffled response as the voice on the other end wanted to know who was calling.

'This is Riddick and I want you people to take your fingers out of your ass and move the first three 17-10s at the head of the line outside. Get them out of the hangar. And I want you to do it now! Put a crew together and set up six scaffolds outside. We're going to need searchlights and power. We're going to roll around the clock with a third eight-hour shift.' Riddick recradled the phone. 'I want you to get me eighty additional pairs of hands, and I need them by ten o'clock tonight to go till morning.'

The personnel man stood watching wide-eyed. 'I'm afraid I'm going to need some paperwork . . .'

Riddick grabbed a sheet of blank paper from a stack,

scrawled his signature on the bottom of it and pushed it over. 'Type anything you want on it. I don't care what you do with it. If you have any problems, don't tell me about them.'

Matt paced the tarmac in front of the maintenance hangar at JFK. Normally he felt comfortable on the broad, grease-streaked space here where a man could have some elbow room and enjoy the potent impression of Manhattan, available but not overwhelming. Normally the world seemed open here. But today Matt was hemmed in by his watch and his blood pressure and Manhattan's spires leaned over the dusky horizon like a long row of fangs.

Abruptly he headed for the hangar. Just inside on the maintenance shift foreman's desk was a phone. The foreman recognized him. Without a word Matt punched the number.

'This is Aspinwall. Any inbounds?'

The dispatcher on duty knew exactly what he was after.

'Nosir.'

Matt jammed the cutoff button with his thumb, let it up and dialled again.

'This is Aspinwall. I want a telex to go out at once.' He barked a number. 'It's a personal communication.'

'Yessir.'

'Just say, "Reference contract. Deliveries overdue. Payment stopped." Sign it "Aspinwall." That's all.'

'Yessir.'

Matt nodded to the foreman and strode from the office. The rangy old mech with the clipped white hair had never been closer to the CEO than the one-column picture which leaned earnestly over the monthly pep talk in his *World Watch*, the company newspaper. He wasn't offended by Aspinwall's curtness; on the contrary. He was subdued by the ominous weight of the conversation he'd

360

overhead. Too big for hangar-floor rumours. He did notice that Aspinwall looked a lot older and more haggard than his photo, and the state of his ruddiness was a little alarming.

Matt reached his office in fifteen minutes. His private secretary could see at once without being told that he was not to be disturbed. She could also see he was in no mood for meditation. She had already placed the response unembellished on his desk. Matt shut the door and held the TWX out at arm's length without fishing for his glasses.

'RETROFIT BEING EXPEDITED AS PER CONTRACT MODIFICATION. EXPECT DELIVERY S/N 009 36 HOURS. WE EXPECT IMMEDIATE RESUMPTION OF PAYMENT.'

He jabbed the squawk box. 'Angela!'

'Yes, Mr Aspinwall.' Her coolness tended to alter perspectives and calm him. Reliable Mrs Sisson. For close on nineteen years now, steady and faithful. A little dowdy at times but always gritty inside, wishing just as fervently as he for the next leap forward.

'Angela,' he began again, hoping he didn't sound quite so desperate. 'Send a telex. The private number. Make the text read, "Require two aeroplanes in twenty-four hours. Payment remains halted under original terms. No contractual rights will be surrendered by Air World." I want that emphasized. "Contract mods you mention are unilateral." Sign my name.'

'Thank you, sir.'

'OK, Angela . . . and . . . thank you.'

Matt slumped in his chair and rubbed his eyes. Then refocusing, he stared through the glass towards Jamaica Bay. A United 727 was rolling out. A Varig DC-10 was lurching towards Cedarhurst, pregnant with fuel. Matt didn't notice. He saw only visions of phantom 17-10s against distant skies which were sodden grey with overcast.

* * *

On the West Coast Fenton Riddick glowered at the Xerox copy of the Air World TWX brought down by messenger from Hollis's office to him, and spat out a string of curses. He punched on the red CONFERENCE IN SESSION light to prevent interruptions. His thick copy of the revised production schedule jammed in his hip pocket was already badly smudged. He tossed it into the wastebasket and grabbed the morning's update from his IN basket with only a glance at the heading. He doubled it lengthwise and ran his fist along the crease, then thrust it absently into his pocket.

Riddick wiped the stubble next to his mouth. He filled the basin in the corner with cold water and splashed double handfuls over his face. Then he dried off, threw the used towel in the corner and pushed his pocket shaver into the worst of the stubble. It pulled and stung but removed the hangover look. OK. Now he could deal with Air World.

He stood by the window to reread the telex and remaining standing, scribbled his reply in the margin. He wrote it out at once, with no hesitation.

'UNABLE TO COMPLY. REFERENCE NEGOTIATIONS UNDER CURRENT CONTRACT AMENDMENT 6 SPECIFYING 17-10B COMPONENT RETROFIT INTO 17-10A AEROPLANES S/N 004 THROUGH 018.' He then scribbled a shorthand list of technical design differences, jotting them from memory, a replay of last week's tortured hours between 2 and 5 A.M. reprocessed at high volume. The last item was 'MODIFIED ELEVATOR ACTUATOR AS PER CURRENT BUTTRESS CHANGE ORDER.' Riddick looked thoughtfully out the window, rubbing his sandpaper chin, then quickly added, 'AS A CONCESSION, CERTAIN NEW COMPONENTS WILL BE PROVIDED AT NO EXTRA COST.'

Matt read the telex with disgust. He summoned Moudon and told him to set up a meeting. He then let himself sag for a moment in complete silence, facing his control-tower glass window, but unaware of the airport activity outside. Presently he closed the curtains. The squawk box sounded.

It was Angela with a message.

'Go ahead.' He reproached himself for sounding abrupt. Matt didn't mean it that way, of course –

'It's a call from *The Wall Street Journal*, Mr Aspinwall.'

'Yeah? – Tell 'em to wait.' There he goes again, just after resolving to calm down. *The Wall Street Journal?* Christ, what could they want? Matt looked around his office with the furtive, half-desperate glance of a man who sought a scroll of gold in the autumn forest.

It was no good. He punched the intercom.

'Go ahead.'

He recognized the voice: the senior aviation editor, calling from the Wings Club . . . heard some disturbing rumours of trouble between Buttress and Air World . . . about cancelling your contract – about not making payment – suggestions this is what's behind the recent signs of sickness in your common stock – seeking confirmation. Care to make any comment?

Matt fought back the painful sensation that rose up in his chest. His irritation and the threats expressed in his telexes had leaked. Or maybe one of Hollis's Georges on the *Scorpion II* was a spy for the press. Should've known. Never did like useless people hanging around in the middle of negotiations.

'That's interesting. Why don't you come over and have lunch sometime this week with my public-relations man and me and we'll talk about it.'

'I'd like to shoot for tomorrow – and, Mr Aspinwall, could we leave the PR man out of it?'

'Talk to my secretary about a date. We don't want you folks in the business press to get the wrong idea about the normal, healthy, sound relationship between Buttress and

Air World – a relationship that extends back almost forty years . . .' Somehow he'd squelch the rumours, keep them out of print.

'I wasn't sure if there was a story here, but I'd appreciate your time.'

Good, he had the bastard on the run. 'Fine, look forward to seeing you. I'm in a meeting, can't give you any more time right now. Goodbye.' Matt held the disconnect button for the briefest moment. When he let it up he barked a rapid-fire stream of chopped-off instructions to Angela, his earlier recriminations forgotten and gone without trace in the blunt morning currents. So much for *The Wall Street Journal*.

The meeting Moudon had been told to arrange got under way in the executive dining room. Legal and contract experts were there with stuffed briefcases. Vic Moudon had completed comparison parametric studies of 17-10B and European Consortium Skybus weight/power/performance figures. 'We'd like to dump the whole 17-10 programme back in Buttress's lap. But we can't. We already have 17-10 hardware.' It was a four-hour head-to-head session of Aspinwall and his principals. This time the middle-management staff flunkies weren't told to vamoose, and tension rippled through the room. Matt laid it on the line. 'We can pull that unilateral crap as well as they can. I'm not interested in improvements in the basic 17-10. *Not now*. We've still got the Big Season primed and I'm not going to let them screw that up.' Then he turned to Moudon. 'You can handle 17-10B negotiations at staff level. Report to me.' Again Matt insisted on the use of the undisclosed position paper. 'If those bastards want to keep us on the string, they've got to produce the performance in the B model two years earlier than they're promising. Otherwise it's the Skybus. The A might get us through this Big Season. But the road doesn't stop there. I want a telex sent: "17-10B contract does not repeat does not apply to current deliveries. Furthermore Air World disagrees with 17-10B contract specifications, to wit." List the problem areas. Lousy specific air range. Insufficient payload. You know what they are. Use your technical jargon. I want that message to be there by three this afternoon.'

'Yessir.'

'An oyster for Hollis Wright's luncheon table.' Matt smiled.

Riddick reread the telex three times through his rage. It was 2055 local time and Buttress was at work. Lights glowed ceaselessly up and down the production bays. Riddick unlocked a metal cabinet inside his inner office and began removing heavy blue books, hefting them out with both hands and tossing them on to his conference table in the adjoining room, half-foot-thick binders bloated with stacks of enormous graphs accordion-folded like maps. It was the 17-10 certification data and it bulged in great square clumps across the polished mahogany. Half a dozen men had taken their places around the table amid an aura of weariness and resignation. Riddick tossed clean yellow pads from another cabinet unceremoniously at each of them. They landed on the table in staccato succession that cut the atmosphere with slaps of acid.

'We've got some problems to solve and nobody leaves until we know where we stand.' Riddick rubbed his bloodshot eyes. The gathered men remained silent. Riddick turned to the one nearest the head of the table, the production foreman, pudgy and pink as if straining at stool.

'Everybody on board for the fix?'

The pudgy man smiled through his strain. 'If Miller can get his design out by morning, we'll proof-test the prototype by the end of the week.'

'Thank God for that.'

'Of course – '

'Of course what?'

The pudgy man hesitated. 'We still need time to integrate the production flow . . . and if there are any modifications – '

'Jesus Christ, we don't have time for all that goose-stepping!'

The production man looked glum. It was no use trying to justify the immutable laws of gravity to a wild-eyed boss who gave the impression of lunging like a cornered bull as he leaned over the head of the table.

Riddick clumped to the square metal coffee jug in the corner, levered a healthy squirt into a paper cup, and clumped back to his chair.

'OK, there's a lot to do and not much time. Let's get down to it.'

It was long after midnight, someone noted, and several additional trips to the coffee jug, before the group completed the message for Air World and sent it down to communications for transmission. It was 0700 the next morning when it began to arrive in Matt's inner office, a twelve-foot TWX spelling out new contract proposals. It rolled from the teletype machine for minute after minute, a dozen feet of gibberish. Matt just stood and stared, holding a double paper cup of hot Tanzanian coffee suspended in his hands, as the rolls of yellow typescript cascaded in ribbonlike piles at his feet. He knew it was a deflection and it brought back the glassy-eyed anger of the dockside. The harsh even chatter of the keys spelled out a reminder that other airlines would be given open options on early-delivery blocks of the new 17-10B. Matt chucked his coffee into the wastebasket nearby and turned to Moudon, whose face was wreathed in consternation.

'They're trying to bluff me,' said Matt. 'Maybe they'll

let me have a one-season exclusive. Maybe not. Then everybody else up and down the street will have the B and we'll be sucking hind tit.'

Moudon didn't respond.

'We'll see about that,' Matt muttered, and without waiting for the clacking teletype machine to finish, without reading a word of the technical proposals, he went to his desk, ripped a single sheet from the telephone pad, and in broad strokes with his felt-tip, wrote two lines. They were barely legible.

'Send this,' he said, shoving it at the transfixed Moudon.

It read: 'THIS AEROPLANE UNACCEPTABLE ECONOMICALLY AND UNSAFE OPERATIONALLY.'

The words boiled across the torn sheet. Moudon gaped at them then up at Matt. 'You sure you want to send this?'

Matt's response made him draw back. 'You're goddamn right I do!'

'But – this part about being unsafe – '

'Send it!' Matt ordered. 'And follow it up with a call to Riddick. I want an immediate response. One I can read and understand. Not this,' and he kicked the scroll at his feet, ripping the paper with his shoe.

Moudon hustled from the office.

Several hours passed before the answer came, at 2115 West Coast time. It was past midnight in Moudon's office at Kennedy. Moudon reached Matt at home. Matt was wide awake.

'Looks like they were on a fishing expedition,' Moudon ventured.

'What'd they say?'

'Well, they conceded that the performance will be provided at no cost.' Moudon was gloating as if he personally had snatched the victory cup. 'They didn't mention the safety – '

367

'Read it to me!'

Moudon began to read from the jumbled collection of typed lines on the sheet he held. '"Your attention invited to amended 17-10B contract proposals with particular reference to upgraded performance provided by increased use of graphite-epoxy in 17-10B weight-reduction programme – "'

'The bastards are blowing smoke at us!' Matt yelled. 'I'm not convinced it's a good idea to use all that graphite-epoxy in the B. I was never completely sold on the idea it was needed on the planes we already got. I've been listening to that bullshit for eight years now. But tell me why NASA is still running safety tests on that stuff. Hollis wants me to be grateful the weight is down, but I've already got more than half a billion dollars tied up in this programme and no way are we going to pay any more for his or anyone else's experiments. I've got passengers lined up to buy tickets and I don't have enough decent aeroplanes to carry them on. But TWA does. I'm not in business to give TWA my business!'

Matt's impatience was becoming all-consuming. He sat down on the edge of the bed as he talked and clung to the hope that it wasn't that serious out at Buttress; because if he travelled west again so soon it would be an admission that he'd reached the pass where he must have his final heart attack. Matt understood he needed help – he had known it for a long time – but he hadn't wanted to relinquish a particle of control and yet his chest was filled with exhaustion. Inescapably he knew he must now entrust the first acre of his domain.

'Vic?'

'Sir?'

'I've never seen you as VP material but that's only a reflection of my own stubbornness. Put your things together and we'll find you a corner room and stick a new title on it. I don't know if I'm right in doing this but I've got to rely on it. From here on forward you call me "sir" and I'll kick your ass. What d'you say to that?'

'You bet your ass, sir.'

Matt laughed, gratified.

Moudon waited without a word, signalling he was comfortable with his response and wasn't going to retrieve it.

Matt liked that. 'I want you to head out to Buttress and go nose to nose with them – walk into the middle of their creative-writing class and yank them back to reality.'

'I can be on their turf by sunup.'

'Walk in unannounced. Type out an order for the Skybus and stick their noses in it.'

Moudon was about to reply.

Matt was too quick for him. 'Flight Eight Six One. The nonstop freighter. Leaves at 2 A.M. Put you in there before five. You've got a no-bump priority first class. Shove your shaver in a bag and get going! I want some answers back before lunch tomorrow.'

Moudon managed to nap through three restless hours on the grimy cargo aeroplane and suffered the taxi ride to the Coolidge Hotel on Grand Avenue. The sixth-floor corner suite with its broad living room was intimately familiar, the subdued scene of pitched corporate battles, and entering, Moudon felt the bleak isolation that came with revisiting yesterday's foxholes, empty but awesome in the desolate misty silence. Air World had an exclusive on the sixth and seventh floor corner suites overlooking the bay through old lace curtains, sites of past advances and retreats, corporate regroupings and new assaults amid the white-shirted armies augmented in relays, with millions in jet-plane sales the prize. He went into the bathroom with its chipped white tile floor and old four-pronged faucets labelled H and C. He stood there and regarded the future and regarded too the four small pills in his palm. And he filled a glass with water and used it to chase the Placytol. The new technology diet, he brooded, a granular substance to veil the environment and maybe dissipate the unease he suffered over Buttress. And perhaps – his mind flared with a kind of desperate glee – perhaps it would work for all the delusive volcanoes of new technology. Then, fitfully and in awful fragments, he slept.

The first clue Buttress might be in some disarray came with a cryptic phone call informing Vic Moudon the meeting couldn't be held at the Coolidge Hotel as in the past. He dressed and with new trepidation he went to the plant. At first Riddick's secretary kept him waiting, which he took as an open disclosure of heavily suppressed urgency. Then he was told Riddick was unavailable. It was not until nine forty-five that he was ushered into a room filled with people he didn't know.

Moudon was on the phone to Matt by ten-thirty West Coast time. Matt was eating lunch in his office, a salad sent down from the executive dining room. Moudon heard him crunching the lettuce over the phone.

'Buttress replaced their chief contract negotiator – '

'Who's the new man?'

Moudon mentioned a name.

Matt laughed. It was a tacit concession that the tone of negotiations would change. The *substance* might change too. 'The bastards are coming around. I knew they would. It's a new ball game, Vic. Stay in there. And get back to me.'

Moudon was back on the line four and a half hours later. 'The Buttress senior comptroller has been promoted to senior vice-president – '

'So they finally moved *that* asshole off the organization chart! Time someone told him to stick to his books.' Matt was gloating. He stood up and paced his office. It was music to his ears. 'Go on.'

'. . . and the manager, Cruise Missile Division, has

been named to the position of assistant general manager, Civil Transport Division. Directly under Riddick. The 17-10B will be delivered as promised.'

There was a pause. Matt's voice came back with a new note of gravity. 'It's a smoke screen. Maybe we're winning. Maybe not.'

'Buttress insists the reason for our 17-10A being held up now is still tied in with the 17-10B contract.'

'We've got to get it back on track. Don't let 'em give you that. Drop the axe if you need to. Our contract for the 17-10Bs isn't signed yet. *Remember that!*'

It was shortly after that the tone began to change in the West Coast meeting from one of forced cordiality; the first shades of testiness became apparent. Moudon began to feel the panic: it nudged him like a bulldozer. That and the pressure and fatigue. Air World needed at least eighteen 17-10s to ensure the Big Season and there wasn't much time 'eft. Moudon transmitted the message from Aspinwall's no-letterhead position paper. 'Air World has been paying Buttress on time – a hundred and seventy-five million dollars so far up front and all of it transmitted on the day it was due. There's another thirty-five million due next Tuesday and you can be sure that it will be in your comptroller's hands by 10 A.M. that day – *provided* the next two 17-10s roll into our hangar by nightfall. We don't care how you do it, but we must rely on the contractual delivery dates.' The new Buttress negotiator said he understood Air World's sense of urgency, 'but you must also realize certain occurrences which were unpredictable must now be taken care of . . . certain shortfalls in performance . . . minor ones but irritating in a time sense . . . By the way, the other airlines are coming along with their orders for 17-10s, especially the B. They're going to be the beneficiaries of your farsightedness in initiating the 17-10 project.'

Moudon studied the man and said evenly, 'If I were in

your place I'd be sure not to cross Air World on being the first to launch an entire fleet of 17-10s. The others can take off just as soon as ours are operational. You'll find the details of that condition on page one thirty-two paragraph six, the last three lines in the contract dated November seventeenth.'

The Buttress negotiator looked at Moudon and said softly, 'Let's hope we won't have to renegotiate.'

Moudon took a long sip of water from the glass on the table and said, 'Let's hope we won't have to go to London.' Within five minutes he had Matt on the line.

'They can't live up to the contract.'

'Keep the pressure on those cocksuckers. Don't let up *one inch*.'

'Something big is going on, Matt. It's like wartime out here.'

14

Guy had been startled by the call from Doug Moss, who had said that he'd decided to keep their meeting. The forty-eight hours were up, he'd said, and he had something he wanted to give Guy. And so it was, on the next morning, that Guy found himself bounding up the steps at Penn Station in New York and on to Seventh Avenue, where he hailed a cab.

'Head up Eighth,' he said to the driver, fishing in his pockets. 'I've got to find the address.' After leaving Moss at La Guardia, he'd thought no more of his quickly spoken threat to him to return with something concrete within forty-eight hours. He'd been venting umbrage; but perhaps Moss's ride in the T-34 had been a cathartic after all. What was it Moss had for him? Moss had refused to discuss it over the phone. Perhaps it would be important enough to take to the New York *Times*. Perhaps Moss had a gun instead and was going to pay him back for the ride. There was no way to tell who was and who wasn't crazy any more.

The cab moved slowly past sleazy storefronts advertising 'Love Teams' and peep shows with private stalls where middle-aged visitors in search of renewal could sit with their pants open looking through a piece of glass at a woman lying naked on a turntable. The restaurant was a narrow Szechuan eat-in and takeout palace with a false brick front, dirty glass and red neon beer logos. Guy paid the driver and moved quickly past three bare-chested blacks in leather vests on the lookout for whatever was next. Guy knew that hurrying past would provoke them.

'Better move, motherfucker! We gangsters, motherfucker!' one yelled and they all laughed.

Inside Guy shrugged off his leather jacket by the alcove next to the two purple-lit cigarette vending machines and handed it to an underdressed girl cooped in the cloakroom. He pushed through into the bar.

Moss was seated in a booth nursing a half-full beer and working his way through a plate of rice and chop suey. Guy sat down opposite him.

'What's this, your regional office? You take all your clients here?'

Moss straightened the napkin that was tucked into his shirt. 'I'm not here under duress. I want you to know that.'

'Of course you're not. You're a born-again bureaucrat. You've made a decision for ethics.' Moss glowered at him. Anders smiled. 'Don't pick up on it. I'm here in friendship and gratitude. You're here with glad tidings. What are you going to do, pass them under the table?'

The waiter leaned in, lifted the glowing candle and cleaned the table in front of Guy. 'Want a menu?'

Guy demurred. The waiter dried the surface and left.

Moss scooped a forkful of scalding vegetables into his

373

mouth and chewed carefully. 'Your hands clean?' he asked. Guy didn't answer but watched as Moss reached into his coat pocket and produced a white business envelope. He held it for a moment, then handed it over and wiped his mouth. Guy slit it open with the back of Moss's spoon, and slowly removed the two folded sheets that were inside. The first was a subpoena. It had his name on it. The second was an FAA Notice of Proposed Certificate Action against him.

He'd been very neatly sandbagged. He'd just been served. The subpoena demanded his presence before the NTSB in its continuing probe of Air World Six, and the Notice of Proposed Certification Action recommended that his pilot's licence be suspended for endangerment to life and property during certain aerobatic manoeuvres in violation of the Federal Air Regulations over Long Island Sound.

Moss sat chewing rapidly with small mincing bites as though he had just discovered an unusual taste treat.

Guy pocketed the subpoena, then took the notice of proposed certificate action, touched its corner to the lit candle, rotated it slowly to let the flames race up its sides and stuck it into Moss's beer. The fire went out with a hiss. A short plume of smoke shot up between them and drifted away.

Moss tried to appear disinterested. 'I didn't want you to walk away from our last meeting feeling you had it dicked. See, without your silver aeroplane and the stripes on your sleeve, you're just another stiff in a Chinese restaurant.'

Guy leaned closer. 'There are three motherfuckers outside looking for something to do. If I give them ten dollars apiece, the only way you'll get out of here is disguised as a takeout order.' Moss was about to reload with another forkful when Guy suddenly reached across the table, clamped his hand across Moss's jaw, and squeezed. Half-chewed rice spewed across the table. He

374

held Moss's face up on its flexed neck like a carved owl atop a totem. 'You better think twice about cold-cocking me on my licence, mister. Because if you and your friends ever put me where I have nothing left to lose, I might want to look you up and go for broke. So don't do that. Even the Russians know that.'

Moss became alarmed at the blank vengeance in Anders's expression. In the smoky light Guy Anders had the look of a terrorist caught in the half-tone greys of a tabloid blowup.

Guy let go of Moss's face. 'So much for your ambush. Now you'd better start combing your brain for something I can use. You conducted an investigation. You had blanks to fill in. I want to know what you wrote!'

Moss began to rise, his face gaunt with wrath and humiliation. The spectre of Anders's raw malevolence checked him for the moment, and he stayed his impulse to lash back. He considered his answer. 'It hasn't been proofed.'

'Try your memory.'

'I have something else.' Moss adjusted his collar and reached into the other side of his jacket. He took a deep breath to steady his voice. 'And I brought you a copy. There are some things going on and it's hard to get a lock on how they might turn out.' Moss produced a folded memo and held on to it.

'What things?'

Moss shrugged. 'Cloakroom things.'

Guy waited for the waiter to pass them. 'You mean . . . hidden things. A little cigar smoke behind the barn,' he prompted.

'Backstage stuff,' Moss agreed.

Guy stared at him. 'That's a synonym for cover-up.'

'Not my words.'

'They're my words, they're my words, but there's a cover-up.'

'I don't ever want it said that I wasn't on the side of justice.' Moss's voice was subdued. 'So I have something for you. It isn't much but it beats a kick in the ass.' He shoved the memo across to Guy.

'First a subpoena, then a notification to rip up my ticket and now justice.'

'Oh, it's really got nothing to do with you,' Moss said archly as he finished his tea and wiped his moustache. 'You see, I'm buying a head start on the future just in case things . . . go the other way.'

Guy stared at him unbelievingly. 'My God, the reincarnation of Rudolf Hess has flown over to the Allies! I thought for a moment you'd scared up a conscience! But it isn't your conscience at all: you're applying for a credit line!'

Moss unfolded the memo and resumed eating. 'Read what it says.'

The text was double-spaced on a pale-green sheet, standard eight-and-a-half-by-eleven size, reproduced in brief paragraphs under the letterhead which stretched across the top in innocuous small black letters: NATIONAL TRANSPORTATION SAFETY BOARD. Guy had to sit back and refocus in the dim light before his eyes could ferret out the crucial words:

INTERNAL MEMO. NOT FOR RELEASE

As the result of additional technical information recently made available to the Board's engineering staff in conjunction with the incident involving Buttress model 17-10 aeroplane US registry number N1711AW at John F. Kennedy International Airport, Jamaica, New York (Air World Flight 6), it is recommended that the Board temporarily delay issuance of final determination as to the probable cause of said incident pending further limited evaluation of certain aspects of the aeroplane's fly-by-wire flight-control system. In particular this evaluation should be directed to a determination of the integrity of certain electrohydraulic components in the pitch circuit, namely . . .

At the bottom of the page the signature stood out in bold isolation: 'Douglas R. Moss.'

'Have you filed this?'

'Last night.' Moss didn't meet Guy's eyes.

Guy exhaled. He could picture Fenton Riddick in his closed dining chamber reading the memo, his jugulars standing out like purple stems. At last, here before him lay the first reversal in the battle to gain a foot-hold. And Doug Moss, from within this no-man's-land might rise up to be an ally – one of convenience – but an ally nonetheless.

'Is that all?' Guy shoved the memo into his shirt pocket.

Moss placed a couple of bills next to his unfinished meal and was sliding from the booth to go. 'What the hell else do you want, Anders?'

'It's a start. But there's more.'

The clamour of the street was hard-edged and hostile as the two men pushed outside. Guy took Moss's elbow and steered him into an alley ten yards farther on that opened on to a parking lot. 'You don't want to walk on Eighth,' he said. Moss wasn't sure if it was a friendly gesture or not. He tried to slip free of Guy's grip but Guy tightened his hold. The air stank with diesel fumes. They continued in silence for a dozen steps before Guy stopped him. 'Now tell me more about the cover-up.'

'But I just gave you – '

'That was very nice but I'd rather talk about the cover-up. See, it's different for me. I don't have all that time to plan for the future like you do. My future is this afternoon.' Guy backed him up against a partly demolished wall. 'So who's in this cover-up? How far in is Buttress's finger? Who's at the end of the string? I want to hear about the daisy chain, the IOUs, the payoffs, and I don't want it in instalments! I want you to get it out of your system right now. Go back home with your head nice and light. Now either you talk or I'm going to start winding you up. Let go. I'm not hearing anything.'

Guy was leaning nose to nose, close and graphic, just like it was for Moss in the T-34. Moss tried unsuccessfully to swallow the discomfort that rose up and choked him. He looked helplessly from side to side but the pedestrians that slouched by were too far away.

'No names. I won't give you names.'

'Then we'll move on to current events – the very latest things you know about. We'll start with that.' Guy's fist squeezed Moss's collar hard against the dark brick and this time it made Moss catch his breath. 'Come on, Rudolf, I want it now before a newspaper digs it out of a pyre, before somebody on a flight deck somewhere gets handcuffed because of it!'

Moss felt his pulse quicken and he wanted to take Anders on, but he couldn't impel himself to do it. The unpleasant realization that he really wanted to be on the other side rose up to invade his jammed throat. He'd always known it, never had been able to keep it completely buried, although he'd got fairly good at a long-standing obligation to hold his ground. He'd even built a career on it, poking and kicking his way through charred and smoking aeroplane wreckages down the years, collating and numbering pieces of human bodies. Only once had he puked on the go team . . . yet, grudgingly, he understood Guy's plight and bitterly envied him his battle. He closed his eyes. 'I want you to get your hands off me. Then we'll talk.'

Guy complied.

'They have – there's a 17-10 research simulator – on the BGR premises . . .'

The stale air of the alley suddenly smelled pungent.

'I must have missed that,' Guy said quietly.

Moss's face was downcast. 'It's part of an ongoing improvement programme . . .' He stopped, looked back up the alley.

'Goddamn considerate,' said Guy.

'They're trying to investigate some conditions – '

'Let me guess – '

' – that might occur in extremely improbable circumstances – '

'Such as might happen to the 17-10 if it were jammed.'

Moss looked up. 'No one's going to jam a transport.'

'By a thunderstorm,' Guy went on calmly, 'by the pulse of an electric storm like the one we ran into on our way to New York. Maybe they're also looking into free fibres released from the graphite-epoxy beams and spars – high-technology dust that can worm its way into the computer. That's classified stuff,' Guy smiled. 'Now how would you rate that as a guess?'

'No one can say I told you that!' Moss's eyes were wide.

'Douglas, what's so special about your mortal ass that you're spending all this time protecting it? That's god-damn un-Christian. All this time there's this dumb co-pilot saying something's gone wrong and all this time Douglas Moss is in the sub-basement looking to subpoena his licence.' Guy checked the alley. 'It's my guess that all of Buttress's fly-by-wire computers are vulnerable – the ones stashed in F-19s and in 17-10s. What would be your professional judgment on that?'

Guy pushed Moss hard up against the brick wall.

'The problem is,' Moss offered, 'they're only vulnerable sometimes – when a stray signal gets in. Like the flux from a storm.'

'Or graphite-epoxy fibres.'

'Graphite-epoxy fibres,' Moss conceded.

'Stray neutrons.'

'Cosmic rays,' Moss added.

'They're vulnerable to everything except the captain's hat.'

'Something gets inside, sits frozen like a bug on a windowpane, then runs wild through those chips like a thumb on a keyboard.'

379

'We're not going to forget any of this, are we? We might want to crank all this up for a future hearing.'

Moss blanched.

'If your mind is feeble, we can get you down on tape two blocks from here. What do you think?'

'I'm late for an appointment.'

'You going to remember?'

'We'll both have to see.'

'Now tell me about this simulator.'

Moss fought back his exasperation. 'Holy shit.'

'Don't you get holy on me now.'

'It's in the wing next to the F-19 chamber – the one we were in. They're trying to duplicate what you and Cosgrove went through. I don't know how far they've gone. I still think it's premature – that's the truth.' Moss slumped. 'That's current,' he said.

'Suppose I said I wanted you to make that public?'

'They'd kill me.'

'Who'd kill you?'

'Certain parties.'

'Is that "party" or "parties"?'

'It's not exactly killing. It's accidents. A pilot who can't see can't be a pilot. An investigator who can't walk is out of work.'

'What about that mechanic cut in two and Melissa found with her head rolling free on Montauk Highway? What about Natalie Mason? What was that? Was it Riddick?'

'I don't know. No one knows.'

They stared at each other.

'Those things are bought,' said Moss.

'By who?'

'My guess is no business is turned away. It's part of our service industry.'

Guy brushed some chalk from Moss's sleeve. 'You didn't have to tell me any of this, did you? You were free to stand there and bullshit me.'

Moss stepped away from the wall and clear of some rubble. 'I give to things like the Red Cross . . . just in case.'

'Wise. No one ever knows when they may need some blood.'

'I've also been known to root for the underdog. But don't ever lay a hand on me again.'

He let Moss go. This new development at BGR sounded like a promising target of opportunity.

Miller left the plant walking slowly. The day was sunny and warm, people were in shirt sleeves, laughing. It was a good day. The fix was complete. Summer had begun for Buttress, even Riddick was in a festive mood, and Miller was buoyed by it. At last the 17-10 was behind him.

The receipt of Buttress's annual shareholders' meeting notification in the mail always came as one of life's arresting improbabilities to Ben Reese. He'd been put on the mailing list, he surmised, sometime before when he'd first launched his coverage of the Buttress scene, and though it should have become obvious that he had not the slightest interest in ever becoming a Buttress shareholder, it was equally obvious that the computer hadn't yet eliminated his name. But the letter's arrival was fortuitous because it gave him one of the best ideas he'd had since his wipe-out in Paris.

It gave him the way to get rid of Jasovak.

He let the idea grow over the remaining length of his dwindling stogie. At length he got up and rummaged through a pile of junk in his closest until he found Buttress's last annual report. He flipped through it two times, searching. The information he sought was printed vertically at the bottom of the inside rear page, almost hidden in the crease beneath the staple. Smiling, he poured himself a hefty slug of rye, decided he harboured no doubts about the idea, and called United to book a seat to the Coast.

Nine hours later put him on the red-carpeted corridor towards the Avis reservations counter at Los Angeles International. According to Buttress's form letter, the shareholders meeting was scheduled in a month's time. That meant the new annual report was already complete or in dummy form just prior to being printed. Either way he would have to move fast.

He noticed nothing out of the ordinary when he was handed the rental sheet at the red-and-white counter. The Avis shuttle bus dropped him off in front of a freshly washed car.

Ben's flight had been delayed and he'd have to hurry. He removed his jacket, threw it on to the passenger seat and slid behind the wheel. As he did, his attention was attracted by a wide rubber band placed precisely around the equator of the gearshift knob. He started to slip it loose, then, feeling a chill of premonition, lowered the window and looked behind him. The parking area was deserted except for a young couple struggling to jam their luggage into the trunk of another car. Ben worked the rubber band free and held it in the palm of his hand, puzzled. He turned it over, studying it. It seemed exceptionally dirty on one side. On an impulse he placed his thumbs inside its loop and pulled. There, in small but clear block letters along the stretched rubber, Ben read: 'YOU'RE IN THE CROSS HAIRS.'

Sonofabitch.

The ignition switch had become ominous; he decided to leave the car where it was. Carefully be opened the door, retrieved his jacket and stepped back into the afternoon heat. The sun reflected from the roofs of shimmering cars around him, and bore in on him from alongside the

382

intersection of frames that carried the airport's elevated restaurant, a glass-enclosed flying saucer suspended beneath sweeping legs arching high above it. Ben couldn't make out details clearly with the sun directly behind its uppermost spine but his instinct told him that he was being watched from there.

He shut the car door, crossed through the triple lane of parked cars and broke into a trot. Suddenly it occurred to him that he'd been lured into the open, made vulnerable, just what the message intended. He needed distance. He sped up, running hard, his lungs surging with exertion, the scenery blending into streams. Dodging through a sparse row of palm trees and across the access highway, he emerged on to an airline cargo ramp. He felt exposed, the lone figure running on the far end of a football field while the hushed crowd watched the sniper raise his telescopic sight to the base of his neck.

Ben stopped to slow his heartbeat and his thoughts. Reaching his destination in Pasadena required wheels. Right now he needed to make a call. A battered phone booth stood crookedly at one end of a low cargo building, and Ben pushed himself through the partly jammed door, slipped a coin into the slot, dialled Buttress's main number and waited. Deep in the shadows of the adjacent cargo dock he spotted two loaders begin the onerous task of hefting a closed metal coffin from the back of a hearse. The Buttress line continued to ring. Ben peered over his shoulder at the four curved spider legs with their elevated glass body, now partly hidden, standing in the airport's central meadow which was bathed in yellow light. Atop the spider Ben saw the indistinct silhouette of . . . beams. Or was it a tarpaulin and a crutch?

Awareness flooded his brain but before he was able to move the bullet slammed into the upper panel of the phone booth door, shattering the glass, and left a three-inch hole in the vertical metal frame.

Ben sank to his knees amid a shower of glass slivers, shouldered his way free, and loped the few yards into the cool safety of the loading dock. The noises there had muffled the sound of the bullet's impact. He checked over his shoulder, shaking the dust and glass free. Mopping his brow gingerly with a sleeve, he made for the hearse driver, who had just shut the tailgate and was folding his paper work.

The figure atop the elevated restaurant lay flat against its uppermost dome, one foot hooked around a thin smoke vent for support, and waited. Almost directly below, a groundskeeper manoeuvred a mower. Just beyond, accumulating afternoon traffic jolted in torrents along its endless clockwise procession. The man atop the restaurant readjusted his weapon, peering past its silencer. Several minutes went by before the hearse eased into the sunlight and drove up the narrow ramp on to the main access road.

The hearse driver pressed a switch under the dashboard. An antenna emerged from the left rear fender. Ben lay flat on his stomach inside the rear compartment holding a phone, the cord extended as far as it would go.

'We use it when we carry somebody big around and we gotta get on the phone,' said the driver. 'I want you to know no one ever used this as a cab before.' He shrugged. 'Listen, it's your money. Now take the guy who was just in here, choked to death on a piece of meat. He was over here on some cultural deal . . .'

Ben put a finger in his ear and heard the Buttress phone ring. Then the pickup.

'Buttress Aerospace.'

'Advertising, please.' Ben kept his face to the floor.

'Listen, take your time,' said the driver. 'We ain't got nobody in the freezer.'

'Advertising.'

Truck traffic suddenly closed in around them. Ben cupped his hand around the mouthpiece. 'Listen, this is Ted McGillicutty of the Advertising Council over in Des Moines and we want to invite the people in the advertising department at Buttress to this year's regional conference of aviation advertisers.'

'Yes.'

'And I want to check the names we'll be sending invitations to. Maybe you can bring me up to date on that. Have there been many changes?'

'Since when?'

'Well, maybe you could run through the names while I check it against what we had last year.'

'Mr Dunlevy is still the director.' The voice was barely audible.

'That's Michael Dunlevy.'

'No, Robert.'

'We had that wrong. And next?'

'There's James Bartholomew, Celia Alderhaus . . .'

'We didn't have her.'

'She's been with us for two years. There's Willard Jenkins.'

'Yes, we have him.'

'And Arthur Moore and I guess Anthony Calzone. That's about it.'

'Calzone, Anthony,' Ben repeated laboriously. 'Appreciate your help.'

'No problem.'

Ben reached over and replaced the phone. He rolled over and looked up at the sky. 'This is a pretty comfortable ride.'

'We don't get too many complaints.'

Ben inched up on his elbows and glanced to the rear. Gauze curtains partially obscured his view but no one appeared to be following. He sat up, worked his wallet loose, edged the bent photograph of Anton Jasovak free and slipped it into his shirt pocket. Then he balled his jacket into a pillow and decided to get some rest.

It was nearly five when the hearse pulled up to the main entrance of Atherton-Healy Printing, which was housed in a single-storey building that extended a full block behind a residential Mexican façade. Wedged in at the end of the block Ben noted several small industrial shop fronts. One had a large sign identifying it as PEACE MESSENGERS; a bearded, middle-aged hippie, his day apparently done, sat out front on a metal chair next to a parked motorcycle, his garishly painted helmet and folded leather jacket alongside as he fed a scrawny cat.

The timing was perfect.

'Park it around the side and keep the meter going,' Ben instructed the hearse driver.

The girl at reception was putting on her pumps to leave when Ben told her that he needed to see someone who had responsibility for the Buttress account. She pressed the desk-top intercom and without sitting up, hollered, 'George or Dimitri, up front!'

The pneumatic sounds of presses slapping and pumping sheets of paper against typeface rippled through the building. A stubby, mid-thirtyish man with an open, dark face appeared. He was wearing a pinstripe apron and drying his hands with a paper towel. 'Yeah?'

'George?' Ben asked.

'No, Dimitri.'

'Dimitri, we got a problem.'

'Yeah? On what? Here it's five o'clock and we got a problem,' he told the receptionist.

'On the Buttress job. On the annual report.'

Dimitri turned to a wall stacked high with cardboard boxes. 'You got a big problem,' he smiled. 'The last of that job's finished. Two hundred thousand copies.'

'We may have to do it over. We left something out.'

Dimitri stood stock still studying Ben's face. He dried

his neck and carefully rubbed the towel over each of his fingers.

'I'm going home,' said the girl.

Dimitri finished his pinky. 'I think we better get George in on this,' he said. 'I didn't get your name.'

Ben ignored the challenge and walked past him. 'How well do you know Bob Dunlevy?'

'Not personally.'

'We had to let him go. Screwed up. We're going to straighten this out before anything reaches the chairman.'

'What are we talking about here? Something on the cover, on the front or the back?'

'In the middle.'

Dimitri had a finger on the intercom. 'George, up front.'

'George left early!' a young voice boomed back.

Dimitri let go of the button. 'Can this keep?'

'I wouldn't be here if it could.'

'The job turned out beautiful.'

'Something of a delicate nature was left out.'

'Who was it left it out?'

'Who did you work with on this?'

'Hey, we only do the job,' Dimitri begged off. 'We don't hang nobody.'

'Will Jenkins, Arty Moore, Tony Calzone?' Ben persisted.

'Tony, mostly Tony and the girl.'

'Celia?'

'That's it.'

Ben figured his credentials were intact.

Dimitri threw the towel into the wastebasket. 'I'm going to need to see some authorization.'

'I want us to get going on it tonight.'

'Tonight! We can't just go ahead like this. We're closed.'

'No you're not.'

'We're a union shop. When the little hand's on the five and the big hand's on the twelve, we go home.'

'You're confused. Buttress isn't some subchapter S outfit looking for fifty sheets of letterhead! I'm sorry to upset your plans and if you feel we're too much of a burden, if we make you nervous, we'll take our action somewhere else! So maybe you want to take a few seconds with your mouth closed to think about that!'

Dimitri's expression was grim. 'I need a purchase order. You're talking about overtime.'

Ben swung the phone around and dialled Buttress. 'Give me purchasing.'

'They've gone home.'

'I don't care. Ring it anyway.'

A young, breathless voice came on the line. 'Yes, hello?'

'Listen, do me a favour and look up the PO on the annual report made out to Atherton-Healy.'

'Who's this?'

Reese lowered his voice. 'Bob Dunlevy.'

'We're all locked up.'

'I need it as a favour.'

Dimitri picked up a line and dialled an extension. 'Tell Angelo, Dwyer and the kid to stick around. We've got a problem.'

'The number is 13-462-418-7.'

'Have a nice evening.' Ben threw the phone down. 'Here's your number.' Dimitri picked up a pencil. '13-462-418-7*A*.'

Ben took the old dog-eared photograph of Anton Jasovak he'd carried for the better part of two years from his shirt pocket and smoothed it against the desk. Dimitri raised his eyebrows.

'That's a pretty beat-up photograph,' he said, looking at it doubtfully.

'I want you to print it with a black border around it.'

The printer picked it up and held it against the light. 'Jesus,' he said. 'Young guy. When did he die?'

'In a few days.' Ben looked up with his best sorrowful expression. 'He's terminal.'

'I don't know that we can get a run on this till Tuesday.'

'Now, come on, Dimitri, you're pulling my prick. I need it by the morning.'

'By the morning?' Dimitri was shouting.

'Seventy or eighty proofs.'

'What the hell for?'

'Advance copies, VIPs, family, admirers.'

'Do you understand what's involved? You realize what I got to go through?'

Ben smiled and took the photograph back. 'First we got to find the page to put it on, then we got to scale it and lay it out and your artist is going to make a nice black border, then we'll shoot and screen it, strip it into the old form and burn a new plate. Then we'll run the page front and back and we'll get on our hands and knees and pull staples. You can't horseshit me. You're looking at a frustrated news-paperman.'

'I still don't know your name.'

'Willis Wright,' Ben said without flinching. 'I'm the nephew.'

Dimitri was momentarily taken aback. 'Well, I'll work with you, Mr Wright.'

'You'll find when you get to know me I'm a real patsy.'

'I don't guarantee nothing. This may take most of the night.'

'I'll hang around.'

It was almost nine o'clock that evening when Ben noticed a second car pull up outside the plant and from what he could see, both drivers remained behind their wheels. The sedan was a Caprice, the other looked like a Fiat but Ben wasn't sure. The driver of the hearse had gone out earlier for some Chinese food for the crew and was inside now with his feet up on the reception desk watching the tube. Ben shut it off.

'Job finished?' the man wanted to know.

Reese motioned him over near a window and turned off the light. 'Look out there. See those two cars?'

'The Caprice and the Triumph?'

'Do I look like a paranoid?'

'No, weird. You're closer to weird.'

'They're here to kill me.'

The hearse driver studied the scene, first the cars outside, then Ben. He moved away from the window. 'You better level with me. I mean, I got nothing against the mob, you understand. We have a good professional association . . . but are you – is this –'

'I'm not with the mob. Do you think you can lose them?'

The driver peered at the two vehicles again. 'I drive an ambulance Sundays.' He turned away from the window and studied Ben. 'How much money you willing to spend?'

'Whatever's in my wallet and whatever my cards'll carry.'

'Then I've got a better idea. What you want to do is get rid of them, right?'

'That's what I had in mind.'

'Give me the phone.' The driver reached seven of his associates and came up with four takers. Within thirty minutes four hearses had circled to the rear of the building and backed up against the darkened loading platform. Minutes later all five hearses tore out of the driveway and headed in different directions. The two cars burst into life and rolled out in tentative pursuit, each heading a different way.

For additional safety, Ben locked himself in the john. Dimitri knocked on the door about midnight and told him the new annual reports would be ready by dawn.

* * *

390

Dick Miller entered his office, which seemed small in the darkness. His palm fumbled along the side of the door searching for the light switch, but three passes up and down failed to locate it. Impatience twisted the droop around his mouth. Then his hand swept the wall wildly and with a click the fluorescent tubes blinked on, buzzing faintly. He went quickly to his file cabinet, where his hands fastened on to the folder he wanted in the third drawer down, and, leaving the drawer open, he lurched back towards his chair to leaf through it. The corner of his desk seemed to reach out and nick his hip with a reproachful jab.

Sitting there he placed the unopened folder on the surface before him and gazed towards the pane of glass across the room as blank and black as the far side of his soul. There's no way to look through that window and see the sun come through the same way any more. It couldn't break up and refract in the red tones that once would fall so gently on a little anvil that he had at the corner of his shop. And he used to love looking at that high anvil with the refracted light on it because it had a rich brown in the metal edged with gold tint. Now the sun glares off white walls.

With a grunt Dick pushed his chair back and shuffled into the silent outer office where the secretaries worked. He sat down at the first desk he came to and removed the cover from its large electric typewriter. Opening the bottom right drawer, his eyes sought the plain bond. The first he pulled out had engraved Buttress letterhead; in the adjacent slot he found what he wanted. Holding the white sheet as straight as he could he turned the roller and switched on the machine. The carriage jumped and it startled him. When the paper appeared centred, he began to type. The first words were:

MEMO
TO: G. HOLLIS WRIGHT
FROM: RICHARD S. MILLER, FLIGHT-CONTROL DESIGNER

At that point he stopped and pored over what he'd typed. His scan travelled past the name to a place behind it where he struggled to deal with himself, where his perception of himself was that of a painted actor whose grievous inner weakness remained hidden from view . . . He licked his lips and with two fingers punched the keys. They sounded like rifle shots as one by one they formed the words:

I FEEL COMPELLED TO WRITE YOU THIS WARNING

He brought himself back, inspected the message so far. Slowly he removed the sheet, crumpled it and threw it away. Like a man lost on a pitching deck in a storm he tottered towards his office, reaching out and missing. His hand shot out to grab a book that appeared to be falling, and knocked it to the floor. Dick remained immobilized; he could almost hear the babble of people who would fill these offices tomorrow, people talking in terms of computer programs, people who never mentioned *aeroplanes* any more. All babbling about things that had nothing to do with what he did.

He regained his balance and moved away from the cabinet, reaching up to brush his eye with the back of his hand. Standing, gripping his chair hard as if to steady himself, his eyes clenched tightly shut, he listened, as if in a dream. From outside came the sound of a car's wheels on gravel, a horn blared, muted by the distance. Cars arriving . . . cars were beginning to arrive already . . . he could hear the babble outside. Could it be the generals arriving? But he wasn't ready yet. He could visualize the sleek Lancejet still waiting behind closed curtains in the bay three floors below. They'd have to get their white coats on. Jesus Christ, where was his? He couldn't remember where he'd left it. The extension was 876 . . . 1 . . . no, 8176. He opened his eyes, the room seemed much smaller to him. He checked his watch. My God, there won't even be time to go home. He reached for the phone and dialled the familiar extension. A strange voice answered. Miller began to speak but his words caught. He cleared his throat and tried again.

'Andy?'

'Who?'

'Is this 8176?'

'Yes, it is.'

'Is Andy Cromer there?'

'Who?'

'Andy Cromer. Where is he? Do you have another number for him?'

'Who is this?'

'Miller. He wasn't transferred was he? What time is it? Maybe he went home.'

'Dick?'

'Who's this?'

'Burt –'

'Burt, I think I'll stay overnight, sleep on the floor. The roll-out's six hours away. They're downstairs shining her up now. Tell Andy. I want him to call me back.' Dick paused. 'Leave him a note.' There was joy in Dick's eyes. Chin forward, he felt himself surging in the wind.

'Dick?' Burt struggled to make sense out of the words. 'Dick . . . for Christ's sake, Andy Cromer's been dead for ten years.'

'What?' Dick was hoarse, suddenly impatient. 'What the hell are you talking about?'

'Dick? . . .'

Miller hung up and sat with a glazed expression, holding on to the edge of the desk to quiet its sudden pitching. He reached for the phone again, pushing his arms through nets to touch it and finally lift it from its cradle again and dial information. But it was after hours and no one answered. He let the receiver fall to the desk top and suddenly alarmed, pushed himself to his feet.

'My God, we have a roll-out in the morning . . .'

He went quickly back into the corridor and headed towards the office he knew was situated across the production bay. Someone appeared around the corner and bumped into him.

'Excuse me – oh, hi, Dick.'

'There's a roll-out in the morning. Tell everyone.'

'What?'

But Dick had stumped away, filing along the corridor's edge with quickening pace. He turned towards the door that led to the catwalk across the vast production bay.

When he had crossed the threshold it was as if he had entered a dark theatre in which a malevolent opera was already under way, and he was in the eaves, backstage, looking down on to a performance played by great empty hulls with webbed green insides which floated by, dull silver ships without water, attended to by crews of black, Lilliputian figures. The noise assaulted him and slowed his steps and the massive vibration in the air rose up in his body in strident whispers that shrieked into his skull building one on top of the other until he stopped and grabbed the rail and pulled his chin in tight against his chest so he could force all the pressure down his legs and out towards the tips of his toes, waiting until the chorus had ended. But it didn't end, it rose up around him like a waterfall in a chasm he was straddling and he felt the moisture on his body from it, the heat from this demonic cascade, and he knew he had to get to the other side, over to the side where he could open his eyes and look up at the friendly wooden rafters and tin roof with eyes heavenward neck craning vision straining sunbeam dust dangling dazzling smell of dope ball peen hammer stammer . . .

There's a roll-out in the morning . . .

Dick's eyes clamped shut again, he grabbed on tight.

Hand over hand on the rail he pulled himself across the abyss opening his eyes to see hangar-door cliffs whirling lights reeling on roller-coaster tracks. He moved he had to get to Cromer's side where he could have spent the rest of his life going inward on his lovely Lancejet but computers were coming and like a child at the wall with a crayon he was yanked away too soon too soon.

There's a roll-out in the morning . . .

The sign man found him like that, struggling with the door, both his hands on the knob jerking it back and forth, his face contorted. Before the sign man could speak Dick begged him, 'You gotta get that door open for me. We have a roll-out in the morning . . .' He wiped his mouth with his sleeve. 'We're not even ready . . . Andy and I have to get together on it.'

The sign man's cart was filled with the blue placards that dangled over the doors, 17-10B AVIONICS, 17-10B FLIGHT-CONTROL SYSTEMS, 17-10B HYDRAULICS, and he was changing them because the plant was doubling up, going into overdrive. He consulted his list.

'This office belongs to Llewelyn. What number do you want?'

'Andy Cromer's office . . . Lancejet project office . . .' Dick was out of breath. He began to sob. 'Jesus Christ, you gotta help me out.' And he began to sag to the floor, sobbing, his fingers slipping down the doorjamb.

The sign man looked around in alarm. He hesitated but then reached down and tried to hold Dick up by the shoulders.

'It's late, mister. C'mon, we'll get some coffee.'

The sign man held him as he staggered a few more yards down the hall into a cubbyhole with vending machines and sat him down on a crate nearby. Coins jangled in one of the machines and soon Dick felt the paper cup at his lips as the sign man fed him some black coffee. Dick blinked and looked into the sign man's face. 'What time is it?'

'It's after ten.'

Dick struggled to his feet.

The sign man was peering closely at him. 'You wanna sit down a little longer?'

Dick's eyes were glazed. He paused, looking away. 'It's . . . OK.' Without another word he stood and walked slowly down the long corridor, past the locked office, and turned from view, back towards his side of the building.

The Santana rolled across the high desert with the scorch-breath of a thousand locomotives, enveloping all before it in clutching gloves of heat that seethed into distant canyons and stretched husk-dry westward towards the Pacific. Its fingers scooped Don Devlin's hair and roused Hollis Wright's too out there on the desolate test range. Don Devlin, the FAA's Northwest Region chief, had turned his back on Hollis Wright: he was actually walking away from him. No one walked away from Hollis Wright, not even the President, yet Hollis watched as if petrified, a pillar with carved features, the ridges in his cheeks as deep as the ravines on stark mountains fifty miles away.

Hollis sprang to life and went for Devlin, the patriarch after the lackey. But Devlin didn't stop. He was headed for the battleship-grey Chevy marked US GOVERNMENT – OFFICIAL. He reached the door and opened it when Hollis came up, white hair out of place, rising in the wind. The sun broiled the flat open miles where secret aeroplanes flew and Hollis paused, more surely a part of this place than human.

But Devlin was not intimidated. He entered the car. 'I'm through with the conversation, Mr Wright. I'm not going to sign it.'

Hollis had to restrain an urge to yank Devlin back from the car by the cords of his neck.

Devlin looked at Hollis Wright, one hand on the open car door. 'Your aeroplane doesn't need a new actuator. It needs to be unravelled and rebuilt.' He paused, seeing the anger blaze up around Hollis Wright's collar. But the man kept it subdued and Devlin was impressed; a tiger in a tuxedo, he thought.

Finally Hollis spoke. 'A man's a member of a larger group, Mr Devlin,' he said shrewdly. 'It's like a family . . . there are interrelationships, responsibilities – '

'I've never been a member of the club. The only cheques I get arrive on Fridays.'

'We won't settle for that.' Hollis's tone was parched. 'We're on every runway in the free world and we have a right to be there.'

'Maybe.'

'This engineering change is pro forma. You've been instructed to sign it.'

'I won't do that because I don't have enough answers.'

'What kind of answers are those?' It was a threat. 'I'll give you whatever answers you want right here.'

'The incident at Kennedy. Nobody in your shop wants to talk about it. And I sign nothing until I've had that conversation.'

'Your people have been in and out of our computer like cockroaches.'

'Flight Six caught fire at nine thousand feet over Deer Park.'

'You'll have to check with the engine manufacturer on that.'

'Or maybe a fuel line broke instead. You people don't know how to read and interpret your own data. Flight Six began shaking itself apart seventeen miles before it crossed the centre of a thunderstorm over Long Island. That's a problem.'

'We have a cure. We're going to retrain the crews on how to read the flight manual.'

397

'I'm more interested in correlation between thunderstorms and the Flight Six control vibrations.'

'There's no proof of correlation.'

'The lights went out in Cedarhurst as Flight Six passed over on its final approach to runway thirty-one left.'

'A rat got into the substation. There was a dog that blew out half of Queens the week before.'

Devlin pointed at Hollis's chest. 'I think it's time you people got off the pilot's back,' he said, his voice unexpectedly deep with fury. 'There's a story going around at NASA that says when the graphite-epoxy you're using in the tail of the 17-10 catches fire, it sheds microscopic fibres that can penetrate concrete and screw up everything from the local utility to the IRS computer in Denver. It can even gum up the on-board flight-control computer. That's what NASA says.'

'NASA doesn't take the responsibility.'

'Buttress submitted an incomplete FMEA. Your people ignored electronic corruption! You couldn't identify the connection between the computer output and possible null bands in the servos!'

'Don't you goddamn get insolent with me!'

'The pressure bulkhead holding all three hydraulic lines should be rebuilt. You make a joke of fail-safe. Your 17-10 should never have been certificated in the first place! You've got to start thinking redesign!' Devlin reached into his pocket, grappling with a piece of paper that had jammed into the crease. He pulled it free. It was Moss's memo and he thrust the green sheet under Hollis's nose. 'The NTSB may be thinking along the same lines. According to Doug Moss, they want to have another look at the hardware!'

Hollis swept the page from Devlin's hand and let it fly, whipping on the hot desert gale. 'There's no way you people are going to lay another year on something that already took us eight years to create,' Hollis rumbled hoarsely. 'All the money's been spent. We put the new actuator in and we did that on our own hook – no directives.'

'I think your new actuator is a decoy. In fact, I think it's a lot of public-relations crap!'

Hollis felt the sweat in his palms and inwardly recited a five count, watching Devlin with street-fighter eyes. He stood, aware he'd become something of a monument as he regarded Devlin's dungarees; then he clamped down, accepting that the game had taken on a broader, more deadly dimension. He welcomed the final grapple. For a long sweeping moment he was the technician on the verge of initiating the sequence for a nuclear strike and he wondered if he had the ability to regain control . . .

Devlin noticed the occasion, fleeting as a hot breath, that widened Hollis's eyes for just an instant. But he wasn't interested in pursuing it. 'If you don't like the call,' he said, 'maybe you'd better get a new umpire.'

'Oh yeah?' Hollis laughed. 'Is that right? A new umpire, huh? Well, we're going to hold a party for you. Invite all your friends. Because you're a real pisser.' Hollis stepped back and was speaking lightly now. 'I think you ought to be commended for being – so straightforward. And your boss ought to know what a good job you do. It's not every day a man on your – level can make such an outstanding decision. In line – in synchronous tone with your conscience – and do such a fine job for our United States Government. So we're going to throw a party for you. We need more people like you . . .'

Devlin looked up at Hollis Wright uncertainly. He shut the door. 'I gotta go.' He started the engine.

'Something like this shouldn't be forgotten . . . characters like you should be – memorialized.'

Pausing as the engine idled, Devlin saw Hollis Wright as a flinty obstinacy set against the silent thunder of the desert, and for a moment he was immobilized, trying to repel the deep-seated feeling that he had just been sentenced.

15

It was a soft spring morning and Anja had insisted: for one whole day the 17-10 must not be mentioned. It was her dictum . . . spoken as a plea.

'There's something I want to show you,' she said. 'It isn't perfect but it's close. It'll do for the moment.'

Guy had no idea what she was talking about but climbed into a pair of jeans as she suggested. Jamie was in school. She would do the driving.

A Western Union messenger had his hand poised to ring the bell as Guy opened the front door. Guy took the envelope, ripped it open and fished out the folded page. The message read: 'COMPANY MAIL ADDRESSED TO ME AT BUTTRESS OFC JFK. HAVE A RED RIBBON NOT YOU PICK IT UP. YOU'LL HAVE TO TAKE IT FROM HERE. N.M.'

The Western Union man got back into his car and pulled out of the driveway. Guy reread the words, 'Have a red ribbon . . . pick it up.' Natalie Mason was still somewhere – but her last line sounded all too final and, waiting there in the still morning air, Guy stood awash with a terrible sense of foreboding.

'Who was it?' Anja asked, coming up from behind.

'There's something I'd like you to do for me,' Guy said. 'At JFK.'

Anja shrugged. 'OK, it's a detour but only a little out of the way.'

At Buttress's JFK office, Anja located the narrow company mail room and, as "Natalie Mason", asked for "her" West Coast mail. The young clerk finished shaking the contents out of a grey canvas sack and said, 'West Coast mail's not in yet. Why'n't you check back at two.'

Less than an hour later Guy and Anja stopped within sight of the Atlantic Ocean. Guy had said little on the drive out, wary of the folded telegram in his pocket, not knowing what to make of it. He searched the distant beach; white sand dunes with tall clumps of grass stretched on both sides. To the left sat a sparse line of small wooden cottages.

'What do you think?' Anja was smiling proudly. She got out first. Guy followed. He let his shirt hang open as they walked across the dunes that fronted the string of bay shacks. Most of the old structures were run-down, several with their windows and doors smashed, but there was one, a small, peeling white clapboard cottage with faded red trim which, from the distance, seemed in perfect condition. Guy watched the clumps of tall reeds that surrounded a small pond sway and heard the ocean roll beyond the bay shack row. Anja put her hand into his.

'Come on,' she said softly, 'squatter's rights. I found it.' She pulled him over the last dune. The wooden steps to the house were broken and slanted into the drifting sand which sloped against the porch. Anja went ahead of him and pushed the door aside. It was quiet – the beckoning quiet one hears from the core of a seashell.

'OK,' he smiled. He carefully moved a couple of old bottles to one side. 'What do we call it?'

The living room was dusty with broken baseboards and the settled-in grey from too many wet seasons. Flotsam and jetsam of abandonment littered the space. A brass bed lounged awkwardly against one wall, the mattress covered by an off-white chenille spread. An ancient lace curtain curled languorously in the breeze. It was tattered but revealed a previous charm.

Outside in the pond two ducks glided, their bodies motionless as they circled their iridescent universe, a

401

hushed presence separate from the race against time. Slowly Guy crossed to the other window, the one on the ocean side, where he could still see, far away, a piece of his world. The great jets wheeled in their approach pattern to Kennedy over Howard Beach as they turned inbound, the twinkling lights on their wings in procession through the grey haze like diamonds slanting slowly down a string. The rumble of their engines followed and reached him like the beat of distant surf. He stood like that, continuing to watch, for a long time. He tried to envision his plan to break into BGR, fly the 17-10 simulator Moss had mentioned, but the more he tried to give it shape the faster it receded until it vanished. Anja was real . . . her presence evoked long-buried memories, back to his first girl in high school with skin like hers, skin like powdered sunshine, smooth, resilient, and cinnamon hair swept loosely back . . . her eyes open with anticipation, eager for fulfilment, serene in its expectation . . .

Anja studied Guy; he seemed more lined than she remembered. He would become more rugged, she thought. He would age well. At that moment his attention was pulled outward, to the sky above Howard Beach.

He tried to thread through the incongruity of having been on fire over Howard Beach with the fact that he was now standing observing the inbound pattern from the calm of a sand dune. He turned away. He felt her fingertips on his arm. He saw her looking into his eyes with a placid yet urgent expression that glowed from the core of her.

Slowly she took his face in her hands; her breath was warm and the sound of the sea thudded in his ears. Her lips and tongue were as sweet fruit, her skin warm velvet, the fragrance of her enveloped him as gently he laid her down. Her breathing mingled with his kisses. She rolled hungrily over his body, he felt the current flow along the stretched-out length of them and lifted her slightly to gaze in rapt wonder at the perfection of her nakedness.

Now Anja guided him. They both gasped at the first exquisite moment, he at the splendour of the wet warmth that surrounded him, she at the completeness that he brought into her.

Pale shadows danced on their entwined bodies, the muted sun catching the gold in the erect fleece of her skin, and he held her to him while wordless noises rose up from the pit of her, hot broken sounds to race with the pulsing of the sea nearby. He was safe again and whole, at peace . . . She felt the intensity of her body as it was roused to the edge of sensation; he moved with her, deeper, and felt himself rise up to empty and drain and fill her to overflowing.

He held her close and imagined how it might be with her on a day still to come . . . on her white sands, the two of them spinning through trails of dappling sunshine, laughing, drifting suspended in peaceful sundowns . . . the image had brilliance and a shuddering beauty to it. Now as he looked at her he saw possibilities that hadn't crossed his mind since his wife died, and for the first time the thought had no betrayal in it.

The dunes were almost shadowless in the waxing sun and the bay shack too was washed with light. Inside, Anja looked over at Guy from where she lay and reached out and twirled his hair slowly in her fingers. When she spoke it was with the languor of intoxication.

'This will be gone soon,' she said.

She was leaning across the pillow, holding her head in the manner that was a private statement to him. 'But it won't matter.' She turned slightly away from him and cocked her head as though trying to hear something. 'This is only the first room of my wonderland. I can travel endlessly from here all the way inside a dewdrop and sit with the tall grass outside and watch it bow towards the sea.'

He barely perceived her words which floated in whispers behind his memory.

403

'Everything around us is pulling the other way, isn't it . . . ?'

Lying there, the sun spoking through the broken windowpane, he appeared much younger, and she could imagine the two of them isolated in a world of unconcern, where parting was unthinkable; yet his statement was playing and replaying between them. Even before she spoke she already sensed the vision of him hurtling outward. The earth receding . . . the meaning of having owned this moment with him growing fainter, then disappearing beyond recall.

He fell asleep. The house became silent except for the steady rhythm of his breathing. A wind sprang up and it grew darker. The rustling curtains lifted, throwing strong shadows across the bed, corporeal fingers of net clutching at his body. She shuddered, seeing him again caught in webs of metal shards, struggling to breathe. She wanted to touch him, to shelter him, but she remained still. Only the curtains stirred.

He awoke and lay still while looking about to reorient himself. She was still by his side, watching in silent vigil. Outside, the trickle of the inlet rang in a litany of little bells. He felt shunted off balance by the quiet, the momentum of his struggle still pounding inside him. At last he let go and that tempo became still to dwindle and it left a searing ache, like knotted muscles in the aftermath of an emergency. He had been living with twentieth-century signals but deaf to himself. How long had it been? From the first shriek of his Air Force fighter the industrial growl had been unending. His senses were returning, it seemed, for the first time in years and he began to hear the brush of the curtain on the sill and see the shadows curling on the white bed, extending and diminishing, leaving a blank spot in the eye.

He propped himself up on an elbow and tried to visualize the simulator at BGR . . . he couldn't . . . and gave up. He flopped back into the coolness of the pillow.

'You make it difficult for me. I like it here better.'

Outside a contrail bore doggedly forward and the distant rumble of other Kennedy departures drifted towards them.

Several hours later, at JFK, Anja returned to Guy waiting in the metered parking lot carrying a brown letter-sized envelope. Guy opened the door and she slid in.

'Success,' she said.

Guy took it from her. It was a crisp interoffice envelope, its front blackened by rows of scratched-out names, except for the most recent entry, a scrawled notation, 'Natalie Mason, JFK.' Guy unwound the red tie string and opened the flap. A plastic-coated Buttress ID card fell into his palm. He turned it over and felt his scalp go electric. The face peering back at him from the one-inch-square photo on the card was that of Fenton Riddick.

FAA Administrator Nicholas Muskgrave sat watching the planes diminish as they flew over the Pentagon, each descending in turn to land at Washington National Airport just beyond. He fixed his gaze on a spot high on the smeared window where each plane would appear and he was pleased to see how many sliced precisely through the stain he'd picked out. Only one swooped in from the side several inches wide of the mark and seemed to struggle to get in line in the short distance remaining. It was eleven in the morning and muggy but he felt chilled and pulled the sheet close around him. The rumble from the aeroplanes overhead seemed to make his teeth chatter until finally he was unable to keep his eyes open any longer and he let himself fall asleep.

Hollis Wright had been trying to reach Muskgrave for four days – ever since he'd seen Devlin – but the administrator hadn't been in his office or at home. The people who should've known where he was were acting non-committally, but Hollis wasn't used to being put off. Despite Devlin's rebuff, the fact that FAA headquarters hadn't yet acted on Miller's fix had left him only minimally concerned; but the fact that FAA Administrator Nick Muskgrave had suddenly disappeared altogether had begun to interfere with the chairman's sleep and so in the middle of the fourth night he turned on the light and ordered his crew to the field, where he met them, and they were airborne and headed east before three.

At Washington National the early morning air was already steaming. But in Hollis's private compartment the processed air from the engine bleeds was so cool as to be almost chilly. The chairman pulled the curtains aside, saw they were already down to perhaps fifteen hundred feet over the Potomac on final approach, one corner of the Pentagon just passing out of view beneath the window's edge. He glanced at his watch, knew it was probably too early, but punched the numbers on his private phone anyway.

The woman who answered for the FAA sounded like a man. 'Sir, I'm sorry, but Mr Muskgrave won't be in today.' Now how in hell would she know that – unless . . . 'Would you care to speak to someone else?' she asked.

'Put me through to his deputy.'

A man named Chuck Poloff identified himself. He was brusque. 'Who's this?'

'This is Hollis Wright, Mr Poloff. I'm ten minutes from your office and I want to know where your boss is.'

Poloff let a moment of stunned hesitation get ahead of him. 'I knew you called yesterday, sir –'

'Where is he, Poloff? Is he in the building?' There was no answer. 'Is he in the can? If he is, I'll wait. Is he in conference somewhere?'

'Sir, he's out of town.'

'Which town would that be, Poloff?'

'He's been called away.'

'I'm at the airport right now and if he's somewhere I can fly to, you tell me that now. Our engines are still spinning. Where is he, Poloff?'

'I'm not certain I can tell you that, sir.'

Hollis felt the blood pounding against his collar and yet the man's answer pleased him. It made him feel he was back in the street where he had begun, with the doors being slammed in his face. He had relished yanking each door open, shoving the corporate ass kissers aside and battering his way to the top. He slipped the receiver gently into its receptacle and waited until the taxiing aeroplane came to a stop. In moments he'd taken the aluminium stairs two at a time and reached an orange-and-black cab that had just pulled to the curb. He felt certain it was going to be a good day.

On the eighth floor of the FAA building, Chuck Poloff heard Hollis Wright's name mentioned outside his office door and quickly busied himself with the latest copy of the *Congressional Record*. It was a futile way of protecting his sovereignty and he knew it but there was nothing else at hand. Then his door was thrust ajar and he saw his two office girls standing apprehensively in the shadows. The door opened further and Hollis Wright stepped inside.

'All right, goddammit, where is he?' Hollis demanded and he kicked the door shut.

Poloff's face went red. He closed the *Congressional Record* and shook his head. 'You know, I've really not been at liberty at all – ' His voice rose weirdly but Hollis cut him off.

'Now you listen to me, you creep. I'm not going to play twenty questions with you. What's his number?' He stirred some papers around on Poloff's desk. 'Find his number.'

'You're making a spectacle.'

'Is he on annual leave? Is he away overnight? Is he back on the oil? Huh? Did he get himself boiled?'

'I'm under no obligation.'

'You're under every obligation, Mr Poloff,' Hollis retorted menacingly. 'Let's not be under any illusions as to what goes on around here. There isn't a government peckerhead in this building who can't be shitcanned by two o'clock daylight saving time and that includes you! We can get someone else to sit in your chair and jerk off five days a week by making a phone call! So you're under every obligation! Where is he, Poloff?'

'I'm a loyal man, Mr Wright.'

'He's shitfaced, isn't he?'

'He's having personal problems.'

'With his wife? Is it family?'

'No.'

'Is he home?'

'No, he's not home.'

'Where is he?'

Poloff stood looking at the mess on his desk. The game was over. 'If you promise – '

'Nobody's gonna know,' Hollis snapped impatiently. 'Just you and me.'

'He's at the motel across from the Pentagon. He's registered under the name of John Nicholas.'

The DC cabby lounged at the wheel with his arm over the back of his seat and said he wasn't going to take Hollis to that address. 'You got to wait for a Virginia cab,' he said.

'Is that right?' Hollis pulled a fifty-dollar bill free, placed it on top of the seat next to the driver's arm, climbed in and slammed the door.

The driver took off like a drag racer.

Hollis lowered the window and let the warm breeze catch him full in the face. The city was already cooking and it wasn't even noon. Off to the right the Potomac sparkled and just beyond the sun pressed down on the Pentagon. The tyres whined as they threaded on to another ramp. Hollis wished they were headed for the Pentagon instead. He visualized the portraits of generals hanging along the corridors. The Mall entrance to the Defence establishment was passing just off to the right. Hollis had friends inside the Pentagon and his visits there had always been comfortable. He hadn't noticed when the cab finally stopped at the motel or paid any attention to the costumed doorman's melodious welcome. He knew only that he was walking briskly through the padded gold-fringed darkness of the motel lobby, intensely anxious to face Muskgrave head on. He lifted the gold house phone and, like a fighter waiting for the bell, felt invigorated at the prospect of confrontation. He asked the operator for John Nicholas's room number and was told it was against the motel's policy to divulge room numbers.

'Then put me through.'

The steady pattern of ringing began. It continued, over and over, it seemed to go on for minutes. Hollis waited grimly. Finally he heard the phone being taken from its hook.

'Nick?'

There was a protracted silence. 'Who's this?'

'This is Hollis. I'm downstairs in the lobby.'

There was no answer.

'Where are you, Nick? I want to talk with you.'

'Leave me alone.' The voice was weak and infinitely weary.

'No, I want to talk with you, Nick. Just give me your room number.'

'Go away.'

'If you don't give me your room number I'll tear every fucking door off this place until I find you.'

There was a long pause. Hollis could sense Muskgrave trying to muster himself. Then, very softly as if from outer space, his voice came through. 'Four twelve . . .' It trailed off with ennui and utter defeat.

Hollis strode past the elevators and took the emergency stairs two at a time. The hallway on the fourth floor was dark and clammy and littered with midday carts carrying folded sheets and disinfectant. A set of passkeys sat atop a pile of folded towels. Hollis took the key ring, marched past the fire extinguisher and located 412. He tried keys in the lock until he found the passkey that fitted, and pushed the door ajar, encountering a resistance. Muskgrave had wedged a chair against the knob from the inside. Hollis hefted his weight against the door and shoved it open. A maid emerged from the room adjacent and stood gaping at him.

'Security,' he confided, tossing the ring of keys back to her and entering the room.

The odour hit him first: the room reeked of vomit and booze, foul and powerful. Then he saw FAA Administrator Muskgrave in bed, knees drawn up tight against his chest, a sheet wrapped around his shoulders, hunched over as though he were watching TV. But the room was silent except for the sounds of outside traffic and the aeroplanes overhead on final approach.

Muskgrave was aware of Hollis standing in the doorway bringing with him the fresh new air of the outside world. He saw him dimly in his peripheral vision but couldn't find the strength to turn his head. His ears were ringing. Hollis closed the door behind him and surveyed the debris. He could see instantly that Muskgrave had puked his guts out, and it was obvious the administrator hadn't let anyone inside for days. Spilled ashtrays and crusted plates of half-eaten food lay scattered on the floor around the bed and empty bottles had been tossed everywhere. The motel's complimentary bowl of fruit lay upended and shrivelling on the bureau and all the lights were on. Muskgrave's countenance was like that of a corpse, his

410

artificial ruddiness gone, replaced by the grey pallor which remained under the ghastly sheen. His hair hung in matted clumps. Hollis lifted the broken chair away from the door and set it aside.

'Jesus Christ, Nick.'

Muskgrave nodded unseeing, his glassy stare fixed directly ahead of him. 'Hollis,' he acknowledged. His voice which the industry knew for a trumpet was now a whisper, hoarse as though he'd been yelling. Hollis switched off the lights and retrieved an open wallet from the floor. What terrifying shouts had rung from these walls? How many hard fists of despair and anguish had they felt? Muskgrave sat unmoving.

Muskgrave reached into the hazy recesses of his mind for the resources he sensed he'd need. He knew he was up against the man who could play it with a violin or a pistol, and he knew too why he'd come. That single thought was clear in his mind but the idea of dealing with Hollis Wright fatigued him immeasurably. He could no longer focus. He closed his eyes. And as he huddled there, head bowed, there came over him an odd but certain knowledge, it came with the explosive power born of primeval instinct, and he knew what it was like for the hunted animals of the jungle. He recalled the wounded zebra he'd once encountered, throat already mangled and bloody, fully conscious but no longer able to react. And now he knew – no, he was – the very embodiment of that exquisite terror, waiting for the lion to close in again.

Hollis sat down on the bed next to him.

'My God, the way you look.' He took Muskgrave's wrist, felt his pulse. It was rapid and weak. 'What'd you do this to yourself for? Why didn't you call me? What the hell are people supposed to be friends for?' Hollis's cheeks deepened.

Nick Muskgrave was scarcely breathing.

Hollis stood up and opened the small wood-grained

411

refrigerator. It was empty except for a forlorn bag of potato chips. Even the ice trays were gone.

'I'm going to get some ice,' he said and moved towards the door. Muskgrave had no reaction. As Hollis opened the door, a passing chambermaid cast a furtive glance inside, her face expectant with wonder, then moved quickly away. Before she could enter the room across the hall, Hollis intercepted her. 'Honey, we need a bucket of ice.'

'There's ice around the corner on the other side of the elevators,' she announced.

'I know there is but I want you to get it for me.'

'I don't get ice for nobody,' she said, standing her ground. A second maid joined them. Hollis steered her aside to let a guest go by.

'Look, there's a man in four twelve who's in very bad shape.'

'That's one man? I thought it was a group,' grinned the one who'd just come along.

Hollis pressed a ten-dollar bill into her hand. 'I need a bucket of ice and a couple of fresh towels.' He crossed back to 412 and went inside.

Muskgrave, his head hanging on his chest, was leaning heavily on one elbow. Hollis pulled him to a sitting position and jammed a chair cushion behind his back.

'You got to get on top of this, Nick. Make up your mind to it. Shut it down or you're going to start puking blood.'

Muskgrave dragged a badly swollen hand across his mouth. His flesh had the consistency of boiled chicken. 'You bastards stole the certification,' he piped hoarsely.

A look of mock consternation spread across Hollis's face. He was intrigued by the challenge. 'You been seeing any mice or bats come out of the wall? Huh? Seen any rats walking on the ceiling?' Hollis waited, then smiled. 'You mustn't talk like that.'

The door opened slightly. The maid with the ice hesitated on the threshold, reluctant to enter.

412

'Lord Jesus,' she said as she surveyed the room.

Hollis took the plastic bucket and the towels and thanked her. Muskgrave watched him tight-roll several cubes of ice into a hand towel, then spasmed when Hollis pressed the ice roll into the nape of his neck and eased his head back. 'You're no good to anyone this way, are you?' Hollis said to the administrator gently.

Muskgrave felt bewildered. Not only had he failed to control Buttress but here he was, a casualty being rescued by the other side. He shut his eyes and grimly resolved to fight back.

Hollis went into the bathroom with the second towel. He filled the sink, soaked the cloth in cool water, wrung it out. He came back to sit on the edge of the bed. Muskgrave didn't resist when Hollis rubbed the cloth across his forehead. He did it with surprising tenderness. Muskgrave's skin was nearly translucent. After five days he wasn't just on a drunk anymore, he was close to shock. Hollis wiped Muskgrave's face with the gentleness of a new mother, bathing the crust away from his four day's growth of stubble. The stubble itself, unlike Muskgrave's hair, was pure white with the hue of an old and tired man.

Hollis pulled the brown blanket from the foot of the bed and draped it around the administrator. He tucked the edge under the mattress and spoke softly. 'This is a shit town, isn't it? It's always been a shit place.' He opened Muskgrave's wallet and shook its contents loose. Credit cards and pictures of Muskgrave's family spilled on to the bed. 'I've always seen you as a decent man,' Hollis went on. 'I've always liked you. Your family too. So we don't want to let any of this get too big.' He tossed the empty wallet aside, put the cloth down and leaned very close to Muskgrave. Somehow he buried his menace and managed to control the quaver in his voice.

'Were you aware that Devlin wasn't a team player?'

The administrator didn't answer. He seemed to be

weaving across the centre line between lucidity and languor. His head bobbed.

'I didn't know that either,' Hollis continued in mock repetition. 'You can imagine how that's tied things up.'

Hollis adjusted the ice pack. 'You know, it's funny, when you're younger you never think that the world would ever get this tough. As a kid I'd see a guy go on a binge and I'd ask myself what could there be in a world so great, with so many wonderful things in it, that would make him do a thing like that to himself?' The chairman stood and pulled the plastic night drape farther back. 'Is this enough light for you?'

Muskgrave, head back, didn't respond.

'There's something I want you to look at.' Hollis waited at the window and removed an envelope from his inside coat pocket. He stuck a pen in his mouth and pulled the cap free. 'All it needs is your signature.'

Again there was no response.

'Nicholas, can you hear me?' Hollis took the plastic breakfast menu from the dresser and smoothed the papers that had been inside the envelope against it. He pulled the last sheet free. 'We've been out looking for you for four days now, Nicholas. The fix is complete and it's a good one. We just need your approval of what we've done.' Hollis watched from the side of the bed and held the ballpoint out to Muskgrave. 'So we need your signature. I'll hold your wrist if you like.'

Muskgrave moved his head away from the towel. His left eye opened and it stared at Hollis. It was black and deep like the entrance hold of a funnel and it was naked with hatred. 'I won't put my name on it.'

Hollis didn't move.

Muskgrave held his mouth shut to keep his teeth from chattering.

'What the hell do you mean, you won't put your name on it?'

414

'Because it's a shit aeroplane. I don't read much any more, but Devlin wasn't wrong. I think you built a shit aeroplane.'

Hollis walked to the window and gazed back into the room. 'But Nicholas, it's your full endorsement that appears on the original type certificate – and now suddenly it's a "shit aeroplane"? The Administrator of the Federal Aviation Administration is sitting here with his guts poisoned offering us his considered judgment that the 17-10 is a *shit aeroplane?* Well, pardon me but you'd better think about that, you goddamn closet drunk! You better think about that!' With a swift motion of his foot Hollis kicked a pile of newspapers and clothes. He upended a case of toilet articles, which skittered across the floor, and tossed the empty case contemptuously against the wall. 'There's a story about you hanging around urinals at Penn Station looking at dicks. Page-one stuff for every tabloid in every supermarket in the country. You don't want to let it all end the way it did for that poor bastard on Wall Street, the one they found sucking some guy off in a public toilet.'

Muskgrave could barely piece together the effort to face Hollis's calumny. But he tried. He hoisted himself on his pillow and, reeling slightly, challenged his tormentor.

'What you need, Hollis, is someone to put a letter in the mail to the Attorney General before the hearing starts covering the last fifteen years of our lives!'

Hollis was stopped in his tracks, flexed as though struck by a sledgehammer. His eyes groped in disbelief at the unlikely source of it.

Muskgrave in his drunkenness scarcely realized he'd thrown down the gauntlet, only that another dimension to his intoxication suffused his head, a fresh exhilaration that now aroused and propelled him. He rolled across the bed and staggered free, ripping at the sheet which twisted around his ankles, at last finding his feet. Lurching against

415

his feebleness, he headed for the window. 'That's what the people . . . ought to hear about!' he shouted, impelled by his sense of sweet irrationality.

Hollis recovered quickly and made a grab for him. Muskgrave reached the handle and tried to wrench the window open. '. . . Tell them how I signed off shit . . . how I protected your proprietary interest!' The administrator's voice trembled. His face was contorted with rare release.

Hollis grappled with the stumbling form. It was heavier and harder than he expected.

'You made promises and you didn't keep them!' Muskgrave seethed through gritted teeth, giving up on the window.

Hollis hauled Muskgrave's sagging body up like an unhinged mannequin and pinned it against the wall. He grunted, struggling to obtain a hold on the larger man; finally succeeding, he marched him back to the bed. Muskgrave sat down heavily, dizzy and exhausted. 'A long letter . . .,' he murmured with strange resolve, 'telling them about the last fifteen years of our lives . . .'

Hollis felt the sweat build under his shirt. His scalp itched. Muskgrave sank back into the gold canvas headboard and languished to one side, his face again dark and sullen. Hollis stepped away, gathering his concentration, attempting to arrest the warning that was welling up inside him. Perhaps Muskgrave in his wretched state would be prepared after all to crucify and bury a relationship of years. As Hollis stood considering the unspeakable, he gradually began to understand just what he faced. Could Muskgrave in his degeneration be imbued again with a sense of fellowship? Hollis might still reassure him, begin to repair his ravaged sense of worth. But the limits of Hollis's own anger were expanding beyond his reach and he went to the bathroom to try to gather them in.

'We've sung some . . . incriminating good harmony!'

Muskgrave called after him drunkenly. Then he swallowed back a rising urge to retch and raised himself up. 'If I can get the letter there before Wednesday,' he chanted in an eerie crescendo of strength, 'it'll all be over by Thursday.'

No sound returned from the bathroom and Muskgrave, with his pulse pounding behind his ears, watching the ceiling slowly gyrate, couldn't tell whether Hollis had left or not.

He held his breath and listened.

It seemed that several minutes had passed, the room had returned to its previous state of inertia. Muskgrave almost forgot Hollis in his slow drift towards slumber. Then, with a chill, he heard a definite sound that burst through the tight space of the room. Muskgrave tried to make it out: glass, scraping on tile, its delicate metallic timbre whispering once, and again. The unmistakable sound of broken glass slipping as from a groping hand. Muskgrave caught his breath.

Slowly Hollis Wright emerged from the bathroom. The lividness of his face was concealed by the shadow in the foyer but Muskgrave, through his swirling vision, could perceive a gleaming thin device in Hollis's hand. Hollis stepped solemnly into the room. Involuntarily Muskgrave pushed himself with effort to sit up, jamming himself against the headboard, feet pedalling under the sheet. Hollis was hunched over, head down, holding the broken remnant of a vodka bottle with one long edge sharp as a scalpel, flashing like a diamond. A small amount of fluid remained trapped within its top curve; Hollis tipped it up, letting the contents spill out in a fine trickle, watching the liquid slip through the serrated edge on to the floor. He didn't look directly at Muskgrave as he lowered the glass and in a strange half crouch took a restrained step towards the bed.

Widening stripes of consciousness spread rapidly

417

through Muskgrave's brain. His eyes cleared, he saw that Hollis's face was chalk-white and that his body was shaking. He also saw that Hollis was still holding the broken bottle by the neck, its long thick sliver pointed towards the ceiling. Muskgrave's tongue felt keen prickles as his throat clamped down on the traces of his bile. He blinked in wonderment as Hollis, barely breathing, shifted his grip on the broken bottle and let his fist close around the bottle's neck so that the sharp end was now pointed down. Like a dagger.

Muskgrave didn't move from the tangled heap at the head of the bed. He watched aghast as Hollis struggled, constricted in the voltage of his appalling idea, and he forced himself to meet the chairman's eyes, which were unyielding. There was a long moment of sharpening realization. Muskgrave's mouth opened with the sanctity of a hymn.

'Oh – my God . . .,' he whispered.

Hollis stood with the slack expression of a dead fish, only his eyes alive, peering as if from behind bars at the base of Muskgrave's blotched and puffy neck.

Then his face began to quiver and with supreme effort he loosed his grip on the bottle and turned his back. There was a long pause before he spoke.

'You want to be careful to think like that,' he muttered finally and he let the broken glass go, resting it on the air-conditioning unit, where it rocked and came to a standstill. 'You're liable to think yourself right into prison.'

He turned towards Muskgrave again. His colour was back and he'd returned to his normal height. He pointed a stern finger at the administrator. 'Don't sign it. Don't put your name on it. Instead, we'll drag you outside and have the press take a look at you, take a few pictures. Maybe we can get them to join us here!'

Hollis circled the bed and picked up the phone. As he

did, he tossed the last page of the Service Bulletin on to Muskgrave's lap and threw the pen after it.

'Within one hour you're going to be holding a press conference announcing your resignation and you're going to tell everybody about your liquor bill and how you've been screwing the government afternoons and how you've been willing to exchange your signature for cash to get your half-wit son through school.'

'That's not true.'

'We have it on tape.'

'I wasn't myself.'

'You were a hundred proof and eloquent! Your next stop is the Bowery Mission, you ungrateful bastard! We're through fronting for you! Give me information, please. See if I'm bluffing. You're going to sell a lot of newspapers tonight. Hello, the number for the Associated Press.'

Muskgrave fingered the edge of the page lying before him but he couldn't focus on it. So he looked out the window at the 727 dipping below the far side of the Pentagon by the smear on the windowpane and he wondered why he'd ever come to Washington. Was it the decision he'd made in his twenties? How terrifying those decisions were, he thought. For he no longer cared a damn about aviation or Washington or Washington's official functions. He desperately wanted out. He wanted to lie down somewhere in a glen, but the game wasn't over. He had a year to do before retirement. He felt for the pen Hollis had thrown at him but couldn't find it.

'I need a pen.' His mouth moved but he was barely audible.

Hollis kept the phone to his ear, disconnected the line and unclipped his gold pen. He placed it in Muskgrave's upturned hand, which lay fallow on the sheet beside him. Hollis spoke courteously. 'Forget about dating it.' He flicked on the bedside light and watched Muskgrave close

419

his fingers over the pen, pull the page closer, and slowly, laboriously, write his name across the bottom of the page.

Noiselessly Hollis reset the phone and took the pen and the page and studied the signature. The tightly wrapped ice pack slipped to the floor as Muskgrave settled back with a plaintive groan, exhausted. The chairman blew on the signature, then folded the page into the rest of the sheaf and slipped it into his inside coat pocket.

'You know, maybe you ought to get away for a while, leave the States, go sit on the sand in St Tropez and watch some bare tits go by. Maybe it'll remind you what life's supposed to be all about.'

On his way to the door, Hollis picked up a vodka bottle from the dresser and, without changing his pace, lofted it into the bathroom. The bottle twisted slowly in a graceful arc, then exploded with a clatter of broken glass against the white tile.

At the front desk he motioned to the manager and pulled a wad of currency from his pocket. 'The man in four twelve – go in there, clean him up, put his hat on his head and get him home.' Hollis was scribbling rapidly on the back of a register blank. 'Here's his address – in Arlington. This is his phone number. Call his wife but don't tell anybody else about it.'

The manager glanced back and forth to see that no one else was within earshot. 'We sure are grateful, sir. We didn't know what to do next. There were some pretty bad things going on in there.'

Hollis pushed the money towards him. 'This should cover the breakage.'

'It's been quite an ordeal, sir.'

Matt Aspinwall held his horn-rimmed glasses in one hand and rubbed his eyes with the other. He replaced the glasses and fixed on Angela Sisson, a brief helpless moment at the end of the day.

'It's time to go home,' she said quietly. 'It's time for both of us to go.'

Darkness had come. The airport was a sea of tiny coloured specks of light, green taxiway centre-line lights under Matt's window, red beacons and blue strobes on the taxiing planes, the white haze of Manhattan spires in the distance.

Matt nodded. He scooped up four piles from various corners of his cluttered desk, arranged them into a half-foot-thick stack and shoved them into his briefcase. He could squeeze only one latch shut. Angela looked at him disapprovingly. 'Homework,' he said simply. He grabbed his mackintosh, wadded it under his arm, and left the office.

Matt walked slowly down the concrete fire-exit stairs, gripping the steelpipe rail. It was the only physical motion he'd engaged in all day and he knew he needed more. He grimaced and felt the hard bulge of the vial containing nitro tablets knocking through his trousers pocket against his leg. He shoved into the horizontal bar that pushed the heavy outer door open, uncomfortably conscious of his gut for the briefest moment, then welcomed the cool night air. Tall cluster lights, the type that lit baseball diamonds, shed streaks over the parking lot. Next to the building ten yards away a shadow moved, detached itself from the main mass of darkness and approached him.

Matt vaguely recognized the man – one of the thirty-five-year veteran mechanics. An older man with string-bean neck, leathery skin, and hair slicked back behind a wave he'd pushed up with his first two fingers. One of the old timers who could still remember unbuttoning cowlings on DC-4s. Christ, Matt thought, here it comes, more personnel problems. The mech stepped forward, into the light, and waved.

421

Matt was distressed but he realized it took a special kind of courage for the man to approach him personally, the kind that renounces the taunts of his buddies on the hangar floor. The old fellow had his Windbreaker on to neaten himself. Matt could see that as he surveyed him in the partial light, and he saw too that the mech had lowered his cuffs to cover his white socks.

'Hello,' Matt offered. His office door's always open, for Chrissakes, he'd told the troops that, and he forced a smile, trying not to reveal a trace of surprise. 'What can I do for you?'

'It may be none of my business, Mr Aspinwall, I'm just a grease monkey on the line' – Matt detected a certain pride there, despite the self-effacement – 'but I can see you're buying a load of shit and I don't know if anyone's telling it to you. If you'll excuse me, sir.'

Matt considered the words. He felt a chill on his arms. Nights were still cool. Be that way this year till mid-June probably. Matt could see the concern on the old man's face. The mech had never experienced the soft hush of the gold-emblazoned tower. Matt could sense that too. Probably make him ashamed of his grimy coveralls up there, like he was soiling the carpet.

'Do you want to elaborate on that?'

The employee swallowed, looked past the chairman's eyes. 'Hydraulic leaks when service it – things we don't expect.'

'Like what?'

'I know I'm talking out of turn, Mr Aspinwall. But you should know, sir . . .' The rangy old voice acquired conviction. 'I mean, my wife and daughter, they're flying to Rome next week – and –'

'What *exactly* have you found?'

'There's a lot of hydraulic fluid back there . . . up near the elevator actuator –'

'That's being redesigned. They're taking care of it.'

422

'It's all over the place – in 'most every ship that comes in.'

Matt pushed aside, smiling distractedly. 'I'll make a note.'

The old mech stood rooted, groping in his head. 'I wanted to say that I won't let my family on a 17-10,' he called. Matt walked away slowly. *'None of the boys will ride in one!'*

Matt eased his Mercedes on to the expressway but his hands were shaking. Vaguely he noticed the traffic was light, Christ, was it that late? Headlights were moving past aggressively. Brakes squealed, a horn blared. He'd wandered halfway across the adjacent lane. Almost too abruptly he pulled over, feeling the raw shudder as the right wheels scrubbed the edge.

He could feel the pulse in his neck and the distension of his abdomen. He'd felt naked back there without Moudon to turn to – funny admitting that – but he could virtually hear the scratchy quality of Moudon's voice saying, 'Well, a lot of material comes across my desk, we must get close to fifty service bulletins a week . . . always something we can make improvements on. But none of it's in the *basics* . . .' There was a service bulletin on the DC-10 cargo door that opened over Paris, a nonmandatory change, Matt reflected. That was basic and no one caught it. Well, this isn't like that . . . Then there was that asymmetric stall problem on the DC-10 at Chicago O'Hare. Jesus! Matt gritted. The lights ahead blurred into the smears on the windshield. Moudon's voice returned. '. . . I didn't see anything recently that particularly triggered me . . . I'll certainly look into it if you want me to – '

Headlights grabbed Matt by the temples. He swerved . . . a whine as the other car rocketed past, fitting into the inches between his door and the retaining wall, then the strange Doppler effect as its horn dropped from shrill to mournful.

Ever since that close call W. B. Cosgrove had recently everything has gone off the track. Buttress was changing the actuators, dammit – even Hollis Wright had acknowledged the new work – but just as adamantly he vowed it was cosmetic, not really necessary. The problem – if there ever was a problem – should be solved. The problem was nonexistent. Nothing should recur. Yet the threat of a fleetwide grounding loomed while they waited for Buttress to engineer something new. And then it would be too late. He could have the perfect aeroplane and it would be *too goddamn late!*

Matt closed his eyes; the only physical sensation was the rumble of the highway plates under the tyres. Christ, he couldn't afford it, none of them could, besides we already had our quota, they had to head off any hysteria.

A harsh squeal of brakes as Matt mashed the middle pedal. Asleep again, he rebuked himself, and jumped the divider into his exit with a lurch that threw the wheel hard over. Damn! Didn't see the truck already in his lane. A shriek as the truck headed for the shoulder. Headlights twirled in the rearview mirror . . . Thank God, he saved it! Matt felt cold all over and humble as he silently praised a truly expert piece of driving, totally undeserved, by the unknown in the truck with whom, in one split second, he might have shared the most devastating moment of his existence on a bloody curbstone. Got to pay attention. And he gripped the wheel hard with both hands as if it were a lifeline.

Should've been calmer back there. Don't get a mechanic with the balls to approach the CEO every day. The issue must have seemed important to him . . . '*Thanks* for coming to see me. Thanks for your concern. I'll call the chief engineer right away and we'll jump right on it.' Why couldn't he have said that? Reassure the fellow. 'My door's always open. Don't forget it.' That's the way we do business with the ranks. The simplest lesson, the one most disregarded. Doesn't cost a nickel, reaps a million dollars. And he'd been too preoccupied.

Too preoccupied. His wife noticed it the moment he walked through the front door. She merely looked up but he could read her face. She was in the large chair knitting. Quietly he placed his briefcase next to the desk, on the far side, trying not to disturb her, and went to the bedroom to get out of his shoes, find his slippers.

At that moment the phone went off.

Matt jumped for the desk, a curse on his lips. His wife raised a hand to calm him. 'There's no hurry, darling.' She desperately wanted to unravel the knot that had been so visibly tightening inside him since the yacht trip, but she was perplexed, it was all getting beyond her.

Matt reached the phone on the third ring. She saw him grab it as though he were cuffing it, he couldn't help it, she knew that. 'Hello,' he said. It sounded like a threat. Then she saw his eyes widen and he sat down thickly.

'Hollis?'

Matt didn't move, eyes fixed straight ahead. His wife began to knit more energetically.

In his Washington hotel suite Hollis Wright had spread the copy of *Newsweek* on the table before the telephone. It was open to the full-page full-colour Air World spread advertising 17-10 space-smooth service to Europe. Cleverly placed on the adjacent page was an article accompanied by a photo of Air World's chief pilot, looking good, endorsing the 17-10. Straight teeth and crooked smile. The page margins were dark from Hollis's doodling, heavy angular symbols with marks that criss-crossed the print. Next to the table was a bucket of iced champagne. Hollis had been refilling his glass when Matt picked up the phone. He took a sip and held the pale-gold fluid up to the light.

'Matty, I'm holding a glass of Dom Pérignon. I'm not

425

saying another word until you get yourself a glass. Go ahead.'

Matt looked around his living room, a little unsure of himself. The desk was littered and next to it his briefcase stood open, still filled with the stacks from the office. In the corner easy chair his wife had hunched before the nervous annoying revolutions that her hands made knitting another turtleneck. He turned back to the phone.

'What is it?'

'You got your drink?'

Matt sensed from the tone in Hollis's voice he meant it. With the idea already forming as a glow of warmth in the base of his head, even before any mental words came, he began pouring a large tumbler of bourbon from the crystal decanter on the desk. His wife looked up with a wan, alarmed expression.

'Yeah, I got a drink.'

'You're a liar and a sonofabitch, Matty, but you deserve to hear some good news for a change. Your 17-10 has been OK'd – a service bulletin, that's all it is. I have a copy of the signature here, the FAA administrator himself signed it this morning. It went into the file less than an hour ago. So take your time with the retrofit if you want – keep 'em flying instead. We're releasing the production line. And the paperwork'll be in your office by morning.'

Only the background static of the phone line could be heard.

'Matty, you're on your way.'

Aspinwall gulped a deep draft of whiskey, feeling it scald his throat, feeling a wave of elation pour through him. He felt the pain in his shoulders drop away. He looked at his wife's uncomprehending features, dimming behind the spontaneous film of tears forming in his eyes.

'By the way, Matty, your new ads are terrific. We're one team after all.'

426

'We love you, Hollis,' Matt blurted. 'Betty and I,' nodding vigorously at her. 'My God . . . it's approved?'

'Go to sleep, Matty. You're going to have the Big Season we promised. Good night.'

Ben Reese, chewing determinedly on a wad of bubble gum, clumped to the rear of the elevator at the Buttress hexagon and adjusted his sunglasses. The garishly painted motorcycle helmet jammed on his head and the leather coat with PEACE MESSENGERS embroidered on the back with yellow wings were a little tight but he didn't care and he let his face show it. He set the heavily bound carton of annual reports containing Jasovak's black-bordered photograph down at his feet and checked his watch. It was still minutes before nine. Employees racing to get in under the wire bounded on board, pressed their destinations and stood with their heads tilted towards the grid of numbers above the door. One balding man in glasses who had been shoved to the back glanced over at Ben, frowned, momentarily puzzled, studied the floor and stared at him again. Ben pressed a squat finger against the bridge of his sunglasses. He remembered the fellow vaguely – an engineer on the F-19, or an employee in avionics R & D – he wasn't sure – but he'd probably run into him when he'd first launched his abortive foray into the F-19 story more than a year ago.

Ben let his eyes wander in weary midfocus, worked his tongue behind the mass of pink gum, blew a bubble and let it snap against his lips. The balding man turned away. He got off at the third floor.

Hollis Wright's enclave was on six, an unmistakable aura of quiet power, controlled and absolute, behind closed mahogany doors. A hushed aliveness exuded from the walls and was conveyed by the luxurious deep pile of meadow-green carpet that led from the elevator to the glass-enclosed outer vestibule on the right. Ben's chin strap dangled against his collar as he plodded towards the central office. He pushed past the door marked CHAIRMAN and strode into the centre of a wood-panelled anteroom that connected Hollis Wright's inner office on one side to the polished boardroom on the other. Several efficient matrons and a drab executive who had not quite made it were checking dispatches, sorting mail, attending the percolator, awaiting the chairman's arrival. No one bothered to acknowledge Ben. Three women were engaged in making dainty pleasantries, gathered around a humming Xerox machine. Ben glanced around, parked the bubble gum to one side and hollered, '*Anybody named Wright around here?*'

The reaction was vital and lightninglike and more pronounced than Ben expected. Staff members' faces were smashed flat with the force of a physical shock wave. Ben could swear he saw a dress flutter and a pair of wing tips leave the floor. He savoured the reaction and decided to try again. He peered down at the label on the package as though to double-check the name and corrected himself.

'Anybody here called Hollis?' he roared.

The woman who appeared to be most senior stood thunderstruck. Painfully she broke past her wounded sanctimony and like a sour librarian homing in on a noisy troublemaker, she stuck her birdlike neck out and hissed at him.

'Oh, I see it!' Ben assured everyone in the room and barged straight through into Hollis Wright's private inner office.

'My God, you can't go in *there!*' the woman gasped and stumbled after him.

'You don't want to try and lift this here box!' Ben shouted over his shoulder.

Before she could enter, Ben had already slammed the

428

package down on the chairman's empty desk and was busy splitting the wrapper. The woman rushed in after him and stood in the doorway wavering in the shadow as Ben pulled one of the fresh annual reports free.

'You must leave at *once!*' The senior secretary was breathless and indignant.

Ben opened the annual report to the page bearing Jasovak's black-framed photograph, flattened the booklet's centre crease with the heel of his hand so that the fold would stay open and pulled a receipt from his leather coat.

'Sign this, sweetheart.'

He ambled past into the peopled anteroom, where he held the crumpled paper flat against a corner desk ready for her signature. She quietly closed the chairman's door, declined the pen Ben offered; instead she picked up a pencil lying on the desk, signed with a fastidious initial and straightened herself imperiously. Ben folded the receipt and whistled softly at the posh surroundings.

'The guy who works here, he's got it made, huh?' Ben fixed the secretary's frozen countenance and dropped one eyelid in a slow, knowing wink.

The secretary walked to the glass door and held it open for him.

He gestured back towards the closed inner office. 'What do you figure a guy like that makes a year?' Ben asked, goading her with mock innocence, aware from the corner of his eye of that loose, unspoken liberty his irreverence had fleetingly granted to the wing tips waiting by the Xerox machine.

'Thank you for the delivery,' the senior secretary said, her stony face averted.

'I'll see myself out,' Ben smiled and resumed ostentatious chewing of his bubble gum.

Outside, he once again adjusted to the still-novel experience of sitting uphill on the low-slung motorcycle, his feet above his rump. He slowed the chopper at the gatehouse and held out his visitor's pass.

The guard looked at him without interest.

'Like, peace, man,' Ben grinned. He twisted the throttle and, leather coat trailing, sputtered off into the early morning traffic.

16

Ed Boice appeared with two cups of coffee. He put them down and fussed with the items at the side of the office, looking over at Dick Miller. The walls opposite the windows blanched white in the unimpeded sunlight.

'You take it sweet, as I remember. And a lot of cream.' Ed poured a long stream from the jar of powdered cream substitute and stirred vigorously with a plastic spoon. He was all smiles and cracker-barrel humour. 'There's nothing like the first team! You and me and Buzz just like it used to be. You did it, Richard. My clutch hitter. We're past the FAA. We're *launched!*' Ed came over to present Dick his coffee and slung a beefy arm around Dick's slightly stooped shoulders. Dick didn't look up. He was arranging and rearranging his drafting tools into neat rows inside the open desk drawer before him. With his free hand Ed hoisted his cup and took large swallows from his own coffee. 'Now that it's over, we can be glad,' he said. 'Sure we're beat, but these are the struggles that are part of any creative effort. Any collaboration like ours has within it the seeds of divergent ideas that must be put to the test and then blended into great sculpture!'

Ed moved away, troubled by the image of the dejected figure. Dick Miller looked drained. Ed softened his tone.

'You gotta go on up to the falls, the salmon there are gonna jump right in your pockets. I'll square the time for you. Cross out the whole month, tell the company to shove it.'

Miller didn't want a vacation. Right now a vacation would frighten him: it would be like falling off the edge of a cliff.

'It can wait . . .'

Miller thought about falling off the edge of a cliff, hurtling into a windless canyon, breaking away permanently from all his obligations – an irretrievable vacation of peace . . .

'Either way, we're going to miss you around here.'

Dick glanced up, startled that perhaps Boice had read his mind. He waited for Ed to continue.

'You're being reassigned.'

Ed tossed his empty cup six feet into the centre of the wastepaper basket and moved across the room. His shadow, etched with precision on the wall, moved with him, separated by two feet, as though he were moving in duplicate. Both Ed Boices lounged against the file cabinet across from the desk. Dick shut his eyes. 'You've done everything that was asked of you,' Ed went on. 'It's time you reaped the benefit. We're sending you back to your peashooters,' he beamed. 'You're moving across to the F-19A.'

Dick peered towards the sun in its white bowl beyond the window and squinted.

Ed pushed away from the file cabinet and broke the cellophane wrapper on a large cigar. He lit it with a certain ceremony, inspecting the end for the proper glow, and sent a cloud of blue smoke halfway across the office. Shadows from the smoke danced in patterns on the wall.

'We're going out to lunch, you and me,' Ed said expansively, grinning, residual smoke oozing from between his teeth. 'Then we're gonna get ourselves a couple broads and get our pipes blown out. There's going to be nothing but Sundays around here from now on!'

431

Miller suddenly associated a pleasant image with the heavy sweetness of Ed's cigar. He looked up for the briefest instant. 'We were good once, weren't we . . . ?'

'We were the best. You've been our ace. We're going to wrap up your office and send it to the Smithsonian! Get your coat, Dick.'

'No . . . you go, Ed. I gotta clean up around here.'

'You're coming out to lunch.'

'No . . . You go ahead . . .'

Ed Boice dragged on his glowing stogie as he stood, feet apart, one bare arm protruding from its rolled-up sleeve across the top of his gut, and contemplated his star engineer. From the adjacent room someone had turned up a radio. It was Sinatra. Strains of big bands of another era filled Dick's head and reminded him of the sweetness of his courtship of Sandy. And he missed her.

'We still have one more piece of business to talk about,' Ed Boice was saying. 'It's a final hurdle,' he continued in a serious vein. Then he smiled. 'Everything's all wrapped up . . . All we gotta do is tie the final ribbon on it.' He paused. 'Flight-Control Design got an invitation to visit the Peck-Searington hearing. The consumer advocates want to talk to the team that handled the fix.' Ed waved the implication aside with his cigar. 'We're all of us mentioned by name. So we're going to need you to go to bat one last time.'

Miller remained still.

'There are going to be some questions asked by people who don't know an actuator from an airfoil. They're going to need a little reassurance.'

Dick had no comeback. He sat, his vision fixed upon something trifling inside his open drawer. He seemed to focus all his concentration on whatever it was. Anguish like steam that might geyser out was unable to push itself past the rigid plug of his shame. All the fists were turned inward, mutely pummelling with each word Ed Boice spoke.

'All that would be asked of you is to answer a couple of

questions about the – enhanced reliability – of the 17-10 flight-control system . . . just a little sweetener for our request for the loan extension. Tell them how improbable it is that we'd ever see a repeat of Air World Six. Let them hear *that* from the man who put it together.' Ed blew a long puff and took two steps closer to Dick's desk.

Dick was shaking his head from side to side. He'd gone pale. 'There's no way I could do that . . .'

Ed regarded the dejected form. He studied his cigar, gathering in his impatience before placing his hand on Dick's shoulder. He adopted a fatherly tone. 'We figure they'll ask why we did still more work on the aeroplane after certification. And of course we're going to say we only *improved* it – and you can live with that. It isn't a lie. We *have* improved it!'

Dick looked at the floor, slowly shaking his head. No words came.

'We'll all be there and we'll be dealing with facts. I don't have to reel off the stats to you on how remote a recurrence of the Kennedy incident is. We don't have to convince you! Hell, the senators, you, me, all of us want the same thing. The dollar is garbage and the people we beat in forty-five are now on tour here to see the ruins. All of us are pulling for the state of this country and even whether there'll *be* a country if our position in the marketplace slips any further!'

Miller didn't react.

Ed's teeth crunched into the cigar. 'Look, Dick, I don't want to use abrasive words, and you know how highly we think of you, but the past notwithstanding, it's important for you to understand that your job at Buttress is riding on those hearings.' Ed's fingers had tightened on Dick's shoulder. But the shoulder had begun trembling. The sensation made Ed pull his hand away. 'Millions of jobs are at stake. You want to be responsible for that? For the first time in eight years we're home free! We only need to cross the plate!' Ed was about to touch Dick again but the prospect provoked a tinge of awkwardness, so he took a long pull on his cigar instead. 'Come on, it's the last of the ninth and we're ahead. We're the ones who invented fly-by-wire, for Chrissakes. *It's the Answer* . . . Tell 'em we're putting capital *A*'s on the Answer to Arab extortion – that it's the only route left to a two per cent profit *after* we ransom the goddamn fuel.' Ed tried a broad grin but it was out of sync and he became concerned that perhaps Miller hadn't heard him at all.

Dick pushed his stool back, but kept his back to Ed and resumed straightening the items in his drawer.

'All they need is reassurance,' Ed said.

'. . . Did you see what I did with my large template?'

Ed mashed the cigar out in the ashtray atop the file cabinet. The dying smoke rose in vertical ropes, projected on the wall by the sun, which had shifted ever so slightly in the sky. The walls weren't so bright any more. Ed's voice was smooth, remote.

'We're counting on you . . . We don't plan to forfeit anything now . . . You don't want to let yourself down either.' Ed frowned. 'And when you come right down to it . . . if you think about it . . . as the father of the fix, you don't have too much of a choice!'

Senator Elton D. Osborne didn't trust the scramble phone to call the State Department from the embassy in Germany because there was no doubt in his mind he was dealing with a full-blown emergency. The Germans had been unswervingly clear to him. They were about to do something with the 17-10 but they wouldn't reveal precisely what. Elton only hoped they wouldn't pull the plug before the Peck-Searington hearing or, worse, during it.

So with barely a night's sleep he flew directly to Washington – the fog at Rhein-Main turned it into a thirteen-hour door-to-door marathon – and took a two-hour nap in his Georgetown apartment before cabbing it to the State Department.

He didn't often get to see the Secretary of State's inner office and today, as on earlier occasions, his surprise was renewed. He was never quite prepared to encounter the setting, perpetually less grand than he had a right to expect. Of all the offices in Washington, this place especially should be properly pretentious; certainly more so than his own quarters in the Senate Office Building. Yet it wasn't. And it certainly didn't begin to approach the sumptuousness of Hollis Wright's office. In fact, it was a trifle shabby. The walls had little smears in the corners and it needed a fresh coat of paint. Elton Osborne became peevish about such imperfections, and these annoyed him for he had long nurtured an image of himself behind this particular desk, in this particular room, the way it should be, with all the glitter appropriate to the Central Executive Suite at Foggy Bottom.

Yet he had long ago convinced himself that he bore neither animosity nor resentment towards the tall spare man who stepped forward to face him across the broad desk.

'I don't mean to jam myself into your day this way.'

The Secretary of State regarded Elton Osborne as though meeting him for the first time. One of the affectations of power. 'How bad is it, Elton?'

'Unofficially, all the Luftwaffe F-19s are grounded. Norvenich, Hopsten, Jever, Leck – *grounded*. Fürstenfeldbruck, *grounded*.'

'Defence isn't unduly concerned . . .' The Secretary was ruddy, composed.

'The Luftwaffe is ready to fly their F-19s in formation once around the Washington Monument and dump them into the Potomac. I don't have to tell you the implications of that.'

The Secretary ignored Osborne's forced tone of arrogance and said with a hint of sarcasm, 'No one at Defence has informed me. Perhaps they don't know this.'

'They know it, they know it. There are eight colonels and a brigadier general with their noses in a thesaurus right now checking for words they can use on the Chief of Staff. There's a strong group inside DLG, the German state airline, that wants the 17-10 out too, off the premises.'

The Secretary lapsed into silence and faced the window. Outside, pleasant shadows played around the windowsill. The office darkened and the area where the two men stood became like an old Dutch painting, grim and austere and serious.

Osborne spoke again, imploringly, his voice jittery. 'They want certain concessions. They know when the hearing starts. They know they can use it as a crowbar. They see Buttress as an arm of State and Defence and so they want to be sure the Administration is willing to back the warranty.'

'What does that mean?'

'They want their money back and they may not give us too much time to think that over.'

There was no talk for several minutes. Just the heavy clock ticking. The Secretary of State stood at the window, staring at the white government buildings and the broad lawns, regenerating with the placidity of an Ivy League college yard on an amiable spring day. Next to the window was a framed eight-by-ten colour photo of the Secretary's wife dressed in white shorts about to hit a tennis ball. She must be at least fifteen years younger than the Secretary, Osborne reflected in a spare corner of his mind. He noticed she had nice legs. She looked incongruous there, backdropped with the furled flags of the United States and the State Department, and especially next to the greying, bespectacled Secretary, who, Elton knew, used to be a university chancellor, a man from the agricultural Mid-west where he'd been nothing more than the director of a couple of banks. A mere transient – who could do – what? And here, surrounded by the peeling paintwork of the inner-office walls, insulated from the bustling world out-side, Elton Osborne worked to restrain his impatience.

The Secretary turned and regarded Osborne over the tops of his glasses. 'They can't seriously expect us to equip their state airline for nothing.'

'They're not too high on what we produce here any more, Aaron. They point to all the Mercedes parked in our shopping centres and they'll tell you their own people haven't been buying too many Cadillacs lately. I'll lay out the choices we have and you tell me what to do because I need to have some direction.'

'Maybe you're giving it too much energy,' the Secretary said calmly. 'Maybe they see you as vulnerable.' The Secretary smiled. 'Are you vulnerable, Elton?'

The taunt keyed a shot of anxiety inside Osborne. For an instant he felt as though he were standing there without his pants on. Osborne kept his eyes down as if party to some ill-defined insubordination and pushed the words out.

'We pay for the whole fleet – all their 17-10s – and they may condescend to keep it for the moment. I didn't say they'd put it into service! Or we don't pay for it and they send every one of those jumbos back before the weekend with an appropriate note to the press.'

'I don't think we ought to go into a knee jerk every time a German raises his voice. That's what the Teutonic mentality thrives on.'

'I need a fallback position. If they light the fuse, I have to have an answer. Maybe we can work something out with Defence.'

'What sort of figures are you talking?'

'A billion nine, two billion three.'

437

'Maybe Buttress should be nationalized. Maybe the territory is getting too big for free enterprise.'

Osborne stood feeling abandoned in the wash of what he hoped was an irrelevant remark. He waited for the Secretary to return to the present.

'We can't keep bailing out free enterprise and then pretending we're not involved. Is what's good for Detroit good for the country? Maybe it is. I don't know. I do know what's good for Buttress is also good for Elton Osborne.' The Secretary made a mental note of Osborne's involuntary reaction. 'But maybe we ought to give Bonn *less* of a response, Elton. Maybe we ought to give them no response. You see, they don't have all that much room to manoeuvre. I mean, who the hell else are they going to form an alliance with?' And the Secretary laughed.

'We have to talk to the President.'

'Our hand isn't that bad, you know. We can deploy our new guided-missile tank to France and the Netherlands first. Let the Chancellor go through next winter thinking of Ivan's T-73 tank divisions sitting in Magdeburg. We might also be able to get some indiscreet noises started up on the Hill about new trade barriers – offer them a picture of Volkswagens and schnapps falling off the docks at Bremerhaven.'

'That's irresponsible.'

'So is two billion three.'

'They spoke very directly about 17-10s being forbidden to fly in German airspace or being used by other airlines to operate inside their country.'

'Do they want the Skybus?'

Osborne was thrown off stride. He considered the Secretary's question, tried to read his train of thought. 'Not necessarily. They're not one of the consortium nations. It's not a political decision. It's a technological decision. They're refusing the 17-10 on technical grounds. I've been insisting on it not on technical grounds but on

438

political grounds. And they don't like the flavour of that ice cream.'

The Secretary stood quite still, thumbs hooked in his belt, and pondered. 'And if we don't answer?'

'Then it's show and tell, Monday morning at zero eight hundred Greenwich mean time, just in time to hit the street on the opening day of the Peck-Searington hearing. If that happens, we might as well tell everybody to stay home. Because that's the end of the hearings, the end of the loan extension, the end of Buttress, the end of my state – the F-19 stops – it's over.'

The Secretary stepped closer, put a hand on Osborne's shoulder. Osborne retracted beneath his shirt at the physical touch of strong fingers, but managed to stand motionless, revealing no outward sign. He could smell the lotion the Secretary wore and his breath, smoky and masculine. The Secretary spoke intimately.

'Elton, we have to keep a low profile. You see, I think they've set up the F-19 and maybe the 17-10 as a trade-off for what they really want – a little tactical nuclear autonomy. No F-19?' The Secretary shrugged. 'They've been disenchanted with their NATO partners for years, and this may just be their best chance to angle for their own nuclear arsenal as a stopgap, at least until we can replace it with the F-20 or F-30 fighter plane or whatever the hell is out there next. But tactical nuclear autonomy wouldn't be a stopgap. It would set a new tone . . . The negotiation involves more than economics, I want you to understand that – '

'I understand perfectly.'

'OK. We're talking politics on a grand scale. Now the German must never have that autonomy. I'd expect he won't give up until he gets it. He doesn't need the money. He wants something else and he figures he has us over a barrel.'

'What's the reading on the loan going through?'

The Secretary loosened his grip on Osborne's shoulder. 'That's not a priority problem at the moment. I don't expect to see anything get off the track there.'

'Then you must have a *quid pro quo* in mind.' Osborne began slowly to smile.

The Secretary walked to his desk, filled his pipe and lit it.

'What's the price, Aaron? How much do we pay the krauts to buy 17-10s?'

'We can't talk about bilateral landing rights or support for the dollar when it comes to the 17-10. We can't talk about NATO or reduced costs this next fiscal year in exchange for whatever, we can't do any of those things.'

'Suppose the negotiation is about aeroplanes after all? Suppose their price for keeping the 17-10 and F-19 is that we foot the bill? Where do we get the funds to pay for that?' Osborne wouldn't let go.

The Secretary of State had seen Osborne once briefly with the President: tough, hard as nails, the consummate pragmatist. But he'd also seen him supine, innocuous, a virtual nonface who could force those around him unwittingly to sell themselves. He'd seen Osborne, when reproached, aligning himself with all of Buttress, smiling as a thief might smile at a bleeding victim who looked down to discover the blood running from the knife in his shirt and begin to protest, and Osborne would be the one to say engagingly, '*Me?* No, *you* did that . . . you did it' to *yourself*,' and keep smiling with the steel shimmer in his eyes.

The Secretary smiled mysteriously at Osborne in return. 'I'm not authorized to tell you just what's being considered – '

'But if it comes to the crunch, the President won't argue the point. Am I right?'

'You'll have to find a way of conveying the assurance that we *might* come up with something for them without committing us to anything definite. That's the politics you're good at. You may not go on record, of course.'

Osborne frowned. 'I need more than that. You'll have to get me the President's OK at least.'

The Secretary took a long drag on his pipe and struck another match to relight it. 'I know the President's mood. And the pressure he's under. It's something I must convince him of privately. First, of course, I have to sit down with the Secretary of Defence and the Budget Director – '

'Jesus, you're talking about days and weeks . . .'

The match flickered and finally went out. 'Give me forty-eight hours . . . See if we can't arrange to have some of our new tanks jump ship at Le Havre, beef up the French first.'

'The krauts aren't the poker players they used to be. They're better.'

'Get some distance on it, Elton. Go home.' The Secretary rubbed his neck, a wry world-weary expression on his face. 'But stay near the phone. And it might also be a good idea to keep your bag packed.'

Jamie hadn't said anything to Anja on the ride to NYU's law library in the Village. They found a place to park at a jammed thirty-minute meter on Ninth Street and ran through the pelting rain under the portal and up the glistening steps of the red-brick building.

It was still early. The Lincoln Research Room was lightly populated. A man with a green raincoat held the door and entered after them, shook the water from his hat, and removed his glasses to wipe them. His hair was dyed and it was apparent he was blind in one eye. He peered towards the main reading room, rummaged in his coat pocket and produced three quarters, which he placed inside the potted fig tree standing next to the entranceway.

Anja hurried up the steps into the main reading room, Jamie walking slowly behind her watching drops of water spill in a crooked line from the end of his yellow poncho.

The librarian was in his early thirties, modest and unhurried. Anja took off her rain hat and shook her hair loose. The action made him look up and for a moment he just watched her.

'I was the one who called earlier,' she smiled.

'Acceptable risk.'

'Yes.'

The librarian led her to a wall of shelves packed with manuals and hardbound volumes. He pointed to a thick book titled *British Civil Air Regulations* and to a copy of the *European Joint Airworthiness Regulations*. 'Both of these get into quantifying what's likely and unlikely. You're going to find the terms "improbable" and "extremely improbable" mean different things to different people.'

'Thanks for the trouble.'

The young man looked back at her and a hint of longing clouded his eyes. 'No trouble.'

Across the room at a long, lacquered table adjacent to the fire exit, the one-eyed man sat and spread a newspaper before him. It was hard to tell if he'd seen Jamie standing diffidently behind one of the bookshelves. The boy noticed that the lower lid of the man's left eye drooped all by itself, showing the red there, the same way he'd pull his lower lid down with his fingers in the mirror. Jamie watched as the man quietly built a pile of quarters as tall as his hand and carefully placed a handkerchief over it. The boy moved a step closer, into the light. The man shut his eyes, concentrating on the covered stack of coins. All at once, he lifted the handkerchief and the stack was gone. Jamie's eyes grew huge. The man pretended to search the floor but popped up quickly and smiled. Jamie, caught grinning back, turned away.

Anja had opened the copy of the *British Civil Air Regulations* to section D (Aeroplanes) and in chapter D1-2 she came across several terms such as *frequent, recurrent, remote, extremely remote, extremely improbable*, each with a specific numerical equivalent. She searched for an explanation as to how the definitions had been arrived at and she thought, how can you *prove* that the likelihood of a foreseeable event occurring is 'extremely improbable'?

She turned to a section in the *European Joint Airworthiness Regulations* and on the fourth page found that 'improbable' failures were those which were 'not expected' to occur during the operation of an individual aeroplane, but *were* expected to occur during the total operational life of all aeroplanes of the type. Anja reviewed the words, frowning at their vaguely contradictory ring. She cross-referenced to the British regulations; there the almost identical definition applied to 'remote' failures: these might occur 'several times' during the total operational life of 'a number' of aeroplanes of the type. Each such failure might occur once during each one hundred thousand hours of flight. On the other hand, 'extremely improbable' failures (a wing falling off? yes – it says so: an event resulting in 'the loss of a number of lives and/or the destruction of the aircraft') may occur less often, by a neat factor of exactly ten thousand.

A paragraph in the *Advisory Circular – Joint*, number 1, stated that the remote event is 'allowed to occur once in 100,000 hours of flight'. *Allowed to occur* – permission granted, sanctioned by law. She recalled the image of a white-coated university physician working with laboratory animals asking a photographer who had come by to take pictures whether it would help his spread if he were to 'sacrifice' one of the animals on camera. 'It would be legal,' he said.

Jamie circled the man in the green coat warily and tried

443

not to look up at him. Instead he concentrated on the smudges his shoes left on the heavily waxed floor. He glanced at Anja, who was in the smaller room with the glass wall. She was alone, concentrating on several thick books. Jamie could feel the magician at the table staring at him. He'd first noticed him outside when they were crossing through the park. The man had held the door for them and his hand was dirty, not at all like a magician's.

Jamie, now hiding in the shadows of the bookshelves, watched the magician for several minutes. He looked like a man Jamie had seen on a late TV movie who sat in a room alone, waiting for morning to arrive. It had been a scary movie, the man had been cruel. The magician beckoned him; his voice was low like the man in the movie. He was telling Jamie that three of the coins under the handkerchief had found their way into the plant across the room. Jamie tried not to listen . . . but the prospect was tempting. The man watched the boy mull it over. Jamie decided to saunter past the plant – but he wouldn't stop and look into it. Yet even from ten feet away he saw the coins glittering in the black dirt. He stared in wonder. They were quarters. He reached in and picked them up.

Allowed to occur, read the document – whether during the billionth hour or the hundred thousandth hour or the thirty-third, that didn't matter. The principle had been established, the moral rampart breached, by those three words: *allowed to occur*.

Anja wrote down the words 'Russian Roulette'. The crew of Air World Six pulled the trigger on one of the first 17-10s – and the gun went off! But that doesn't mean on the next million flights Guy or the others in the cockpit get to keep the empty gun. By definition they're handed a new loaded pistol the next time they climb aboard, one with a new live bullet in its chamber somewhere. And that new bullet is just as likely to be close to the top as to the bottom. If the gun went off the next time the trigger was pulled, would that still be within bounds? At what point do you decide to rebuild the aeroplane?

She turned towards the bearded librarian who was approaching hopefully with still another book. 'Who decided all this?' she queried. 'Who has the right to decide all this?'

'We've got shelves full of stuff like that.'

'Isn't there anyone who disagreed with this? This is an arrangement for the financial convenience of the manufacturer.'

'If anyone ever filed a suit, it's clear from what's on these shelves they didn't win.'

'Who certified the 17-10?'

'The Federal Aviation Agency. They're in Washington.'

Anja stood. 'Do you mind if I use your phone?'

'That line doesn't go outside. You'll have to use the pay phone.' The librarian pointed to a row of coin booths. 'The area code is 202.'

Anja took her handbag and looked around for Jamie. There was no sign of him. 'If a small boy pops out of a bookcase,' she said with a solicitous smile, 'he belongs to me.'

Anja headed for the back of the room and dug into her purse for change.

Jamie stood several feet from the long, shiny table and tried hard to examine the magician's face. He locked his gaze on to the glass eye and the raw red drooping skin beneath it. The magician refolded his newspaper and turned his face far to the left, a cyclops scanning the area. Jamie followed his stare. Anja had left the table. When Jamie looked back, the magician's smile had disappeared and his voice was more commanding. He motioned for Jamie to come closer. The boy stood stock-still, eyes large. The man's head seemed to float like a clump of wet straw washed against a pier, jamming itself into the turned-up green collar.

'The rest of the coins are outside,' the man said, and smiled again at the boy.

Anja got the number from Washington information and was put through to a dry male voice at the FAA. She skipped introducing herself and went directly to the point. 'I want to know who certified the 17-10.'

There was a pause before the voice adopted a patronizing tone and said, 'Certification is a lengthy process – '

Anja snapped, 'Who signed it?' She didn't feel like getting into any roundabout gamesmanship.

'Ma'am?'

Anja raised her voice. 'Whose name appears on the 17-10 certificate? The one clearing the 17-10 to carry passengers. I assume there has to be a name.'

'May I know who I'm talking to?'

'My name isn't a prerequisite to receive information from the FAA, is it?'

'I'll be glad to send you a copy of the FAA directive which discusses the administration's procedures – '

'Don't do this.'

'What?'

'I'm asking a simple question. Who certified the Buttress 17-10? Question mark.'

'The FAA did.'

'Who specifically?'

'I don't have that information in front of me but I assume it was the Northwestern Region chief. Since that region handles all transport category certification.' As if she should know, of course.

'Does he have a telephone?'

'Just a minute please . . .'

'Wait! Don't switch – ' But the line had already gone dead. She hovered between hanging on and slamming the receiver into its cradle. She held on until still another voice came on the line.

'Hello? Is there something I can do for you?'

446

Anja brought the phone down on its hook. She re-dialled the FAA main switchboard.

'FAA,' said the distant anonymous voice.

'I'm calling from outside. Would you give me the number for the Northwestern Region chief?'

'Just a moment, please . . . it's on the West Coast . . . area code 206 . . . the number is 555-2770.'

'And his name again?'

'You mean Mr Devlin?'

'His first name?'

'Donald.'

'Thank you.'

Jamie stood at the front door, which the one-eyed man held ajar. The rain was smacking down, little bounces of water fragmenting and collecting into puddles which over-flowed into the street. It was supposed to be a spring day but the raw cut of winter was still in the air. Jamie stared at the sidewalk but couldn't see the coins from where he was standing. He wanted to stick his head out farther but wasn't going to do it. The hiss and sight of the splattering rain dancing in little inverted umbrellas made him stare.

'I'm not going to go out there,' he said finally.

'Why not?'

Jamie looked up into the magician's face so close above him, seeing where the whiskers had been gashed clean on the side not darkened by the shadow of the half-open door. 'Because you're a kidnapper.'

Anja stepped clear of the booth and caught sight of Jamie in his yellow poncho silhouetted by the brightness of the street outside. The door being held by the stranger in the green coat was wide open.

'*Jamie!*' she called.

The boy jerked into the air. The three quarters flew out of his hand and hit the stone floor with a broken ring. He ducked down and scrambled after one of them, which was rolling across the hall.

447

Anja came down the marble steps from the main reading room. Jamie picked the last coin from the floor as she reached him. He wanted to put his face into her coat but waited for her to touch him instead.

'What were you doing?'

He didn't look at her when he said, 'Nothing.'

Just beyond them the front door sank shut. The figure in the green coat was gone.

Hollis Wright considered personally shredding the annual reports that had been left on his desk but he knew there were others so he didn't bother. Instead he instructed the compromised company executive to prepare for an immediate flight out of the country, not by conventional means where his physical existence might still be established, but by trans-oceanic flight of the first two-seat F-19 scheduled for delivery to Saudi Arabia. The Middle East, Hollis explained, would permit a man to drop entirely out of sight much as if he had never existed at all. Upon the personal solicitation of the board chairman himself, chief test pilot Gus Helmsdorf had agreed to fly the mission and his inexperienced passenger had been granted final internal clearance and completed the proper briefings. The fighter now crouched on the broad concrete acres outside, a sleek bomb-coloured machine, netted and held subdued by minigantries and other support machinery, awaiting its release; but Hollis chose not to observe the activity around it. Instead he retreated to sit alone at the head of the deserted table in the ghostly Buttress boardroom, an unlit cavern with an atmosphere as dank as the inside of an Egyptian pyramid.

There was a sudden short burp high over the Sierra desolation and a sharp rush of cold air behind Helmsdorf's neck as first the aft canopy went followed by the ejection seat behind him. It was all automatic: the aneroid kicked the body free, then activated the chute, which was set to open at ten thousand feet. The F-19 pirouetted, dancing in the sky, beautiful, like a stingray, while Anton Jasovak dangled helplessly from his parachute, a tiny orange fish in the wide blue sea. Helmsdorf was the only man who had the skill in the F-19. Jasovak's body grew larger in Helmsdorf's gunsight reticle. The fine green-and-orange diffraction patterns of cross hairs seen through the fighter's windshield were focused far out in front, where the target floated. Helmsdorf adjusted the sight like a careful surgeon. For a moment he recalled the same scene, the dangling legs of the P-51 pilot hanging in a mottled white chute over Koblenz, then the sudden splatter over the windscreen of his Me.109 as the rattling prop chewed hunks out of the American. But today it would be almost gentle, a silent windswept approach.

Jasovak was still stunned from the unexpected blow of the ejection charge up his spine. And in that chin-crushing instant he knew it was over. They hadn't told him the back seat could be fired from the front cockpit. For a long moment he hung in the limitless void as his chute swished gently overhead, as helpless as if pinned to a board, and from two miles beneath him came the faint mournful whistle of a train on the ground. He knew he'd never reach the ground . . . He thought of Ben Reese, and in spite of where he was he couldn't resist a sardonic smile.

Jasovak had lost sight of the fighter but heard it overlapping the diminishing noise from the train. It was not so far away and he heard the echo too of its engines, a frothy rumble growing and rising from the ravines below. He twisted in his chute, then caught sight of the fighter's exhaust, a light pencil tracing just above the horizon. The pencil point lifted, then plunged into the purple profile of a distant mesa and Jasovak lost sight of it again.

Jasovak's body wasn't visible to Helmsdorf from the

outer circumference of the turn, just the chute which was no longer a fish but had become an orange speck against the mountains, a bright-winged insect crawling slowly past brown corrugation. Helmsdorf turned down the intensity of the reticles in his windshield gunsight display until they were razor-thin green cross hairs and he watched as they slid slowly on to the insect, fixing it as though through a microscope. The auto guidance fire control system was tracking perfectly and the active fly-by-wire control system was keeping the F-19 on a precise, even trajectory. Six seconds out he would make the tiniest correction, readjusting the aim so that it locked on to the inverted apex where the fine web of the insect's legs converged in a point just below its body.

Jasovak tried to relocate the F-19 from the other side. It was unmistakable, hooded and venomous from a distance and it circled flat, unyielding, sitting comfortably in its pattern. It slipped to the right, settled and lined up. Jasovak took a deep breath but didn't close his eyes. Instead, with a sudden desperation, he grabbed one riser and prepared to pull down with all his strength – perhaps at the last instant his racing brain had shouted, he could spill his canopy and change the rate of fall just enough to spoil Helmsdorf's aim and put the huge nylon shroud into his jet intake instead. But he hadn't counted on the monstrous speed of the fighter. It had swept swiftly behind him; he tried frantically to twirl in the choking straps of the chute harness to catch sight of it and judge the timing of his effort . . . It was almost impossible to twist with his legs dangling helplessly, his arms stuck out like a child's in a snowsuit and the exertion forcing his breath into short, shallow spasms. Slowly the chute began to twirl in the sky. With strenuous effort Jasovak hauled on the risers. The engine sounds rose like demented thunder to surround him as the chute bobbed and swayed . . . When he saw the F-19 again it was head on, almost upon him, and he forgot everything in his fascination with its exploding evil leer.

Jasovak's silhouette grew in the electronic windshield cross hairs, it grew arms, a head. Lead angle, deflection, were perfect, Helmsdorf noted with satisfaction. How did one kill another man? At four hundred knots it takes an angle just so.

It lasted only an instant. Helmsdorf plugged in the two afterburners, felt the F-19 force itself ahead, there was only a microsecond of a silent gargle through the glass, Helmsdorf saw the razor-edged wing was aimed right at the navel. Then a slapping sound like a birdstrike and only the slightest bump.

At that moment in New York, Ben Reese tried to force himself to hold on to his fitful sleep. He sensed it was past noon: the sounds on the street below his apartment were no longer the before-nine kind, clipped and fresh, but had compressed into the midday amalgam of shoppers and workers spilling on to the sidewalk in search of respite and meals. Ben had been up until five, writing the first article of what he planned would establish his comeback. But something hadn't fitted and now, as his mind, suspended somewhere between sleep and wakefulness, sought a clue, he found himself amid a group of nervous feline things, roaming through his head, jostling and snarling and crowding for space, emitting low moans and finally, evaporating, waking him fully with their last furtive howls. He rolled over groggy and scratchy and swore at the effort it took to locate his watch. The top sheet was jammed into a crushed heap along one edge of the bed and faint images of fleeting dreams dissipated unidentified, just beyond recall, into the shadows cast by bleak outside light. But something had been left behind, some faintly iridescent footprint from those dark prowlers of his subconscious to ebb and glow there, and it troubled him.

451

Ben was contemplating the raw physical energy necessary to heave himself upright for a visit to the bathroom and wondering if it was worth it when suddenly he sat bolt upright. He closed his eyes and the footprint from his dream expanded into the letter he'd found in Paris. He saw it through the mental screen as sharply as if it were focused behind a magnifying lens and he fixed his attention towards the bottom, on to the mark there, struggling to see something he'd previously rejected – something he'd subconsciously tried to dismiss but which still nagged him. The letters rolled in his head, 'James Somebody – ' Who the hell was *James Somebody?* With a thrill of foreboding that originated deep in that dreamland and rose like unwanted bile to the surface, Ben knew who it was.

He padded to the closet, his hands were clumsy and he swore again and finally found his shirt. Groping until he pulled free the two items he wanted, he was already chastising himself for having been so blind. He took the items to the window above the radiator and tilted them towards the light. First he unfolded the flimsy carbon copy letter, then he placed the old signed photo, the one he'd carried in that pocket for more than two years, the one Dimitri had used, alongside. Even the writing was the same. *JAS.* That's not *James Somebody*, for God's sake, that's *Jasovak!* Jasovak himself was the Buttress lawyer turned adventurist who had set up the perfumery. Ben bent his head over the flat radiator shelf and brought his fist down with such force that the metal lid jumped.

Realization exploded into action. Ben almost tore his shirt in his haste to put it on. He had no time to lose: he would somehow collar Jasovak and bring him in alive, sit him down and force him to spill his guts.

Then Ben stopped. He didn't know how to do it. For the first time in his life Ben Reese didn't know where to start. Without realizing it, he slumped half dressed on the edge of the bed, hands rigid, staring into the empty room. The last vestige of his dream returned: the glossy image of the black-bordered photograph in the doctored annual report. It had blown Jasovak's cover and Ben knew conclusively in that moment that he'd done it too soon. A coldness crawled over his body. He was aware that a certain tension had just vanished from his life and for the first time in weeks he felt alone. Anton Jasovak, the skier, the lawyer, the smooth dealer in international cosmetics, the man who'd blackmailed his employer's critics into silence and had found his way into countless other high- and low-level arrangements, was already dead. Of that, Ben knew, though he had no proof, there could be no doubt.

He raised his head and a crooked smile creased his face despite the loss of his quarry. It was the smile of respect and shared awareness one gladiator reserves for another. And Jasovak, by not being available to verify the letter, had given Ben the final fuck-you – posthumously.

Helmsdorf pulled back hard and the F-19 took four miles of sky in one enormous gulp. Far on the horizon the majestic battlements of a giant thunderhead reared heavenward. He reached the mighty cumulonimbus in moments to skirt the edges for a freshwater washdown. Get rid of any traces, he thought with a mental shrug. Then he returned to Buttress Field, where Hollis Wright waited in his hushed boardroom, and landed.

17

Anja stood in Jamie's old bedroom wearing Levi's shorts and one of Guy's frayed shirts. She had nearly finished painting the entire room a light pastel beige and she decided she liked it. The time at home had been pleasant and yet she was disconcerted. She tried to trace it. Guy had gone off to Air World's Flight Training Centre, he'd said, to get something he'd have to have in the next few days. He was supposed to have been back by now and she realized she was vaguely irritated because he wasn't and Jamie had snubbed her on the way to school and as small as he was, she'd felt like shaking him. The impulse had nearly got away from her. She'd watched him walk off to the main entrance and, as she'd relocked the car door, she'd sensed somehow by the droop of his gait that he was disappointed too that she hadn't intercepted him. It was then, just a few hours ago, that she decided she would put an end to his living apart. She was keyed up about it and looked forward to his coming home. It was already nearly three and she'd grown alert for the sound of the returning school bus.

She was also angry about something else but she didn't know what it was. She stood in his room, paint roller and brush in her hands, the vaguely medicinal sting of latex biting her throat, and she drew back for a perspective of her handiwork, but her attention drifted into the stillness of the house. She forced her gaze on to the lush scene outside the window and it seemed to blanch and turn grey as she watched. Two small clouds stopped in their passage and remained locked above the neighbour's garage. To Anja it seemed as though the main voltage of life had suddenly shut off around her. For a moment the only sound was that of her pulse coursing at the back of her ears. Slowly she began to fathom that it wasn't the wind or the leaves that had stopped. No. She had plunged into contact with her own unspoken anger at Guy for not having broken the standoff with Jamie sooner himself, and as she came to grips with that, she nearly blanked out. Opening the window further, she drew in cool air slowly and the landscape blushed back into colour. Perhaps the problem wasn't Guy's. Perhaps *she'd* been the impediment, always giving advice and never realizing she was the one who hadn't made her feelings clear to the boy. She placed the tools aside and was on her way to the kitchen when the phone rang. She answered it on the third ring. There was no response. Seconds passed. Anja was certain the line was live, that there was someone waiting on the other end.

'Hello?' she repeated.

Two clicks signalled the disconnect.

Guy's flight bag stood next to the front door precisely where he'd left it so many days ago. A thin layer of dust already had built up on the lid. She pictured him now, in the abstract as she had so vividly before, airborne, hunched against the pristine dome, pinioned by shards of metal and glass trying to pull two delicate strands of a broken silver link apart, yet not hearing her tell him that it had already been decided without his consent or even his presence that his life and those of his passengers were expendable and that there was a law on the books that endorsed it.

She recradled the phone, took hot coffee into the living room and sipped it, rearranging the clutter of law review books and journals strewn about the couch and floor. She caught sight of the piece of paper she'd used as a bookmark on which she'd written the name of the FAA's Northwest Region chief, Don Devlin, and beneath it his phone number. The 17-10 originated in his jurisdiction, the librarian had said. This man Devlin must have some knowledge of the precept of *acceptable risk* he was paid to enforce. She would still call him . . .

She pictured Guy again insisting on his cross plots, on all the missing specifics. But the *problem* wasn't only the incident at Kennedy or even any identifiable flaw in the 17-10. It was the subtle *drift in philosophy* which said with some impatience that life and health could be used as part

455

of the price paid for a decent annual report and there were few men willing to fight it because most had taken refuge in the corporate temple, economically trapped into equivocation.

Reverence for life had become a pain in the ass.

And in industry, it would continue to be cheaper to hang the monkey on the dead pilot's back and sap outrage by means of 'the law's delays' and 'the insolence of office' than to do it right in the first place. The staggering cost of aeronautical technology had begun to outpace the supply of investable capital needed to patrol it, and this demanded in turn that certain time-honoured impressions about life be . . . adjusted.

She heard the growl of the school bus outside. With an odd sense of guilt, she snapped on the radio to dispel her lingering mood and felt her shoulders tighten. A curdled radio voice bloomed in midsentence, exhorting listeners to hurry before it was all too late, and she shut it off. There was silence. The front door opened. Jamie stood in the doorway eyeing her.

'Take a look at what's happened to your room,' she said. Jamie charged past, up the stairs, without answering, and locked himself in the attic.

Anja returned to the kitchen, took a deep gulp of her coffee, slammed the mug down on the counter and went after him.

On the second floor she reached into his room for the extension pole she'd used to paint the ceiling and took it with her the rest of the way. She stood in the semidarkness facing the black-lacquered attic door. Nothing stirred from within. She could see along the crack of backlight at the edge of the frame that the deadbolt had been closed.

'I was talking to you down there!' She closed her eyes, feeling very much the blasphemous intruder now, standing on carpeting someone else had selected, knowing the wallpaper had been one of his mother's very last projects.

456

Her voice overruled her misgivings. 'Jamie, I'm not going to ask you to open the door because this time we're getting rid of it! So get out of the way!' And with that she held the extension pole over her shoulder like a battering ram and drove it against the top right panel of the door. It bounced back and stung her hands. The pole wasn't going to do it. She looked around for something heavier and pulled the dust-covered fire extinguisher from the wall. It was heavier than she expected.

Inside Jamie stood by the window, listening, uncertain about what she was doing.

Anja held the red extinguisher by the neck and swung it sideways. It struck the wood with a watery gong and bounced away. Twice more it sprang away, but on the fourth try she caught the weakness in a bottom panel and felt it splinter. Without let-up she swung again and again and finally knocked most of the two bottom panels out and cracked the centre cross bar. She could have reached in at this point and retracted the dead-bolt but instead she came down hard on the upper half and splintered it. She saw Jamie holding on to the curtain next to the far window staring at her wide-eyed. Anja pulled on the latch and it fell out of its housing and swung down dangling from the last anchored screw. She set the extinguisher down, removed a wood fragment from her hair and pushed the still-attached debris aside on its hinges.

'You're going to get it for that. You're going to get fired,' the boy said quietly, his face pale, his amazed expression unaltered.

Anja stood uncertainly facing him, short of breath from the exertion. 'You don't have to like me,' she said, and she swallowed, 'but you're not going to be rude to me again.'

The boy backed up as she entered. Staring at her, he stopped, stood still. He liked the look of her bare legs.

Anja picked a pair of binoculars from the floor.

'You're going to be in trouble,' the boy said.

Anja reached over to his bed and yanked the covers off, spilling a couple of stuffed animals that were perched on one side on to the floor. Jamie bounded away from the window and slid to a stop on his knees at the head of the bed, where he clutched the sheets. Anja heaved the blankets and pillow into a bundle and threw them down the steps.

'It's all over up here,' she announced breathlessly. 'You're moving south where things are a little warmer.' She tore at the top sheet but the child held on.

'No, you're not going to!' he exclaimed, gritting his teeth. She grabbed for his pyjama trousers instead but he caught the waistband and scrambled to his feet. Anja tried to tear the garment free but the boy's one-handed grasp was tenacious; he threw his other arm around the leg of his desk and held on. She folded the end she held hand over hand and knelt down in front of him to pry his hand open.

'If you think I'm going to put up with this and have you insult me any longer, you're crazy.' As she broke his grip he brought his other hand up to snatch the folded pyjamas and ripped them. She dropped the trousers, turned away from him and yanked the sheets free. Panting and glaring, he watched as she tossed them out of the door. She then went for the mattress but the boy dived for it and Anja, feeling her adrenalin surge, swung the bedding across the floor with the boy sliding along behind it.

'You've got plenty of time to decide to be a hermit, but you're going to try being normal first!'

As she slowed near the doorway he pounced on to the mattress and swung his leg to kick her hand free but she clutched at his ankle and held it, and quickly caught his other leg as he brought it around. He tried to sit up but she rolled him over on to his stomach and with a grimace of effort held him there.

'I have a rough idea why you want to stay away from me up here,' she said, 'but don't offer me an explanation. It's too late. We're fresh out of new doors.' She released his feet. 'Now get out! And march!'

Jamie spun around and backed away from her. Anja pulled the mattress free and shoved it out of the door, where it slid along the floor and tumbled to the landing below. Jamie seized the back of his desk chair and sent it spinning on its casters towards her. She let it crash into the wall.

'I'm not asking your permission,' she warned.

Jamie hoisted one side of his desk until it teetered. The drawers slid out, spilling with a clatter, and it fell to the floor with a crash. Anja stepped around it and reached for him. He took a toy truck from the floor and, holding it by the pull cord, swung it at her. It caught her on the hip. She twisted the lanyard out of his hand and yanked him to his feet. A muffled cry rose in the boy's throat but he kept his mouth shut. He broke loose, flailing wildly, and she took a blow to her ear before she could pin both his arms. Jamie struggled to break her grip and he looked down at her hand on his chest. Anja saw it.

'If you bite my hand,' she breathed, 'I want you to know that I'm going to knock your head off.'

Jamie's nose was running and she could feel him swallowing back the rising flood.

'Let's go now.'

'No!' A muffled whimper slipped away from him.

Anja shook the loose hair from her eyes, got a lock on his wrists and pulled him towards the shattered door. The boy dropped to his knees.

'This isn't your house!' he blurted. 'You only have a job!'

'I'm a human being!'

She hauled him through the doorway and he let himself be dragged from the room that way, his legs bumping down the stairs. She tripped over the end of the mattress but managed to hold her balance and with great effort she slung him across the threshold of his freshly painted room and let go. Jamie landed on his back and slid into the ladder but he jumped to his feet at once, looking for a way out. Anja blocked the door and waited. Tiny pearls of perspiration had begun to build under her eyes and around her lips.

'You and I are going to give your dad a surprise,' she said. Jamie put his head down and charged. Anja caught him. 'We're going to give him one less thing to worry about.' And she sent him sprawling back to the centre of the room. His legs churning, Jamie found his feet and in his fury, upended the folding ladder which hit the floor with the slap of a gunshot. He was crying openly now, the sobs breaking from his throat, his lungs struggling for air. He grabbed the old shower curtain covering a stack of books, angrily ripped it aside, kicked the pile of books in, sending several skittering to the wall, and crawled to the wide paintbrush lying on the roller tray. With a new look on his face, he picked it up slowly, stood with it and came at her. Anja moved to deflect his arm but he was too quick. A twisting braid of paint arced overhead as the slinging, dripping brush moved ahead of it and landed hard against her temple. It startled her and this time he'd hurt her. The edge of the metal holding the bristles had dug into her skin. Suddenly she was no longer the adult, the teacher. She sank to her knees and the image blurred as her own tears filled her eyes. She went for the outline of his hand, took the brush, pried it loose and slapped him hard across the face with its bristles. His head snapped back from the force of the blow, a wet beige imprint covering his cheek and ear. A defiant, angry shriek burst from him and he picked up the tin roller tray with its layer of wet paint and swung it at her. An elliptical blob of latex turned once in the air and landed on her shirt as the metal pan bounced off her shoulder and hit the wall behind her. She brushed the tears from her eyes to see more clearly and her hand flicked out and cracked him hard across the left cheek. Anja waited as he looked for his next weapon. He flung the roller at her and as quickly she smacked him on the other side of his face. She tasted the paint at the corner of her mouth and the hot salt from her eyes and waited again. He sat opposite her with paint dripping from his ear and chin, a hum of anguish droning in his throat and slowly, head down, he pushed away from her, sliding backward until he had reached the far corner, where he sat crying to himself. All at once he looked small and humiliated.

A sob finally burst from Anja as she watched him. Finding a towel, she wiped her hands. A car passed by outside, fanning spokes of sunlight across the ceiling. The house was still and she came to him and knelt. Gently she touched the towel to his cheek. Neither of them spoke. The sound of a piece of wood hitting the floor upstairs broke the silence. A mixture of a laugh and a sob shot from the boy but he couldn't look up. The moan continued in his throat.

Her voice was halting. 'You do know if I could bring it all back the way it was for you I would . . . and I wouldn't be here . . . don't you know I'd do that?'

Jamie didn't answer, though he wanted to. He was aware of her coming closer and reaching in under his arms to bring him to her but he held his hands near his face to keep her away. She caught his eye and smiled.

'I don't know how we're going to explain this.'

The boy wiped the sniffle from his nose but smeared paint on it instead. Again a grudging laugh broke through and he let his hands drop. She nestled her head against his shoulder and she felt her own tears run down her face. She spoke softly.

'My name is Anja. You can call me Miz or Anja or Hey

461

You and I'm not going to mind that one bit. We don't have to solve that right away but for the time that we know each other, I want it to be something.' She shut her eyes, her cheek against the paint on his neck and held him tight against her.

And she noticed that he was holding her too.

The car that had slowly passed the house minutes before now backed up and parked directly across the street. The driver removed his sunglasses, surveyed the neighbourhood with his good eye and shut the engine off.

Anja had the bucket of water on the flagstones next to the garden table and she daubed at the paint that streaked her face and arms in long stiffening stripes. Her hair was matted with it, her shirt ruined. She worked at the job of removing the paint with steady patient effort despite her emotional exhaustion from the confrontation with Jamie. But a kind of rejoicing had begun to surge through her as she worked and it reinforced her determination to sustain what had been set into motion. She halted, the hand holding the wet cotton suspended in midair; and coming upon her in a rush was a new feeling, the realization of being strangely akin to the rhododendron blossoms that faced the sun with a kind of bravery she'd never stopped to notice before. It was the bravery of being new, the kinship with life facing new possibilities.

She noticed the telephone on the redwood table and began to dial a West Coast number. It was the one scribbled on the bookmark she'd used during her day at the law library. Without too much delay she was put through and, with an ease she had no right to expect, suddenly heard him on the line.

'Devlin.'

She examined the face that flashed before her. She pictured him gruff and tanned with a broad nose and a roll at the back of his neck trying to reach retirement before his emphysema got ahead of him.

'I hesitate to start this conversation because I know it's going to turn into an argument and I don't want you to hang up on me.'

Devlin hung up on her.

Anja laughed and redialled. Her image of him began to change. Again he picked up.

'Suppose I didn't call back?' she demanded.

'Then I would have won the argument.'

'You're not going to hang up on me again, are you?'

Devlin hung up. Anja whooped with laughter. She redialled.

'Listen, you're plugged into a federal agency and it's been a bad day around here,' he declared.

'I attended the public hearing on Air World Six. I'm a friend of the co-pilot.'

'We've just had a farewell lunch here, so I can't promise anything.'

'Are you sober?'

'Unfortunately.'

'I've studied the law, but I wish you'd justify why it's written the way it is. Tell me why an air disaster is considered legally acceptable.'

He didn't answer right away. 'Let me be sure I understand your question. What law are you talking about?'

'The law that covers airworthiness. Federal Air Regulation, Part 25.'

'That's pretty broad. Can you be more specific?'

'Specifically, paragraph 25.671(c) assumes a failure in the controls will be "extremely improbable" – but a failure did occur! On Air World Six. Well before it should have!'

'Even so, 671(c), just like the rest of the code, requires

that the aeroplane – after any failure – be capable of continued safe flight *and landing*. And I seem to recall Air World Six successfully – '

'Without requiring exceptional piloting strength or skill,' she parried. 'Not luck.'

'I know what it says.'

'Good, then how can that law – or any of your laws – decide for the flying public that it's legally acceptable for a certain number of them to die? No one has ever checked with them to see if they agree with that!'

Devlin took stock of her challenge. 'All the federal airworthiness law says is that the level of reliability we try to impose must correspond to the consequences of failure. If a certain piece of an aeroplane breaks and that would cause an accident, then we demand high reliability to ensure that that piece doesn't break too often. On the other hand, if the piece that breaks isn't too important, we're prepared to accept its breaking more often. That may allow it to be built lighter – '

'Or cheaper.'

'As you will.'

Her mental picture of him changed further. Gone was the struggling coach, now transformed into someone lean and more academic. She imagined him now with black hair. His expression still eluded her. 'How do you select that level beyond which it is acceptable to take a fatal risk? Buttress claims there will be only one crash due to aircraft failure in ten million flights. The DC-10 already disproved that!'

Devlin paused. 'In the real world, assumptions have to be made. Obviously we can't go out and try something ten million times. And neither can anybody go out and bang up an aeroplane to examine just where the edge of safety lies. But despite my own critical view of what goes on around here, we do run extremely thorough tests, and the record isn't bad. We can't just throw additional money or weight into the mix if there haven't been any crashes to warrant it –'

'What I hear you saying is it takes a little death to locate the dollars.'

'You have to take a certain amount on faith just as when you cross the street you're shooting dice or when you sit down in a tub. You can check John Glenn on that. Flying is safer than climbing into a tub.'

'For some people.'

'For most people.'

'Most isn't all.'

'Aha! The argument is joined!'

'I'm talking about the ones left out, the ones the industry can afford to cremate.'

'It's the only workable way to write the law. We have to set a standard – '

'How can a standard that gives a jumbo jet the legal right to fail be supported?'

'The odds are overwhelmingly against it failing.'

'Tell it to the crew of Air World Six.'

'The standards weren't selected haphazardly.'

'They were selected without my permission.'

Devlin tried to plod through the minefield she was laying step by step. 'Without them we couldn't function. They're designed to be within the realm of possibility.'

'Change that to read the realm of profit! The margin of safety is related to the degree of profit. Zero deaths would intrude on profit.'

'Don't knock profit. It pays for the technology needed to buy more safety.'

The driver of the car parked across the street stepped up to the front door and checked the knob. The door was locked. He rang the bell.

Anja heard the chime but stayed with her pursuit.

'It's not used to buy more safety. It's used to buy more expansion to generate more complexity to create more profit and the concept of acceptable risk says you can get away with it. Mr Hollis Wright can sit on a yacht because the law allows him to limit his obligation! He has a cheaper way out! Settlements can be made on the people the industry kills instead!'

'The crash is never acceptable,' Devlin said with remarkable calm. 'The risk is.'

'How magnanimous. After due deliberation the industry has decided it can afford to risk my neck!'

'Obviously it can *afford* it! Be realistic! It can afford a lot more than that!'

'Because the industry never has to do the bleeding!'

Devlin brushed his hand through his long blond hair. 'I want you to know that I'm not on the profit-making side of this business. I'm a cop!'

She shut her eyes, gathering in her argument, reducing it to a single point. 'Would you say a plane which depends entirely on a computer for its ability to fly is acceptable?'

'If it can match a reliability factor of ten to the minus seventh – '

'On Sunday, a computer in the North American Air Defence Command – '

'Oh, boy, here it comes.'

' – signalled the whole defence network that the Soviets had launched a first strike. A sergeant caught it before your missiles lifted off. Page four of the *Post*, bottom left-hand corner. I think handing my only life over to a computer while I'm inside an aeroplane is a risk I should not be required to take.'

'Planes without computers have been known to break up in flight.' He realized at once he had fallen into her trap.

'And the people who bought tickets on them went down long before the law of acceptable risk said they should have!'

'Let me put it another way – '

466

'Don't! You just told me you couldn't even enforce the law when you were dealing with simpler planes.' Anja leaned back and waited.

Devlin heard her idealism, and despite his own similar convictions, *idealism* came across as an anachronism. Perhaps most people still felt a friendship towards idealism, but a self-conscious one now, as when children are sometimes the self-conscious friends of old people, not wishing to be seen with them in their decrepitude. He gripped the phone and swept his gaze across the cluttered room. 'Despite what you're saying, I do try to enforce the law in areas where I see enforcement's called for. That's why I wouldn't approve the 17-10 fix. Because, in my view, it wouldn't – '

'The what?'

'Huh?'

'What about the 17-10?'

'The fix on the 17-10. The plane your friend flies.' Every soft purling of leaves and whirring of bee's wings suddenly seemed amplified, projected through bullhorns.

'A fix?'

'On the 17-10.'

Anja squinted into the sun. 'They fixed the 17-10?'

'It doesn't meet the stringency of the law as I see it . . . but I was overruled.' He fingered the unopened folder, then tossed it aside and swung around to turn his back on the desk. Unseen by Anja, his shoulders slumped. Weariness and detachment gripped him. 'If you'd called a month from now, you'd have had to fight someone else. The way it looks from here, I'll likely be down on all fours checking centre-line stripes on runways in Ecuador because I wouldn't go along with that fix. I'm really no longer here.' He laughed wistfully. 'Hey, I don't know if I helped you any . . . And you know what?'

'What?'

'I would have preferred to argue the case from your side.'

467

Anja's mental picture of Devlin became slightly jumbled. All she could see now was a face dominated by sympathetic eyes.

'Mr Devlin? Don?' Her voice was gentle.

'Ma'am?'

'It's not that crashes aren't inevitable,' she said. 'I suspect they are. It's that they are *accepted*. The logic of acceptable risk says that life is something less important than other considerations. And it tells those of us who refuse to go along with that to be "realistic".'

Devlin sat mute. The argument had grown more serious than he had anticipated and he began to comprehend the depth of respect he had for her words. All he could say finally was, 'I appreciate your calling.' His sincerity registered on Anja. And somehow she perceived, though she couldn't see him, that he wasn't prepared to hang up.

Anja replaced the phone and pushed it aside. She wasn't aware of time passing till she heard the front door open. Peering at her reflection in the window, she burst out laughing. Tufts of hair protruded in mottled beige antennae, paint smudges like vivid bruises scarred her face. She'd removed most of the paint but not all. For an instant she thought of the mental picture she'd had of Devlin and wondered if he'd formed one of her. She giggled at how erroneous it must have been and at an image of him suddenly confronting her as she was, strident, demanding, leading with her beige-coloured hair.

Guy heard her laughter, then saw her coming through the back door. The sight stopped him dead in his tracks. 'First or second coat?' he queried, sizing her up. Taking a closer look, he reached out, touched her hair.

'Who was the guy leaving the house?'

'What guy?'

'Someone left just as I pulled up.'

'I was on the phone,' she said.

Guy went out front. The street was deserted. The mailbox was empty.

'I meant to answer it,' Anja said when Guy returned.

'Maybe good you didn't.'

Anja concentrated on rubbing a crust of paint from her hand. 'I'd forgotten about that for a moment. There were other things going on.'

'That's as plain as the paint on your nose.'

'There's a metamorphosis going on upstairs. The hornet's coming out of the attic.'

Guy waited at the bannister for an explanation but she gave none. Curious, he returned to the foyer and headed upstairs. His son, carrying a broken record player, was on his way down. Guy smilingly tried to engage him, but Jamie pushed by. As the top of the boy's head passed him, Guy could count the strands of hair matted with paint, could see the little stuck-out ear sporting the same shade of beige, and he was instantly aware of a new tone in the boy's bearing. He thought about cuffing Jamie playfully but he didn't yet have his son's unspoken invitation to do so. Left standing midway between floors, Guy hesitantly reached out to him with a greeting, surprised by the sound of his own misgiving.

'Uh, what do you think, do we send her back to Europe or does she stay?'

Jamie stopped and turned towards him but, after considering, didn't look up. He was not ready to acknowledge to his father that the time had now come to let the magic that he had once shared with his original family go altogether. Guy was touched by the boy's quality of privacy, which, behind the reluctance and the paint, revealed an unspoken need to avow on his own terms and in his own time whatever new magic he'd just discovered. Guy stood helplessly on the step and watched as Jamie paused on the landing and passed him. He went into the master bedroom and threw the report he'd been carrying on to the bed. He peeled off his coat and it followed.

Anja joined him, motioning towards the first item. 'What's that?'

On the bedspread lay an inch-thick manual clasped in a stiff, blue paper folder. Its pasted-on label had a typed inscription: '17-10 SIMULATOR FLOW CHART.' 'A little homework, that's all. Picked it up at flight training. You look like you could use a bath. I could use one too. Why don't we conserve water – '

'Soap up with a friend?'

'The environmentalists recommend it.'

'I'll start the water.'

'Make it hot. I need to loosen up.'

'I'll take care of that,' she smiled.

He went back down to the dining room while she undressed and poured himself two fingers of twelve-year-old single malt whiskey, returned to the bedroom and stripped, then took the whiskey and telephone into the bathroom.

'What are you going to do with that?' she demanded, looking at the telephone from within the rapidly filling bathtub.

'One call,' he said, testing the water with his foot. 'Aiy-yai! I said hot, but – '

'Get in, sissy boy.'

Guy tossed his clothes into the hamper. 'I don't know, maybe I ought to start thinking of doing something else for a living. Maybe buy a business or teach weekend jocks how to fly.' He manoeuvred himself gingerly into the tub, lowering himself inch by inch, until he was seated facing Anja. He leaned his head back, eyes closed, and savoured the searing relaxation that rose up to his neck and enveloped him. The grime and hurry of the day floated free. After a long sip of scotch he took the phone and began to dial.

'Turn around,' she said.

Guy twisted in the water, holding the phone receiver aloft with one hand to keep it dry. Anja got on her knees behind him and began to knead his shoulders while he finished dialling.

'Hardware store might be the thing,' he said as the sound of ringing came through.

'A hard-on store,' she mused. 'What a novel idea,' and she reached around to his penis.

'BGR Computer Group,' answered the distant switchboard operator.

'Well, how're you doing?' Guy grinned from ear to ear and tried to think of what to say next. He focused on a broken tile but Anja had put her fingers around him and squeezed him gently. Guy shut his eyes. 'Listen there, how are you?'

'Hello?' came the puzzled reply.

'I'd like to get through to somebody in your, ah . . .' Guy laughed.

'Yes?'

'Are you folks, uh, running a night shift?'

'The facility's closed, sir.'

'Yeah, well, what time does it close?' Guy roared.

'Five-thirty.'

'Listen, you've got to forgive me for laughing but I'm at the dentist's here with laughing gas. Is that every day at five-thirty?'

'Monday through Friday.'

Guy convulsed as Anja reached down with her other hand and pinched him underneath the water, making him jump. The water splashed. 'That's helpful,' he wailed.

'What's that?' The person on the other end chuckled self-consciously.

'That's what I called about!'

'Yes, sir,' the woman cackled.

'Appreciate your help!' Guy yelled and set the phone

down, shaking with laughter. For a full minute he let the pent-up stress break away from him, finally able to feel the consoling warmth of the water again. He stroked her legs. 'Oh, man, that was good.'

'Who was it?'

'BGR. I had to be sure they're not working nights.' His tone changed.

Anja raised the water cupped in her hand and let it trickle on to his hair. 'Want to tell me about it?'

'It's something I'm not going to be able to do on my own.'

'Would someone like me be suitable?'

'Would require someone highly motivated.'

Slowly he relaxed against her and felt the tips of her breasts slippery against him and her slightly rounded tummy in the small of his back just beneath the water as she softened his shoulders. He draped his arms over the sides and let her massage him.

The sound of furniture moving came from the attic.

'He's got a lot to do,' Anja said.

'Somebody in this room is going to get ravished.'

'Don't be in such a hurry,' she whispered gently, using her fingertips on his neck. 'They decided to make a change on the 17-10.'

He reached up and took a slow sip of scotch.

She waited for a response and began to wonder if he'd heard what she'd said. But she could see the muscles in his arms growing taut, and a patch of paint on the heel of one of her hands scratched him.

He asked, 'Shall I get on my knees and beg for the rest of it?'

'If you don't mind.' She patted the red mark on his shoulder where she'd scratched it.

'Anja?'

'In good time.' She was enjoying the advantage.

'What change, Anja?'

472

She turned serious. 'The FAA. Buttress has been at work on a fix for the 17-10.' She sensed his astonishment and she savoured the punch line. 'But the FAA – the Northwest Region chief – wouldn't buy it.'

'They wouldn't *what?*' Guy twirled around in the tub. Water sloshed over the sides in cascades. 'What fix? What are you talking about?'

'I don't know what I'm talking about; I didn't know what questions to ask.'

'Of whom?'

'A decent man in the FAA who's being mowed down at the knees.'

Guy searched her eyes.

'The Northwest Region chief. He didn't approve the fix.'

Guy was still hunting for the telltale sign of a joke. Had he missed the buildup? 'You just said the *FAA*'s man in the West didn't approve a . . . *fix?*'

'Yes.'

'You're . . . *dead certain?*'

'It was a clear connection.'

'Right.'

Guy shook his head from the effect of the jolt, slinging a small fountain from glistening sheets of his hair. He drained the scotch, reached over the side for the phone and dialled.

'But he was overruled.'

His dialling finger stopped in midsweep. 'Did he call *here?*'

'I called him.'

'Jesus . . . What made you call him?'

Anja had no time to answer. Guy had completed dialling and was already talking his way through the ALPA switchboard in Washington until he had Toby on the line. 'I don't want you to hold your breath, Toby, but Buttress is into some sort of rebuild on the 17-10!'

'If you're talking about the service bulletin that just came out, it's only a beefed-up elevator actuator. Nothing mandatory for the airline, no time limit. They can wait till after Christmas to put it in if they want. It's benign.'

'Not so. The Northwest Region chief refused to approve it!' He was watching Anja, who was nodding. 'But he was overruled!'

'That's hard to believe.' Toby sounded distant; it was more than the telephone separation. Guy was puzzled by his diffidence.

In Washington, Toby sat somewhat stiffly behind his desk, holding the phone loosely, his attention fixed on an article in *The Wall Street Journal* which lay open before him. The two-column headline read, 'DLG TAKES OPTIONS ON 25 BUTTRESS 17-10BS.' The lead paragraph explained that, according to G. Hollis Wright, the Germans had just given the 17-10 a clean bill of health and intended to purchase more.

'Don't take my word for it,' Guy insisted. 'Check it!'

Toby was silent.

Guy waited. 'You still there or did you die?'

'This morning the Germans took options on twenty-five 17-10Bs.'

'Where'd you hear that?'

'Front page, *The Wall Street Journal*.'

It was an ambush and it dumbfounded Guy. He had to stop long enough to absorb the news. Almost absently he lifted the glass of scotch and upended it over his head, letting the ice cubes tumble into the bath water.

'Holy – shit.' Guy's eyes were tightly shut. 'Toby, let's take one thing at a time. As a favour to me, will you call the Northwest Region chief and ask him why he wouldn't sprinkle his holy water on Buttress?'

'How do you know that's true?'

'Call him.'

'And he's going to spill his guts outside the office, get

474

fired and kiss all the time he's piled up goodbye. What, are you kidding me? The administrator signed something off and you want me to go snooping around in the field behind his back? I'll be slamming doors in our faces!'

'You can't expect me to paint in all the squares for you. You got to come to me part of the way.'

'Realistically, I don't think there's anything ALPA can do under these circumstances.' The words were flat and strained.

Guy tried to relocate his bearings. He might have expected refusal but not indifference. He exploded. 'Jesus, Toby, I'm getting goddamn tired of being polite to you! If you're not going to be satisfied till you see some gristle and bone, then it's time you excused yourself and got out! I know you want to be meticulous, but you owe me and the other people who pony up the annual dues more than that!'

'The 17-10 isn't the only thing we have to think about around here. We can't stop what else we're doing because you and Cosgrove made one successful emergency landing!'

'I recommend you shift gears and get on this and I'm putting it in a letter so that it gets on record. I recommend you first call Buttress and find out what specifically needs fixing and why and then you call the FAA and find out why the Northwest Region chief was overruled and then you get back to us, and if it doesn't stick together, the membership is to be given ballots to decide whether to fly the 17-10 or not. You see, because the loan-guarantee hearings are round the corner now and every effort is going to be made to freeze the 17-10 in a bed of roses. The FAA and the NTSB and Hollis Wright have been cornholing each other for years. And right now they're corkscrewing down like clams in the sand and taking everything that's been going on down with them and if you don't jump in after them now, we'll be too late. The fact that one

contrary Northwest Region man has just been counter-
manded has got to tell you something!'

'I'll put in a call, Guy. I'll do that for you. But I'm going
to get a "no comment",' Toby warned.

'The time has come to twist some arms.'

'Just as long as you don't twist mine.'

'Then you better be sure you leave me a choice.' Guy
threw the phone down.

At virtually the same instant – the bells were still toning
from the curt hang-up – the instrument rang again. With a
graceful swoop, Anja swept it from the floor before Guy
could reach it and held it away from him.

'One of the first things I'm going to do when I get
enough guts is to twist every phone I see out of its socket.'

Guy went for it as it rang again but Anja kept it beyond
his reach.

'With deep respect for the phone company, I don't want
to hear from anyone at the other end of the world or talk
after five when it's cheaper or react to someone else's
need to bother me.' She spoke louder to outdo the
continuing jangle. 'I don't want to be woken up, startled,
canvassed, pestered, interfered with, interrupted in the
middle of making love – '

'Anja.'

'No. I don't want my privacy invaded' – and she smiled
– 'except by invitation.' She lifted the receiver an inch in
the air and smacked it down again, disconnecting the call.
Slowly she lowered the dead phone back on to the
bathroom floor.

'You disconnected it!'

'It's a burglar machine – gets inside without a key and
orders sensible people to stop the sensible things they're
doing to pay attention to the problems that wouldn't be
theirs if the caller couldn't get through in the first place!'
Anja struck a triumphant pose. Then her face softened.
With sheepish irony she remembered that as part of her

476

Plan she herself had a call to make: the irreverent senator from New York who would sit on the Peck-Searington Select Senate Committee; for the moment she made a mental note. It would have to keep.

'Suppose that was important, and I'm serious.'

'I am too.' She watched him for a moment. 'There are times when that ring scares me half to death because – I guess I've been afraid that one day it's going to change my life . . .'

There was a pause during which the only sound was the slow trickle of water. But the phone rang again. Anja crossed her arms and stared at Guy, who waited stoically through the third shrill bell without making a move.

In his office, Matt Aspinwall stared at Guy Anders's phone number and held the receiver to his ear waiting for it to ring a fourth time. He surveyed the advertisement emblazoned across a full page of the New York *Times*: 'Air World Is Ready to Whisk You to Europe on the Space-Smooth 17-10 . . . With 191 Pilots at Your Disposal,' all in bold black type like hand grenades across the page. Matt had insisted on the ad impulsively, bulldozed it through, and now, in the hush behind the tinted glass of his office, he knew why the agency men had cringed and accused him of being defensive. He should never have called attention to Air World's leftover problem in the press because now the press wouldn't leave him alone. 'Shouldn't it be *192* pilots, Mr Aspinwall?' they taunted. It was a stinging barb that accorded Guy Anders a particular, unanticipated dignity. And so, Matt decided, almost as impulsively, he wanted him back. The hardware was secure; at last the aeroplanes were arriving from Buttress. Another had pulled in just before lunch, its smooth aluminium skin like a mirror, the Air World logo riding the rudder huge and fresh and scrubbed. But the public's curiosity that lingered in the aftermath of Guy Anders's well-publicized refusal to fly the 17-10, that still hurt. It was the last thorn needing to be plucked. Matt Aspinwall chewed down some pride and waited.

It was not until the start of the sixth ring that Guy picked it up. He watched Anja and tried to sound offhand. 'Who's this?'

'Guy Anders?'

'That's me.'

'This is Matt Aspinwall.'

When Guy recognized what he'd just heard, he straightened up and rubbed his face with a towel to remove the perspiration. He wiped his ear. But in that instant, because the call had come to him, because there was an undeniable quality of harassment about the voice on the other end, Guy sensed that *this* was the turning point. The moment when at last he was about to be granted his first real grip on the axe handle of some authentic leverage. Right here, naked in a bathtub.

'I'm the cocksucker you figured ought to be sent to the outback to teach jigaboos how to fly,' Guy said easily.

There was a pause while Matt worked to ignore the remark. 'You feel any different about flying the 17-10 today?'

'No, I don't feel any different about it.'

'I want you to know that Buttress has undertaken a fix as a consequence of Flight Six.'

'I didn't hear it was as a consequence of Flight Six, but I did hear it's been accorded all the weight of a service bulletin – somewhere on the scale of importance between a loose magazine rack and a cracked sun visor.'

'The assumption has to be it isn't worth more than that.'

'My assumption is that if it related to Flight Six, it's worth a hell of a lot more than that. Let me ask you this. What do you know about the German report?'

'I know all about that report.'

'Have you seen it?'

'No. A fellow in Bonn I know wrote it and his assignment is to see how the Fatherland can be first with the 17-10 and break our grip. I'm not about to give up first place. Guy, you don't realize it but you've been used against your own and my best interests. I want you to read me correctly on this. You've cost me a lot of money. I can't document that, but you've hurt the cash register. I suspect your aim was at Buttress but you missed by a country mile and hit us instead and we're the ones who pay your goddamn mortgage.'

'Well, if we had dumped your goddamn aeroplane in Jamaica Bay, it would have cost you – '

'Just shut up and let me finish.' Guy let the discourtesy pass; he was more interested in Matt's struggle for the words. 'On the other hand I do come up with a feeling of . . . respect for you sometimes. It isn't often, but I have experienced it. Right now you're the only black mark I've got left on the Big Season. It's like walking around with one shoelace untied and I aim to convert it. I want you back on the line.'

Guy didn't answer.

'Now how long do you figure you're going to have to watch others fly the 17-10 before you decide it's safe?' Aspinwall continued.

'Is there an innuendo there?'

'No, there isn't. That's me, pure Aspinwall, tactless as hell but certain about what he wants. Read the article on me in *Time*. It explains everything.'

It was pure Aspinwall but it lacked the customary bravado. The faint quality of an entreaty had begun to colour his tone as he went on.

'Your buddies think you're grapefruit. You want to come off that reputation before it sticks, Anders.' He was making light of things but the halting effort it took was detectable. Guy recognized it and felt sorry for him. And as Matt spoke, Guy visualized Air World crews in their black uniforms, checking in without him, placidly gather-

479

ing in the distance on identical flight decks, seated in long limos heading for temporary rooms; abstractly, Guy saw them wearing headsets . . . waiting . . . and suddenly he caught the first glimmer of an idea he knew could bring Buttress to its knees – an idea involving Toby and Reese – and requiring that he go back on the line.

Guy wasn't certain how long Matt had stopped talking. He considered calling him 'Mr Aspinwall', but the need for it was gone.

'Matt?'

'Did you hear what I said?' Matt asked.

Guy settled back and let the warm water enclose him. 'Look, Matt, you and I don't have an argument. Aside from your overseas plans for me, I have no quarrel with Air World. So maybe we ought to get together.'

'This week.'

'There are a couple of things I'm involved in.'

'It doesn't have to be this afternoon.'

'In a few days, then.'

'I would look forward to it,' said Aspinwall. 'Call me or Angela and you set it up.'

'Fine.'

'Nice talking to you.'

At that moment in a Paris clearinghouse, a certain night clerk red-flagged the perfumery cheque for twenty-five thousand dollars made out to Guy Anders. The clerk matched the cheque against the description in his instructions and brought it to his supervisor, a stern-faced man perched within a glass-enclosed cubicle. The supervisor studied the cheque, turned it over to inspect the endorsement, then reached for his telephone. 'I want to make a call to the United States,' he said. 'Person to person. To Mr G. Hollis Wright.'

* * *

Guy had replaced the receiver and taken a big gulp of air. He looked again at the phone and at Anja and reached over to take the receiver off the hook and drop it alongside, on the tile floor. He threw a towel over it and turned back to her. The water was slippery, slidy, more comfortable than ever.

A knowing half smile formed slowly on her lips. She drew one thigh back under the water and he moved closer.

Dick Miller was reluctant to lock the front door. The luggage was packed for the trip to Washington, all the errands had been accomplished, nothing remained to be done except to get in the car and drive to the airport. Yet he hesitated. On some imaginary pretext he began to push the front door open again as if to re-enter the small house in which he'd spent so many years, paying mortgage instalments since before he could remember, each one of those instalments he'd originally thought of as a step upward, but so many steps had accumulated they'd become lost and meaningless and still they stretched upward in front of him, steepening into the indistinctness ahead, an endless row of little steps.

He felt Sandy's hand, thin and cool, close over his own, gently restraining him, and he stood there by the shut front door and stared at her. It wasn't a vacant stare exactly but she could tell his mind was somewhere else. Despite the white sunshine and overheated air she felt a chill and gooseflesh rose on her arms. For one lucid instant she sensed how it would be when this house, which she'd always thought of as permanent, as rock-solid as an endless calendar whose pages followed one upon another, would be turned over to unknowns; and it was an idea she found abhorrent. Not from the inevitable invasion of strange furniture or alien tastes, but from their indifference to, their ignorance of all the accumulated private hours cradled by these special walls.

'Come on, Richard, let's go,' she said a little tartly.

He looked around blankly. Then, as if rousing himself, he stooped and hoisted the large suitcase. His knuckles shone.

'Oh, Richard . . . must we go?' She stood apart, appealing to him. 'Is it necessary?'

He halted, perhaps analysing the implications of her question. At last he nodded, woodenly. And it occurred to both of them in their respective silence on that porch that they didn't know where this place was and probably never did. Had there really been laughter here? Screen doors slamming? Through the coldness she strained to hear an atom of it and the bushes lay limp under the fever heat.

When Dick Miller moved off, along the walk, it was nevertheless with a certain resoluteness.

18

Ben Reese was standing outside the Mayflower Hotel in Washington eating peanut brittle and staring at the three-column headline across the top right side of page one of the morning paper: 'AIRLINE PILOT IN PAYOFF.' As jaded as he had become and as prepared for this event as he was, the brazenness of it caught him. Just as he had envisioned, Guy Anders was smeared across and down the front page. Ben scanned the subheads and first couple of paragraphs; the words fell in predictable order:

AIR WORLD FIRST OFFICER ACCUSED
OF TAKING BRIBE FROM EUROPE

'Paid Delivery Boy'
Said to Be Desperate
to Mask Role in Recent
Landing Incident, Played
into Hands of Intense
International Competition

Special from Combined Wire Services – It was revealed on the West Coast late yesterday by a spokesman for the Buttress Aerospace Corporation that Air World First Officer Gavin Anders has allegedly accepted at least $25,000.00 for the purpose of making statements prejudicial to the major US aeroplane and defence contractor, Buttress . . . Anders issued a recent statement widely reported in the press in which he refused to fly aboard 17-10 aeroplanes, alleging they all contain a major design flaw as yet uncorrected. This view so far has received no support . . . The pilot's alleged acceptance of money enabled the European Consortium, builders of the Skybus, the 17-10's main competitor, to make Anders the pawn in a major international aerospace battle for future airline and military sales. At stake are billions in production work . . . When questioned if Buttress intends to bring charges or file suit against pilot Anders, the Buttress spokesman commented the matter was in the hands of its attorneys. Buttress retains the services of the Washington law firm Kolmar, Swinburne & Stapleton . . .

Ben scanned to the end. Not surprisingly, there was no acknowledgment of the coincidence that the story had broken minutes before the Peck-Searington hearing on Buttress's loan extension was due to start. Despite the gravity of the words in black print Ben found himself grinning: if now he could tie the smear conclusively to Buttress, he'd have the journalistic upset of the decade.

Ben checked his watch; then through the glass of the hotel's revolving door he noticed the characteristically purposeful gait of the editor, the close-cropped peppery head and the familiar slouch of his frame. Striding across the lobby alone, heading for the opposite door. With one adroit move Ben was stationed by the exit directly behind the doorman, who was busy accepting currency in a neat backhand through the open rear door of a taxi. The editor was emerging, glancing with nervous chops of the eyes back and forth for the next cab, unaware of Ben, who had resumed his nonchalance. Ben spotted the cab first and pushed off. His timing was exact. In a single motion the taxi pulled up and Ben, with a flourish, had its rear door open. The doorman, grunting like a foghorn, wedged in to take charge, but Ben gave him an elbow to the midsection which rebounded. With the other hand he grabbed his former boss's arm.

'We'll go halves.'

Ben was stronger and had the leverage and with a shove moved the editor inside the cab. Flashing a broken grin, he tipped the doorman the last of his peanut brittle as he piled in, scooping the door shut behind him. 'The Old Senate Office Building.'

The editor was already slouched in the opposite corner, braced with his back against the side window, focusing on Ben with a mixture of estimation and long-suffering. 'Well, if it isn't the re-embodiment of Ben Reese,' he said with some wonder but with the tone he'd use to a vagrant.

Ben smiled, a long slow smile, savouring the moment. 'I trust we're headed for the same sideshow.' Then his grin faded and his face settled into serious pleats. 'That stuff you printed about Anders this morning is crap.'

'We have two sources.'

'Buttress and the National Association of Industrial Stickbuddies.'

'We have a photostat of the cheque.'

'That cheque came from a perfumery in Paris organized by the same Washington law firm that handles the Buttress account.'

The editor seemed to compress as though privately to sift for a worthy response to a particularly provocative insult.

'But you didn't know that,' Ben went on.

'Benny, you and I have had our day. I don't want to chase down that track.'

'You can't afford to ignore it.'

'Another spine-tingling hunch, Benny?'

In unspoken response Ben pulled free a Xerox copy of the letter he'd found in Paris, unpeeled it and held it in front of the editor's face. As the editor reached for it, Ben placed it deliberately across his lap. 'Read it and mourn . . . just because you blew it – and without my help – and second, because you can't have it. Go on, read it.'

The editor lifted it at the corner as though it were contaminated, but the cab lurched and he had to take hold of the page with both hands. He studied it for half a dozen blocks and didn't look up when at last he spoke. 'This is authentic?'

'As the Dead Sea Scrolls.'

'Could be a coincidence, couldn't it?'

'On the other hand, reality may have got too taxing for you.'

'Why did Anders endorse the cheque?'

'I told him to so we could work our way back to the source of it.'

'The source of it is stacked with notables from Europe's aviation industry.'

'All at the peak of their senility – and all planted there by Buttress.'

Shadows flitted across the editor's face. He glanced up at Ben and indicated the letter. 'This isn't the original.'

'Perceptive.' Ben's eyes twinkled. 'The fellow who wrote it is dead. That's also a reasonably reliable assumption.'

The editor frowned quizzically.

'I blew his cover,' Ben responded. 'He was a man with a violent mission. I have a shoe full of blood to prove it.'

'Where did you get this?'

'None of your business.'

Cars in the right lane sped up nearly preventing the cab from making a right turn. The driver swore.

'I know a stickup when I see one, Benny. Your unemployment run out already?'

'You're not doing anything to ingratiate yourself.'

The editor faced him. 'How much do you want for this? Name the amount.'

Ben's voice was firm. 'I want back on as a roster player. You owe me nothing except expenses and a chair in the press room.'

'You're disreputable.'

Ben fingered a knob of broken threads that once had held a button. 'I'll get a needle and thread. You won't have to print what I write but when you do you're going to have to pull up a chair and dig into an order of crow. That's how I'd like to be reinstated.'

The editor studied the sheet again. Ben settled back and noticed that the traffic to the Hill had begun to thicken.

'Of course, what I should do is take it to the *Times* or the *Free Press* but that wouldn't be right. I want you to have a chance to expiate your sins.' Ben faced the editor, beaming. 'I want you to rehabilitate me.'

'This letter doesn't mean much.'

'You know better.' Ben gestured significantly through the front window where the Capitol dome could be seen riding the treetops. 'The Peck-Searington hearing's fixed. You know that, too.'

'I don't know it.'

'Your nose knows it.'

'Instinct isn't news.'

'It used to be a place to start. You're no longer using the First Amendment the way it was meant to be used. You're writing ad copy for the status quo. You're writing defensively as though you'd been warned.'

'Thanks to you, we have.'

'Get your nitpicking lawyers away from the copy desk and open the windows. You have my word I won't shoot my mouth off without your say-so. But that hearing is fixed. That's me talking to you. It's a gang bang. They're going to sodomize the taxpayer.'

'Not necessarily.'

'Then you tell me why the big banks won't touch Buttress. Because they know something we don't. So they're going to take the little guy who humps a desk or carries a lunch pail and prime him to prop up Hollis Wright. And if Hollis goes belly up, the GoGetum Evening News Team will tell the great panting legions watching the box one night that their taxes will have to go up again, not because of Buttress but because of inflation. And those taxes will never go down, even after the debt's been paid.'

The cab slowed as it approached the Hill.

'I'll take this letter the way it is but without attribution. Your name is poison.'

Ben didn't react.

'I need to know what kind of dollars we're talking about,' the editor said.

'You pay nothing down.' The cab stopped before the ornate entrance to the Old Senate Office Building. 'I need a clean set of credentials to work the hearing and if you have to think it over, have the grace to pass on it now. There are others out there willing to commit murder for my brain.'

Even as he spoke, the editor was aware of his expression changing; the vagrant had acquired a certain measure of respectability. Ben's former boss had never been good at hiding the phenomenon of his own face softening at the recognition of having been sold. The driver waited expectantly.

The editor announced, 'Your vouchers'll be in the press room in half an hour.'

487

Ben slipped the letter out of the editor's hands. He smiled. 'This was just to get your heart started. You're entitled to more than that.' He folded it and put it away. 'You don't want to go with this anyway. It's circumstantial. Won't hold up. Any half-wit lawyer will tell you that.'

'That's three dollars and forty cents,' said the driver.

Ben reached over and patted the driver's hand. 'Of course it is. But we have an agreement back here and that's his department.'

Ben got out and fell in behind a TV news crew heading up the Old Senate Office Building steps.

The start of the Peck-Searington hearing was already a half-hour behind schedule. Five of the six senators who would sit to hear for their peers the request to extend and increase the government loan guarantee to Buttress Aerospace Corporation arrived late and now, as the packed gallery waited, took a long time to sit down, conferring with staff, greeting each other, posturing in weighty preamble. It was more than being in the august presence of the senators themselves or reconciling the incongruity of easy mannerisms on faces seen in newspapers that caused the general hush to prevail over the ranks of spectators. It was also a universal awe before the grandeur of the Senate Caucus Room itself in which the Peck-Searington committee would sit. Encompassed by its Corinthian marble columns towering to the majestically coffered and gilded ceiling from which stately curtains descended in silent maroon cataracts, the senators sat stern and imposing like a row of steel-engraved images risen from within the arabesque volutes of old bank notes.

Two prosperously dressed lawyers had taken their places behind G. Hollis Wright, who sat at the broad mahogany table directly across from the senators. The stouter of the lawyers passed Hollis a yellow legal pad with scribbled notes but Hollis brushed it away; instead his gaze examined the senators as they took their places. Senator Albert Searington, white-haired and commanding, sat motionless, a little weary perhaps, but still the gamecock. Alongside him E. Harlowe Peck, the committee's co-chairman, lean, gaunt New Englander with silver-copper hair like the notched edge of a coin, seemed as remote as a Puritan schoolmaster. Indeed, he'd got his start that way, on an astringent school board, and he still wore the plain brown suit and green bow tie of another era. Elton Osborne's chair was vacant and the briefest tightening of expression flickered across Hollis's face. In the last seat, even the senator from Alaska, the firebrand Democrat bush pilot Bob Burch didn't look out of place despite his youth. Still in his thirties, he had a young-old face, pink and soft, which occasionally went haggard between shaggy temples already grey. His dossier in Hollis's briefcase was thin. He'd been against the pipeline but was often strongly pro-aviation. On the other side of Searington, Eugene McDermott, husk dry, blown to Washington by the winds that rolled off the Great Plains, was thin-lipped and against the loan. Alongside him, at the opposite end of the long dais, was Senator Constantine Zakowski of New York, conspicuous in his factory warehouse suit, new to the Senate, having been catapulted directly from the House seat of his Bronx congressional district. He now sat blinking at the lights and perhaps too at the ceremonial splendour of the setting. Hollis had read about him in *Newsweek*, a short piece describing the man's beginnings as a colourful boardwalk politician. Hollis had dismissed him as a lightweight.

The murmur in the room subsided as Senator Peck pounded the gavel. In the rear Ben Reese glanced at the one vacant chair on the dais. He'd been surprised to learn Osborne was absent. Buttress would certainly want Osborne present; the senator's own re-election virtually depended on Buttress support. Something was amiss.

Senator Peck leaned forward slightly. 'Before we begin, I have one announcement.' He stopped to clear his throat as if pained. 'We must apologize for the absence of Senator Elton Osborne today. It was hoped he could take his seat on the committee for the opening of the hearing, but he was unavoidably detained on urgent business abroad.' Peck quickly completed a general welcome and the perfunctory opening remarks but it was obvious he wanted to focus all attention on one of the established supranational potentates of the aviation industry, and rather more quickly than expected he concluded his introductions. Senator Zakowski, leaning forward suddenly, scowled and grappled with his microphone. Senator Peck thought only that Zakowski wanted to straighten out some minor procedural matter, and nodded almost absently to recognize him.

'I have an opening remark,' Zakowski rasped.

'The distinguished gentleman may proceed.'

'I just want to remind this committee that ever since the fiery landing of Air World Six, a number of my constituents living near JFK have become convinced that under certain conditions – as when the wind dictates the use of runway twenty-two or Canarsie approaches are in progress – they're living under a potential *umbrella of death!*'

Searington was suddenly wide awake but too stunned to retort. Peck hesitated. The abruptness of the remark had prevented its full impact from filtering through the great room. Mild buzzing could be heard from a few people still murmuring in the background.

'Now they would be wrong if Flight Six had been a fluke – a one-in-a-hundred-million possibility – but Flight Six happened on Air World's sixty-first landing of a 17-10 at JFK! So my constituents are a little excited – maybe you might say overexcited about seeing a 17-10 break up over their homes – but they're not out of their senses. Now we could talk about that here, but I don't want to.' Zakowski's gaze was fixed dead on Hollis. 'I expect we'll get to that.'

'Senator Zakowski, is this an opening remark or a position paper?' Albert Searington challenged. Before Zakowski could answer, Searington continued, 'I would like to point out to the gentleman from New York that we have an agenda and he will have sufficient time for his full remarks.'

'Mr Co-chairman, I would like my remarks to be construed and entered into the record as preceding the agenda because there's something wrong with the tone of this Senate hearing right from the opening gong. And I don't want us to get off on the wrong foot.'

'Will the distinguished gentleman yield?' Senator Peck asked uncertainly.

'Mr Co-chairman, I know there's a lot of yielding and deferring that goes on as part of the parliamentary procedure. I was not always the model of convention in the House of Representatives, and I guess it will be said of me here that I'm not much of a tiptoe artist. It interferes with honesty and I just want to say something about how my people feel about us holding this meeting. Now I don't think that calls for yielding. I don't think anyone will get a nosebleed if I'm permitted to finish my remarks.'

A single laugh began somewhere in the gallery, triggering a ripple of guarded hilarity. Senator Peck gavelled for order.

Hollis Wright leaned towards his microphone and broke through the diminishing laughter. 'Mr Co-chairman,' he boomed, 'I don't mind if Senator Zakowski wishes to set the tone for this hearing.' Hollis was convinced he recognized a jackal, and sat back fascinated.

Zakowski nodded towards the witness table. 'I'm grateful, Mr Wright. And I want to assure this distinguished body that I mean no disrespect. Now we could talk about your aeroplane, Mr Wright, but I don't want to do that now. We could also talk about how Mr Hollis Wright, who's come for his second fix from the public treasury, makes five hundred fifty thousand dollars a year, and that my working constituents average fourteen thousand in this inflation and in this economy. But I don't want to talk about that either.' He saw Hollis redden ever so slightly but remain controlled. Zakowski's gaze travelled past Hollis Wright. He searched the gallery and continued, 'I want to tell you about several thousand friends of mine who, for one reason or another, found themselves with more bills payable than accounts receivable. You know who they are: the lone operators – two brothers who get together, or a man whose wife works as the bookkeeper six days a week with the seventh left over for worrying. And when the payout began to exceed the take in, the banks looked on without so much as a word of encouragement. So they did what has to be done, took the beating, and looked to see if they could get in on the fun again with a snappier service or a better product. Now that's the nature of our system as I understand it. It isn't always pleasant; neither is the Rose Bowl when you lose it. Free enterprise is synonymous with taking a shot – going out on a limb. If you win, you can win it all. If someone beats you to it, you either redouble your effort and retake the lead or you take a bath. What you can't do in free enterprise is go run to the government when you get blown out of the saddle! My unfortunate constituents couldn't find anybody in the government who wanted to talk to them. That's not too thrilling but that's reality. Now if that's the reality out on the sidewalk for so many of my friends, how come it isn't Hollis Wright's reality? *His* people gummed it up. Yes they did! His boys said, boss, we're going to make you the F-19 for x and they made it for x plus the shirt off our backs! Then they said, boss, we're going to

492

make you the 17-10 fly-by-wire, light-in-the-tail civilian transport for *y* plus *z* because it's a new-technology aeroplane and now they're into the Chinese alphabet!'

Again laughter broke out in the gallery.

'Point of order!' Senator Peck shouted, smacking the gavel. 'Senator Zakowski, you're in contempt of the rules!' Peck's remark was partially lost in the laughter.

'No, that's not funny!' Zakowski spoke sharply into his microphone, ignoring Peck. 'A year ago Buttress opened a six-hundred-and-fifty-million-dollar credit line with the People's Republic of China! Which is just a drop in the bucket of what it needed to stay afloat. But instead of Hollis Wright paying the consequences, he made a call to Washington and got a loan guarantee! Now he wants that loan extended because he's in no position to cover his obligations! This might even become a yearly reunion. But if you ask him, he'll tell you he wants less government interference – less restrictions and meddling and regulation. And if you ask him, he'll make a speech about free enterprise. He's given it lots of times to the Junior Achievement and at conventions and at political rallies! He's an armchair free enterpriser – a real commando for our system provided the government covers his flanks!'

Hollis Wright sat looking at Zakowski with the imperturbability of a lion staring at his prey between meals.

'Is the senator finished?' intoned Peck flatly.

Zakowski turned towards Searington. 'I just want to be sure, Mr Co-chairman, that we all understand if this committee recommends extension of a two-point-three-billion-dollar loan guarantee, we will have signalled in ten figures our government's commitment to go to bat for the elite sector of our economy on an exclusive basis. I think the people in the gallery and anyone buying a newspaper have a right to know that.'

Searington pushed his notes aside and glared down along the burdensome years at Zakowski. 'This isn't a shooting gallery where we gather to hurl insults at the very people who have had the enterprise to *build this country*.' His gravelly voice came across as though his throat had been stepped on, but his eyes were alight with the messianic vision of the Commander. 'If we did that here, we'd be throwing in with the unwashed rabble that never did a day's work and has never built anything, itching to tear down what has taken raw guts and generations to put together. They would tear the marble pillars off this building in the name of something better when there *is* nothing better!' Spontaneous applause burst from the gallery. Impassive, Senator Searington waited for it to die down. 'We'd be doing *their* cowardly work. That doesn't mean questions cannot be asked and testimony given, but I don't care for the tone of Senator Zakowski's remarks. Buttress and a lot of other people were there when the mass murderers of Germany and Japan came for our throats and they've kept us suited up in the type of hardware that has kept the other side at least partially sober. We're here to go eye to eye with facts. That's how I understand it. Hollis Wright is here to make his case. He's not on trial. At least as far as I know he's done nothing to result in his indictment. I trust it's not too much to insist that we extend some rudimentary courtesy, however much out of character that may be.'

'Do you plan to continue to run interference for Mr Wright, Senator?' queried Zakowski, raising the stakes.

Searington didn't move. His face was dark like an ancient iron mask. 'I intend to block calumny, Senator.'

'I just want to be sure this hearing won't be limited to a guided tour.'

'I trust we can now proceed with our agenda.'

'I reserve the right, Mr Chairman, to get more annoying and a lot more technical further on.'

Albert Searington took off his glasses and cleaned them during a spattering of enthusiastic applause. 'Do you have any further comments?'

'No, sir, and I thank the chairman and Mr Wright for their indulgence.'

'Sticks and stones,' Ben Reese muttered to a colleague in the press section. 'But morality isn't the issue, is it?'

'The gentleman from New York was only clearing his throat,' whispered the colleague. 'There's more.'

Ben neatly folded a fresh Xerox copy of the perfumery letter signed by Jasovak and sealed it in a news service envelope. He turned it over and in large block letters wrote across the front 'G. HOLLIS WRIGHT.' 'Save my seat,' Ben said and left.

'As suggested, I have noted the previous remarks as being outside the agenda,' Senator Peck was saying, 'and further wish not to be associated with the remarks of the gentleman from New York.' He looked around earnestly as though to reorient himself, locating the figure waiting to open the proceedings, and smiling, introduced him. With that, Hollis Wright had the floor.

He spoke as though Zakowski's outburst had never occurred.

'Senator Peck, Senator Searington, Senators, ladies and gentlemen. It is a pleasure to speak before you this morning on the matter of the proposed government loan extension to Buttress Aerospace Corporation. Let me begin with a little comparison. Back in 1930 the Ford Tri-Motor took thirty-four hours to fly coast to coast. It made sixteen stops en route. The fare for such a trip would cost more than a thousand in today's dollars. The Buttress 17-10 presently flies coast to coast in one sixth the time and passengers can buy tickets at one fifth the cost. In terms of fatalities per passenger-mile, the airlines – even before the new technology of the 17-10 – are more than forty times safer.' Hollis had hunched over the table. He was speaking earnestly. 'This progress came about very simply because the portion of the nation's gross national product devoted to aviation technology accelerated for twenty-five years. Today, however, that portion is woefully low. We may never see the equivalent level of investment in the aviation industry achieved again. A Ford Tri-Motor cost fifty thousand dollars. A 17-10 costs more than seventy million. Couple this with the fact, sad but true, that today's economic climate discourages risk taking. Despite several emerging technologies that offer bright promise, the consequences of fallback are just too expensive for private investors. Without massive help from the public sector, the next half century will not see nearly the same degree of improvement as the last.'

Senator McDermott began cleaning his glasses.

Hollis Wright continued. 'Since 1945 there have been only two main shifts in the type of transport plane delivered to the airlines. Both of these shifts accrued primarily because of large advances in engines. The two shifts were simply piston to jet and jet to fan-jet. The changes to aeroplanes these shifts allowed us to make – first to swept-back wings and then to widebodies – could not be applied retroactively to the older aeroplanes on a cost-effective basis.

'Today, Senator, we at Buttress foresee only one new equivalent shift of such magnitude. This time it won't come from new engines. Engines have reached a plateau. Instead, it's coming from digital computers – and from new nonmetal materials. These two developments allow us to chop off the tail, make the wings thinner, do things that again cannot be applied retroactively. With that we can squeeze direct operating costs down and push return on investment – what Air World and the German airline DLG and all our other customer airlines are interested in – up more than ten per cent. That's not peanuts, gentlemen. That's oxygen to an industry that's being choked by stifling costs! But it means we *must* succeed. And since success has important implications for all of us, we need the means to carry out our efforts with some certainty, with reasonableness, with little speculation on our part as to the outcome.'

Hollis Wright had caught his stride. His hands were wide apart, clenched. Several senators sat transfixed by the urgency of his persuasiveness. 'Consider the 707 programme, which ran for almost a quarter century – longer if you count the prototype development. Disregarding military versions, from 1958 its builder turned out an average of close to one aeroplane a week for nearly twenty years – *continuous production*. We look forward to that kind of programme with the 17-10, gentlemen.' Hollis Wright smiled and stopped to sip water from the glass at his elbow. A young black girl in a page uniform entered the arena, cautiously placed Ben's envelope next to Hollis Wright's hand and withdrew. The Buttress chairman didn't acknowledge the delivery nor reveal any particular interest in it. Instead he observed Ed Boice on his flank facing straight ahead like a platoon leader in the turret of a tank riding alongside, loyal and eager, but the man's presence worried him. He had his sergeant with him instead of his brigadier, who was still back West wrestling with the plugged production line.

'It should be pointed out,' he continued, 'that the 17-10 delivers better environmental impact, far less fuel consumption, far less noise. Everybody appreciates that. Yet in the course of doing business it's not uncommon for an industry dedicated to solving a common dilemma such as the continuation of an economically viable transportation system to find itself beset by vilification. During my tenure, we have been accused of everything from causing a chicken who camped too close to a runway to go bald to causing a loss of hearing on the ground. We've been confronted but never convicted.' Hollis's face softened at the tittering that passed through the gallery. 'We've been taken to task for putting limits on capacity in jumbo jets that need power for takeoff, then criticized by the same people about inadequate safety when we've agreed to a reduction of that power in the interest of noise relief. That's a little like criticizing the lack of mass transit, then standing on the third rail in wet shoes to make a case against the energy lobby!'

Laughter broke, built and cascaded through the hall. Neither Peck nor Searington made a move to stop it; instead they sat back to enjoy it. Hollis Wright began to laugh too, taking the moment to open the envelope which had been placed beside him. He removed the single sheet, unfolded it and stared at the contents. Watching him, Ben could see the flash point of an explosion take place then darken as the board chairman, exposed as he was in the spotlight, worked within the confines of his head to contain his reaction. He reminded Ben of a bomb truck surrounding and muffling a detonation: his body moved slightly like the wheels under the steel cage of the vehicle as it absorbed the shock.

The senators had turned back and were ready for him to continue. Hollis refolded the paper and slipped it into its envelope. It was a masterful conquest on his part, Ben acknowledged, though it could be only momentary; the sole clues to the chairman's struggle were his eyes, which darted once around the room to see if any traces needed retrieving. They slotted on to Ben Reese behind the shadows of the press section and almost imperceptibly widened. Ben simply returned the chairman's stare. Hollis fed the missive into his inside coat pocket, took a sip of water and smiled. Ben smiled too.

'I just want to say, Mr Chairman, that confrontation has become part of our life-style. This is neither harmful nor should it be construed as conclusive in the plaintiff's favour.'

Then Hollis drew himself up, mustered himself for the conclusion. His final phrases chopped the air like machetes. 'Our position in the industry didn't come free,'

498

he boomed. 'With respect to the 17-10, we've amortized our development costs over a twenty-year lifetime of a fleet of four hundred and fifty 17-10s. That's a lot of input. We're now looking to you for the temporary backup to justify this considerable investment. If you falter or equivocate in this area, it is at our peril. And since Buttress leads the nation in aerospace defence production, it becomes a matter of national peril.' Hollis deliberately softened his tone. 'I don't think it would be prudent to lose sight of that.' Hollis took his watch off and placed it before him. 'I will be pleased to answer questions, Mr Chairman.'

Dick Miller stood at the base of the white marble steps watching the tourists in their multicoloured outfits filing by towards the Capitol. He turned and watched several taxis as they came up the slope crowding in behind each other. He hoped his wife would step out of one of them. She'd wanted some extra time at the hotel to put herself together and had suggested that Dick go to the hearing ahead of her; he wasn't due to testify before the committee until the end of the morning session; she'd catch up with him later. He wanted so much to see Sandy right then and there, to greet her and to hold her hand and walk into the Senate Office Building with her by his side. Dressed up she always looked regal, as though some special warm quality of light found joy in escorting her. Her hand would be familiar and its warmth would fill him and at least for that small transition in time it would calm the ache that had begun to well in his throat. He tried to picture her coming up the street and he concentrated on that thought as though by his will he could force her to materialize. He remembered he had tried to conjure her that same way so very long ago when he was trying to meet her for the first time. He had spotted her on the trolley going to work in the building next to his and he had stood in the street waiting for her to reappear at the end of the day. Miller smiled at the recollection. Weeks had gone by. Each day he'd returned to stare at that dark glass entrance and he'd wished so hard and finally she'd stepped into the sunlight and, partly holding his breath to block his fears, he'd introduced himself and she'd been so pleased. Her voice had been friendly, he had wanted to burst out with an aria, do something that wasn't expected, but he didn't know music and he walked with her wanting more than anything just to listen to her.

A siren wailed somewhere below in the distance. He hadn't noticed her enough since that walk; there had been so many other things. He refocused and searched the grey mall. All the cabs were gone. It was finally time to find the Caucus Room.

The news alleging that the European Consortium of Aircraft Manufacturers had paid co-pilot Anders to call Buttress's design of the 17-10 into question reached London, Paris, Rome and Amsterdam at 1400, European time. An urgent conference call among the parties of the consortium was booked to begin at 1430. The press and international wire services, clamouring for a reaction, were promised a combined statement by 1500 hours, in time for them to get into print before the evening rush.

Dick Miller surveyed the gallery, peering above the heads of people clustered near the door. The setting intimidated him. For a moment he couldn't make himself push through, and tottering on the threshold, diminished by the high-vaulted cavern of marble and mahogany, he suffered intense ambivalent waves of repulsion and attraction. Scattered words wafted to him like small floating magnets. He allowed himself hesitantly to be drawn in, his neck extended as though to stay above the waterline. Far across through the haze, the remote row of patriarchal jurors sat elevated on their massive gates.

For an instant Miller was stunned by the realization that the man whose back he faced was the legendary G. Hollis Wright in person, for so many years distant master of his own uncertain destiny, a man even more remote to him than the senators, whose faces he recognized from news magazines. Miller watched, dazzled by the sight, the old man's white hair and the blue of his suit too brilliant under the lights; yet he seemed so much smaller in real life than Miller had expected, almost shrunken in his isolation.

Next to Ed Boice two seats were vacant. Miller took the one farthest from his boss, leaving the one between them for Sandy. And as he waited, he sat huddled and still, hearing without listening, absently peeling his knuckles, head bowed as if in some neopagan prayer.

Alarmed by Miller's distress, Ed Boice sought to distract him. Miller's colour was that of wet chalk and it wasn't because of the lights.

'It's all going well.' Boice tried to sound offhand.

Miller didn't respond.

'There's some ice water here and there's some coffee and Danish next door . . .'

Feelings of teetering above the metal chasms of Buttress swept over Dick Miller, the fright of a man losing his balance as the edge of the abyss crumbles away beneath his feet, and he sat jittery and afraid the chair would topple over. It made him clear his throat twice, urgently, with a shuddering sort of cough. Frowns formed in a halo around him, taking shape from the evanescent regions of his reverie; slowly he realized where he was. The frowns were real people displeased with the noise he'd made. Ed Boice had moved over and was in the chair Dick had left for Sandy.

'How about some aspirin, Richard?' Boice spoke out of the side of his mouth.

'I'll be OK,' Miller said under his breath.

Senator Zakowski had his hand cupped over his microphone and was listening to Gene McDermott, who sat next to him. Finally he took his hand away. His expression was sclerotic.

'Mr Wright. I'm not sure we don't have alternatives available to us. There are other companies fully capable of absorbing Buttress's unfinished work. After a short lag it seems reasonable to assume – '

'No, it isn't,' Hollis cut him off. 'It's impossible for anybody to duplicate what Buttress is doing, Senator Zakowski. We got there by instituting the development, by taking the risk. No one else in this business was willing to do that. Not until now. But now they're years behind. We only ask that now, when the results are becoming apparent, you share in that – with us.'

Senator Searington thrust his neck clear of his shirt collar. 'It's quite clear to me,' he said testily to Zakowski, 'that Buttress must continue to manage the production of its own aeroplanes. If it does not, if it fails, the real gross national product would decline at least four per cent. Still-higher interest rates would result. The stock market would be more unstable than it is now. Worse, the Buttress share of the market would go not to other American manufacturers, but to foreign builders. This nation simply cannot tolerate the worldwide loss of jumbo-jet orders to the European Consortium. The loss of the F-19 would strip us of vital defence and would cost us devastating reversals in the balance of payments, in national security – '

'That's far too pessimistic a view,' Senator McDermott broke in firmly. 'If I may, I'd like to ask the distinguished gentleman from Buttress one or two questions.' He waited quietly, with something approaching a mild expression,

502

while Peck and Searington bent their heads together. Finally Senator Peck glanced up.

'Go ahead.'

'Pardon me?'

'The distinguished gentleman from Nebraska may proceed.'

McDermott consulted his notes and spoke without looking up.

'How much did Buttress lose in the first quarter, Mr Wright?'

'Our most recent financial analysis is printed in our revised annual report which was unexpectedly delayed but which is a matter of public record – '

'If you would give it to me straight, Mr Wright.'

'Two hundred and ninety-six million – subject, of course, to final audit.'

'The rescue you are seeking here – '

'Temporary assistance, Senator.'

'I don't care what you call it,' McDermott snapped. 'Whatever it is, I submit, will cost the people of this nation more than the cost of letting your company fail. In short, the cure is worse than the sickness.'

'If Buttress fails, Senator,' Hollis shot back, 'an economic earthquake will rumble across this land.' He saw Searington nod vigorously. The senator from Alaska, who hadn't spoken yet, looked worried.

'Many don't agree with you, Mr Wright,' lectured McDermott. 'The financial experts on my staff have assured me your assets would be sold and not to foreigners. Your military-products divisions would simply be reorganized. Your workers would be hired by your competitors, who would then expand. I'm quite convinced in the end there would be very little impact on the economy.'

'Already several of our twenty-four thousand one hundred and thirty-six suppliers – who last year supplied Buttress with an aggregate thirteen point thirty-six billion dollars' worth of goods and services, if I have my figures right – have bought insurance to cover their accounts receivable with us. That means they're plenty worried. Our commercial paper has lost credit standing. We must turn to the commercial banks at crushing interest rates.'

'I would like to suggest to this committee that all that's beside the point,' McDermott said with deliberate patience.

Miller sat listening to the exchange. It called up the vision of a battle going on far above him somewhere. He thought of the moment he would be summoned to stand in the ring. 'What are they going to talk about?' He tried to make it sound casual.

Boice leaned forward. 'They're going to be respectful. They just want a chance to meet the artist.'

'How do we know you're not going to be back to the government next year, Mr Wright?' McDermott was saying.

Senator Searington raised a commanding hand and smiled tolerantly at his colleague. 'We're only talking about a single situation, Senator McDermott, not the collective ruination of the Republic.'

'I haven't yielded, Senator Searington – '

'But, sir,' Searington rumbled, 'I'm merely suggesting that in the real world, excursions from what we hold dear happen. That may not make us feel good all over all the time, but if they're occasional and the cause is inherently just, I see no danger to our survival.'

'I wish the distinguished co-chairman would make himself clear,' McDermott urged.

'I'm only saying the company and the government are not entirely unrelated – '

'It sounds to me like you're saying some industries should be *insulated* from capitalism.'

'*That's precisely what I am saying.*'

A horrified silence fell across the room. One or two

reporters scampered out. Ben Reese half rose in his seat, looking over heads for the editor. Merle Tarpender sat pensively thinking about the possibility of becoming a tennis pro. Hollis Wright regarded the suddenly faltering wall of hesitant senators with the disgust and helpless fury of a beleaguered field marshal.

Ed Boice took the moment to steer Dick Miller into the marble corridor outside the Caucus Room. Miller had become exceedingly pale and hadn't objected to being lifted and jostled past the intimidating threshold. Now, as he stood in the hall, he appeared lost.

Boice fumbled deep in a pocket, came up with a small bottle of aspirin. 'There's a fountain over there. Take three of these,' he coaxed.

Dick stared blankly at Boice's hand holding the tablets out to him. He made no move to take them. He noticed then that his loathing of Ed Boice was so intense it had become euphoric; he was staring past Boice's hand, oblivious to all Boice's efforts at persuasion. He turned his head, casting his view across the echoing corridor. Where was he? What was this place? Scenes blended, the scenes of his life which were no longer separated by time.

He reeled. His legs vibrated and he wanted to butcher Boice, annihilate him. Slowly shaking his head at the imaginary scene of Boice sprawled dead at his feet, he sensed what a humiliation it would be for Sandy and he couldn't leave her with that. Besides, the company store owned his whole being and he knew it. He'd sold them his twenty-seven years of good behaviour, his laughter and his pleasantries, in exchange for a steady stream of groceries and car payments, and although he hated Buttress, he didn't want to lose its approval.

'Our mission is to paint in all the technical squares,' Boice quietly briefed. 'Just show them the quality of our thinking.'

Miller turned towards him with startled eyes.

Boice smiled. 'Whoever scouted that group in there ought to get run out of town. They're not fooling around, are they?'

Absently Miller swallowed the pills Boice shoved at him. Maybe the act of swallowing would somehow remove the unpleasant presence of Ed Boice from his midst. All the rest was meaningless. Even stray recollections which filtered past like distant muted horn calls in a dark forest, the countless midnight incursions of panic, sweating, knowing the prospect of the inevitable void . . . endless, stretching . . . but that was all gone now. Awakening, feeling life with all its wonder and mystery, that too, that music a hollow echo, evaporated . . .

He figured Sandy must be getting into a taxi by now. He'd better get ready to go onstage.

19

Miller worked his way into the echoing chamber and found the chair Boice provided for him. His eyes were watery from the glare of the light. So he concentrated on Hollis Wright's voice as it wafted through the space around him.

'The government is already deeply involved in private enterprise, Senator McDermott. The Economic Development Administration grants loans to companies day in and day out with far less technical justification than ours. You must not forget that Buttress builds more than the 17-10. It builds submarines. Cruise missiles. It builds the F-19.' Hollis became comradely. 'We readily acknowledge the civil transport division is going to lose money on the first three hundred and fifty 17-10s built. But we have full confidence the division will begin to show a substantial profit after that. First we have to *get* that far. And it's absolutely essential that we not lose out to the European Consortium for the current round of new-technology jumbo-jet orders that are sure to come from every major airline in the world. The market is staggering. Then comes the follow-on benefit because that, in turn, will enable us to maintain our F-19 programme. And our conservative estimate is that the worldwide market for fighters over the next twenty years is in excess of four thousand planes – something on the order of *seventy-five billion dollars!*' Hollis cleared his throat while the figure sank in. 'We certainly don't want to jeopardize *that*, gentlemen.'

He'd stopped the entire committee cold. Even McDermott was hushed for the moment.

Hollis continued calmly. 'Now suppose we put this in perspective.'

Miller was keeping time with Hollis's words, which beat like a cadence, rhythmically . . . They rose and fell away and returned to hammer a hard series of blows, then fell away again, diminishing into a long stillness. When he focused, he was startled to see that Hollis was gone. It was as if an hour had passed, for there was Ed Boice sitting at the witness table. Miller hadn't seen the exchange and he realized he had been searching the gallery for a sign of his wife, but had found it difficult to distinguish faces. And there was Eddie Boice, upright like a stumpy Napoleonic mortar, ruddy, alert, expectant, facing the senators. Two people from Buttress's legal department were next to him.

Senator Zakowski had the floor. He waited until some members of the press were seated.

'Mr Boice, you're here to respond to the technical issues. Why do we need the 17-10?'

Boice hesitated as though replaying the question to himself. 'What?'

'Why must we play your technological game?'

Boice blinked back at Zakowski, unwilling to answer.

'Because it's there?' Zakowski prompted.

Boice frowned into the polished tabletop before him. 'Two reasons. First, the old generation wears out. Second, better gas mileage. Economic necessity.'

'Maybe we don't need the 17-10 at all. Maybe there are other choices.'

'I wouldn't know what they are.'

'Can you imagine the world without any of this new technology?'

'No, I can't.'

'Well, I can.'

'Attaché cases gonna get awful wet in those rowboats.'

Laughter acclaimed Boice's quickness. He sat like a proud child who had just delivered himself of a portentous BM.

'Is the 17-10 the last word in technology?' Zakowski persisted quietly.

'Of course not.'

'It will go on.'

'Yes, I believe it will.'

'Do you feel we need it?'

'Definitely.'

'Is that the only choice?'

'As soon as we conceive of anything new in technology, we no longer have a choice.'

'We don't?'

'No, sir. Not in technology, Senator.'

'If that's true, Mr Boice, then we're trapped, like galley slaves blindly stoking the engines of a ship with no bridge.' Zakowski noted Boice's face had gone flat. 'I just wanted to make that point, Mr Chairman,' Zakowski said. 'Let us now continue with our mortal concerns.'

'Thank you, Senator,' said Peck, straightening his posture. 'There's concern the 17-10 may have a hidden weakness.' He barked the statement directly into his

508

microphone, then cupped his hand over it as he turned aside to confer with an aide. Ed Boice could smell the doubt that was crawling back and forth along the senatorial bench, and spoke with assurance, as though he had Peck's complete attention.

'That's entirely fallacious, Senator, the result of over-reaction and exaggerated press accounts – '

'Then what went wrong at Kennedy, Mr Boice?'

Miller noticed the question came from Senator McDermott, who seemed angry.

'Ah . . . you mean Air World Six . . . ah – *nothing* went wrong, Senator. On the contrary, the Air World Six incident is proof of what I'm saying. Even though the flight crew failed to follow established procedures – and, as we read it, this has already been determined by the NTSB public hearing – nevertheless, the 17-10 landed safely. The pilot's task was complicated by an engine fire, which for some unknown reason the crew also failed to extinguish, and still they came in safely. I mean, if we're here talking about reliability . . .'

Dick Miller saw the co-chairmen lean towards each other and sensed what was coming. The entire scene played instantaneously as he sat, hands passive but his mind in a tumult as if a door were banging open inside his skull revealing lines of script scrawled on interior walls, and he could recite the entire script even before reading it. He heard Ed Boice, saw the very lines he would speak, they stood out from the mass of script to glow fiercely on the screen of his mind: '. . . and let me remind this committee, the FAA has imposed no mandatory changes to the 17-10 design. Not one . . .' And more doors were rushing open around some deep cavernous circle, knocking his head from side to side with their force. He noted that Senator Peck wasn't smiling.

'Why didn't Buttress issue an Alert Service Bulletin relating to Air World Six?'

'We put out an Operational Occurrence Report. We felt that to be entirely sufficient.'

. 'Surely you must have wanted to alert Air World to make inspections –'

'Not so. The 17-10 is new, it's sound. We didn't judge the Air World Six incident to be of significance.'

. 'You just finished testifying that Buttress made alterations to an elevator actuator –'

'Well, that one is going out as a Service Bulletin. It's just been – ah, finalized.' Ed Boice glared at Senator Peck, as if watching him from behind a rock. 'Senator, I should remind you, we've embarked on a new method of aeroplane design and construction, a new philosophy . . .'

Miller tried to follow Boice's words. It was the litany they'd developed over eight years, but all he heard was the crescendo of his own pulse beating in his ears.

'. . . and the aeroplane itself has enough residual aerodynamic stability for any reasonably competent airline pilot to manage a perfectly safe arrival and landing in any mode of failure we could possibly envision. Air World Six proved that even less-than-competent pilots are protected. Look, the entire aviation industry is being forced to rely on advanced electronics and computer technology to compete in today's marketplace. We are not alone in that assessment. Lockheed, McDonnell Douglas, Boeing, not to mention the European competition we face, are all going the same way.'

'Then tell this committee, Mr Boice, how have you assured the level of reliability required? Your 17-10 is the first to fly with these features. Have you flight-tested for every reasonable failure possibility?'

Dick Miller drifted in and out, frightened by the belligerence in the room, barely hearing Ed Boice's words, hearing them only as faintly familiar echoes, a dialogue reconstructed from some revolving nightmare . . .

'Senator, we're certainly not about to take a seventy-million-dollar aeroplane out there and shut off part of the stability and go hunting for a potentially dangerous situation. That would be foolhardy. You don't test the Empire State Building by starting a fire in the basement. We don't need to take such risks. We have massive computers in our design office where we can program everything from a screw backing out to a major burst hydraulic line, one by one and in combinations – '

Senator McDermott broke in. 'But no one yet has told me if what you're doing is really worth it!'

Really worth it? The question jangled with paralyzing vibrations through Dick Miller's arms and hands. All those years! Worth it? Boice was answering. 'Senator, let me answer you this way. We can now accomplish the same job, carry the same passengers the same distance, for twenty-two per cent less fuel. *Ten thousand gallons less* for each North Atlantic crossing! In today's economy, you must agree, that's worth it!'

'Mr Co-chairman!'

Somewhat reluctantly, Searington granted Zakowski the floor.

'Now, Mr Boice, worth it or not, I have a constituent who has a particularly keen interest in what's happening here today and she has asked me to put a few questions to you. Are you familiar with the concept of *acceptable risk?*'

Ed Boice sat hunched like a coach with a one-point lead watching a midcourt shot go sailing towards his basket in the last two seconds of the game. The lights bothered him again and his neck itched under the collar. 'I'm familiar with it,' he muttered.

'Suppose as part of the deal that may ultimately be made with the government, we find some way of getting rid of it?'

'We couldn't accept that.'

'Why not?'

'It would force us into infinite expenditure. Make us reach for the stars.'

'Well, let's say if we just made it so you'd have to reach for more stars than you do now.'

'We reach far enough now to be able to say that the risk of a serious problem will only occur once in ten million times.'

'You can say it if you wish, but Flight Six kind of fouled up that sweet expectation by nearly coming apart on the sixty-first landing in New York of a 17-10! That's a little early, isn't it?'

Miller stared at the floor. He felt as though he were a visitor to a foreign country, not knowing the ritual of the ceremony that surrounded him.

'Acceptable risk is within the well-established realm of statistics.'

'I submit that the realm of statistics is a fairyland of hope! It's no real indicator of an aeroplane's predictable airworthiness!'

'I disagree.'

'Did it predict accurately in the instance of the Lockheed Electra? I seem to recall something about the wings falling off early in its career and that it took some farmer's howling dog to provide the experts with the clue that there was something wrong with the plane's vibration. It's a good thing the dog didn't know about statistics or he wouldn't have believed his ears and maybe he wouldn't have howled. Did the statistics of acceptable risk accurately predict the airworthiness of the DC-10 or did the DC-10 point out the flaw in the statistic . . . several times?'

'I think the senator is being entertaining.'

'Wouldn't it make sense, Mr Boice, to sharpen our act, go the extra mile, build in more safety to achieve a better relationship between reality and statistics?'

'Certain limits are dictated by forces in the marketplace.'

'I believe you're speaking about profits.'

'It's part of our reality,' Boice smiled. 'It's the only thing that allows us to pay back our loans.'

'But I don't think profit is more important than lives.'

'Personally I may not either, Senator, but you're not seeing it from the standpoint of the corporate imperative.'

'Mr Boice, you're entirely wrong about that. Why, I've already been one of your partners for over a year, and now I'm being asked to believe that you want to deepen our relationship! Unless I've been misreading all your advances, you've come to Washington to try to stay in bed with us, and now you're telling me I'm not seeing it just from your viewpoint! Certainly if we aren't to have anything to say about how the money is spent, then maybe we ought to put an ad in the paper as to how you've left our bed and board and that now you're responsible for all your own bills!'

Laughter played through the gallery. Senator Searington rapped his gavel.

'I want to be on record here that I do not support the gentleman's comments.'

Boice decided not to wait for the next query. He was angry. 'Senator Zakowski, I would like to interject here that I do not feel my company deserves to be ridiculed. I believe I know the source of your questioning. I make no accusation, but it has the bite of someone out to hang us.'

'Who did you have in mind?'

Boice bristled. 'The co-pilot of Air World Flight Six, whose reasons for maligning us are documented in this morning's newspaper!'

The reaction was instant. The people in the press section who had settled back in comradely comfort came to sudden, startled life.

'I want to say, Mr Boice,' boomed Zakowski, 'that your implication borders on slander. I trust you're not impugning my motives by association.'

Boice tried to break in.

513

'No, I'm not finished,' Zakowski admonished. 'You have a right to your surmise, though it is not necessarily a correct one, and the documentation you refer to in the matter of the co-pilot is not documentation at all but is an allegation. I have no idea whether it is as the papers say or not, nor is that the issue here. We're here in part to examine the fitness of the Buttress product, to see if it's worthy of another transfusion, and in line with that I want to ask about the fix undertaken as a consequence of Flight Six into Kennedy International.'

'Point of clarification!' shouted Searington, almost falling from his chair.

'I'd like to hear Mr Boice answer, if the distinguished co-chairman will allow it,' Zakowski lashed back.

Boice grabbed his microphone. 'There is no narrow relationship between Flight Six and any improvements we may have made on the aircraft,' he interjected quickly.

'That is the point I wish to reinforce, Senator Zakowski,' said Searington. 'There has been no fix as I understand it. I believe it would be more correct to confine our remarks to an *improvement*.'

Zakowski turned to face Ed Boice, waving a handful of papers. 'I don't really care what you call it. I have here a summary from the FAA computer bank – maintenance reports on hydraulic leaks in the tail – in the elevator to be exact.'

'Does the FAA say there's a trend?' Boice shot belligerently.

'No, they don't. What is your expert opinion, Mr Boice? In aeroplanes not so improved, isn't there still a problem?'

Before Boice could answer, Senator Peck broke in. 'I understand that an alteration has been made to the aeroplane and that as we have requested, your key design person responsible for this alteration is here and prepared to brief us on the precise nature of it. Is that correct?'

'Yes, sir.'

'Then I believe it's appropriate that we speak with that spokesman. A Mr Richard Miller. Is he here?'

'Yes, sir, he's here.'

Senator Peck shielded his eyes against the lights and scanned the darkness. 'Mr Miller, sir, if you would be good enough to come forward and speak with us, the committee would be grateful.'

Dick Miller stood up in the lights. He answered, 'Yes, sir – ' but being without a microphone, the words fell in front of him, inaudible even to the people nearby. He made his way mechanically to the witness table, the crepe soles of his shoes making him appear to lope slightly.

Eddie Boice was holding the empty chair for him.

'Please have a seat, Mr Miller.'

Dick Miller slowly sat down, staring at the lights at first, then past them, searching for Sandy. He wished he were sitting in the kitchen with her. Boice returned to the sidelines. Senator Peck thanked Miller for coming to 'educate us ignorant senators who have more faith than knowledge when we go up in an aeroplane!'

Miller stated his name and job title and the years he'd put in. Along the row of Buttress people in the gallery the mood was tense. Miller touched the water glass, then realized it was empty. The pitcher, so apparent when Hollis Wright was testifying, was gone. One of the men who had attended the Buttress chairman noticed it and came quickly alongside Miller to fill his glass. Dick Miller closed his eyes and took a long cool drink. The slaking of his thirst was a delicious sensation. Ends of hair over his temples had gone stringy from perspiration during his wait.

Ben Reese sat down slowly, watching Miller, whom he had known in the past, and he felt unmistakably as though he had come upon a casualty, alone among the unafflicted. Ben was scared.

Senator Searington faced Dick Miller. He could see the shadows beneath Miller's eyes, the deep gouges there. He began gently, determined to guide Miller along the thorny briar path of interrogation. The senator smiled, a warm, fatherly prelude to their exchange.

'I understand, Mr Miller, that you have collaborated as a flight-control design engineer on the creation of some of our worthiest achievements in fighter aeroplanes.'

Miller sat too far from the microphone, so he was not heard clearly when he said, 'I worked on the Lancejet.'

'Sir?' Searington raised his eyebrows, smiling encouragingly.

Miller leaned forward. 'The Lancejet, sir,' he said and coughed once.

Searington stared out at the room to further sharpen the attention directed towards the dais. 'Having been on active duty with the Air Force during that period, I'd like to say that we all fondly recall the Lancejet as a remarkable answer in a time of national need. We are proud to have you with us, sir.' Searington sat back, content that he had delivered a conclusion.

'Will the chair yield?' It was McDermott.

'I'm not sure,' said Searington darkly.

'With due respect, I'd prefer to hear about a fix, and I understand this man – '

'Fix what?' Searington retorted, his anger rising. 'Nothing was broken specifically that needed a fix. Even Air Force One, the President's own 17-10, is intact. What has been fixed specifically?'

'That's what I'd like to hear from Mr Miller.'

'If you don't mind,' Searington said soothingly, 'we were talking about the general nature of the way these aircraft are improved – always under constant improvement, and that's – '

'This man wouldn't be here today, Mr Co-chairman, unless there was a fix – F-I-X.'

516

'I thought we'd been all through this.'

'I want to hear about a fix and I'd like to put it in the record that we're talking about a fix and not an improvement.'

Senator Searington threw up his hands, looking out across the gallery with the air of a wronged coach helpless before the fulminations of an unreasoning umpire.

'Mr Miller, I'm afraid I have to ask it this way' – Miller licked his lips and under the edge of the table resumed peeling his raw knuckles – 'but it's the consensus of this body. Is that fix on the 17-10 in the nature of an improvement?'

Miller, embarrassed, looked away from the grim-faced McDermott.

'Yes, sir, I suppose you could say it is, sir.' He cast his eyes down. In the gallery Ed Boice began to sweat.

'I wasn't finished, Mr Co-chairman,' said Senator McDermott. 'Mr Miller, I have only three more questions for you. Isn't it true that high-technology aircraft break down more often than aircraft of a previous generation?'

Miller leaned in towards his microphone, as he had seen Hollis Wright and Ed Boice do, and searched for Boice. Those weren't the kinds of questions he had come all the way to Washington to answer. He located Boice, who sat looking at him the same way the others did. Boice frowned back at him as though to say he didn't understand what was wrong.

'Mr Miller, is that a fair statement?' McDermott's voice crackled. Miller turned around guiltily as though he'd been caught cheating. He ducked in towards the microphone.

'I didn't come prepared with any numbers, sir.' He heard his answer over the speaker system but felt as though he were still sitting on the sidelines listening to someone else. He glanced back at Boice, who had his elbows on his knees again, staring at the floor. Boice was displeased. It was a reprimand. Dick hadn't done well at all.

'Mr Miller, why did Buttress recently feel it necessary to stop the 17-10 production line?'

Dick sat looking at the inside of his hand and noticed a patch of sweat gathering into a brightly reflecting drop. He raised his head to locate McDermott but saw only a halo of light.

Boice crossed himself. Nothing happened. He looked up and saw Miller grinning – but also that Miller's head was shaking ever so slightly as though he were struggling to contain a palsy. Miller held his grin as he spoke. His voice sounded metallic and he tried to say it the way Boice had told it to him.

'Overzealous adherence to a level of perfection which had already been achieved but had not yet been fully appreciated.'

Boice had to restrain himself from letting the breath he'd been holding escape too obviously. Deep inside his head he began thanking God.

McDermott placed his notes aside and leaned on his elbows. He spoke quietly so that Reese had to strain to hear him.

'I'm not sure I believe what you're saying. What I don't understand, Mr Miller, is how an unimportant improvement can stop an entire production line. Would you tell us about that?'

There was a long pause. Ed Boice reminded himself that he'd always been a fatalist. Dick Miller studied the individual ribs on the microphone very intently, trying with all his might to divine the answer. Finally he spoke.

'Those are executive decisions, sir. People have to make assumptions.'

He barely heard McDermott continue.

'I'm sorry I have to ask you a fourth question, Mr Miller. After this assessment was made, and in your

518

expert opinion, sir, was this improvement recently engineered under your cognizance in fact so routine in terms of the aeroplane's safe operation that it deserved no more than a Service Bulletin?'

A long silence ensued. Hushed breaths filled the gallery, all waiting for Miller's answer. Ed Boice's hands were tense as compressed granite as they clenched the arms of his chair. Every eye was fixed on Dick Miller, who suddenly seemed wounded, with all the sadness of a broken bird, yet obstinate too, protecting his remaining dignity by offering them his presence. He sat round-shouldered, dwarfed by the dark mahogany chair and table and huddled under the huge stone columns which seemed to be leaning inward, over him, waiting too for his answer.

He murmured something, looking down.

'Sir, I'm afraid I cannot hear you,' Peck said gently.

Ed Boice shut his eyes.

Dick Miller looked up with anguish carved into his face, as stony white as the Corinthian columns. His eyes were focused past Searington and McDermott, they looked deep into the shadows beyond the long bench and lights. When he spoke, his voice was hoarse but clearly audible.

'Yes, sir . . . deserved no more than a Service Bulletin.'

Searington squinted across the distance, leaning out of his chair like a mandarin doll.

Miller sensed Boice's impatience. 'Yes, sir,' he repeated, his voice echoing throughout the cavernous Caucus Room.

'Thank you, Mr Miller,' Searington said quickly. From the corner of his eye he observed Zakowski preoccupied with scribbling something on his notes. 'You are dismissed, Mr Miller. Thank you.'

Ed Boice's eyes widened. He was beginning to smile broadly but still gripping the arms of his chair. There was a noticeable stir around him. Miller slumped as if someone had ripped him open and let all the stuffing out. He glanced for the first time towards the Buttress people in the gallery, with the wild look of a cornered animal. But no one noticed. He turned uncertainly back towards the row of senators, unmindful of the tears beginning to crease his cheek.

As he did, Ed Boice stood to intercept him and tried to grab his hand as he walked by. 'Jesus Christ, Dick . . . we're a goddamn *team*.' Miller brushed him aside as order was called. People in the gallery, sensing a recess, began shuffling. But Boice was recalled to resume his testimony. Enjoying himself after Miller's blessing on the fix, he made his way like a champion towards the witness table. Just at that moment the rear door opened again; it was Sandy Miller, who stood slightly embarrassed, surveying the vast room, looking for her husband.

Outside the Caucus Room, the tears running down his face, Dick Miller walked aimlessly along the marble corridor, his footfalls echoing hollowly. A guard lounged next to a barren table adjacent to the water fountain. Dick came up alongside him and bent to drink. Through the corner of his blurred vision he saw the top of the guard's pistol, the two wood halves of the handle clamped flush to the black steel centre frame, the trigger housing below it and the trigger reflecting curved glints from the overhead lights. Miller let the water run across his teeth and then with a sudden stabbing motion unsnapped the holster's straps and yanked the pistol free. He stumbled away, waving the gun at the startled people nearby. Groping behind him, he found the door to the men's room, pushed it open and disappeared inside. Several moments of hesitation ensued; people up and down the hall gaped in growing alarm but no one was ready to follow him in. Then, all at once, sharp but definite, over before realization had a chance to begin, there came the report of a shot being fired. It echoed through the Caucus Room and stopped Senator Searington in midsentence.

Dick Miller had fallen forward, twisting to avoid the unyielding edge of the toilet so that his left arm, straight out, had glanced off the stall divider and hit the sourness of the heel-smudged tile floor first. The body had bounced slightly, then humped, bending the head back against the base of the toilet. The teeth showed in a broken, frozen grin. The barrel of the pistol was still burrowed deep between them.

There was bedlam. Sandy Miller sat down in the chair next to the one her husband had occupied in the gallery. But all the chairs around her were empty. She'd known at once her husband was dead.

She didn't scream but just let it out, crying softly as she talked. No one recognized her, but she kept talking anyway, long, bitter self-reproaches. She'd known it was coming. She'd arrived too late. There were times, she sobbed, when I could soothe him. No one was listening; people had clustered at the entrance door in a frenzied rush. I'd hold him in my arms and rock him like a baby and make him put so much of the world's ugliness out of his mind. And then he would sleep and feel better . . .

She raised her eyes like those of a tragic Madonna in anguished pleading. No one noticed, no one knew who she was. Only Ben Reese, who spotted her from across the gallery. Transfixed, he watched from the other side of the room. But he made no move towards her. He merely watched, ashen-faced, as she cried.

20

Guy's reaction to the suicide was strangely detached, his mood banked by the darkening gravity the 17-10 embodied. Something monstrous had been breaking through the corporate veneer for weeks but Miller's death was more poignant. A part of Miller had tried to help the crew as Flight Six approached Kennedy out of control but his passion had receded, twinkling to vagueness by the time Guy had faced him directly.

Guy and Anja had both been untalkative, Guy spending the afternoon boning up on the 17-10 flight-simulator manual. Anja had been particularly pensive. Finally he'd tossed the manual aside.

'How would you like to reclaim a little sanity and have dinner out with a turncoat pilot who claims he's been smeared and whose friend Ben Reese can't prove it?'

'Yet.'

'Yet could be infinite and Reese isn't going to live that long.'

Anja arranged for a sitter, brought the girl back to the house and settled close to Guy on the bed in his room, watching him change his clothes. She spoke again about Miller.

'Why didn't he just quit?'

'What, and give up job security?' Guy visualized the sharp-edged Buttress complex in the hard western crosslight and recalled Fenton Riddick's threat to him. Now Miller had slowed the 'nation-state' Riddick had warned about and made it vulnerable. Guy glanced at the simulator manual lying on the bed. 'They're going to come psyched up for booby traps when the hearing continues. But this time they're going to hear what Miller forgot to say.'

It was almost dark outside but neither had bothered to turn on the lights. Anja saw the sitter standing uncertainly in their bedroom doorway.

'I don't know if your son's fooling around or not,' the girl said, 'but he's saying there's a kidnapper outside.'

Anja was smiling at her, not sure whether it was a cute observation or whether she meant it.

'He says he's seen him before.'

'Where outside?' Guy asked.

'He was gone for a while but now he's back out front.'

Guy's shirt was still open as he crossed to the bedroom window. A few lights were on in the neighbourhood. A teenager was pedalling his bike past, his hands behind his back. A second figure was standing across the street with a leash in one hand as though waiting for his dog to return.

'When did Jamie say he saw him?' Anja asked.

'I don't know,' said the sitter. 'He's hiding behind a chair.'

Guy buttoned his cuffs. 'I want you to keep the lights out.' He stepped away from the window and headed for the stairs. 'Both of you stay with Jamie.'

'Guy . . .'

Guy stopped in the doorway. 'I don't know, Anja – dinner may have to keep.'

He decided to go out the back and came up along the side of the house. The neighbourhood was uncommonly still, more like dawn than sundown. Guy stepped out on to the front lawn, checked the street for a lone animal to go with the leash the man was holding, but the block was deserted in both directions. He faced the stranger who stood on the far curb.

'Lose your dog?' Guy called.

The man turned slowly as though uncertain he were being spoken to. He faced Guy with an oblique pinched stare.

'You lose something?' Guy repeated.

Unhurriedly, the man assessed the quietude behind him and casually stuck his free hand into his jacket pocket.

Guy stepped off the curb. He heard a window being shoved open behind him.

'You want to tell us what you're doing here?' Guy challenged as he headed across. An inner twitch told him he'd made a mistake, that the man was armed, but it was too late. In that same instant he realized he'd seen him before. He heard Anja call out to warn him. The startled figure scanned the windows with only one side of his face, then bolted up the street. All at once the weeks of frustration and outrage compressed in Guy's temples and exploded. '*No you don't*, you bastard!' and he knew he was going to nail him.

'Guy!' Anja called after him but he was off in pursuit.

The figure broke into the open down a street wet from lawn sprinklers, then cut between two houses. A German shepherd enclosed in a run went wild, nearly scaling its six-foot cyclone fence. Guy realized his quarry could stop, spin, drop to one knee and hit him several times. But there'd be shots, witnesses, perhaps no way out for him – drawbacks. He felt borne by the invulnerability of his rage; perhaps the fugitive had sensed this too and it provided Guy with the momentary psychological advantage between them. The figure ahead cut left towards the shopping mall built in a broad hollow below the residential streets, crashed through an uneven line of scrub trees and skidded down the weed-and-rubble-strewn embankment. Guy was behind him, his shoes filling with sand and stones. Both men landed in the parking lot surrounded by squared-off shops, most of which had already closed. The fugitive, coat flapping, was headed for a parked car in the centre of the mall. Abruptly the man wheeled in the direction of a shuttered filling station. In the gathering dusk he didn't see an oil slick. His feet nearly shot out from under him but he recovered and dived for the cover of a row of gas pumps. There he crouched and drew his pistol.

Guy felt as though he were skimming the ground on a cushion of air as he reached out blindly and made contact, bowling the stranger over backwards and scraping his head on the concrete. He saw the glint of the Magnum pass at the right corner of his eye and he brought his weight down on the man's forearm, sending the pistol skittering against the pump platform. In a single fluid move, Guy had the fugitive on his feet and ran him backwards up against the garage door.

'You better produce the dog that belongs to that leash or a good alibi,' he panted. 'You want to do something to me, you do it now!'

The intruder glared back with a contorted, sweat-streaked face. 'Lay off,' he breathed.

'Who wants me to lay off?'

The stranger brought both his arms up hard and with a grunt broke Guy's hold. He ducked and staggered forwards to ram Guy but Guy caught his arm and bent it up behind his back. He tore through the man's pockets and yanked the dog leash free. For one wild moment he considered using it to garrote the stranger.

'Talk to me now or I'm going to drag you into the police station on all fours. Who covers your rent?'

Several people emerged from a distant drugstore. Guy noticed them and never saw the air-pressure hose with its brass nozzle coming at him. It hooked once around his neck, the metal end smacking into his cheekbone. The welt of pain roused his fury. He dropped the leash and came up with a crushing punch to the flat of the man's jaw and pinned him. 'I'm warning you, friend . . .'

The intruder spat full in Guy's face. Guy retaliated with a stinging jab to the mouth which dropped him to his knees. Guy stepped back and wiped the spit and blood from his face as the stranger struggled to regain his feet, circling Guy with widening step to get closer to the gun lying on the pavement. When he made a move for it, Guy caught him in the face with his foot, a perfectly placed punt that sent the man reeling backwards. Simultaneously a hard object seemed to launch from his head. It arched and fell to the ground, landing in a pool of oil. Guy lunged for the man but was numbed by a stiff-armed sidewinder that ploughed into his solar plexus. He backed off, struggling for air, slipped to the ground and picked up the pistol.

The people from the drugstore were closer and Guy jammed the weapon into his pocket. The fugitive, holding one side of his face, stumbled to the lone brown sedan parked thirty yards away. Guy crawled to the small recess of the service-station doorway. Painfully he pulled himself to his feet, removed his shirt, bundled it and towelled his face, wincing as he pressed the wound inflicted by the brass-tipped air hose. The sedan burst into life, swerved, its headlights carving a circle across the parking lot, and headed for the exit in the opposite direction. Guy stepped clear and knelt beside the small pool of oil. Despite the darkness, he saw the glistening oval form of a bloodied plastic eye.

Waves of light played across the aluminium gas pumps, reflecting, and swung across him, blinding him – was it the police? When the glare receded he saw it was Anja behind the wheel of his car.

'Guy?'

Guy rose halfway, tried to fill his lungs, but his solar plexus still curled in spasm and he couldn't speak. He kneeled and retrieved the false eye. It was lighter than he expected. He wrapped it in his shirt.

Anja reached across the front seat and threw the passenger door open. 'You left a trail of open mouths back there.' She looked terrified. 'My God, you OK?'

Guy ached horribly but managed to stretch to his feet,

cross the elevated pump island and sag into the seat beside her, fighting for breath. He pulled the door shut, bunched the shirt up and shoved it between his feet.

'Guy, what'd he do? You're cut!'

Guy put his head between his knees and felt the blood pound his temples. Anja raised the window.

'Leave it open,' he gasped. 'Drive around there,' he waved, indicating the mall. The late shoppers had stopped in their tracks bewildered by the spectacle of the man holding his face, driving off, his car bounding over the shopping-mall curb.

Anja pulled onto the road. 'I called the police,' she said, trying to see Guy more clearly. He let his head fall back against the headrest.

'Jamie saw him at the library and never opened his mouth. That was before we got to talking.'

'What'd the cops say?'

'They'll be around as soon as they finish dinner.'

Guy slipped the gun out of his pocket. 'The bastard came prepared. This'll blow a hole through a man the size of a baseball.'

'Great. It's great he had a gun,' she continued. 'That's terrific.'

She drove through the changing light and swung around the corner. 'It's Buttress, isn't it?'

'It isn't the IRS. They only threaten.'

They entered a poorly lit street blocked by an aging car moving slowly ahead of them.

'What are we doing?' she asked.

'Depends. He can't be feeling too hot either.' Guy squinted at the vehicle in front. 'He takes an evening stroll, deals, returns out here for his car and nobody's a licence plate wiser. OK, that isn't him. Let's head back.'

Anja pressed the accelerator and passed the slower vehicle. 'I get the feeling I should never have given you any pointers on anger. You do all right on your own.'

'Annie, you're under no obligation to stay.'

'I like it better when you say "Anja". I know it's a job. *Au pairs* are never permanent, are they? Well, I kept my promise about Jamie, so there's less than two weeks to go.'

'I cannot insist that you listen to what I'm going to say next. But I worry about you. I have a habit of worrying about the people I care about. So I'd be pleased if you paid attention.' Guy examined the Magnum, released the chamber and spilled the bullets into his hands. He closed both hands around the grip and took aim at the windshield. 'If an outsider ever breaks in while I'm out, take Jamie up to the bedroom with you, kneel down at the corner diagonally across from the door, hold this in front of you, grab it with both hands and the instant the door opens, squeeze.' He pressed the trigger. The hammer fell with a dull slap.

Anja started and gripped the wheel tighter. Guy slotted the bullets back into the pistol.

'A lot more's been happening than you've told me about, hasn't there?'

'What makes you say that?'

'There's some dried blood in one of your shoes but there's no cut on your foot. I looked.'

As they came back through the neighbourhood he guided her to the police station.

'We're going to park it here. Less chance for anyone to fool with it.'

'What kind of fooling?'

'Explosions. There have been a couple of incidents.' He didn't want to say more but it was too late to keep it from her. 'Benny and I have had to duck a couple of times.'

Anja paused to consider the words.

'You know what I wish?' said Anja.

'What?'

'I wish I were as tough as my mouth.'

Guy picked up his shirt. 'Let's go.'

Inside the precinct house Guy made a statement of the event to a detective, then unwrapped the eye and placed it on the table. The cop stared at it, fascinated. It was one thing he hadn't seen before.

'If anyone shows up for this, throw a net over him and introduce me,' Guy said in parting.

The mall was deserted and there, in the nearly tar-black arena, Guy had the distinct feeling he had just entered the window of Riddick's long-threatened dogfight. They would rendezvous, his perfect childhood dream of flight opposed, his right to possess it challenged. He saw beyond the shopping mall to the mechanic caught in the jaws of the wheel well, to Melissa, to Natalie Mason, now obscured to him; and he realized he had become curiously comfortable with the violence that now had fully emerged.

Their footsteps were too loud, blocking all other sounds. Guy stopped to be certain they weren't being tailed. The only thing moving was a lone attendant in the gloom of a distant gas station with a lit Avis sign in its window.

'I'm usually less scared if I'm doing something,' Anja said. 'So let's do something.'

'My adrenalin's about to come out of my ears. You want to know what I want to do?' Guy checked for blood at the side of his face. 'I want to hit their goddamn simulator right now – that's what I want to do.'

'Now?'

'I think we better change cars. You up to breaking and entering?'

She swallowed. 'Do you think you could find someone else?'

'Offhand, I'd say the choice would be fairly slim. It being night and all,' he added apologetically.

'. . . And with such short notice,' she agreed with mock concern.

Guy smiled with a hapless shrug. She took his arm and they headed for the Avis sign.

The night guard at BGR's main gate seemed civilized enough. He had his transistor tuned to WQXR and when Guy described the reason for returning to work as 'a little executive OT,' he said, 'Well, all we need is your birth certificate and a small stool sample.'

Guy slipped the plastic ID Natalie sent to JFK out of his wallet and handed it over. It bore a new photograph.

'OK, Mr Riddick,' the guard smiled. 'Now I wish I could be more accommodating to you tonight and I know you're not going to like this, but I can't let you in, sir.'

Guy felt his shoulders tighten as he rummaged around in his back pocket in the hope of finding some magical artifact that would reverse the call. He did his best to look perplexed. 'Why not?' It was a shade short of indignation.

'Well, sir, Mr Riddick, on account of your card here is no good. It's expired,' explained the guard with a hound-dog expression, handing the ID back. 'Thirty-one March,' he indicated with his thumb. 'Right there.'

Guy visualized a corrugated steel door descending across his hopes. 'The new card's on the dresser,' he offered.

'If I could, I'd go look at it on your dresser but I'm emotionally involved with my salary, such as it is. So, how long do you figure the round trip is going to take you?'

'The dresser's on the West Coast.'

The guard winced as though he'd been bitten and frowned sympathetically.

Guy spotted the corporate phone book, yanked it free, riffled to the West Coast section and ran his finger down to Riddick's name. 'This edition's current.'

530

The guard held out his hand for the ID, compared the spelling of the names, noted 'vice-president' after Riddick's name in the book and sniffed a short nervous sniff.

'I'm here on loan,' Guy declared.

'We've always been kind to immigrants.' The guard studied the raw gash at the side of Guy's face, then pointed to the sign-in log. Guy forged Riddick's signature, handed the pen back, retrieved the card and went inside.

It took him longer than he expected to locate the rear loading dock. Feeling his way around in the dark, he struggled and cursed to unlock the loading dock's huge double doors. When at last the latch logic became apparent, the doors separated vertically, retracting into the floor and ceiling.

As they did, an amber signal appeared on a master console a city block away.

Anja, who had been waiting in the shadows outside, gingerly stepped across the threshold. Guy pulled her clear of the steel opening and inched the door down until it met the other half that emerged from the floor. Inside, the BGR computer complex was cloaked in blackness. Guy slid his hand along the wall, turned the corner and located the long panel of light switches. He hoped the closest switch would light only the local area but when he flipped it, the long empty hall ahead flared into brilliance.

They stepped into the open. The walls were bare, the white-tile ceilings did nothing to blunt the explosions of their footfalls as they headed into the building's depths along freshly waxed tile floors. They passed the glass entrance door to the F-19 electronic jamming room where Guy had confronted Pierce and turned the corner at the sliding door to the adjoining wing. Guy stopped and listened. Only the overhead fluorescents hummed. The door opened more easily than he expected.

They stepped into a sterile room with the hard, slightly narcotic smell of wet hemp and the atmosphere of a

531

hellborn foundry where aeroplanes were cloned. Mounted two storeys up in the room's centre was the distorted front end of a 17-10 suspended above what seemed like an oversized surgical floor with hydraulic fluid spilling red and yellow in slow rivulets towards main waste gates. This was the enormous jumbo-jet flight deck lopped off just beneath the cockpit-floor level, half swallowed above by the angular housing for the apparatus that projected visual scenes in front of the windshields. Fitted behind the pilot stations was an operator's area enclosed inside a space the size of a small house trailer. The base of this entire assembly was mounted atop a tilted set of hydraulic jacks giving the impression of crossed spider legs; their pistons, like long trombone slides, were able to push and heave the cab to give the occupants strapped inside the complete sensations of flight. From the cab's flat base the dozens of trunk-thick cables for instruments and controls emerged between its steel legs in fountains of rubber that spilled into great gutters in the floor for ducting to the computer consoles nearby.

'Unless everyone here is dead, no way I can light that up without setting something off.'

'It's like a brontosaurus,' she answered. She was awe-struck. Next to the main computer consoles stood a pale-green wooden cupboard with rows of mail slots, each containing a stack of computer punch cards. The program memory cores were slotted in vertical metal-and-glass cabinets where the program data were stored. Near one of the upright cores and attached to it was a card hopper where punch card data could be transferred to memory.

There was a smaller area which enclosed a desk-sized typewriter used to produce fresh cards from sheets of program instructions. On the wall next to it was another bin of green mailboxes. Notations under each compartment identified its stack of cards: 'hydraulic interface validity program', 'stabilizer trim ratio change program',

532

several titles stacked up, one above the other, 'ride smoother gain mod program', nothing out of the ordinary. Then he felt his eyes being teased by something familiar, and suddenly he locked on to one stack whose label leaped at him the way one's name can leap out from a page crowded with hundreds. Its pencilled stub, half folded under the thick rubber band, read '*Electronic Corruption Program*'.

The thick silence of the room lay undisturbed, but there was a roar in his head at the sight of the strange term first heard in England, now facing him inside the manufacturer's own compound. Guy removed the label and held it out for Anja to see.

'Archaeologists and cops are the only ones who can know what this feels like,' he exulted.

When he threw the master switch, ranks of lights burst into a splendid blaze, a silent scream for doors to be thrown open and the two of them surrounded. A soft whine emanated from somewhere deep in the building. Or was it closer? Guy steered Anja to the foot of the metal ladder below the huge cab dominating the room.

'Don't look down on the way up,' he said as he led the way.

Two floors up he stepped on to the small metal platform and pushed the cockpit door ajar. The interior was illuminated by a soft glow from the rows of half-lit switches and dials which had been powered at the same time as the main computers. It was a cockpit ready for flight, accurate in every detail.

Anja was standing slightly behind him, wide-eyed. Guy motioned to her.

'I'm going to need a second pair of hands. I won't be able to see you from up here and I want to show you why.'

Fascinated, Anja stooped to peer past the centre throttle pedestal, over the instrument-panel glare shield, out through the forward cockpit windows. The vivid lights of runway 31-left at JFK stretched towards a point in the distance; miles away the horizon was aglow with Manhattan's jewelled towers. She was speechless with wonder and amazement at the incredible fidelity. Carefully she nudged herself in behind the first officer's yoke to get a better look, facing the rows of Promethian instruments, readouts and warning lights.

'If you wave at me from the floor I won't see it. We'll be on headsets. If I tell you to cut the power, cut it or this thing's going to take a hike.'

'I'm not mechanical.'

'Come on down.'

Anja followed him to the main computer console, where Guy plugged in her headset. Next he fed the electronic corruption card stack into the hopper and pressed 'start'. With the regularity of train wheels clicking over loose track, the cards followed each other in jerky procession. Guy reclimbed the ladder to the simulator cab. He noted that while it resembled the standard 17-10 training simulator, it had been designed to process a wide spectrum of research conditions. He found the fast-start feature as well as latitude-longitude freeze and altitude slew. Turning his attention, his hands raced over the flight engineer's panel, fuel valves open, pumps on. Then to the throttle pedestal between the pilots' seats, start levers to 'on'. He hit 'fast-start' on the operator's console and heard the unmistakable whine of the huge turbofan engines spooling up. N1 and N2 gauges came off the peg, exhaust-gas temperatures rose nicely to 450°C. At the flight engineer's panel again he snapped on generator switches, saw the monitor lights and indications fall into proper order. Hydraulic pumps on, pressure gauges normal. Control verification check, normal and alternate systems. Main AFCS computer verification, self-test, and monitors cross-checked, everything looked good. He was inside a living 17-10, ready for takeoff.

He left the cab, clambering down the ladder, back to the main computer consoles. The last punch cards were travelling through the hopper. Earlier Guy had noticed three controls in close proximity below the hopper, labelled 'research program insert', 'program validity check' and 'research program run'. He faced them now, and waited impatiently for the last card to jerk through its slot. When it did he punched 'research program insert', saw the square button light up green. Without hesitation he pressed 'program validity check'. And watched. Anja was watching too. 'I don't know what the indications should be but nothing's turned red. I'm going upstairs. When I tell you, hit this switch – "program run".'

'What do I do when the guard walks in?'

'Tell him you're from Europe.'

It was flip but she had to admire it. She was taken by his aplomb in the bizarre situation. A kind of weightlessness swept over her; it always did when he seemed so certain of himself.

Guy left her standing below, stopped at the operator's console and pressed 'motion on'. The cockpit lurched as the hydraulic rams underneath the cab came to life to lift it on its elongated jacks, pushing it to the awesome height of three stories. He selected a takeoff weight of 500,000 pounds, at which the aeroplane should be light and responsive. Then he strapped into the captain's chair, checking speed brake lever forward, flaps selected to 18 degrees for takeoff, leading edge devices extended and locked, stabilizer trim set, caution panel lights out. He took a deep breath, released the parking brake and pushed the four throttles smoothly forward. The engines bellowed, the acceleration was terrific, the seat back pressed into his spine. Outside the window the runway rushed at him in blurred streams. At 140 knots indicated airspeed he eased back on the yoke; there was a reaction of gusto as he sensed the 17-10 leap into the air. The feel

535

was uncanny. Gear up; a slight groan and bump signalled retraction and locking into place. One thousand feet. Flaps 8. Speed V_2 plus sixty, flaps up. Every kinesthetic nerve end was alive to the subtle vagaries of feel in the yoke. The trim change was just as he knew it. He pulled a throttle to idle, smoothly feeding in rudder with his right foot. The fidelity was fabulous, much more finely tuned than the Air World simulator. He restored power on number one, advanced all four throttles to climb thrust and accelerated to cruise speed. A quick scan of the instruments showed all was in order. It was now time to get what he had come for. He snapped on the autopilot, left his seat to go back to the operator's console where he pressed 'altitude slew'. The instrument needles and digital readouts twirled in their black whorls as the computed altitude ran quickly up to thirty-five thousand feet. The indicated airspeed fell off – he had the throttles well forward – but the Mach increased. Soon it was at 0.9 – nine tenths the speed of sound, max cruise speed. The readings stabilized, fell into normal cadence. Guy pressed the mike switch. 'Start the program.'

With a certain relish Anja pressed the master button labelled 'research program run' and marvelled as a dozen lights on the main computer console by her side flashed green. On the captain's panel up in the cockpit the instruments remained steady. Guy grasped the yoke, snapped off the autopilot. The yoke felt light, responsive. So far it was precisely like any normal flight, smooth, untroubled. Gently he banked as if to begin a shallow turn.

The first tremor was light but unmistakable and though he had prepared himself for it, a wave of anxiety swept across the pit of his stomach. The next tremor jolted him upright. Then he felt it again, as if the rear end of his car had shot out on an icy road. Suddenly he wasn't in a simulator any more, he was sitting across from W.B., the

536

old man wrestling the writhing, struggling thing loosed in the cockpit with them. And for the first time Guy felt the acutely horrifying sensation of useless controls that Cosgrove had known.

Below, next to the master console, Anja's eyes widened. She brushed her hair back from her eyes, she could only stare with distrust and growing fright as the huge box three stories above her pounded on its spindly jacks so hard it seemed it must topple off. The whole room was shaking, the red 'high voltage' signs quaking in their mounts, a couple of fluorescent tubes in the ceiling sputtered and went out. There was a piercing shriek as the joint on a hydraulic pipe near the wall let go, sending pressurized streams of fluid to puddle on the concrete floor in wrinkled pools.

Anja had already drifted a few paces away from underneath the enormous white keg being shaken like a toy in a giant fist. On the nearby console, ranks of jittery lights were now flashing wildly. The simulator cab tilted steeply to one side and suddenly the whole massive room was seized by such a vengeance of buffeting that Anja staggered and slipped to her hands and knees. She crawled for the door, which was hanging loosely ajar, banging against its jamb.

Inside Guy could take no more. The instrument panel seemed ready to jump from its mount, the blur of the dials overlapped in rippled shadows, all the readings had tumbled. The altimeter was unwinding, indicating a steep dive towards the ground, the overspeed bell blared. In consternation he tried to roll the aeroplane upright, to ease off the plummeting rate of descent, but the controls had gone haywire; it was hard to grasp the yoke which wrenched his hands in bruising shocks. The computer had taken over, the simulator was on the verge of self-destruction. Guy suddenly feared for his safety.

Leaning far back in his seat he strained with exasperation to reach the computer program circuit breakers on the overhead panel, but it was no use. 'Cut the power!' he bellowed into the microphone but he was certain Anja was unable to hear him. All at once he undid his straps, grasped the chair back and pulled himself free, knowing he must reach the operator's inside control console without being thrown down. He braced his feet and hung with one hand on to the empty flight engineer's chair, trying to shake the stray impression that Hanks must have bailed out, and he stretched for the console. His fingers found the simulator's red-guarded emergency power switch; it was safety-wired. He gave it a brutal wrench to knock it free and lift the toggle.

There was a long sigh of relieved hydraulics and the simulator gradually became still. Soon it reposed as hushed as a mounted coffin, an odd utensil with no hint of flight, incongruous in its walled-in cell. All the bulbs in their rows on the master console had extinguished.

Guy threw the simulator door open and stepped on to the steel stairs. The yellow light in the room burned his eyes. His first sight was of Anja sprawled on the floor against the far door.

'Hey, you OK?' he shouted. He raced down the ladder and helped her to her feet.

'I'm going to be honest with you. I'm a little bit frightened,' she said in a shaken voice.

'All we need is the printout.' Guy punched off the computer switches, replaced the stack of cards and stuffed the printout sheets under his arm. 'Let's get out of here!'

They retraced their steps through the leering corridors as a clump of feet raced down the corridor above them. Release washed over both of them with the black night air waiting outside the freight entrance. Soon they had crept through no-man's-land and extricated themselves from the outermost chain-link confines and bid good night to BGR. Anja buckled into the seat next to him as Guy started the rented car.

'Let's get you home.'

'Just me?'

'I've got to get this to Toby by sunup.'

Guy reached the outskirts of Washington at sunup. His hair had gone lank, his mouth tasted like cotton, stubble covered his face. When he accosted Toby's car at the entrance to the ALPA building's underground parking lot, Toby didn't recognize him. Guy spotted him first and stood to block the driveway, hand raised. To Toby, the shadowy figure fitted exactly his imagined version of a mugging. He tried to quell his fright and lurched to a stop. Guy went to the driver's window, thrust his head inside. Toby was taken aback.

'I've got the crossplots you say you need.' He pushed the BGR simulator printout sheets through the window, across Toby's lap. The stack landed heavily on the passenger's seat.

'Jesus, Anders.'

'That's a carbon copy of what happened to us going into JFK. And proof that Buttress is studying electronic corruption on the 17-10!'

A quizzical gust passed across Toby's face. 'Where'd you get it?'

'Read it.'

'Is this something else you're bringing in from Europe?'

'I flew it myself six hours ago! The 17-10 simulator at BGR – using a Buttress program. She went ape! Total loss of control and this time, if it hadn't been a simulator, we'd have creamed every last passenger.'

Toby was about to shift into gear but Guy was halfway through the window and wouldn't let go.

'I came through for you!'

539

'You have leprosy around here.'

'I just drove from Connecticut nonstop. I left a ten-million-dollar cockpit standing on broken legs. It's like a meltdown back there! For Christ's sake, Toby, how much more do you guys need to get off your dead asses around here?'

Toby glared at him.

'You honestly *believe* I took money from the Europeans? Don't you understand? It's a smear. And for insurance the bastards have been trying to kill me!'

A car on the driveway behind them honked. The echo reverberated.

'This is real, Toby.'

'You didn't get their permission?'

'What permission?'

'You didn't go into BGR without permission?'

Guy was aghast. The car behind honked again.

'There are no invitations in this game! There's nothing moral about it! We had an agreement, you and I, and that's the hottest piece of paper this union's ever seen this close up!'

'Simulators aren't enough,' Toby announced. 'Simulators can be faked. What you need is *operational* evidence.'

The honking behind them grew insistent.

'Otherwise,' Toby shouted, 'there's no point in discussing it.' He slammed the gears and pulled away, spinning Guy free.

Guy ran behind Toby's tail-lights through the grey of the underground lot. Toby had screeched into his spot and was trying to make it to the elevator before Guy could reach him again.

'This isn't enough?' Guy demanded.

'No.'

'*Operational* proof?'

'And maybe not then.'

540

'If I can get it to you, on both the F-19 and how it links up with the 17-10, will that prove the point?'

Toby hesitated.

'It won't be American data,' Guy warned.

'German?'

'Will you take it?'

'Can you prove you were smeared?'

'Listen, you dumb bureaucrat, you call up Buttress! *You* ask them about a 17-10 research simulator at BGR! *You* ask them about electronic corruption! Ask them what's really in the F-19 report from Germany! I sent you the first eight pages.'

'I read them,' said Toby. 'There's no letterhead! It could have been written from a hotel!'

'Did you ever bother to find out why the FAA Northwest Region chief wouldn't buy the Buttress fix?'

'Muskgrave himself –'

'Have you ever asked anyone what the NTSB wants to look at in the tail end?' Guy was waving Moss's green internal memo in his fist. 'Have you ever checked to see why the fire in Air World Six started in the fuel shroud drain?' He brandished the folded eight-by-ten photo the gnome reporter had handed him the night of the incident. 'Ask them about a perfumery in Paris where they launder their payoff money! Ask them who the hell Anton Jasovak is! Goddammit, Toby, ask them some *real* questions!'

Toby, who had been studying his shoes, spoke in calm tones. 'OK, you're right, you're right. Let's do it your way. You have good questions. I'm going to go out and face the other side and I'll put it to them. I'll ask them who the hell is this Jasovich – or whatever his name is – and I want you people to explain the fuel shroud drain and what the blackened area around it signifies – and I'll ask them about that perfumery in Paris. I'll ask them how they launder their money. See, I'm going to come at them from your side.'

'Now you're talking,' Guy said, grinning.

'. . . And they're going to ask me, Tobyhana, who's your source, Tobyhana? And I'll have to tell them – fellow named Gavin Anders. You fellows remember Guy Anders. And I'm going to get the same non-answers you've been getting. But if it'll make you feel any better, I'll hold this simulator printout as backup.'

Guy swiped it away. 'You bastard, no you don't!'

Palms up, Toby said, 'OK, have it your way . . . Look,' he added placatingly, 'I am running into a couple of things that lead me to believe that maybe you're not as full of crap as I once thought you were. But I can't go into the ring with your second-best punch.'

'I'll get the operational information.'

Toby saw the pain behind Guy's determination. 'Guy, I want to believe you. But what am I supposed to do with the stuff in the papers? The planes are showing up clean. Shit, I've been prepared to stand on top of the ALPA building with you or hijack the President's plane for publicity. I want to be a part of what you're saying but I don't know where the scrimmage line is. I don't know what colour jersey you're wearing.'

The elevator opened. Toby stepped in and pressed '7'. Guy followed.

'OK, I'll deliver the German operational report.'

'How?'

'I'll get it.' But he didn't know how. Guy flipped the alarm switch, stopping the elevator. The bell rang far below them.

'What the hell are you doing?'

'I don't want you getting away that fast. This time I want us to be sure we understand each other. If I produce it, you're going to call a stand-down on the 17-10.'

'Stand-downs are up to the membership.'

'Then line up their addresses.'

'They'll want to see evidence.'

542

Guy smiled at him encouragingly. Their faces were inches apart. Toby reached for the switch but Guy cupped his hand over it. 'You've never taken a position on anything before so they're going to take your word on this. Your credibility is unassailable.'

'Not if you're my source.'

'I may be respectable by then.' Aspinwall's sudden interest in his rejoining the line ran through his head. He let go of the alarm. The elevator moved. 'I may even be famous.' He said that because the second thing that ran through his head was the word *mutiny* . . .

Toby stepped out, bewildered. Guy pressed 'lobby'. Before the doors closed, he glimpsed a man standing behind Toby. Guy tried to place him. Somebody from his college days . . . a teacher? No. A former airline captain? . . . No. Guy exited at the lobby, considered going back up to Toby's floor, then thought better of it. He paced for forty minutes before the elevator opened and the white-haired man stepped out. Guy now knew where they'd met.

'It's real good to see you again,' he greeted the man, falling into step alongside. 'You're quite a way from home.'

The English accent was distinctive, brisk. 'Ah, Mr Anders. Our spectrographic analysis of your cockpit voice tape didn't do you much good, I fear.' The professor from the Chelmsford electronic laboratory led the way through the double-glass doors, on to Massachusetts Avenue. The professor's long-gaited stride was rapid; he wasn't about to slow down.

'Are you here by invitation?' Guy queried.

'I'm afraid there was no marine band,' the professor smiled.

'You're not here as an exchange student, either.'

'Nor am I here as an individual. Actually, it's in behalf of – larger interests – '

543

'Including your government.'

'Yes . . .' The professor maintained his pace. 'The impression that we paid to have the 17-10 discredited casts our Skybus in a poor light. We want no association with that. Quite obviously we do not need to resort to that. Our effort is superior to begin with. I'm here to make that point.'

'Is anybody listening?'

The professor stopped. 'They can ill afford to delude themselves. You see, the Germans are trying very hard to drop the axe on the 17-10 but your State Department has them in a hammerlock.'

'How do you know this?'

'The Germans have been holding exhaustive trials on the 17-10 above the North Sea and we've had a peek at some of their analyses. They're a meticulous lot, you know. And ever since they've lost faith in your country's ability to defend them, they've been less inclined to hold their tongues. I cannot tell you more than that.'

'Who in Germany? Give me a name.'

'There are many. I don't believe I should go into it any further with you for fear someone else will say we're spoon-feeding you to do things for us. But if you were to get it through your own American sources, that would be quite different, wouldn't it? This is the suggestion I made to your colleague Toby, and it's one I'm happy to repeat to you. So if you wish to follow through, I'd suggest you have a talk with a rather tacky fellow on your own safety board named Moss. Maybe you've heard of him.'

Guy searched the professor's eyes for the gag.

'He's trying to get the German paper discreetly – through channels.'

Guy ran the several blocks to the NTSB offices, the hot early sun making his shirt feel as though it were baked on.

He raced past the receptionist and found Moss in a meeting with two others.

'I can't talk to you now,' Moss said, looking a little feverish.

'I should think you'd want to be related to me.'

Moss stepped into the corridor. 'We can meet after work,' he whispered. He seemed to tremble. 'I've been relieved of anything related to Flight Six.'

'Who's got it?'

'Tarpender. All of it, the whole file, under lock and key.'

'Does it contain anything?'

'We were just getting started – '

'Sure you were.' Guy smiled. 'I've got some eye-popping reading for you right here.'

Moss watched as Guy removed the simulator printout sheets from his coat pocket. 'But you don't get to see it till you quash the subpoena and the notification of proposed certificate action we left behind in your beer.'

Moss reached for the sheets. 'You have my word.'

'I need collateral.'

Moss walked into the adjoining empty office and picked up the phone. 'Read me the number.' Guy took a tightly pressed document from his wallet, unfolded it and spoke. Moss wrote the information down and dialled an outside exchange. He was unequivocal with his contact, and ordered the originals of both documents delivered to his office by hand. He hung up. 'You're going to own the only copies.'

Guy unfolded the simulator printouts. 'If you'd done a straightforward job on Flight Six instead of kissing Buttress's ass, this wouldn't be news to you! Read it! You'll see there are several points at which the graph scoots off the page.' He handed the packet to Moss. 'It's a virtual repeat of our seat-of-the-pants letdown into JFK produced by Buttress's own punch cards.'

Moss noticed the small BGR logo at the edge of the sheet. 'The 17-10 research simulator . . .' He blanched.

'When you're done with that, go across town and interpret it for Senator Zakowski so he can sound intelligent about it when they restart the loan hearing.' He handed Moss a pen and a piece of paper. 'And you take this down. Go on, write it! You tell him to find out why Buttress is using an electronic-corruption program in a 17-10 research simulator at BGR. And why the FAA Northwest Region chief, Don Devlin, wouldn't buy Miller's fix and whether that's got anything to do with his sudden transfer!'

'Jesus, keep your voice down.'

'And you tell him to ask Buttress why the fire in Air World Six started in the fuel shroud drain. And if that fire had anything to do with the lights going out in Cedarhurst –'

'Huh?' Moss kept his head down.

'Have him mention microscopic fibres that shed from the graphite-epoxy composite and have him ask Buttress to explain it.'

Moss scribbled.

'There's a perfumery in Paris Buttress uses to launder payoff money. Ask them to talk about that. Tell him to drop the name Anton Jasovak in their laps and to ask Riddick or Hollis Wright to explain who he is.' Guy was soaring. Anja's pug-nosed face with her defiant eyes appeared to him almost as a vision. Her expression was one of definite approval.

'You're assuming a hell of a lot, aren't you?' Moss simpered.

'I'm assuming you're smart enough to know that it's time to jump ship. You're going to need me to vouch for your soul. We're allies, Moss. You've got a chance to be a hero.'

'And if we're in over our heads?'

'Then you'll die someday with your personal résumé intact.' Guy smiled knowingly. 'I understand you're digging through channels.'

'It's at the highest level. They've run a full operational trial on the 17-10 and rounded out the report.'

'I know that,' said Guy.

'I might owe W. B. Cosgrove an apology.'

'I know that too.'

'They held up signing the final draft until they could get a look at Miller's fix. Now they've included their opinion of that. Jesus Christ, I understand it's murder.'

'Who's your source?'

'They've got a document, three hundred pages stuck between blue plastic covers, thirteen thousand man-hours. They want the right to return the whole order or they're going to print the entire report in paperback and drop it on newsstands. I'm trying to get a copy of the 17-10 stuff from State but it's been classified.'

'Who else has access to it?'

'The Germans.'

'OK.'

'And Senator Osborne. He's working with them trying to modify it, cut it down.'

'And you know for a fact he's in Germany?'

'In Bonn "on an errand of mutual advantage relating to the manufacture of F-19s in Germany in exchange for additional import quotas over here" – according to *The Wall Street Journal*.'

'You're the wave of the future, Douglas. Any other names on the scorecard?'

'I can only tell you there's a mass burial going on in a number of places right now.'

'Cover-up.'

'It's going to succeed.' Moss was very pale. 'They'll field these,' he said, looking at the page of scribbled questions which was fluttering in his hand.

'You just make sure you get to Senator Zakowski.'

'I'll see Zakowski.'

'You're going to be a national sensation. Unless, of course, I don't get possession of the subpoenas.'

Guy realized he would have to go to Germany to take the report away from Osborne. He left the NTSB with Moss looking very sincere.

The last two nights had been rough for Matt. Miller's suicide had gnawed at him and now reports of several hydraulic leaks on the newest operational planes had landed on his desk. Moudon came bursting into his office with a tale about the Germans preparing a public blast on both the 17-10 and the F-19 and it had taken Matt two fretful hours to chase the story down.

'Why the hell am I the first to plunk down my cash and the last to find out when something goes wrong?' he bellowed.

'Nothing's gone wrong yet, Matt,' Moudon placated, trying to sound like a VP who could handle pressure with grace.

'We're wound tighter than a winch to launch the Big Season, we got the silverware sparkling like mirrors and you come in here telling me this horseshit! What am I supposed to do with it, cancel my life? Because that's what that boils down to!'

'Matt, I only wanted you to know.'

'And what do you want in return, a pat on the head? Don't come in here dumping on me! This isn't a goddamn clinic! You come to me with *answers* so that I have some room to move around in!'

He sat heavily in his chair, alternately staring at the airport beyond and at the thermometer tube displays on the wall.

'Give me the gist of it.'

'There's a man named Locker who's filling in for Miller. He said there was a flap about it out at Buttress.'

'*All* of Buttress? Everybody? *All* the employees milling around on the goddamn campus, babbling about it?'

'No.'

'Then be specific. I want to know how big it is.'

'There was a discussion between Hollis Wright and Riddick and they cut Locker out of it. There was some shouting between Riddick and Wright but he got enough to tell me there's some pressure building from the Germans.'

'Which Germans? The state airline?'

'Bonn.'

'That's political. Or you better pray to your God on your bare fucking knees it *is* political. Get Osborne on the line.'

When he heard the senator was 'away from his office', Matt began calling friends on the Hill, keeping it light in the hope that it would also disarm any lurking bad news.

'So you've heard nothing around town that would get in the way of our launch?' he continued with Moudon.

'Only the Miller suicide and that's bound to be forgotten.'

When he'd exhausted calling the names he'd scribbled on the pad before him, he settled back, not entirely satisfied, but at least minimally secure that the picture was not as bleak as he'd thought. To bolster himself further he instructed Angela Sisson to get Hollis Wright on the phone. Angela found the board chairman at his home.

'I'm packing,' Hollis said. 'What the hell do you think, you're my only client?'

'I want you to tell me what this business with West Germany is all about and give it to me without filtering the words. Don't waste my time with bullshit. Have they found anything they can make stick?'

'If they have they haven't told us about it.'

'But it can't just be frivolous! Even if it's a ploy it's got to be bolted to something concrete!'

549

'Maybe they think the wings ought to be bigger.'

'What do *you* think?'

'I think you ought to stop torturing yourself. Osborne is over there and he's got the State Department bellying up behind him and you've got to know we're ready for them.'

'I've got one foot out the door, Hollis. I leave for LA at two this afternoon to set up our launch for Monday. I'm shooting my whole bankroll on this, you know that? I'm going for broke.'

'I wish I had a chunk of your action. Your stock is going to go through the roof.'

'I'll pray for that prophecy.'

'We're rooting for you.'

Matt shut his eyes. 'This is the biggest thing I've ever done.'

'I'm going to drink to you on Monday. I'm going to think about you.'

'It's been some collaboration, hasn't it?' Matt was still seeking reassurance.

'Like a war. We've had our differences but I wouldn't want anyone different in the line with me.'

'Have a good trip, wherever you're going.'

'It's going to be a great summer, Matty.'

Hollis sounded very reassuring and Matt decided he felt a lot better. He was glad he'd called. And Angela looked brighter, too. She was always relieved when Matt appeared happier but this time it was something else. She was holding a TWX in her hands and smiling.

'See, things do turn out for the better, don't they?'

'What's that?'

She flattened the curling page on his desk. His eyes flicked across the date-time group. The source was London. Then he dug into the meat. It was addressed to:

MATTHEW T. ASPINWALL, ESQ., CHAIRMAN AIR WORLD JFK, NY. DEAR SIR, IF ANYONE EVER PROVES AIR WORLD FIRST OFFICER ANDERS OR

ANYONE IN HIS FAMILY OR EMPLOY EVER RECEIVED ANY PAYMENT FROM ANY MEMBER OR REPRESENTATIVE OF THE EUROPEAN SKYBUS CONSORTIUM WE WILL GIVE AIR WORLD ONE FULLY EQUIPPED EIGHTY MILLION DOLLAR FLY-BY-WIRE SKYBUS ENTIRELY FREE OF CHARGE.

It was signed 'E. E. Halstead and F. T. Chamoneaux, Co-chairmen, Skybus, For the Consortium, London, England/Paris, France.'

'Jesus H. Christ. That's what you call putting your money where your mouth is. My God,' he whistled. He sat rereading it.

'Doesn't that help?'

When he got to the signature line again, he said, 'I don't know. I don't know. This is no bluff. This says our man is clean.'

'That's what I thought was so good,' Angela said, frowning hopefully.

'So what is Anders bitching about? He hasn't come up with a thing. What the hell is his motive?'

Angela knew she wasn't equal to the conversation and that it wasn't her place but she decided to mention the obvious. 'Could there *be* something wrong?' She was surprised when Matt didn't take offence at it.

'I've asked everybody, Angela. People get affected in different ways, you know. You don't walk away from a Flight Six the way you walk into it. Nobody ever does. W. B. Cosgrove is still out on his soybean farm. Anders is walking around like he's been mugged. That's how I see it. He's looking under beds.' Matt stood at the window. 'That's a beautiful ship out there.' He was admiring the newest shining 17-10 jumbo he would soon ride to the Coast.

Angela waited uncertainly. 'Well,' she said, trying to sound light-hearted, 'the Skybus is nicer to look at but I'm sure you've made the best decision.' She knew at once she'd said the wrong thing. She was going to add

551

'nice to look at from the woman's point of view', but didn't. She saw the droop in her boss's posture and his voice was tight when he said, 'Get Hollis back on the line. Let's find out who's paying who what.'

In a moment she signalled him. Matt picked up. Hollis was irritated.

'Now what?'

'Did you people plant money on Anders to smear him?'

There was a delay before Hollis said, 'What?' Matt found the delay significant.

'You heard me!'

'Matty, I don't know if Valium will help but maybe you ought to give it a try.'

'All right, never mind. I'll put it to you another way. If I can *prove* you had money laid on Anders, if I can prove your people smeared him, will you give me one 17-10 free of charge?'

This time the silence was more pronounced. Finally Hollis spoke.

'Legitimate concerns are one thing but I don't like getting crank calls from you or anyone else!' Hollis's voice was shaking. 'What the hell's wrong with you?'

'There's nothing wrong with me. But you better go back to your store and jerk your legal troops into overdrive!' Matt slammed the phone and buzzed Angela.

'Sir?'

'Locate Guy Anders and you figure some way for him to meet with me before we take off.'

21

High above western Pennsylvania, Air World Flight Twenty-eight, Buttress 17-10 coast-to-coast service, slowly banked left. Fenton Riddick watched the prisms of light turning on his window and sipped his scotch. He let the swirl of whiskey go through his head as the 17-10 completed its slight course alteration, positioning itself for an eventual approach into New York's Kennedy Airport. He still had a two-hour respite before he'd have to confront the executive committee of Intercarrier Life and Casualty. The threat to cancel Buttress's equipment and product liability insurance was a new thumb vice. Riddick shut his eyes and his thoughts strayed, careening about until they settled on what he might do – after Buttress . . . Abruptly he squeezed the button that put his chair in an upright position and tried to correct the image. He never heard the seat belt chime or the change in engine tone as the plane left its cruising altitude. Instead the cabin seemed to darken for him and he felt as though all his private holocausts had just jumped out and were dancing in front of him, murals of blinding sleeplessness punctuated by the shrieks of a red hair ribbon . . .

Guy could no longer make a direct connection to Frankfurt or Bonn but he took a cab to National Airport anyway to book space to Germany from New York. He didn't want to chance doing it by phone, he wanted the ticket in hand, and this time he didn't look for available crew space but used his American Express card and paid full fare, purposely respelling his name 'Andress' for listing in the reservations computer – a mistake that could be attributed to a ticket clerk should the name be checked against his passport. He didn't want to signal the international reservations computer of his intentions. When he called home, Anja answered. There had been one phone call.

'It was Matt Aspinwall.'

'Certainly not in person.'

'You never called him back.'

'I know.'

'That's what his secretary said.'

'What else did she say?'

'Matt got on the phone. He said it was urgent.'

'That's it?'

'Except he hoped someday to meet me. He wants to see the kind of woman who would spend time with an anarchist. He said it sweetly.'

'How urgent is urgent?'

'He'd appreciate it if you could get to his office by two.'

Matt Aspinwall left the Air World complex at JFK and was on his way across the tarmac towards the newly arrived 17-10 when Guy caught up.

'I'm grateful for your promptness,' Matt greeted him. Guy wasn't sure if he meant it in the context of the most recent phone call or the one prior.

'Sorry if I held you up. But then I've had doubts about meeting a man who entertained the idea of me walking the plank.'

'As I remember it, you were the one who turned tail. You'll notice we've never docked your pay for that. I figured we owed you something for Flight Six even if you do shoot your mouth off.'

They had reached the truck-mounted stairs leading to the first-class cabin.

'Your message said this was urgent,' Guy prompted.

Matt unfolded the TWX from his shirt pocket. 'Come on up. There's something here you're entitled to see.'

Guy hesitated.

'Well, don't stand there. I'm not going to hijack you!' Matt led the way into the first-class lounge. They were greeted by two flight attendants who became solicitous in deference to the CEO. The flight crew, jackets and hats off, were already on the flight deck, which was visible through the partly open cockpit door. Guy recognized the

554

elderly captain as a talkative fellow he'd flown with before. He didn't know the other two. Matt pointed Guy to a chair and told the steward to serve two glasses of red wine.

'Read that,' he said, handing Guy the TWX. Three company photographers clambered on board with their gear. Matt waved them through. 'Park it in the back and pour yourself whatever you want.' He watched Guy's face and waited for him to finish reading.

'I'd like a copy of this,' Guy said.

'That is a copy. It's yours.'

'Have you got a second TWX saying where the money *did* come from?'

The steward placed two full glasses on the table between them. Matt stuck a finger in the wine to check its temperature.

'Hollis Wright coins a billion and a half a year because he's able to sweep aside the minor irritations most people get snagged on. You're a minor irritation. That doesn't mean he gave you the money. But the fact that he's pointing an accusing finger at people who are prepared to back their innocence with eighty million dollars has me interested. It supports your innocence. But then what in the hell kind of a peckerhead goes ahead and cashes such a cheque?'

'It was the only way to trace it back to Hollis Wright, who some people saw as the source.'

'What people is that?'

'Ben Reese.'

Matt screwed up his face.

'You'd have been a lot better off if you'd read him instead of Buttress's love notes,' Guy declared.

'You don't cross four billion dollars,' Matt levelled at him. 'There isn't a human being anywhere that's worth that.'

'I disagree.'

555

'I have to admire you for your guts.' It was said ungrudgingly. But it didn't quite come off as a compliment.

'I'm no priest. But I had no choice.'

'I'm here to tell you that's all changed now.'

'You ought to stop and take a good hard look at the tiger you've grabbed on to.'

Matt struggled to shed the feeling of having been tackled from behind. Assaulted with an echo of the insurance company's alert that Anders did have damning evidence – uncertain whether he had dreamt it or whether it had actually occurred – assaulted with an echo of his own angry telex to Fenton Riddick. Too loudly he blared, 'Anyone trying to take apart something with this many economies vested in it needs allies. I don't see too many on your side of the line.'

Guy noted the bravado in the comeback. 'You're right.'

Matt flushed. 'I'm talking about a Big Season that's going to start on schedule. I'm talking about raw reality. Not about what they teach in the Harvard Business School.'

Guy sipped his wine. He saw small beads of moisture lodged in the forehead creases of the man sitting next to him and incongruously he was reminded of a sombre scene replayed from a long-ago baseball game. Guy felt sorry for Matt Aspinwall the same way the fans had felt sorry for Lou Gehrig. He understood Matt's obstinacy. His mind blazed with a ringing challenge to Matt: 'Do you really buy the FAA sign-off?' But he didn't voice it. Matt, fists clenched, hadn't touched his own wine. Whatever it was he was grasping so tightly, he could not let go.

Still, Guy wondered if there wasn't some way to slow Matt down, back him up, reposition him at an earlier crossroad. He chose his words carefully.

'It seems to me what you have to weigh is the higher risk of flying the 17-10 and the fatal black eye that could

556

accrue to the whole fleet or, say, taking a breather right now and going with a different manufacturer.'

The suggestion was so far removed from what Matt wanted to talk about that at first he couldn't respond at all. He put a hand through his hair and spoke calmly.

'Time is always endless to observers. It may be that there will always be better choices in retrospect. But at a certain point, every man has to lock down his bet. Either that or you got to get the hell away from the gaming tables. Now you're looking at a man who's beaten the house for the past thirty years.'

Matt had formulated his position and like some shellfish had taken refuge inside it. Guy watched, sadly aware that Aspinwall with his weary eyes had suddenly crossed the line into old age and would not be coaxed away from the immediate objective in which he resided.

'You've been a winner, Matt. That's the reason you're head of this operation. Other people didn't see it your way but you were right.'

'You and I are not that far apart,' Matt Aspinwall responded in a conciliatory way. 'I took on the odds and I don't look back on that as having been a foolish thing. Now you're taking on the odds. Unfortunately, I'm part of your odds.' Matt smiled. 'But now it's up to all of us to get this thing through, and we can't panic.' Matt regained some composure, a curt moment of recovery. 'Nobody else is complaining, Anders. Only you.'

'The aeroplane is certificated and you're legal.'

Matt sidestepped the verbal jab and became grudgingly apologetic. 'We're still working out flight procedures – strict orders to hold in the event of thunderstorms within twenty-five miles of destination . . .'

'Oh?'

'We're considering limiting the cruise airspeed to another ten per cent below Buttress's flutter margin speed; besides, we're not treating the new actuator as a

Service Bulletin, that was done that way just to avoid bad publicity. Legally you're right, I can fly one hundred per cent right now, but Air World isn't like that, we're insisting we have only the best and all our 17-10s will have the new actuator before they fly. You have my personal guarantee on that.'

'But we both know it won't make any difference no matter how many actuators you shove into it – don't we?'

'We're going to fly it with one foot on the brake for a while. Crawl all over it between trips to check it out, put more crews on it as we go. But the way you change the situation,' he barked, 'is you come on board and you work *with* us, you work from *within*.' His cheeks spasmed. He contemplated his untouched wine.

Guy waited.

With his eyes still fixed on the glass before him, Matt continued, 'People make mistakes, but they're there to be corrected.' Matt knew he was asking in his most civilized tones for help. And Guy knew it hurt. It was most definitely not Matt's style. Matt met Guy's eyes and said, 'Every one of us, you, me, Buttress, is out to perpetuate himself. I don't want to see you stand in the way and get mowed down. Because they're not going to let anything stand in their way. That's simple business. And that's how you grow up; you learn these things. You need to square things and I need you back in the right-hand seat. I need you because you've given me a pain in the ass publicity-wise.' Matt said it openly, reaching out to put a heavy paw on Guy's shoulder. 'We're going to open the Big Season with our blue-ribbon Los Angeles–London nonstop on Monday. The press will be there. I want you on board.'

Guy smiled, started to speak. Matt held a finger up.

'If you fly, you won't have to fly forever.'

'Just until the outback?'

Matt laughed. 'I'm talking about getting away from aeroplanes. Kick off the flying boots, put on a pair of spats. You're a smart young man. Lots of indignation. I like that. Shouldn't be allowed to go flat in a cockpit. You see,' he said confidentially, leaning closer, 'I need allies too.'

Guy didn't comment but he reflected that the media event he had promised Toby had just grown far beyond what he originally had in mind.

'You have my word that if you come back on the line, reverse some of this lousy publicity, I won't forget it.'

Guy was watching a downed ace, a Jap hanging from the trees in the Luzon jungles, naked and wounded but still taking aim, a proponent of raw power and at the same time a victim of it.

'OK, Matt,' he said softly. 'One foot on the brake for the Big Season inaugural – '

'Right,' Matt expounded loudly. 'You and I both know we're committed to passengers and we both know that if we pull back on the old schedules a little bit it'll be all right.' He grinned, the nervous elixir salesman closing a deal. 'Next season we'll have the B's – or the Skybus – we'll trade the A's back in if we have to. We'll have an option to be altruistic – or moralistic – and tell Buttress to shove them all up their ass, tail first. I'm on your side.'

'I'm ready to help you on your terms then. I'll fly first officer for the inaugural.'

'Well, that's great,' Matt said unabashedly. 'That's fine.' For the first time he seemed to relax. He downed half his wine with one swallow and turned away, facing the broad expanse of JFK through the passenger window. 'I'll be counting on you,' he said.

It took Guy two hours to locate Ben by phone, who was about to leave for New Mexico.

'What are you going there for?'

'There's a plane overdue and it has something to do with you.'

'What plane is that?'

'Twin Beech. It may have gone down in the desert near Tula Rosa, so I want to get out there.'

'I don't get it.'

'Don Devlin was at the controls.'

Guy accepted it with no greater shock than if he'd heard it about a stranger on the news.

'My instinct tells me I ought to get out there.'

'Try to resist that.'

'What for?'

'Because a few hours from now you're going to West Germany and a few hours after that you and I are going to hang these bastards.'

'I don't know what you're talking about.'

'Of course you don't. How soon can you get to JFK?'

'Did you say West Germany?'

'I was set to go myself, Benny, but there's a new development and my end will have to be played from here. I'll explain it later.'

'Check Delta's arrivals at Kennedy. I'll be on one of them.'

Lights from within the Air World terminal at JFK shone brightly against the blood red of sunset. Inside, Guy, Anja and Ben were striding in a group through the long corridor, towards the boarding gates. Ben was in his safari suit, the unironed army-navy special; he was checked in for the first evening departure to Frankfurt. He'd shoved the yellow boarding pass underneath one epaulet, his canvas carry-on bag hitched over the other shoulder. Anja, in her jeans and button-down shirt, was walking between them, holding each by the arm. Hordes of people filled the corridors.

'You look like you're off to bag a tiger,' Anja said.

'It's a disguise,' Ben retorted.

'Now look, no half-assed discoveries or flimsies or papers that you come by in a trash can,' Guy said.

'The reason you got me doing this is because I'm the braver of the two of us – '

'You've been selected out of loyalty – not bravery or intelligence.'

'Start talking, Anders. I can't give you much time,' Ben said as they wedged between a large group of waiting people.

'Your target is the German report. Osborne's been editing it day and night. Don't go snooping around your old haunts looking for thrills. *The Wall Street Journal* says he's in Bonn "on an errand of mutual advantage relating to the manufacture of F-19s in Germany in exchange for additional import quotas over here". Translated that means Osborne's spreadeagled over three cities like a rubber suit on a torture rack, trying to hold it all together.'

'How come my plane is never at the first gate?' Ben groaned.

'Get yourself to Bonn and find Osborne. Find out which hotel has the heaviest security. One way or another you've got to get next to him. The report he has is so sensitive that there's a better-than-even chance he's lying on top of it – like a man on a hand grenade.'

'It's in blue ink,' Ben said, repeating what he thought Guy had told him earlier.

'No – a blue cover. Repeat what I told you.'

'What do I know?'

'You'll come back with a goddamn menu.'

They reached the crowded boarding area. Ben unhitched his shoulder bag and stood looking through the glass at the jumbo jet nuzzled in, awaiting its passengers. Resolve lay behind his eyes and, as well, a kind of devotion. Seeing that, Guy couldn't speak. Ben's gritty features had the quality of an old spectator pressed into the lineup in place of the quarterback.

Softly Guy began, 'Benny, this is right down your alley. It has nothing to do with gathering facts. It has to do with breaking noses. You'll feel right at home. It's going to take adrenalin. We've finally got a window to climb through. But it's only going to be open a short time. You've got less than sixty hours and no room for digressions. You must be at Los Angeles Airport with that report under your arm and in one piece by noon, Los Angeles time, on Monday.'

'You're talking about rough stuff.'

'If you make it, we'll end up blowing the lid off on national TV. If you don't, the industrial buggering alliance will work up some other scheme – using a new stack of megabucks – to keep the lid on and BS their way through another month.' Guy handed Ben his ticket. 'You're looking for a three-hundred-page report bound in blue plastic; it describes 17-10 operational flight trials that were run over the North Sea. I'll be at Los Angeles looking out the window.' Guy produced a folded scrap of paper. 'Here's my hotel. When you get there, you and I are going to hand it over to Toby. Telegrams will be released, phones will start humming. The 17-10 will be grounded by sunset. The strike will be on and the inaugural will never take off.'

'And if I don't make it?'

'If you don't make it, Toby will go back to DC and climb into his desk – and I will have aborted the inaugural takeoff for whatever publicity it might get us, but then I'll have to do the rest in handcuffs.'

The first boarding call for the Frankfurt passengers was announced. A line formed at the door leading to the aeroplane.

'If I get it too late for LA,' Ben asserted, 'I'll make a lateral pass to wherever it'll do the most good.'

'If anyone's on to you, you'd be dead before you could make that move. Speed is your only ally. And if you keep your hat down over your ears, they may not know who you are till you reach LA. Once you're standing next to Toby, you're home free because the other side would never risk the connection after that. But if you're late and get here alone . . .' Guy shook his head.

'What is this, one-upmanship? You used to be naïve,' commented Ben.

'Will I have to worry about you?' Anja asked Ben.

'It's not required but I'd feel better if you do.'

Anja hugged his arm. 'When you get back we're all going to go to a Jacuzzi and gloat. And maybe after that I'll move on. Then you both can come to my island and we'll repeat it every ten years . . . out West.'

Guy reacted to her statement, trying to deal with the idea of a final farewell. He covered his feelings with small talk.

'As you can see, Reese and I are pretty tough *hombres*. If you ever need help keeping the bulldozers out, you might want to give us a call. I think we could handle that.'

Ben was puzzled. 'What island is that?'

'Private property,' Guy said. Anja smiled.

The lounge was almost empty as the line of embarking passengers stepped through smartly. Ben stooped to hitch up his shoulder bag.

Suddenly Anja put her arms around Ben's neck. 'You're a lovely and a beautiful man,' she said, her eyes beginning to glisten. She reached into her bag and fished out a sheaf of papers. 'I want you to have these.' She placed them in his hand. 'My handwriting stinks, but I think you'll be able to read it.'

Ben held the sheaf uncertainly.

'Read it,' she urged.

'What is it?'

'Facts.'

Ben shoved the papers into his shoulder bag and took both her hands in his, smiling gently. 'The only thing that's been more elusive to me than facts is a beautiful woman – like you.'

The gate agent was motioning to them. It was time to go. Guy clapped Ben on the shoulder. 'Watch yourself, huh?'

'Oh, hell . . .' Ben shrugged. 'It's just another deadline.'

Three hours after Ben's plane had taken off, Guy's flight to Los Angeles was due to depart. Anja sat in a corner of the waiting lounge as other passengers accumulated, filling the room. Guy was at a nearby pay phone, talking to Toby.

Anja watched the passengers as they gathered. She studied something in their faces – a reflection of her own face, she expected, and she thought of her red tote bag and of her maps. She thought of her island and of Guy's and of getting there. He stood in the distance with the carriage and stateliness of the senior captain he would one day be, tall, enclosing the circle around him with a certain dignity. She watched him and thought of an hour from now. There settled over her the gentle quality of an ineffable sadness.

He was back alongside her. She was faintly surprised at the strong feeling of comfort that gave her.

'Will you still be here when I get back?' he asked.

She thought of the day at the bay shack. She wanted him, she knew that, and she knew it was selfish. But she also knew herself well enough to know that if he came to her on just those terms she would no longer be touched by him. She stared into space, recalling the endless string of lights slanting down out the window there.

He looked at her face, her eyes like two pale opals, feisty, yet innocent. A throb of loneliness beat inside him.

She was trying to visualize herself alone, on her island

. . . but she knew she'd still respond to him, even there. And now she felt giddy as if there were an unseen zipper down the middle of her, inside, and it had just been unzipped all the way down. But she was tough for all that and tried not to let it show.

'I won't leave Jamie in the lurch – but I still have my maps.'

'Will I know how to find you?' he asked.

'I'm not sure yet if I'll want you to . . .'

She reached into her purse and took something out. She held it towards him. His hand touched a small sealed envelope.

'Read this . . . when you can. I hope you realize I was never your enemy . . . even on the night after that landing.'

Staring at the blue blankness outside the aeroplane window, thinking of Anja, Guy took her envelope from his pocket and opened it. A small plain card fell into his palm. On it were two handwritten lines. They read simply, 'There may be no more islands left except the ones we make ourselves.'

Anja took a piece of stationery and a pen from Guy's desk and picked a clean spot on the kitchen table to write. Jamie sat eating a jam sandwich he'd made and watched. Anja steadied her hand, then positioned the blank sheet. She gazed at the gaping hole in the wall left from the evening following Air World Six, then returned her attention to the paper. Slowly she wrote.

'Wanted – *au pair* with adventurous ideas to take care of small person whose attractive father is an airline pilot . . .'

She studied it and crossed it out.

'Whatcha doin'?'

'Nothing.'

Anja began again.

'Wanted – widowed airline pilot requires – '

She stared at the shadows playing against the window and saw a mixture of images, a kaleidoscope of the past few weeks; she wrote 'requires' again, noticed it, crossed it out and added 'young woman.' She was surprised to see the words on the page. She'd meant to write 'young *au pair.*'

Jamie watched her fold the page in half and crumple it. Anja became still, turned her head to watch the doorway and seemed not to notice he was there. She was thinking about the inaugural never taking off – visualizing Guy and his son on a beach out West afterwards – taking time out, spending whole days together. And she wondered what it would be like out there.

'You want the rest of my jelly sandwich?'

Jamie's voice startled her. She smiled. 'Later maybe,' she said.

On the evening of the second day – the day before the Big Season inaugural – Ben was becoming concerned. All his leads had run into dead ends, all his ploys collapsed. He was unable to home in on Osborne. He had to back off and get a perspective. So he pulled off the autobahn and thought. They had the senator well camouflaged. Ben hadn't been able to spend any of his bribe money, informers were not to be had. He'd prowled around the airline's corporate offices, he'd tried the hotels. He'd been to the government offices in Bonn. He'd collared news-papermen, old colleagues, and that was most discouraging of all. They knew the senator was in town but they didn't know where. Ben riffled through the cards, bills and notes that had grown slick and round-edged in his wallet since

Dien-bienphu and, after intense study, came up with something new. He watched the traffic as it sped by. He'd have to return to Bonn.

As dusk gathered, he pulled on to the roadway in his rented white BMW and headed west. Once in the capital city he made his way to the government press office in the Bundestag. He was after an acquaintance whose address he'd finally deciphered in his smeared address book.

Despite the hour, it didn't take long for Ben to locate and buttonhole his former colleague behind a paper-strewn desk. The West European correspondent for one of the large US daily newspapers greeted him cautiously.

'You're looking at a man in a bind,' Ben informed him fervently, 'and you won't see the face here but there's another man in a bind back in the States. We've got to help him. You and I.'

'We do?'

'If we don't help him, I'll write a detailed exposé of a man who could have made a difference to a great many lives – and didn't.'

'Last time you wrote an exposé around here, I seem to recall it was about a certain fighter plane – '

'Don't finish,' Ben said, holding up his hand. He fished some folded papers from his shirt pocket. They were his new credentials. 'Here, what do these look like, soap coupons? I'm rehabilitated.'

The colleague wasn't impressed.

'I'm looking for Elton Osborne. There's an official report that's highly critical of the 17-10. I have to see him about it.'

The man made a pretence of sucking on his pipe. His expression was noncommittal.

'I can do without Osborne if I can see the report. It's very recent,' Ben nudged. 'About three hundred pages. Trials over the North Sea.' He watched the correspondent's face for a clue. 'What do I have to do to get my own copy? I don't have time to wait in hearing rooms or rummage through wastepaper baskets.'

'I can't say that I don't know anything.'

'But if you tell me, it could get rough for you.'

'Yes, something like that.'

'I see,' Ben mused. 'It's big, huh?' he prodded. His blue eyes watched from within the seamed brows. 'Is that big like in Bonn-big?'

'Like in Chancellor-big,' his friend said quietly, filling the gap. Ben whistled softly. 'That's all I can say,' the man finished.

'Then interest in that report must be high in the Bundestag. Since Osborne *is* here, there might even be a conference going on right now,' Ben opined brightly.

The colleague shook his head. He picked his way through the next sentence. 'Nothing's going on right now. The Chancellor himself is out of town. That's the truth. Whatever is going on is being handled by the national airline. There's a meeting being held in the morning.'

'Where?'

The colleague shook his head. 'They'd have my neck.'

'When?'

'Early. But don't expect to see anything about it in the papers.'

'The airline's headquarters are in Cologne . . . The Chancellor's office – in Cologne? – '

'*Benny* . . . Aviation's not my beat. Let's leave it, huh?'

Ben scratched his chin thoughtfully, still at an impasse. 'Thanks for trying,' he nodded, turning for the door.

'Ben . . .' his colleague called after him. 'Follow the helicopter.'

Barges plied the Rhine even at this early hour beneath the twin Gothic spires of Cologne's Dom Cathedral. Ben raced north from Bonn, leaning often to squint over the steering wheel for any sign of a helicopter overhead, still puzzled over his friend's parting shot. Jesus Christ, what kind of helo? Large – or small? What colour? What make? He chastised himself; he'd done it again: he'd raced off without the facts.

He needed a lookout point, one with instant access to his car, and yet a promontory from where he could enjoy a broad view. The helicopter's destination could be anywhere . . . and it would be plausible to expect it to want to throw off suspicion by circling and coming at the city from any direction. Ben entered the traffic circle which provided access to the first of several main ring roads that enclosed central Cologne in a series of half-moon-shaped patterns. The crumpled street map open on the seat next to him indicated that halfway around the ring he would reach the broad boulevard that was the Aachenerstrasse, an axis running due east and west from the centre of the city. It fronted the huge Friedhof Melaten cemetery – broad, grassy and open – with a view both north and south. Ben proceeded north on the Bonnerstrasse, closer to the city, until he intercepted the ring road which would take him to Aachenerstrasse and the cemetery. With one eye on the road and one on the empty sky, he weaved through the morning rush.

In a quarter hour Ben was perched high up one of the grave markers, a tall marble monument which afforded a good view of the sky over the entire city.

For more than thirty minutes, he sat listening to the hiss and rattle of early morning traffic and only gradually became aware that there was a change in the tempo. All at once the thump-thump of a helicopter's rotor came from behind him. Ben twisted on his observatory. He complimented himself on his tactical skill. A small helo was coming from the west like an overgrown dragonfly on a course straight down the broad boulevard. Ben piled down from the tall grave marker and into the BMW. He made a smoking U-turn and tore away eastward as the helo appeared just above his front windshield. Progress through the city was tortuous, past the Neumarkt and along Cäcilienstrasse. The helo pulled majestically ahead, diminishing in the direction of the river. Finally Ben reached the shore. His face fell. The helo was perched on the broad flat deck of a river barge, rotor idling. Two fellows in workmen's clothes were getting in.

Wrong helo.

In twenty minutes he was back atop his marble lookout. It was already past eight in the morning. The situation was getting a little thin. Guy would be asleep in Los Angeles, the sixty hours now cut down to barely ten. And here he was, still not past square one, hanging on a gravestone in the city of Cologne, on a wild-goose chase . . .

Even if there were another helo, it could have come and gone during his diversion. Ever since his press colleague had made the cryptic remark, Ben had considered and discarded several speculations as to the scenario and what part a helicopter could play in it. Police? Press? Private interests? Ben's best guess was that the chopper would be carrying the Chancellor or his representative to a secret meeting place, or if that were too visible, it would have on board covert security for him. Grimly Ben hung on, trying to shut out the possibility he'd missed it. In another half hour he'd be too late – he'd fail.

He was beginning to wonder if he'd heard his colleague's late-evening remark at all.

Ten minutes passed. Nothing. Ben was becoming cramped. Then from far away a heavier sound than before – the thrumming beat of air. Ben was almost blind from squinting . . . and suspicious. Maybe this would be another false alarm. Then he saw it, a speck far off to the south, boring in low from the southeast where the huge Köln-Bonn airport was, on a straight course with no pretence at being cute.

570

Ben was instantly back in the BMW, roaring through the district of Lindenthal, past the university, hoping he wouldn't cream a bicycle. The helo was now ahead of him in the distance, scooting from his right to his left, getting closer. Ben pulled up at the intersection where Luxemburgerstrasse crossed; the chopper was dead ahead now, perhaps half a kilometre away. Ben watched as it skimmed northward just ahead of his car. As it went by he could see its rotor blades chopping briskly. It had plain markings. The traffic light changed. Ben threw a look over his shoulder at the oncoming horde of traffic, jammed his foot to the floor and swerved across several lanes in a left turn. Two vans had to slam brake. Ben ignored the shouts and the third fingers as he roared into the boulevard, scattering traffic, trying not to lose sight of the chopper. He saw it clearly again, off to his right. It had slowed somewhat and appeared to be descending. Ben braked the BMW almost to a crawl. Traffic behind was piling up on his rear bumper, but Ben in his concentration didn't hear the horns and shouts. Damn. He was going to lose it.

He tromped on the gas to get quickly through the railway underpass, hollering at the slower traffic, frantically searching as he emerged, and respotted his quarry. Damned if it didn't appear to be setting up for a landing. He'd have to hurry again. He screamed into Trierstrasse; that was a mistake: it afforded a right turn only on to the Salierring, and in dismay Ben saw the chopper pass directly over his car flying in the opposite direction. He was swearing at the top of his lungs, forgetful his head was out the window. A group of pedestrians shied back, certain he was a certified lunatic. Another red light ahead. Ben clenched his gum, picked a slot, and tyres shrieking, ran the light to muscle into a U-turn, avoiding a splendid collision with a Porsche by millimetres. He was steaming into the Barbarossaplatz with the helicopter about to dip completely behind the buildings and trees. He needed to go hard right, the street was one way against him. He started up the Hohenstaufenring at high speed, then wrenched the car into the first right he came to. It was a 135-degree turn and Ben almost lost control. He recovered, straightened the drift, and roared into a narrow crowded side street called Friedrichstrasse. Just before he lost sight of the helo for good it was again dead ahead – and not more than half a kilometre away. After forcing his way through crossing traffic at two busy intersections Ben emerged on Am Weldenback, and there, directly in front of him, was a park approximately three hundred metres in extent dominated by a cloister and a church. He grabbed his map. It was the St Pantaleon Kirche.

A church . . . A quiet refuge situated in a large area of green; plenty of open space under the trees for men to stroll out of earshot . . . or hide cars . . . or even land a helicopter. Ben slowly circled the park. The chopper had come down in an open area a hundred metres to the north of the church and was just then disgorging a harried-looking, long-haired young man in a crumpled pinstripe suit. The man ducked his head under the whirling rotors and loped along a path leading back to the church itself. Almost at once the chopper's door shut and it jumped from the grass, swung around in a nimble circle below treetop level and took off. Ben pulled the BMW into Walsenhausgasse, and left it pointed south towards the ring road two blocks away. He prowled once slowly around the church. The young man in the pinstripe suit had disappeared within. Ben fished a tie from his hip pocket, uncrumpled it and knotted it on. Keeping his flanks covered with glances back and forth, he walked up the steps and pushed his way inside.

* * *

572

Elton Osborne was ashen. His lower jaw stuck out in pure livid rage; somehow he restrained his voice. 'I hope that's just a very bad joke.'

'I assure you, Senator, we are this time quite serious.'

Osborne nervously faced a grim official across a broad desk in a plush, modern office in the DLG airline's corporate tower. Jet lag accentuated the dark bags under Osborne's eyes; the harsh alarm clock before seven – 1 A.M. Washington time – had jolted him severely. The ungodly hour and the tenor of the meeting landed like a couple of haymakers before the bell. Osborne summoned himself to rally.

'You people realize,' he blustered, 'if anything goes off the track, the break – the arrangement – Germany is getting on its F-19 purchases – and perhaps other military hardware – will be severely endangered.' He saw the rejoinder coming and stopped it with a raised hand, forcing a false show of bravado. 'Of course, with just a few weeks' more effort it might be possible for – well, for my government to reassure Bonn with respect to certain cost reductions on the F-19.'

'That is a matter for the Chancellor.'

Osborne continued loudly, 'As for your concerns regarding the 17-10, Buttress is making measurable progress – or, I should say, the Buttress computer facility BGR – we've gone beyond our beefed-up actuator – '

'The Chancellor's man will see you within the hour.'

Osborne, fully awake, glanced at his watch.

'The meeting will be held here, in Köln,' continued the German. 'Herr Hollis Wright will arrive in person as well. Perhaps at that time he will talk about another "fix" for the 17-10. Perhaps he knows of one . . .'

Osborne slumped, the wind gone from his sails. Next to his elbow on the table lay a marked-up three-quarter-inch-thick document with the typed title OPERATIONAL ANALYSIS OF THE INTERACTION OF ELECTRO-HYDRAULIC

FLIGHT-CONTROL COMPONENTS WITH ELECTRONIC CORRUPTION OF THE AFCS COMPUTER IN THE BUTTRESS 17-10 TRANSPORT AEROPLANE. Osborne had tried to edit it out of the comprehensive German report that featured the F-19 but he'd been unsuccessful.

'I'm sorry, Senator, but we cannot alter our conclusions through the choice of more conciliatory words.'

And now, Osborne realized with a rush, the Chancellor's representative himself was coming to tell both Buttress and the US Government – through him personally – that the Germans were rescinding their order of twenty-five 17-10Bs – and were poised to ground the rest of their fleet. Osborne slipped the blue-bound report into his attaché case and snapped the lid. 'As you know, Senator,' the German official continued, 'the F-19 has special control protection and antijamming installed. The extra weight has imposed a terrible reduction in combat effectiveness – and has not completely solved all inherent problems. These protections the 17-10 does not have . . . because Buttress never assumed faults would exist in both the computer and the servo outputs. And they never considered electronic corruption being so important for a transport. Moreover, in our view, with expanded use of graphite-epoxy, the problem in the future will be even worse. And it is aggravated by the hydraulic lines and the fuel line being routed through a common bulkhead.' He paused, then delivered the *coup de grâce*.

'Unless Mr Wright has something new, the state airline will ground its 17-10s.'

'Where is the meeting with the Chancellor's representative to take place?' Osborne asked dejectedly.

'It must be discreet, you realize.'

'Yes, I realize.'

'Therefore, it won't be here. But nearby. Where no one should notice. In church.'

* * *

574

Ben had always been a little in awe of the mysterious things that went on inside churches. He stood somewhat uncertainly in the transept, contemplating the altar, watching as a young priest in long vestments glided noiselessly by, stopping to genuflect. Two or three people were sitting quietly in pews. To his right Ben saw an old woman kneeling in the last row; adjacent in the corner was a piece of furniture, an ancient wooden desk or lectern perhaps four feet high. Attached to it was a metal sign soliciting alms which had surely been there fifty years. With a hoarse '*Entschuldigen, bitte*' to the old woman, Ben removed the candle from the stand, gently placed it on the floor, saying, 'Forgive me, Lord, I haven't got time to explain . . .' Then he lugged the stand towards the main entrance. It was much too heavy to lift, and Ben struggled, wincing at the scraping noises. The old woman cowered as he loped back past her to inspect several items hanging from a row of wall pegs. From the various vestments Ben pulled one dusty item free. It was a green-felt Bavarian greatcoat. It wasn't perfect but it would hide his army-navy accoutrement: it would have to do.

The young man with long hair and rumpled pinstripe suit he'd seen emerge from the helicopter bounded towards him. Ben was struggling into the long coat, at least two sizes too small, but he stepped forward, supremely imposing with his face like the side of a mesa in the sunset, cleared his throat, and with a guttural word of German stopped the man, who took him at once to be someone official.

Ben dropped his voice an octave, tucked his chin in. 'Who are you?' he asked in German.

'PR . . . Advance man.' The young man searched the church, looked back at Ben, puzzled. 'The meeting is to be discreet,' he said.

'Last-minute security,' confided Ben. 'And discreet,' he agreed with a conspiratorial wink.

575

'They'll be here momentarily.'

'*Ich weiss*,' Ben rasped.

Poor old guy's probably got throat cancer, thought the young man.

Ben meanwhile was involved with stabilizing his stand, which wobbled on the uneven stone floor.

'The meeting will be at the back,' advised the advance man. 'Two pews have been set aside. So we must keep everybody else out of that section.'

'*Aber natürlich*,' said Ben, still fussing with one leg of his stand.

'*Alles in Ordnung*,' said the young man to himself with one final glance around. Then to Ben, 'The Chancellor's representative will enter over there . . . The Americans, on the other hand, will enter here – except for Herr Hollis Wright, who's arriving by special car.'

Ben raised his eyebrows. Hollis Wright?

The first cars were already pulling up, drivers deftly opening doors, people emerging. Ben had steadied the stand at an acute angle to the entrance door. The first three men were at the door, walking in.

Ben spoke up officiously. 'Attaché cases, *bitte*,' he rumbled and slapped the lectern twice with his hand.

The first German stopped dead, the natural reflex to authority Ben was counting on, and obeyed by placing his attaché case on the lectern. Ben could have leaned across and kissed the German soundly for halting so unquestioningly, but instead he quickly unsnapped the case, raised and lowered the lid with a sharp glance inside, snapped it shut and handed it back. He followed the same perfunctory routine with the next two men. Shuffling in the line towards Ben's post were two bodyguards. Strongarms trying to appear inconspicuous are like bureaucrats trying to appear useful, Ben reflected. The first one was before him. When he placed his leather shoulder bag on the lectern, Ben saw that it was bulging, probably with radio transmitters, magazines of ammo and like parapher-nalia. Ben half nodded to the growing question on the man's face, gave him a knowing wink and with a slight gesture, motioned him to pass. Ben could not afford to begin a search for he'd have to complete it, and a body frisk was out of the question. Both bodyguards were wearing pistols; they'd never let him close enough. Ben could see the first bodyguard wasn't entirely convinced by the setup; maybe the man's Teutonic proclivity for rigid obedience would delay his challenging the disguise. Mentally, Ben kept his fingers crossed.

Then he recognized the gaunt Senator Elton Osborne striding up the steps.

When Ben tapped the lectern indicating he wanted the senator to make his attaché case available for inspection, Osborne objected.

'I'm Senator Osborne,' he assured the man in the green coat.

'He's the American senator,' the bodyguard muttered privately to Ben.

'Ya, *you* know that,' Ben whispered back in German. 'I have my orders.'

The guard paused uncertainly at the impasse and smiled ingratiatingly at Osborne. 'It's all right, Senator, to show him the bag.' With self-deprecation he added, 'We Germans have an unfortunate way of being like this.'

Osborne agreed with a thin smile, lifted his case, twirled dials on both ends and lifted the lid.

There, on top, facing Ben was the bright-blue binder with its typed title. Sideways Ben couldn't make out the words but saw the figures '17-10.' He peered over the open attaché case lid, smiled at the deadpan senator, grabbed the report and bolted for the door.

For five full seconds the confounded Osborne couldn't comprehend what was happening. The bodyguard nearby didn't know whether to shout after Ben or shout at all because he was in church. Osborne regained his wits but by then others were coming up the steps. The senator shoved the first one aside as he let out an angry bellow. All activity stopped as Osborne's shouted curse pealed through the church.

Ben's footfalls were scrunching on the gravel, pounding into the distance, past the black cars that had been pulled back.

'Jesus Christ, *stop him*,' Osborne gargled, almost incoherent with rage.

Overhead Ben noticed the hovering helicopter. No doubt just as he'd surmised: real security for the Chancellor's man, whose car had not yet appeared. Or perhaps for Hollis Wright, who at that moment, though Ben didn't know it, was crossing the Deutzerbrücke with a case that contained close to fifty million dollars – Buttress's hand-delivered cash offering for Germany's stopgap order of twenty-five 17-10Bs – in other words, a different kind of fix.

Ben was already behind the wheel of the BMW, which blasted to life and left a long trail of rubber as it streaked away in the direction of the ring. Osborne and his staff assistant with the two bodyguards were piling into their black Mercedes. Doors slammed, rubber squealed as it took off in pursuit. Running up to the other car was the chief state airline official. As his car dug out, he grabbed a mike from the dashboard and issued a terse command to the chopper overhead.

The engine whined in Ben's BMW. He'd got a jump but not as much as he would have liked. Already the black Mercedes was visible in his rearview mirror. Ahead was a yellow *Umleitung* detour arrow and the red-and-white candy stripes of roadblocks. Too late to turn, Ben swerved through the barrier on tortured rubber, sending street markers flying and just missing the gaping dirt hole in the roadway. Behind him the Mercedes took the sidewalk, bouncing road markers in front of it like ten pins. A bicyclist hit the ditch. The car's rear wheel caught the lip of the hole coming out, the car rocked violently but the driver saved it. Through the glass Osborne's wizened face had the ghastly expression of a prisoner behind bars.

The airport was six miles ahead. German drivers, used to no speed limits on their autobahns, were astonished as first the white blur of Ben's BMW, then the black blur of the pursuing Mercedes, rocketed past. Ben was working his lights furiously, blinking slower drivers aside, throwing wary glances at the rearview mirror, afraid his engine would melt.

Unseen by Ben, the chopper was almost directly overhead, barrelling just behind the two screaming cars at 140 mph. Tree branches swayed in its rotor wash. The pilot had relayed a message to the Luftwaffe operations centre at the airport. Buttress's latest F-19 demonstrator sat parked on a hardstand only three hundred yards from the boundary fence. A figure burst from the low-slung grey building nearby and scrambled up the ladder into the cockpit. The auxiliary power cart whined . . .

Even as scenery belted past in globs of blurs, a part of Ben's mind could dwell on Anja and the gift she had made to him. A quick check assured him her notes were safe. In his mind's eye he could already see the headline of his first story about acceptable risk – and the first paragraph:

There's a passenger I know . . . a young woman . . . who was as perplexed as this reporter by two words used by a Buttress spokesman at the recent NTSB hearing on the near-disaster of Air World Flight 6. The words: *acceptable risk*. My fellow passenger found the risk Buttress was willing to impose upon unsuspecting users of its products – people like you and me – to be, by any logical reckoning, entirely *un*acceptable. Since I had been recalcitrant in providing you, the reader, with a means to glean facts from among my agitated opinions, I want my forthcoming series of articles to present the absolute proof of the manufacturer's culpability . . .

Ben patted the bright blue 17-10 report which lay snuggled in the seat cushions next to Anja's notes, and which Guy – and now he – would use with devastating effect. Ben was excited by the prospect. He wanted to stop and scribble the lines while they were still new in his head.

Ben saw the airport turnoff ahead – too late. He braked hard, threw the wheel over, felt the friction let go, then the sickening sideways whip as the car spun. He heard shots. His car was pointed back towards the turnoff road, Ben mashed the accelerator, his tyres whirled, gripped concrete. The black Mercedes, throwing gravel from the shoulder, shot by Ben's car. Ben saw a cruel face partly hidden by sunglasses and a fatter man in the back leaning, pointing a pistol over his shoulder. The Mercedes was swerving to block him, to force him to stop. At that moment, half a mile away, the tracking system locked on to the first car – the one apparently being chased – and while the man inside was trying to get a bead through his open window with the pistol aimed straight at Ben, the dual three-beam array of the F-19's pulsed electric-discharge Krypton-fluoride laser burped its terrible light streams. Pencil-thin, razor-straight bolts of lightning slashed across the morning, and the black Mercedes in front of Ben lofted as gently as if it were a handkerchief in a breeze. It disintegrated with the swiftness of a soufflé collapsing into little black clouds of metallic dust. Eerie pink-green shadows accentuated the jagged edges of the exploding cloud in relief. Two angular pieces spewed from the cloud, the iron-rigid knuckle of a car axle and a single broken human torso, each jerking end-over-end in divergent arcs propelled by the force of massive energy. Then the laser stopped. It had missed Ben, who slammed on his brakes wide-eyed and swallowed his gum. But all earthly traces of Senator Elton D. Osborne, his driver, his bodyguards and his limousine had been vapourized to smithereens.

The laser had left a gaping hole in the stout metal fence that surrounded the airport. Ben wasted no time and gunned the BMW swiftly across the grass and into the still-smoking opening. Thoughts of Guy's admonition to keep moving were with him as the tyres rumbled over the rough ground; the space was too narrow, jagged bits of hot wire mesh gashed out the right side of the car as Ben sped through. The car hurtled into a shuddering drift as Ben swerved away at a sharp angle, hoping to be out of the line of fire before the operator in the F-19 realized he'd zapped the wrong target. Chocked in its hardstand with the external electrical power cart alongside plugged in, its engines not running, the F-19 could not re-aim its fixed laser gun. In one hundred metres Ben would be safe; with a bump he drove up on to the inside perimeter road that circled the airport and pulled in directly behind an airline catering truck. Keeping his front bumper just inches from its tailgate, Ben slowly proceeded towards the main terminal complex.

Then as he passed the general aviation area, he saw it: a sleek Learjet parked apart. A fuel truck had just pulled away. Ben made a quick left, leaving the shelter of the catering truck, and raced across the tarmac to pull up next to the Lear. It was decorated with blue-and-green diagonal striping and the words CONTINENTAL EXPRESS MESSENGER. The pilot was leaning against one wing-tip fuel tank as Ben braked to a halt. Ben leaped from the BMW, shed the green overcoat which he piled into the back seat, grabbed Anja's notes and the blue report together with his shoulder bag and with a flushed expression turned to face the somewhat startled pilot.

'What was that?' the pilot asked, nodding towards the scene Ben just left.

'How does a blowout strike you?'

'It was louder than that,' the German pilot enunciated meticulously.

'It was all four tyres.' Ben's eyes carried a warning. 'I see you just took fuel.'

'I'm off to Copenhagen – '

'No you're not. I have urgent business for Paris.' Ben pulled a thick wad containing three kinds of currency from the recesses of his shoulder bag. 'How much does Continental Express charge per pound?'

The pilot, eyeing the money, started a quick mental calculation. 'You got a package?'

'Yes, I do.'

'How many pounds is it?'

'Two hundred and sixteen – with shoes.'

'You'll have to fill out a shipping label.'

'I'll slap it on my neck after we take off.'

'It'll cost you six marks a pound to Paris . . . plus a five-hundred-mark surcharge for schedule disruption.'

'Let's go.'

22

PARIS: 1000 G.M.T.: 0800 NEW YORK: 0400
LOS ANGELES: 0100
PLACE: VISTA PACIFIC HOTEL, LOS ANGELES
INTERNATIONAL AIRPORT

Guy, wearing a fishing hat and dark glasses, approached the hotel's front desk. An attractive woman, already bored with the midnight shift, appeared behind the counter and welcomed him.

'Yes sir?'

'I have a reservation.'

'Your name, sir?'

'Hector McCardle.' Guy met her mildly puzzled expression with an unflinching fisheye. She checked the indexed reservation ledger.

'It says here you have the governor's suite, Mr McCardle.'

Guy completed the registration card. 'That's right. Could you see if a Mr Anders has checked in yet?'

Her fingers flicked through the plastic tabs on the reservations roster. 'I see no record, sir.'

'Check under Air World crew.'

She rethumbed the ledger. 'He's flagged here as a late arrival. He's not in yet.'

'I'd like to leave him a note.'

The receptionist placed a pen and memo pad in front of him. Guy wrote: 'Guy, I got here early. I'm at the Santa Monica Plaza. Come to the parking lot. Don't look for me. I'll find you. Ben Reese.'

Guy sealed it in an envelope which the woman slipped into the slot marked 202. Guy figured the note would be read before sunup, and the Santa Monica Plaza parking lot would serve as a reasonable detour. Guy held up a valise. 'Do you think you could leave this in Mr Anders's room? He'll be looking for it and I'd prefer not to hang around for his arrival.'

'No problem,' said the receptionist.

That's good, he thought. Two detours.

Upstairs in the governor's lavish suite, Guy filled the oversized tub after shaking a generous amount of bubble bath from the complimentary toiletries displayed on the sink. He settled back, letting the luxurious suds envelop him, and closed his eyes. Eleven hours to go. Suddenly he was scrambling out, leaving a trail of soapy water across the living room carpet as he ran to turn up the TV volume. It was an unconfirmed report that Senator Elton Osborne had just been killed in an explosion in Germany.

Details were not yet available, said the comely woman on the TV screen, but she would be back as soon as they were.

Guy was agog. Did that mean Ben had murdered the senator? Or did it mean that Ben himself was also . . . or perhaps caught? Using the phone wouldn't be smart. He dried himself and fine-tuned the TV. It would be like waiting for the results of a biopsy.

Toby's expression was glazed when, an hour later, he arrived with two ALPA attorneys and stacks of envelopes, stick-on address labels and stapled press releases on ALPA letterhead explaining the 17-10 pilot stand-down. The cabdriver from the airport informed them that terrorists had dynamited Osborne's limousine in West Germany and that it had something to do with a group demanding an end to Germany's ties to NATO.

'Is there more than that?' Toby asked Guy. 'Has your courier got anything to do with this?'

'Why ask me? Watch the set.'

'Because I've got a gnawing sensation.'

'That's your peptic ulcer.'

'Your operational evidence is German, isn't it? It comes from Germany, doesn't it?'

'Why the hostility, Toby?'

Toby shuffled awkwardly. 'Because I'm terrified. I have a phobia about prisons. I also come from a long established line of chickens.'

'I sent you a Xerox of a cable that was sent to Aspinwall.'

'I received it.'

'Well, you must have had it verified or you wouldn't be here.'

'I'm satisfied you were smeared.' Toby was abashed. 'But . . . if this involves murder, you lose ALPA.'

'You're not dealing with murderers.' Guy said it with conviction but it was only a hope. 'Toby, the report – if it

584

gets here – originates in Germany. It's going to be stolen property.' He held up his hand. 'No, and don't even think of laying a morality trip on me about that.' He opened a bottle of single malt whiskey and poured Toby a drink. 'We're co-conspirators at this point,' Guy continued. 'Isn't that right?' He grinned at the lawyers. 'Go on, tell him the law!'

'If the document isn't here by tomorrow . . .' Toby coaxed.

'You'll just be another one of Matt's happy well-wishers and I'll be on my own again.'

'There's something else I want understood,' said Toby. 'If the document doesn't appear and you abort the takeoff to underscore your beef, that's going to come as news to us. Nothing gets put in the mail, no telegrams go out, and you'll be terminal.'

'And be put in bad standing.'

'Don't make light of it.'

'There's one final matter,' said one of the lawyers. 'How will we know the report is authentic?'

'The way you test that is when Toby gets it, let him take a walk with it by himself in the open.'

The point wasn't pursued and the lawyer confirmed that the private security people Guy had recommended had been hired and were already in their rooms.

Guy toasted Toby. 'You snuggle up real close to them,' he advised.

The lawyers opened their attaché cases and settled down to brief Guy on ALPA policy and on contingencies that might arise in a give-and-take with the press. Toby removed his tie and rolled up his sleeves to stuff envelopes. The 'America Tonight' show was interrupted by an update on the explosion in Cologne. A young man with a British accent speaking from the Köln-Bonn airport confirmed that it was Osborne who had been killed. 'The explosion of the senator's vehicle,' said the reporter, 'was unusually intense and is under investigation by German pyrotechnics experts.'

No mention whatever was made of Ben Reese.

PARIS: 1045   G.M.T.: 0845   NEW YORK: 0445
LOS ANGELES: 0145
PLACE: CHARLES DE GAULLE AIRPORT, PARIS

From his shoulder bag, which had been shoved in partly behind the co-pilot's seat, Ben Reese pulled a creased schedule and flipped through it. Air France Flight One, the supersonic Concorde to New York, was due to take off at eleven. It was already past ten-thirty.

'You gotta put this jet scooter on the ground in less than fifteen minutes,' he told the pilot.

The young German glanced sideways, obviously irritated with Ben.

Air Traffic Control issued orders for them to slow down.

The pilot grunted.

Ben grabbed the hand-held microphone and barked into it, 'We'd like to keep our speed up. We have a tight connection to make.'

ATC relented. 'Keep your speed up for twenty more miles.'

The pilot threw Ben a scowl. 'Tighten your seat belt, then.'

'Give me Air France's operations frequency,' Ben snapped into the radio.

An Air France flight ahead of them called back with the freq.

'Which is your number two radio?' Ben queried. The pilot pointed and punched the appropriate transmit selector. Ben twirled in the channel and called Air France ops.

'We have a priority VIP passenger for Air France Flight One arriving in a Learjet,' he announced. 'Confirm a booking for Rieser, party of one. And we'd like the OK to taxi alongside to expedite the connection. We'll expect you to set that up for us.'

'We'll do our best,' came the response. 'But you'll have to meet our schedule, m'sieur.'

Ben checked the clock on the instrument panel and swore. 'Keep your pedal to the metal,' he urged the pilot.

ATC slowed the Lear down to sequence it behind a Singapore jumbo and two other transports, all landing on runway 27. Ben swore again. Passengers would already be boarding the Concorde. 'Ask them if we can expedite by using the other runway,' he growled impatiently. '*Ask them.*'

The German called the controller. 'We'd be grateful if you would give us runway twenty-eight. We're running a little late.'

'Unable. Departure traffic.' Like why did you bother.

'Shit.' Ben retracted, gripping the armrests, watching the tiny white hands on the round black clock before him crawl.

They touched down at last, turned off at taxiway Sierra, belting along southward. Ben caught sight of the Concorde nuzzled up to its terminal. It hadn't started engines yet.

'Head for that!' He punched the pilot's shoulder, urging him on. There was no time to think of where he was, or what had happened, how long the day had been, how much longer there was yet to go. He gripped his shoulder bag, a shadow flashed by; he glanced up. The Learjet crunched to a halt under the nose of the Concorde. Gendarmes surrounded the interloper. With an agility that surprised the Lear pilot, Ben sprang from the co-pilot's seat and, grasping his shoulder bag, he headed aft, crouched as if to tumble like a parachutist through the

587

open cabin door. The Lear pilot next saw him waving his ticket under the Concorde cockpit. The only access on board was through the long jetway tunnel which extended to its side two stories above. Two gendarmes apprehended Ben on the open ramp, pinning his arms, and seemed on the point of marching him away. A hand was signalling thumbs up through one of the Concorde cockpit windows far above. Ben motioned agitatedly with his head. Finally one of the gendarmes looked up. They released him, stepped back and bowed as he raced through a nearby door towards a flight of stairs that led up to the boarding area. Last-minute passengers had already embarked and Ben didn't stop running until he was through the main cabin door, which shut behind him.

Air France Flight One was less than ten minutes late when it lurched under the prod of the push-back tug. It would be in New York before 9 A.M., New York time. Ben's mind was already leapfrogging to the connection with the 10 A.M. 747 to the coast, which in turn, barring en route delay, would have him in Los Angeles just after noon – only two hours later (on the local clock) than now!

The sleek delta didn't waste time traversing the distance to the runway end. Spindly, spiky like a thin old maid tiptoeing, it wheeled into position. Pilots and passengers in the two planes next in line saw four lavender plumes erupt from yawning tailpipes, heard the noise rise, watched as it gathered speed to achieve rare grace, rotate sharply and pierce the haze, a slender white arrowhead riding its thunder into the sky.

The coast of France slid behind just moments later and all of England, an afterthought in the widening blue, fell away. Soon the cabin gauge flickered past Mach 2. Ben sat back, sipped his wine and wondered about Guy.

* * *

PLACE: VISTA PACIFIC HOTEL, LOS ANGELES
INTERNATIONAL AIRPORT

The mess in Guy's hotel room had been straightened, the
envelopes to be mailed were arranged in neat stacks and
rehearsals as to how to deal with the press were completed. The lawyers had been specific with respect to the
thin line between allegation and libel and had left with
Toby an hour before. Now Guy was in bed, struggling to
slow the gyrations inside his head. He tried to focus on
calmer things, on the serenity of the bay shack, but he
could no longer conjure it. Burrowing his head into a
cooler part of the pillow, he concentrated on the pinpoints
of light rippling down the insides of his eyelids . . . but
anticipation of what lay ahead broke his attention. He
couldn't quell the growing anxiety that no word whatever
had come from Ben. He projected ahead and visualized
aborting the takeoff; it would be mutinous and punish-
able. It would also produce full tabloid headlines and give
him his second swipe at Buttress in public, allow him to
proclaim the unanswered questions he'd told Moss to put
to Zakowski, but he wasn't ready yet to settle for that.

He turned on the bedside light, jerked the phone on to
the blanket, dialled New York. No answer. It occurred to
his fogged brain that it would be past 10 A.M. in New York
– no telling where anyone was. He hung up and wondered
about the concept of mutiny. It was a second choice, a
backup strategy, and as far as he could divine, while Ben
might not make it, there was no way the second strategy
could fail. He thought about Osborne . . . and he wondered whether he might have accorded Ben too many
youthful qualities. Somehow he'd always pictured Ben as
indefatigable and, although frequently blistered, also in-
vulnerable. At first buoyed by Ben's departure from JFK,

589

always confident in Ben's ability to hold up his end of the double play, Guy now had to consider whether he might have done Ben a disservice. Sleep, like a seductive drug, pulled him down and he lay back. His mind spun, unravelling; the tension, the barriers to stray thoughts disintegrating. He thought of Ben again and, as sleep was about to shut him off, he grew alarmed to realize he had come to fear for Ben's life.

PARIS: 1600   G.M.T.: 1400   NEW YORK: 1000
LOS ANGELES: 0700
PLACE: JOHN F. KENNEDY INTERNATIONAL
AIRPORT, NEW YORK

At JFK Ben saw the headline announcing Osborne's death on the newspaper held by an airport employee and knew he had to call Guy. But there was no time. Air traffic backed up by a night of rain had delayed the Concorde's arrival and there were only minutes left to make his connection. He was jogging when he passed the wall phone outside the combined customs and immigration hall – it seemed to reach out and beckon – but he kept on moving. Barely aware of the throngs surging in the opposite direction, Ben opened the distance between himself and the cluster of passengers who had disembarked with him. Casually he checked over his shoulder and was shocked to see a man shoving his way through the pack of amblers as if intent on pursuing him. Ben tightened his grip on the shoulder bag and broke into a dead run. His shoes slid on the polished surface; he moved next to the wall to let his fingers brush against it for balance. The feet behind him increased their tempo; Ben tried to match their pace but couldn't. He picked out the spot in the hall ahead where his life would end. There would be the jab of a knife or the dart at the end of an umbrella slipped into his ribs, or the plop of a silencer, a bullet smashing his spine; and his shoulder bag gone before anyone knew why he was sprawled on the floor.

The smack of shoes rose up and came alongside. Ben contracted and slowed. The running figure passed him, racing towards the gate of a flight that had just closed. Ben wobbled to a stop, his scalp prickling with sweat, his lungs sucking to slow his heart. He wiped his face and crossed to an overhead TV display of arrivals and departures. He stepped on to the moving rubber walkway that led part way to his departure gate, walking slowly like a horse cooling down after the Preakness. The far end was blocked by a group of businessmen in well-tailored greys and pinstripes. They stood before a broad window and behind them Ben could see his California-bound 747. But something was wrong. He squinted to shake the illusion – no, it wasn't illusion: a squat tug was pushing the flight away from the gate.

Ben knew he was now in hip-deep. He examined the unruffled senior members of the power elite before him. No observer would mistake Ben for them, but he could speak their language fluently.

'Gentlemen,' he purred from the back of his throat, 'how are you this morning?' He was feeding back the meaningless warble of executive words which, like remote military formalities, inspired unspoken fuck-yous from enlisted men.

The assembled murmured their salutations through curt smiles, let Ben pass, and continued their sonorous communion.

Ben loped away from them; he had no direction in mind but he couldn't remain still. His running was no longer as beautiful to watch as it once had been, one leg hitched as he ran and it bothered him. He spoke to God. 'If you're good to me now, I'll explain the candle in Cologne.' Instantly ashamed, he cancelled the deal and became aware again of the pinstripers behind him and of their counterparts at Buttress. 'Business is war,' he would now write of their brotherhood. 'It has generals and chiefs of staff and NCOs, soldiers and spies and turncoats. It has divisions and task forces and blind loyalties. It has fuck-ups, it has executions. It has no pity.'

The boarding gate directly ahead of him was marked DALLAS–FORT WORTH/LOS ANGELES. Passengers were already boarding. Ben reopened his conversation with God. The flight was due to arrive at Los Angeles forty minutes after the nonstop. And in a way it was an improvement. No one would figure him taking the long way around.

PARIS: 1800   G.M.T.: 1600   NEW YORK: 1200
LOS ANGELES: 0900
PLACE: LOS ANGELES INTERNATIONAL AIRPORT

Guy slipped a coin into the turnstile to the observation deck. He'd managed to sleep for an hour. When he awoke, he put on a T-shirt and dungarees, repacked his uniform, left by way of the fire stairs and took all the night's paper work to a desk safe at ALPA's office in Los Angeles. Toby had promised to meet him for breakfast but when Guy called his room, the best he could get was a weary grunt and the suggestion that Guy go on ahead. Now, as he fingered the key to the safe, he watched planes take form, growing from distant black specks approaching LA's parallel runways from the west. He pictured Benny seated inside one of those dots, looking down on the blue Pacific below, anticipating the touchdown. But it was still too early for the day's arrivals from Europe or the East Coast. Guy stared at the sky and took comfort from the fact that Ben's name had not been connected with Osborne's death.

On the south side of the terminal wing below him stood the Big Season inaugural 17-10, polished and gleaming, its speed striping brightening as the sun appeared briefly through a break in the overcast. It sat well back from the terminal building in resplendent isolation befitting the importance of the occasion. Large bleachers more than a dozen levels high had been erected on the open ramp on either side of the aeroplane, facing its nose, lending the area around it the bravura quality of a football game. Orchestra members had already taken their seats behind tiered music stands. Red-and-white bunting fluttered. Ten-foot-wide red carpets connected the terminal building to the circle of festivities; they lay across the grimy ramp. London-bound passengers would be warmly greeted in the waiting lounge inside; when called, they'd follow the red carpet downstairs and outside, across the ramp, in front of the bleachers, to the boarding steps. Despite efforts to rid the concrete of grease and oil, wet black stains were already soiling the red carpet's edge.

Two technicians were stapling microphone cables to the wood bleacher frame, leading them back to a bank of amplifiers. Behind them two TV cameras stood on their wheeled tripods under plastic shrouds. The air was clammy; the iron-grey edge of the front that had pin-wheeled the area hung in livid sacks to the north.

A frazzled female reporter startled him on his way down the stairs.

'Is there a Guy Anders up there?' She looked puzzled as though following an uncertain lead.

'Anders?'

'Yes.'

'He just left,' Guy countered.

'Aw, shoot,' said the woman.

On his way back to ALPA's office, he stepped into the makeshift newsroom and picked up an Air World press kit. The honoured guests were listed as:

G. Hollis Wright and Mrs Wright, Chairman and Chief Executive Officer, Buttress Aerospace Corporation
The Secretary of Transportation
Senator and Mrs Elton Osborne
The Deputy Secretary of State
The Deputy Secretary of the Interior
Nicholas Muskgrave, Administrator of the Federal Aviation Administration
The Chairman of the Civil Aeronautics Board
The Mayor of Los Angeles
Fenton Riddick, Executive Vice-President and General Manager, Commercial Transport Division, Buttress Aerospace Corporation
S. Helmsdorf and Mrs Helmsdorf, Director, Flight Operations, Buttress Aerospace Corporation
The Curator of the National Air and Space Museum

The captain of the inaugural flight to London was listed as Roger Beaucamp.

PARIS: 2015   G.M.T.: 1815   NEW YORK: 1415
LOS ANGELES: 1115
PLACE: ABOARD TRANS-GLOBE EN ROUTE
DALLAS–FORT WORTH TO LOS ANGELES

Ben watched as the flight attendant slotted dirty trays into the narrow metal trolley, mashing napkins and plastic cups into the open spaces and trundling the cart into the dumbwaiter to send it below. He held a drink in one hand; the other rested on his shoulder bag containing the German report. In his fantasy he visualized a twenty-year-old hostess massaging his temples with long cool fingers for the rest of the flight. But this one looked more like the father of the girl he had in mind. He was well aware his thoughts were sexist, and although he didn't mean them that way, they derived from his staunch and undisputed male instinct which no amount of consciousness-raising or

594

political campaigns (with which he was heartily in sympathy) would ever alter.

Ben pulled the fold-down jump seat away from the wall. 'Mind if I sit here?' He closed the curtain.

'It's against the rules,' the woman informed him.

'Most things that are good for people are against somebody's rules. You sit down too. Go ahead. Where I can see you.'

She didn't, but regarded him pleasantly.

'We should have met in high school,' Ben said to her with a trace of genuine sadness. 'Just think how much fun we could have had together by now.'

'Would you like me to freshen that drink?'

'No, that's all right.'

She was a nice person, Ben decided. His fantasy expanded. They'd go well together in a retirement home, which, if he didn't get to Los Angeles on time, would be his next address anyway. 'How far out are we?'

The woman leaned towards the window hoping for a glimpse of the Sierras. 'There's a lot of bad weather below. Hard to tell.'

'You have any influence with the cockpit?'

'It depends on what needs influencing.'

'I'd like a current ETA.'

'We haven't really slowed down yet. So the captain's first estimate should hold up.'

'What about detours? Seems like we've been making a few detours.' Ben took a deep swallow from his glass. 'Under what conditions can your boss land in front of the traffic ahead of him?'

'Medical emergency.'

Ben thought it over. Perhaps a temporary coronary would be just the thing. What the hell, with the on-board food being what it was, who would indict him for getting an attack that would later turn out to be a case of heartburn? 'I'd appreciate it if you would tell your captain to stop playing with himself up there and crank it up a notch.'

'You feeling ill?'

'You're looking at a desperate man. My watch says there's forty-five minutes to go. The point I'm making is it can't be *more* than that.'

At that moment the jumbo was jolted by some particularly rough air. Almost simultaneously the chime indicated the FASTEN SEAT BELTS sign was lit and the PA crackled with the captain's voice.

'Ladies and gentlemen, I'd appreciate it if you would return to your seats and fasten your seat belts. We have to tiptoe through some lousy weather here and we don't want anyone getting a bump on the head.'

'That means you,' said the attendant to Ben.

Ben stood up to return to his seat. The captain came on again. 'Flight service, suspend your service and take your seats.'

'I wouldn't lay any bets on our on-time arrival,' said the stew sympathetically.

Ben heard the rain lash the ship and thought about what a coronary looked like.

PARIS: 2030   G.M.T.: 1830   NEW YORK: 1430
LOS ANGELES: 1130
PLACE: ABOARD TRANS-GLOBE 747 EN ROUTE
NEW YORK TO LOS ANGELES

The young flight attendant stowed the screen on which the economy-class movie had been shown and made her way to one of the toilets in the aft section. She knocked on the door, which had been shut for some time, and a little boy wearing Junior Pilot Wings came out. The flight attendant reached through the galley curtains for a soft drink and handed it to him as she returned him to his seat. Jamie clambered on to his chair, careful not to awaken the sleeping figure next to him. The flight attendant straightened him out and fastened his seat belt. The click of the metal clasp woke Anja. She adjusted herself, smiled at him, and went back to sleep.

PARIS: 2030   G.M.T.: 1830   NEW YORK: 1430
LOS ANGELES: 1130
PLACE: AIR WORLD DISPATCH OFFICE, LOS ANGELES INTERNATIONAL AIRPORT

The TWA dispatcher was polite but not helpful. Over the phone he gave Guy the ETAs of all inbounds from Europe and New York, but none of the flights would arrive early enough. Guy thanked him and punched the internal number for the United dispatcher. He was using the wall phone with the five-digit airport phone numbers. Same story: no inbounds – at least none that would have Ben in Los Angeles on time. Guy's list was getting short. He'd been frustrated to learn the nonstop Germany–Los Angeles flights were all late-afternoon arrivals. So he reckoned Ben would have to come via New York. Yet if he'd done that, why had there been no call? Guy fought a cold feeling of being abandoned as he dialled Trans-Globe.

They had one inbound from New York, a nonstop due to land at noon. Flight plan ETA was 1914Z – quarter past noon local time. Airline Flight Control couldn't come up with passenger names. Ben was probably travelling incognito anyway.

'We have one other inbound coming from Dallas–Fort Worth which originated in New York,' said the dispatcher helpfully.

'Did it connect with an arrival from Europe?'

'Not with us, but there are other possibilities. Gotta be at least seven or eight connections . . .'

'Thanks anyway,' said Guy and hung up. It was now or never, that one nonstop or nothing. He wondered about Ben and considered again the remarkable prospect of actually being out on his own . . .

His own Air World dispatcher was trying to say something.

'What?'

'Weather here.' The man seemed very insistent, barging through Guy's distraction. 'We got two sigmets already on this cold front and the third one's just coming off the machine.'

Guy stared at the strips of teletype paper. Slowly the message registered.

'A line of buildups along the coast, tops to flight level 390.'

Here by the dispatch office counter Guy was again in his former world of the blue serge and gold braid, black humour and red faces, crew members lounging nearby, paper cups and cellophane from used cigarette packs scattered around, men talking of mundane matters, rumours, the latest irreverent graffiti decorating the bulletin boards, or just staring ahead with that same blank stare forty-one thousand feet pastes on to a man's face, when the eyes automatically focus to a distance of three feet simply because there's nothing to adjust to outside the cockpit window. Captain Roger Beaucamp walked through the pilots' lounge door and stepped past a group of pilots straight up to the counter. A few clapped him on the shoulder, wishing him well on the Big Season inaugural. He peered at Guy but didn't smile. Neither had seen the other since their trip to London together. Picking up the flight folder from its clipboard, Beaucamp appeared not to want to speak.

Guy threw one of his kid grins. Beaucamp, groping for a certain accurate insight, suspected it as false.

'Looks like you stepped in shit again, Roger,' said Guy.

'So I heard – from the chief pilot. Can't say it pleases me.'

'Maybe we'll have better luck this time. There's an old saying: time mellows all things.'

'I was after a perfect flight today, Anders, but I guess that won't be possible.'

'What a pity, Roger. Only perfect flight I ever heard about was one a while back, when the engineer got laid, the first officer got a landing – and the captain had a bowel movement.' Leaving Beaucamp walled off, Guy walked out.

Beaucamp continued shuffling through the computer printout flight plan and weather folder as if to reconfirm his own total control. The chief pilot had personally selected Beaucamp to fly the Big Season inaugural, a flight he might have taken himself; but it was the bouquet, the small gesture with which Beaucamp was bought off and even allowed to preen for a moment, and now the coveted wreath around the star on his wings was forgotten as he was left alone at the counter.

PARIS: 2115   G.M.T.: 1915   NEW YORK: 1515
LOS ANGELES: 1215
PLACE: LOS ANGELES INTERNATIONAL AIR-
PORT

The music had begun outdoors promptly at noon; it was the indomitable sound of the big band – solid with a heavy bass beat and featuring superb brass. They'd done 'New York' and 'California' and were giving 'My Kind of Town' its second big ride and it was gooseflesh stuff. The TV cameras were lit, technicians were sorting the cables and speaking into their headsets. Arriving guests were assembling on the red carpet, mingling in front of the bleachers; the mayor of Los Angeles, surrounded by a tight entourage, was trying again to respond to a woman holding a microphone but the trumpets and trombones blared their harmony and drowned him out a second time. The mayor threw back her head and laughed. Other dignitaries were climbing the reviewing bleachers, matching numbered invitations against numerical designations fastened to red-velvet pillows which dotted the stands. Everyone had BIG SEASON buttons like campaign buttons on their lapels and dresses, and Big Season baggage stickers were slapped on to attaché cases.

Guy, now in uniform, surveyed the gathering crowd from a ground-floor doorway, spotted Blasingame and Helmsdorf with their wives and saw Matt making his way towards Toby, who was barely visible behind half a dozen bodyguards.

There was one sombre note. The American flag atop the arrivals building was flying at half mast.

Matt squeezed Toby's arm and put his mouth next to Toby's ear. 'Just want to tell you it's awful nice of you ALPA boys to show up!' he shouted. 'You're a pain in the ass every three years and sometimes in between too, but we couldn't jerk all that iron around without you people!' He winked at the men standing close to Toby. 'I guess we'd all be in the slaughterhouse without ALPA! Make sure you get yourselves some champagne! And there's plenty of lobster back there, too! Don't pass that up!'

Matt made his way back into the building, took the stairs two at a time and waded into the crowded lounge. Uniformed Air World flight attendants with flowers in their hair passed through the passengers with trays of champagne in real crystal glasses. 'No paper cups today!' Matt chortled, roaming through the crowd, shaking hands, clasping shoulders, doling out souvenirs. 'Our girls have plenty more! Take some home for the kids, help yourselves!'

Outside, Guy made his way next to Toby. The two

attorneys, slightly uncomfortable in the glare of hoopla, were standing nearby, holding stuffed attaché cases.

'How do I play this?' Toby was pale.

'Just keep your eye out for Reese.'

'They're running late here already – '

'There's a lot of champagne to get through. And Matt still has to anoint the aeroplane.'

Guy worked his way back inside to see if he couldn't get another ETA on the next direct inbound from New York but was stopped by a wall of people. Waiters holding trays of food manoeuvred through the tightly packed lounge. Several London-bound passengers were singing along with the richly orchestrated medley that penetrated the walls from just outside. The Big Season was being heralded in a hundred ways. Matt spotted Guy through the crowd, reached him and took his hand as he would that of a young son. Guy wished Matt had remained in the finance world because underneath he was quite a decent guy, but Matt had become an unsuspecting passenger himself – and by his own hand. Guy could think of no way to save him and he regretted that.

'Come with me a minute,' Matt said. 'You still got plenty of time.' He led Guy to an assortment of press people cleaning off a tray of hors d'oeuvres. 'Fellows,' he announced, 'you been on my tail for weeks. Many nights I had to go to sleep reading your bum reviews. But I want you to know we got our team back together. This young man here has put his act back together and thinks enough of our 17-10 to come back on the line and fly our inaugural.' He beamed at Anders. 'Am I putting words in your mouth?'

Guy took his hand away and, with a broad grin, responded, 'Did you people ever hear of an employee who would contradict what his boss had to say?'

One reporter didn't smile. 'Where does the European bribe figure, Matt?'

'It was a hoax. We've got the proof.'

Another reporter pulled a pen from his shirt. 'Would you be inclined on this festive occasion to give a struggling writer a break?'

'Come see me at the hotel.' Matt winked at the group and turned to Anders. 'Go on out there and find your key and wind her up. And call me when you get to Heathrow!'

As he left, Guy heard Matt ask, 'Has anybody here seen Hollis Wright?'

Guy ran down the hall to a monitor lit with departures and arrivals. The nonstop flight from New York was identified as 'delayed'. The flight from Germany to California wouldn't be in for another two hours. If the German report was to ride the crest of this one-and-only high-visibility media wave and accord Guy's plan the indisputable national reverberations it needed, it must arrive on the nonstop flight. Otherwise the outcome might be in doubt for months, possibly never to be resolved.

Guy saw Fenton Riddick with a woman whom he took to be his wife coming towards him.

'Hey, Riddick!' he called before reaching him. 'Big day for Buttress, huh? Say, I've been meaning to ask you something.'

Riddick tried to push on past but his wife restrained him.

'Whatever happened to Natalie Mason?'

Riddick's features compressed. 'Maybe we ought to get together and talk about it.' The words were laced with threat.

'Buzz, you know, I'm going to follow up on that.' Guy nodded to the woman and returned outdoors to single Toby out one more time.

'I guess you're on your own again.' Toby said it with some reluctance.

'There's a flight coming in from New York in twenty or thirty minutes – maybe less. If Reese is not on that, go home. Meanwhile, stay put. I've got to get out to the plane.

602

If he shows, you're going to have to do the press thing instead of me.'

'Shit, Guy,' Toby commiserated.

'Well, my friend, when was the last time we had a mutiny in the cockpit?'

'Jesus.' Toby swallowed hard.

'Yeah, I know, but that's where the line of scrimmage is. So long as they don't put the cuffs on me till I've had a chance to talk.'

Guy saw that Roger Beaucamp was already seated in the cockpit and he headed for the aeroplane.

More passengers accumulated to join the jovial throng in the departure lounge until people no longer could find any place to stand. Matt was trying to keep the party alive, confident he'd created an atmosphere identical to that which accompanied, in a more genteel era, the launching of a proud ocean liner. The public address crackled. There was an instant collective polarity towards red-carpeted stairway doors. Then a pause. Matt Aspinwall had stepped to the check-in desk to offer an official welcome from the chairman of the board. Flashbulbs popped. Like a circus barker, Matt bawled, 'C'mon up and shake hands with a happy man.' His exuberance boomed across the lounge. He shook hands with the first passenger in line, a rangy westerner, and into the PA said, 'Welcome, welcome to the Big Season! First-class passengers please use doorway A at your convenience. Those seated in economy rows thirty-eight to fifty-seven should now also go on board. Use doorway B. Goodbye now, we love you all! Have a nice flight.' He handed the mike back to the beaming traffic agent.

Matt was at centre stage. He was at the very threshold of success, his throat about to burst.

Passengers filed across the open ramp and up the red-carpeted boarding steps, through the aeroplane's metal doors, as impregnable as the hatches of a bank vault.

Smiling cabin attendants in their new space-motif uniforms offered their greeting from each open cabin door. The soft fragrance of perfume and strains of upbeat music filled the air.

Leaning to peer across the passenger by the window, Ben Reese could just make out enough of the view below to recognize Santa Monica and Santa Barbara on the coast, barely perceivable through the milky skein that choked the LA basin. The flight attendants had allowed him to take a first-class seat next to the door so he could be the first to leave.

Guy arranged the straps and armrests and climbed into the right-hand cockpit seat. He wedged his flight bag in next to the cockpit wall, adjusted the seat position by working the electric controls next to his left thigh, horizontal, vertical, recline and tilt. He attached his earpiece to the light-weight headset, checked the cords and jacks, and when he had established interphone communication, pulled the quick-don oxygen mask from its overhead receptacle.

'Got a sanitary towel handy?' he said over his shoulder to the engineer.

The engineer handed up a packet from which Guy removed a small paper towel saturated with disinfectant; with it he wiped out his oxygen mask. He pulled the mask over his head, checked oxygen pressure and flow and communications through the mask mike. He restored the mask into its ready position above his head. So far he had not glanced over at Beaucamp. Neither man had spoken to the other. Through his front window Guy could see the throngs of well-wishers and, above them, massifs of distant cloud. The engineer behind them grew eager to break the tension which had grown palpable in the cockpit.

'Fellow on a golf course had his pockets stuffed,' he began haltingly to the backs of the two men seated just ahead of him. 'This chick, she sees it and says to him, "What's that in your pocket?" "Golf balls," he says. "Oh, yeah, is that anything like tennis elbow?"'

It fell flat. The engineer turned disconsolately towards his panel and settled back for a very long flight.

Guy couldn't figure it. The nonstop New York–LA inbound was only a quarter hour out. Yet no calls, no messages for what seemed like a week. Ben knew the schedule and the importance of it. This wasn't like him. *For Christ's sake, Reese!* Guy yelled it in his head.

The purser barged into the cockpit and addressed the flight engineer. 'Call Commissary, would you, we're short three vegetarian meals.' Guy sensed a reprieve, a slim chance for Ben still to arrive.

But Beaucamp peremptorily dashed the possibility. 'There's no time. Talk to that new stew with the big boobs. Maybe she'll let 'em feed on those instead.'

The purser drew back at Beaucamp's distinct lack of grace.

'Let's get this show on the road,' the captain shot with finality.

A man in grimy blue coveralls followed the purser into the cockpit. He held a smudged pink chemical-copy paper towards the flight engineer. 'Fuel sheet, Chief.' The engineer scanned the figures scrawled there, checked them against the eight fuel gauges and weight-and-balance form in the folder on his desk. He pencilled an initial on the pink sheet and the grimy man took off.

Green lights blinked on the overhead panel. 'Inertial navigation system's aligned,' the engineer said offhandedly.

'Inertials to nav,' said Beaucamp, reaching up with effort to twist three rotary selector knobs. Somewhere in the dark hold beneath them the nav computers hummed.

605

Guy called ground control, which issued clearances to start engines and push back. As he did so, he leaned forward, scanning the crowd, hoping to lock on to Ben's sudden appearance. But the only people visible were those waving as the band struck up with 'The Olympiad'. Guy shut his mind to what might have been.

A click in the headphones. The ground man three stories below had plugged his phone cord into the receptacle jack on the massive nosewheel trunnion. 'Ground to cockpit, how do you read?'

'Hello, Ground,' said Beaucamp, 'number four A and B hydraulic pumps are off, interconnects closed, clear to push.' The captain was acknowledging that nosewheel steering was not powered, a condition which could have disastrous consequences during pushback. The giant tow bar, thick as a thigh and made from solid steel, could be snapped like a matchstick. Men had been killed by such careless mistakes.

'We're ready for start,' said the ground man, confirming that the acreage to the rear of the 17-10 was vacant. Once running, the huge jet engines could topple aeroplanes and small structures.

'We have start clearance from the tower,' confirmed Guy.

'Turn one,' said Beaucamp.

Guy saw Matt Aspinwall standing by a music stand, a microphone in his hand, speaking to the assembled guests.

The engineer twisted the start switch. The first of four giant turbines began to spin with a shuddering growl, at first reluctant, but which grew quickly to a deep-bellied whine. Beaucamp moved the fuel lever on the throttle pedestal. 'Fuel flow normal. Light up.' The 17-10 lurched as the gruff pushback tug laboured. The aeroplane rolled backwards, away from the terminal.

'Twenty per cent,' intoned the engineer. 'Thirty per cent. Forty per cent.' The engine accelerated. Beaucamp watched the rise of exhaust-gas temperature, alert for any sudden abnormal jump. 'Release. Normal start. Turn two.'

'Parking brake set, Chief,' commanded the man by the nosewheel outside.

'Brakes set.'

The tug unhitched. All four engines were running.

'Why don't you get taxi clearance?' queried Beaucamp impatiently.

'Air World One, taxi,' radioed Guy.

'Follow the Clipper 747 right to left, taxi to runway two five left,' the electronic voice responded.

'Taxi checklist,' muttered Beaucamp. They were under way.

Ben raced across the parking lot separating the two main terminal complexes. His flight from New York and Dallas–Fort Worth had deposited him about as far as it was possible to be from the Air World departure area. Fleeting memories of Jasovak intruded as he ran under the arches supporting the elevated restaurant. He gripped the German report, dodging cars as he ran through two red lights. Overhead a 747 which had just taken off moaned.

Ben caught up to the long line shuffling through passenger security, cut to the front and fished out his press card. It cut no mustard. One of the waiting passengers let him break in line, and for the first time since he'd left Cologne he let the shoulder bag containing the report out of his sight as it went through the X-ray screening device. Ben stepped quickly through the metal detector to retrieve it but was stopped by the warning tone. He emptied his pockets, handing keys and change to an attendant, and stepped through again. Clean. Stuffing keys and spilling change, he grabbed the shoulder bag from the conveyor belt and bolted away, feeling for the shape of the report. Toppling an ashtray and scattering luggage, he barged through corridors until he came to the crowded Air World departure lounge. People fell out of his way as he double-timed towards the staircase leading outdoors on to the apron. He flew down the carpeted steps, touching only two of them before he hit the landing, and raced past a security guard. Outside he was confronted with the bunting-draped bleachers; all he could see for the moment was a cobweb of crisscross frames and feet. Cheers arose from the people just above him and blended with the triumphant notes of 'The Olympiad'; rising above it all was the growing whine of jet engines. Ben shook the guard off with his press pass, stepped around the bleachers and found himself facing the empennage of the inaugural 17-10 a hundred yards away, its rudders flopping stiffly back and forth.

'Oh, Lord – oh no . . .' For the first time since he'd been a kid, Ben felt tears blot his view. 'Oh, shit . . .'

He ran absently past Toby, directly in front of the bleachers, his leg beginning to hitch, past the august assembly of dignitaries as the 17-10 bellowed to accelerate along the taxiway. Eyes snapped away from the receding aeroplane to the lone crumpled man out in front. Ben headed for Toby, whose dark suit lent him the aspect of a mortician against the surfeit of flowered shirts and dresses. He felt a gust of jet wash blow against him.

The 17-10 was given clearance to line up and hold. Beaucamp taxied on to the broad runway.

'Air World One, cleared for takeoff.'

Beaucamp advanced the four throttles. The massive turbines growled. Slowly, against the inertia of its raw weight, its four hundred eighteen passengers and baggage, its 140 tons of fuel, the massive jumbo began to move. Guy's airspeed needle quivered nervously once, then came off the peg and began to crawl stiffly around the dial. Beaucamp's left hand was on the nosewheel steering tiller, his right resting lightly on the throttles as the engineer, leaning forward between the two pilots, made his last fine adjustments of power. Time languished; speed gathered with effort. The 17-10 trundled along its three miles of runway, seemingly as far removed from flight as a mountain of lead.

'Eighty knots.'

Beaucamp released the nosewheel tiller – at this speed the rudders were effective – and took the yoke with his left hand. Second by second more speed was added. The turbines screamed in unison. Centre-line stripes were rushing at them. But the soaring grace of flight still seemed interminable miles ahead.

The airspeed needle slowly crept past 100 knots; 110; 120. A faraway hint of fleetness manifested itself. The controls were alive. 130. The 17-10 was racing towards the midway point, its fourteen fat tyres whirling in frenzied circles, bulging under the awesome dead weight of three quarters of a million pounds. 140. Still twenty knots below V_1.

Then Guy acted. With the abrupt suddenness of a cannon shot he reached over and slapped the throttles closed underneath Beaucamp's hand. *'Abort the takeoff!'* he hollered.

Beaucamp had been trained for years to react by raising his feet to the tops of the rudder pedals to mash down the toe brakes, at the same time yanking the lift spoiler lever to its 'extended' position. For when any cockpit crew member said 'Abort', it meant he'd observed something seriously wrong, something the others might have missed but which affected the integrity of the ship; it meant they were not fit to fly.

As in the simulator rides he'd busted, Beaucamp did not react as prescribed. He reacted viscerally to Anders, to this fresh intrusion. His right arm shot out, slamming Guy's head sideways against the steel post of the starboard window. Almost simultaneously Beaucamp shoved the throttles full forward. With tortured screams of protest the massive turbines slam-accelerated to well past 105 per cent. Airspeed caught up, surged past V_1, touched V_R. Beaucamp pulled back roughly on his yoke. The 17-10 reared back, its landing gear legs extending – shuddered – and hauled itself ponderously into the sky.

'*Gear up!*' Beaucamp yelled.

The end of the runway, the far approach lights on their iron-rail stanchions, flashed underneath.

Guy slumped in a half stupor, dreaming of his first flight, a fourteen-year-old boy in a Piper Cub, the glorious sensation, the crosswind, the wrenching swerving ground loop. For a moment he was aware of a warm wet trickle behind his right ear and felt himself being thrust upwards as though on a swing. The lightness of the feeling pleased him, as did the idea of going to sleep.

Beaucamp had reached across and yanked the landing gear lever angrily to the 'up' position. With metallic straining noises the fourteen wheels buried themselves into the hull. The flight engineer sat wide-eyed and speechless as the giant jet groaned for height.

At Los Angeles six men piled unannounced into the common IFR room and stood uncertainly in the gloomy darkness lit only by radar-scopes glowing like giant portholes. Toby, holding the blue-bound German report, stepped ahead of Ben and the four security men to identify himself. Toby was shaken – the inaugural takeoff had not been aborted – and Toby didn't understand. Maybe Guy wanted to call off the whole plan. 'Jesus Christ, what're you doing?' Ben blurted. 'The media's hauling ass out the gate.'

'I need thirty seconds on the radio to Air World One,' Toby said to the Air Traffic Control representative who accosted them.

The woman eyed the group warily. 'You'd better come with me. Not the others.'

Ben piped, 'We're related.'

'Is Departure Control still handling Air World One?' Toby asked. He'd followed the woman over to the supervisor who stood behind the controller working the flight along with four dozen others. 'We need to give the crew of Air World One a short call,' Toby announced.

'Sorry, can't allow it,' said the controller. 'United Three Twenty-Seven, turn right direct Salinas, climb to eight.'

'Roger, Three Twenty-Seven up to eight, direct Salinas . . . We'd like to deviate a few miles south to avoid a couple of cells.'

'Deviation approved.' The controller adjusted his radar return. 'I'm not painting the weather.'

'Well, they're isolated,' said United Three Two Seven, 'but building over the hills up to the north.'

'Personal messages have to go by way of Air World company radio,' explained the supervisor. 'Sorry, but that's hard and fast and I've got four kids at home.'

The Trans-Globe 747 crossed the white runway threshold stripes and despite the seat belt fastened around him, Jamie managed to push himself high enough to see the concrete streak past. Anja had her head back and felt the thump as the main landing gear settled smoothly on to Los Angeles's runway 25R.

Guy perceived himself in wartime London, floating through black-and-white pictures he'd seen as a kid with the searchlights combing the ragged clouds as around him engines growled and a dull thudding boomed in the distance. He wanted to turn over and sleep on his other side and change dreams but when he moved he hit his hand on something cold and hard. He opened his eyes a crack, the way he did to read the alarm clock before it rang, and thought he saw a gash of lightning but it was almost totally dark so it had to be searchlights piercing the blackout in London. The trembling ground he was standing on jerked sideways and he wished the cannonading would stop so he didn't have to tense his legs to keep from falling.

Captain Beaucamp couldn't make up his mind whether to turn the flight around or not. Anders had been clearly insubordinate and had caused a dangerous situation. Beaucamp restudied his mental image of the takeoff and could recall no reason for the abort. The plane had responded well enough on climb-out. The flight engineer had said nothing . . . in fact, the engineer was sliding his chair forward. Alarm registered on the engineer's freckled features. He was placing a gauze pack behind Guy's ear.

Beaucamp glowered at his first officer. Maybe he should turn back for medical reasons. But he'd have to negotiate the coastal weather disturbance first.

Beaucamp knew he was letting the jumbo slip deeper into the turgid clouds. Ahead was a clear hole with bright light streaming from its centre. It was as if the airliner were slipping sideways, slewing on a course that would miss the clearing. The darkness of the cloud seemed somehow to promise security, a heavy blanket more comforting than the brightness . . . The impulsive punch to Anders's head had been correct but it left a terrible ringing in Beaucamp's ears that he wanted to swallow away so that he could concentrate again. He needed just a minute or two, one hundred twenty seconds to sort out what he'd done in the cockpit – the first time ever – then he'd put the whole show back on course for England. His wrist throbbed where it had slammed Guy; his attention was on it as the jumbo slid deeper into the boiling darkness. During a quick glance at the engineer, he saw the man's wide eyes staring at him, his mouth moving,

612

calling attention to something – the radio, which was chattering insistently. Well, screw 'em and the engineer too. He'd answer them all as soon as he collected himself. Meanwhile he'd keep track of the seconds and let the ringing in his ears and the pressure of what had happened wear off. He had enough altitude to step outside himself for a detached perspective. Besides, it was impossible to fly while Anders was slumped against the control column. He made himself look at Anders again and was surprised to see that he was lying back, nowhere near the controls. So what had Anders done to the yoke? The sonofabitch had to have done something to the yoke . . .

Beaucamp wished he were a pitcher on the mound, all suited up for an important game, looking in for the sign, enjoying that fine moment before he'd have to prove it all with the first pitch . . . It was *that* moment he loved; and in that fantasy he hoped the game would never start . . .

He heard the engineer's grating voice again. This time he was saying something about the heading. Beaucamp saw him crack an ammonia ampule under Anders's nose.

'Where the hell are you taking this?' the engineer yelled at Beaucamp.

The aeroplane slid sideways through pustulent clouds that rose up in dark piles, filled with silent white fire.

Beaucamp's hands were wet as he reached for the transponder button when the controller repeated his request for an ident the third time.

The sector controller who had taken over from Los Angeles departure motioned to the supervisor. 'Something may be wrong here.'

The supervisor bent to get a closer look.

The controller pointed. 'First he went steaming out of here twenty degrees off the departure heading. Now he's over here. Air World One, ident again.' Both men were peering at one edge of the huge round scope.

'Air World One, say your altitude.'

Beaucamp didn't answer.

'Air World One, if you read, ident.'

'That's the weirdest goddamn – There, it stopped.'

'American Nineteen, climb to one seven thousand, contact centre on one three five point four five.'

'Seventeen thousand, thirty-five, forty-five, going over,' answered American Nineteen through the speaker.

'There it goes again.' The controller was studying a set of green electronic numerals floating alongside the blip that was Air World One. They were cycling and returning to an altitude designation Air World One should have left several minutes ago.

'Air World One, please say your altitude and recheck your mode C squawk.'

The sky around Roger Beaucamp was dark. He hadn't yet turned off the seat-belt sign. That seemed a shame on the inaugural flight, where everything should be ideal. The flight engineer was jabbering about an apparent glitch in the transponder and saying something about altitude. Mostly he was talking to Anders and stinking up the cockpit with ammonia.

The aeroplane wasn't gaining altitude on the autopilot. The engineer had seen it, and silently checked the circuit breakers. They were all in.

'Try it manually!' suggested the engineer.

'What?' blinked Beaucamp.

'I think the autopilot is malfunctioning. Why don't you snap it off?'

Beaucamp couldn't deal with the prospect of having to fly nine more hours without autopilot . . . He snapped it off . . . Jesus . . .

Then a thrill of fear coursed through his body. The yoke had gone stiff. Freckles stood out on the engineer's glistening face.

'Hey, let's get this thing on the ground . . . Whaddaya say, Roger?'

Perspiration stained the armpits of Beaucamp's shirt; his jowls and forehead were sweating freely.

The engineer made his choice. He took his own mike and spoke directly to Los Angeles Centre. 'This is Air World One. Say the nearest airport.'

The call sent a ripple of alarm through the radar room at the air route traffic control centre. 'That would be Sacramento, Air World One . . . Say the nature of your difficulties.' The sector controller ran an electronic cursor to the blip on his scope that was Air World One while his supervisor leaned over his shoulder to see.

'Let's put her down in Sacramento, Roger,' said the engineer. 'Let's, for Chrissakes, get a vector! Centre,' he said into his mike, 'give us a vector to Sacramento.'

Beaucamp roused himself and tightened his grip on the yoke. Sacramento? Christ, Los Angeles had longer runways. '*I* have command up here,' he barked. 'Cancel that, Centre,' he said into his mike.

'Say again.'

'That's negative on Sacramento . . . we'll take a vector back into Los Angeles instead.' It was a thin show of bravado.

More than a hundred miles away, Air World One wheeled in a giant arc, away from its route towards the north and London.

Something somebody said bothered Guy. He opened his eyes, suspicious at first of the racket in his vicinity. He sat as still as he could trying to decipher it, waiting for the shape of his surroundings to be revealed. His right ear ached horribly. The scene shifted; slowly he realized he was airborne, that time had elapsed, and he knew he wanted to murder Roger Beaucamp. It took several more minutes to understand that Beaucamp was not in command of the situation. Instead of skirting the ominous anvil-topped thunderheads, Beaucamp was riding along-side them. Guy picked out the altimeter. Their altitude had to be low – perhaps as much as ten thousand feet too low. He placed his hands on the yoke, his feet on the rudder pedals, and watched the attitude director indicator swimming in the instrument panel. He applied slight back pressure; instead of the normal response he hoped for, the control column remained rigid. Beaucamp felt Guy's touch on the yoke and went through the role of retaining command.

'I'm going to bring you up on charges.'

Guy ignored him and put it to the engineer. 'I want our exact position. I want you to stand by to jettison fuel.' Turning to Beaucamp he ordered, 'I want you to take your hands and feet off the controls. I am relieving you of command. Do you understand that clearly?'

A spasm of shuddering shook the plane, then retreated. The flight seemed to settle down.

Beaucamp fingered the trim switches on his yoke but offered no resistance.

'I would prefer that you let me hear your agreement out loud so that it can be heard on the cockpit voice tape.'

Beaucamp didn't answer.

Guy spoke into the PA. 'Ladies and gentlemen, this is the pilot. Please remain in your seats with your seat belts fastened.' Next he chimed a member of the cabin staff to pick up the phone.

The purser came forward. 'What's going on?'

Guy cut him off. 'I want all those champagne glasses stored. I want any passengers wearing glasses to take them off. I want you to hand pillows out and I want you to keep them calm.'

The purser ducked out.

Guy turned to the engineer. 'Call company dispatch on the number two radio. Ask for an urgent phone patch through to Buttress. I want a Mr Edwin Boice on the horn. Pronto.'

Guy gripped his yoke. Sacramento was far behind; they were committed to Los Angeles. Beaucamp, sallow-faced, was leaning close to his window as if studying the weather to provide an incisive interpretation. The stubbornness in the controls became stronger; it was the precise moment all over again before the simulator went berserk.

'OK, Centre, Air World One. *Mayday!*' Guy spoke sharply into his mike.

Roger Beaucamp sat frozen, colour draining from his slack chins, his eyes beginning to cloud with bewilderment.

'Confirm you're declaring an emergency,' said Centre.

'That's affirmative. We have an emergency. I want a straight in to the nearest airport.'

'That's Los Angeles, Air World One. Your present heading looks good.'

The first hint Vern Locker had that the day might not go well was when he heard his name paged to report to the flight-control design coordinating room. Puzzled, he scraped his chair aside and spun through the open door to his office. When he arrived, Ed Boice was just plugging in the extension jacks from a phone receiver into positions connecting four terminals. His face was white. Vern knew better than to interrupt. Apprehension blooming through his head, he waited at the door, not moving. Boice scarcely noticed him.

Air World One sank rapidly through towering floes of cloud towards the distant smoky smear that marked the Los Angeles basin. For Ed Boice it was a dream he'd long dreaded recurring.

Guy turned to the flight engineer. 'Pull the circuit breaker on panel seven – Elevator Program A!'

'Which one?'

'Both of them – programmes A and B. Do it now, god-dammit!'

The flight engineer pulled himself up from his seat, gripping the edge of his desk for support.

'Make sure you get the right ones!' Guy shouted, struggling to adjust the radio, needing to grip the shivering yoke with both hands to control the worsening gyration. He mashed the mike switch under his right forefinger. 'Buttress! Do you read Air World One?'

A wild irrational hope that the developing reality over the phone would go away consumed Boice. Choked as though informed of a terrible verdict, he said nothing into the phone receiver; instead he clutched it behind his raised shoulder, as if hiding, waiting to hear the calm and normal tones that might follow.

Vern Locker snapped on the desk speaker.

'Buttress!' came Guy's electronically filtered voice. 'We're forty-five miles out on final! We've just pulled all the elevator programme circuit breakers but we can't disconnect the faulty computer channel –'

Boice refused to answer.

'Buttress! Are you there?'

Boice remained immobilized.

A full twenty seconds passed, the speaker crackling. Vern Locker took a step closer and held out his hand for the phone.

Los Angeles tower had been advised of the emergency in progress and had established radar contact with the stricken ship. The airport was closed to all other traffic. Fire trucks bellowed at full speed to line the runways.

Boice was shaking. He stared at Vern Locker, containing his awful realization, staring through the broadened whites of his eyes. But he wouldn't let go of the phone.

Locker still had his hand out.

'Transmitting in the blind, thirty miles out . . .' It was Guy again. 'We're losing too much altitude! I can't control the pitch!'

Suddenly Locker made his move. It started from the very tips of his toes and like a visible bolt of lightning moved up through his entire body to concentrate in the extension of his fist, which cracked directly on the side of Boice's wide-open left jowl. Boice seemed to lift half a foot; his entire body lengthened sideways and with a crash his head and shoulders took out half the partition behind him. The close air was ripped by music as the divider disintegrated, showering splintered glass across the room.

The phone flopped with a clunk to the floor. With his good hand, Vern grabbed it.

'Air World One, this is Vern Locker at Buttress. How am I getting across?'

The crackling response from Air World One was too garbled to be understood. He switched the backup radio to LA tower frequency.

' – say your altitude, Air World One.'

'Five thousand!'

'Climb immediately and maintain – '

'I can't keep the nose up!'

Vern gripped the mike. 'Air World One, this is Buttress transmitting in the blind. If you read, follow these instructions. Do exactly as I say!'

An awful muttering came from Ed Boice, who was heaped against the wall.

Vern Locker ignored him. 'Go down into the electronics bay beneath the cockpit and find the cable above the elevator-mode receptacle on the main AFCS computer. It's the third cable up, labelled YZ3614 – '

'OK, Buttress.' Guy's voice came through with startling clarity.

'On the end of that cable is a cannon plug; you have to pull the cable out of the receptacle to get to it – '

'Roger, go ahead – ' ·

'You have no fail-safe now! All the redundant hydraulic lines are routed through one common bulkhead: if it shakes loose, everything will go – the fuel line as well. If a fire starts, the regional computer will be corrupted by graphite-epoxy fibres at the tail. You have to bypass the main elevator-control servo circuit and stop the vibration before you lose everything!' Vern Locker was transported. The problem with the 17-10 and F-19 too was now out in the open. Ed Boice put his hand on the cracked wall post behind his head, struggling to haul himself up to stop Locker, but couldn't; and sat back down again.

Then Guy came through. 'Tell me how, Locker!'

'You have to create a contact between two pins in the twenty-four-pin receptacle at the elevator-mode cannon plug! The two outermost pins at the twelve- and two-o'clock positions!'

'A contact – ?' Guy's voice faded. The phone patch was breaking up. The aeroplane was getting too low for the distance between them.

Ed Boice was on his hands and knees. He heard Locker's instructions to Guy through a fog of disbelief. Where was Riddick, where was Hollis Wright? The boardroom's been empty for days . . .

'You have to bring the two pins into electrical contact!' Locker was shouting. 'The twelve- and two-o'clock-position outermost pins!'

Guy glanced at the engineer, hit his circular lap buckle, which simultaneously loosed his seat belt and shoulder harness. Roger Beaucamp had become no more than a passenger. Guy hauled the pallid flight engineer bodily from his seat.

'Get up there and fly this thing. Just hold her where she is.'

The engineer tried to swallow his panic, not let it show, as he took Guy's seat. Guy grabbed a paper clip from the engineer's desk and, jostled by the spasms of jackhammer tremors, made his way to the hatch leading from the cockpit to the electronics bay below.

In the dark electronics bay, Guy tried to locate the cannon plug on the side of the computer with his flashlight to follow Vern Locker's instructions. Several cables joined the black box but one, larger, stood out; Guy yanked it away, saw the tiny exposed pins there. They were in a diamond pattern, not at all as he'd expected to find them. He jammed the flashlight more firmly under his arm and tried to bend the paper clip to fit. Ripping his tie free to insulate the delicate piece of metal as he held it, he touched its edges across two outside pins. Sparks flew; the jumbo shuddered. But nothing else happened. He touched two more. Nothing. Guy rebent the paper clip. It wouldn't wedge in. In the darkness it was like being in the bowels of a sinking ship and he had a wild stray vision of the furnace stokers on the *Titanic*, helpless when the lights snapped out, trapped in steel crossbeams.

Vern Locker waited for confirmation from Air World One, watching the wall clock, mentally timing the final approach. They'd be down to only two thousand feet now, maybe less . . . maybe inside the outer marker.

Guy bent the clip back the other way; it broke. He dropped the useless pieces on the floor and thrust his hand into his pocket for a coin or a nail clipper. He brought the handful up to the light. Loose change and a car key, no nail clipper. He gripped the key in his tie, studied its indentations and laid it across the cannon plug's diameter.

Instantly Air World One sat straight, flying level. Simultaneously it occurred to Guy it wasn't a car key at all. It was Synova's season's pass, which he'd never used.

Guy fumbled frantically with one hand to release the intercom mike from its stowage compartment and plug its cord into the receptacle by the computer. In it he shouted for the engineer. 'Get down here! Hey! Get down here!' He didn't dare let go of the connection of key and cannon plug. The engineer's head appeared upside down, peering through the open hatch at the top of the ladder.

'What's our altitude?' Guy called.

'Fifteen hundred feet – '

'Get down here and clamp your hand around this!'

The engineer clambered down into the electronics bay; Guy grabbed his pants leg and hauled him down the last three rungs. A spark flew, the ship shuddered. Guy reset the key, pressed the man's hand firmly on top of it, and reached for the ladder.

It wasn't enough. Halfway up the ladder, Guy felt the 17-10 tilt as on his simulator ride. He stumbled. One hand flailed wildly to grab hold, gripping hard, preventing him from having to reconquer the first three rungs.

'You're not holding the right pins!' he shouted.

He fought to regain his seat in the cockpit.

They were too low.

Guy recalled a fragment of a war diary he'd read somewhere, and he huddled together with its author across time and space, a trapped man who had also gazed at the mental image of his beloved and experienced the soul-rending anguish that he'd never touch or smell or taste her again. That she'd be left young and eager for others to invade.

'*Anja . . . oh – Jesus . . .*'

Imperfect memories will linger, coloured by loneliness and grief, until even memory fades, growing dim like dried tears until it's as if memory had never existed – only a layer of dust on an old album never opened . . . then gone   in a blinding instant.

622

Guy saw Beaucamp across from him goggle-eyed, immobilized like a baby with a bib surrounded by the incomprehensibility of a jumbo-jet cockpit as the surface of the sea erupted around the cockpit windows . . . the cataclysmic miasma of grinding destruction, row by row, until all fifty-seven rows of filled passenger seats had shovelled together . . . Dimly Guy heard the engineer shout something in a strangled voice; he saw the scene jerk back a few frames to play again, with the runway so close but off to one side, dozens of people frozen in awe as the silver liner hurtled at them, and he somehow trying to lift the massive weight of it alone as Cosgrove had done, his arms numb with pain, trying to roll into a bank towards the runway, hearing his own faraway scream, 'The pins!' wishing during the scream to see the runway actually slide underneath the cockpit windows, all of it occurring in the last microsecond of life . . .

Guy saw the shallow blue waves off to his right as the giant 17-10 tipped. He found himself marvelling at the water's clarity no more than fifty feet below or perhaps twenty. He had full throttle on the outboards as a last meaningless attempt to raise the nose. He'd even reached to extend the inboard trailing edge flaps.

'Oh, shit . . .' Beaucamp moaned to no one. 'We're going in . . .'

A man climbing on to the deck of his moored yacht saw it and tried to get to the rail to dive away from the oncoming metal behemoth but he didn't make it.

In his last conscious motion at the controls, Guy just managed to keep the nose from ploughing in as the right wing of Air World One slashed across the tops of the waves at better than two hundred knots. The lane Guy had selected for splashdown wasn't wide enough. One wing clipped and scattered boats and clusters of wood and metal pieces before it like billiard balls. One flew into the air spinning sideways as the jumbo lurched to a halt in a great swell and wash, twisting to jolt alongside the pier.

An instant of absolute stillness followed as though nothing at all had occurred. Then a geyser of flame ripped through the cracked fuselage and cascaded across the adjacent parking lot, travelling along the ground like a volcanic eruption.

Ben Reese was running from the terminal building. Toby caught up with him at the far end of the empty bleachers. Fire trucks were heading away across the tarmac. A great stain of coal-black smoke not two miles away was bellying towards the sky. Both men stopped. Toby had a stupefied expression. Ben's knotted face was moving, but only a terrible animal wail grew in his chest. Unconsciously he allowed the German report to pass into Toby's hands. Then he stepped around the pushback tug used a short time ago to ease the inaugural on its way, stuck the police pass to his shirt and headed towards the flaming marina.

Anja heard the crackle of the overhead speakers in the corridor. It was an intrusion which she desperately didn't want to hear and she wondered what to do. She was holding Jamie's hand. Together they disappeared among the waiting people; as they did so, Jamie studied the ceiling, not comprehending why the place had grown so quiet.